Great Esquire Fiction

Great *Esquire* Fiction

The Finest Stories from the First Fifty Years

Edited and with an Introduction by L. Rust Hills
Preface by Phillip Moffitt

THE VIKING PRESS · NEW YORK

Copyright © 1983 by Esquire Publishing, Inc.
All rights reserved
First published in 1983 by The Viking Press
40 West 23rd Street, New York, N.Y. 10010
Published simultaneously in Canada by
Penguin Books Canada Limited

LIBRARY OF CONGRESS CATALOGING IN PUBLICATION DATA
Main entry under title:
Great Esquire fiction.
1. Short stories, American.   2. American fiction—
20th century.   I. Hills, L. Rust.   II. Esquire (New York, N.Y.).
PS648.S5G73   1983   813'.01'08   83-47877
ISBN 0-670-15922-0

Pages 587–88 constitute an extension of the copyright page.

Printed in the United States of America
Set in Times Roman

Preface

The Magic of the Short Story

As you read the pages of this book you will discover it to be filled with the distinct voices of some of America's best short fiction writers of the last fifty years. Each of these voices has its origin in a particular time and place. And you give yourself over to these voices, you are momentarily transported: it is as though you have just had an intimate encounter with complete strangers. At that moment, the senses register new sights and sounds; you experience different textures of life, and the brain analyzes data from a new emotional context. At that moment, your fears shift, sympathies change, and the meaning of it all is magically tilted. And for that brief duration, you are free of the physical and emotional limits of yourself.

It is for this reason that *Esquire* gives over a number of its pages month after month to fiction: the streams of images, the tumbling of words, the depth of the characters and, above all, the force of the author's control. This is the value of the short story. It is a treat, like a rich dessert to be savored slowly.

One of the pleasures of being editor of *Esquire* is the continuous exposure to this literary output and the process of selecting stories that are best suited to the magazine's needs. For me, it is a particular joy to discover emerging young talent and to watch it develop. I am very proud that we have been able to expose so much of this talent to the world. If there is any single criterion for which we examine each piece of fiction, it is this magical power to transport the reader.

This book succeeds brilliantly in that regard. Enjoy it.

—Phillip Moffitt

Contents

CONTENTS

Introduction

*E*squire magazine's tradition of publishing fiction is a long one—as long as its own fifty-year lifetime. The magazine was originally conceived as a men's fashion magazine—"The Quarterly for Men"—intended to be distributed mostly in clothing stores; yet the very first issue contained nine stories, by such writers as John Dos Passos, Morley Callaghan, William McFee, Dashiell Hammett, Manuel Komroff, and, oddly, Douglas Fairbanks, Jr. There was as well Erskine Caldwell's "August Afternoon," a story that even today may seem to the reader startlingly sexual.

An innovative mix of robust sex, elegant graphics, and literature served the magazine well in its early years, and the success of *Esquire* was more or less immediate: it switched to monthly publication after the first issue, and circulation by newsstand and subscription rose to close to 200,000 by the end of the first year, a remarkable achievement given its fifty-cent cover price at a time when America was still deep in the Depression.

The magazine's literary reputation in the 1930s was not based entirely on its fiction. Most of the major writers of the time contributed nonfiction in various forms: articles, essays, reportage, "letters," and columns of review and "opinion." James T. Farrell reviewed books in the first issue. Ezra Pound contributed eccentric essays through the mid-thirties. Saroyan published stories through the late thirties, even though Hemingway attacked his work in a column in 1935—an early instance in the long tradition of *Esquire*'s writers having at one another in our pages. Sinclair Lewis went after everyone in his book reviews in the mid-forties. In the early years there was a category called "Semi-Fiction"; Thomas Wolfe published autobiographical fiction; H. L. Mencken published autobiographical articles. Theodore Dreiser and John Dos Passos were among the many writers who would sometimes publish fiction, sometimes nonfiction, and sometimes something in-between.

That *Esquire* was ever "literary" in the first place was due to the tastes and convictions of its founding editor, Arnold Gingrich. Arnold to some extent created the magazine in his own image. His personal interests were always prominently featured—jazz, travel, fishing, automobiles, and thus also literature. He developed rather close personal friendships with Hemingway and Fitzgerald and others, but especially those two; he collected first editions of their work as a hobby, and he kept them writing for the magazine.

Ernest Hemingway was in the first issue with a letter from Cuba, "Marlin off the Morro," the first of many he was to contribute, including "On the Blue Water" in 1936, which famously contained the germ of *The Old Man and the Sea,* which didn't appear until 1952. There were many pieces by him about Spain during the Civil War, hunting in Africa, living in Paris, Spain, Key West, and so on; but there was also much fiction reflecting the same Hemingway interests. "The Snows of Kilimanjaro," probably both *Esquire*'s and Hemingway's most famous story, appeared in August 1936; but famous means familiar, and for this reason we include instead "The Horns of the Bull," which appeared in June of the same year. The story's title may seem unfamiliar, because when it was collected in *The Fifth Column and the First Forty-Nine Stories* (1938), it was retitled "The Capital of the World."

F. Scott Fitzgerald also published dozens and dozens of pieces in *Esquire* in those years, again in a variety of genres. There was a good deal of "satire," about Princeton or publishing or whatever, some straightforward stories, and a series of stories about Pat Hobby, the Hollywood screenwriter down on his luck who in some respects resembled Fitzgerald at that point in his life. Many of Fitzgerald's articles were autobiographical, and they became more and more personal, culminating in the disclosures of "The Crack-Up" and its companion pieces—"Pasting It Together," "Handle with Care," and "Afternoon of an Author"—all of which appeared in 1936. The short story reprinted here, "An Alcoholic Case" (February 1937), although told from the point of view of a young attendant nurse, indicates vividly both the morbidity and the romance Fitzgerald associated with drinking.

Later in the 1930s three of John Steinbeck's best stories appeared, including the eerie "A Snake of One's Own," retitled "The Snake" when it appeared in his collection *The Long Valley.* Two stories from the early 1940s are reprinted here. "The Eighty-Yard Run" is one of a dozen stories Irwin Shaw has published in *Esquire* over the years, perhaps the best known. Nelson Algren's "The Captain Is a Card" is an early use of a police line-up scene, which appears so often in his work.

Then came a period of literary decline for *Esquire*, a decline that came about for two reasons. During the first half of the 1940s, *Esquire* "went to war"—like Lucky Strike Green. The Varga Girls that followed the Petty Girls into the center gatefolds of the magazine were tacked on every barracks room locker door, and the magazine catered patriotically to the reader in uniform. Even more responsible for the changes in quality of the magazine, perhaps, was the fact that in 1945 Arnold Gingrich left to become one of the first American tourist civilians in Europe after the war ended. He lived in Switzerland, writing, and he didn't return to this country until after 1950, and not to the magazine until 1952.

Throughout the period, the magazine continued to publish fiction—usually six or seven stories an issue, sometimes more—but it was "pulpy" and man-oriented. It was not "formula" exactly, not of course "boy-meets-girl," not slick in the *Saturday Evening Post* and *Collier's* sense, not traditional magazine fiction certainly. But it was not literary either, for with Arnold Gingrich away, the magazine had lost its literary idiosyncrasy.

Toward the end of this period, however, there appeared stories by the two great novelists of World War II—James Jones's "Two Legs for the Two of Us" and Norman Mailer's "The Language of Men." But the full effects of Arnold Gingrich's return to the magazine weren't realized in the pages until as late as 1957.

In the mid-fifties a decision was made at *Esquire*, more or less on a business basis, to "go for quality again"—one of those anomalous good opportunities that rarely but occasionally occur in commerce. To those of us newly arrived there as young, or relatively young, editors—Harold Hayes, Clay Felker, Ralph Ginsburg, and myself (with Arnold Gingrich in charge)—it seemed that we were creating a new identity for the magazine, more like its original one.

Fiction of course played a major role in instrumenting this change of policy. The kind of fiction a magazine publishes affects its image out of all proportion to the amount of fiction published. At first when I went around talking to agents and authors, they found it hard to believe that *Esquire* wanted literary fiction, which itself seems hard to believe now. What we published in the autumn of 1957 made an amazing statement for the magazine. Leslie Fiedler's "Nude Croquet" in September was a first attention-getter: the New York intellectual crowd found themselves not just reading *Esquire* but scathingly depicted in a roman à clef. In October we published Arthur Miller's short story "The Misfits," on which he was to base his screenplay for the celebrated Monroe–Gable–Clift movie—and in the same issue we published for the first time Thomas Wolfe's ten-scene play, "Welcome to Our City," as we were to publish many newly discovered literary works posthumously in the years to come. In November we ran the perfectly wrought story "Goose Pond," by Thomas Williams, who was at the time a graduate student in the Writers' Workshop at the University of Iowa, a place from which we have ever since gotten much of our good fiction by beginning writers. In December, having turned in the expensive pinup centerfold for eight pages of special stock, we ran Gian-Carlo Menotti's libretto for the Samuel Barber opera *Vanessa*, and a month later elegant New Yorkers were in the opening-night audience with copies of *Esquire*, of all things, in their hands. All these literary elements worked together to accomplish a remarkable transition remarkably fast; but to me, as fiction editor, it seemed that those three extraordinary stories, reprinted here—the first scandalous and highbrow, the second both literary and yet to become a film "property," and the third just quietly superb by a new young writer—bracketed the target of what we wanted to do with *Esquire* fiction.

Thereafter, for a while at least, came a flood of fine stories. It was a terrific time to be a fiction editor because most of the writers who have since become well-known and sought after by national magazines had published only in the literary quarterlies and little magazines up to that point. Writers appeared as if out of nowhere. George P. Elliott had published in quarterlies only, until we ran "Among the Dangs," a story so highly imagined it amazed everyone. Stanley Elkin first found his "voice" as Stanley Elkin with "I Look Out for Ed Wolfe." John Barth's second novel produced a wonderfully self-contained excerpt, both crazy and cogent, "The Remobilization of Jacob Horner." We published part of Philip Roth's first novel under the title "Very Happy Poems." And Terry Southern's "The Road Out of Axotle" has since become a classic of Beat writing.

Each of these stories seems to me, or perhaps I should say all of them seem, to break the bounds of any known formula of magazine fiction. And as well, we were able to run fine fiction by more established authors. John Cheever's "The Death of Justina" is a story that's central to his work. Isaac Bashevis Singer's story "The Spinoza of Market Street" is one of his most moving. Bernard Malamud's "Life Is Better Than Death" is characteristically both funny on the one hand and mordant and macabre on the other. Thus, as *Esquire* entered the 1960s it had returned to the fiction policy that had made it successful in the 1930s: a mixture of strong stories by new voices with major work by major authors of the time.

And—or but—the tradition of reportage from literary writers was renewed too, and in an even more vigorous form. What became known as "the New Journalism" flourished in *Esquire* during the sixties; there was a lot to report on, and *Esquire* relished covering it. Some of the New Journalists were fiction writers to begin with— Mailer and Capote and Southern and others. Some used the dramatizing methods of fiction in nonfiction—Tom Wolfe, Gay Talese, John Sack, Michael Herr, and others. Although publishing all this journalism led to a diminishment in the amount of straightforward fiction-as-such in the magazine (often now we were down to one story an issue, and in some rare instances no fiction at all appeared), and although this saddened me, it could scarcely be contested because the work was so good as to seem to be in fact literature itself.

Robert Brown was the fiction editor of *Esquire* from 1964 to 1969, and the fiction tradition continued. Bruce Jay Friedman's "Black Angels" is representative of the many fine stories he's contributed to *Esquire* over the years. Flannery O'Connor's "Parker's Back" was published posthumously. And Barry Targan's "Harry Belten and the Mendelssohn Violin Concerto" became one of the best-loved stories *Esquire* ever printed.

Gordon Lish was fiction editor of *Esquire* from 1969 to 1977, through a succession of editors: Harold Hayes, Don Erickson, Lee Eisenberg, and Byron Dobell. What a remarkable stewardship it was! It was Gordon's opportunity, and perhaps his genius, to find for the magazine a new kind of fiction—which was in fact called "the New Fiction" by academic scholars of the time. So influential and energetic was Lish in his role of fiction editor of *Esquire* that the New Fiction, as such, seemed to begin when he began, to crest as he crested, and to subside when he relinquished his tenure. It was a new wave, and Lish gloriously surfed it! I presume to say that of all of the New Fiction stories none was greater than the two classics, pillars of the genre, that are reprinted here. William Kotzwinkle's "Horse Badorties Goes Out" is the startling, never-to-be-forgotten "dorky, dorky, dorky, dorky" section of his *The Fan Man*. And T. Coraghessan Boyle's "Heart of a Champion" is the notorious account of Lassie in lust.

Of the other excellent fiction first published by Lish and reprinted here, the reader (and posterity) will have to say which stories fall within and which fall outside the New Fiction category. Raymond Carver's "Neighbors" is an early example of that fine writer's completely distinctive and original voice. Gail Godwin's "A Sorrowful Woman" is short but moving, a genuine art-object of the women's movement. Joy Williams' "The Lover" is a fine example of the bizarre bleak-and-comic vision of that talented writer's writer. And Grace Paley's "The Long-Distance Runner" is one of two fine stories she contributed while Gordon Lish was fiction editor.

During that time as well, sections of long-awaited, *still*-awaited novels-in-progress appeared: Harold Brodkey's "His Son, In His Arms, In Light, Aloft" and Truman Capote's "La Côte Basque 1965" (projected as part of his *Answered Prayers*), which caused a sensation when it appeared, as it was said to reveal actual scandal among the socially elite.

Then in 1977 Clay Felker purchased *Esquire*, converted it to fortnightly publication, and I returned. Fiction resided uneasily in the fortnightly *Esquire*, which was otherwise more journalistic than literary. After a shaky start, and some ill-advised and half-hearted (on my part) attempts to have a sort of journalistic fiction "created" for the magazine, it was finally decided (or recognized) that only good strong literary fiction had any place in a magazine called *Esquire*, no matter how unlike the traditional *Esquire* that magazine might be. Of all the good fiction we published in the period that followed, one story in particular stands out: William Styron's "Shadrach," which although it might originally have been conceived as part of the novel *Sophie's Choice*, was not finally included there and exists as an independent short story.

In 1979 the magazine managed to get itself bought again. I realize that I'm beginning to speak of *Esquire* as if it had a sense of its own destiny, and sometimes I think it somehow does. In this case it certainly chose well for itself. Two new young owners, Phillip Moffitt (editor) and Christopher Whittle (publisher), shortly returned the magazine to monthly periodicity, square-backed it again, and made *Esquire* once again a successful enterprise.

From this most recent period, six stories have been selected from among many fine ones. Vance Bourjaily's "The Amish Farmer" is the most recent of much fine work—fiction and nonfiction—that he's contributed to the magazine over the years. Tim O'Brien's "The Ghost Soldiers" is a chilling story of the war in Vietnam. Richard Ford's "Rock Springs" maintains voice marvelously right into the luminous epiphany of its ending. John Updike's "More Stately Mansions" looks back on the 1960s from the 1980s with a wonderfully evocative nostalgia. Joyce Carol Oates's *"Ich Bin ein Berliner"* uses the Berlin Wall as a metaphor in a complex study of isolation and madness. And Don DeLillo's "Human Moments in World War III" meditatively appraises the danger and hope that lie in man's future. These stories show, more clearly than any statement could, how uncompromising is the new commitment to the old tradition of *Esquire* fiction.

The editor of an anthology usually feels called upon to justify his choices. But I have no such feeling in this case. The stories here more than justify themselves. What I worry about, what I feel I ought to have to justify, are my exclusions. It's very painful to me to think of how much good fiction I have had to leave out of this book.

I think, for instance, of work that ran in the magazine that is just too long to reprint here: novellas like Truman Capote's *Breakfast at Tiffany's* and Jim Harrison's *Legends of the Fall*; or long abridgments of novels, like John Gardner's *The Song of Grendel*, Evan S. Connell's *Mr. Bridge*, and Mark Harris's *Wake Up, Stupid*; or long excerpts from novels we ran, for instance from Joseph Heller's *Something Happened*, William Faulkner's *The Reivers*, Thomas Berger's *Little Big Man*, and Leonard Michaels' *The Men's Club*; or simply very long short stories, like Saul Bellow's "Leaving the Yellow House," Reynolds Price's "Waiting at Dachau," Barry Hannah's

"Quadberry," Ivan Gold's "The Nickel Misery of George Washington Carver Brown," James Blake's "The Widow, Bereft," Donald Barthelme's "The Emerald," Robert Coover's "The Magic Poker," and Donald Newlove's "Beautiful Soup." I could go on and on. As fiction editor I'm grateful that *Esquire* has never been afraid to publish long fiction, but that's made my task as an anthologist more difficult than it would otherwise be.

Quite arbitrarily excluded from this book are writers-in-English from abroad—like Kingsley Amis, Graham Greene, Aldous Huxley, D. H. Lawrence, Frank O'Connor, John Wain, and Evelyn Waugh— although *Esquire* published fiction by them all. And I've left out work that was available by such great international authors as Camus, Kundera, Nabokov, Mann, Márquez, Mauriac, Maurois, Moravia, Simenon, and others.

But imagine the plight of the anthologist who has to leave *out* of his book work available from American writers like these (besides those I've mentioned already): Paul Bowles, William Burroughs, James M. Cain, R. V. Cassill, Robert M. Coates, James Dickey, J. P. Donleavy, Richard Fariña, Herbert Gold, Donald Hall, James B. Hall, William Harrison, Edward Hoagland, William Humphrey, John Irving, Jack Kerouac, Ken Kesey, Ring Lardner, Leo Litwak, Thomas McGuane, Robert Miner, John O'Hara, Cynthia Ozick, Dorothy Parker, J. F. Powers, James Purdy, Thomas Pynchon, Tom Robbins, Gilbert Rogin, Hughes Rudd, J. D. Salinger, James Salter, Mark Schorer, Budd Schulberg, Allan Seager, Wallace Stegner, Harvey Swados, Kurt Vonnegut, Jr., Robert Penn Warren, Tennessee Williams, Herbert Wilner, Hilma Wolitzer, Richard Wright, and Richard Yates. These are just *some* among the many American authors whose work I had to choose from.

And I regret most especially omitting work by some of the new young writers we've been publishing recently, whose names are not as yet as well-known as those I've mentioned. *Esquire* is now, more than ever, interested in what is new.

As *Esquire* celebrates its fiftieth-anniversary year, it does so from a position of strength that could scarcely have been imagined a few years back. This revitalization has not been achieved without a considerable investment of talent and energy and perception. Perhaps it is sentimental of me to do so, but I quite often think with considerable emotion of how gratified Arnold Gingrich would have been that these two young men who, having grown up on *Esquire* in the past, are now seeing to it that the magazine lives into the future.

—L. Rust Hills
March, 1983

Great

Esquire

Fiction

ERSKINE CALDWELL

August Afternoon

Vic Glover awoke with the noon-day heat ringing in his ears. He had been asleep for only half an hour, and he was getting ready to turn over and go back to sleep when he opened his eyes for a moment and saw Hubert's black head over the top of his bare toes. He stretched his eyelids and held them open as long as he could.

Hubert was standing in the yard, at the edge of the porch, with a pine cone in his hand.

Vic cursed him.

The colored man raked the cone over the tops of Vic's toes and stepped back out of reach.

"What do you mean by standing there tickling me with that dad-burned cone?" Vic shouted at Hubert. "Is that all you can find to do? Why don't you get out in that field and do something to those boll-weevils? They're going to eat up every pound of cotton on the place if you don't stop them."

"I surely hated to wake you up, Mr. Vic," Hubert said, "but there's a white man out here looking for something. He won't say what he wants, but he's hanging around for something."

Vic was wide awake by that time. He sat up on the quilt and pulled on his shoes without looking into the yard. The white sand in the yard beat the glare of the sun directly into his eyes and he could see nothing beyond the edge of the porch. Hubert threw the pine cone under the porch and stepped aside.

"He must be looking for trouble," Vic said. "When they come around and don't say anything, and just sit, it's trouble they're look-ing for."

"There he is, Mr. Vic," Hubert said, nodding his head across the yard. "There he sits up against that water oak."

Vic looked around for Willie. Willie was sitting on the top step at the other end of the porch, directly in front of the stranger. She did not look at Vic.

"You ought to have better sense than to wake me up while I'm taking a nap. This is no time of day to be up. I've got to get a little sleep every now and then."

"Boss," Hubert said, "I wouldn't wake you up at all, not at any time, but Miss Willie just sits there high up on the steps and that white man has been out there whittling on a little stick a pretty long time without saying anything. I've got scared about something happening when he whittles that little stick clear through, and it's just about whittled down to nothing now."

Vic glanced again at Willie, and from her he turned to stare at the stranger sitting under the water oak tree in his front yard.

The piece of wood had been shaved down to paper thinness.

"Boss," Hubert said, "we ain't aiming to have no trouble today, are we?"

"Which way did he come from?" Vic asked.

"I never did see him come, Mr. Vic. I just looked up, and there he was, sitting against that water oak whittling on a little stick. I reckon I must have been sleeping when he came, because when I looked up, there he was."

Vic slid down over the quilt until his legs were hanging over the edge of the porch. Perspiration began to trickle down his neck as soon as he sat up.

"Ask him what he's after, Hubert."

"We ain't aiming to have no trouble today, are we, Mr. Vic?"

"Ask him what he wants, I said."

Hubert went almost half way to the water oak tree and stopped.

"Mr. Vic says what can he do for you, white-folks."

The man said nothing. He did not even glance up.

Hubert came back to the porch, the whites of his eyes becoming larger with each step.

"What did he say?" Vic asked him.

"He ain't said nothing yet, Mr. Vic. He acts like he don't hear me at all. You'd better go talk to him, Mr. Vic. He won't give me no attention. Appears to me like he's just sitting there looking at Miss Willie on the high step. Maybe if you was to tell her to go in the house and shut the door, he might be persuaded to give some notice to what we say to him."

"Can't see any sense in sending her in the house," Vic said. "I can make him talk. Hand me that stilyerd."

"Mr. Vic, I'm trying to tell you about Miss Willie. Miss Willie's been sitting there on that high step and he's been looking up at her a right long time, Mr. Vic. If you won't object to me saying so, Mr. Vic, I reckon I'd tell Miss Willie to go sit somewhere else, if I was you. Miss Willie ain't got much on today, Mr. Vic. That's what I've been trying to tell you."

"Hand me that stilyerd, I said."

Hubert went to the end of the porch and brought the cotton steelyard to Vic. He stepped back out of the way.

"Boss," Hubert said, "we ain't aiming to have no trouble today, are we?"

Vic was getting ready to jump down into the yard when the man under the water oak reached into his pocket and pulled out another knife. It was about nine inches long, and both sides of the handle were covered with hairy cowhide. There was a springbutton on one end. The man pushed the button with his thumb, and the blade sprang open. He began playing with both knives, throwing them up in the air and catching them on the back of his hands.

Hubert moved to the other side of Vic.

"Mr. Vic," he said, "I ain't intending to mix in your business none, but it looks to me like you got yourself in for a mess of trouble when you went off and brought Miss Willie back here. It looks to me like she's got up for a city girl, more so than a country girl."

Vic cursed him.

"I'm telling you, Mr. Vic, a country girl wouldn't sit on a high step in front of a man, not when she wasn't wearing nothing but that blue wrapper, anyhow."

"Shut up," Vic said, laying the steelyard down on the quilt beside him.

The man under the water oak closed the blade of the small knife and put it into his pocket. The big cowhide-covered knife he flipped into the air and caught easily on the back of his hand.

"What's your name?" he asked Willie.

"Willie."

He flipped the knife again.

"What's yours?" she asked him.

"Floyd."

"Where are you from?"

"Carolina."

He flipped it higher, catching it underhanded.

"What are you doing in Georgia?"

"Don't know," he said. "Just looking around."

Willie giggled, smiling at him.

Floyd got up and walked across the yard to the steps and sat down on the bottom one. He put his arm around his knees and looked up at Willie.

"You're not so bad-looking," he said. "I've seen lots worse looking."

"You're not so bad yourself," Willie giggled, resting her arms on her knees and looking down at him.

"How about a kiss?"

"What would it be to you?"

"Not bad. I reckon I've had lots worse."

"Well, you can't get it sitting down there."

Floyd climbed the steps on his hands and feet and sat down on the next to the top step. He leaned against Willie, putting one arm around her waist and the other over her knees. Willie slid down to the step beside him.

"Boss," Hubert said, his lips twitching, "we ain't going to have no trouble today, are we?"

Vic cursed him.

Willie and Floyd moved down a step without loosening their embrace.

"Who is that yellow-headed sap-sucker, anyhow?" Vic said. "I'll be dad-burned if he ain't got a lot of nerve—coming here and fooling with Willie."

"You wouldn't do nothing to cause trouble, would you, Mr. Vic? I surely don't want to have no trouble today, Mr. Vic."

Vic glanced at the nine-inch knife Floyd had, stuck into the step at his feet. It stood on its tip eighteen inches high, while the sun was reflected against the bright blade and made a streak of light on Floyd's pant leg.

"Go over there and take that knife away from him and bring it here," Vic said. "Don't be scared of him."

"Mr. Vic, I surely hate to disappoint you, but if you want that white-folk's knife, you'll just have to get it your own self. I don't aim to have myself all carved up with that thing. Mr. Vic, I surely can't accommodate you this time. If you want that white-folk's knife, you'll just be bound to get it yourself, Mr. Vic."

Vic cursed him.

Hubert backed away until he was at the end of the porch. He kept on looking behind him all the time, looking to be certain of the exact location of the sycamore stump that was between him and the pine grove on the other side of the cotton field.

Vic called to Hubert and told him to come back. Hubert came slowly around the corner of the porch and stood a few feet from the quilt where Vic was sitting. His lips quivered and the whites of his eyes grew larger. Vic motioned for him to come closer, but he would not come an inch farther.

"How old are you?" Floyd asked Willie.

"Fifteen."

Floyd jerked the knife out of the wood and thrust it deeper in the same place.

"How old are you?" she asked him.

"About twenty-seven."

"Are you married?"

"Not now," he said. "How long have you been?"

"About three months," Willie said.

"How do you like it?"

"Pretty good so far."

"How about another kiss?"

"You've just had one."

"I'd like another one now."

"I ought not to let you kiss me again."

"Why not?" Floyd said.

"Men don't like girls who kiss too much."

"I'm not that kind."

"What kind are you?" Willie asked him.

"I'd like to kiss you a lot."

"But after I let you do that, you'd go away."

"No, I won't. I'll stay for something else."

"What?"

"Let's go inside for a drink and I'll tell you."

"We'll have to go to the spring for fresh water."

"Where's the spring?"

"Just across the field in the grove."

"All right," Floyd said, standing up. "Let's go."

He bent down and pulled the knife out of the wood. Willie ran down the steps and across the yard. When Floyd saw that she was not going to wait for him, he ran after her, holding the knives in his pocket with one hand. She led him across the cotton field to the spring in the pine grove. Just before they got there, Floyd caught her by the arm and ran beside her the rest of the way.

"Boss," Hubert said, "we ain't aiming to have no trouble today, are we?"

Vic cursed him.

"I don't want to get messed up with a heap of trouble and maybe get my belly slit open with that big hairy knife. If you ain't got objections, I reckon I'll mosey on home now and cut a little firewood for the cook-stove."

"Come back here!" Vic said. "You stay where you are and stop making moves to go off."

"What are we aiming to do, Mr. Vic?"

Vic eased himself off the porch and walked across the yard to the water oak. He looked down at the ground where Floyd had been sitting, and then he looked at the porch steps where Willie had been. The noonday heat beat down through the thin leaves overhead and he could feel his mouth and throat burn with the hot air he breathed.

"Have you got a gun, Hubert?"

"No, sir, boss," Hubert said.

"Why haven't you?" he said. "Right when I need a gun, you haven't got it. Why don't you keep a gun?"

"Mr. Vic, I ain't got no use for a gun. I used to keep one to shoot rabbits and squirrels with, but I got to thinking one day, and I traded it off the first chance I had. I reckoned it was a good thing I traded, too. If I had kept it, you'd be asking for it like you did just now."

Vic went back to the porch and picked up the steelyard and hammered the porch with it. After he had hit the porch four or five times, he dropped it and started out in the direction of the spring. He walked as far as the edge of the shade and stopped. He stood listening for a while.

Willie and Floyd could be heard down near the spring. Floyd said something to Willie, and Willie laughed loudly. There was silence for several minutes, and then Willie laughed again. Vic was getting ready to turn back to the porch when he heard her cry out. It sounded like a scream, but it was not exactly that; it sounded like a shriek, but it was not that, either; it sounded more like someone laughing and crying simultaneously in a high-pitched voice.

"Where did Miss Willie come from, Mr. Vic?" Hubert asked. "Where did you bring her from?"

"Down below here a little way," he said.

Hubert listened to the sounds that were coming from the pine grove.

"Boss," he said after a while, "it appears to me like you didn't go far enough away."

"I went far enough," Vic said. "If I had gone any farther, I'd have been in Florida."

The colored man hunched his shoulders forward several times while he smoothed the white sand with his broad-soled shoes.

"Mr. Vic, if I was you, the next time I'd surely go that far."

"What do you mean, the next time?"

"I was figuring that maybe you wouldn't be keeping her much longer than now, Mr. Vic."

Vic cursed him.

Hubert raised his head several times and attempted to see down into the pine grove over the top of the growing cotton.

"Shut up and mind your own business," Vic said. "I'm going to keep her till the cows come home. Where else do you reckon I'd find a better-looking girl than Willie?"

"Boss, I wasn't thinking of how she looks—I was thinking how she acts."

"She acts that way now because she's not old enough to do different. She won't act that way much longer. She'll get over the way she's doing pretty soon."

Hubert followed Vic across the yard. While Vic went towards the porch, Hubert stopped and leaned against the water oak where he could almost see over the cotton field into the pine grove. Vic went up on the porch and stretched out on the quilt. He took off his shoes and flung them aside.

"I surely God knowed something was going to happen when he whittled that stick down to nothing," Hubert was saying to himself. "White-folks take a long time to whittle a little piece of wood, but after they whittle it down to nothing, they're going to be up and doing."

Presently Vic sat upright on the quilt.

"Listen here, Hubert—"

"Yes, sir, boss."

"You keep your eyes on that stilyerd so it will stay right where it is now, and when they come back up the path from the spring, you wake me up in a hurry. Do you hear?"

"Yes, sir, boss," Hubert said. "Are you aiming to take a little nap now?"

"Yes, I am. And if you don't wake me up when they come back, I'll break your head for you when I do wake up."

Vic lay down again on the quilt and turned over on his side to shut out the blinding glare of the early afternoon sun that was re-flected upon the porch from the hard white sand in the yard.

Hubert scratched his head and sat down against the water oak facing the path from the spring. He could hear Vic snoring on the porch above the sounds that came at intervals from the pine grove across the field. He sat staring down the path, singing under his breath. It was a long time until sundown.

[Autumn 1933]

WILLIAM SAROYAN

Little
Miss Universe

There were three authorities on the horses at The Kentucky Pool Room, number One Opera Alley, in San Francisco: Mr. Levin, a fat gentleman of fifty, affectionately called *The Barrel* because he resembled one: San Jose Red, a nervous, thin person of sixty-five; and a neatly dressed young man of twenty who was known as Willie. These three gentlemen knew more about thoroughbreds than any other three people living, or for that matter, as someone had suggested, more than the horses themselves knew. Nevertheless, they were almost always broke. Each kept an accurate record of what he would have won if he had had money with which to bet, and the profit for each day was fairly amazing; for a month it was breathtaking. A month ago, for example, if Willie had had a half dollar to bet on the nose of *Panther Rock,* today he would be worth— well, to be exact (he opened a small book full of neatly written figures)—ten thousand, two hundred and eighty-six dollars and forty-five cents.

"And," said Willie, "I could use it, too."

Willie had a system. He looked up the horses in every race and chose the one with the worst record. "That horse," he explained, "has been loafing. He has been going around the track as a spectator, watching the race from a good position. But he'll win today. Even a horse has got to break the monotony. He'll win out of sheer boredom. His mother was *Ella Faultless,* and you know what she did."

"No," somebody said. "What did she do?"

"Well," said Willie, "five years ago she started twenty times and wasn't once in the money. She ran beautifully but never exerted herself. Then all of a sudden she woke up and won six races in a row."

Willie looked into the faces of his small audience with an expression of profound wisdom, as if by divine grace he alone of all mortals had been blessed with the faculty of understanding such a remarkable performance.

"Bang," he said with emotion.

"One.

Two.

Three.

Four.

Five . . . SIX!

In a row. Think of it." He spoke the small words distinctly, sending them from his mouth with the precision of a hen producing an egg.

"Somebody must have got the horse mad," said a young gambler named Blewett. He was a barber by profession.

Willie smiled at Blewett and whispered confidentially, "That's just it—some horse must have got her mad. We can't figure these things out because they're not in the dope sheets. But it's a cinch one horse can get another horse sore. Remember *Mr. Goofus?* He was a card."

"What'd he do?" asked Mr. Blewett.

"There was a horse," said Willie. He paused to catch his breath for the remarkable statement he was about to make. "There was a horse," he repeated, "that was almost human."

"Ridiculous," said D. L. Conrad, an accountant who had passed out cards to several of his pals of the pool room. "Who ever heard of such a thing? How can a horse be almost human?"

"Let me explain," said Willie with the imperial air of a duke addressing a peasant. "It is characteristic of human beings to compete, is it not? In athletics. In commerce. In life itself."

"Granted," said Mr. Conrad, the accountant. "But what has that to do with *Mr. Goober,* or whoever it was you mentioned?"

"Allow me," said Willie impatiently. "If you will let me proceed for a moment, you will soon know. Now then: I said *Mr. Goofus* was almost human. I mean just that. There was a horse that had the soul of a man. In short, he was vicious. He was a bully. Don't interrupt me. If *Mr. Goofus* was leading the field and another horse tried to overtake him, why, he would turn around and bite the horse. It made him mad to have another horse pass him. He didn't like it. Of course they disqualified him a couple of times, but that didn't matter. He had all the horses scared, and it wasn't often they would try to get in front of him. He had a terrible eye, they say. One look and it was all over. *Mr. Goofus* won a lot of races and he beat horses that were much faster than him. You've got to work on horse personalities. That is an element almost always overlooked by handicappers. Psychology. Horses have it. No use being oldfashioned. There isn't a single race horse that hasn't better breeding than the average man. You can't expect such beasts to remain uncivilized for long. They're bound to get vicious after a while."

"Nuts," said Mr. Conrad with a laugh. "A horse is a horse. Tell me who's going to win the third at Arlington and we'll have a beer together."

"I do *not* tout," said Willie with pride. "I like *Miss Universe.*"

Mr. Conrad made an ugly face. "Why," he said, "that horse has started eleven times in the past month and hasn't once been better than sixth."

"I know," said Willie. "I am aware of the facts. Nevertheless, I like her just the same."

"I'm playing *Polly's Folly,*" said Mr. Conrad. This horse was a hot favorite; her odds were a paltry six to five to win, whereas the odds on *Miss Universe* were twenty to one. Nevertheless, Willie said:

"I hope you have luck."

Willie sat at a table and produced his note-book and a pencil. Under the classification "Tired Horses" he wrote the name *Polly's Folly.* Among other names under this classification was that of the great *Equipoise.* In Willie's humble estimation this horse was tired of everything; of winning, of racing, of the whole routine in general. Let it be known then that Willie, himself a superior by nature, disliked superior horses and cherished fondly those whom most bettors despised. For example, of the millions of pony-players in America he alone had hopes for the ultimate success of the two-year-old maiden *Miss Universe.* To Willie this horse was not merely another horse. She was something more subtle, more mystical. Along with the success of *Miss Universe* would date the success of Willie himself. She was his pet. He loved her passionately. He had a special alibi for each of her miserable performances, a psychological alibi. Also: the name was beautiful. It was poetry. No other horse in the history of racing had had such a glorious name. Such a horse could not fail. It would be unnatural.

Mr. Levin, called *The Barrel,* also had a system. It was externally more complicated than Willie's, but a good deal less subtle. Willie's system was centrifugal, working outward from the brain, the soul, and the personality of the horse. The hub of Mr. Levin's system was the great panorama of the earth itself. To him the horses were mere puppets, helpless and a bit foolish. His desire was to discover the dark secrets of owners, jockies, and wise gamblers. His system took into consideration all the physical facts involved in a race: the distance, the weight and talent of the jockey, the tendencies of the owner and trainer of the horse, the weather at the track, the weather in Iowa, the number of people at the track, carload shipments of raw products, progress of the N R A, the state of his own private stomach, and the amount of money on the person being touted.

In short, everything.

Mr. Levin was a drab realist while Willie was a mystic.

Which brings my document (for this is a document, as I shall soon show) to the case of M. San Jose Red. I have said he was a thin, nervous person of sixty-five. Do not imagine, however, that San Jose Red was an old man, for he was not. (A young man once addressed him innocently as "Pop" and was severely reprimanded for the indelicacy. "Don't call me Pop," said San Jose Red. "I don't like it. I go out of this joint every day with five hundred dollars.") This was a preposterous exaggeration, but San Jose Red apparently had the idea that if a man made money on the races he could not possibly be old. He had the slim figure of a boy, the voice of a boy, and, alas, the sense of one. He was Irish. He was angry. He puffed at his pipe with defiance. He uttered one fantastic falsehood after another, innocently, sinlessly, since he himself believed his most atrocious lies. He was never known to have a dime. Nevertheless, he maintained vigorously that he won no less than five hundred dollars per week, net. If you got him angry enough he announced, as I have already said, that he earned this sum *every* day. He was extravagantly careless with these sums, and threw vast figures about him with the heedlessness of the born spend thrift. Nothing definite was known about him, though from his name it is to be inferred that at one time he lived in or near the city of San Jose, sixty miles south of San Francisco, in Santa Clara Valley.

San Jose Red also had a system. It was the laughing stock of The Kentucky Pool Room, but San Jose Red believed in it implicitly.

After every race this fiery old codger would swiftly scribble the name of the winner on a small sheet of cardboard, and, flourishing this document wildly, rush through the crowd, grumbling insanely, but with a beatific smile on his magnificent Irish face, "See? *Black Patricia.* I told you. Why, I picked that horse last night." And then he would go on to tell a stranger how much he cleaned up every day.

This system of course is nothing short of infallible; in fact, it is a good deal more than infallible, for there has not yet been a horse race in which at least one horse has not won. Under the circumstances, it must be designated a philosophical (and perhaps scientific) system, and San Jose Red must be identified as both a philosopher and a scientist, something in the nature of Albert Einstein with a bit of Oscar Spengler, Walter Lippman, and the Associated Press thrown in for good measure. His philosophy accelerates on this scientific basis: one waits until a thing happens, and then declares that it happened. You can't go wrong; science, statistics, legal documents, and everything else is on your side. It is, in its way, the only system known to man worth a tinker's toot, or whatever it is. But you've got to be unimaginative to fool with it. Or else, like San Jose Red, you've got to believe in the retrogression of events. In plainer terms, you've got to confuse the outcome of an event with the state of affairs immediately preceding the outcome. Or in still simpler terms, you've got—well, you've got to be sixty-five and Irish and broke and angry and frustrated and mad at the world. You've got to give yourself all the odds, a million to one, or to use figures generally related to the age of light years (or something), sixty trillion to one.

Now, perhaps, you are beginning to see that this *is* a document, and a profound one at that; a document with stupendous implications. For the unsubtle reader, and for children, I shall hint one of the implications.

Gambling, betting on horses, among other things, is a way of life. The manner in which a man chooses to gamble indicates his character or his lack of it. In short, gambling is a game, a philosophy, just as in Spain bull fighting is these things, as Mr. Hemingway has pointed out in five hundred pages of small print and two or three dozen photographs. Of course this document would be richer if I accompanied it with photographs of San Jose Red, Mr. Levin, and Willie in various poses and at various crucial moments. I should like to have you see, for instance, an actual photographic reproduction of

San Jose Red frantically flourishing the name of the latest winner, or one of Mr. Levin standing humbly behind his belly telling a boy of eighteen how to play the ponies, or yet another of Willie in his elegantly-pressed twelve-dollar suit elucidating on the subtle make-up of horse-brains; but I regret that I cannot produce these pictures. Not that these men are not real flesh-and-blood people (You can go down to number One Opera Alley any day and see for yourself that they are), but that the light in The Kentucky Pool Room is dim indeed, and furthermore that my camera lies now in hock.

My document ought, properly, to end at this point, but such an ending would be artless. Subscribers to this magazine would write letters to the editor complaining; one or two would cancel their subscriptions. "What sort of a story do you call that?" readers would be saying to themselves. "No plot, no outcome, no climax, nothing exciting."

All right then. I will proceed to a plot. I will manufacture an outcome, a climax, and produce excitement. (Mind you, nothing ever happens at The Kentucky Pool Room. Bets are made, a few lucky fellows collect, but in the long run everybody loses. These are the facts. Day in and day out Willie and Mr. Levin and San Jose Red arrive and wait for the races, but nothing ever happens, so if I make a tale, it is not my fault, but the fault of art.)

Well, Willie is sitting at a table. The next race is the third at Arlington. Mr. Levin is rolling a cigarette of borrowed paper and tobacco. While he does so he is telling the man from whom he has borrowed the tobacco that a horse named *Wacoche* is going to win the race. "He's going to win by six lengths," says Mr. Levin, feeling miserable and lonely.

San Jose Red is out of sight. He comes in after the race. No one knows where he goes between races, but he is always out of sight until the winner is announced.

Let the matter rest here for a moment. Anyone can see for himself that any number of tales are now possible. I could say, for instance, as a young man once actually said, speaking of himself, that Willie, in an idle moment, thrust his thumb and his forefinger into his upper right-hand vest pocket, an act of habit, and there felt a heavy coin, which instantly set his heart to beating and proved to be a *bona fide* American half dollar. I can go on to say that Willie rushed up to Smithy, the bookie-clerk, and bet the whole half dollar right on the nose of *Miss Universe,* and that furthermore *Miss Universe* came to life and won the race, thereby placing in Willie's neat trousers the vast sum of ten dollars. And I could continue, saying that Willie's luck, as he himself dreamed, began at this point and that from this meagre beginning in less than a week he became the possessor of four hundred and sixty-two dollars and eleven cents. I could say, for the sake of romance, that he was in love with a beautiful young stenographer who would not marry him until he earned enough money to buy a license and a cheap ring. And so on.

About Mr. Levin and San Jose Red I could say all sorts of things that would make this tale interesting and exciting, but, forgive me, I *cannot.* It is impossible for me to lie, even though Mr. Kipling has declared that writers can never lie, that even when they do so, they unconsciously reveal even more profound truths. But about these men I cannot make pastry. Their stories are exciting enough in themselves. Let us try to be content with the paltry romance which lies pathetically in the ugly truth.

So we return. It is Thursday. One twenty-four P.M. In about six minutes the third race at Arlington will be run.

There's the lay-out.

Now the fun begins.

I am strolling along Third Street, a melancholy-looking young writer seeking material for a tale. It is a bright day, the sun is warm, and even the forelorn men of this drab street seem to reflect the brightness of the day in their unshaved faces. I am idly eating California peaches, when suddenly I notice three men hurrying in quick succession through a narrow doorway marked "Cairo Club, Gentlemen." There is something exciting about their haste. I decide to find out where they are going and why. In less than half a minute another man passess swiftly and impatiently through the same portal. Then another. Then yet another. This last fellow is in a terrific hurry; he is nervously jingling two coins in his right hand. I follow him at a trot and find myself stampeding down a narrow and dark corridor, close on the heels of my guide. We make two turns, open as many doors, and finally emerge into the gloom of a paved crevice between the Winchester Hotel, Rooms 35c and Up, and the Westchester Hotel, same rates.

It is Opera Alley!

I read the sign "Number 1 Opera Alley" over the swinging doors of The Kentucky Pool Room, and hasten to enter. Number One Opera Alley is a large, dark, square room containing five tables, fourteen chairs, six benches, and thirteen spittoons; not to mention sixty-three men including Mr. Levin and Willie. (San Jose Red, as I have said, is out of sight for the moment.) I am there. I myself, the writer. I see that Mr. Levin is sadly longing for someone to tout. And I see Willie seated at the table, impeccable, his face glowing with lack of character, his entire physical being a picture of graceful lack of purpose. Still, he is the neatest person in the room, so I take the chair beside him.

In precisely four minutes and twelve seconds *Miss Universe,* in company with seven other horses, will begin to scramble around the track at Arlington Park, in Chicago. There is no time to lose, but I know absolutely nothing about horses or horse racing.

Fully fifteen seconds I do not hear so much as an idle word from the lips of my contemporary. (Nine out of ten gamblers are habitual talkers-to-themselves. But not Willie.) I decide to offer him a cigarette. He replies:

"Thank you, I do not smoke."

I am astounded. What character. What discipline. Not to smoke in that atmosphere of hope and dread and spiritual fidgetiness. It is incredible.

Although I am aware of what is going on, I say to Willie in order to make conversation:

"What is going on here, anyway?"

He looks at me with eyes that are suddenly transformed. I detect in them the roar and surge of great hope. I am, bluntly, a greenhorn, and perhaps after all Willie will be able to bet on *Miss Universe*— with *my* money. Nevertheless, he is a subtle performer.

"I beg your pardon?" he says with elegance.

I repeat my question and Willie relates to me the entire history of horse racing, the tricks of owners, the habits of jockeys, the idiosyncrasies of horses, and the thoughtlessness of most gamblers. And while he speaks with an air of great leisure, he nevertheless imparts all this information in something less than twenty seconds flat. A thoroughbred himself.

In the meantime I have dispatched my right hand to my vest pocket where it is timidly thrilling at the feel of my last dollar, the dollar which is to keep me with food in my stomach another long week.

By this time, I have developed implicit confidence in the mystical omnipotence, etcetera, of Willie, and am itching to have him make a bet for me.

"There is one horse in this race," says Willie, "that is all but human. She hates to lose; it breaks her heart. She has been trying for all she's worth and today's her day. She is the daughter of *Lady Venus* by *The Wop,* and you know what *Lady Venus* did."

Of course I have no idea what *Lady Venus* did, and I say so.

"Everything," says Willie. "She did everything."

"Well," I say, "who is the horse?"

Willie bends to whisper into my ear, so that no one will learn the good news. *"Miss Universe,"* he says passionately.

"God, what a beautiful name," I think, and the next thing I know I have given Willie my last dollar. He rushes up to Smithy, the bookie-clerk, and plasters it on the nose of *Miss Universe*—and none too soon either, for no sooner had Smithy scribbled the bet on a slip than the race began.

You see, everything worked perfectly and precisely.

Well, there I am in The Kentucky Pool Room, and about two thousand miles away, in Chicago, eight horses are running around a track, one of them *Miss Universe.* And there beside me is Willie, neat and clean, piously hopeful.

"A beautiful name," I keep thinking. "A glorious name."

The phone clerk calls: "At the quarter: *Stock Market, Dark Mist, Fiddler."* This means these horses are leading the field in the order named.

Willie is pale. I'm paler. Willie says, "She's running fourth. She starts slow but she'll come up." Then for an instant he is overcome and shouts to himself "Come on, *Miss Universe!"*

I do the same.

The phone clerk announces: "At the half: *Stock Market, Dark Mist, Fiddler."*

Willie is a little paler. I'm just a shade paler than he is.

"Her mother," Willie gasps, "lost eleven races before she got out in front. This is *Miss Universe's* eleventh race. You watch her tear loose in a minute."

The phone clerk, his voice rising (he knows everyone is excited and he wants to be sympathetic; he knows small histories are being made and unmade; he is not heartless and he *can* shout), shouts:

"At the three-quarters: *Stock Market,* a neck, *Fiddler,* a half-length, *Dark Mist* five lengths."

"*Cute Face* is running fourth," he declares apologetically.

Willie is visibly nervous and a bit paler than before. I resemble a well-dressed ghost.

"Come on, *Miss Universe,*" Willie whispers madly.

"Yes," I say to myself. "Come on, darling, please come on, please, please, that's all the money I have and I have a terrible appetite."

It was a prayer, I admit. All horse-bettors are religious.

The phone clerk pauses dramatically and shouts:

"This next is the winner."

Then he says:

"Number 57, *Fiddler,* wins—by a neck. 51, *Stock Market* is second—by three lengths. 53, *Dark Mist* is third."

There you have it: the story. Nothing added, nothing taken away, like pure mayonnaise.

But wait: what's this. A madman is tearing through the crowd. He is small and Irish, and he is shouting, "See. Didn't I tell you? *Fiddler. Fiddler.* Why, I had him picked last night." He is holding a slip of cardboard on which is written the name of the horse.

It is San Jose Red, but of course you knew it.

Willie is ill with disappointment. He falls exhausted into a chair.

"I'm sorry," he says. "Her father was never much to speak of."

"It's all right," I reply.

Now I am walking up Third Street with an empty pocket, and I am telling myself, "There is still half a loaf of rye bread, a quarter pound of coffee, a bit of cheese, and eleven cigarettes. *Miss Universe.* What a beautiful name. If I have one slice of bread twice a day and a cup of coffee for breakfast—well, I can make it, I suppose."

[December 1934]

ERNEST HEMINGWAY

The Horns of the Bull

Madrid is full of boys named Paco, which is the diminutive of the name Francisco, and there is a Madrid joke about a father who came to Madrid and inserted an advertisement in the personal columns of *El Liberal* which said *Paco meet me at Hotel Montana noon Tuesday all is forgiven papa* and how a squadron of Guardia Civil had to be called out to disperse the eight hundred young men who answered the advertisement. But this Paco, who waited on table at the Pension Luarca, had no father to forgive him nor anything for the father to forgive. He had two older sisters who were chambermaids at the Luarca, who had gotten their place through coming from the same small village as a former Luarca chambermaid who had proven hardworking and honest and hence given her village and its products a good name, and these sisters had paid his way on the auto-bus to Madrid and gotten him his job as an apprentice waiter.

He came from a village in a part of Extremadura where conditions were incredibly primitive, food scarce and comforts unknown, and he had worked hard ever since he could remember. He was a well built boy with very black, rather curly hair, good teeth and a skin that his sisters envied and he had a ready and unpuzzled smile. He was fast on his feet and did his work well and he loved his sisters, who seemed beautiful and sophisticated, he loved Madrid, which was still an unbelievable place, and he loved his work which, done under bright lights, with clean linen, the wearing of evening clothes, and abundant food in the kitchen, seemed romatically beautiful.

There were from eight to a dozen other people who lived at the Luarca and ate in the dining room but for Paco, the youngest of the three waiters who served at table, the only ones who really existed were the bull fighters.

Second rate matadors lived at that pension because the address in the Calle San Jeronimo was good, the food was excellent and the room and board was cheap. It is necessary for a bull fighter to give the appearance, if not of prosperity, at least of respectability since decorum and dignity rank above courage as the virtues most highly prized in Spain, and bull fighters stayed at the Luarca until their last pesetas were gone. There is no record of any bull fighter having left the Luarca for a better or more expensive hotel; second rate bull fighters never become first rate; but the descent from the Luarca was swift since anyone could stay there who was making anything at all and a bill was never presented to a guest unasked until the woman who ran the place knew that the case was hopeless.

At this time there were three full matadors living at the Luarca as well as two very good picadors, and one excellent banderillero. The Luarca was luxury for the picadors and the banderilleros, who, with their families in Seville, required lodging in Madrid during the spring season; but they were well paid and in the fixed employ of fighters who were heavily contracted during the coming season, and the three of these subalterns would probably make much more apiece than any of the three matadors. Of the three matadors one was ill and trying to conceal it; one had passed his short vogue as a novelty, and the third was a coward.

The coward had at one time, until he had received a peculiarly atrocious horn wound in the lower abdomen at the start of his first season as a full matador, been exceptionally brave and remarkably skillful, and he still had many of the hearty mannerisms of his days of success. He was jovial to excess and laughed constantly with and without provocation. He had, when successful, been very addicted to practical jokes but he had given them up now. They took an assurance that he did not feel. This matador had an intelligent, very open face and he carried himself with much style.

The matador who was ill was careful never to show it and was meticulous about eating a little of all the dishes that were presented at the table. He had a great many handkerchiefs which he laundered himself in his room and, lately, he had been selling his fighting suits. He had sold one, cheaply, before Christmas and another in the first week of April. They had been very expensive suits, had always been well kept and he had one more. Before he had become ill he had been a very promising, even a sensational, fighter and, while he himself could not read, he had clippings which said that in his debut in Madrid he had been better than Belmonte. He ate alone at a small table and looked up very little.

The matador who had once been a novelty was very short and brown and dignified. He also ate alone at a separate table and he smiled rarely and never laughed. He came from Valladolid, where the people are extremely serious, and he was a capable matador, but his style had become old-fashioned before he had ever succeeded in endearing himself to the public through his virtues, which were courage and a calm capability, and his name on a poster would draw no one to a bull ring. His novelty had been that he was so short that he could barely see over the bull's withers, but there were other short fighters, and he had never succeeded in imposing himself on the public's fancy.

Of the picadors one was a thin, hawk-faced, gray-haired man, lightly built but with legs and arms like iron who always wore cattleman's boots under his trousers, drank too much every evening and gazed amorously at any woman in the pension. The other was huge, dark, brown-faced, good-looking, with black hair like an Indian and enormous hands. Both were great picadors although the first was reputed to have lost much of his ability through drink and dissipation, and the second was said to be too headstrong and quarrelsome to stay with any matador more than a single season.

The banderillero was middle-aged, grey, short, cat-quick in spite of his years, and, sitting at table reading the paper, looked a moderately prosperous business man. His legs were still good for this season and when they should go he was intelligent and experienced enough to keep regularly employed for a long time. The difference would be that when his speed of foot would be gone he would always be frightened where now he was assured and calm in the ring and out of it.

On this evening everyone had left the dining room except the hawk-faced picador who drank too much, the birth-marked faced auctioneer of watches at the fairs and festivals of Spain, who also drank too much, and two priests from Galacia who were sitting at a corner table and drinking, while not too much perhaps enough. At that time wine was included in the price of the room and board at the Luarca and the waiters had just brought a fresh bottle of Valdepeñas to the tables of the auctioneer, then to the picador and finally to the two priests.

The three waiters stood at the end of the room. It was the rule of the house that they should all remain on duty until the diners whose tables they were responsible for should all have left, but the one who served the table of the two priests had an appointment to go to an Anarcho-Syndicalist meeting and Paco had agreed to take over his table for him.

Upstairs the matador who was ill was lying face down on his bed alone. The matador who was no longer a novelty was sitting looking out of his window preparatory to walking out to the café. The matador who was now a coward had the older sister of Paco in his room with him and was trying to get her to do something which she was laughingly refusing to do. This matador was saying "Come on little savage."

"No," said the sister. "Why should I?"

"For a favor."

"You've eaten and now you want me for dessert."

"Just once. What harm can it do?"

"Leave me alone. Leave me alone I tell you."

"It is a very little thing to do."

"Leave me alone I tell you."

Down in the dining room the tallest of the waiters, who was overdue at the meeting, said "Look at those black pigs drink."

"That's no way to speak," said the second waiter. "They are decent clients. They do not drink too much."

"For me it is a good way to speak," said the tall one. "There are the two curses of Spain, the bulls and the priests."

"Certainly not the individual bull and the individual priest," said the second waiter.

"Yes," said the tall waiter. "Only through the individual can you attack the class. It is necessary to kill the individual bull and the individual priest. All of them. Then there are no more."

"Save it for the meeting," said the other waiter.

"Look at the barbarity of Madrid," said the tall waiter. "It is now half-past eleven o'clock and these are still guzzling."

"They only started to eat at ten," said the other waiter. "As you know there are many dishes. That wine is cheap and these have paid for it. It is not strong wine."

"How can there be solidarity of workers with fools like you?" asked the tall waiter.

"Look," said the second waiter who was a man of fifty. "I have worked all my life. In all that remains of my life I must work. I have no complaints against work. To work is normal."

"Yes, but the lack of work kills."

"I have always worked," said the old waiter. "Go on to the meeting. There is no necessity to stay."

"You are a good comrade," said the tall waiter. "But you lack all ideology."

"Mejor si me faltan eso que el otro," said the older waiter (meaning it is better to lack *that* than work). "Go on to the *mitin."*

Paco had said nothing. He did not yet understand politics but it always gave him a thrill to hear the tall waiter speak of the necessity for killing the priests and the Guardia Civil. The tall waiter represented to him Revolution and revolution also was romantic. He himself would like to be a good Catholic, a revolutionary, and have a steady job like this while, at the same time, being a bull fighter.

"Go on to the meeting Ignacio," he said. "I will respond for your work."

"The two of us," said the older waiter.

"There isn't enough for one," said Paco. "Go on to the meeting."

"Pues me voy," said the tall waiter. "And thanks."

In the meantime, upstairs, the sister of Paco had gotten out of the embrace of the matador as skillfully as a wrestler breaking a hold and said now angry, "These are the hungry people. A failed bull fighter. With your tonload of fear. If you have so much of that use it in the ring."

"That is the way a *puta* talks."

"A *puta* also is a woman, but I am not a *puta."*

"You'll be one."

"Not through you."

"Leave me," said the matador who, now, repulsed and refused, felt the nakedness of his cowardice returning.

"Leave you? What hasn't left you?" said the sister. "Don't you want me to make up the bed? I'm paid to do that."

"Leave me," said the matador, his broad good-looking face wrinkled into a contortion that was like crying. *"Puta."*

"Matador," she said, shutting the door. "My matador."

Inside the room the matador sat on the bed. His face still had the contortion which, in the ring, he made into a constant smile which frightened those people in the first rows of seats who knew what they were watching. "And this," he was saying aloud. "And this! And this!"

He could remember when he had been good and it had only been three years before. He could remember the weight of the heavy fighting jacket on his shoulders on that hot afternoon in May when his voice had still been the same in the ring as in the café, and how he sighted along the point dipping blade at the place in the top of the shoulders where it was dusty in the short-haired, black hump of muscle above the wide, wood-knocking, splintered-tipped horns that lowered as he went in to kill, and how the sword pushed in as easy as into a mound of stiff butter with the palm of his hand pushing the pommel, his left arm crossed low, his left shoulder forward, his weight on his left leg, and then his weight wasn't on his leg. His weight was on his lower belly and as the bull raised his head the horn was out of sight in him and he swung over on it twice before they pulled him off it. So now when he went in to kill, and it was seldom, he could not look at the horns and what did any *puta* know about what he went through before he fought? And what had they been through that laughed at him? They were all *putas.*

Down in the dining room the picador sat looking at the priests. If there were women in the room he stared at them. If there were no women he would stare with enjoyment at a foreigner, *un ingles,* but lacking women or strangers he now stared with enjoyment and insolence at the two priests. While he stared the birth-marked auctioneer rose and folding his napkin went out, leaving over half of the wine in the last bottle he had ordered. If his accounts had been paid up at the Luarca he would have finished the bottle.

The two priests did not stare back at the picador. One of them was saying, "It is ten days since I have been here and all day I sit in the ante-chamber and he will not receive me."

"What is there to do?"

"Nothing. What can one do? One cannot go against authority."

"I have been here for two weeks and nothing."

"We are from the abandoned country. When the travel money runs out we can return."

"To the abandoned country."

"One understands the action of our brother Basilio."

"Madrid is where one learns to understand. Madrid kills Spain."

"If they would simply see one and refuse."

"No. You must be broken and worn out by waiting."

"Well we shall see. I can wait as well as another."

At this moment the picador got to his feet, walked over to the priests' table and stood, greyheaded and hawk-faced, staring at them and smiling.

"A *torero,*" said one to the other.

"And a good one," said the picador and walked out of the dining room, grey-jacketed, trim-waisted, bow-legged, in tight breeches over his cattleman's boots that clicked on the floor as he swaggered quite steadily, smiling to himself. He lit a cigar and tilting his hat at an angle in the hallway went out to the café

The priests left immediately after the picador, hurriedly conscious of being the last people in the dining room, and there was no one in the room now but Paco and the middle-aged waiter. They cleared the tables and carried the bottles into the kitchen.

In the kitchen was the boy who washed the dishes. He was three years older than Paco and was very cynical and bitter.

"Take this," the middle-aged waiter said and poured out a glass of the Valdepeñas and handed it to him.

"Why not?" the boy took the glass.

"*Tu,* Paco?" the older waiter asked.

"Thank you," said Paco.

The three of them drank.

"I will be going," said the middle-aged waiter.

"Good night," they told him.

He went out and they were alone. Paco took a napkin one of the priests had used and standing straight, his heels planted, lowered the napkin and, with head following the movement, swung his arms in the motion of a slow sweeping veronica. He turned and, advancing his right foot slightly, made the second pass, gained a little terrain on the imaginary bull and made a third pass, slow, perfectly timed and suave, then gathered the napkin to his waist and swung his hips away from the bull in a media-veronica.

The dishwasher, whose name was Enrique, watched this critically and sneeringly.

"How is the bull?" he said.

"Very brave," said Paco. "Look."

Standing slim and straight he made four more perfect passes, smooth, elegant and graceful.

"And the bull?" asked Enrique standing against the sink, holding his wine glass and wearing his apron.

"Still has lots of gas," said Paco.

"You make me sick," said Enrique.

"Why?"

"Look." Enrique removed his apron and citing the imaginary bull he sculptured four perfect, languid, gypsy veronicas and ended up with a rebolera that made the apron swing in a stiff arc past the bull's nose as he walked away from him.

"Look at that," he said. "And I wash dishes."

"Why?"

"Fear," said Enrique. *"Miedo.* The same fear you would have in a ring with a bull."

"No," said Paco. "I wouldn't be afraid."

"Mierde," said Enrique, "everyone is afraid. But a torero can control his fear so that he can work the bull. I went in, in an amateur fight and I was so afraid I couldn't keep from running. Everyone thought it was very funny. So would you be afraid. If it wasn't for fear every bootblack in Spain would be a bull fighter. You, a country boy, would be frightened worse than I was."

"No," said Paco. He had done it too many times in his imagination.

Too many times he had seen the horns, seen the bull's wet muzzle, the ear twitching, then the head go down and the charge, the hoofs thudding, and the hot bulk pass him as he swung the cape, to re-charge as he swung the cape again, then again, and again, and again, to end winding the bull around him in his great media-veronica, and walk swingingly away with bull hairs caught in the gold ornaments of his jacket from the close passes, the bull standing hypnotized and the crowd applauding. No, he would not be afraid.

Others, yes. Not him. He knew he would not be afraid. Even if he ever was afraid he knew that he could do it anyway. He had confidence. "I wouldn't be afraid," he said.

Enrique said the word again that meant contempt. Then he said, "If we should try it?"

"How?"

"Look," said Enrique. "You think of the bull, but you do not think of the horns. The bull has such force that the horns rip like a knife, they stab like a bayonet, and they kill like a club. Look," he opened a table drawer and took out two meat knives. "I will bind these to the legs of a chair. Then I will play bull for you with the chair held before my head. The knives are the horns. If you make those passes then they mean something."

"Lend me your apron," said Paco. "We'll do it in the dining room."

"No," said Enrique, suddenly not bitter. "Don't do it Paco."

"Yes," said Paco. "I'm not afraid."

"You will be when you see the knives come."

"We'll see," said Paco. "Give me the apron."

At this time while Enrique was binding the two heavy-bladed razor-sharp meat knives fast to the legs of the chair with two soiled napkins holding the half of each knife, wrapping them tight and then knotting them, the two chambermaids, Paco's sisters, were on their way to the cinema to see Greta Garbo in *Anna Christie*. Of the two priests, one was sitting in his underwear reading his missal and the other was wearing a night shirt and saying the rosary. All the bull fighters except the one who was ill had made their evening appearance at the Café Fornos where the big, dark-haired picador was playing billiards. The short serious matador was sitting at a crowded table before a coffee and milk, along with the middle-aged banderillero and other serious workmen.

The drinking, grey-headed picador was sitting with a glass of cazalas brandy before him staring with pleasure at a table where the matador whose courage was gone sat with another matador, who had renounced the sword, to become a banderillero again, and two very house-worn looking prostitutes. The auctioneer stood on the street corner talking with friends. The tall waiter was at the Anarcho-Syndicalist meeting waiting for an opportunity to speak. The middle-aged waiter was seated on the terrace of the Cervezeria Alvarez drinking a small beer. The woman who owned the Luarca was already asleep in her bed where she lay on her back with the bolster between her legs, big, fat, honest, clean, easy-going, very religious and never having ceased to miss or pray daily for her husband dead, now, twenty years. In his room, alone, the matador who was ill lay face down on his bed with his mouth against a handkerchief.

Now, in the deserted dining room, Enrique tied the last knot in the napkins that bound the knives to the chair legs and lifted the chair. He pointed the legs with the knives on them forward and held the chair over his head with the two knives pointing straight ahead, one on each side of his head.

"It's heavy," he said. "Look Paco. It is very dangerous. Don't do it." He was sweating.

Paco stood facing him, holding the apron spread, holding a fold of it bunched in each hand, thumbs up, first finger down, spread to catch the eye of the bull.

"Charge straight," he said. "Turn like a bull. Charge as many times as you want."

"How will you know when to cut the pass?" asked Enrique. "It's better to do three and then a media."

"All right," said Paco. "But come straight. Huh torito! Come on little bull!"

Running with head down Enrique came toward him and Paco swung the apron just ahead of the knife blade as it passed close in front of his belly and, as it went by, it was, to him, the real horn, white tipped, black, smooth and as Enrique passed him and turned to rush again it was the hot, blood-flanked mass of the bull that thudded by, then whirled like a cat and came again as he swung the cape slowly. Then the bull turned again and, as he watched the onrushing point, he stepped his left foot two inches too far forward and the knife did not pass but had slipped in as easily as into a wine skin and there was a hot scalding rush above and around the sudden inner rigidity of steel and Enrique shouting, "Ay! Ay! Let me get it out! Let me get it out!" and Paco slipped forward on the chair, the apron cape still held, Enrique pulling on the chair as the knife turned in him, in him, Paco.

The knife was out now and he sat on the floor in the widening warm pool.

"Put the napkin over it. Hold it!" said Enrique. "Hold it tight. I will run for the doctor. You must hold in the hemorrhage!"

"There should be a rubber cup," said Paco. He had seen that used in the ring.

"I came straight," said Enrique, crying. "All I wanted was to show the danger."

"Don't worry," said Paco. "But bring the doctor! Bring, bring the doctor."

In the ring they lifted you and carried you, running with you, to the operating room. If the femoral artery emptied itself before you reached there they called the priest.

"Advise one of the priests," said Paco holding the napkin tight against his lower abdomen. He could not believe that this had happened to him, nor did his voice sound his own.

But Enrique was running down the Carrera San Jeronimo to the first aid station and Paco was alone, all through it, first sitting up, then huddled over, then slumped on the floor, until it was over, feeling his life go out of him as water empties from a bathtub when the plug is drawn. He was frightened and he felt faint and he tried to say an act of contrition and he remembered how it started but before he had said, as fast as he could, "Oh my God I am heartily sorry for having offended Thee who art worthy of all my love and I firmly resolve—" he felt too faint and could not remember and he was lying face down on the floor. It was over very quickly. A severed femoral artery empties itself faster than you can believe.

As the doctor from the first aid station came up the stairs accompanied by a policeman who held on to Enrique by the arm, the two sisters of Paco were still in the moving picture palace of the Gran Via where they were intensely disappointed in the Garbo film which showed the great star in miserable low surroundings when they had been accustomed to see her surrounded by great luxury and brilliance. The audience disliked the film thoroughly and were protesting by whistling and stamping their feet. All the other people from the hotel were doing almost what they had been doing when the accident happened, except that the two priests had finished their devotions and were preparing for sleep, and the grey-haired picador had moved his drink over to the table with the two houseworn prostitutes. A little later he went out of the café with one of them. It was the one for whom the matador who had lost his nerve had been buying drinks.

The boy Paco had never known about any of this nor about what all these people would be doing on the next day and on other days to come. He died, as the Spanish phrase has it, full of illusions. He had not had time to lose any of them nor even time to complete an act of contrition. He had not even had time to be disappointed in the Garbo picture which disappointed all Madrid for a week.

[June 1936]

F. SCOTT FITZGERALD

An Alcoholic Case

"Let—go—that—oh-h-h! Please, now, will you? *Don't* start drinking again! Come on—give me the bottle. I told you I'd stay awake givin it to you. Come on. If you do like that a-way—then what are goin to be like when you go home. Come on—leave it with me—I'll leave half in the bottle. Pul-lease. You know what Dr. Carter says—I'll stay awake and give it to you, or else fix some of it in the bottle—come on—like I told you, I'm too tired to be fightin you all night. . . . All right, drink your fool self to death."

"Would you like some beer?" he asked.

"No, I don't want any beer. Oh, to think that I have to look at you drunk again. My God!"

"Then I'll drink the Coca-Cola."

The girl sat down panting on the bed.

"Don't you believe in anything?" she demanded.

"Nothing you believe in—please—it'll spill."

She had no business there, she thought, no business trying to help him. Again they struggled, but after this time he sat with his head in his hands awhile, before he turned around once more.

"Once more you try to get it I'll throw it down," she said quickly. "I will—on the tiles in the bathroom."

"Then I'll step on the broken glass—or you'll step on it."

"Then let go—oh you promised—"

Suddenly she dropped it like a torpedo, sliding underneath her hand and slithering with a flash of red and black and the words: SIR GALAHAD, DISTILLED LOUISVILLE GIN.

It was on the floor in pieces and everything was silent for awhile and she read *Gone With the Wind* about things so lovely that had happened long ago. She began to worry that he would have to go into the bathroom and might cut his feet, and looked up from time to time to see if he would go in. She was very sleepy—the last time she looked up he was crying and he looked like an old Jewish man she had nursed once in California; he had had to go to the bathroom many times. On this case she was unhappy all the time but she thought:

"I guess if I hadn't liked him I wouldn't have stayed on the case."

With a sudden resurgence of conscience she got up and put a chair in front of the bathroom door. She had wanted to sleep because he had got her up early that morning to get a paper with the Yale-Harvard game in it and she hadn't been home all day. That afternoon a relative of his had come in to see him and she had waited outside in the hall where there was a draft with no sweater to put over her uniform.

As well as she could she arranged him for sleeping, put a robe over his shoulders as he sat slumped over his chiffonier, and one on his knees. She sat down in the rocker but she was no longer sleepy; there was plenty to enter on the chart and treading lightly about she found a pencil and put it down:

Pulse 120

Respiration 25

Temp 98—98.4—98.2

Remarks—

—She could make so many:

Tried to get bottle of gin. Threw it away and broke it.

She corrected it to read:

In the struggle it dropped and was broken. Patient was generally difficult.

She started to add as part of her report: *I never want to go on an alcoholic case again,* but that wasn't in the picture. She knew she could wake herself at seven and clean up everything before his niece awakened. It was all part of the game. But when she sat down in the chair she looked at his face, white and exhausted, and counted his breathing again, wondering why it had all happened. He had been so nice today, drawn her a whole strip of his cartoon just for the fun and given it to her. She was going to have it framed and hang it in her room. She felt again his thin wrists wrestling against her wrist and re-membered the awful things he had said, and she thought too of what the doctor had said to him yesterday:

"You're too good a man to do this to yourself."

She was tired and didn't want to clean up the glass on the bath-room floor, because as soon as he breathed evenly she wanted to get him over to the bed. But she decided finally to clean up the glass first; on her knees, searching a last piece of it, she thought:

—This isn't what I ought to be doing. And this isn't what *he* ought to be doing.

Resentfully she stood up and regarded him. Through the thin delicate profile of his nose came a light snore, sighing, remote, incon-solable. The doctor had shaken his head in a certain way, and she knew that really it was a case that was beyond her. Besides, on her card at the agency was written, on the advice of her elders, "No Alco-holics."

She had done her whole duty, but all she could think of was that when she was struggling about the room with him with that gin bottle there had been a pause when he asked her if she had hurt her elbow against a door and that she had answered: "You don't know how people talk about you, no matter how you think of your-self—" when she knew he had a long time ceased to care about such things.

The glass was all collected—as she got out a broom to make sure, she realized that the glass, in its fragments, was less than a window through which they had seen each other for a moment. He did not know about her sisters, and Bill Markoe whom she had almost mar-ried, and she did not know what had brought him to this pitch, when there was a picture on his bureau of his young wife and his two sons and him, all trim and handsome as he must have been five years ago. It was so utterly senseless—as she put a bandage on her finger where she had cut it while picking up the glass she made up her mind she would never take an alcoholic case again.

II

Some Halloween jokester had split the side windows of the bus and she shifted back to the Negro section in the rear for fear the glass might fall out. She had her patient's check but no way to cash it at this time of night; there was a quarter and a penny in her purse.

Two nurses she knew were waiting in the hall of Mrs. Hixson's Agency.

"What kind of case have you been on?"

"Alcoholic," she said.

"Oh yes—Gretta Hawks told me about it—you were on with that cartoonist who lives at the Forest Park Inn."

"Yes, I was."

"I hear he's pretty fresh."

"He's never done anything to bother me," she lied. "You can't treat them as if they were committed—"

"Oh, don't get bothered—I just heard that around town—oh, you know—they want you to play around with them—"

"Oh, be quiet," she said, surprised at her own rising resentment.

In a moment Mrs. Hixson came out and, asking the other two to wait, signaled her into the office.

"I don't like to put young girls on such cases," she began. "I got your call from the hotel."

"Oh, it wasn't bad, Mrs. Hixson. He didn't know what he was doing, and he didn't hurt me in any way. I was thinking much more of my reputation with you. He was really nice all day yesterday. He drew me—"

"I didn't want to send you on that case." Mrs. Hixson thumbed through the registration cards. "You take T.B. cases, don't you? Yes. I see you do. Now here's one—"

The phone rang in a continuous chime. The nurse listened as Mrs. Hixson's voice said precisely:

"I will do what I can—that is simply up to the doctor. . . . That is beyond my jurisdiction. . . . Oh, hello, Hattie, no, I can't now. Look, have you got any nurse that's good with alcoholics? There's somebody up at the Forest Park Inn who needs somebody. Call back, will you?"

She put down the receiver. "Suppose you wait outside. What sort of man is this, anyhow? Did he act indecently?"

"He held my hand away," she said, "so I couldn't give him an injection."

"Oh, an invalid he-man," Mrs. Hixson grumbled. "They belong

in sanitaria. I've got a case coming along in two minutes that you can get a little rest on. It's an old woman—"

The phone rang again. "Oh, hello, Hattie. . . . Well, how about that big Svensen girl? She ought to be able to take care of any alcoholics. . . . How about Josephine Markham? Doesn't she live in your apartment house? . . . Get her to the phone." Then after a moment, "Jo, would you care to take the case of a well-known cartoonist, or artist, whatever they call themselves, at Forest Park Inn? . . . No, I don't know, but Doctor Carter is in charge and will be around about ten o'clock."

There was a long pause; from time to time Mrs. Hixson spoke: "I see. . . . Of course, I understand your point of view. Yes, but this isn't supposed to be dangerous—just a little difficult. I never like to send girls to a hotel because I know what riff-raff you're liable to run into. . . . No, I'll find somebody. Even at this hour. Never mind and thanks. Tell Hattie I hope the hat matches the negligee. . . ."

Mrs. Hixson hung up the receiver and made notations on the pad before her. She was a very efficient woman. She had been a nurse and had gone through the worst of it, had been a proud, realistic, overworked probationer, suffered the abuse of smart interns and the insolence of her first patients who thought that she was something to be taken into camp immediately for premature commitment to the service of old age. She swung around suddenly from the desk.

"What kind of cases do you want? I told you I have a nice old woman—"

The nurse's brown eyes were alight with a mixture of thoughts—the movie she had just seen about Pasteur and the book they had all read about Florence Nightingale when they were student nurses. And their pride, swinging across the streets in the cold weather at Philadelphia General, as proud of their new capes as debutantes in their furs going in to balls at the hotels.

"I—I think I would like to try the case again," she said amid a cacophony of telephone bells. "I'd just as soon go back if you can't find anybody else."

"But one minute you say you'll never go on an alcoholic case again and the next minute you say you want to go back to one."

"I think I overestimated how difficult it was. Really, I think I could help him."

"That's up to you. But if he tried to grab your wrists."

"But he couldn't," the nurse said. "Look at my wrists: I played basket ball at Waynesboro High for two years. I'm quite able to take care of him."

Mrs. Hixson looked at her for a long minute. "Well, all right," she said. "But just remember that nothing they say when they're drunk is what they mean when they're sober—I've been all through that; arrange with one of the servants that you can call on him, because you never can tell—some alcoholics are pleasant and some of them are not, but all of them can be rotten."

"I'll remember," the nurse said.

It was an oddly clear night when she went out, with slanting particles of thin sleet making white of a blue-black sky. The bus was the same that had taken her into town but there seemed to be more windows broken now and the bus driver was irritated and talked about what terrible things he would do if he caught any kids. She knew he was just talking about the annoyance in general, just as she had been thinking about the annoyance of an alcoholic. When she came up to the suite and found him all helpless and distraught she would despise him and be sorry for him.

Getting off the bus she went down the long steps to the hotel, feeling a little exalted by the chill in the air. She was going to take care of him because nobody else would, and because the best people of her profession had been interested in taking care of the cases that nobody else wanted.

She knocked at his study door, knowing just what she was going to say.

He answered it himself. He was in dinner clothes even to a derby hat—but minus his studs and tie.

"Oh, hello," he said casually. "Glad you're back. I woke up a while ago and decided I'd go out. Did you get a night nurse?"

"I'm the night nurse too," she said. "I decided to stay on twenty-hour duty."

He broke into a genial, indifferent smile.

"I saw you were gone, but something told me you'd come back. Please find my studs. They ought to be either in a little tortoise shell box or—"

He shook himself a little more into his clothes, and hoisted the cuffs up inside his coat sleeves.

"I thought you had quit me," he said casually.

"I thought I had, too."

"If you look on that table," he said, "you'll find a whole strip of cartoons that I drew you."

"Who are you going to see?" she asked.

"It's the President's secretary," he said. "I had an awful time trying to get ready. I was about to give up when you came in. Will you order me some sherry?"

"One glass," she agreed wearily.

From the bathroom he called presently:

"Oh, nurse, nurse, Light of my Life, where is another stud?"

"I'll put it in."

In the bathroom she saw the pallor and the fever on his face and smelled the mixed peppermint and gin on his breath.

"You'll come up soon?" she asked. "Dr. Carter's coming at ten."

"What nonsense! You're coming down with me."

"Me?" she exclaimed. "In a sweater and skirt? Imagine!"

"Then I won't go."

"All right then, go to bed. That's where you belong anyhow. Can't you see these people tomorrow?"

"No, of course not."

"Of course not!"

She went behind him and reaching over his shoulder tied his tie—his shirt was already thumbed out of press where he had put in the studs, and she suggested:

"Won't you put on another one, if you've got to meet some people you like?"

"All right, but I want to do it myself."

"Why can't you let me help you?" she demanded in exasperation. "Why can't you let me help you with your clothes? What's a nurse for—what good am I doing?"

He sat down suddenly on the toilet seat.

"All right—go on."

"Now don't grab my wrist," she said, and then, "Excuse me."

"Don't worry. It didn't hurt. You'll see in a minute."

She had the coat, vest and stiff shirt off him but before she could pull his undershirt over his head he dragged at his cigarette, delaying her.

"Now watch this," he said. "One—two—three."

She pulled up the undershirt; simultaneously he thrust the crimson-grey point of the cigarette like a dagger against his heart. It crushed out against a copper plate on his left rib about the size of a silver dollar, and he said "ouch!" as a stray spark fluttered down against his stomach.

Now was the time to be hard-boiled, she thought. She knew there were three medals from the war in his jewel box, but she had risked many things herself: tuberculosis among them and one time something worse, though she had not known it and had never quite forgiven the doctor for not telling her.

"You've had a hard time with that, I guess," she said lightly as she sponged him. "Won't it ever heal?"

"Never. That's a copper plate."

"Well, it's no excuse for what you're doing to yourself."

He bent his great brown eyes on her, shrewd—aloof, confused. He signaled to her in one second, his Will to Die, and for all her training and experience she knew she could never do anything constructive with him. He stood up, steadying himself on the wash basin and fixing his eye on some place just ahead.

"Now, if I'm going to stay here you're not going to get at that liquor," she said.

Suddenly she knew he wasn't looking for that. He was looking at the corner where she had thrown the bottle this afternoon. She stared at his handsome face, weak and defiant—afraid to turn even half-way because she knew that death was in that corner where he was looking. She knew death—she had heard it, smelt its unmistakable odor, but she had never seen it before it entered into anyone, and she knew this man saw it in the corner of his bathroom; that it was standing there looking at him while he spit from a feeble cough and rubbed the result into the braid of his trousers. It shone there . . . crackling for a moment as evidence of the last gesture he ever made.

She tried to express it next day to Mrs. Hixson:

"It's not like anything you can beat—no matter how hard you try. This one could have twisted my wrists until he strained them and that wouldn't matter so much to me. It's just that you can't really help them and it's so discouraging—it's all for nothing."

[February 1937]

JOHN STEINBECK

A Snake of One's Own

It was almost dark when young Dr. Phillips swung his sack to his shoulder and left the tide pool. He climbed up over the rocks and squashed along the street in his rubber boots. The street lights were on by the time he arrived at his little commercial laboratory on the cannery street of Monterey. It was a tight little building, standing partly on piers over by the water and partly on the land. On both sides the big corrugated iron sardine canneries crowded in on it.

Dr. Phillips climbed the wooden steps and opened the door. The white rats in their cages scampered up and down the wire, and the captive cats in their pens mewed for milk. Dr. Phillips turned on the glaring light over the dissection table and dumped his clammy sack on the floor. He walked to the glass cages by the window where the rattlesnakes lived, leaned over and looked in.

The snakes were bunched and resting in the corners of the cage, but every head was clear; the dusty eyes seemed to look at nothing, but as the young man leaned over the cage the forked tongues, black on the ends and pink behind, twittered out and waved slowly up and down. Then the snakes recognized the man and pulled in their tongues.

Dr. Phillips threw off his leather coat and built a fire in the tin stove; he set a kettle of water on the stove and dropped a can of beans into the water. Then he stood staring down at the sack on the floor. He was a slight young man with the mild, preoccupied eyes of one who looks through a microscope a great deal. He wore a short blond beard.

The draft ran breathily up the chimney and a glow of warmth came from the stove. The little waves washed quietly about the piles under the building. Arranged on shelves about the room were tier above tier of museum jars containing the mounted marine specimens the laboratory dealt in.

Dr. Phillips opened a side door and went into his bedroom, a book-lined cell containing an army cot, a reading light and an uncomfortable wooden chair. He pulled off his rubber boots and put on a pair of sheepskin slippers. When he went back to the other room the water in the kettle was already beginning to hum.

He lifted his sack to the table under the white light and emptied out two dozen common starfish. These he laid out side by side on the table. His preoccupied eyes turned to the busy rats in the wire cages. Taking grain from a paper sack he poured it into the feeding troughs. Instantly the rats scrambled down from the wire and fell upon the food. A bottle of milk stood on a glass shelf between a small mounted octopus and a jellyfish. Dr. Phillips lifted down the milk and walked to the cat cage, but before he filled the containers he reached in the cage and gently picked out a big rangy alley tabby. He stroked her for a moment and then dropped her in a small black painted box, closed the lid and bolted it and then turned on a petcock which admitted gas into the killing chamber. While the short soft struggle went on in the black box he filled the saucers with milk. One of the cats arched against his hand and he smiled and petted her neck.

The box was quiet now. He turned off the gas for the airtight box would be full of gas.

On the stove the pan of water was bubbling furiously about the can of beans. Dr. Phillips lifted out the can with a big pair of forceps, opened the beans and emptied them into a glass dish. While he ate he watched the starfish on the table. From between the rays little drops of milky fluid were exuding. He bolted his beans and when they were gone he put the dish in the sink and stepped to the equipment cupboard. From this he took a microscope and a pile of little glass dishes. He filled the dishes one by one with sea water from a tap and arranged them in a line beside the starfish. He took out his watch and laid it on the table under the pouring white light. The waves washed with little sighs against the piles under the floor. He took an eyedropper from a drawer and bent over the starfish.

At that moment there were quick soft steps on the wooden stairs and a strong knocking at the door. A slight grimace of annoyance crossed the young man's face as he went to open. A tall lean woman stood in the doorway. She was dressed in a severe dark suit—her straight black hair, growing low on a flat forehead, was mussed as though the wind had been blowing it. Her black eyes glittered in the strong light.

She spoke in a soft throaty voice. "May I come in? I want to talk to you."

"I'm very busy just now," he said half-heartedly. "I have to do things at times." But he stood away from the door. The tall woman slipped in.

"I'll be quiet until you can talk to me."

He closed the door and brought the uncomfortable chair from the bedroom. "You see," he apologized, "the process is started and I must get to it." So many people wandered in and asked questions. He had little routines of explanations for the commoner processes. He could say them without thinking. "Sit here. In a few minutes I'll be able to listen to you."

The tall woman leaned over the table. With the eyedropper the young man gathered fluid from between the rays of the starfish and squirted it into a bowl of water, and then he drew some milky fluid and squirted it in the same bowl and stirred the water gently with the eyedropper. He began his little patter of explanation.

"When starfish are sexually mature they release sperm and ova when they are exposed at low tide. By choosing mature specimens and taking them out of the water, I give them a condition of low tide. Now I've mixed the sperm and eggs. Now I put some of the mixture in each one of these ten watch glasses. In ten minutes I will kill those in the first glass with menthol, twenty minutes later I will kill the second group and then a new group every twenty minutes. Then I will have arrested the process in stages, and I will mount the series on microscope slides for biologic study." He paused. "Would you like to look at this first group under the microscope?"

"No, thank you." He turned quickly to her. People always wanted to look through the glass. She was not looking at the table at all, but at him. Her black eyes were on him but they did not seem to see him. He realized why—the irises were as dark as the pupils, there was no color line between the two. Dr. Phillips was piqued at her answer. Although answering questions bored him, a lack of interest in what he was doing irritated him. A desire to arouse her grew in him.

"While I'm waiting the first ten minutes I have something to do.

Some people don't like to see it. Maybe you'd better step into that room until I finish."

"No," she said in her soft flat tone. "Do what you wish. I will wait until you can talk to me." Her hands rested side by side on her lap. She was completely at rest. Her eyes were bright but the rest of her was almost in a state of suspended animation. He thought, "Low metabolic rate, almost as low as a frog's, from the looks." The desire to shock her out of her inanition possessed him again.

He brought a little wooden cradle to the table, laid out scalpels and scissors and rigged a big hollow needle to a presssure tube. Then from the killing chamber he brought the limp dead cat and laid it in the cradle and tied its legs to hooks in the sides. He glanced sidewise at the woman. She had not moved. She was still at rest.

The cat grinned up into the light, its pink tongue stuck out between its needle teeth. Dr. Phillips deftly snipped open the skin at the throat; with a scalpel he slit through and found an artery.

With flawless technique he put the needle in the vessel and tied it in with gut. "Embalming fluid," he explained. "Later, I'll inject yellow mass into the venous system and red mass into the arterial system—for blood stream dissection—biology classes."

He looked around at her again. Her dark eyes seemed veiled with dust. She looked without expression at the cat's open throat. Not a drop of blood had escaped. The incision was clean. Dr. Phillips looked at his watch. "Time for the first group." He shook a few crystals of menthol into the first watch glass.

The woman was making him nervous. The rats climbed about on the wire of their cage again and squeaked softly. The waves under the building beat with little shocks on the piles.

The young man shivered. He put a few lumps of coal in the stove and sat down. "Now," he said, "I haven't anything to do for twenty minutes." He noticed how short her chin was between lower lip and point. She seemed to awaken slowly, to come up out of some deep pool of consciousness. Her head raised and her dark dusty eyes moved about the room and then came back to him.

"I was waiting," she said. Her hands remained side by side on her lap. "You have snakes?"

"Why, yes," he said rather loudly. "I have about two dozen rattlesnakes. I milk out the venom and send it to the anti-venom laboratories."

She continued to look at him but her eyes did not center on him, rather they covered him and seemed to see in a big circle all around him. "Have you a male snake, a male rattlesnake?"

"Well it just happens I know I have. I came in one morning and found a big snake in—in coition with a smaller one. That's very rare in captivity. You see, I do know I have a male snake."

"Where is he?"

"Why right in the glass cage by the window there."

Her head swung slowly around but her two quiet hands did not move. She turned back toward him. "May I see?"

He got up and walked to the case by the window. On the sand bottom the knot of rattlesnakes lay entwined, but their heads were clear. The tongues came out and flickered a moment and then waved up and down feeling the air for vibrations. Dr. Phillips nervously turned his head. The woman was standing beside him. He had not heard her get up from the chair. He had heard only the splash of water among the piles and the scampering of the rats on the wire screen.

She said softly, "Which is the male you spoke of?"

He pointed to a thick, dusty grey snake lying by itself in one corner of the cage. "That one. He's nearly five feet long. He comes from Texas. Our Pacific coast snakes are usually smaller. He's been taking all the rats, too. When I want the others to eat I have to take him out."

The woman stared down at the blunt dry head. The forked tongue slipped out and hung quivering for a long moment. "And you're sure he's a male."

"Rattlesnakes are funny," he said glibly. "Nearly every generalization proves wrong. I don't like to say anything definite about rattlesnakes, but—yes—I can assure you he's a male."

Her eyes did not move from the flat head. "Will you sell him to me?"

"Sell him?" he cried. "Sell him to you?"

"You do sell specimens, don't you?"

"Oh—yes. Of course I do. Of course I do."

"How much? Five dollars? Ten?"

"Oh! Not more than five. But do you know anything about rattlesnakes? You might be bitten."

She looked at him for a moment. "I don't intend to take him. I want to leave him here, but—I want him to be mine. I want to come here and look at him and feed him and to know he's mine." She opened a little purse and took out a five dollar bill. "Here! Now he is mine."

Dr. Phillips began to be afraid. "You could come to look at him without owning him."

"I want him to be mine."

"Oh, Lord!" he cried. "I've forgotten the time." He ran to the table.

"Three minutes over. It won't matter much." He shook menthol crystals into the second watch glass. And then he was drawn back to the cage where the woman still stared at the snake.

She asked, "What does he eat?"

"I feed them white rats, rats from the cage over there."

"Will you put him in the other cage? I want to feed him."

"But he doesn't need food. He's had a rat already this week. Sometimes they don't eat for three or four months. I had one that didn't eat for over a year."

In her low monotone she asked, "Will you sell me a rat?"

He shrugged his shoulders. "I see. You want to watch how rattle-snakes eat. All right. I'll show you. The rat will cost twenty-five cents. It's better than a bull fight if you look at it one way, and it's simply a snake eating his dinner if you look at it another." His tone had become acid. He hated people who made sport of natural processes. He was not a sportsman but a biologist. He could kill a thousand animals for knowledge, but not an insect for pleasure. He'd been over this in his mind before.

She turned her head slowly toward him and the beginning of a smile formed on her thin lips. "I want to feed my snake," she said. "I'll put him in the other cage." She had opened the top of the cage and dipped her hand in before he knew what she was doing. He leaped forward and pulled her back. The lid banged shut.

"Haven't you any sense," he asked fiercely. "Maybe he wouldn't kill you, but he'd make you damned sick in spite of what I could do for you."

"You put him in the other cage then," she said quietly.

Dr. Phillips was shaken. He found that he was avoiding the dark eyes that didn't seem to look at anything.

He felt that it was profoundly wrong to put a rat into the cage, deeply sinful; and he didn't know why. Often he had put rats in the cage when someone or other had wanted to see it, but this desire to-night sickened him. He tried to explain himself out of it.

"It's a good thing to see," he said. "It shows you how a snake can work. It makes you have a respect for a rattlesnake. Then, too, lots of people have dreams about the terror of snakes making the kill. I think because it is a subjective rat. The person is the rat. Once you see it the whole matter is objective. The rat is only a rat and the terror is re-moved."

He took a long stick equipped with a leather noose from the wall. Opening the trap he dropped the noose over the big snake's head and tightened the thong. A piercing dry rattle filled the room.

The thick body writhed and slashed about the handle of the stick as he lifted the snake out and dropped it in the feeding cage. It stood ready to strike for a time, but the buzzing gradually ceased. The snake crawled into a corner, made a big figure eight with its body and lay still.

"You see," the young man explained, "these snakes are quite tame. I've had them a long time. I suppose I could handle them if I wanted to, but everyone who does handle rattlesnakes gets bitten sooner or later. I just don't want to take the chance." He glanced at the woman. He hated to put in the rat. She had moved over in front of the new cage; her black eyes were on the stony head of the snake again.

She said, "Put in a rat."

Reluctantly he went to the rat cage. For some reason he was sorry for the rat, and such a feeling had never come to him before. His eyes went over the mass of swarming white bodies climbing up the screen toward him. "Which one?" he thought. "Which one shall it be?" Suddenly he turned angrily to the woman. "Wouldn't you rather I put in a cat? Then you'd see a real fight. The cat might even win, but if it lost it might kill the snake. I'll sell you a cat if you like."

She didn't look at him. "Put in a rat," she said. "I want him to eat."

He opened the rat cage and thrust his hand in. His fingers found a tail and he lifted a plump, red-eyed rat out of the cage. It struggled up to try to bite his fingers and failing hung spread out and motionless from its tail. He walked quickly across the room, opened the feeding cage and dropped the rat in on the sand floor. "Now, watch it," he cried.

The woman did not answer him. Her eyes were on the snake where it lay still. Its tongue flicking in and out rapidly, tasted the air of the cage.

The rat landed on its feet, turned around and sniffed at its pink naked tail and then unconcernedly trotted across the sand, smelling as it went. The room was silent. Dr. Phillips did not know whether the water sighed among the piles or whether the woman sighed. Out of the corner of his eye he saw her body crouch and stiffen.

The snake moved out smoothly, slowly. The tongue flicked in and out. The motion was so gradual, so smooth that it didn't seem to be motion at all. In the other end of the cage the rat perked up in a sitting position and began to lick down the fine white hair on its chest. The snake moved on, keeping always a deep *S* curve in its neck.

The silence beat on the young man. He felt the blood drifting up in his body. He said loudly, "See! He keeps the striking curve ready. Rattlesnakes are cautious, almost cowardly animals. The mechanism is so delicate. The snake's dinner is to be got by an operation as deft as a surgeon's job. He takes no chances with his instruments."

The snake had flowed to the middle of the cage by now. The rat looked up, saw the snake and then unconcernedly went back to licking his chest.

"It's the most beautiful thing in the world," the young man said. His veins were throbbing. "It's the most terrible thing in the world."

The snake was close now. Its head lifted a few inches from the sand. The head weaved slowly back and forth, aiming, getting distance, aiming. Dr. Phillips glanced again at the woman. He turned sick. She was weaving too, not much, just a suggestion.

The rat looked up and saw the snake. He dropped to four feet and backed up, then—the stroke.

It was impossible to see, simply a flash. The rat jarred as though under an invisible blow. The snake backed hurriedly into the corner from which he had come, and settled down, his tongue working constantly.

"Perfect!" Dr. Phillips cried. "Right between the shoulder blades. The fangs must almost have reached the heart."

The rat stood still, breathing like a little white bellows. Suddenly he leaped in the air and landed on his side. His legs kicked spasmodically for a second and he was dead.

The woman relaxed, relaxed sleepily.

"Well," the young man demanded, "it was an emotional bath, wasn't it?"

She turned her misty eyes to him. "Will he eat it now?" she asked.

"Of course he'll eat it. He didn't kill for a thrill. He killed it because he was hungry."

The corners of the woman's mouth turned up a trifle again. She looked back at the snake. "I want to see him eat it."

Now the snake came out of his corner again. There was no striking curve in his neck, but he approached the rat gingerly, ready to jump back in case it attacked him. He nudged the body gently with his blunt nose, and drew away.

Satisfied that it was dead, he touched the body all over with his chin, from head to tail. He seemed to measure it and to kiss it. Finally he opened his mouth and unhinged his jaws at the corners.

Dr. Phillips put his will against his head to keep it from turning toward the woman. He thought, "If she's opening her mouth, I'll be sick. I'll be afraid." He succeeded in keeping his eyes away.

The snake fitted his jaws over the rat's head and then with a slow peristaltic pulsing, began to engulf the rat. The jaws gripped and the whole throat crawled up, and the jaws gripped again.

Dr. Phillips turned away and went to his work table. "You've made me miss one of the series," he said bitterly. "The set won't be complete." He put one of the watch glasses under a low power microscope and looked at it, and then angrily he poured the contents of all the dishes into the sink.

The waves had fallen so that only a wet whisper came up through the floor. The young man lifted a trapdoor at his feet and dropped the starfish down into the black water. He paused at the cat, crucified in the cradle and grinning comically into the light. Its body was puffed with embalming fluid. He shut off the pressure, withdrew the needle and tied the vein.

"Would you like some coffee?" he asked.

"No, thank you. I shall be going pretty soon."

He walked to her where she stood in front of the snake cage. The rat was swallowed, all except an inch of pink tail that stuck out of the snake's mouth like a sardonic tongue. The throat heaved again and the tail disappeared. The jaws snapped back into their sockets, and the big snake crawled heavily to the corner, made a big eight and dropped his head on the sand.

"He's asleep now," the woman said. "I'm going now. But I'll come back and feed my snake every little while. I'll pay for the rats. I want him to have plenty. And sometime—I'll take him away with me." Her eyes came out of their dusty dream for a moment. "Remember, he's mine. Don't take his poison. I want him to have it. Goodnight." She walked swiftly to the door and went out. He heard her footsteps on the stairs, but he could not hear her walk away on the pavement.

Dr. Phillips turned a chair around and sat down in front of the snake cage. He tried to comb out his thought as he looked at the torpid snake. "I've read so much about psychological sex symbols," he thought. "It doesn't seem to explain. Maybe I'm too much alone. Maybe I should kill the snake. If I knew—no, I can't pray to anything."

For weeks he expected her to return. "I will go out and leave her alone here when she comes," he decided. "I won't see the damned thing again."

She never came again. For months he looked for her when he walked about in the town. Several times he ran after some tall woman thinking it might be she. But he never saw her again—ever.

[February 1938]

IRWIN SHAW

The Eighty-Yard Run

The pass was high and wide and he jumped for it, feeling it slap flatly against his hands, as he shook his hips to throw off the halfback who was diving at him. The center floated by, his hands desperately brushing Darling's knee as Darling picked his feet up high and delicately ran over a blocker and an opposing linesman in a jumble on the ground near the scrimmage line. He had ten yards in the clear and picked up speed, breathing easily, feeling his thigh pads rising and falling against his legs, listening to the sound of cleats behind him, pulling away from them, watching the other backs heading him off toward the sideline, the whole picture, the men closing in on him, the blockers fighting for position, the ground he had to cross, all suddenly clear in his head, for the first time in his life not a meaningless confusion of men, sounds, speed. He smiled a little to himself as he ran, holding the ball lightly in front of him with his two hands, his knees pumping high, his hips twisting in the almost-girlish run of a back in a broken field. The first halfback came at him and he fed him his leg, then swung at the last moment, took the shock of the man's shoulder without breaking stride, ran right through him, his cleats biting securely into the turf. There was only the safety man now, coming warily at him, his arms crooked, hands spread. Darling tucked the ball in, spurted at him, driving hard, hurling himself along, his legs pounding, knees high, all two hundred pounds bunched into controlled attack. He was sure he was going to get past the safety man. Without thought, his arms and legs working beautifully together, he headed right for the safety man, stiff-armed him, feeling blood spurt instantaneously from the man's nose onto his hand, seeing his face go awry, head turned, mouth pulled to one side. He pivoted away, keeping the arm locked, dropping the safety man as he ran easily toward the goal line, with the drumming of cleats diminishing behind him.

How long ago? It was autumn then and the ground was getting hard because the nights were cold and leaves from the maples around the stadium blew across the practice fields in gusts of wind and the girls were beginning to put polo coats over their sweaters when they came to watch practice in the afternoons . . . Fifteen years. Darling walked slowly over the same ground in the spring twilight, in his neat shoes, a man of thirty-five dressed in a double-breasted suit, ten pounds heavier in the fifteen years, but not fat, with the years between 1925 and 1940 showing in his face.

The coach was smiling quietly to himself and the assistant coaches were looking at each other with pleasure the way they always did when one of the second stringers suddenly did something fine, bringing credit to them, making their $2,000 a year a tiny bit more secure.

Darling trotted back, smiling, breathing deeply but easily, feeling wonderful, not tired, though this was the tail end of practice and he'd run eighty yards. The sweat poured off his face and soaked his jersey and he liked the feeling, the warm moistness lubricating his skin like oil. Off in a corner of the field some players were punting and the smack of leather against the ball came pleasantly through the afternoon air. The freshmen were running signals on the next field and the quarterback's sharp voice, the pound of the eleven pairs of cleats, the "Dig, now, *dig!*" of the coaches, the laughter of the players all somehow made him feel happy as he trotted back to midfield, listening to the applause and shouts of the students along the sidelines, knowing that after that run the coach would have to start him Saturday against Illinois.

Fifteen years, Darling thought, remembering the shower after the workout, the hot water steaming off his skin and the deep soap-suds and all the young voices singing with the water streaming down and towels going and managers running in and out and the sharp sweet smell of oil of wintergreen and everybody clapping him on the back as he dressed and Packard, the captain, who took being captain very seriously, coming over to him and shaking his hand and saying. "Darling, you're going to go places in the next two years."

The assistant manager fussed over him, wiping a cut on his leg with alcohol and iodine, the little sting making him realize suddenly how fresh and whole and solid his body felt. The manager slapped a piece of adhesive tape over the cut and Darling noticed the sharp clean white of the tape against the ruddiness of the skin, fresh from the shower.

He dressed slowly, the softness of his shirt and the soft warmth of his wool socks and his flannel trousers a reward against his skin after the harsh pressure of the shoulder harness and thigh and hip pads. He drank three glasses of cold water, the liquid reaching down coldly inside of him, soothing the harsh dry places in his throat and belly left by the sweat and running and shouting of practice.

Fifteen years.

The sun had gone down and the sky was green behind the stadium and he laughed quietly to himself as he looked at the stadium, rearing above the trees, and knew that on Saturday when the 70,000 voices roared as the team came running out onto the field, part of that enormous salute would be for him. He walked slowly, listening to the gravel crunch satisfactorily under his shoes in the still twilight, feeling his clothes swing lightly against his skin, breathing the thin evening air, feeling the wind move softly in his damp hair, wonderfully cool behind his ears and at the nape of his neck.

Louise was waiting for him at the road, in her car. The top was down and he noticed all over again, as he always did when he saw her, how pretty she was, the rough blonde hair and the large, inquiring eyes and the bright mouth, smiling now.

She threw the door open. "Were you good today?" she asked.

"Pretty good," he said. He climbed in, sank luxuriously into the soft leather, stretched his legs far out. He smiled, thinking of the eighty yards. "Pretty damn good."

She looked at him seriously for a moment, then scrambled around, like a little girl, kneeling on the seat next to him, grabbed him, her hands along his ears, and kissed him as he sprawled, head back, on the seat cushion. She let go of him, but kept her head close to his, over his. Darling reached up slowly and rubbed the back of his hand against her cheek, lit softly by a street-lamp a hundred feet away. They looked at each other, smiling.

Louise drove down to the lake and they sat there silently, watching the moon rise behind the hills on the other side. Finally he reached over, pulled her gently to him, kissed her. Her lips grew soft, her body sank into his, tears formed slowly in her eyes. He knew, for the first time, that he could do whatever he wanted with her.

"Tonight," he said. "I'll call for you at seven-thirty. Can you get out?"

She looked at him. She was smiling, but the tears were still full in her eyes. "All right," she said. "I'll get out. How about you? Won't the coach raise hell?"

Darling grinned. "I got the coach in the palm of my hand," he said. "Can you wait till seven-thirty?"

She grinned back at him. "No,"she said.

They kissed and she started the car and they went back to town for dinner. He sang on the way home.

Christian Darling, thirty-five years old, sat on the frail spring grass, greener now than it ever would be again on the practice field, looked thoughtfully up at the stadium, a deserted ruin in the twilight. He had started on the first team that Saturday and every Saturday after that for the next two years, but it had never been as satisfactory as it should have been. He never had broken away, the longest run he'd ever made was thirty-five yards, and that in a game that was already won, and then that kid had come up from the third team, Diederich, a blankfaced German kid from Wisconsin, who ran like a bull, ripping lines to pieces Saturday after Saturday, plowing through, never getting hurt, never changing his expression, scoring more points, gaining more ground than all the rest of the team put together, making everybody's All-American, carrying the ball three times out of four, keeping everybody else out of the headlines. Darling was a good blocker and he spent his Saturday afternoons working on the big Swedes and Polacks who played tackle and end for Michigan, Illlinois, Purdue, hurling into huge pile-ups, bobbing his head wildly to elude the great raw hands swinging like meat-cleavers at him as he went charging in to open up holes for Diederich coming through like a locomotive behind him. Still, it wasn't so bad. Everybody liked him and he did his job and he was pointed out on the campus and boys always felt important when they introduced their girls to him at their proms, and Louise loved him and watched him faithfully in the games, even in the mud, when your own mother wouldn't know you, and drove him around in her car keeping the top down because she was proud of him and wanted to show everybody that she was Christian Darling's girl. She bought him crazy presents because her father was rich, watches, pipes, humidors, an icebox for beer for his room, curtains, wallets, a fifty-dollar dictionary.

"You'll spend every cent your old man owns," Darling protested once when she showed up at his rooms with seven different packages in her arms and tossed them onto the couch.

"Kiss me," Louise said, "and shut up."

"Do you want to break your poor old man?"

"I don't mind. I want to buy you presents."

"Why?"

"It makes me feel good. Kiss me. I don't know why. Did you know that you're an important figure?"

"Yes," Darling said gravely.

"When I was waiting for you at the library yesterday two girls saw you coming and one of them said to the other, 'That's Christian Darling. He's an important figure.' "

"You're a liar."

"I'm in love with an important figure."

"Still, why the hell did you have to give me a forty-pound dictionary?"

"I wanted to make sure," Louise said, "that you had a token of my esteem. I want to smother you in tokens of my esteem."

Fifteen years ago.

They'd married when they got out of college. There'd been other women for him, but all casual and secret, more for curiosity's sake, and vanity, women who'd thrown themselves at him and flattered him, a pretty mother at a summer camp for boys, an old girl from his home town who'd suddenly blossomed into a coquette, a friend of Louise's who had dogged him grimly for six months and had taken advantage of the two weeks when Louise went home when her mother died. Perhaps Louise had known, but she'd kept quiet, loving him completely, filling his rooms with presents, religiously watching him battling with the big Swedes and Polacks on the line of scrimmage on Saturday afternoons, making plans for marrying him and living with him in New York and going with him there to the night-clubs, the theatres, the good restaurants, being proud of him in advance, tall, white-teethed, smiling, large, yet moving lightly, with an athlete's grace, dressed in evening clothes, approvingly eyed by magnificently dressed and famous women in theatre lobbies, with Louise adoringly at his side.

Her father, who manufactured inks, set up a New York office for Darling to manage and presented him with three hundred accounts and they lived on Beekman Place with a view of the river with fifteen thousand dollars a year between them, because everybody was buying everything in those days, including ink. They saw all the shows and went to all the speakeasies and spent their fifteen thousand dollars a year and in the afternoons Louise went to the art galleries and the matinees of the more serious plays that Darling didn't like to sit through and Darling slept with a girl who danced in the chorus of *Rosalie* and with the wife of a man who owned three copper mines. Darling played squash three times a week and remained as solid as a stone barn and Louise never took her eyes off him when they were in the same room together, watching him with a secret, miser's smile, with a trick of coming over to him in the middle of a crowded room and saying gravely, in a low voice, "You're the handsomest man I've ever seen in my whole life. Want a drink?"

Nineteen twenty-nine came to Darling and to his wife and father-in-law, the maker of inks, just as it came to everyone else. The father-in-law waited until 1933 and then blew his brains out and when Darling went to Chicago to see what the books of the firm looked like he found out all that was left were debts and three or four gallons of unbought ink.

"Please, Christian," Louise said, sitting in their neat Beekman Place apartment, with a view of the river and prints of paintings by Dufy and Braque and Picasso on the wall, "please, why do you want to start drinking at two o'clock in the afternoon?"

"I have nothing else to do," Darling said, putting down his glass, emptied of its fourth drink. "Please pass the whiskey."

Louise filled his glass. "Come take a walk with me," she said. "We'll walk along the river."

"I don't want to walk along the river," Darling said, squinting intensely at the prints of paintings by Dufy, Braque and Picasso.

"We'll walk along Fifth Avenue."

"I don't want to walk along Fifth Avenue."

"Maybe," Louise said gently, "you'd like to come with me to some art galleries. There's an exhibition by a man named Klee—"

"I don't want to go to any art galleries. I want to sit here and drink Scotch whiskey," Darling said. "Who the hell hung those goddam pictures up in the wall?"

"I did," Louise said.

"I hate them."

"I'll take them down," Louise said.

"Leave them there. It gives me something to do in the afternoon. I can hate them." Darling took a long swallow. "Is that the way people paint these days?"

"Yes, Christian. Please don't drink any more."

"Do you like painting like that?"

"Yes, dear."

"Really?"

"Really."

Darling looked carefully at the prints once more. "Little Louise Tucker. The middle-western beauty. I like pictures with horses in them. Why should you like pictures like that?"

"I just happen to have gone to a lot of galleries in the last few years . . ."

"Is that what you do in the afternoon?"

"That's what I do in the afternoon," Louise said.

"I drink in the afternoon."

Louise kissed him lightly on the top of his head as he sat there squinting at the pictures on the wall, the glass of whiskey held firmly in his hand. She put on her coat and went out without saying another word. When she came back in the early evening, she had a job on a woman's fashion magazine.

They moved downtown and Louise went out to work every morning and Darling sat home and drank and Louise paid the bills as they came up. She made believe she was going to quit work as soon as Darling found a job, even though she was taking over more responsibility day by day at the magazine, interviewing authors, picking painters for the illustrations and covers, getting actresses to pose for pictures, going out for drinks with the right people, making a thousand new friends whom she loyally introduced to Darling.

"I don't like your hat," Darling said, once, when she came in in the evening and kissed him, her breath rich with Martinis.

"What's the matter with my hat, Baby?" she asked, running her fingers through his hair. "Everybody says it's very smart."

"It's too damned smart," he said. "It's not for you. It's for a rich, sophisticated woman of thirty-five with admirers."

Louise laughed. "I'm practicing to be a rich, sophisticated woman of thirty-five with admirers," she said. He stared soberly at her. "Now, don't look so grim, Baby. It's still the same simple little wife under the hat." She took the hat off, threw it into a corner, sat on his lap. "See? Homebody Number One."

"Your breath could run a train," Darling said, not wanting to be mean, but talking out of boredom, and sudden shock at seeing his wife curiously a stranger in a new hat, with a new expression in her eyes under the little brim, secret, confident, knowing.

Louise tucked her head under his chin so he couldn't smell her breath. "I had to take an author out for cocktails," she said. "He's a boy from the Ozark mountains and he drinks like a fish. He's a Communist."

"What the hell is a Communist from the Ozarks doing writing for a woman's fashion magazine?"

Louise chuckled. "The magazine business is getting all mixed up these days. The publishers want to have a foot in every camp. And anyway, you can't find an author under seventy these days who isn't a Communist."

"I don't think I like you to associate with all those people, Louise," Darling said. "Drinking with them."

"He's a very nice, gentle boy," Louise said. "He reads Ernest Dobson."

"Who's Ernest Dobson?"

Louise patted his arm, stood up, fixed her hair. "He's an English poet."

Darling felt that somehow he had disappointed her. "Am I supposed to know who Ernest Dobson is?"

"No, dear. I'd better go in and take a bath."

After she had gone, Darling went over to the corner where the hat was lying and picked it up. It was nothing, a scrap of straw, a red flower, a veil, meaningless on his big hand, but on his wife's head a signal of something . . . big city, smart and knowing women drinking and dining with men other than their husbands, conversation about things a normal man wouldn't know much about, Frenchmen who painted as though they used their elbows instead of brushes, composers who wrote whole symphonies without a single melody in them, writers who knew all about politics and women who knew all about writers, the movement of the proletariat, Marx, somehow mixed up with five-dollar dinners and the best looking women in America and fairies who made them laugh and half-sentences immediately understood and secretly hilarious and wives who called their husbands "Baby." He put the hat down, a scrap of straw and a red flower, and a little veil. He drank some whiskey straight and went into the bathroom where his wife was lying deep in her bath, singing to herself and smiling from time to time like a little girl, paddling the water gently with her hands, sending up a slight spicy fragrance from the bathsalts she used.

He stood over her, looking down at her. She smiled up at him, her eyes half closed, her body pink and shimmering in the warm, scented water. All over again, with all the old suddenness, he was hit deep inside him with the knowledge of how beautiful she was, how much he needed her.

"I came in here," he said, "to tell you I wish you wouldn't call me 'Baby.'"

She looked up at him from the bath, her eyes quickly full of sorrow, half-understanding what he meant. He knelt and put his arms around her, his sleeves plunged heedlessly in the water, his shirt and jacket soaking wet as he clutched her wordlessly, holding her crazily tight, crushing her breath from her, kissing her desperately, searchingly, regretfully.

He got jobs after that, selling real estate and automobiles, but somehow, although he had a desk with his name on a wooden wedge on it, and he went to the office religiously at nine each morning, he never managed to sell anything and he never made any money.

Louise was made assistant editor and the house was always full of strange men and women who talked fast and got angry on abstract subjects like mural painting, novelists, labor unions. Negro short-story writers drank Louise's liquor, and a lot of Jews, and big solemn men with scarred faces and knotted hands who talked slowly but clearly about picket lines and battles with guns and leadpipe at mineshaft-heads and in front of factory gates. And Louise moved among them all, confidently, knowing what they were talking about, with opinions that they listened to and argued about just as though she were a man. She knew everybody, condescended to no one, devoured books that Darling had never heard of, walked along the streets of the city, excited, at home, soaking in all the million tides of New York without fear, with constant wonder.

Her friends liked Darling and sometimes he found a man who wanted to get off in the corner and talk about the new boy who played fullback for Princeton, and the decline of the double wing-back, or even the state of the stock market, but for the most part he sat on the edge of things, solid and quiet in the high storm of words. "The dialectics of the situation . . . the theatre has been given over to expert jugglers . . . Picasso? What man has a right to paint old bones and collect ten thousand dollars for them? . . . I stand firmly behind Trotsky . . . Poe was the last American critic. When he died they put lilies on the grave of American criticism. I don't say this because they panned my last book, but . . ."

Once in a while he caught Louise looking soberly and consider-ingly at him through the cigarette smoke and the noise and he avoided her eyes and found an excuse to get up and go into the kitchen for more ice or to open another bottle.

"Come on," Cathal Flaherty was saying, standing at the door with a girl, "you've got to come down and see this. It's down on Fourteenth Street, in the old Civic Repertory, and you can only see it on Sunday nights and I guarantee you'll come out of the theatre singing." Fla-herty was a big young Irishman with a broken nose who was the law-yer for a longshoreman's union, and he had been hanging around the house for six months on and off, roaring and shutting everybody else up when he got in an argument. "It's a new play, *Waiting for Lefty,* it's about taxi-drivers."

"Odets," the girl with Flaherty said. "It's by a guy named Odets."

"I never heard of him," Darling said.

"He's a new one," the girl said.

"It's like watching a bombardment," Flaherty said. "I saw it last Sunday night. You've got to see it."

"Come on, Baby," Louise said to Darling, excitement in her eyes already. "We've been sitting in the Sunday *Times* all day, this'll be a great change."

"I see enough taxi-drivers every day," Darling said, not because he meant that, but because he didn't like to be around Flaherty, who said things that made Louise laugh a lot and whose judgment she accepted on almost every subject. "Let's go to the movies."

"You've never seen anything like this before," Flaherty said. "He wrote this play with a baseball bat."

"Come on," Louise coaxed. "I bet it's wonderful."

"He has long hair," the girl with Flaherty said. "Odets. I met him at a party. He's an actor. He didn't say a goddam thing all night."

"I don't feel like going down to Fourteenth Street," Darling said, wishing Flaherty and his girl would get out. "It's gloomy."

"Oh, hell!" Louise said loudly. She looked coolly at Darling, as though she'd just been introduced to him and was making up her mind about him, and not very favorably. He saw her looking at him, knowing there was something new and dangerous in her face and he wanted to say something, but Flaherty was there and his damned girl, and anyway, he didn't know what to say.

"I'm going," Louise said, getting her coat. "I don't think Fourteenth Street is gloomy."

"I'm telling you," Flaherty was saying, helping her on with her coat, "it's the Battle of Gettysburg, in Brooklynese."

"Nobody could get a word out of him," Flaherty's girl was saying as they went through the door. "He just sat there all night."

The door closed. Louise hadn't said good-night to him. Darling walked around the room four times, then sprawled out on the sofa, on top of the Sunday *Times*. He lay there for five minutes looking at the ceiling, thinking of Flaherty walking down the street talking in that booming voice, between the girls, holding their arms.

Louise had looked wonderful. She'd washed her hair in the afternoon and it had been very soft and light and clung close to her head as she stood there angrily putting her coat on. Louise was getting prettier every year, partly because she knew by now how pretty she was, and made the most of it.

"Nuts," Darling said, standing up. "Oh, nuts."

He put on his coat and went down to the nearest bar and had five drinks off by himself in a corner before his money ran out.

The years since then had been foggy and downhill. Louise had been nice to him, and in a way, loving and kind, and they'd fought only once, when he said he was going to vote for Landon. ("Oh, Christ," she'd said, "doesn't *anything* happen inside your head? Don't you read the papers? The penniless Republican!") She'd been sorry later and apologized as she might to a child. He'd tried hard, had gone grimly to the art galleries, the concert halls, the bookshops, trying to gain on the trail of his wife, but it was no use. He was bored, and none of what he saw or heard or dutifully read made much sense to him and finally he gave it up. He had thought, many nights as he ate dinner alone, knowing that Louise would come home late and drop silently into bed without explanation, of getting a divorce, but he knew the loneliness, the hopelessness, of not seeing her again would be too much to take. So he was good, completely devoted, ready at all times to go anyplace with her, do anything she wanted. He even got a small job, in a broker's office and paid his own way, bought his own liquor.

Then he'd been offered the job of going from college to college as a tailor's representative. "We want a man," Mr. Rosenberg had said, "who as soon as you look at him, you say 'There's a university man.'" Rosenberg had looked approvingly at Darling's broad shoulders and well-kept waist, at his carefully brushed hair and his honest, wrinkle-less face. "Frankly, Mr. Darling, I am willing to make you a proposition. I have inquired about you, you are favorably known on your old campus, I understand you were in the backfield with Alfred Diederich."

Darling nodded. "Whatever happened to him?"

"He is walking around in a cast for seven years now. An iron brace. He played professional football and they broke his neck for him."

Darling smiled. That, at least, had turned out well.

"Our suits are an easy product to sell, Mr. Darling," Rosenberg said. "We have a handsome, custom-made garment. What has Brooks Brothers got that we haven't got? A name. No more."

"I can make fifty, sixty dollars a week," Darling said to Louise that night. "And expenses. I can save some money and then come back to New York and really get started here."

"Yes, Baby," Louise said.

"As it is," Darling said carefully, "I can make it back here once a month, and holidays and the summer. We can see each other often."

"Yes, Baby." He looked at her face, lovelier now at thirty-five than it had ever been before, but fogged over now as it had been for five years with a kind of patient, kindly, remote boredom.

"What do you say?" he asked. "Should I take it?" Deep within him he hoped fiercely, longingly, for her to say, "No, Baby, you stay right here," but she said, as he knew she'd say, "I think you'd better take it."

He nodded. He had to get up and stand with his back to her, looking out the window, because there were things plain on his face that she had never seen in the fifteen years she'd known him. "Fifty dollars is a lot of money," he said, "I never thought I'd ever see fifty dollars again." He laughed. Louise laughed too.

Christian Darling sat on the frail green grass of the practice field. The shadow of the stadium had reached out and covered him. In the distance the lights of the university shone a little mistily in the light haze of evening. Fifteen years. Flaherty even now was calling for his wife, buying her a drink, filling whatever bar they were in with that voice of his and that easy laugh. Darling half-closed his eyes, almost saw the boy fifteen years ago reach for the pass, slip the halfback, go skittering lightly down the field, his knees high and fast and graceful, smiling to himself because he knew he was going to get past the safety man. That was the high point, Darling thought, fifteen years ago, on an autumn afternoon, twenty years old and far from death, with the air coming easily into his lungs, and a deep feeling inside him that he could do anything, knock over anybody, outrun whatever had to be outrun. And the shower after and the three glasses of water and the cool night air on his damp head and Louise sitting hatless in the open car with a smile and the first kiss she ever really meant. The high point, an eighty-yard run in the practice, and a girl's kiss and everything after that a decline. Darling laughed. He had practiced the wrong thing, perhaps. He hadn't practiced for 1929 and New York City and a girl who would turn into a woman. Somewhere, he thought, there must have been a point where she moved up to me, was even with me for a moment, when I could have held her hand, if

I'd known, held tight, gone with her. Well, he'd never known. Here he was on a playing field that was fifteen years away and his wife was in another city having dinner with another and better man, speaking with him a different, new language, a language nobody had ever taught him.

Darling stood up, smiled a little, because if he didn't smile he knew the tears would come. He looked around him. This was the spot. O'Connor's pass had come sliding out just to here ... the high point. Darling put up his hands, felt all over again the flat slap of the ball. He shook his hips to throw off the halfback, cut back inside the center, picked his knees high as he ran gracefully over two men jumbled on the ground at the line of scrimmage, ran easily, gaining speed, for ten yards, holding the ball lightly in his two hands, swung away from the halfback diving at him, ran, swinging his hips in the almost girlish manner of a back in a broken field, tore into the safety man, his shoes drumming heavily on the turf, stiff-armed, elbow locked, pivoted, raced lightly and exultantly for the goal line.

It was only after he had sped over the goal-line and slowed to a trot that he saw the boy and girl sitting together on the turf, looking at him wonderingly.

He stopped short, dropping his arms. "I ..." he said, gasping a little though his condition was fine and the run hadn't winded him, "I ... Once I played here."

The boy and the girl said nothing. Darling laughed embarrassedly, looked hard at them sitting there, close to each other, shrugged, turned and went toward his hotel, the sweat breaking out on his face and running down into his collar.

[January 1941]

NELSON ALGREN

The Captain Is a Card

The undersized man at the head of the first line of the evening had just been brought in off the street, and wore an oversized army overcoat dragging past his knees; its hem was frayed and caked with mud, as though he'd been sitting on a curb with the hem in the gutter. The coat's top button dangled loosely and he twisted it tenderly; feeling perhaps that the last vestige of his respectability dangled with it. If you took him seriously he looked like the original tough-luck kid, and if you didn't he looked like Amateur Night at the nearest burlesque.

What was he doing in a police lineup anyhow, the Captain wanted to know.

"Just here for protecting myself is all," the little man explained. Then he glanced uneasily toward the Captain's shadowed corner as though fearing he had, so soon in the questioning, given a wrong answer.

"Don't look over here. Tell your story to the mike."

The oversize overcoat looked into the amplifier with the face of an aging terrier searching forever, with brown-eyed weariness, a world of shadowed corners. Of padlocked poolrooms, bootleg bookies, curtained brothels, darkened sidestreets and unlit, littered alleys. He looked like he hadn't walked down an open street in daylight, nor had a friendly nod of recognition in his life. He looked lost.

"Do you ever go around looking for trouble?"

"No sir. I don't like trouble."

"Then what are you doing in front of a tavern at two in the morning with a Luger under your coat? Don't you know those things go off?"

"I'm a veteran."

NELSON ALGREN

"What's that got to do with it? I'm a veteran too. But I don't go prowling around taverns with artillery under my clothes."

The veteran eyed the Captain's corner furtively before he answered.

"He shoved me," was the explanation.

"Who's 'he'?"

"A feller I never seen him before. He bought me a drink. Because I'm a veteran."

"Then what happened?"

"He told me to go home."

"Then he slugged you?"

"No sir. He just shoved me was all."

"Then what?"

"Then nothing. That's all. I went home like he told me."

"And picked up a Luger and came back to blow his head off?"

"Yes sir. Naturally." As though that had been understood all along.

"Naturally? Don't you realize that if the officer hadn't happened along to take that thing off you, you'd be standing there for murder now?"

Silence. "Well?"

"Yes sir. I realize."

"You're pretty cool about it."

"Yes sir. I'm a veteran."

"What the hell *has* that got to do with it?" The Captain was exasperated at last. "I saw as much over there as you did."

The little man found the Captain with his eyes at last. And snapped like a mongrel held where it cannot move.

"It wasn't you what got shoved. It was *me."*

"Oh." The Captain lowered his eyes as though he were, suddenly, the guilty man. Then he grinned. *"Man,"* he said quizzically, half sympathy and half surprise, "I'd hate to have you get mad at me for something worth getting mad about."

The next man was half-leaning, half-crouching against the black-and-white lines of the wall. He was a blond of perhaps twenty-two.

"Stand up there!" The Captain sounded like a public-school principal on examination day.

The blond stood as best he could. The knuckles were clenched

64

whitely; the lips were bloodless. And the tip of the nose as white as new snow. The Captain relented.

"You must be hitting it pretty hard."

The boy's lips moved inaudibly toward the mike; it was hard to tell whether he was trying to speak or merely wetting his lips in preparation for saying something.

"What do you take?"

The answer could not be heard; the lips could not be read.

"Speak up, son. Do you sell it too?"

This time the answer came faintly, from somewhere in Cloudland.

"Once—upon—a—time."

"How's last Tuesday afternoon—is that once upon a time?"

The boy nodded solemnly, dreamily, with a slow-motion gravity all his own.

Yes.

Any Tuesday afternoon in Cloudland was once upon a time.

The next man in line was a high yellow in his early thirties.

"What you here for?"

"Havin' whiskey in my home."

"You too? I thought they repealed that law. You don't carry a gun, do you?"

"No sir."

"Do you keep one on the premises?"

"I just keep it. I don't carry it. I leave it on the premises."

"But there was a .38 on the premises?"

"I wasn't nowhere near it."

"I didn't ask you how close you were. I asked whether it was there."

"Yes sir. That's what they claims. I'm in business. I got to have one."

"I thought you said it was your home. Now it's a business. Make up your mind, you can't beat both raps. It'll go lighter on you if you stick to the whiskey story. What you using a private home for business for anyhow? *What* business?"

"The True-American."

"What's *that?*"

"Social 'n athletic club."

"With five women?"

"That's the social part."

"I see. Was afraid you'd tell me they were lady wrestlers."

The woman in the back giggled at the Captain's humor.

"No sir. A mixed club, *that's* what we got."

"I see. Good clean fun and lots of sunshine?"

"Yes sir. Meets in my home. We go on hikes."

"Now it's a home again. You're not selling whiskey there then after all?"

"Oh no sir. I *give* it away. They my *guests.*"

"Which one of your guests filed the numbers off that .38 for you? One of the lady wrestlers?"

"Nobody. I bought it that way."

"Now we're getting somewhere for a change. Ever been in trouble before?"

"No sir," the high yellow declared.

The Captain shook his head sadly, to indicate his resignation at human mendacity. "You know, I'll begin to think you aren't telling the whole truth to these people. You're down here for strongarm robbery on June 1, 1934. Did that happen on one of your hikes?"

"I paid a fine."

"Did you pay a fine for that no-bill for murder in 1928?"

The high yellow started almost imperceptibly. The Captain had reached him where he lived—in his courage. You could see him visibly trying to pull that courage together, like a fighter holding his guts with one hand while arranging a fixed grin for his opponent to show he isn't hurt. You can tell when they're hurt when they try to smile.

"I didn't kill her."

"You know what I mean though?"

"It's a different case."

"You know what I mean though."

The Negro's face seemed burned a rust-yellow across the forehead and nose, the way a man's face is left when he is lifted out of the chair. He stared straight into the mike, deep shadows under the eyes and the eyes themselves two yellow flares.

"Yes sir," he said at last. And waited tensely for the mike to move. The yellow flares began to die down in the eyes; when they were faded to pinpoints the Captain spoke leisurely, like a man with nowhere to go and the whole night to kill.

"Tell us more about it."

Silence.

"If you don't tell it I'll read it."

The Negro's eyes were dead embers now, and his voice a dying man's voice. He spoke without emphasis, in a dead-level monotone, and—at the first moment—with the dead woman's voice:

"Us two live t'gether 'n we sort of separated 'n got t' goin' t'gether again 'n we were drinkin' t'gether 'n I wanted t' go home n' figures I'd bluff her, teach her a lesson, scare her so's she wouldn't run off 'n always come home with me when it was time. I pulled the gun 'n leveled it 'n she grabbed for it 'n it went off 'n shot her in the stomach 'n when I went t' see her at the hospital she took my hand 'n say, 'Honey, you shouldn't a done it,' 'n that was all she ever say."

"You're a bad man. You been going wrong fifteen years."

The mike was moved to the next man.

Next was a redheaded Irish boy of eighteen, with teeth like piano keys.

"What's your trouble, Red?"

"Left a jimmy in a gas-station door."

"At night?"

"No sir. Daytime."

"Didn't have criminal intent, did you?"

"No *sir.*"

"You weren't going to break into that station when it got dark, were you?"

"I just had it on my mind."

"Where were you arrested?"

"I was walkin' on the rocks off 39th. The park officer called me over."

"Where were you going when he called you?"

"Home."

"Then you got it off your mind?"

The redhead grinned amiably. He had it off his mind.

While the mike was being moved the Captain turned to his audience with the deliberation of a sideshow barker at a county fair.

"I want you to look close at this next man, ladies 'n gentlemen. This, let me tell you, is a sweetheart. Folks, meet Hardrocks O'Connor. Meet the folks, O'Connor."

A flat-faced felon in his late fifties, with no bridge to his nose and a bulge for a forehead. The voice hoarse from a hundred cells. You could tell he hit the bottle hard and you could tell he'd done his time the hard way. In the hard places. And still trying to make it the hard way. It was in his posture and in his voice; in the lean set of the jaw and across his punched-in mug like a brand.

"Tell us about yourself, Morning Glory."

O'Connor's mouth split when he said:

"Take 'em west yerself."

The Captain knew when he had a prize: he took Hardrocks west for five solid pages. Danbury, Waupun, Jeff City, Wetumpka, Leavenworth, Huntsville. For a phony bunco game. For a dice game with 'missouts.' For violation of the Narcotics Act. For forgery, for the pocketbook game, for the attention racket, for using the mails to sell a pair of missouts, for bigamy, for vag, for impersonating an officer, for breach of promise, for contributing to delinquency of a minor, for defrauding an innkeeper, for indecent exposure, for tapping a gas main. And for the phony bunco game, right back where he'd started a lifetime before.

Two years, ten days, six days, six months, thirty days, a year and a day, fifty-dollar fine, given a floater out of the state in Lubbock, only to run into two years at hard labor on the pea farm at Huntsville for taking a rancher with a phony roulette wheel at a McAllen County fair.

"Why didn't you get out of the state like they gave you a chance to do at Lubbock instead of running on down to McAllen?" The Captain was merely curious.

"Had a deal on down there."

The Captain turned to his listeners.

"Five more pages, ladies 'n gentlemen—'n not one a crime of violence. He'll sell you a little dope, take a little hisself, sell you an oil-well 'r take a merry widow for a ride on her insurance money. But he won't use a gun. He'll spot a beggar paddlin' down the street when he has t' get out of town in a hurry—but he'll stop 'n try t' take the beggar." This spectacle of a man who could steal for a lifetime without once doing so by force affected the good Captain as an obscenity. "C'mon down here," he ordered. "Let the people see you so's they'll remember you. How'd you get your nose bust, Hardrocks? Trying to take the same sucker twice?"

O'Connor paused on a step from the stage to rub the place where the bridge of his nose had once been.

"Had the bone took out when I was twenty. Wanted t' be a fighter." He hesitated as though he were about to add something.

"Keep movin', Hardrocks. No speeches. All the way down front. There, that's as near as we want you. Take off that cap. That's how he looks without a cap, folks. Now put it back on. That's how he looks with it on. Walk around, Daffodil. We want to see how you look when you walk."

O'Connor began a deliberate pacing: five steps forward and five steps back. And turned heavily at an imagined door. His life was a bull-pen, and he turned within it like a gelded bull: five dogged steps forward and five dogged steps back.

"That's enough of that, O'Connor. Now stand still and turn around with your cap in your right hand."

The old man turned, the sheen of his worn brown suit showing in the glare from above like light on an aging animal's hide.

"That's how he looks with his back turned, folks. Put your cap on, Hardrocks. No, don't turn around yet. That's how he looks when he's walking away with your money. All right, O'Connor, back on the platform."

O'Connor returned slowly to his position before the mike.

"What did you say you were arrested for, Hardrocks? Stealing from a blind man?"

"I wasn't arrested. I walked into the station 'n give myself up. I can't make it no more. I want 'em t' come 'n get me, I want 'em all t' come 'n get me. Anyone who wants me, tell 'em t' come 'n get me. I can't make it no more."

The woman in the back stopped tittering. The Captain cocked his head to one side in mild surprise. The young men, on either side of the hardest one of them all, looked straight out over the lights as though the old man was speaking for their futures as well as for his past.

"I been a stumblin' block, I been a obstacle to the Republic. I done it all wrong, I got hard-boiled too young. I got kicked around too soon. I was a orphan 'n got kicked around. I'm an old man, I got nobody, I can't make it no more—" Hardrocks O'Connor was crying.

The next man was a young Negro in a gabardine, heavy in the shoulders and lean in the shanks.

"What you here for, Ready-Money?"

"Don't know."

"Then you'll need a lawyer to tell you. How old was the girl?"

"She looked like sixteen."

"Yeah. But she was eleven. Are you on parole?"

"Yes sir."

"Goodbye."

The last man in the line was a dwarf with the head and torso development of a man of average height. He stood two inches short of the four-foot mark on the black-and-white diagram behind him and looked to be in his early forties. An ugly specimen.

"What's it for, Shorty?"

"Just a pickup."

"Pickup for what?"

"Don't know. Suspicion I s'pose."

"What you sit seven years in Stateville for, Shorty?"

"Suspicion."

"Isn't seven years on suspicion a little severe?"

The dwarf's voice was as shrill as a ten-year-old's.

"Yes *sir*. It *was* severe."

"Ever get boosted through a transom, Shorty?"

"Yes *sir.*"

"Who boosted you?"

"A frien'. He's still settin'."

"How many places you rob that way, Shorty?"

"I ferget."

"You shouldn't. You're still in the business. How much time you done?"

"Year 'n a day once 'n once three years."

"You don't count Stateville?"

"You said that one."

The women tittered their enjoyment of the little man's confession. A dwarf, standing between a seven-year-long shadow and a new shadow just as long. Perhaps it was funny to be so little while transoms were so high. And shadows were so long. Perhaps they saw no shadow. Perhaps they saw no man.

Next was a middle-aged Serb, splayfooted, with the hands of a stockyards skinner. He stood with his naked forearms folded.

"What you here for this time, Rutu?"

"Neigh—bors complain."

"Again? What about?"

"Same ol' t'ing. I fight."

"Who were you fighting with this time?"

"Same ol' t'ing. Wid wife."

"Hell, that's no crime neither. Next."

"I went and let somebody use my car."

"That puts you in, too. Next."

"What's your trouble, next man?"

"I beg your pardon?"

"Don't beg my pardon," the Captain quipped. "Beg the pardon of the woman whose purse you snatched."

"I didn't snatch it."

"How'd the officers find it in your room?"

"I stole it."

"Oh, that's different. I beg *your* pardon. *Dis*charged."

The next man was a paunchy character with the professionally friendly aspect of a floorwalker or beauty-shop operator. His iron-grey hair had been recently marcelled.

"What you here for, Flash?"

"Just riding in a cab is all."

"What did you have in your pocket?"

"Just a toy cap pistol was all."

"What was that for—Fourth of July?"

"I was on my way to give it to my little nephew in Hammond for a Christmas present."

"How many cabs you take with that toy gun, Santa?"

"Just the one I was riding in. I don't know what come over me."

"Come off it, Coneroo. How many you hold up altogether?"

"Nine."

"I said altogether."

"Oh. Altogether. Twenty-eight."

"You know what happens to habituals in Michigan?"

"Yes sir. They get life."

"Too bad you didn't wait to get to Chicago to stick up that driver. We call that a misdemeanor here. Do you think crime pays?"

The floorwalker retired gracefully from the mike and adjusted his cravat.

The last man was a Negro of perhaps nineteen, in a torn and

bloodstained shirt and with one arm in a cast. He had Mongolian features, the cheekbones set high and widely—to protect the eyes—the eyes slanted slightly and the skin like tawny parchment. The Captain explained.

"This is the sweetheart who shot Sergeant Shannon Friday night. Tell it to the people the way you told it to us, Memphis."

"Ah was out look'n fer somebody t' stick up 'n had m' gun handy 'n he come along, that's all."

"Where was this?"

"South side of 59th Street. Ah was crossin' over t' the north side when ah saw Shannon, he wasn't in uniform."

"Did he call after you?"

"Yes sir. He say 'Hey Buddy, wait a minute'. 'N he had somethin' in his hand. It looked like a gun 'n ah pulled out m' pistol 'n stahted t' fire. He shot 'n hit me in the right ahm 'n ah ran 'n tried t' find some place t' hide."

"You're sure you weren't out gunning for Sergeant Shannon?"

"Oh no sir."

"But you knew him from before?"

"From a lo-o-ong time."

"You know he may die?"

"That's what they tell me."

"Aren't worried much about it though, are you?"

"It was me 'r him."

"How'd they find you?"

"Ah leaned on a mail-box, ah was bleedin' pretty bad. Ah left stains on th' box 'n some of m' own people seen them 'n tol' a officer." The boy seemed more saddened by that single circumstance than by either the imminence of Shannon's death or his own. Like a thing repeated many times in an effort to believe and accept:

"My *own* people."

And his voice was heavy with shame for them.

"How do you feel about getting the chair, Boy?"

"Don't care one way 'r another. Don't feel nothin', good 'r bad. Just feel a little low is all. Knew ah'd never get t' be twenty-one anyhow."

The line turned and shuffled restlessly through the door to the cells. The overhead lights went out one by one, till even the tittering women were gone. And nothing remained in the showup room but the sounds of the city, coming up from below.

The great trains howling from track to track all night. The taut and telegraphic murmur of ten thousand city wires, drawn most cruelly against a city sky. The rush of city waters, beneath the city streets.

The passionate passing of the night's last El.

[June 1942]

JAMES JONES

Two Legs
for the
Two of Us

"No," said the big man in the dark blue suit, and his voice was hoarse with drunkenness. "I cant stay. I've got some friends out in the car."

"Well, why didnt you bring them in with you, George?" the woman said in mock disgust. "Dont let them sit out in the cold."

George grinned fuzzily. "To hell with them. I just stopped by for a minute. You wouldnt like them anyway."

"Why, of course I'd like them, if they're your friends. Go on and call them."

"No. You wouldnt like them. Let the bastards sit. I just wanted to talk to you, Sandy." George looked vaguely around the gayness of the kitchen with its red and white checkered motif. "Jesus, I love this place. We done a good job on it, Sandy, you know it? I used to think about it a lot. I still do."

But the woman was already at the kitchen door and she did not hear. "Hey out there!" she called. "Come on in and have a drink."

There was a murmur of words from the car she could not understand and she opened the screen door and went outside to the car in the steaming cold winter night. A man and woman were in the front seat, the man behind the wheel. Another woman was in the back seat by herself. She was smoothing her skirt.

Sandy put her head up to the car window. "George is drunk," she said. "Why dont you go on home and leave him here and let me take care of him?"

"No," the man said.

"He's been here before."

"No," the man said sharply. "He's with us."

Sandy put her hand on the door handle. "He shouldnt be drinking," she said. "In his condition."

The man laughed. "Liquor never bothers me," he said.

"Poor George. I feel so sorry for him I could cry."

"No, you couldnt," the man said contemptuously. "I know you. Besides, it aint your sympathy he wants." He thumped the thigh of his left leg with his fist. It made a sound like a gloved fist striking a heavy bag. "I pawned one myself," he said.

Sandy moved as if he had struck her. She stepped back, putting her hand to her mouth, then turned back toward the house.

George was standing in the door. "Tom's a old buddy of mine," he grinned. "He was in the hospital with me for ten months out in Utah." He opened the screen.

Sandy stepped inside with slumped shoulders. "Why didnt you tell me? I said something terrible. Please tell him to come in, George, he wont come now unless you tell him."

"No. Let them sit. We got a couple of pigs from Greencastle with us." He grinned down at her belligerently through the dark circles and loose lips of an extended bat.

"Ask them all in, for a drink. I'm no Carrie Nation, George. Tell them to come in. Please, George. Tell them."

"All right. By god I will. I wasnt going to, but I will. I just wanted to see you, Sandy."

"Why dont you stay here tonight, George?" Sandy said. "Let them go on and I'll put you to bed."

George searched her face incredulously. "You really want me to stay?"

"Yes. You need to sober up, George."

"Oh." George laughed suddenly. "Liquor never bothers me. No sir by god. I aint runnin out on Tom. Tom's my buddy." He stepped back to the door. "Hey, you bastards!" he bellered. 'You comin in here an have a drink? or I got to come out and drag you in?" Sandy stood behind him, watching him, the big bulk of shoulder, the hair growing softly on the back of his neck.

There was a laugh from the car and the door slammed. The tall curly-haired Tom came in, swinging his left side in a peculiar rhythm.

After him came the two women, one tall and blonde, the other short and dark. They both smiled shyly as they entered. They both were young.

"Oh,"said the short one. "This is pretty."

"It's awful pretty," the blonde one said, looking around.

"You goddam right its pretty," George said belligerently. "And its built for utility. Look at them cupboards."

George introduced the girls by their first names, like a barker in a sideshow naming the attractions. "An this here's Tom Hornney," he said, "and when I say Hornney, I mean Hornney." George laughed and Tom grinned and the two girls tittered nervously.

"I want you all to meet Miss Sandy Thomas," George said, as if daring them.

"Sure," Tom said. "I know all about you. I use to read your letters out in Utah."

George looked at Sandy sheepishly. "A man gets so he cant believe it himself. He gets so he's got to show it to somebody. That's the way it is in the army."

Sandy smiled at him stiffly, her eyes seeming not to see. "How do you want your drinks? Soda or Coke?"

"They want Coke with theirs," Tom pointed to the girls. "They dont know how to drink."

"This is really a beautiful place," the blonde one said.

"Oh my yes," the short one said. "I wish I ever had a place like this here."

Sandy looked up from the drinks and smiled, warmly. "Thank you."

"I really love your place," the blonde one said. "Where did you get those funny spotted glasses? I seen some like them in a Woolworth's once."

George, laughing over something with Tom, turned to the blonde one. "Shut up, for god sake. You talk too much. You're supposed to be seen."

"Or felt," Tom said.

"I was only being polite," the blonde one said.

"Well dont," George said. "You dont know how."

"Well," said the blonde one. "I like that."

"Those are antiques, dear," Sandy said to her. "I bought them off an old woman down in the country. Woolworth has reproductions of them now."

"You mean them are *genuine* antiques?" the short one said.

Sandy nodded, handing around the drinks.

"For god sake, shut up," George said. "Them's genuine antiques and they cost ten bucks apiece, so shut up. Talk about something interesting."

The short one made a little face at George. She turned to Sandy and whispered delicately.

"Surely," Sandy said. "I'll show you."

"See what I mean?" Tom laughed. "I said they couldnt hold their liquor."

Sandy led the girls out of the kichen. From the next room their voices came back, exclaiming delicately over the furnishings.

"How long were you in the army?" Sandy asked when they came back.

"Five years," Tom said, grinning and shaking his curly head. "My first wife left me three months after I got drafted."

"Oh?" Sandy said.

"Yeah. I guess she couldnt take the idea of not getting any for so long. It looked like a long war."

"War is hard on the women too," Sandy said.

"Sure," Tom said. "I dont see how they stand it. I'm glad I was a man in this war."

"Take it easy," George growled.

Tom grinned at him and turned back to Sandy. "I been married four times in five years. My last wife left me day before yesterday. She told me she was leaving and I said, Okay, baby. That's fine. Only remember there won't be nobody here when you come back. If I wanted, I could call her up right now and tell her and she'd start back tonight."

"Why dont you?" Sandy said. "I've got a phone."

Tom laughed. "What the hell. I'm doin all right. Come here, baby," he said to the blonde one, and patted his right leg. She came over, smiling, on his left side and started to sit on his lap.

"No," Tom said. "Go around to the other side. You cant sit on that one."

The blonde one obeyed and walked around his chair. She sat

down smiling on his right thigh and Tom put his arm clear around her waist. "I'm doin all right, baby, ain't I? Who wants to get married?"

George was watching him, and now he laughed. "I been married myself," he said, not looking at Sandy.

"Sure," Tom grinned. "Dont tell me. I was out in Utah when you got the rings back, remember? Ha!" he turned his liquorbright eyes on Sandy. "It was just like Robert Taylor in the movies. He took them out in the snow and threw them away with a curse. Went right out the ward door and into the snowing night.

"One ring, engagement, platinum, two carat diamond," Tom said, as if giving the nomenclature of a new weapon. "One ring, wedding, platinum, diamond circlet.—I told him he should of hocked them."

"No," Sandy said. "He should have kept them, then he could have used them over and over, every other night."

"I'll say," Tom said. "I'll never forget the first time me and George went on pass in Salt Lake City. He sure could of used them then."

"Aint you drinkin, Sandy?" George said.

"You know I dont drink."

"You used to. Some."

"That was only on special occasions," Sandy said, looking at him. "That was a long time ago. I've quit that now," she said.

George looked away, at Tom, who had his hand up under the blonde one's armpit, snuggled in. "Now this heres a very fine thing," Tom said, nodding at her. "She's not persnickity like the broads in Salt Lake."

"I didnt really like it then," Sandy said.

"I know," George said.

"George picked him up a gal in a bar in Salt Lake that first night," Tom said. "She looked a lot like you, honey," he said to the blonde one. The blonde one tittered and put her hand beneath his ear.

"This gal," Tom continued, "she thought George was wonderful; he was wearing his ribbons. She asked him all about the limp and how he got wounded. She thought he was the nuts till she found out what it was made him limp." Tom paused to laugh.

"Then she got dressed and took off; we seen her later with a marine." He looked at George and they both laughed. George went around the table and sat down beside the short one.

"You ought to have a drink with us, Sandy," George said. "You're the host."

"I dont feel much like being formal," Sandy said.

Tom laughed. "Me neither."

"Do you want something to eat?" Sandy asked him. "I might eat something."

"Sure," Tom said. "I'll eat anything. I'm an old eater from way back. I really eat it. You got any cheese and crackers?"

Sandy went to one of the cupboards. "You fix another drink, George."

"Thats it," Tom said. "Eat and drink. There's only one think can turn my stommick," he said to the blonde one. "You know whats the only think can turn my stommick?"

"Yes," said the blonde one apprehensively, glancing at Sandy. "I know."

"I'll tell you the only thing can turn my stommick."

"Now, honey," the blonde one said.

George turned around from the bottles on the countertop, pausing dramatically like an orator.

"Same thing that can turn my stommick."

He and Tom laughed uproariously, and he passed the drinks and sat down. The blonde one and the short one tittered and glanced nervously at Sandy.

Tom thumped George's right leg with his fist and the sound it made was solid, heavy, the sound his own had made out in the car.

"You goddam old cripple, you."

"Thats all right," George said. "You cant run so goddam fast yourself."

"The hell I cant." Tom reached for his drink and misjudged it, spilling some on the tablecloth and on the blonde girl's skirt.

"Now see what you did?" she said. "Damn it."

Tom laughed. "Take it easy, baby. If you never get nothing worse than whiskey spilled on your skirt, you'll be all right. Whiskey'll wash out."

George watched dully as the spot spread on the red and white checked tablecloth, then he lurched to his feet toward the sink where the dishrag always was.

Sandy pushed him back into his chair. "Its all right, George. I'll change it tomorrow."

George breathed heavily. "Watch yourself, you," he said to Tom. "Goddam you, be careful."

"What the hell. I dint do it on purpose."

"Thats all right, just watch yourself."

"Okay, Sergeant," Tom said. "Okay, halfchick."

George laughed suddenly, munching a slab of cheese between two crackers, spraying crumbs.

"Dont call me none of your family names.

"We really use to have some times," he said to Sandy. "You know what this crazy bastard use to do? After we got our leather, we use to stand out in the corridor and watch the guys with a leg off going down the hall on crutches. Tom would look at them and say to me, Pore feller. He's lost a leg. And I'd say, Why that's turrible, ain't it?"

Sandy was looking at him, watching him, her sandwich untouched in her hand. Under her gaze George's eyebrows suddenly went up, bent in the middle.

"We use to go to town," he said, grinning at her. "We really had some times. You ought to seen their faces when we'd go up to the room from the bar. You ought to see them when we'd take our pants off." He laughed viciously. "One broad even fainted on me. They didnt like it." His gaze wavered, then fell to his drink. "I guess you cant blame them though."

"Why?" Sandy said. "Why did you do it, George?"

"Hell," he said, looking up. "*Why?* Dont you know *why?*"

Sandy shook her head slowly, her eyes unmoving on his face. "No," she said. "I dont know why. I guess I never will know why," she said.

Tom was pinching the blonde one's bottom. "That tickles mine," he said. "You know what tickles mine?"

"No," she said, "what?"

Tom whispered in her ear and she giggled and slapped him lightly.

"No," George said. "I guess you wont. You aint never been in the army, have you?"

"No," Sandy said. "I havent."

"You ought to try it," George said. "Fix us one more drink and we'll be goin.'"

"All right, George. But I wish you'd stay."

George spread his hands and looked down at himself. "Who?" he said. "Me?"

"Yes," Sandy said. "You really do need to sober up."

"Oh," George said. "Sober up. Liquor never bothers me. Listen, Sandy. I wanted to talk to you, Sandy."

Under the red and white checked tablecloth George put his hand on Sandy's bare knee below her skirt. His hand cupped it awkwardly, but softly, very softly.

"I'll get your drink," Sandy said, pushing back her chair. George watched her get up and go to the countertop where the bottles were.

"Come here, you," George said to the short dark one. He jerked her toward him so roughly her head snapped back. He kissed her heavily, his left hand behind her head holding her neck rigid, his right hand on her upper arm, stroking heavily, pinching slightly.

Sandy set the drink in front of him. "Here's your drink you wanted, George," she said, still holding the tabled glass. "George, here's your drink."

"Okay," George said. "Drink up, you all, and lets get out of this."

The short one was rubbing her neck with her hand, her face twisted breathlessly. She smiled apologetically at Sandy. "You got a wonderful home here, Miss Thomas," she said.

George lurched to this feet. "All right. All right. Outside." He shooed them out the door, Tom grinning, his hand hidden under the blonde one's arm. Then he stood in the doorway looking back.

"Well, so long. And thanks for the liquor."

"All right, George. Why dont you stop drinking, George?"

"Why?" George said. "You ask me why."

"I hate to see you ruin yourself."

George laughed. "Well now thanks. That sure is nice of you, Sandy girl. But liquor never bothers me." He looked around the gayness of the kitchen. "Listen. I'm sorry about the tablecloth. Sorry. I shouldnt of done it, I guess. I shouldnt of come here with them."

"No, George. You shouldnt."

"You know what I love about you, Sandy girl? You're always so goddam stinking right."

"I just do what I have to," Sandy said.

"Sandy," George said. "You dont know what it was like, Sandy."

"No," she said. "I guess I dont."

"You goddam right you dont. And you never will. You'll never be . . ."

"I cant help the way I'm made."

"Yes? Well I cant neither. The only thing for us to do is turn it over to the United Nations. Its their job, let them figure it out."

Tom Hornney came back to the door. "Come on, for Christ sake. Are you comin or aint you?"

"Yes goddam it I'm comin. I'm comin and I'm goin." George limped swingingly over to the countertop and grabbed a bottle.

Tom stepped inside the door. "Listen, lady," he said. "What the hells a leg? The thing a man wants you dames will never give him. We're just on a little vacation now. I got a trucking business in Terre Haute. Had it before the war. There's good money in long-distance hauling, and me and George is goin to get our share. We got six trucks and three more spotted, and I know this racket, see? I know how to get the contracks, all the ways. An I got the pull. And me and George is full-time partners. What the hells a leg?"

George set down the bottle and came back, his right leg hitting the floor heavy and without resilience. "Tom and me is buddies, and right or wrong what we do we do together."

"I think thats fine, George," she said.

"Yeah? Well then, its all all right then, aint it?"

"Listen, lady," Tom said. "Someday he'll build another house'll make this place look sick, see? To hell with the respectability if you got the money. So what the hells a leg?"

"Shut up," George said. "Lets go. Shut up. Shut up, or I'll mash you down."

"Yeah?" Tom grinned. "I'll take your leg off and beat you to death with it, Mack."

George threw back his head, laughing. "Fall in, you bum. Lets go."

"George," Sandy said. She went to the countertop and came back with a nearly full bottle. "Take it with you."

"Not me. I got mine in the car. And I got the money to buy more. Whiskey never bothers me. Fall in, Tom, goddam you."

Tom slapped him on the back. "Right," he said. And he started to sing.

They went out of the house into the steaming chill February night. They went arm in arm and limping. And they were singing.

> "Si-n-n-g glorious, glorious,
> One keg of beer for the four of us,
> Glory be to God there's no more of us,
> 'Cause . . ."

Their voices faded and died as the motor started. Tom honked the horn once, derisively.

Sandy Thomas stood in the door, watching the headlights move away, feeling the need inside, holding the bottle in her hand, moisture overflowing her eyes unnoticed, looking backward into a past the world had not seen fit to let alone. Tomorrow she would change the tablecloth, the red and white checkered tablecloth.

[September 1951]

NORMAN MAILER

The Language of Men

In the beginning, Sanford Carter was ashamed of becoming an Army cook. This was not from snobbery, at least not from snobbery of the most direct sort. During the two and a half years Carter had been in the Army he had come to hate cooks more and more. They existed for him as a symbol of all that was corrupt, overbearing, stupid, and privileged in Army life. The image which came to mind was a fat cook with an enormous sandwich in one hand, and a bottle of beer in the other, sweat pouring down a porcine face, foot on a flour barrel, shouting at the K.P.'s, "Hurry up, you men, I ain't got all day." More than once in those two and a half years, driven to exasperation, Carter had been on the verge of throwing his food into a cook's face as he passed on the serving line. His anger often derived from nothing: the set of a pair of fat lips, the casual heavy thump of the serving spoon into his plate, or the resentful conviction that the cook was not serving him enough. Since life in the Army was in most aspects a marriage, this rage over apparently harmless details was not a sign of unbalance. Every soldier found some particular habit of the Army spouse impossible to support.

Yet Sanford Carter became a cook and, to elaborate the irony, did better as a cook than he had done as anything else. In a few months he rose from a Private to a first cook with the rank of Sergeant, Technician. After the fact, it was easy to understand. He had suffered through all his Army career from an excess of eagerness. He had cared too much, he had wanted to do well, and so he had often been tense at moments when he would better have been relaxed. He was very young, twenty-one, had lived the comparatively gentle life of a middle-class boy, and needed some success in the Army to prove to himself that he was not completely worthless.

In succession, he had failed as a surveyor in Field Artillery, a clerk in an Infantry headquaters, a telephone wireman, and finally a rifleman. When the war ended, and his regiment went to Japan, Carter was still a rifleman; he had been a rifleman for eight months. What was more to the point, he had been in the platoon as long as any of its members; the skilled hard-bitten nucleus of veterans who had run his squad had gone home one by one, and it seemed to him that through seniority he was entitled to at least a corporal's rating. Through seniority he was so entitled, but on no other ground. Whenever responsibility had been handed to him, he had discharged it miserably, tensely, overconscientiously. He had always asked too many questions, he had worried the task too severely, he had conveyed his nervousness to the men he was supposed to lead. Since he was also sensitive enough and proud enough never to curry favor with the noncoms in the platoons, he was in no position to sit in on their occasional discussions about who was to succeed them. In a vacuum of ignorance, he had allowed himself to dream that he would be given a squad to lead, and his hurt was sharp when the squad was given to a replacement who had joined the platoon months after him.

The war was over, Carter had a bride in the States (he had lived with her for only two months), he was lonely, he was obsessed with going home. As one week dragged into the next, and the regiment, the company, and his own platoon continued the same sort of training which they had been doing ever since he had entered the Army, he thought he would snap. There were months to wait until he would be discharged and meanwhile it was intolerable to him to be taught for the fifth time the nomenclature of the machine gun, to stand a retreat parade three evenings a week. He wanted some niche where he could lick his wounds, some Army job with so many hours of work and so many hours of complete freedom, where he could be alone by himself. He hated the Army, the huge Army which had proved to him that he was good at no work, and incapable of succeeding at anything. He wrote long, aching letters to his wife, he talked less and less to the men around him and he was close to violent attacks of anger during the most casual phases of training—during close-order drill or cleaning his rifle for inspection. He knew that if he did not find his niche it was possible that he would crack.

So he took an opening in the kitchen. It promised him nothing except a day of work, and a day of leisure which would be completely at his disposal. He found that he liked it. He was given at first the job of baking the bread for the company, and every other night he worked till early in the morning, kneading and shaping his fifty-pound mix of dough. At two or three he would be done, and for his work there would be the tangible reward of fifty loaves of bread, all fresh from the oven, all clean and smelling of fertile accomplished creativity. He had the rare and therefore intensely satisfying emotion of seeing at the end of an Army chore the product of his labor.

A month after he became a cook the regiment was disbanded, and those men who did not have enough points to go home were sent to other outfits. Carter ended at an ordnance company in another Japanese city. He had by now given up all thought of getting a non-com's rating before he was discharged, and was merely content to work each alternate day. He took his work for granted and so he succeeded at it. He had begun as a baker in the new company kitchen; before long he was the first cook. It all happened quickly. One cook went home on points, another caught a skin disease, a third was transferred from the kitchen after contracting a venereal infection. On the shift which Carter worked there were left only himself and a man who was illiterate. Carter was put nominally in charge, and was soon actively in charge. He looked up each menu in an Army recipe book, collected the items, combined them in the order indicated, and after the proper time had elapsed, took them from the stove. His product tasted neither better nor worse than the product of all other Army cooks. But the mess sergeant was impressed. Carter had filled a gap. The next time ratings were given out Carter jumped at a bound from Private to Sergeant T/4.

On the surface he was happy; beneath the surface he was over-joyed. It took him several weeks to realize how grateful and delighted he felt. The promotion coincided with his assignment to a detachment working in a small seaport up the coast. Carter arrived there to discover that he was in charge of cooking for thirty men, and would act as mess sergeant. There was another cook, and there were four permanent Japanese K.P.'s, all of them good workers. He still cooked every other day, but there was always time between meals to take a break of at least an hour and often two; he shared a room with the other cook and lived in comparative privacy for the first time in several years; the seaport was beautiful; there was only one officer, and he left the men alone; supplies were plentiful due to a clerical error which assigned rations for forty men rather than thirty; and in general everything was fine. The niche had become a sinecure.

This was the happiest period of Carter's life in the Army. He came to like his Japanese K.P.'s. He studied their language, he visited their homes, he gave them gifts of food from time to time. They worshiped him because he was kind to them and generous, because he never shouted, because his good humor bubbled over into games, and made the work of the kitchen seem pleasant. All the while he grew in confidence. He was not a big man, but his body filled out from the heavy work; he was likely to sing a great deal, he cracked jokes with the men on the chow line. The kitchen became his property, it became his domain, and since it was a warm room, filled with sunlight, he came to take pleasure in the very sight of it. Before long his good humor expanded into a series of efforts to improve the food. He began to take little pains and make little extra efforts which would have been impossible if he had been obliged to cook for more than thirty men. In the morning he would serve the men fresh eggs scrambled or fried to their desire in fresh butter. Instead of cooking sixty eggs in one large pot he cooked two eggs at a time in a frying pan, turning them to the taste of each soldier. He baked like a housewife satisfying her young husband; at lunch and dinner there was pie or cake, and often both. He went to great lengths. He taught the K.P.'s how to make the toast come out right. He traded excess food for spices in Japanese stores. He rubbed paprika and garlic on the chickens. He even made pastries to cover such staples as corn beef hash and meat and vegetable stew.

It all seemed to be wasted. In the beginning the men might have noticed these improvements, but after a period they took them for granted. It did not matter how he worked to satisfy them; they trudged through the chow line with their heads down, nodding coolly at him, and they ate without comment. He would hang around the tables after the meal, noticing how much they consumed, and what they discarded; he would wait for compliments, but the soldiers seemed indifferent. They seemed to eat without tasting the food. In their faces he saw mirrored the distaste with which he had once stared at cooks.

The honeymoon was ended. The pleasure he took in the kitchen and himself curdled. He became aware again of his painful desire to please people, to discharge responsibility, to be a man. When he had been a child, tears had come into his eyes at a cross word, and he had lived in an atmosphere where his smallest accomplishment was warmly praised. He was the sort of young man, he often thought bitterly, who was accustomed to the attention and the protection of women. He would have thrown away all he possessed—the love of his wife, the love of his mother, the benefits of his education, the assured financial security of entering his father's business—if he had been able just once to dig a ditch as well as the most ignorant farmer.

Instead, he was back in the painful unprotected days of his first entrance into the Army. Once again the most casual actions became the most painful, the events which were most to be taken for granted grew into the most significant, and the feeding of the men at each meal turned progressively more unbearable.

So Sanford Carter came full circle. If he had once hated the cooks, he now hated the troops. At mealtimes his face soured into the belligerent scowl with which he had once believed cooks to be born. And to himself he muttered the age-old laments of the housewife: how little they appreciated what he did.

Finally there was an explosion. He was approached one day by Corporal Taylor, and he had come to hate Taylor, because Taylor was the natural leader of the detachment and kept the other men endlessly amused with his jokes. Taylor had the ability to present himself as inefficient, shiftless, and incapable, in such a manner as to convey that really the opposite was true. He had the lightest touch, he had the greatest facility, he could charm a geisha in two minutes and obtain anything he wanted from a supply sergeant in five. Carter envied him, envied his grace, his charmed indifference; then grew to hate him.

Taylor teased Carter about the cooking, and he had the knack of knowing where to put the knife. "Hey, Carter," he would shout across the mess hall while breakfast was being served, "you turned my eggs twice, and I asked for them raw." The men would shout with laughter. Somehow Taylor had succeeded in conveying all of the situation, or so it seemed to Carter, insinuating everything, how Carter worked and how it meant nothing, how Carter labored to gain their affection and earned their contempt. Carter would scowl, Carter would answer in a rough voice, "Next time I'll crack them over your head." "You crack 'em, I'll eat 'em," Taylor would pipe back, "but just don't put your fingers in 'em." And there would be another laugh. He hated the sight of Taylor.

It was Taylor who came to him to get the salad oil. About twenty of the soldiers were going to have a fish fry at the geisha house; they had bought the fish at the local market, but they could not buy oil, so Taylor was sent as the deputy to Carter. He was charming to Carter, he complimented him on the meal, he clapped him on the back, he dissolved Carter to warmth, to private delight in the attention, and the thought that he had misjudged Taylor. Then Taylor asked for the oil.

Carter was sick with anger. Twenty men out of the thirty in the detachment were going on the fish fry. It meant only that Carter was considered one of the ten undesirables. It was something he had known, but the proof of knowledge is always more painful than the acquisition of it. If he had been alone his eyes would have clouded. And he was outraged at Taylor's deception. He could imagine Taylor saying ten minutes later, "You should have seen the grease job I gave to Carter. I'm dumb, but man, he's dumber."

Carter was close enough to giving him the oil. He had a sense of what it would mean to refuse Taylor, he was on the very edge of mild acquiescence. But he also had a sense of how he would despise himself afterward.

"No," he said abruptly, his teeth gritted, "you can't have it."

"What do you mean we can't have it?"

"I won't give it to you." Carter could almost feel the rage which Taylor generated at being refused.

"You won't give away a lousy five gallons of oil to a bunch of G.I.'s having a party?"

"I'm sick and tired," Carter began.

"So am I." Taylor walked away.

Carter knew he would pay for it. He left the K.P.'s and went to change his sweat-soaked work shirt, and as he passed the large dormitory in which most of the detachment slept he could hear Taylor's high-pitched voice. Carter did not bother to take off his shirt. He returned instead to the kitchen, and listened to the sound of men going back and forth through the hall and of a man shouting with rage. That was Hobbs, a Southerner, a big man with a big bellowing voice.

There was a formal knock on the kitchen door. Taylor came in. His face was pale and his eyes showed a cold satisfaction. "Carter," he said, "the men want to see you in the big room."

Carter heard his voice answer huskily. "If they want to see me, they can come into the kitchen."

He knew he would conduct himself with more courage in his own kitchen than anywhere else. "I'll be here for a while."

Taylor closed the door, and Carter picked up a writing board to which was clamped the menu for the following day. Then he made a pretense of examining the food supplies in the pantry closet. It was his habit to check the stocks before deciding what to serve the next day, but on this night his eyes ranged thoughtlessly over the canned goods. In a corner were seven five-gallon tins of salad oil, easily enough cooking oil to last a month. Carter came out of the pantry and shut the door behind him.

He kept his head down and pretended to be writing the menu when the soldiers came in. Somehow there were even more of them than he had expected. Out of the twenty men who were going to the party, all but two or three had crowded through the door.

Carter took his time, looked up slowly. "You men want to see me?" he asked flatly.

They were angry. For the first time in his life he faced the hostile expressions of many men. It was the most painful and anxious moment he had ever known.

"Taylor says you won't give us the oil," someone burst out.

"That's right, I won't," said Carter. He tapped his pencil against the scratchboard, tapping it slowly and, he hoped, with an appearance of calm.

"What a stink deal," said Porfirio, a little Cuban whom Carter had always considered his friend.

Hobbs, the big Southerner, stared down at Carter. "Would you mind telling the men why you've decided not to give us the oil?" he asked quietly.

" 'Cause I'm blowed if I'm going to cater to you men. I've catered enough," Carter said. His voice was close to cracking with the outrage he had suppressed for so long, and he knew that if he continued he might cry. "I'm the acting mess sergeant," he said as coldly as he could, "and I decide what goes out of this kitchen." He stared at each one in turn, trying to stare them down, feeling mired in the rut of his own failure. They would never have dared this approach to another mess sergeant.

"What crud," someone muttered.

"You won't give a lousy five-gallon can of oil for a G.I. party," Hobbs said more loudly.

"I won't. That's definite. You men can get out of here."

"Why, you lousy little snot," Hobbs burst out, "how many five-gallon cans of oil have you sold on the black market?"

"I've never sold any." Carter might have been slapped with the flat of a sword. He told himself bitterly, numbly, that this was the reward he received for being perhaps the single honest cook in the whole United States Army. And he even had time to wonder at the obscure prejudice which had kept him from selling food for his own profit.

"Man, I've seen you take it out," Hobbs exclaimed. "I've seen you take it to the market."

"I took food to trade for spices," Carter said hotly.

There was an ugly snicker from the men.

"I don't mind if a cook sells," Hobbs said, "every man has his own deal in this Army. But a cook ought to give a little food to a G.I. if he wants it."

"Tell him," someone said.

"It's bull," Taylor screeched. "I've seen Carter take butter, eggs, every damn thing to the market."

Their faces were red, they circled him.

"I never sold a thing," Carter said doggedly.

"And I'm telling you," Hobbs said, "that you're a two-bit crook. You been raiding that kitchen, and that's why you don't give to us now."

Carter knew there was only one way he could possibly answer if he hoped to live among these men again. "That's a goddam lie," Carter said to Hobbs. He laid down the scratchboard, he flipped his pencil slowly and deliberately to one corner of the room, and with his heart aching he lunged toward Hobbs. He had no hope of beating him. He merely intended to fight until he was pounded unconscious, advancing the pain and bruises he would collect as collateral for his self-respect.

To his indescribable relief Porfirio darted between them, held them apart with the pleased ferocity of a small man breaking up a fight. "Now, stop this! Now, stop this!" he cried out.

Carter allowed himself to be pushed back, and he knew that he had gained a point. He even glimpsed a solution with some honor.

He shrugged violently to free himself from Porfirio. He was in a rage, and yet it was a rage he could have ended at any instant. "All right, you men," he swore, "I'll give you the oil, but now that we're at it, I'm going to tell you a thing or two." His face red, his body perspiring, he was in the pantry and out again with a five-gallon tin. "Here," he said, "you better have a good fish fry, 'cause it's the last good meal you're going to have for quite a while. I'm sick of trying to please you. You think I have to work—" he was about to say, my fingers to the bone—"well, I don't. From now on, you'll see what chow in the Army is supposed to be like." He was almost hysterical. "Take that oil. Have your fish fry." The fact that they wanted to cook for themselves was the greatest insult of all. "Tomorrow I'll give you real Army cooking."

His voice was so intense that they backed away from him. "Get out of this kitchen," he said. "None of you has any business here."

They filed out quietly, and they looked a little sheepish.

Carter felt weary, he felt ashamed of himself, he knew he had not meant what he said. But half an hour later, when he left the kitchen and passed the large dormitory, he heard shouts of raucous laughter, and he heard his name mentioned and then more laughter.

He slept badly that night, he was awake at four, he was in the kitchen by five, and stood there white-faced and nervous, waiting for the K.P.'s to arrive. Breakfast that morning landed on the men like a lead bomb. Carter rummaged in the back of the pantry and found a tin of dehydrated eggs covered with dust, memento of a time when fresh eggs were never on the ration list. The K.P.'s looked at him in amazement as he stirred the lumpy powder into a pan of water. While it was still half-dissolved he put it on the fire. While it was still wet, he took it off. The coffee was cold, the toast was burned, the oatmeal stuck to the pot. The men dipped forks into their food, took cautious sips of their coffee, and spoke in whispers. Sullenness drifted like vapors through the kitchen.

At noontime Carter opened cans of meat and vegetable stew. He dumped them into a pan and heated them slightly. He served the stew with burned string beans and dehydrated potatoes which tasted like straw. For dessert the men had a single lukewarm canned peach and cold coffee.

So the meals continued. For three days Carter cooked slop, and suffered even more than the men. When mealtime came he left the chow line to the K.P.'s and sat in his room, perspiring with shame, determined not to yield and sick with the determination.

Carter won. On the fourth day a delegation of men came to see him. They told him that indeed they had appreciated his cooking in the past, they told him that they were sorry they had hurt his feelings, they listened to his remonstrances, they listened to his grievances, and with delight Carter forgave them. That night, for supper, the detachment celebrated. There was roast chicken with stuffing, lemon meringue pie and chocolate cake. The coffee burned their lips. More than half the men made it a point to compliment Carter on the meal.

In the weeks which followed the compliments diminished, but they never stopped completely. Carter became ashamed at last. He realized the men were trying to humor him, and he wished to tell them it was no longer necessary.

Harmony settled over the kitchen. Carter even became friends with Hobbs, the big Southerner. Hobbs approached him one day, and in the manner of a farmer talked obliquely for an hour. He spoke about his father, he spoke about his girl friends, he alluded indirectly to the night they had almost fought, and finally with the courtesy of a Southerner he said to Carter, "You know, I'm sorry about shooting off my mouth. You were right to want to fight me, and if you're still mad I'll fight you to give you satisfaction, although I just as soon would not."

"No, I don't want to fight with you now," Carter said warmly. They smiled at each other. They were friends.

Carter knew he had gained Hobbs' respect. Hobbs respected him because he had been willing to fight. That made sense to a man like Hobbs. Carter liked him so much at this moment that he wished the friendship to be more intimate.

"You know," he said to Hobbs, "it's a funny thing. You know I really never did sell anything on the black market. Not that I'm proud of it, but I just didn't."

Hobbs frowned. He seemed to be saying that Carter did not have to lie. "I don't hold it against a man," Hobbs said, "if he makes a little money in something that's his own proper work. Hell, I sell gas from the motor pool. It's just I also give gas if one of the G.I.'s wants to take the jeep out for a joy ride, kind of."

"No, but I never did sell anything." Carter had to explain. "If I ever had sold on the black market, I would have given the salad oil without question."

Hobbs frowned again, and Carter realized he still did not believe him. Carter did not want to lose the friendship which was forming. He thought he could save it only by some further admission. "You know," he said again, "remember when Porfirio broke up our fight? I was awful glad when I didn't have to fight you." Carter laughed, expecting Hobbs to laugh with him, but a shadow passed across Hobbs' face.

"Funny way of putting it," Hobbs said.

He was always friendly thereafter, but Carter knew that Hobbs would never consider him a friend. Carter thought about it often, and began to wonder about the things which made him different. He was no longer so worried about becoming a man; he felt that to an extent he had become one. But in his heart he wondered if he would ever learn the langauge of men.

[April 1953]

LESLIE A. FIEDLER

Nude Croquet

"**D**on't you ever get tired of being right!" Howard snarled ritually, jamming the brakes down hard as the house rose up from a tangle of runty pines and bushes just where Jessie had said it would be. They had been arguing for twenty minutes about the last turn, he with all the desperate passion of a man without a sense of direction.

"Won't you ever learn how to stop a car!" Jessie snapped back automatically; then, counting the crazy turrets castellated and masked with iron filigree, "Seven! Bernie wasn't exaggerating for once." And at last, "I'm so damn tired of being right, I could *puke!*" She stared miserably at the bats sliding down the evening sky over the slate roofs—her face very pale in the last light. "It'll be raining in half an hour," she added. "There goes your swim."

"Don't sound so happy," he answered, cutting the motor and putting an arm around her shoulder. "Look. Let's turn right around and go home. There's no point in this whole—I mean, what do we have in common any more, Leonard and Bill and I, except our remembered youth—and that's only a reproach. It's just that—I—" He gave up finally, waving his free hand at the grounds before them: the offensive acres of plants and flowers that neither of them could have named, the lily-infested pond barely visible beside the porte-cochere, the untidy extravagance of the great house itself.

Jessie shook herself free of his arm and thrust her face forward, viciously, almost into the mirror on the sun visor. "I look so old—so goddamned *old!*" She touched the creases on her cheek that had once been dimples, the vein-riddled crescents under her eyes, the ungenerous mouth that had sunk inward, pulling her nose and chin closer together.

"You *are* old. *We*'re old. Forty-three, forty-five—that's not young. What do you want?" Howard turned slowly to look at the face he seldom saw.

"At least my hair's a good color this time." She lifted a lock of it in her bony hand—very red against the white. "But *you* look like a baby. It isn't fair. A spoiled baby!"

He tried to concentrate on her hair, but could not resist glancing a little smugly at his own face in the glass, baby pink and white under the baby yellow curls, luxuriant and untouched by grey. His face had always been plump and never handsome, but its indestructible youthfulness had managed finally to lend it a certain charm.

"A spoiled baby—and I'm the one who spoils you. I must want you to look young. Why the hell do I want that, Howard? I know why *you* like it; it makes other women feel sorry for you, yoked to such a hag! But why do I want it, Howard, *why?*"

"I don't know. You're just a good American girl, I guess." He could hear the sea walloping the rocks, realized that he had been hearing it for a long time: *thump—thump—thump.* Like a man in an empty house, he thought sadly, banging a table, banging a table and shouting into the darkness that—

"Do I really look so old, Howard? *Do* I?" she interrupted. "What would you think if you just met me for the first time?"

He examined her for a moment with his careful painter's eye. "Yes," he answered at length, "you do." He was quite serious; after much devious thought, he always ended up telling the truth, the simplest truth. It was a kind of laziness. "I always tell the truth," he explained, trying to embrace her again. "It's a kind of laziness."

"A bon mot!" she cried bitterly. "Save it! Save it for your friends and their twenty-year old wives." She tried vainly to light her cigarette at the car lighter in an intended gesture of nonchalance; and he flipped a match with finger and thumb.

"Listen, Jess, I'm not kidding. Let's turn around. It's bound to be gruesome—six men who never loved each other to begin with, and two brand-new wives. Besides, you're upset. We can call up later and say I got lost. Everyone knows I always get lost. Let's keep going to Atlantic City; a man can die without having been in Atlantic City and this may be our only chance. The kid's in camp and—"

She had not even been listening. "I suppose you intend to play the fool again tonight the way you always do. That's the difference between you and an ordinary fool; you always plan it in advance. Which one will you make a pass at tonight? Which twenty-year-old? Which ingénue: Molly or Eva?"

"Ay-vah," he corrected her. "She says it 'Ay-vah' not 'Eva.' It makes Leonard mad when—"

"To hell with Leonard. He's a worse fool than you are. Giving up a girl like Lucille for a—"

"Please, Jess, don't yell at me. Take it up with Leonard. I'm not the one who divorced his wife. I just said—"

"You just *said.* You just sit there preening in the mirror and thinking what-a-good-boy-am-I because you didn't divorce your wife like Leonard or Bill. Many thanks."

"You're welcome."

"Oh, no, you don't divorce her; you only make a fool of her by slobbering over somebody else's twenty-year-old wife, because you're too lazy and too spoiled and too irresponsible even to be the first-class kind of bastard Leonard is. But don't think you just make a fool out of me. You make a worse fool out of yourself. After all, you *are* forty-five—forty-five and foolish and fat, just like in the comic strips." She took the fold of fat over his belt between two fingers and pinched it hard. She was crying. "The shame of it is that it's such a pattern, so stupid, so *expected.* Everyone knows what Howard Place, boy abstractionist, is going to do at a party, and everybody watches and waits for him to do it. Who will it be tonight? Which sleazy bitch or celebrity-happy sophomore from Bennington?"

"All right, then, we'll—"

"All right, then, we'll *what?* You don't even bother to protest any more, do you? You won't even lie to me."

"Okay, so let's get out of here." Clumsily and in anger, he began to slew the car around.

But Jessie had changed her mood, though her tears were not yet dry. "At least we can still argue. That's a good sign, Howard, isn't it?"

"It sure is." He kissed her tentatively.

"Then don't turn around. How can you be such a fool? Don't you think I want to see the inside of the house, too? I want it to be so vulgar and stupid that—"

"Look, darling—"

"Oh, you poor, helpless bastard, just lie to me a little, that's all. I *love* you, you know." She leaned over to return his kiss—not very hard.

"That's just because I'm going to be in next year's Biennale. You don't want to lose a winner."

"It helps." She kissed him again, and he held her to him almost with passion.

"I love you, too, Jess. God have mercy on us." It was the simplest truth, and yet he was already thinking how Eva (Leonard's wife whom he had seen only once) and Molly (for whom Bill had left Elaine and whom he had not yet met) would be to touch or taste, their flesh not much more subdued by love or time than his fourteen-year-old daughter's.

The drive led them past two tennis courts and wound now beside the pond, around which they could see the white gleam of marble statues, emperors and fauns, athletes and nymphs, carefully mutilated to look like recovered antiques. It had begun to rain, and over Jessie's shoulder he could see drops glistening on a slender, high-breasted Venus who was arched across a shell in the middle of a pool, with her head tossed arrogantly back. "Aphrodite at the gates. It's a good omen." Howard whooped helplessly, abandoned to laughter, while Jessie said, "For pity's sake, what's so funny? Look, it's Bill himself."

It *was* Bill, at the door—unmistakably Bill, playing squire in this place created by his rich wife's grandfather, waving a Martini glass in their direction and yelling what must have been a fond greeting. Three years (was it only three since they had sat in the Piazza del Popolo choking on Camparisoda?) had done something cruel and comical to him. It was not merely that he had grown fat. He looked somehow as if he had been blown up by a kid with a bicycle pump: the skinny, bewildered face still skinny but *inflated,* the once half-starved body ballooned out under the unbleached-linen jacket.

"I'm not rich for nothing," he said. "Imagine it, me rich." He raised a plump arm with visible effort to indicate his domain. "Sixty-two bedrooms—we even have a ghost, but unfortunately on Sundays ghosts don't—" He seemed to remember for the first time the dark-haired girl with the pale eyes who stood beside him. Everything about her was tiny except for her breasts, which, thrust forward by her sway-backed stance, gave her the overweighted air of an eighth-grader who has not yet grown up to her body. "And this is the secret of my success, Molly-o, my wife." A deprecatory grin fought to take shape in the tight, round blank of his face. It was impossible to say if he changed expression when he added with scarcely a pause, "Did you know Irving's dead?"

Molly reached a hand toward Howard first, very brisk and businesslike, though her pale eyes fluttered coyly. They were green, he thought, if they were any color at all.

"Place," she said, greeting him by last name as if she were a man. "Delighted. I recognized you from the picture in *Harper's Bazaar.*"

He touched her cheek lightly, ignoring the hand. "Delighted, too. I recognized you from the picture outside Minsky's."

"Pardon?" Molly asked uncertainly. Her lids moved up and down frantically over the ambiguous green.

"Oh, for pity's sake," Jessie exclaimed, "she's only a child." Then, giving her a hug and a large kiss, "I love you, you know. I love all of Bill's wives."

"He only had *two,*" Molly answered, moving uneasily in Jessie's embrace. "I mean, I'm the second, that is—"

"I said Irving's dead," Bill tried again. "Irving's dead. Irving's dead." He was constitutionally incapable of shouting, but he pounded Howard's back with a pudgy hand to claim his attention.

"I know he's dead," Howard answered at last. "Irving's been dead for years. I keep telling him so. He never got out from under the influence of Hoffman. But where the hell is he? I haven't seen—"

"No! No!" Bill insisted, dancing up and down in exasperation. "He really died two nights ago. He was supposed to be here tonight with Esther—"

"Sarah, you mean," Jessie interrupted.

"I thought it was—to hell with it. The important thing is, he's dead."

"You mean *dead,*" Howard yelled, registering at last. "Irving? Irving Posner? Dead?"

"He died two nights ago," Molly said, "the fourteenth, at 7:30 P.M. in the arms of his wife, of a heart attack." This at least, she obviously believed, was a solid fact to be hung on to, to be asserted in the midst of references that baffled her and slippery insults. This was what she knew, what she could tell the others.

In his distress, Howard had not noticed Marvin and Achsa, who were coming toward them out of the house, Marvin as usual carefully not looking at his wife, who followed him fiercely, like a dog on a fresh scent. Molly tried to continue; but Marvin leaned down toward her from his immense height, almost touching her pony tail with his chin.

"You sound like a newspaper," he said in his flat, unpleasant voice; "the kind of newspaper I never read. You ask me how I know what kind of newspaper it is, if I never read it; I answer I know that you read it, and knowing you I deduce—"

"Excuse *me,* Mr. Solomon," Molly retorted with schoolgirl iciness, "I wasn't aware that you were eavesdropping." Marvin had withdrawn again to his full height, lifting his dark, melancholy face back into its customary loneliness; and she had to tilt her own head back perilously to glare at him.

"Why don't you call me Marvin," he said. "That would make me more uncomfortable yet."

"For the love of Jesus, shut *up,*" Achsa cut in. "You're not even drunk." She did not try to engage his eye, shouting instead with all the hopeless rage of one whose worst enemy has remained out of range for twenty years. At that moment, she caught sight of Jessie and, screaming her name, flung herself with equal though opposite passion from her husband toward her friend.

"Achsa! Achsa! What have you heard from Lucille and Elaine? You never write." Jessie had not so much forgotten Molly as not yet taken her into account.

"I have no time for writing. I'm working full time again—in the same office with Lucille. You should see her; she looks like a ghost— skin and bones and eyes, that's all. She's back to social psychiatry— what she was doing in Minneapolis—when Leonard was working on his first book, remember, the proletarian one. Proletarian!"

"For Christ sake, Achsa—Irving is dead. Have a little decency." Howard found he had his arm around Molly, in a gesture of solidarity he had not really thought out.

"I know," Achsa said. "Thirty-eight years old. A tragedy for the Jewish people. It couldn't be worse if we lost Sholem Asch. I never liked that little twerp Irving and you know it, Howard. Why should I be a hypocrite now? The last time we saw him he was going to *shul*— couldn't even stop to talk. He's a faker, Howard, admit it. First a Marxist, then a Jungian, then an Orthodox Jew—what's the use, Howard; dead or alive, he was a fake!"

"How do you do, Achsa? I'm very glad to see you again after all these—"

"Ah, you see Howard's offended because I didn't kiss him. Aren't you? Isn't that sweet! You always were a *much* sweeter fake than poor Irving." She pecked him meaninglessly on his nearest cheek, her eyes swinging feverishly from face to face.

"And you, Marv? How are you?" It was an idiotic thing for Howard to say out of his complicated feelings, but he could think of nothing else. It was Marvin who had first taken him to an art museum, Marvin who had made him read Marx, and now—

"Sufficiently lousy." Marvin inclined his head wearily toward him without visible affection. "But she's right after all, though God knows how." He avoided his wife's name, using the simple pronoun in referring to her. "A mountebank, a bankrupt comedian. At least you've learned to come to terms with your badness and be popular."

"Thank you, Marvin," Howard answered, scarcely realizing that he imitated Marv's toneless Brooklyn voice as he spoke. "The tribute of your envy is worth more to me than being chosen for the Biennale." It was the simplest truth again, and he wished there were some way for Marvin to know it.

"Oh, please come *in* everybody, come in and have a drink. Please. All you intellectuals I've read about all my life, and you don't know enough to come in out of the rain." Molly urged and pushed them inside, aided by Howard to whom her stupidity and her not-quite-green eyes seemed equally charming. But what does her voice remind me of, he asked himself, that polite, private-school New York voice, so unlike the voices of anyone I ever knew or hated or slept with, the voice (he had it at last) of F.D.R., a Fireside Chat!

A thin stream of blue water rose and fell from the marble basin rimmed with palms in the entrance hall, and in the shallow pool great, slow, golden carp hung as if asleep. Howard could see into the immense living room, with its balcony for musicians and the mirrored walls on either end that reflected back and forth into a haze of plane-less images and ivory Buddhas, the carved oaken bishop's throne, the twisted iron lamp stands and the faces of Achsa, Marvin, Jessie, Bill Ward—so improbably there. Rain beat stupidly against the leaded window panes, and the room was oppressive after the chill, full of smoke and dead air and rock-and-roll music blaring mercilessly from a pair of speakers in opposite corners of the ceiling.

"It's too damn hot. I can't stand it!" Achsa screamed and, grabbing a Cinzano bottle, hurled it through one of the windows at the point where, above a scarlet shield, the motto read: *Ad astras per aspera.*

"Real vermouth," Bill commented, while Molly giggled, obviously feeling that this was more like what she had read about writers and painters in novels, more like a real party at last.

The sound of breaking glass startled the couple on the other side of the room into turning around. They had stood clutched together heedlessly when the others first came in, not really dancing but making little rubbing motions against each other in time to the music. It was Leonard and his new wife, Howard knew even from the backs of their heads, his black and a little grizzled, hers blonde, the hair hanging straight to her shoulders. She was very slim and a little taller than Leonard even in her flat ballet slippers; and when she whirled around, her eyes still large and her mouth a little open, a large gold cross swung lazily between her breasts. Leonard had grown a beard and looked handsomer than ever, almost masculine despite his short legs and tiny feet, his soft, girlish body.

"Disgusting!" Achsa said, not troubling to make clear whether she meant the cross, the beard, the public caresses, or all three; and in the confusion of kissing and greeting that followed, no one cared. It was a full ten minutes and a drink later before they could hear each other saying what they had all been unable to stop thinking: "Thirty-eight." "Poor Irving." "Dead."

"Thirty-eight," Jessie managed to make herself heard above the rest. "Thirty-eight! The youngest of us and the first with a reputation—the first one whose name anyone knew but *us*. We're all a little dead now. What are we doing here anyway? Why don't we lie down like good corpses and—"

"What else was there for him to do?" Achsa asked mercilessly. "A painter who couldn't paint any more. It's better than praying, isn't it, more honest to die!" Irving had been her lover once, Howard was aware, but whatever tenderness she may have felt had long since dissolved in her scorn. "You don't *have* to die of a heart attack. It's an act of cowardice. Look at Marvin. He's had three already, three attacks, but he doesn't die, and what kind of hero is he?"

"You're kidding," Jessie cried out. "For pity's sake, you don't mean to say that—"

But at the same moment Howard was saying, "He wouldn't give you the satisfaction, Achsa." Turning to Marvin, he winked, but looked away again, seeing the sudden terror in Marvin's loosened lip and staring eye. "Old revolutionaries never die," he went on, just to keep talking. "If the last Trotskyite in America conked out from a twinge of the heart, it would be sacrilege or lèse-majesté or something. . . ."

Howard filled his glass again and gulped it down, feeling very sorry for himself. But why *himself?* He could imagine Irving's pinched, dark-bearded face before him, peering out from behind the tortoise-shell glasses as from behind a mask; and playing whatever part he had temporarily chosen, sage or revolutionary or prophet or kindly old uncle with all the furious commitment of a ten-year-old. "I loved him." Perhaps that was it.

"In 1935, he was the most talked about painter in America. A way out of the cubist academy. And for the last five years he never touched a brush—"

"He had the dignity of failure," Marvin said suddenly. "Nothing else matters."

"The dignity of failure," Achsa screamed, closing in on her husband as if she intended to bite him. She, at least, was drunk. "You should be an expert on that, Marv, a real expert. But I don't understand it, not even after twenty-one years of postgraduate study. Just how dignified is it to be the only spokesman of failure, *pure* failure, in a room with a painter who's going to be one of the five Americans in the next Biennale—"

"Four," Jessie corrected her, while Howard winced.

"Plus the winner of the *Prix de Rome* for literature—the only poet in America married to an escapee from a convent!"

For a moment, it seemed as if Eva's mouth was shaping a protest, but she contented herself with pressing it against Leonard's sleeve, snuggling up to him even closer.

"Not to forget our host, the author of *All Buttoned Up,* which not only got the Drama Critics' Circle Award, but even won him as a special bonus Molly-o, complete with the highest-class sanitarium in the marshes of New Jersey." Achsa spilled the rest of her drink on Molly, bowing exaggeratedly in her direction.

"Hardest buck I ever made," Bill said, giggling. He obviously hoped it was a classic remark—and was resolved to find Achsa merely funny.

"And what do *you* have to offer, Marvin, to this distinguished group of repentant Marxists-on-the-make besides the purity of your principles? Twenty-seven years of conversation everyone admires and no one remembers! Twenty-seven years of nail-biting and insomnia—including twenty-one years of *me*. No book. No prize. No new bride. Only me. How do you like me, Marvin? Am I a dignified enough failure for you?"

"You see what I mean," Leonard cut in with his shrill, somewhat fruity voice. He was not addressing the rest of them, really, only Eva, continuing the one dialogue that was important to him. "Conjugal love. Punishing each other for punishing each other. Eating each other, because each one is sure the other's the only true poison. This is what it was like with *me* and—"

"Say Lucille's name and I'll leave this stupid party!" Jessie cried out. "How did she poison you? How? By letting you sit year after year writing poems no one would print, while she worked for twenty-five lousy bucks a week. By letting you weep on her shoulder after each of your 'little affairs' and wipe away your tears until the next one. By—"

"Forgiving is a poison, too, Jessie," Leonard answered mildly. "It's habit forming. After a while, you get so you—"

"Put down that poisoned toothpick, Leonard! No one hurts my Jessie!" They had not heard Bernie Levine's Cadillac pull up on the cinders outside or seen him and Beatie come through the open front door; but he bounded now from one to the other, the last guest, fat and bald and incredibly ugly, kissing Jessie, lifting Achsa high into the air, thrusting a finger into Bill's middle to see if it was real, patting Eva's behind. "What a *tuchas!* What a *tuchas!* You're a lucky boy, Leonard. What a poet can do with this, I don't know, but a cloak-and-suiter like me! When do we eat? What a dive—my God, the heating bill alone!"

Beatie had been standing behind him through his whole act, grimacing and shaking her head back and forth in her cradled hands to express mock horror; but now she smiled the slow, sweet smile Howard remembered out of her too-big, noble head under its fasionably cropped grey bob.

"Howard, you're just beautiful. And you're famous, my oldest

104

son tells me, my fifteen-year-old, imagine it! He saw it in *Time* Magazine. Kiss me already." Pulling her close, Howard saw the tears in her eyes; they had known each other since they were three. "It's terrible, no? And it'll be worse before it's over? What an idea!" She gestured with her head to indicate she meant the whole party. "What can you expect in such a house. No self-respecting ghost would haunt it. Absolutely. Ah, poor Howard—and Jessie! Jessie!"

They embraced warmly, not speaking. "I'm really tired, I didn't realize it. What a summer—my mother-in-law's been with me for three weeks. Why don't we eat? Thanks. Thanks." She waved off Bill who approached with a glass. "We stopped on the way for a drink. To tell you the truth, for three drinks. That's why we're late."

"Are we ready?" Bill asked, turning to Molly.

"Ready for what?"

"To eat. It's nearly half-past nine."

"Eat!" She said the words with exaggerated contempt, and leaning toward Bill, whispered furiously into his ear.

"Urge them?" he asked, scratching his behind in a mild panic. "But what should I urge them to—what do you mean?"

"You don't even remember. And it was going to be the High Point!"

"The High Point?"

"We were going to *swim!*" There were tears in her eyes, darkening the elusive green.

"But it's raining, sweetie," Bill protested, "and it's cold and late and—"

"It's *best* in the rain."

"What? What?" Bernie shouted. "She wants to swim? The young lady wants to swim? So let her swim; it's a constitutional right. I personally will grease her down. I have in the back of my car—"

"You'll swim with me, won't you, Bernie?"

Howard found himself resenting the "Bernie" (he had been coldly "Place"), as he resented the way Molly-o snuggled up to Bernie now, one breast nudging his solar plexus.

"Me? You mean *me* swim? Excuse me, my dear, this is another question entirely. After all I just ate two olives in my last Martini. Otherwise I'd be glad to oblige."

"Really, dear, it's out of the question," Beatie added with a heavily matronly air that even Howard could scarcely abide. "Besides, we have no bathing suits. Bill didn't say anything when he called about—"

"But that's just it. We don't need any bathing suits. It's no fun if it's not spontaneous. We have a lovely private beach, and I thought we would all just slip out of our clothes and— It was going to be so *exciting!* I mean, I remember when I was in college, a bunch of us kids sneaked off to a quarry with a case of beer and— Oh, everybody was so beautiful that night, so free and beautiful in the moonlight!"

"Moonlight!" Howard could not help breaking in, though he did not want to seem to stand against her with the veteran wives and their scared husbands. "Just look at the moonlight!" He pointed through the splintered pane to the sky whose murkiness an occasional lightning flash showed without dispelling.

"It'll be wonderful! We'll be like ghosts in the lightning. *Nude* ghosts." Noo-oo-oo-oode, she said it, lingering dreamily over the vowel of what was for her a magic word. "Nude ghosts."

"And now *listen!*" Howard persisted, hushing them so that they could hear the noise of the sea on the rocks. "It would tear you to pieces."

"Oh, how can you all be so sensible! I wish your precious Irving was here. At least he *knows* he's a corpse!" And shedding clothes as she ran, she headed out the door into the rain and toward the roar of the ocean. Her brassiere she flung back over her shoulder as she disappeared in a final, theatrical gesture.

"Bravo!" Marvin shouted, clapping his long, thin hands together. "Bravo!"

"What'll I do?" Bill asked, starting to follow her, and then turning irresolutely back.

"You can show me the silent-flush toilets," Beatie answered, taking Bill's arm. "Leave her alone. Don't you know *anything*, even the second time around?"

"Well, I can go wading at least while my wife consoles abandoned husbands in bathrooms." Bernie had taken off his shoes and socks and was heading for the marble fishpond in the entry hall. "This is more my speed. Oy! it's cold!" He jumped out, then, with a shudder, back in again. "Look at me! Free and beautiful! Hoo-hah, I'm F. Scott Fitzgerald!"

But no one even listened. Leonard and Eva were necking again, she utterly abandoned to an inner rhythm of desire, he glancing up occasionally, vaguely troubled, in search of an O.K. from his old friends. Marvin, with no one to talk to, drank in silence, pacing nervously, while Achsa drifted behind him without being aware she followed. Suddenly Howard realized that the darkness before the house to which he had pointed an instant before was blazing with light, through which the slowing rain ran stitches like a sewing machine gone mad. Someone (it must have been Molly-o through all her tears) had switched on a bank of floodlights under the eaves. But why, Howard wondered; and he pressed his face against the window, staring out into the pointless glare.

Molly had apparently not gone swimming at all, but was sitting quite naked on a stone bench just at the verge of the last dune. She was set in absolute profile, her knees drawn up before her, her arms braced behind, and her head thrown back so that her hair fell onto the stone seat. Howard had not realized that it was so long and full, caught up in the pony tail she usually wore. In that excessive light and at that distance, all color was bleached from her body, leaving her perfectly black and white. She appeared no more or less real than the marble Venus, which also stood in Howard's direct line of sight, naked above the lily pads and under the faltering rain. Tintless and eyeless, without motion and with her hair down, Molly was the twin of the statue, another Aphrodite.

Howard knew she was aware of his watching her as surely as he knew his wife was watching his watching; and he turned away with a sigh.

In ten minutes, Molly was back with them again; she had changed into riding breeches and a man's plaid shirt, but was barefoot. "Soup's on," she said grinning, and lifting her arms over her head, she stretched until the shirt was taut from nipple to nipple. She could not have been wearing a brassiere.

She led them into the adjoining dining room where, around a bowl of fresh-blood-colored flowers, tall silver monks held up lighted candles that set the table silver winking and flashing. "That's Oswald," Molly said, tapping one of the monks on his tonsured head. "He's my favorite. Isn't he a darling!"

Dinner began eventlessly enough and was probably excellent,

but everyone was too drunk to taste it. Only Eva did not drink, raising to their occasional half-mocking toasts ("The Critics' Circle Award!" "The Biennale!" "The *Prix de Rome!*") a depressingly white glass of milk. Bernie, who sat beside her, kept pretending to shy from the glass, raising one hand to his eyes as if to shield them from the glare.

"Revolt!" he kept telling her. "That's the last symptom of Momism. Let go of the titty, Eva."

"Ay-vah," Leonard pronounced it for him, irked at the way Bernie kept kneading his wife's arm.

Howard had managed to sit beside Molly; but she had drenched herself with some almost acrid sandalwood perfume after her imaginary swim, and he was actually relieved whenever she rose to go down to the kitchen in pursuit of something forgotten or overlooked. She walked with greater and more perilous dignity each time, until the trip which brought her screaming back with a bloody rag wrapped about the forefinger of her left hand.

"Oh, Bill, I cut it! I *cut* it!" she howled. "I'll bleed to death all because of your silly friends and their silly socialist ideas. Everybody *knows* we have help! What could one person do with a house this size, even for just a summer place. Why did I have to send Ellen and Janet to the movies? So I could chop my finger to pieces? It's snobbery, that's what it is, silly socialist snobbery. They *like* being servants and I like having them and I—oh, Bill—it's all over my shirt—I'm all *bloody*, Bill." Looking down at the red-stained rag she screamed again.

"Really, I—Really, I—" Bill's mouth opened and closed, opened and closed, as if he were trying to say something, though it became clear finally that he was only laughing soundlessly.

"Bill just sent them away to protect them from Bernie," Howard began, feeling somehow that what would surely seem a good joke when they were sober, they might as well laugh at now.

But Molly was crying again. "I can't help it if I need servants, can I? Don't make me send them away again. *Promise!* I'm just stupid, that's *all*. Oh, *Bill!*" She held her wounded finger under his mouth until he made kissing noises in its general direction, glancing all the while at Marvin to see how strongly he disapproved and making indistinct remarks about the superiority of Bandaids to kisses.

Marvin, on the other hand, looked happy for the first time that night; his long head moving up and down like a horse eating sugar from a child's hand, he began to speak. "Sending servants away, this is more than a symptom of insecurity; it is clearly a symbolic action—but symbolic of what? What is the objection to a maid from people who have sold out their principles, their former friends, their past. To make jokes for hire about everything you believed in once, this is apparently all right, as long as it's in verse." He bowed toward Leonard, showing his crooked yellow teeth in the nearest thing to a smile he could manage. "To sign a loyalty oath to a state with a law against miscegenation in order to keep a job teaching schoolboys to draw vases and plaster casts, this is kosher." He nodded at Howard. "To live off a stupid mother-in-law who believes in 'Art,' but fortunately does not know what it is—who would object? Not our host, who objects to servants or should I say to displaying his servants to former comrades. Do you follow this?"

A chorus of "no's" answered him, though they had all stopped to listen. He was the only one of them able to compel the attention of the others.

"Please, *I*'d like to say something," Bill said, holding his hand up like a boy in school. He still had the corkscrew in his clenched fist. "Marvin, you don't understand. About the servants, I won't say anything because it's—well, I just won't. And as for my mother-in-law, whatever help she gave me and for whatever reasons, I don't need it any more. With what I made on *All Buttoned Up*, I'm independent—for five years now I can—never mind. You know how many people have seen *All Buttoned Up*. And sure they go out laughing at Roderick, the revolutionary bum. But the gimmick is all the time I'm laughing at them for being sucked in. I get them coming and going, Marv, don't you see. I—"

"I won't stand for it," Marvin broke in, pounding the table before him with his loose, hairy fist until the glasses rattled. "I warn you I won't stand for it. I drank your toasts to the Critics' Circle Award and *Prix de Rome*, but only on the understanding that no one plays games with me. You're petty-bourgeois conformists. You're whores. Okay, these are the facts. Now, I'm not too proud to sit with whores; I'll even let a whore buy me a drink. But only on the condition that he wears his identification ticket: I AM A WHORE—and underneath it, I LIKE IT! or HOW UNHAPPY I AM! This much is optional; but no *principles*, for God's sake! That's my department. You have everything else: money, prizes, new wives, admiring coeds. I don't resent it. Only admit what you are. I warn you, I won't stand for it!"

"What'll you do, Marv?" Howard asked mildly. "Write an article?" He pretended he could not hear Jessie who whispered at him from across the table, "The man is sick, Howard. For pity's sake, he's sick."

Marvin refused to dignify his challenge with an answer and Bill, nonplused, had sunk back into his seat, his mouth working soundlessly. The rest stared at each other, unwilling or unable to pick up the conversations they had dropped to listen to Marvin, when Eva's voice rang out astonishingly distinct in the hush. It was the first thing they had heard her say. "Do you understand all this, darling?" She blew into Leonard's ear, bit the lobe gently. She had refused to sit anywhere except beside him, despite Molly-o's outraged protest.

"Certainly."

"But it's ridiculous, darling."

"Of course it's ridiculous, but that's not the point. This is a language for unhappy people—a way of pretending that unhappiness is virtue. Once I talked this language, too."

"But now you're happy and sensible, aren't you, Leonard? And lucky, too, because it *pays* to be happy in America, to give up crazy talk about classes and conformity and discuss the New Criticism or transubstantiation or how many angels can dance on the head of a Thomist poet." Marvin glared first at Leonard, then at Eva's crucifix.

"Why do you all *listen* to him, then? Why do you sit there apologizing to him, as if he were a fuehrer or something?" Eva had risen to her feet, brushing a long, blonde lock of hair out of her eyes with the back of one hand. She was very red, and her lower lip trembled as if she might break into tears at any moment. "Don't you see, he's not only silly, he's vicious—a diseased man tearing at everything that's healthy. I suppose you all read his asinine article *Fanny Freud at the Harpsicord,* and snickered over it, and thought how smart he was and how smart you were for knowing it. Well, Leonard doesn't care a hoot for what Mr. Marvin Solomon says about his poetry. After all, Leonard writes it, and Marvin is just a mad dog baying at the—at the—*whatever* it is." Her voice, tremulous throughout, broke, and she retreated behind her glass of milk, again scarlet and trembling.

"Take a tranquilizer," Bernie advised her. "Beatie swears by them."

"Never mind," Howard said. "It is refreshing to find a wife ready to defend her husband. But Leonard needs no defense. Who reads what Marv writes any more? Not even us. . . ."

He had, of course, read carefully through Marvin's attack on Leonard, as he read (and the rest with him) each rare piece he wrote, his writing obviously blocked now except when malice moved him to snarl at some younger and more successful friend. It had become clear to everyone long since that Marvin would never write the long epic poem on the Wobblies or the immense study of American culture in four volumes that he had talked about all his life. But how to explain this to the girl with her cross and her glass of milk; how to make clear the sense in which Marvin (though only two or three years older) had been the father of them all, the model for the insolence and involution that they had learned from him to think the hallmarks of the revolutionary intellectual. "Boddhavisata," they had called him when they were in high school, and they had quoted his remarks to each other, passing them from hand to hand until they were worn out—their chief inheritance.

Howard knew that Marv clung to the old counters still, the inviable clichés of Marxism, not because he believed in them, but because they had once been tokens of his power to compel love and respect. In a sense, he held them in trust for them all, their one-time papa, now the keeper of the museum of their common past. He felt an obligation to insult Marvin publicly as Marvin in the first place had taught him to do, to respond to Marv's insults as if they mattered. It was the last possible gesture of respect; to have greeted his sallies with silence would have been to reveal pity, and that Marvin could never have stood.

"Never mind," Howard repeated to Eva. "Nobody takes Marv seriously anyway, a man who writes from rage and out of weakness in a magazine no one sees, except the wives and friends of the author he's giving the treatment. What do you call it again, Marvin, that journal for boys who never grew up? *Peter Pan, Boy's Life, Our Sunday Messenger?*"

"*Contempt,*" Achsa answered for her husband. "*Contempt,* you clown!"

"Ah yes, *Contempt, or the Fountain of Youth.* No forty-year-old ex-post-Marxist can read it without sobbing to his image in the mirror, 'They're playing our song!' Believe it or not, I think Marvin really knows that an attack from him under such auspices helps a book, and since he's fast becoming a kindly old man—"

"Listen, Howard—"

"Listen, Howard—"

"Listen, Howard—"

Marvin, Achsa and Bernie, all three beginning at precisely the same moment and in precisely the same way, collapsed in laughter, while Jessie groaned aloud. She thinks I'm showing off for Molly-o, Howard told himself; and maybe I am, maybe I am. . . . But Molly was not even listening.

"Quiet, *please,*" Bernie announced into the hubbub, pounding his glass with a fork. "Everyone's too melancholy. I'm going to tell a joke!"

"I thought that's what Howard was doing," Jessie said.

"Well, since you all insist, reluctantly I'll do it. It seems that one day Mendel meets his old friend Sidney on the street and says to him, 'Sidney, where've you been? For two weeks I haven't seen you in the office, on the street. . . .' 'I've been on my honeymoon!' 'Don't kid me,' Mendel says. 'You've been married already for—' 'Twenty-five years,' Sidney finishes. 'A second honeymoon. We went back to the identical hotel in Atlantic City, took the identical room—' "

"Wouldn't you say this is a little long, Bernie?" Achsa asked.

"Sh! I guarantee you you'll love it. Where was I? So, Sidney says to Mendel, 'Everything exactly the same. We had the same waiters; we ate at the same table, the same chopped liver, the same chicken soup—' "

"Do you have to recite the whole menu?" Achsa broke in again.

"Look," Leonard said. "There are at least two people here who've listened to this rigamarole three times before. I for one won't sit through it again." He was pale with anger. "If it's an appropriate joke you want, I know one that's shorter at least."

"I can never remember them," Molly said. "I hear some really cute ones, but—"

"This man and his wife were making love," Leonard persisted, "when suddenly he says—"

"Oh, Leonard, not that *nauseating* one," Jessie cried. "It's exactly what I knew you were going to—"

"This is the ghost at the feast, isn't it?" Leonard screamed. "Irving isn't the only victim of heart failure. It's the disease of us all without benefit of doctors: failure of the heart, failure of the genitals, failure of love. This is the critical fact of our lives—the specter that's haunting New Jersey and Westport and Paducah and Brooklyn. But we don't tell, do we? Not in Bill's plays or my poems or Howard's paintings—only in Bernie's crummy jokes. Ha-ha!"

"Please, Leonard darling," Eva implored him.

"I'll be damned if I'll let them sit around for the rest of the night sniffing at you and me." His voice rose even more shrilly. "Well, I broke out of the trap, and so did Bill; that's what they'll never forgive us for. That's why they're sitting there right now cooking up nasty little stories about us that will last through a whole year of parties. Am I right, Bill?"

Bill was sound asleep at the head of the table, his head cradled in his arms, and the corkscrew, symbol of authority, lying beside him.

"Well, *I* know about it anyhow. *I* know what it is to lie side by side with a woman you've made love to so many times you feel sick and silly when you add up the total—and each of you dead to the other. Such things may not happen to you, Achsa and Marvin, or you, Jess and Howard, or you, Beatie and Bernie; for you the honeymoon may last twenty years. You'll just have to take it on faith that it happened to me, to me and Lucille, who—"

"I told you, Howard, if he mentioned my friend's name in the same room with that silly little girl, I'd—" Jessie wove around the table and stood behind her husband's chair, straddle-legged, her fists on her hips.

"What do you want me to do? Hit him? Should I knock him down for you, Jessie, because he offended divorced American womanhood?"

"She may not have been good enough for you, Leonard," Achsa interrupted him impatiently, "but she's so much more of a woman than you'll *ever* be a man that it's a scandal. You and your masculine-protest type beard that doesn't fool anybody for one minute! She was a splint for your poor feeble masculinity, Leonard, a splint. Don't think that I don't know that before her, you couldn't even—"

"Achsa, what's the point of dragging up all the bedroom gossip you ever heard? All I'm trying to say is—"

"I wasn't the one who started bringing up bedroom gossip,

Leonard, but since you began it, I'll just finish. I'm sure this will all be very educational for your new wife, who's been getting your special version of things. I'm sure she'll appreciate knowing that without Lucille you couldn't—"

"Hell's bells, I'm not trying to justify myself against Lucille, Achsa. I'm a bastard, I know."

"You can say that again," Achsa screamed triumphantly, working her way slowly around the table to put an arm around Jessie's waist. "Now tell us exactly what *kind* of a bastard you are. I have a few little anecdotes to contribute that you may have forgotten."

"All I mean is, what else can you do when—"

"You can shut up, Leonard. So much you can always do." Beatie moved as she spoke toward the other two women, finally taking up a position on the other side of Jessie, though not yet touching her—like a last reserve. "We love you still, Leonard, believe it nor not; but don't you see what an offense it is to bring that poor, sweet girl here and sit smooching with her. I wish you a hundred good years with her and a dozen children, but only—"

" 'Poor, sweet girl,' with that ridiculous voodoo charm around her neck. I tell you—"

"Never mind the voodoo charm, Achsa. We all have our idiocies and that's not the worst. Leonard, all I say to you is this: go sit in a corner like a good boy and hold your Eva's hand, but leave us grown-ups alone."

"Beatie, I can talk to *you*. You're no fishwife. What do you *do* Beatie, when you lie side by side with somebody, two people seeing each other naked, knowing each other by heart, as they say, but without love. It's not tolerable, Beatie. What do you *do?*"

"Lie side by side with the dignity of failure. There is no love." Marvin rose at last with the air of one contributing the final wisdom; he spoke more slowly than any of the others and from his greater height, very pale above their heads.

"Marvin, I tell you right now that if you say 'failure' or 'dignity' again tonight, I'll—I'll throw a water pitcher at your head. I'll—I'll—" Beatie put an arm around Achsa now, soothing her, while Jessie on her other side squeezed her waist without a word. "All right," Beatie kept saying over and over, "all right, all right."

Coffee had been set before everyone, and tasting it now, they discovered it had grown cold. The cognac they dutifully swallowed without tasting, but no one was capable of getting any drunker. Suddenly they had nothing more to say, and they looked away from each other in pained silence, like Leonard's perhaps legendary husbands and wives, wondering what dead and irrecoverable passion had left them stranded in an association that, without it, was merely absurd.

"Oh, let's *dance!*" Eva cried at the top of her voice, sensing that only a shout could break so deep a silence. She made her way to the hi-fi set in the mirrored room, fiddling with the knobs until music assailed them again from the corners.

It was as if not their images only, bedraggled and dim-eyed, but the sound, too, was reflected from glass to glass across the immense room. Bernie and Leonard had carried Bill in, sagging between them, to deposit him in the bishop's chair, where he rolled over once and sank back snoring. Jessie, Achsa and Beatie sat side by side on a sofa, leaning their heads together and whispering like conspirators, while Marvin pulled down book after book from the wall shelves, glancing briefly and disapprovingly in each.

Molly-o had flung herself on the floor, gazing meditatively down between her breasts, her back nestled down into a white bearskin rug. "I'm too warm—and too full—and I drank too much," she announced mournfully, unbuttoning two more buttons of her shirt and smoothing her breeches across the hips.

Bill once dropped, Leonard had taken Eva in his arms, and they were moving together again in their slow un-dance off in one corner. No one joined them.

"We have squash courts in the basement," Molly said without much conviction, snuggling even more sensually into the white fur, "and ping-pong tables—and sixty-two bedrooms, if anyone is inclined to—"

"The only game that interests me is craps," Bernie said. "If some of you gentlemen—"

"What about Guggenheim?" Marvin asked.

"Guggenheim!" Achsa cried scornfully. "Next it'll be charades."

"I can't play any of those category games," Molly said, looking quite pleased with herself all the same. "I'm too stupid."

"The only thing I ever played in my life," Howard put in from the doorway, where he stood gulping the damp, cold air by way of therapy, "was croquet. I was at Yaddo in '49, and all the time we weren't at the race track, we were playing—"

"You mean that stupid game for children with wooden balls?" Achsa asked.

"I never knew a child with— Isn't there some danger of splinters—" Bernie began, whooping with delight.

"Were you at Yaddo, *too?*" Molly-o inquired, slowly easing herself over, then rising to sit on her feet like a Japanese. She looked admiringly at Howard as if she had just discovered his most dazzling distinction. "Bill was there once. Long, long ago in '38."

"That's not so long ago," Howard objected. "It was that year that the Museum of Modern Art bought my—"

"I was six years old," Molly said, casting her eyes down modestly.

"Oy! Oy! Oy!" Beatie cried out. "It's the only answer. Oy! Oy! Oy! Imagine it, six years old."

"Bill says that in '38, they used to play *nude* croquet!" Molly lingered over the vowel of the magic word again. "You know, at night when the middle-aged prudes were asleep. There were lots of interesting people there that year. I don't remember their—"

"Marianne Moore and T. S. Eliot," Marvin suggested. "They'd look good at nude croquet."

"And Henry James," Jessie added.

"We have a croquet set somewhere, don't we, Bill?" In her mounting excitement, Molly ignored their quips. "Don't we? Don't we?" She ran over, silent on her bare feet, and shook her husband until he opened his eyes, staring at her unseeingly. "*Don't* we have a croquet set? We can play it *nude,* just like you used to do at Yaddo, can't we, Bill? It'll save the whole party! Howard, why don't *you* go down into the basement and look just behind the steps. I'm sure you'll find it, in a big cardboard box that says—"

"Croquet, I'll bet," Howard finished for her, while Bill, blinking sightlessly, repeated, "Nude ... nude ... nude...." and fell back again onto the seat snoring.

"Oh, Bill!" Molly sighed, then turning once more to Howard, "Well, we'll just have to play without him!"

"It's raining again," Howard said by way of answer. He had been holding one hand outside the door, cupped under the dripping eaves; and he wiped it off now on Molly's plump cheek. "Wet! It's a bog out there. You'll have to make it water polo."

"Oh, we're not going to play out there, silly. We'll play in here where it's all comfy. Right *here!* Just move some of these chairs back—and turn off that ridiculous music, and we're all set." As she snapped it off Leonard and Eva stood gasping in the sudden silence, like a couple of sea creatures hauled out of their element. "Well, get it, please. Go and get it," she insisted, laying a hand on Howard's arm.

"Howard," Jessie warned him, rising to her feet. "Let's not commit ourselves to anything childish. Really, it's late already and we have a long way to go."

"It's only eleven-thirty-seven," Howard answered, consulting his watch. What he would have done if his wife had not intervened he was not sure; but there was nothing to do now but go after the croquet set and see what would happen.

He found himself wishing that it would not be there, but, of course, discovered it immediately (he who could never find anything at home) at the bottom of the steps where Molly had said it would be. He wrestled the clumsy cardboard box up the steep stairs, tearing a chunk of flesh out of the back of one hand on the doorjamb and scarcely feeling it. "It's here," he said triumphantly, casting it down at Molly's feet and sucking the bleeding place. He liked the taste of his blood. "Strip already!"

He had thought he was joking, but before he could laugh or try to stop her, Molly had stripped off her shirt, leaving herself bare to the waist. "Think fast!" she said, tossing the checkered blouse at him and beginning to fumble with the buttons of her riding breeches.

Bill, still asleep, writhed on the oaken chair, calling out in a choked voice, "Please, please, please. . . ." and Bernie rushed toward Molly-o in sudden panic, pulling off his jacket to put around her shoulders. "What is this? Minsky's?" he yelled, flushing and paling by turns. "We're not going to go through with this craziness, are we? What are we anyway, high-school children who think you're only living when you take off your clothes? Howard, you tell her—you're an artist, naked women are your bread and butter. A joke is a joke, but I'm forty-four years old—forty-four—an underwear salesman."

"What are you getting so excited about?" Howard calmed him, feeling superior to them all. "Let's be reasonable about this and—"

"Reasonable!" Molly flung Bernie's jacket contemptuously aside, and stepping out of her breeches now, confronted them in a pair of pale green pants (the color of her eyes), covered with tiny red hearts. "Well, what are we waiting for?" Her skin was smooth and tight, unmarred by childbearing and unmarked even by the crease of brassiere or girdle. On shoulder and thigh, breast and belly alike she was tanned the rich brown of one who turns patiently under the sun lamp, reading a fashion magazine and loving nothing more than her own flesh.

"Just because Bill married a *nudnick,* do I have to play the bohemian in my old age? Nude croquet! I don't know which is worse, the nude or the croquet! Listen, Howard, God knows we've got nothing to show each other by letting down our pants. We're naked enough now, for Christ's sake!"

"Bernie's right," Marvin said, looking directly at Molly who had gone on undressing and stood now with her underpants hanging delicately from silvered thumb and forefinger; if he saw her, he registered nothing. "It would be more to the point to put on steel masks and lead drawers, to hide in all decency a nakedness we can no longer pretend is exciting or beautiful. All our compromises are hanging out, out withered principles dangling obscenely. We can't even remember to button our flies!"

"My God, what *difference* does it make!" Achsa cried out. "Let's show what we can't hide anyway. Let these children look at what they have to become, what they are already, even if their mirrors aren't ready to tell them yet. I only wish I could take off my *skin,* too." Her dress and slip, her brassiere with the discreet padding, the girdle she wore only to hold up her stockings, she had off in a moment, rolling them into a ball and heaving them at her husband's head. He did not even lift a hand to block them, but bowed as they went past him, smiling obscurely to himself. Achsa was almost completely breastless, skinny and yellow with strange knobby knees and two scars across her flat, flaccid belly.

"You've all gone nuts," Bernie protested. "Nuts! I'm geting out of here before I find myself galloping bare-ass like a kid. What are we doing, grown men and women? Maybe it's kiddie night in the bughouse! Beatie, come on." He had picked up his rumpled, Italian-silk jacket, stuck his panama on the back of his bald head. "Well, come on!"

"I'm not coming, Bernard," Beatie answered quietly, bending over and beginning to unlace the sensible shoes into which her solid, unlovely legs descended. "I'm going to stay."

"You're going to play nude croquet—*nude* croquet? Are you crazy, too?"

"No—only a little drunk. Nude croquet, nude pinochle! Achsa's right, what difference does it make. Listen, Bernie, I manage to get one night in three months away from the kids—away from a house of flu and measles and diaper rashes. Well, this is the night and here I am and so I intend to stay at least till I've done something I'm sorry for. Do you understand? Excuse me, Bernie, but tonight I don't go home early."

"You're not only drunk," he screamed, pulling her by the arm. "You're crazy, plain, ordinary crazy."

"So, I'm crazy. Just let go of me, Bernie. *Let go of me!*" She turned on him, her usually mild gaze now coldly ferocious, staring at him until he dropped his hold, then bent down to pull off her stockings. "Go home Bernie, and when you get there, wake up little David and tell him his mama says—tell him I say—'Merry Christmas.' "

Everyone laughed and Molly shouted, "Hooray!"

"I'm giving you one more chance, Beatie." Bernie stood at the door, his nylon shirt dark with sweat, his coat dangling from his hand. "I for one will not—"

"Oh, *go* already," she sobbed. "Go! Can't you see I'm living it up? A real orgy." She flung her head down onto Jessie's lap weeping. She did not even see Bernie when, a moment later, he stuck his head back through the door, glowered around the room and, crying, "To hell with you all!" disappeared for good.

"Why don't *you* go, too?" Achsa asked, whirling on her husband. But Marvin was already undressing without a word, placing his black shoes, his socks with the garters attached, his pants folded neatly onto a bookshelf which he had cleared by throwing the books on the floor. His limp, usually almost unnoticeable, grew more evident as he stripped.

Beatie meanwhile had staggered to her feet again, her shoes in her hand, and was making her way to the door, yelling, "Wait, Bernie. I'm coming. Wait! What am I doing here?"

"He's gone," Howard said, stopping her and whirling her around. He was one drink past the simplest truth, and so he lied to her without thinking, though he could still see through the window the red gleam of Bernie's Cadillac, in which he must have been sitting in sullen indecision and self-pity. "It'll do him good to spend a few hours imagining you in a game of nude croquet."

"I don't know what got into me," Beatie sobbed. "You don't understand, Howard. He's in trouble, bad trouble, and I should stand by him. What else can a wife do but stick with her husband? It's her duty, isn't it, no matter what? I just don't know what got into me. I—" She dissolved once more into tears, Howard patting her head uncertainly, until all at once she looked up and winked. "It's all a joke, right, Howard? 'Duty,' 'husband,' 'stand by'—a *joke*! That's what's so hard to remember." She sat sprawled on a gilt and brocade chair that looked frail and ridiculous under her, her legs spread wide and one hand on her heart. "I'm here and I'll play if it kills me. Jessie, come here and help unbutton me."

"Oh, *good*," Molly shouted, clapping her hands. "Good for you. You're a real sport!"

"Some sport," Beatie responded ruefully. "Poor Bernie!"

"And what about those two?" Achsa pointed to one corner where Leonard and Eva stood staring at each other mutely, their hands clasped. Then, even as she spoke, they began to undress each other, still without a word, moving in a slow pantomime that converted each unbuckling or tug of a zipper into a caress.

"And you, Jessie?" Howard turned deliberately toward his wife, wondering exactly how angry she was. He had already taken off his shirt and his T-shirt revealed his fat chest, the thick blond prickles which covered it.

"Whatever you say, Howard." She was apparently going to try the tack of patient submission. "If you want me to join in this—"

"Certainly. You're only young once."

She sighed a little; she had never looked so haggard, so ugly. "Tell me, Molly, is there a room on this floor where I could undress? I'm in poor shape for climbing stairs."

"A room! To undress!" Howard protested, feeling the request as somehow an intended rebuke. "But we're all going to be playing in here together in a minute, without a—"

"What harm does it do you, Howard? I'm willing to stand naked side by side with these young things and let you make comparisons, since it amuses you to torture yourself in this way. But getting undressed is a private matter for me. For pity's sake, indulge me a little. You can stay here with your—"

"I'll come with you," Howard volunteered, not quite knowing why.

"There's a room in there," Molly-o said, shrugging her shoulders a little contemptuously so that her breasts bounced. She pointed a tapering, tanned arm toward a door on her right. "A music room we hardly use any more."

Howard followed Jessie into the darkness, though she had walked off without even looking back in his direction and he knew he would be able to find nothing to say to her. When he reached for the wall switch, Jessie put a hand over it to prevent him; but she had left the door open a little so that in the mitigated gloom he could make out a dozen or so spindly chairs hunched under dust covers around the walls, a love seat also protected from the dust, a piano and, behind it, a harp.

"It's a harp!" Jessie said wonderingly, touching the strings lightly until they responded with a tingling and humming that filled the shadowy room. "Let's go home, Howard. Let's get out of here. You said before—"

"A ghost of a harp. No. It's too late now." He hung his pants on the harp, muting the strings. "Oh, Lord, now that we've decided to stay, I've got to go."

"There's another door on the other side of the room. I imagine that somewhere through there— Can you see all right in the dark? Please. Howard, couldn't we just—"

"No, no, no. I can see fine." But he lurched and stumbled in the darkness, nearly tripping over one of the hooded chairs, and staggered finally into a lighted corridor, flanked by the john.

Coming out again, he almost walked into Molly-o, who flung her arms around his neck and kissed him briskly. Her breasts were astonishingly firm despite their size, the nipples, not brownish or purple but really pink as a child would paint them, hard enough to press uncomfortably into his soft flesh. Jessie's, he thought dimly, had never been like this even when she was quite young. "Oh, *thank* you, Howard," Molly said breathlessly. "You saved the party. I thought we were going to have to sit there and *talk* all night. I had you all wrong. I—"

He grabbed her again, returning the kiss hard, his hands slipping down her back until he held her around the hips. Her mouth fell open all the way under his and he could feel her knees bend, her body sag, though whether from passion or alcohol he could not tell. I'm just doing this to shut her up anyway, he told himself; I'm not even excited. . . .

He jumped suddenly under a resounding smack on his right buttock, and Molly skittered off, smiling at him vaguely over her shoulder. Beatie stood behind him, grinning broadly and quite naked. *"Shmendrick!"* she said. "Big Brother is watching. Do you call this croquet?"

She had not called him *shmendrick,* Howard realized, since they were both fifteen and they had fumbled their way into what was the first affair for both of them, more like friends playing than lovers. Then Beatie had really fallen in love for the first time and—somehow thirty years had gone by! "Thirty years!" he said, perhaps aloud, but Beatie did not respond. He looked incredulously at her body, a girl's body when he had touched it last, now all at once full-blown, the muscle tone gone, the legs mottled blue-black with varicose veins— like someone's mother.

"I was just—" he stuttered. "That is—"

"Never mind," Beatie answered. "Before you lie to me, I believe you. Go find Jessie."

As he turned around confusedly, looking for a way back into the music room, Howard had the impression that the door through which he had come was closed softly, as if Jessie had been watching him, too, and was now withdrawing. But when he entered, she was lying face down on the love seat, her naked back rising and falling regularly.

"Are you asleep?" he whispered.

"Asleep!" she answered, rolling over. "You bastard, come here." She pulled him to her, winding her arms around him with a ferocity that astonished him. She had not clung to him so desperately in years.

"Oh, hold me, Howard, and for God's sake don't say anything. Tight, tight, *tight!*"

When they rejoined the others, they discovered that someone had set the record player going again, and that the overhead lights had been turned off. Only two huge gilded and twisted candlesticks illuminated the big room now, one set before each of the wall-length mirrors; and reflected back and forth, from glass to gleaming body to glass, the points of light were multiplied to thousands. Leather-bound folios, opened to the middle and set spine up, did duty for wickets. The others were already bent over the varicolored balls, mallets in hand. They had begun to scream insults and encouragement at each other, at ease in the friendly dark that camouflaged their bulges and creases and broken veins.

After a while, he could begin to make them out more clearly through the flickering shadows: Leonard, vaguely hermaphroditic, pudgy and white; Eva, her cross falling just where her pancake makeup gave way to the slightly pimpled pallor of her skin (there was the mark of a bite on one small breast); Jessie, whose body was astonishingly younger than her lined, witch's face, but whose grey below betrayed the red splendor of her hair; Achsa, tallow-yellow and without breasts; Beatie, marked with the red griddle of her corseting and verging on shapelessness; Marvin, sallow and unmuscled beneath the lank black hair that covered even his upper arms. He dragged more and more wearily behind him a withered left leg, creased from hip to knee by a puckered and livid scar, testimony to the osteomyelitis that had kept him in bed through most of his childhood. Only Molly pranced and preened, secure in her massaged and sun-lamped loveliness. To each of the others nudity was a confession, a humiliation. Yet they laughed louder and louder, though no one knew precisely what he was doing; and the crack of mallet on ball punctuated their chatter.

Once in the hubbub, Beatie drew Howard aside into the music room where he and Jessie had undressed. She was crying abandonedly once more, snorting and heaving and dripping tears that seemed somehow ridiculous above the expanse of her nakedness. "What's going to be with me and Bernie, Howard?" she asked, not in hope of an answer, he knew, but because the question had to be spoken aloud. "He's in bad trouble, sicker than anyone knows—under analysis. Don't tell anyone, Howard, not even Jessie. He doesn't want—and I let him go away alone. He couldn't any more take his clothes off in front of these people, than—I don't know—than finish the novel he's been working on secretly since he was in high school."

What did he have to tell her, what wisdom for all his forty-five years? He may have kissed her then, for he had come always to kiss women when he was at a loss with them—another laziness.

All other episodes, however, faded into the confusion of the endless and pointless game, and into the mockery of Marvin which finally became its point. All the rest, varyingly drunk and skillful, slapped an occasional shot through an improvised folio wicket, or successfully cracked an opponent's ball away from a favorable spot; but Marvin, incredibly unco-ordinated, could do nothing. Sometimes, his leg buckling under him, he would miss the ball completely, denting the hardwood floor with his mallet or catching it under a Persian rug; sometimes the ball would skid off the edge of his hammer, trickle two or three inches to one side and maddeningly stop. Once the head of his mallet flew off at the end of a particularly wild swing, just missing Molly's eye.

After a while, they were all trailing after him, Achsa leading the pack, like the gallery of a champion golfer, roaring at every stroke, while Marvin said nothing, only more grimly and comically addressed the ball. The real horror, Howard felt, was that Marvin now *wanted* to smack the elusive object before him squarely through the wicket, to win the applause of his mockers. For all that he knew it to be nonsense, Marvin had been somehow persuaded that it *mattered*—reliving, Howard supposed, the ignominy of his childhood, when in the street and to the jeers of his fellows he had failed at caddy or stoopball or kick the can.

Drawing the stick back between his scarred and rickety legs, Marvin delivered a stroke finally with such force and imbalance that he toppled over onto his face. He lay there for a little while motionless, his pale, skinny buttocks twitching, while they all laughed and hooted and cheered. They could not afford to admit that it was anything but a joke.

Only Eva, who had screamed at him earlier, was moved to protest.

"Oh, don't!" she cried, whirling on the rest with tears in her eyes. "Please, *don't!* Can't you see he's like a fallen king—a fallen king!" She took a step toward him, but could not bring herself to touch his pale, sweaty body, and ended covering her eyes with the hand she had reached out toward him in sympathy.

"A fallen king!" Achsa repeated contemptuously, sensing the others were slipping away from her, beginning to feel shame and pity. "Why don't you get up, your majesty, and say a few words about the dignity of failure?" She was hopelessly drunk and the efforts of Jessie and Beatie to quiet her only seemed to infuriate her more.

"He likes it down there on the floor and in the dark," she continued. "Don't disturb him, my fallen king. He's working out Canto 24 of the Epic, volume three of the Cultural History. Don't laugh so loud. You might wake him and American literature will suffer." She leaned over and tapped her husband lightly on the side of the head with the flat of her mallet. "Get up! Get up, Marvin, and try again. You're holding up the game. Get up!" He rose slowly into a sitting position, very pale and avoiding her eyes. "Maybe you'd like to make a statement," she insisted. "Maybe you'd like to—"

"Give me a hand, Howard," he said. "I guess I'm higher than I thought. I need a—"

"I'll give you a hand," Achsa screamed before Howard could move; and she held out the end of her mallet toward Marvin who made no move to lay hold of it. "Here, *take* it!" she cried in rage, drawing it back and smashing it full force across his left cheek. "How come you don't say 'Thank you,' Marv? Say 'Thank you' to the nice lady!" She hit him harder this time on the other side of the head; and when he remained silent, harder and harder still, first right, then left, then right. She could hardly breathe. "Why don't you talk to me, Marvin? Why don't you *talk* to me? Say 'Thank you,' Marvin. Why don't you say 'Thank you'?"

Howard, who had stood by paralyzed with the rest, grabbed her under the arms, dragging her backwards with her feet in the air, and hanging on grimly though she leaned over to sink her teeth into the back of his hand.

"Smack her, Howard," Jessie advised him. "For pity's sake, slap her. She's hysterical." But he did not dare shift his hold, for fear of losing his purchase on her damp and squirming flesh.

Meanwhile, Marvin had risen very slowly to his feet, a thin trickle of blood running out of one corner of his mouth and down over his chin. "I—I—" he began twice over. "I—" then sank to his knees, moaning. "Achsa," he yelled in terror. "Achsa, for God's sake, the pills in my pocket—my right—It's another attack, another—" His words burbled away into incoherence; then, grasping his upper left arm in his right hand and lifting his chin into the air, he cried out in agony. His mouth was drawn back, his teeth shown in what may have been a smile, and his wordless cry may have turned again into Achsa's name before he pitched forward on his face again; but Howard could not be sure.

"Let me go! Let me go!" Achsa begged him, kicking and scratching. "What are you doing to him? My Marvin! Let me go!" He finally released his hold at the moment the overhead lights were switched on again, fixing them all in their nudity and helplessness, caught for one everlasting instant as in a flashlight still.

Molly had begun to scream, a single note, high and pure, that seemed as if it would never end; and whirling about, they all stared at her in the hard light, even Bill, startled back to awareness on his bishop's throne. One arm concealing her breasts, the other thrust downward so that her hand hid the meeting of her thighs, Molly-o confronted them in the classic pose of nakedness surprised, as if she knew for the first time what it meant to be really nude.

[September 1957]

ARTHUR MILLER

The Misfits

Wind blew down from the mountains for two nights, pinning them to their little camp on the desert floor. Around the fire on the grand plateau between the two mountain ranges, they were the only moving things. But awakening now with the first pink of dawn they heard the hush of a windless morning. Quickly the sky flared with true dawn like damp paper catching fire, and the shroud of darkness slipped off the little plane and the truck standing a few yards away.

As soon as they had eaten breakfast they took their accustomed positions. Perce Howland went to the tail, ready to unlash the ropes, Gay Langland stood near the propeller, and both watched the pilot, Guido Racanelli, loading his shotgun pistol and stowing it under the seat in the cockpit. He looked thoughtful, even troubled, zipping up the front of his ripped leather jacket. "Sumbitch valve is rattling," he complained.

"It's better than wages, Guido," Perce called from the tail.

"Hell it is if I get flattened up there," Guido said.

"You know them canyons," Gay Langland said.

"Gay, it don't mean a damn thing what the wind does down here. Up there's where it counts." He thumbed toward the mountains behind them. "I'm ten feet from rocks at the bottom of a dive; the wind smacks you down then and you never pull up again."

They saw he was serious so they said nothing. Guido stood still for a moment, studying the peaks in the distance, his hard, melon cheeks browned by wind, the white goggle marks around his eyes turning him into some fat jungle bird. At last he said, "Oh, hell with it. We'll get the sumbitches." He climbed into the cockpit calling to Gay, "Turn her over!"

Perce Howland quickly freed the tail and then the wing tips and Gay hurried to the propeller, swung the blade down and hopped back. A puff of white smoke floated up from the engine ports.

"Goddam car gas," Guido muttered. They were buying low octane to save money. Then he called, "Go again, Gay-boy; ignition on!" Gay reached up and pulled the propeller down and jumped back. The engine said its "Chaahh!" and the fuselage shuddered and the propeller turned into a wheel in the golden air. The little, stiff-backed plane tumbled toward the open desert, bumping along over the sage clumps and crunching whitened skeletons of winter-killed cattle, growing smaller as it shouldered its way over the broken ground, until its nose turned upward and space opened between the doughnut tires and the desert, and it turned and flew back over the heads of Gay and Perce. Guido waved down, a stranger now, fiercely goggled and wrapped in leather. The plane flew away, losing itself against the orange and purple mountains which vaulted from the desert to hide from the cowboys' eyes the wild animals they wanted for themselves.

They had at least two hours before the plane would fly out of the mountains, driving the horses before it, so they washed the plates and the cups and stored them in the aluminum grub box. If Guido did find horses, they would break camp and return to Bowie tonight, so they packed up their bedrolls with sailors' tidiness and laid them neatly side by side on the ground. Six great truck tires, each with a rope coiled within, lay on the open truck bed. Gay Langland looked them over and touched them with his hand, trying to think if there was anything they were leaving behind. Serious as he was he looked a little amused, even slightly surprised. He was forty-six years old but his ears still stuck out like a little boy's and his hair lay in swirls from the pressure of his hat. After two days and nights of lying around he was eager to be going and doing and he savored the pleasurable delay of this final inspection.

Perce Howland watched, his face dreamy and soft with his early-morning somnambulist's stare. He stood and moved, bent over the tires and straightened himself as effortlessly as wheat, as though he had been created full-grown and dressed as he now was, hipless and twenty-two, in his snug dungarees and tight plaid shirt and broad-brimmed hat pushed back on his blond head. Now Gay got into the cab and started the engine and Perce slid into the seat beside him. A thin border collie leaped in after him. "You nearly forgot Belle," he said to Gay. The dog snuggled down behind Gay's feet and they started off.

Thirty miles ahead stood the lava mountains which were the northern border of this desert, the bed of a bowl seven thousand feet in the air, a place no one ever saw excepting a few cowboys searching for strays. People in Bowie, sixty miles away, did not know of this place.

Now that they were on the move, following the two-track trail through the sage, they felt between them the comfort of purpose and their isolation. It was getting warm now. Perce slumped in his seat, blinking as though he would go to sleep, and the older man smoked a cigarette and let his body flow from side to side with the pitching of the truck. There was a moving cloud of dust in the distance, and Gay said, "Antelope," and Perce tipped his hat back and looked. "Must be doin' sixty," he said, and Gay said, "More."

After a while Perce said, "We better get over to Largo by tomorrow if we're gonna get into that rodeo. They's gonna be a crowd trying to sign up for that one."

"We'll drive down in the morning," Gay said.

"Like to win some money. I just wish I get me a good horse down there."

"They be glad to fix you up. You're known pretty good around here now."

Perce tucked his thumbs into his belt so his fingers could touch his prize, the engraved belt buckle with his name spelled out under the raised figure of the bucking horse. He had been coming down from Nevada since he was sixteen, picking up money at the local rodeos, but this trip had been different. Sometime, somewhere in the past weeks, he had lost the desire to go back home.

They rode in silence. Gay had to hold the gearshift lever in high or it would slip out into neutral when they hit a bump. The transmission fork was worn out, he knew, and the front tires were going, too. He dropped one hand to his pants pocket and felt the four silver dollars he had left from the ten Roslyn had given him.

As though he had read Gay's mind, Perce said, "Roslyn would've liked it up here. She'd liked to have seen that antelope, I bet."

Through the corner of his eye Gay watched the younger man, who was looking ahead with a little grin on his face. "Yeah. She's a damned good sport, old Roslyn." He watched Perce for any sign of guile.

"Only educated women I ever knew before was back home near Teachers College," Perce said. "I was learning them to ride for awhile, and I used to think, hell, education's everything. But when I saw the husbands they got married to, why I don't give them much credit. And they just as soon climb on a man as tell him good morning."

"Just because a woman's educated don't mean much. Woman's a woman," Gay said. The image of his wife came into his mind. For a moment he wondered if she was still living with the same man.

"You divorced?" Perce asked.

"No. I never bothered with it," Gay said. It surprised him how Perce said just what was on his mind sometimes. "How'd you know I was thinking of that?" he asked, grinning with embarrassment.

"Hell, I didn't know," Perce said.

"You're always doin' that. I think of somethin' and you say it."

"That's funny," Perce said.

They rode on in silence. They were nearing the middle of the desert where they would turn east. Gay was driving faster now, holding onto the gearshift lever to keep it from springing into neutral. The time was coming soon when he would need about fifty dollars or sell the truck, because it would be useless without repairs. Without a truck and without a horse he would be down to what was in his pocket.

Perce spoke out of the silence. "If I don't win Saturday, I'm gonna have to do something for money."

"Goddam, you always say what's in my mind."

Perce laughed. His face looked very young and pink. "Why?"

"I was just now thinkin'," Gay said, "what I'm gonna do for money."

"Well, Roslyn give you some," Perce said.

He said it innocently, and Gay knew it was innocent, and yet he felt angry blood moving into his neck. Something had happened in these five weeks since he'd met Perce and let him come home to Roslyn's house to sleep, and Gay did not know for sure what it was. Roslyn had taken to calling Perce cute, and now and again she would bend over and kiss him on the back of the neck when he was sitting in the living-room chair, drinking with them.

Not that that meant anything in itself because he'd known eastern women before, and it was just their way. What he wondered at was Perce's hardly noticing what she did to him. Sometimes it was like he'd already had her and could ignore her the way a man will who knows he's boss. Gay sensed the bottom of his life falling if it turned out Roslyn had really been loving this boy beside him. It had happened to him once before, but this frightened him even more and he did not know exactly why. Not that he couldn't do without her. There wasn't anybody or anything he couldn't do without. He had been all his life like Perce Howland, a man moving on or ready to. Only when he had discovered his wife with a stranger in a parked car did he understand that he had never had a stake to which he'd been pleasantly tethered.

He had not seen her or his children for years, and only rarely thought about any of them. Any more than his father had thought of him very much after the day he had gotten on his pony, when he was fourteen, to go to town from the ranch, and had kept going into Montana and stayed there for three years. He lived in his country and his father did and it was the same endless range wherever he went and it connected him sufficiently with his father and his wife and his children. All might turn up sometime in some town or at some rodeo where he might happen to look over his shoulder and see his daughter or one of his sons, or they might never turn up. He had neither left anyone nor not-left as long as they were all alive on these ranges, for everything here was always beyond the furthest shot of vision and far away, and mostly he had worked alone or with one or two men between distant mountains anyway.

He drove steadily across the grand plateau, and he felt he was going to be afraid. He was not afraid now, but something new was opening up inside him. He had somehow passed the kidding point: he had to work again and earn his way as he always had before he met Roslyn. Not that he didn't work for her, but it wasn't the same. Driving her car, repairing her house, running errands wasn't what you'd call work. Still it was too. Yet it wasn't either. He grew tired of thinking about it.

In the distance now he could see the shimmering wall of heat rising from the clay flatland they wanted to get to—a beige waste as bare and hard as pavement, a prehistoric lake bed thirty miles long by seventeen miles wide couched between two mountain ranges, where a man might drive a car at a hundred miles an hour with his hands off the wheel and never hit anything at all.

When they had rolled a few hundred yards onto the clay lake bed, Gay pulled up and shut off the engine. The air was still, in a dead, sunlit silence. Opening his door, he could hear a squeak in the hinge he had never noticed before. When they walked around out here they could hear their shirts rasping against their backs and the brush of a sleeve against their trousers. They looked back toward the mountains at whose feet they had camped and scanned the ridges for Guido's plane.

Perce Howland said, "I sure hope they's five up in there."

"Guido spotted five last week, he said."

"He said he wasn't sure if one wasn't only a colt."

Gay let himself keep silence. He felt he was going to argue with Perce. "How long you think you'll be stayin' around here?" he asked.

"Don't know," Perce said, and spat over the side of the truck. "I'm gettin' a little tired of this, though."

"Well, it's better than wages."

"Hell, yes. Anything's better than wages."

Gay's eyes crinkled. "You're a real misfit, boy."

"That suits me fine," Perce said. They often had this conversation and savored it. "Better than workin' for some goddam cow outfit buckarooin' so somebody else can buy gas for his Cadillac."

"Damn right," Gay said.

"Hell, Gay, you are the most misfitted man I ever saw and you done all right."

"I got no complaints," Gay said.

"I don't want nothin' and I don't want to want nothin'."

"That's the way, boy."

Gay felt closer to him again and he was glad for it. He kept his eyes on the ridges far away. The sun felt good on his shoulders. "I think he's havin' trouble with them sumbitches up in there."

Perce stared out at the ridges. "Ain't two hours yet." Then he turned to Gay. "These mountains must be cleaned out by now, ain't they."

"Just about," Gay said. "Just a couple small herds left."

"What you goin' to do when you got these cleaned out?"

"Might go north, I think. Supposed to be some big herds in around Thighbone Mountain and that range up in there."

"How far's that?"

"North about a hundred miles. If I can get Guido interested."

Perce smiled. "He don't like movin' around much, does he?"

"He's just misfitted like us," Gay said. "He don't want nothin'." Then he added, "They wanted him for an airline pilot flyin' up into Montana and back. Good pay too."

"Wouldn't do it, huh?"

"Not Guido," Gay said, grinning. "Might not like some of the passengers, he told them."

Both men laughed and Perce shook his head in tickled admiration for Guido. Then he said, "They wanted me take over the riding academy up home. Just stand around and see the customers get satisfied and put them girls off and on."

He fell silent. Gay knew the rest. It was the same story. It brought him closer to Perce and it was what he had liked about him in the first place. He had come on Perce in a bar where the boy was buying drinks for everybody with his rodeo winnings, and his hair still clotted with blood from a bucking horse's kick an hour earlier. Roslyn had offered to get a doctor for him and he had said, "Thank you, kindly. But if you're bad hurt you gonna die and the doctor can't do nothin', and if you ain't bad hurt you get better anyway without no doctor."

Now it suddenly came upon Gay that Perce must have known Roslyn before they had met in the bar. He stared at the boy's straight profile. "Want to come up north with me if I go?" he asked.

Perce thought a moment. "Think I'll stay around here. Not much rodeoin' up north."

"I might find a pilot up there if Guido won't come. And Roslyn drive us up in her car."

Perce turned to him, a little surprised. "Would she go up there?"

"Sure. She's a damn good sport," Gay said. He watched Perce's eyes, which had turned interested and warm.

Perce said, "Well, maybe; except to tell you the truth, Gay, I never feel comfortable takin' these horses."

"Somebody's goin' to take them if we don't."

"I know," Perce said. He turned to watch the far ridges again. "Just seems to me they belong up there."

"They ain't doin' nothin' up there but eatin' out good cattle range. The cow outfits shoot them down if they see them."

"I know," Perce said.

There was silence. Neither bug nor lizard nor rabbit moved on the great basin around them. Gay said, "I'd a soon sell them for riding horses, but they ain't big enough. And the freight's more than they're worth. You saw them—they ain't nothin' but skinny horses."

"I just don't know if I'd want to see like a hundred of them goin' for chicken feed, though. I don't mind like five or six, but a hundred's a lot of horses. I don't know."

Gay thought. "Well, if it ain't this it's wages. Around here anyway." He was speaking of himself and explaining himself.

They heard the shotgun off in the sky somewhere and they stopped moving. Gay slid out of the tire in which he had been lounging and off the truck. He went to the cab and brought out a pair of binoculars, blew dust off the lenses, mounted the truck and, with his elbows propped on his knees, he focused on the far mountains.

"See anything?" Perce asked.

"He's still in the pass, I guess," Gay said.

They sat still, watching the empty sky over the pass. The sun was making them perspire now and Gay wiped his wet eyebrows with the back of one hand. They heard the shotgun again. Gay spoke without lowering the glasses: "He's probably blasting them out of some corner."

"I see him," Perce said quickly. "I see him glintin', I see the plane."

It angered Gay that Perce had seen it first without glasses. In the glasses Gay could see the plane clearly now. The plane was flying out of the pass, circling back and disappearing into the pass again. "He's got them in the pass now. Just goin' back in for them."

Now Gay could see moving specks on the ground where the pass opened onto the desert table. "I see them," he said. "One, two, three, four. Four and a colt."

"We gonna take the colt?" Perce asked.

"Hell, can't take the mare without the colt."

Gay handed him the glasses. "Take a look."

Gay went forward to the cab and opened its door. His dog lay shivering on the floor under the pedals. He snapped his fingers and she leaped down to the ground and stood there, quivering as though the ground had hidden explosives everywhere. He climbed back onto the truck and sat on a tire beside Perce, who was looking through the glasses.

"He's divin' down on them. God, they sure can run."

"Let's have a look," Gay said.

The plane was dropping down from the arc of its climb and as the roaring motor flew over them they lifted their heads and galloped faster. They had been running now for over an hour and would slow down when the plane had to climb after a dive and the motor's noise grew quieter. As Guido climbed again Gay and Perce heard a shot, distant and harmless, and the shot sped the horses on as the plane took time to climb, bank and turn. Then as the horses slowed to a trot the plane dived down over their backs again and their heads shot up and they galloped until the engine's roar receded. The sky was clear and lightly blue and only the little plane swung back and forth across the desert like the glinting tip of a magic wand, and the horses came on toward the vast striped clay bed where the truck was parked, and at its edge they halted.

The two men waited for the horses to reach the edge of the lake bed when Guido would land the plane and they would take off with the truck.

"They see the heat waves," Gay said, looking through the glasses. The plane dived down on them and they scattered but would not go forward onto the unknowable territory from the cooler, sage-dotted desert behind them. The men on the truck heard the shotgun again. Now the horses broke their formation and leaped onto the lake bed, all heading in different directions, but only trotting, exploring the ground under their feet and the strange, superheated air in their nostrils. Gradually, as the plane wound around the sky to dive again, the horses closed ranks and slowly galloped shoulder to shoulder out onto the borderless waste, the colt a length behind with its nose nearly touching the mare's long tail.

"That's a big mare," Perce said. His eyes were still dreamy and his face was calm, but his skin had reddened.

"She's a bigger mare than usual up there, ya," Gay said. Both men knew the mustang herds lived in total isolation and that in-breeding had reduced them to the size of large ponies. The herd swerved now and they could see the stallion. He was smaller than the mare, but still larger than any they had brought down before. The other two horses were small, the way mustangs ought to be.

The plane was hurrying down for a landing now. Gay and Perce Howland got to their feet and each reached into a tire behind him and drew out a coil of rope whose ends hung in a loop. They glanced out and saw Guido taxing toward them and they strapped themselves to stanchions sticking up from the truck bed and stood waiting for him. He cut the engine twenty yards away and leaped out of the open cockpit before the plane had halted, its right wing tilted down, as always, because of the weak starboard shock absorber. He trotted over to the truck, lifting his goggles off and stuffing them into his torn jacket pocket. His face was puffed with preoccupation. He jumped into the cab of the truck and the collie dog jumped in after him and sat on the floor, quivering. He started the truck and they roared across the flat clay.

The herd was standing still in a small clot of dots more than two miles off. The truck rolled smoothly past sixty. Gay on the right front corner of the truck bed and Perce on the left pulled their hats down to their eyebrows against the rush of air and hefted the looped ropes which the wind was threatening to coil and foul in their palms. Guido knew that Gay was a good roper and that Perce was unsure, so he headed for the herd's left in order to come up to them on Gay's side of the truck if he could. This whole method of mustanging—the truck, the tires attached to ropes and the plane—was his idea, and once again he felt the joy of having thought of it all. It had awakened him to life after a year's hibernation. His wife dying in childbirth had been like a gigantic and insane ocean wave rising out of a calm sea, and it had left him stranded in his cousin's house in Bowie, suddenly a bachelor after eleven married years. Only this had broken the silence of the world for him, this roaring across the lake bed with his left boot ready over the brake pedal should the truck start to overturn on a sudden swerve.

The horses, at a standstill now, were staring at the oncoming truck, and the men saw that this herd was beautiful.

A wet spring had rounded them out, and they shone in the sunlight. The mare was almost black and the stallion and the two others were deeply brown. The colt was curly-coated and had a grey sheen. The stallion dipped his head suddenly and turned his back on the truck and galloped. The others turned and clattered after him, with the colt running alongside the mare. Guido pressed down on the gas and the truck surged forward, whining. They were a few yards behind the animals now and they could see the bottoms of their hoofs, fresh hoofs that made a gentle tacking clatter because they had never been shod. The truck was coming abreast of the mare now and beside her the others galloped, slim-legged and wet after running almost two hours.

As the truck drew alongside the mare and Gay began twirling his loop above his head, the whole herd wheeled away to the right and Guido jammed the gas pedal down and swung with them, but the truck tilted violently so he slowed down and fell behind them a few yards until they would straighten out and move ahead again. At the edge of their strength they wheeled like circus horses, almost tamely in their terror, and suddenly Guido saw a breadth between the stallion and the two browns and he sped in between, cutting the mare off at the left with her colt. Now the horses stretched, the clatter quickened. Their hind legs flew straight back and their necks stretched low and forward. Gay whirled his loop over his head and the truck came up alongside the stallion whose lungs were screaming with exhaustion and Gay flung the noose. It fell on the stallion's head and, with a whipping of the lead, Gay made it slip down over his neck. The horse swerved away to the right and stretched the rope until the tire was pulled off the truck bed and dragged along the hard clay. The three men watched from the slowing truck as the stallion, with startled eyes, pulled the giant tire for a few yards, then reared up with his forelegs in the air and came down facing the tire and trying to back away from it. Then he stood there, heaving, his hind legs dancing in an arc from right to left and back again as he shook his head in the remorseless noose.

As soon as he was sure the stallion was secure, Guido turned sharply left toward the mare and the colt which were trotting idly together by themselves in the distance. The two browns were already disappearing toward the north, but they would halt soon because they were tired, while the mare might continue back into her familiar hills where the truck could not follow. He straightened the truck and jammed down the gas pedal. In a minute he drew up on her left side because the colt was running on her right. She was very heavy, he saw, and he wondered now if she were a mustang at all. Then through his right window he saw the loop flying out and down over her head, and he saw her head fly up and then she fell back. He turned to the right, braking with his left boot, and he saw her dragging a tire and coming to a halt, with the free colt watching her and trotting beside her very close. Then he headed straight ahead across the flat toward two specks which rapidly enlarged until they became the two browns which were at a standstill and watching the oncoming truck. He came in between them and they galloped; Perce on the left roped one and Gay roped the other almost at the same time. And Guido leaned his head out of his window and yelled up at Perce. "Good boy!" he hollered, and Perce let himself return an excited grin, although there seemed to be some trouble in his eyes.

Guido made an easy half circle and headed back to the mare and the colt and slowed to a halt twenty yards away and got out of the cab.

The three men approached the mare. She had never seen a man and her eyes were wide in fear. Her rib cage stretched and collapsed very rapidly and there was a trickle of blood coming out of her nostrils. She had a heavy, dark brown mane and her tail nearly touched the ground. The colt with dumb eyes shifted about on its silly bent legs trying to keep the mare between itself and the men, and the mare kept shifting her rump to shield the colt from them.

They wanted now to move the noose higher up on the mare's neck because it had fallen on her from the rear and was tight around the middle of her neck where it could choke her if she kept pulling against the weight of the tire. Gay was the best roper, so Perce and Guido stood by as he twirled a noose over his head, then let it fall open softly, just behind the forefeet of the mare. They waited for a moment, then approached her and she backed a step. Then Gay pulled sharply on the rope and her forefeet were tied together. With another rope Gay lassoed her hind feet and she swayed and fell to the ground on her side. Her body swelled and contracted, but she seemd resigned. The colt stretched its nose to her tail and stood there as the men came to the mare and spoke quietly to her, and Guido bent down and opened the noose and slipped it up under her jaw. They inspected her for a brand, but she was clean.

"Never see a horse that size up here," Gay said to Guido.

Perce said, "She's no mustang. Might even be standardbred." He looked to Guido for confirmation.

Guido sat on his heels and opened the mare's mouth and the other two looked in with him. "She's fifteen if she's a day," Gay said. "She wouldn't be around much longer anyway."

"Ya, she's old." Perce's eyes were filled with thought.

Guido stood up and the three went back to the truck, and drove across the lake bed to the stallion.

"Ain't a bad-lookin' horse," Perce said.

He was standing still, heaving for breath. His head was down, holding the rope taut, and he was looking at them with deep brown eyes that were like the lenses of enormous binoculars. Gay got his rope ready. "He ain't nothin' but a misfit," he said. "You couldn't run cattle with him; he's too small to breed and too old to cut."

"He is small," Perce conceded. "Got a nice neck though."

"Oh, they're nice-*lookin'* horses, some of them," Guido said. "What the hell you goin' to do with them, though?"

Gay twirled the loop over his head and they spread out around the stallion. "They're just old misfit horses, that's all," he said, and he flung the rope behind the stallion's forelegs and the horse backed a step and he drew the rope and the noose bit into the horse's fetlocks drawing them together, and he swayed but he would not fall. "Take hold here," Gay called to Perce, who ran around the horse and took the rope from him and held it taut. Then Gay went back to the truck, got another rope, returned to the rear of the horse and looped his hind legs. But the stallion would not fall. Guido stepped closer to push him over, but he swung his head and showed his teeth and Guido stepped back. "Pull him down!" Guido yelled to Gay and Perce, and they jerked their ropes to trip the stallion, but he righted himself and stood there, bound by the head to the tire and by his feet to the two ropes which the men held. Then Guido hurried over to Perce and took the rope from him and walked with it toward the rear of the horse and pulled hard. The stallion's forefeet slipped back and he came down on his knees and his nose struck the clay ground and he snorted as he struck, but he would not topple over and stayed there on his knees as though he were bowing to something, with his nose propping up his head against the ground and his sharp bursts of breath blowing up dust in little clouds under his nostrils. Now Guido gave the rope back to young Perce Howland who held it taut and he came up alongside the stallion's neck and laid his hands on the side of the neck and pushed and the horse fell over onto his flank and lay there and, like the mare, when he felt the ground against his body he seemed to let himself out and for the first time his eyes blinked and his breath came now in sighs and no longer fiercely. Guido shifted the noose up under his jaw, and they opened the ropes around his hoofs and when he felt his legs free he first raised his head curiously and then clattered up and stood there looking at them, from one to the other, blood dripping from his nostrils and a stain of deep red on both dusty knees.

Then the men moved without hurrying to the truck and Gay stored his two extra ropes and got behind the wheel with Guido beside him, and Perce climbed onto the back of the truck and lay down facing the sky and made a pillow with his palms.

Gay headed the truck south toward the plane. Guido was slowly catching his breath and now he lighted a cigarette, puffed it and rubbed his left hand into his bare scalp. He sat gazing out the windshield and the side window. "I'm sleepy," he said.

"What you reckon?" Gay asked.

"What you?" Guido said.

"That mare might be six hundred pounds."

"I'd say about that, Gay."

"About four hundred apiece for the browns and a little more for the stallion. What's that come to?"

"Nineteen hundred, maybe two thousand," Guido said.

They fell silent figuring the money. Two thousand pounds at six cents a pound came to a hundred and twenty dollars. The colt might make it a few dollars more, but not much. Figuring the gas for the plane and the truck, and twelve dollars for their groceries, they came to the figure of a hundred dollars for the three of them. Guido would get forty-five, since he had used his plane, and Gay would get thirty-five, including the use of his truck, and Perce Howland, if he agreed, as he undoubtedly would, had the remaining twenty.

"We should've watered them the last time," Gay said. "They can pick up a lot of weight if you let them water."

"Yeah, let's be sure to do that," Guido said.

They knew they would as likely as not forget to water the horses before they unloaded them at the dealer's lot in Bowie. They would be in a hurry to unload and be free of them, free to pitch and roll with time in the bars or asleep in Roslyn's house or making a try in some rodeo. Once they had figured their shares they stopped thinking of money, and they divided it and even argued about it only because it was the custom of men. They had not come up here for the money.

Gay stopped the truck beside the plane. Guido opened his door and said, "See you in town. Let's get the other truck tomorrow morning."

"Perce wants to go over to Largo and sign up for the rodeo tomorrow," Gay said. "Tell ya—we'll go in and get the truck and come back here this afternoon maybe. Maybe we bring them in tonight."

"All right, if you want to. I'll see you boys tomorrow," Guido said, and he got out and stopped for a moment to talk to Perce. "Perce?"

Perce propped himself up on one elbow and looked down at him.

Guido smiled. "You sleeping?"

"I was about to."

"We figure about a hundred dollars clear. Twenty all right for you?"

"Ya, twenty's all right," Perce said. He hardly seemed to be listening.

"See you in town," Guido said, and turned on his bandy legs and waddled off to the plane where Gay was already standing with his hands on the propeller blade. Guido got in and Gay swung the blade down and the engine started immediately. Guido gunned the plane and she trundled off and into the sky and the two men on the ground watched her as she flew toward the mountains and away.

Now Gay returned to the truck and said, "Twenty all right?" And he said this because he thought Perce looked hurt.

"Heh? Ya, twenty's all right," Perce answered. Then he let himself down and stood beside the truck and wet the ground while Gay waited for him. Then Perce got into the cab and they drove off.

Perce agreed to come back this afternoon with Gay in the larger truck and load the horses, although as they drove across the lake bed in silence they both knew, gradually, that they would wait until morning, because they were tired now and would be more tired later. The mare and her colt stood between them and the sage desert toward which they were heading. Perce stared out the window at the mare and he saw that she was watching them, apprehensively but not in real alarm, and the colt was lying upright on the clay. Perce looked long at the colt as they approached and he thought about it waiting there beside the mare, unbound and free to go off, and he said to Gay, "Ever hear of a colt leave a mare?"

"Not that one," Gay said. "He ain't goin' nowhere."

Perce laid his head back and closed his eyes. His tobacco swelled out his left cheek and he let it soak there.

Now the truck left the clay lake bed and it pitched and rolled over the sage clumps. They would return to their camp and pick up their bedrolls.

"Think I'll go back to Roslyn's tonight," Gay said.

"Okay," Perce said and did not open his eyes.

"We can pick them up in the morning, then take you to Largo."

"Okay," Perce said.

Gay thought about Roslyn. She would probably razz them about all the work they had done for a few dollars, saying they were too dumb to figure in their labor time and other hidden expenses. To hear her sometimes they hadn't made any profit at all. "Roslyn going to feel sorry for the colt," Gay said, "so might as well not mention it."

Perce opened his eyes and looked out at the mountains. "Hell, she feeds that dog of hers canned dog food, doesn't she?"

Gay felt closer to Perce again and he smiled. "Sure does."

"Well, what's she think is in the can?"

"She knows what's in it."

"There's wild horses in the can," Perce said, as though it was part of an angry argument with himself.

They were silent for a while.

"You comin' back to Roslyn's with me or you gonna stay in town?"

"I'd just as soon go back with you."

"Okay," Gay said. He felt good about going into her cabin now. There would be her books on the shelves he had built for her, and they would have some drinks, and Perce would fall asleep on the couch and they would go into the bedroom together. He liked to come back to her after he had worked, more than when he had only driven her here and there or just stayed around her place. He liked his own money in his pocket when he came to her. And he tried harder to visualize how it would be with her and he thought of himself being forty-seven soon, and then nearing fifty. She would go back east one day, maybe this year, maybe next. He wondered again when he would begin turning grey and he set his jaw against the idea of himself grey and an old man.

Perce spoke, sitting up in his seat. "I want to phone my mother. Damn, I haven't called her all year." He sounded angry. He stared out the window at the mountains. He had the memory of how the colt looked and he felt an almost violent wish for it to be gone when they returned. Then he said, "I got to get to Largo tomorrow and register."

"We'll go," Gay said, sensing the boy's unaccountable irritation.

"I could use a good win," he said. He thought of five hundred dollars now, and of the many times he had won five hundred dollars. "You know something, Gay? I'm never goin' to amount to a damn thing." Then, suddenly he laughed. He laughed without restraint for a moment and then laid his head back and closed his eyes.

"I told you that first time I met you, didn't I?" Gay grinned. He felt a bravery between them now, and he was relieved to see that Perce was grinning. He felt the mood coming on for some drinks at Roslyn's.

"That colt won't bring two dollars anyway," Perce said. "What you say we just left him there?"

"Why, you know he'd just follow the truck right into town."

After they had driven for fifteen minutes without speaking, Gay said he wanted to go north very soon for the hundreds of horses that were supposed to be in the mountains there. But Perce had fallen fast asleep beside him. Gay wanted to talk about that expedition because as they rolled onto the highway from the desert he began to visualize Roslyn razzing them again, and it was clear to him that he had somehow failed to settle anything for himself; he had put in three days for thirty-five dollars and there would be no way to explain it so it made sense and it would be embarrassing. And yet he knew that it had all been the way it ought to be even if he could never explain it to her or anyone else. He reached out and nudged Perce, who opened his eyes and lolled his head over to face him. "You comin' up to Thighbone with me, ain't you?"

"Okay," Perce said, and went back to sleep.

Gay felt more peaceful now the younger man would not be leaving him. There was a future again, something to head for.

The sun shone hot on the beige plain all day. Neither fly nor bug nor snake ventured out on the waste to molest the four horses tethered there, or the colt. They had run nearly two hours at a gallop and as the afternoon settled upon them they pawed the hard ground for water, but there was none. Toward evening the wind came up and they backed into it and faced the mountains from which they had come. From time to time the stallion caught the scent of the pastures up there and he started to walk toward the vaulted fields in which he had grazed, but the tire bent his neck around and after a few steps he would turn to face it and leap into the air with his forelegs striking at the sky and then he would come down and be still again. With the deep blue darkness the wind blew faster, tossing their manes and flinging their long tails in between their legs. The cold of night raised the colt onto its legs and it stood close to the mare for warmth. Facing the southern range five horses blinked under the green glow of the risen moon and they closed their eyes and slept. The colt settled again on the hard ground and lay under the mare. In the high hollows of the mountains the grass they had cropped this morning straightened in the darkness. On the lusher swards which were still damp with the rains of spring their hoofprints had begun to disappear. When the first pink glow of another morning lit the sky, the colt stood up and, as it had done at every dawn, it walked waywardly for water. The mare shifted warningly and her bone hoofs ticked the clay. The colt turned its head and returned to her and stood at her side with vacant eye, its nostrils sniffing the warming air.

[October 1957]

THOMAS WILLIAMS

Goose Pond

Robert Hurley's wife died in September, and by the middle of October he had more or less settled everything. His son and daughter were both married and lived far away from New York; his son in Los Angeles, his daughter in Toledo. They came East for the funeral and each wanted him to come and visit. "I'm not about to retire. I won't be an old man in a guest room," he told them, knowing the great difference between the man he looked at fifty-eight and the man he felt himself to be. It had taken Mary six months to die, and during the last few of those months he began quietly to assume many of her symptoms. The doctors noticed it and understood, but his children, accustomed to a father who had always been to them a common-sense, rather unimaginative figure, were shocked by his loss of weight, by a listlessness as unlike him, as unsettling to them as if the earth's rotation had begun to slow down.

But he would do no visiting, even though his business did not need him. "I know what visiting is," he wrote to his son. "I don't do it very well. Please don't call so much. You know how to write leters." "Daddy," his daughter said, long distance. "The children are crazy to have their grandfather come and see them."

And he thought, there is one place I would like to go, and there are no children I know there: "I'm going to New Hampshire, to Leah."

"All by yourself? What for?" She began to get excited, almost hysterical. He could see her biting her lower lip—a habit of her mother's. Afterwards she would be calling Charles in Los Angeles.

"I was born there. Your mother and I lived there before you were born. Do I need any other reason? It's October. Anyway, I'll be back in a couple of weeks."

"But, Daddy, we felt that you shouldn't be alone. . . ."

"I haven't been alone for thirty years," he said. "I want to try it again. Now go back to whatever you were doing. I can hear a baby

145

crying in your house. Go take care of it. I'm going to stay with the Pedersens. Do you remember the old people in the big house on the mountain? If they still take boarders, that's where I'll be." *If they're still alive,* he thought. He wanted to walk in the woods again, but he had other reasons. The sight of his grandchildren, the hundred times a day when their small disasters caused screaming, tears; he couldn't stand it. They were always about to hurt themselves, they nearly fell so many times. They had so many deadly years to make. Automobiles, knives, leukemia, fire. . . . On the afternoon of the funeral he had watched his granddaughter, Ann, and suddenly he saw her having his wife's senseless pain, saw her crying not because of a bumped knee, but at more serious wounds. And the Pedersens? They were so old, they had somehow escaped, and as he remembered them they lived dried-up and careful, in a kind of limbo. He would go to the Pedersens, on Cascom Mountain.

Nana fussed with the Edison lamp, turning the white flame up in the mantle, moving the broad base across the crack made by the table leaf; then with the side of her hand she wiped the shiny surface of the table where it had been. The light shone past the tinted shade, up the glass chimney and sharpened her old face, made her glasses glint for a second until she moved away, tall and always busy, her small eyes always alert. She rarely sat down, and even then seemed poised, ready for busy duty. The old man settled himself cautiously, as he did now, one piece at a time. Nana had his zither out of its case, the light just right, made sure he had his hearing aid, his pick, an ash tray near. In spite of his age, he smoked cigarettes.

Back in the shadows, between a lacy, drooping vine and the narrow window, Nana's older sister, blue dress and high black shoes, composed and fragile face, sat in a rocker and never spoke. Nana herself was seventy-nine. For forty years she had bossed the seven-mile trek down to Leah in the late fall, back up the mountain again to this high old house in the spring. It was Nana who dealt with the world, who shut the windows when it rained, herded great-grandchildren when the family came in the summer, locked the house for the winter. In a few weeks they would be going down to their small apartment in Leah, to take their chances on another winter.

The old man tuned his zither, humming in a dry, crackly falsetto and turning his wrench as he picked the short strings. Tuned against the windy old voice, the crisp notes of the zither were startling, clear and metallic. There seemed to be no connection between the voice and the sounds of the strings, as if the old man heard other notes, the sounds of memory to check his instrument against.

"German *concert* zither," Nana said proudly, still hovering over the lamp. She rearranged his cigarettes, the coffee cup. She spoke from behind him, "He don't hear so good," nodding vigorously. "But he got the hearing aid." She pointed into his ear, where the pink button shone like a flower against brown freckles. "He don't wear it all the time, like he should." She moved quickly away on some sudden errand, and the old man looked up and winked at Hurley.

"Sometimes it makes too much noise," he said, smiling benevolently at his wife. She began to move the table. "It's all right. It's all right!" he said. In his fifty years in America he had mastered the sounds of English, but the rhythms of his speech were Scandinavian. "I'm going to play first a Norwegian song."

Nana poised herself upon a chair, folded her hands firmly, set herself for a moment and then began energetically to smooth her apron down her long thighs. The old lady against the wall stopped rocking. It always startled Hurley when, out of her silent effacement, she responded.

The old man bent over his zither, his shiny face as ruddy as a baby's. His mottled, angular fingers worked over the strings; he swayed back and forth to keep time and snorted, gave little gasps and grunts he evidently did not hear himself, in time with the music. Beneath, occasionally overcoming the sibilant, involuntary breaths, the music was poignantly clear, ordered, cascading, vivid as little knives in the shadowy room. At the end they all applauded, and the old man bowed, very pleased.

That night Hurley climbed the staircase that angled around the central chimney, an oil lamp to light his way, and entered his cold room in moonlight almost as bright as the lamp, but colder, whiter against the lamp's yellow. Two little windows looked down across the old man's garden—"Mostly for the deer," the old man had said of it— then over the one still-mown pasture left to the farm, down the long hills silvery in moonlight to Lake Cascom in the valley, white among black surrounding spruce. Behind, on the other side of the house, he could feel the dark presence of Cascom Mountain.

He wondered if it would be a night for sleep. He was tired enough. In the last few days he had taken many of the familiar trails, especially following those that he remembered led through hardwood. Although the leaves had turned and mostly fallen, here or there one tree flamed late among the bare ones, catching light and casting it in all directions as if it were an orange or soft red sun. He stopped often in the woods, surprised by each molten maple branch, even the smallest bright veins of each leaf golden and precious against a gnarled black trunk or the green twilight of a spruce grove. He walked carefully, resting often, sampling the few cold, sweet apples from the abandoned mountain trees, eating Nana's sandwiches a little at a time. He wanted the day to last as long as possible. At night he thought of his wife.

The high, sloping bed was wide and lonesome as a field of snow. During his wife's illness he could not sleep in their own bed, but slept every night on a studio couch where he could reach the sides, hold himself down, remember exactly where he was and why she was not beside him. If he woke in the night and for a second forgot, he had to learn over again from the beginning that Mary was going to die. It was always the first time over again, when they had left the doctor (the poor doctor, according to Mary) at the cancer hospital and walked together to Grant's Tomb. Mary finally said, "You know? They should pay a man a thousand dollars a minute for having to say those words."

Then the inevitable sequence of hours came through his mind, one after the other, until the afternoon when she was not so brave any more and shook her head back and forth as if to throw off the plastic tube that went into her nose and down, jiggling the clamps and the bottle on its hanger. Tears rolled from the outside corners of her drowned eyes and she cried pettishly, "Help me, help me."

She had taken pain better than most, was better at taking it by far than her husband or her children. When she had the compound fracture of her wrist she had been the calm one, the strong one. And he thought, *My God, how much pain she must have if she is caused to do this—if it is Mary who is caused to do this. . . .*

As they cut nerves, cutting off pain in little bits and pieces, it was as if they cut off her life, too, by shreds—the pain, the possibility of it forever gone; the life forever gone. But new pain took the place of the old. She lived for six months and died almost weightless, ageless, the little lines and wrinkles of her familiar body smoothed as if by a filling pulp. Her arms turned to thin tubes, her forehead waxed as taut, as translucent as a yellow apple. Her eyes, before the final cutting, watched him, blameful as a beaten child's. She whined for help: "What is happening to me?" And being a man only, he could stand, and stand, and stand, helpless at the foot of her crank-operated bed, the simple handle drawing his eyes, mocking, it seemed to him, telling him to crank, to grasp the handle in his strong hands and crank, sweat at it, crank faster and harder, crank until she is well again.

He turned and his hand touched the firm, virginal pillow next to him. The linen smelled country new, of washdays and clotheslines.

At midnight he heard what he first supposed to be a hundred dogs barking in the distance, and as the barking changed on the wind he suddenly knew, in exactly the same way he had known in his childhood, that it was the Canada geese flying over, low here because of the height of the land, streaming over in the darkness. *Lorlorn, lorlorn, lorlorn,* the geese called to each other as they passed. He ran to the window—remembering an old excitement, feet numb on the cold boards—but the geese did not cross the moon. He remembered them well enough that way: the long, wavering files of geese, necks thrust out straight, dark wings arching tirelessly on their long journey over the guns, through all the deadly traps set for them—the weather, the ice, the hunting animals and the traitor decoys. Each one its own warm life deep in the cold sky, and they called to each other, kept close and on course together, facing with disciplined bravery that impossible journey.

He came awake in the indeterminate time when night was breaking and the small windows were luminious squares upon the wall. He lay on his back and watched the light grow, the corners arrange themselves and the moldings darken, wondering at a curved shape above the closet door. As the morning increased (he heard pans banging down in the kitchen, Nana's sharp morning voice) he finally saw that the curved shape was a bow hung on pegs. This room evidently had been a young boy's during the summer: a huge fungus platter hung

between the windows and in the back of the closet he had found a fly
rod enmeshed in kinky leader. Nana had missed a trout hook crusted
with dried worm, stuck high on a curtain.

Before he went downstairs he remembered the bow, took it down
and, wondering at the easy memories of his youth, strung it. He instinctively placed the lower end against the inside of his right foot, his
left hand slid easily up the wood with the string lightly guided by his
finger tips. The string vibrated tautly, and he remembered, too, how a
bow seemed lighter after being strung, the tense pressure communica-
ting energy to the arm. He estimated the pull at sixty pounds—quite a
powerful bow.

"Oh, you found the bow'n arrow!" Nana said when he came into
the kitchen with it. "You going to shoot? Say, how did you cock it?"

He placed the bow against his foot, pulled with his right hand
and pushed with the heel of his left hand, his fingers working the
string out of the notch.

"Nobody could fix it. The children going crazy they couldn't
shoot, nobody could cock it," Nana said admiringly.

"Do you have any arrows?"

The old man had decided to listen. "In the umbrella stand is
some arrows," he said, and Nana rushed out after them. After breakfast she insisted they all go out and watch him shoot, and he was surprised at his own excitement when he fitted the nock of one of the
warped target arrows to the string. He drew and loosed the arrow
across the thirty yards between the driveway and the barn. *Whap* as
the arrow hit the silvery, unpainted wood of the barn and stuck, quivering. A cloud of swallows streamed out of a sashless window, and
shreds of dusty hay fell from between the boards. The old people
were impressed.

As he drew his second arrow the bow split apart above the grip.
Arrow, string, half the bow fell loosely over his arms.

"Ooooh!" the old people sighed. "The wood was too old," the
old man said. "It all dries up and it got no give to it."

"I'll get you another one," Hurley said. They shushed him up,
said it wasn't any good, that nobody could cock it anyway. But later
when he drove his Drive-Ur-Self Chevrolet down into Leah for groceries and the mail, he stopped in at Follansbees' hardware store.

Old Follansbee remembered him from the times he and Mary
had come up to ski, possibly not from the earlier time when Follans-

bee was a young man working in his father's store and Hurley was a boy.

"Do for you?" Old Follansbee's bald head (once covered with black, bushy hair, parted in the middle) gleamed softly, approximately the same color and texture as his maple roll-up desk.

"I'd like to buy a bow—and some arrows," Hurley added in order to specify what kind of bow he meant. In Leah he had always been constrained to come immediately to the point. The old man led him to the sporting-goods corner where rifles and shotguns, fish poles and outboard motors, knives, rubber boots, decoys, pistols lay in cases on counters, hung on racks. He remembered this part of the store and the objects he had fallen in love with as a boy. No girl had meant as much to him at fifteen as had the beautifully angular lines of a Winchester model 62, .22 pump. He even remembered the model number, but from this distance he wondered how a number could have meant so much.

He tried out a few of the pretty, too-modern bows until he found one that seemed to have the same pull as the one he had broken.

"That one's glass," Old Follansbee said. "My boy says it don't want to break."

"Glass? It's made of glass?"

"Correct. Strange, ain't it? What they can do these days? You'll want some arrows, did you say?"

He bought two arrows. When he'd pulled the one out of the barn it came apart in his hands, split all the way up the shaft. He decided to replace it with two, even though he knew the New Hampshire way was to resent such prodigality. He bought a leather arm guard and finger tabs; then he saw the hunting arrows. The slim, three-bladed heads suggested Indians and his youth. The target arrows, beside them, seemed to have no character, no honest function. He bought two hunting arrows and, under old Follansbee's suspicious conventional eye, a bow-hunting license, feeling like a child who had spent his Sunday-school money on a toy.

At the Post Office he found a joint communiqué from his worried children. "We have decided that it would be best. . . ." the words went. He sent two identical telegrams: *Having wonderful time. Tend your business. Love, Dad.* They all believed in the therapy of youth—in this case, grandchildren. He couldn't think of a way to tell them that he loved them all too much.

Nana and the old man walked with him as far as the ledges at the top of the wild orchard, careful in their white tennis shoes. Nana stood splayfooted on the granite, queen of the hill, and surveyed the valley, the advancing forest with a disapproving eye.

"I see Holloways is letting their north pasture go back," she said, shaking her head. She had seen whole hills go back to darkness, many fine houses fall into their cellar holes. She turned toward Hurley accusingly, he being from the outside and thus responsible for such things. "You got to pay money to have them take the hay!"

"Tell me it's cheaper to buy it off the truck," the old man said. "But I told them it don't grow on trucks." He stood beside his tall wife, in his baggy pants and old mackinaw. His new tennis shoes were startlingly white. "I call this 'the hill of agony,'" he said, winking at Hurley.

"You see where the deer come down to eat our garden?" Nana said, pointing to the deer trails through the apple trees. "We tell the game warden to shoot. Nothing. They hang bangers in the trees. All night, 'Bang! Bang!' Nobody can sleep."

"Neither could the deer. They stayed up all night and et my lettuce," the old man said. He laughed and whacked his thigh.

"You shoot me a nice young deer," Nana said. "I make mincemeat, roasts, nice sausage for your breakfast."

He had tried to tell them that he didn't want to shoot anything with the bow, just carry it. Could he tell them that it gave a peculiar strength to his arm, that it seemed to be a kind of dynamo? When he was a boy in these same woods he and his friends had not been spectators, but actors. Their bows, fish poles, skis, rifles had set them apart from the mere hikers, the summer people.

"I won't be back tonight unless the weather changes," he said. The sun was warm on the dry leaves, but the air was crisply cool in the shadows. He said good-by to the old people, took off his pack and waited on the ledges to see them safely back to the house below, then unrolled his sleeping bag and rolled it tighter. The night before he had noticed on his geodetic map a small, five-acre pond high in the cleft between Cascom and Gilman mountains. It was called Goose Pond, and he seemed to remember having been there once, long ago, perhaps trout fishing. He remembered being very tired, yet not wanting to leave; he remembered the cat tails and alders and a long beaver dam, the pond deep in a little basin. He was sure he could follow the brook that issued from the pond—if he could pick the right one from all the little brooks that came down between Gilman and Cascom.

His pack tightened so that it rode high on his back, he carried his bow and the two hunting arrows in one hand. He soon relearned that arrows pass easily through the brush only if they go points first.

Stopping often to rest he climbed past the maples into ground juniper and pine, hearing often the soft explosions of partridge, sometimes seeing them as they burst up and whistled through the trees. He passed giant beeches crossing their noisy leaves, then walked silently through softwood until he came to a granite knob surrounded by stunted, wind-grieved hemlock. To the northwest he could see the Presidential Range, but Leah, the lake and the Pedersens' farm were all out of sight. He ate a hard-boiled egg and one of the bittersweet wild apples he had collected on the way. The wind was delightfully cool against his face, but he knew his sweat would soon chill. At two o'clock the sun was fairly low in the hard blue sky—whole valleys were in shadow below.

He took out his map. He had crossed three little brooks, and the one he could hear a short way ahead must be Goose Pond's overflow. By the sound it was a fair-sized brook. When he climbed down through the hemlock and saw it he was sure. White water angled right and left, dropping over boulders into narrow sluices and deep, clear pools. He knelt down and lowered his head into the icy water. His forehead turned numb, as if it were made of rubber. A water beetle darted to the bottom. A baby trout flashed green and pink beside a stone. It was as if he were looking through a giant lens into an alien world, where life was cold and cruel, and even the light had a quality of darkness about it. Odd little sticks on the bottom were the camouflaged larvae of insects, waiting furtively to hatch or to be eaten. Fish hid in the shadows under stones, their avid little mouths ready to snap. He shuddered and raised his head—a momentary flash of panic, as if some carnivorous animal with a gaping mouth might come darting up to tear his face.

Following the brook, jumping from stone to stone, sometimes having to leave it for the woods in order to get around tangles of blowdown or waterfalls, he came suddenly into the deep silence of the spruce, where the channel was deep. In the moist, cathedral silence of the tall pillars of spruce he realized how deafening the white water had been. The wind stirred the tops of the trees and made the slim trunks move slowly, but could not penetrate the dim, yet luminous greenness of the place.

And he saw the deer. He saw the face of the deer beside a narrow tree, and for a moment there was nothing but the face: a smoky-brown eye deep as a tunnel, it seemed, long delicate lashes, a black whisker or two along the white-shaded muzzle. The black nose quivered at each breath, the nostrils rounded. Then he began to follow the light brown line, motionless and so nearly invisible along the back, down along the edge of the white breast. One large ear turned slowly toward him. It was a doe, watching him carefully, perfect in the moment of fine innocence and wonder—a quality he suddenly remembered—the expressionless readiness of the deer. But other instincts had been working in him. He hadn't moved, had breathed slowly, put his weight equally on both legs. The light sharpened as if it had been twilight and the sun had suddenly flashed. Every detail—the convolutions of the bark on the trees, tiny twigs, the fine sheen of light on each hair of the doe, each curved, precious eyelash—became vivid and distinct. Depth grew, color brightened; his hunter's eyes became painfully efficient, as if each needle-like detail pierced him. The world became polarized on the axis of their eyes. He was alone with the doe in a green world that seemed to cry for rich red, and he did not have time to think: it was enough that he sensed the doe's quick decision to leave him. An onyx hoof snapped, her white flag rose and the doe floated in a slow arc, broadside to him, clear of the trees for an endless second. He watched down the long arrow, three blades moved ahead of the doe and at the precise moment all tension stopped; his arms, fingers, eyes and the bow were all one instrument. The arrow sliced through the deer.

Her white flag dropped. Gracefully, in long, splendid leaps, hoofs stabbing the hollow-sounding carpet of needles, the doe flickered beyond the trees. One moment of crashing brush, then silence. A thick excitement rose like fluid into his face, his arms seemed to grow to twice their normal size, become twice as strong. And still his body was governed by the old, learned patterns. He walked silently forward and retrieved his bloody arrow, snapped the feathers alive again. The trail was a vivid line of jewels, brighter than the checker-berries against their shiny green leaves, unmistakable. He rolled the bright blood between his fingers as he slowly moved forward. He must let the doe stop and lie down, let her shock-born strength dissipate in calm bleeding. Watching each step, figuring out whole series of steps, of brush bendings in advance, he picked the silent route around snags and under the blowdown.

In an hour he had gone a hundred yards, still tight and careful, up out of the spruce and onto a small rise covered with birch and poplar saplings. The leaves were loud underfoot and, as he carefully placed one foot, the doe rose in front of him and crashed downhill, obviously weak, staggering against the whippy birch. A fine mist of blood sprayed at each explosion of breath from the holes in her ribs. He ran after her, leaping over brush, running along fallen limbs, sliding under low branches that flicked his cheeks like claws. His bow caught on a branch and jerked him upright. After one impatient pull he left it. He drew his knife. The brown shape ahead had disappeared, and he dove through the brush after it, witch hobble grabbing at his legs.

The doe lay against a stump, one leg twitching. He knelt down and put one hard arm around her neck and, not caring for the dangerous hoofs, the spark of life, raised the firm, warm neck against his chest and, sighing, stabbed carefully into the sticking place. Blood was hot on the knife and on his hand.

He rolled over into the leaves, long breaths bending him, making his back arch. His shirt vibrated over his heart, his body turned heavy and pressed with unbelievable weight into the earth. He let his arms melt into the ground, and a cool, lucid sadness came over his flesh.

He made himself get up. In order to stand he had to fight gravity, to use all his strength—a quick fear for his heart. His joints ached and had begun to stiffen. He must keep moving. Shadows were long and he had much to do before dark. He followed the blood trail back and found his bow and one arrow. He limped going back down the hill; at a certain angle his knees tended to jackknife, as if gears were slipping.

He stood over the clean body of the doe, the white belly snowy against brown leaves. One hind leg he hooked behind a sapling, and he held the other with his knee as he made the first long incision through the hair and skin, careful not to break the peritoneum. He ran the incision from the breast to the tail, then worked the skin back with his fingers before making the second cut through the warm membrane, the sticky blue case for the stomach and entrails. He cut, and the steamy innards rolled unbroken and still working out onto the ground. A few neat berries of turd rattled on the leaves. He cut the anus and the organs of reproduction clear of the flesh, then found the kidneys and liver and reached arm-deep into the humid chest cavity, the hot smell of blood close in his nostrils, and removed the yellow lungs in handfuls. Then he pulled out the dark red heart. Kidneys, liver and heart he wrapped carefully in his sandwich wrappings, then rose and painfully stretched. Goose Pond lay just below; he could see a flicker of water through the skein of branches, and there he would make camp.

With his belt looped around the neck and front hoofs, he slid the doe down toward the pond. It was dusk by the time he found a dry platform of soft needles beneath a hemlock, next to the water. The doe had become stiff enough so that he could hang it in a young birch, head wedged in a fork. He spread his sleeping bag, tried it for roots and stones, and found none. The last high touch of sun on the hill above him had gone; he had even prepared ground for a fire when he realized that he had no energy left, no appetite to eat the liver of the doe.

Darkness had settled in along the ground, but the sky was still bright; one line of cirrus clouds straight overhead still caught orange sunlight. Across the silver water the alder swamp was jet black, and the steep hill rose behind, craggy with spruce. A beaver's nose broke water and even, slow circles spread across the pond. The dark woods filled with cold, and one of his legs began to jerk uncontrollably. He took off his boots and slid into his sleeping bag.

The doe was monstrous, angular against the sky, her neck stretched awkwardly, head canted to one side. The black hole in her belly gaped empty. He drew his sleeping bag up around his face.

If he were twenty again he would be happy. To have shot a deer with a bow—he'd be a hero, a woodsman, famous in Leah. How it would have impressed Mary! She would have said little about it—she went to great lengths never to flatter him; her compliments had been more tangible, seldom in words. He must think of something else. The world was too empty. The cold woods, the darkening water were empty. He was too cold, too tired to manipulate his thoughts. And the progression of hours began again. Mary's eyes watched him, deep in sick hollows. How could her flesh turn so brown? Why could he do nothing to stop the pain? She watched him, in torment, her frail body riven, cut beyond endurance. The disease had killed her bravery with pain and left her gruesomely alive, without dignity, whimpering like a spoiled brat, asking for help she should have known did not exist. And he stood by and watched, doing nothing. Nothing. He was not a man to do nothing. *Mary, did I do nothing to help you?*

He heard, far away, the lonely cry of the Canada geese. He was alone, hidden in the blind night, high on the stony mass of Cascom Mountain.

And then they came in, circling, calling to each other above the doubtful ground. Perhaps they had seen the reflected circle of fading sky, or remembered; generations remembering that geese had rested safely in the high pond and found food there. The scouts came whistling on their great wings, searching and listening. They sent their messages back to the flock waiting above, then planed down, braking, smeared the water with wind and came to rest in a flash of spray. The flock circled down after, careless now it was safe, honking gaily, giving the feeding call prematurely, echoing the messages of the leaders and landing masters. "Come in, come down and rest," they seemed to call, until everyone had landed safely. Then the voices grew softer, less excited, and only an occasional word drifted across the water.

Robert Hurley lay in the warm hollow of his sleeping bag, where the hours had stopped. He thought for a moment of the doe's death, and of his knife. The geese spoke softly to each other on the water—a small splash, a flutter of wings and the resting, contented voices in the deep basin of the pond. As sleep washed over him he seemed to be among them; their sentinels guarded him. When they had rested well they would rise and continue the dangerous journey down the world.

[November 1957]

GEORGE P. ELLIOTT

Among the Dangs

I graduated from Sansom University in 1937 with honors in history, having intended to study law, but I had no money and nowhere to get any; by good fortune the anthropology department, which had just been given a grant for research, decided that I could do a job for them. In idle curiosity I had taken a course in anthro, to see what I would have been like had history not catapulted my people a couple of centuries ago up into civilization, but I had not been inclined to enlarge on the sketchy knowledge I got from that course; even yet, when I think about it, I feel like a fraud teaching anthropology. What chiefly recommended me to the department, aside from a friend, was a combination of three attributes: I was a good mimic, a long-distance runner, and black.

The Dangs live in a forested valley in the eastern foothills of the Andes. The only white man to report on them (and, it was loosely gossiped, the only one to return from them alive), Sir Bewley Morehead in 1910, owed his escape to the consternation caused by Halley's Comet. Otherwise, he reported, they would certainly have sacrificed him as they were preparing to do; as it was, they killed the priest who was to have killed him, so he reported, and then burned the temple down. However, Dr. Sorish, our most distinguished Sansom man, in the early Thirties developed an interest in the Dangs which led to my research grant; he had introduced a tribe of Amazonian head-shrinkers to the idea of planting grain instead of just harvesting it, as a result of which they had fattened, taken to drinking brew by the tubful, and elevated Sorish to the rank of new god; the last time he had descended among them—it is Sansom's policy to follow through on any primitives we "do"—he had found his worshipers holding a couple of young Dang men captive and preparing them for ceremonies which would end only with the processing of their heads; his godhood gave him sufficient power to defer these ceremonies while he made half-a-dozen transcriptions of the men's conversations, and learned their langauge well enough to arouse the curiosity of his colleagues. The Dangs were handy with blowpipes; no one knew what pleased them; Halley's Comet wasn't due till 1984. But among the recordings Sorish brought back was a legend strangely chanted by one of these young men, whose very head perhaps you can buy today from a natural science company for $150 to $200, and the same youth had given Sorish a sufficient demonstration of the Dang prophetic trance, previously described by Morehead, to whet his appetite.

I was black, true; but, as Sorish pointed out, I looked as though I had been rolled in granite dust and the Dangs as though they had been rolled in brick dust; my hair was short and kinky, theirs long and straight; my lips were thick, theirs thin. It's like dressing a Greek up in reindeer skins, I said, and telling him to go pass himself off as a Lapp in Lapland. Maybe, they countered, but wouldn't he be more likely to get by than a naked Swahili with bones in his nose? I was a long-distance runner, true; but as I pointed out with a good deal of feeling, I didn't know the principles of jungle escape and had no desire to learn them in, as they put it, the field. They would teach me to throw the javelin and wield a machete, they would teach me the elements of judo, and as for poisoned darts and sacrifices they would insure my life—that is, my return within three years—for $5000. I was a good mimic, true; I would be able to reproduce the Dang speech, and especially the trance of the Dang prophets, for the observation of science—"make a genuine contribution to learning." In the Sansom concept, the researcher's experience is an inextricable part of anthropological study, and a good mimic provides the object for others' study as well as for his own. For doing this job I would be given round-trip transportation, an M.S. if I wrote a thesis on the material I gathered, the temporary insurance on my life, and $100 a month for the year I was expected to be gone. After I'd got them to throw in a fellowship of some sort for the following year, I agreed. It would pay for filling the forty cavities in my brothers' and sisters' teeth.

Dr. Sorish and I had to wait at the nearest outstation for a thunderstorm; when it finally blew up, I took off all my clothes, put on a breechcloth and leather apron, put a box of equipment on my head, and trotted after him; his people were holed in from the thunder, and we were in their settlement before they saw us. They were taller than I, they no doubt found my white teeth as disagreeable as I found their stained, filed teeth; but when Sorish spoke to me in English (telling me to pretend indifference to them while they sniffed me over), and in the accents of American acquaintances rather than in the harsh tones of divinity, their eyes filled with awe of me. Their taboo against touching Sorish extended itself to me; when a baby ran up to me and I lifted him up to play with him, his mother crawled, beating her head on the ground till I freed him.

The next day was devoted chiefly to selecting the man to fulfill Sorish's formidable command to guide me to the edge of the Dang country. As for running—if those dogs could be got to the next Olympics, Ecuador would take every long-distance medal on the board. I knew I had reached the brow of my valley only because I discovered that my guide, whom I had been lagging behind by fifty feet, at a turn in the path had disappeared into the brush.

Exhaustion allayed my terror; as I lay in the meager shade recuperating, I remembered to execute the advice I had given myself before coming: to act always as though I were not afraid. What would a brave man do next? Pay no attention to his aching feet, reconnoiter, and cautiously proceed. I climbed a jutting of rock and peered about. It was a wide, scrubby valley; on the banks of the river running down the valley I thought I saw a dozen mounds too regular for stones. I touched the handle of the hunting knife sheathed at my side, and trotted down the trackless hill.

The village was deserted, but the huts, though miserable, were clean and in good repair. This meant, according to the movies I had seen, that hostile eyes were watching my every gesture. I had to keep moving in order to avoid trembling. The river was clear and not deep. The unmutilated corpse of a man floated by. I felt like going downstream, but my hypothesized courage drove me up.

In half a mile I came upon a toothless old woman squatting by the track. She did not stop munching when I appeared, nor did she scream, or even stand up. I greeted her in Dang according to the formula I had learned, whereupon she cackled and smiled and nodded as gleefully as though I had just passed a test. She reminded me of my grandmother, rolled in brick dust, minus a corncob pipe between her gums. Presently I heard voices ahead of me. I saw five women carrying branches and walking very slowly. I lurked behind them until they came to a small village, and watched from a bush while they set to work. They stripped the leaves off, carefully did something to them with their fingers, and then dropped them in small-throated pots. Children scrabbled around, and once a couple of them ran up and suckled at one of the women. There remained about an hour till sunset. I prowled, undetected. The women stood, like fashion models, with pelvis abnormally rocked forward; they were wiry, without fat even on their breasts; not even their thighs and hips afforded clean sweeping lines undisturbed by bunched muscles. I saw no men. Before I began to get into a stew about the right tack to take, I stepped into the clearing and uttered their word of salutation. If a strange man should walk in your wife's front door and say, "How do you do," in an accent she did not recognize, simultaneously poking his middle finger at her, her consternation would be something like that of those Dang women; for unthinkingly I had nodded my head when speaking and turned my palm out, as one does in the United States; to them this was a gesture of intimacy, signifying desire. They disappeared into huts, clutching children. I went to the central clearing and sat with my back to a log, knowing they would scrutinize me. I wondered where the men were. I could think of no excuse for having my knife in my hand except to clean my toenails. So astonishing an act was unknown to the Dangs; the women and children gradually approached in silence, watching; I cleaned my fingernails. I said the word for food; no one reacted, but presently a little girl ran up to me holding a fruit in both hands. I took it, snibbed her nose between my fingers, and with a pat on the bottom sent her back to her mother. Upon this there were hostile glances, audible intakes of breath, and a huddling about the baby, who did not understand any more than I did why she was being consoled. While I ate the fruit I determined to leave the next move up to them. I sheathed my knife and squatted on my hunkers, waiting. To disguise my nervousness I fixed my eyes on the ground between my feet, and grasped my ankles from behind in such a way—right ankle with right hand, left with left—as to expose the inner sides of my forearm. Now this was, as I later learned, pretty close to the initial posture taken for the prophetic trance; also I had a blue flower tattooed on my inner right arm and a blue serpent on my left (from the summer I'd gone to sea), the like of which had never been seen in this place. At sundown I heard the men approach; they were anything but stealthy about it; I had the greatest difficulty in suppressing the shivers. In simple fear of showing my fear, I did not look up when the men gathered around; I could understand just enough of what the women were telling the men to realize that they were afraid of me. Even though I was pelted with pebbles and twigs till I was angry, I still did not respond, because I could not think what to do. Then something clammy was plopped onto my back from above and I leaped high, howling. Their spears were poised before I landed. "Strangers!" I cried, my speech composed. "Far kinsmen! I come from the mountains!" I had intended to say *from the river lands,* but the excitement tangled my tongue. Their faces remained expressionless, but no spears drove at me, and then, to be doing something, I shoved the guts under the log with my feet.

And saved my life by doing so. That I seemed to have taken, though awkwardly, the prophetic squat; that I bore visible marvels on my arm; that I was fearless and innerly absorbed; that I came from the mountains (their enemies lived toward the river lands); that I wore their apron and spoke their language, albeit poorly; all these disposed them to wonder at this mysterious outlander. Even so, they might very well have captured me, marvelous though I was, possibly useful to them, dangerous to antagonize, had I not been unmaimed, which meant that I was supernaturally guarded. Finally, my scrutinizing the fish guts, daring to smile as I did so, could mean only that I was prophetic; my leap when they had been dropped onto my back was prodigious, "far higher than a man's head," and my howl had been vatic; and my deliberately kicking the guts aside, though an inscrutable act, demonstrated at least that I could touch the entrails of an eel and live.

So I was accepted to the Dangs. The trouble was that they had no ceremony for naturalizing me. For them, every act had a significance, and here they were faced with a reverse problem, for which nothing had prepared them. They could not possibly just assimilate me without marking the event with an act (that is, a ceremony) signifying my entrance. For them, nothing *just happened,* certainly nothing men did. Meanwhile, I was kept in a sort of quarantine while they deliberated. I did not, to be sure, understand why I was being isolated in a hut by myself, never spoken to except efficiently, watched but not restrained. I swam, slept, scratched, watched, swatted, ate; I was not really alarmed, because they had not restrained me forcibly and they gave me food. I began making friends with some of the small children, especially while swimming, and there were two girls of fifteen or so who found me terribly funny. I wished I had some magic, but I knew only card tricks. The sixth day, swimming, I thought I was being enticed around a point in the river by the two girls, but when I began to chase them they threw good-sized stones at me, missing me only because they were such poor shots. A corpse floated by; when they saw it they immediately placed the sole of their right foot on the side of their left knee and stood thus on one leg till the corpse floated out of sight; I followed the girls' example, teetering. I gathered from what they said that some illness was devastating their people; I hoped it was one of the diseases I had been inoculated against. The girls' mothers found them talking with me and cuffed them away. I did not see them for two days, but the night of my eighth day there, the bolder of them hissed me awake at the door of my hut in a way that meant "no danger." I recognized her when she giggled. I was not sure what their customs were in these matters, but while I was deliberating what my course of wisdom should be she crawled into the hut and lay on the mat beside me. She liked me; she was utterly devoid of reticence; I was twenty-one and far from home; even a scabby little knotty-legged fashion model is hard to resist under such circumstances. I learned, before falling asleep, that there was a three-way debate among the men over what to do with me: initiate me according to the prophet-initiation rites, invent a new ceremony, or sacrifice me as propitiation to the disease among them, as was usually done with captives. Each had its advantages and drawbacks; even the news that some of the Dangs wanted to sacrifice me did not excite me as it would have done a week before; now, I half-sympathized with their trouble. I was awakened at dawn by the outraged howl of a man at my door; he was the girl's father; the village men gathered and the girl cowered behind me. They talked for hours outside my hut, men arrived from other villages up and down the valley, and finally they agreed upon a solution to all the problems: they proposed that I should be made one of the tribe by marriage on the same night that I should be initiated into the rites of prophecy.

The new-rite men were satisfied by this arrangement because of the novelty of having a man married and initiated on the same day; but the sacrifice party was visibly unmollified. Noticing this and reflecting that the proposed arrangement would permit me to do all my trance-research under optimum conditions and to accumulate a great deal of sexual data as well, I agreed to it. I would of course only be going through the forms of marriage, not meaning them; as for the girl, I took this vow to myself (meaning without ceremony): "So long as I am a Dang, I shall be formally a correct husband to her." More's a pity.

Fortunately a youth from down the valley already had been chosen as a novice (at least a third of the Dang men enter the novitiate at one time or another, though few make the grade), so that I had not only a companion during the four-month preparation for the vatic rites but also a control upon whom I might check my experience of the stages of the novitiate. My mimetic powers stood me in good stead; I was presumed to have a special prophetic gift and my readiness at assuming the proper stances and properly performing the ritual acts confirmed the Dangs' impressions of my gift; but also, since I was required to proceed no faster than the ritual pace in my learning, I had plenty of leisure in which to observe in the smallest detail what I did and how I, and to some extent my fellow novice, felt. If I had not had this self-observing to relieve the tedium, I think I should have been unable to get through that mindless holding of the same position hour after hour, that mindless repeating of the same act day after day. The Dangs *appear* to be bored much of the time, and my early experience with them was certainly that of ennui, though never again ennui so acute as during this novitiate; yet I doubt that it would be accurate to say they actually are bored, and I am sure that the other novice was not, as a fisherman waiting hours for a strike cannot be said to be bored. The Dangs do not sate themselves on food; the experience which they consider most worth seeking, vision, is one which cannot glut either the prophet or his auditors; they cannot imagine an alternative to living as they live or, more instantly, to preparing a novice as I was being prepared. The people endure; the prophets, as I have learned, wait for the time to come again, and though they are bitten and stung by ten thousand fears, about this they have no anxiety—the time will surely come again. Boredom implies either satiety, and they were poor and not interested in enriching themselves, or the frustration of impulse, and they were without alternatives and diversions; and that intense boredom which is really a controlled anxiety they are protected from by never doubting the worth of their vision or their power to achieve it.

I was assisted through these difficult months, during which I was supposed to do nothing but train, by Redadu, my betrothed. As a novice, I was strictly to abstain from sexual intercourse; but as betrothed, we were supposed to make sure before marriage that we satisfied one another, for adultery by either husband or wife was punishable by maiming. Naturally, the theologians were much exercised by this impasse of mine, but while they were arguing, Redadu and I took the obvious course—we met more or less surreptitiously. Since my vatic training could not take place between sunrise and sundown, I assumed that we could meet in the afternoon when I woke up, but when I began making plans to this effect, I discovered that she did not know what I was talking about. It makes as much sense in Dang to say, "Let's blow poisoned darts at the loss of the moon," as to say, "Let's make love in broad daylight." Redadu dissolved in giggles at the absurdity. What to do? She found us a cave. Everyone must have known what I was up to, but we were respectable (the Dang term for it was harsher, *deed-liar*), so we were never disturbed. Redadu's friends would not believe her stories of my luxurious love ways, especially my biting with lips instead of teeth. At one time or another she sent four of them to the cave for me to demonstrate my prowess upon; I was glad that none of them pleased me as much as she did, for I was beginning to be fond of her. My son has told me that lip-biting has become, if not a customary, at any rate a possible caress.

As the night of the double rite approached, a night of full moon, a new conflict became evident: the marriage must be consummated exactly at sundown, but the initiation must begin at moonrise, less than two hours later. For some reason that was not clear to me, preparing for the initiation would incapacitate me for the consummation. I refrained from pointing out that it was only technically that this marriage needed consummating and even from asking why I would not be able to do it. The solution, which displeased everyone, was to defer the rites for three nights, when the moon, though no longer perfectly round, would rise sufficiently late so that I would, by hurrying, be able to perform both of my functions. Redadu's father, who had been of the sacrifice party, waived ahead of time his claim against me: legally he was entitled to annul the marriage if I should leave the marriage hut during the bridal night. And although I in turn could legally annul it if she left the hut, I waived my claim as well so that she might attend my initiation.

The wedding consisted chiefly of our being bound back to back by the elbows and being sung to and danced about all day. At sunset, we were bound face to face by the elbows (most awkward) and sent into our hut. Outside, the two mothers waited—a high prophet's wife took the place of my mother (my Methodist mother!)—until our orgiastic cries indicated that the marriage had been consummated, and then came in to sever our bonds and bring us the bridal foods of cold stewed eel and parched seeds. We fed each other bite for bite and gave the scraps to our mothers, who by the formula with which they thanked us pronounced themselves satisfied with us; and then a falsetto voice called to me to hurry to the altar. A man in the mask of a moon slave was standing outside my hut on his left leg with the right foot against his left knee, and the continued to shake his rattle so long as I was within earshot.

The men were masked. Their voices were all disguised. I wondered whether I was supposed to speak in an altered voice; I knew every stance and gesture I was to make, but nothing of what I was to say; yet surely a prophet must employ words. I had seen some of the masks before—being repaired, being carried from one place to another—but now, faced with them alive in the failing twilight, I was impressed by them in no scientific or aesthetic way: they terrified and exalted me. I wondered if I would be given a mask. I began trying to identify such men as I could by their scars and missing fingers and crooked arms, and noticed to my distress that they too were all standing one-legged in my presence. But I had thought that was the stance to be assumed in the presence of the dead! We were at the entrance to The Cleft, a dead-end ravine in one of the cliffs along the valley; my fellow novice and I were each given a gourdful of some vile-tasting drink and were then taken up to the end of The Cleft, instructed to assume the first position, and left alone. We squatted as I had been squatting by the log on my first day, except that my head was cocked in a certain way and my hands clasped my ankles from the front. The excitements of the day seemed to have addled my wits; I could concentrate on nothing, and lost my impulse to observe coolly what was going on; I kept humming *St. James Infirmary* to myself, and though at first I had been thinking the words, after a while I realized that I had nothing but the tune left in my head. At moonrise we were brought another gourd of the liquor to drink, and were then taken to the mouth of The Cleft again. I did, easily, whatever I was told. The last thing I remember seeing before taking the second position was the semicircle of masked men facing us and chanting, and behind them the women and children—all standing on the left leg. I lay on my back with my left ankle on my right and my hands crossed over my navel, rolled my eyeballs up and held the lids open without blinking, and breathed in the necessary rhythm, each breath taking four heartbeats, with an interval of ten heartbeats between each exhalation and the next inspiration. Then the drug took over. At dawn when a called command awoke me, I found myself on an islet in the river dancing with my companion a leaping dance I had not known or even seen before, and brandishing over my head a magnificent red and blue, new-made mask of my own. The shores of the river were lined with the people chanting as we leaped, and all of them were either sitting or else standing on both feet. If we had been dead the night before, we were alive now. Redadu told me, after I had slept and returned to myself, that my vision was splendid, but of course she was no more permitted to tell me what I had said than I was able to remember it. The Dangs' sense of rhythm is as subtle as their ear for melody is monotonous, and for weeks I kept hearing rhythmic snatches of *St. James Infirmary* scratched on calabash drums and tapped on blocks.

Sorish honored me by rewriting my master's thesis and adding my name as co-author of the resultant essay, which he published in JAFA (*The Journal of American Field Anthropology*): "Techniques of Vatic Hallucinosis Among the Dangs." And the twenty-minute movie I made of a streamlined performance of the rites is still widely used as an audio-visual aid.

By 1939 when I had been cured of the skin disease I had brought back with me and had finished the work for my M.A., I still had no money. I had been working as the assistant curator of the university's Pre-Columbian Museum and had developed a powerful aversion to devoting my life to cataloguing, displaying, restoring, warehousing. But my chances of getting a research job, slight enough with a Ph.D., were nil with only an M.S. The girl I was going with said (I had not told her about Redadu) that if we married she would work as a nurse to support me while I went through law school; I was tempted by the opportunity to fulfill my original ambition, and probably I would have done it had she not pressed too hard; she wanted me to leave anthropology, she wanted me to become a lawyer, she wanted to support me, but what she did not want was to make my intentions, whatever those might be, her own. Therefore, when a new grant gave me the chance to return to the Dangs, I glady seized it; not only would I be asserting myself against Velma, but also I would be paid for doing the research for my Ph.D. thesis; besides, I was curious to see the Congo-Maryland-Dang bastard I had left in Redadu's belly. My assignment was to make a general cultural survey but especially to discover the *content* of the vatic experience—not just the technique, not even the hallucinations and stories, but the qualities of the experience itself. The former would get me a routine degree, but the latter would, if I did it, make me a name and get me a job. After much consultation I decided against taking with me any form of magic, including medicine; the antibiotics had not been invented yet, and even if there had been a simple way to eradicate the fever endemic among the Dangs, my advisers persuaded me that it would be an error to introduce it since the Dangs were barely able to procure food for themselves as it was and since they might worship me for doing it, thereby making it impossible for me to do my research with the proper empathy. I arrived the second time provided only with my knife (which had not seemed to impress these stone-agers), salve to soothe my sores, and the knowledge of how to preserve fish against a lean season, innovation enough but not one likely to divinize me.

I was only slightly worried how I would be received on my return, because of the circumstances under which I had disappeared. I had become a fairly decent hunter—the women gathered grain and fruit—and I had learned to respect the Dangs' tracking abilities enough to have been nervous about getting away safely. While hunting with a companion in the hills south of our valley, I had run into a couple of hunters from an enemy tribe which seldom foraged so far north as this. They probably were as surprised as I and probably would have been glad to leave me unmolested; however, outnumbered and not knowing how many more were with them, I whooped for my companion; one of the hunters in turn, not knowing how many were with me, threw his spear at me. I sidestepped it and reached for my darts and, though I was not very accurate with a blowpipe, I hit him in the thigh: within a minute he was writhing on the ground, for in my haste I had blown a venomous dart at him, and my comrade took his comrade prisoner by surprise. As soon as the man I had hit was dead, I withdrew my dart and cut off his ear for trophy, and we returned with our captive. He told our war chief in sign language that the young man I had killed was the son and heir of their king and that my having mutilated him meant their tribe surely would seek to avenge his death. The next morning a Dang search party was sent out to recover the body so that it might be destroyed and trouble averted, but it had disappeared; war threatened. The day after that I chose to vanish; they would not think of looking for me in the direction of Sorish's tribe, north, but would assume that I had been captured by the southern tribe in retribution for their prince's death. My concern now, two years later, was how to account for not having been maimed or executed; the least I could do was to cut a finger off, but when it came to the point, I could not even bring myself to have a surgeon do it, much less do it myself; I had adequate lies prepared for their other questions, but about this I was a bit nervous. I got there at sundown.

Spying, I did not see Redadu about the village. On the chance, I slipped into our hut when no one was looking; she was there, playing with our child. He was as cute a little preliterate as you ever saw suck a thumb, and it made me chuckle to think he would never be literate either. Redadu's screams when she saw me fetched the women, but when they heard a man's voice they could not intrude. In her joy she lacerated me with her fingernails (the furrows across my shoulder festered for a long time); I could do no less than bite her arm till she bled; the primal scene we treated our son to presumably scarred him for life, though I must say the scars haven't showed up yet. I can't deny I was glad to see her too; for, though I felt for her none of the tender, complex emotions I had been feeling for Velma, emotions which I more or less identified as being love, yet I was so secure with her sexually, I knew so well what to do and what to expect from her in every important matter, that it was an enormous, if cool, comfort to me to be with her. *Comfort* is a dangerous approximation to what I mean; being with her provided, as it were, the condition for doing; in Sansom I did not consider her my wife, and here I did not recognize in myself the American emotions of love or marriage; yet it seemed to me right to be with her, and our son was no bastard. *Cool*: I cannot guarantee that mine was the usual Dang emotion, for it is hard for the cool to gauge the warmth of others; in my reports I have denied any personal experience of love among the Dangs for this reason. When we emerged from the hut, there was amazement and relief among the women: amazement that I had returned and relief that it had not been one of their husbands pleasuring the widow. But the men were more ambiguously pleased to see me: Redadu's scratches were not enough and they doubted my story, that the enemy king had made me his personal slave who must be bodily perfect. They wanted to hear me prophesy.

Redadu told me afterward, hiding her face in my arms for fear of being judged insolent, that I surpassed myself that night, that only the three high prophets had ever been so inspired. And it was true that even the men most hostile to me did not oppose my reentry into the tribe after they had heard me prophesy: they could have swallowed the story I fed them about my two-year absence only because they believed in me the prophet. Dangs make no separation between fact and fantasy, apparent reality and visionary reality, truth and beauty. I once saw a young would-be prophet shudder away from a stick on the ground, saying it was a snake, and none of the others, except the impressionable, was afraid of the stick: it was said of him that he was a beginner. Another time I saw a prophet scatter the whole congregation, myself included, when he screamed at the sight of a beast which he called a cougar: when sober dawn found the speared creature to be a cur it was said of the prophet that he was strong, and he was honored with an epithet, Cougar-Dog. My prophesying the first night of my return must have been of this caliber, though to my disappointment I was given no epithet, not even a nickname I'd sometimes heard before, Bush-Hair. I knew there was a third kind of prophesying, the highest, performed only on the most important occasions in the Cave-Temple where I had never been. No such occasion had presented itself during my stay before, and when I asked one of the other prophets about that ceremony, he put me off with the term Wind-Haired Child of the Sun; from another, I learned that the name of this sort of prophesying was Stone is Stone. Obviously, I was going to have to stay until I could make sense of these mysteries.

There was a war party that wanted my support; my slavery was presumed to have given me knowledge which would make a raid highly successful; because of this as well as because I had instigated the conflict by killing the king's son, I would be made chief of the raiding party. I was uneasy about the fever, which had got rather worse among them during the previous two years, without risking my neck against savages who were said always to eat a portion of their slain enemy's liver raw and whose habitat I knew nothing of. I persuaded the Dangs, therefore, that they should not consider attacking before the rains came, because their enemies were now the stronger, having on their side their protector, the sun. They listened to me, and waited. Fortunately, it was a long dry season, during which I had time to find a salt deposit and to teach a few women the rudiments of drying and salting fish; and during the first week of the rains, every night there were showers of falling stars to be seen in the sky; to defend against them absorbed all energies for weeks, including the warriors'. Even so, even though I was a prophet, a journeyman prophet as it were, I was never in on these rites in the Cave-Temple. I dared not ask many questions. Sir Bewley Morehead had described a temple surrounded by seventy-five poles, each topped by a human head; he could hardly have failed to mention that it was a cave; yet he made no such mention, and I knew of no temple like the one he had described. At a time of rains and peace in the sky, the war party would importune me. I did not know what to do but wait.

The rains became violent, swamping the villages in the lower valley and destroying a number of huts; yet the rainy season ended abruptly two months before its usual time. Preparations for war had already begun, and day by day as the sun's strength increased and the earth dried, the war party became more impatient; and the preparations in themselves lulled my objections to the raid, even to my leading the raid, and stimulated my desire to make war. But the whole project was canceled a couple of days before we were to attack because of the sudden fever of one of the high prophets; the day after he came down, five others of the tribe fell sick, among them Redadu. There was nothing I could do but sit by her, fanning her and sponging her till she died. Her next older sister took our son to rear. I would allow no one to prepare her body but myself, though her mother was supposed to help; I washed it with the proper infusions of herbs, and at dawn, in the presence of her clan, I laid her body on the river; thank heaven it floated, or I should have had to spend another night preparing it further. I felt like killing someone now; I recklessly called for war now, even though the high prophet had not yet died; I was restrained, not without admiration. I went up into the eastern hills by myself, and returned after a week bearing the hide of a cougar; I had left the head and claws on my trophy, in a way the Dangs had never seen; when I put the skin on in play by daylight and bounded and snarled, only the bravest did not run in terror. They called me Cougar-Man. And Redadu's younger sister came to sleep with me; I did not want her, but she so stubbornly refused to be expelled that I kept her for the night, for the next night, for the next; it was not improper. The high prophet did not die, but lay comatose most of the time. The Dangs have ten master prophets, of whom the specially gifted, whether one or all ten, usually two or three, are high prophets. Fifteen days after Redadu had died, well into the abnormal dry spell, nearly all the large fish seemed to disappear from the river. A sacrifice was necessary. It was only because the old man was so sick that a high prophet was used for this occasion; otherwise a captive or a woman would have served the purpose. A new master prophet must replace him, to keep the complement up to ten. I was chosen.

The exultation I felt when I learned that the master prophets had co-opted me among them was by no means cool and anthropological, for now that I had got what I had come to get, I no longer wanted it for Sansom reasons. *If the conditions of my being elevated,* I said to myself, *are the suffering of the people, Redadu's death, and the sacrifice of an old man, then I must make myself worthy of the great price. Worthy*: a value word, not a scientific one. Of course, my emotions were not the simple pride and fear of a Dang. I can't say what sort they were, but they were fierce.

At sundown all the Dangs of all the clans were assembled about the entrance to The Cleft. All the prophets, masked, emerged from The Cleft and began the dance in a great wheel. Within this wheel, rotating against it, was the smaller wheel of the nine able-bodied master prophets. At the center, facing the point at which the full moon would rise, I hopped on one leg, then the other. I had been given none of the vatic liquor, that brew which the women, when I had first come among the Dangs, had been preparing in the small-throated pots; and I hoped I should be able to remain conscious throughout the rites. However, at moonrise a moon slave brought me a gourdful to drink without ceasing to dance. I managed to allow a good deal of it to spill unnoticed down with the sweat streaming off me, so that later I was able to remember what had happened, right up to the prophesying itself. The dance continued for at least two hours; then the drums suddenly stopped and the prophets began to file up The Cleft, me last, dancing after the high prophets. We danced into an opening in the cliff from which a disguising stone had been rolled away; the people were not allowed to follow us. We entered a great cavern illuminated by ten smoking torches. We circled a palisade of stakes; the only sound was the shuffle of our feet and the snorts of our breathing. There were seventy-five stakes, as Morehead had seen, but only on twenty-eight of them were heads impaled, the last few with flesh on them still, not yet skulls cleaned of all but hair. In the center was a huge stone under the middle of which a now dry stream had tunneled a narrow passage: on one side of the stone, above the passage, were two breast-like protuberances, one of which had a recognizable nipple suitably placed. Presently the dancing file reversed so that I was the leader. I had not been taught what to do; I wove the file through the round of stakes, and spiraled inward till we were three deep about The Stone; I straddled the channel, raised my hands till they were touching the breasts and gave a great cry. I was, for reasons I do not understand, shuddering all over; though I was conscious and though I had not been instructed, I was not worried that I might do the wrong thing next; when I touched The Stone, a dread shook me without affecting my exaltation. Two moon slaves seized my arms, took off my mask, and wrapped and bound me, arms at my side and legs pressed together, in a deer hide, and then laid me on my back in the channel under The Stone with my head only half out, so that I was staring up the sheer side of rock. The dancers continued, though the master prophets had disappeared. My excitement; the new, unused position; being mummied tightly; the weakness of the drug; my will to observe; all kept me conscious for a long time. Gradually, however, my eyes began to roll up into my head, I strained less powerfully against the things that bound me, and I felt my breathing approach the vatic rhythm. At this point, I seemed to break out in a new sweat, on my forehead, my throat, in my hair; I could hear a splash; groggily I licked my chin; an odd taste; I wondered if I was bleeding. Of course—it was the blood of the sick old high prophet, who had just been sacrificed on The Stone above me; well, his blood would give me strength; wondering remotely whether his fever could be transmitted by drinking his blood, I entered the trance. At dawn I emerged into consciousnes while I was still prophesying; I was on a ledge in the valley above all the people, in my mask again. I listened to myself finish the story I was telling. "He was afraid. A third time a man said to him: 'You are a friend of the most high prophet.' He answered: 'Not me. I do not know that man they are sacrificing.' Then he went into a dark corner; he put his hands over his face all day." When I came to the Resurrection, a sigh blew across the people.

It was the best story they had ever heard. Of course. But I was not really a Christian. For several weeks I fretted over my confusion, this new, unsuspected confusion. I was miserable without Redadu; I let her sister substitute only until I had been elevated, and then I cast her off, promising her however that she and only she might wear an anklet made of my teeth when I should die. Now that I was a master prophet I could not be a warrior; I had had enough hunting, fishing, tedious ceremonies. Hunger from the shortage of fish drove the hunters high into the foothills; there was not enough; they ate my preserved fish, suspiciously, but they ate them. When I left, it was not famine that I was escaping, but my confusion; I was fleeing to the classrooms and the cool museums where I should be neither a leftover Christian nor a mimic of a Dang.

My academic peace lasted for just two years, during which time I wrote five articles on my researches, publishing them this time under my name only, did some of the work for my doctorate, and married Velma. Then came World War II, in which my right hand was severed above the wrist; I was provided with an artificial hand and given enough money so that I could afford to finish my degree in style. We had two daughters and I was given a job at Sansom. There was no longer a question of my returning to the Dangs. I would become a settled anthropologist: teach, and quarrel with my colleagues in the learned journals. But by the time the Korean War came along and robbed us of a lot of our students, my situation at the university had changed considerably. Few of my theoretical and disputatious articles were printed in the journals, and I hated writing them; I was not given tenure and there were some hints to the effect that I was considered a one-shot man, a flash-in-the-pan; Velma nagged for more money and higher rank. My only recourse was further research, and when I thought of starting all over again with some other tribe—

in Northern Australia, along the Zambesi, on an African Island—my heart sank. The gossip was not far from the mark—I was not one hundred per cent the scientist and never would be. I had just enough reputation and influential recommendations to be awarded a Guggenheim Fellowship; supplemented by a travel grant from the university, this made it possible for me to leave my family comfortably provided for and return to the Dangs.

A former student now in Standard Oil in Venezuela arranged to have me parachuted among them from an S.O. plane; there was the real danger that they would kill me before they recognized me, but if I arrived in a less spectacular fashion I was pretty sure they would sacrifice me for their safety's sake. This time, being middle-aged, I left my hunting knife and brought instead at my belt a pouch filled with penicillin and salves. I had a hard time identifying the valley from the air; it took me so long that it was sunset before I jumped; I knew how the Dangs were enraged by airplanes, especially by the winking lights of night fliers, and I knew they would come for me if they saw me billowing down. Fortunately, I landed in the river, for, though I was nearly drowned before I disentangled my parachute harness, I was also out of range of the blowpipes. I finally identified myself to the warriors brandishing their spears along the shore; they had not quite dared to swim out after so prodigious a being; even after they knew who I said I was and allowed me to swim to shore, they saw me less as myself than as a supernatural being. I was recognized by newcomers who had not seen me so closely swinging from the parachute (the cloud); on the spot my epithet became, as it remained, Sky-Cougar. Even so, no one dared touch me till the high prophet—there was only one now—had arrived and talked with me: my artificial hand seemed to him an extension of the snake tattooed onto my skin; he would not touch it; I suddenly struck him with it and pinched his arm. "Pinchers," I said, using the word for a crayfish claw, and he laughed. He said there was no way of telling whether I was what I seemed to be until he had heard me prophesy; if I prophesied as I had done before I had disappeared, I must be what I seemed to be; meanwhile, for the three weeks till full moon, I was to be kept in the hut for captives.

At first I was furious at being imprisoned, and when mothers brought children from miles about to peek through the stakes at the man with the snake-hand, I snarled or sulked like a caged wolf. But I became conscious that a youth, squatting in a quiet place had been watching me for hours, and demanded of him who he was. He said, "I am your son," but he did not treat me as his father. To be sure, he could not have remembered what I looked like; my very identity was doubted; even if I were myself, I was legendary, a stranger who had become a Dang and had been held by an enemy as captive slave for two years and had then become a master prophet with the most wonderful vision anyone knew. Yet he came to me every day and answered all the questions I put to him. It was, I believe, my artificial hand that finally kept him aloof from me; no amount of acquaintance would accustom him to that. By the end of the first week it was clear to me that if I wanted to survive—not to be accepted as I once had been, just to survive—I would have to prophesy the Passion again. And how could I determine what I would say when under the vatic drug? I imagined a dozen schemes for substituting colored water for the drug, but I would need an accomplice for that and I knew that not even my own son would serve me in so forbidden an act.

I called for the high prophet. I announced to him in tones all the more arrogant because of my trepidations that I would prophesy without the vatic liquor. His response to my announcement astonished me: he fell upon his knees, bowed his head, and rubbed dust into his hair. He was the most powerful man among the Dangs, except in time of war when the war chief took over, and furthermore he was an old man of personal dignity; yet here he was abasing himself before me and, worse, rubbing dust into his hair as was proper in the presence of the very sick to help them in their dying. He told me why: prophesying successfully from a voluntary trance was the test which I must pass to become a high prophet; normally a master prophet was forced to this, for the penalty for failing it was death. I dismissed him with a wave of my claw.

I had five days to wait until full moon. The thought of the risk I was running was more than I could handle consciously; to avoid the jitters I performed over and over all the techniques of preparing for the trance, though I carefully avoided entering it. I was not sure I was able to enter it alone, but whether I could or not I knew I wanted to conserve my forces for the great test. At first during those five days I would remind myself once in a while of my scientific purpose in going into the trance consciously; at other times I would assure myself that it was for the good of the Dangs I was doing it, since it was not wise or safe for them to have only one high prophet. Both of these reasons were true enough, but not very important. As scientest, I should tell them some new myth, say the story of Abraham and Isaac or of Oedipus, so that I could compare its effect on them with that of the Passion; as master prophet, I should ennoble my people if I could. However, thinking these matters over as I held my vatic squat hour after hour, visited and poked at by prying eyes, I could find no myth to satisfy me: either, as in the case of Abraham, it involved a concept of God which the Dangs could not reach, or else, as with Oedipus, it necessitated more drastic changes than I trusted myself to keep straight while prophesying—that Oedipus should mutilate himself was unthinkable to the Dangs and that the gods should be represented as able to forgive him for it was impious. Furthermore, I did not think, basically, that any story I could tell them would in fact ennoble them. I was out to save my own skin.

The story of Christ I knew by heart; it had worked for me once, perhaps more than once; it would work again. I rehearsed it over and over, from the Immaculate Conception to the Ascension. But such was the force of that story on me that by the fifth day my cynicism had disappeared along with my scientism, and I believed, not that the myth itself was true, but that relating it to my people was the best thing it was possible for me to do for them. I remember telling myself that this story would help raise them toward monotheism, a necessary stage in the evolution toward freedom. I felt a certain satisfaction in the thought that some of the skulls on the stakes in the Cave-Temple were very likely those of missionaries who had failed to convert these heathen.

At sundown of the fifth day, I was taken by moon slaves to a cave near The Cleft, where I was left in peace. I fell into a troubled sleep, from which I awoke in a sweat: "Where am I? What am I about to do?" It seemed to me dreadfully wrong that I should be telling these, my people, a myth in whose power, but not in whose truth, I believed. Why should I want to free them from superstition up into monotheism and thence up into my total freedom, when I myself was half-returning, voluntarily, down the layers again? The energy for these sweating questions came, no doubt, from my anxiety about how I was going to perform that night, but I did not recognize this fact at the time. Then I thought it was my conscience speaking, and that I had no right to open to the Dangs a freedom I myself was rejecting. It was too late to alter my course; honesty required me, and I resolved courageously, not to prophesy at all.

When I was fetched out, the people were in assembly at The Cleft and the wheel of master prophets was revolving against the greater wheel of dancers. I was given my cougar skin. Hung from a stake, in the center where I was to hop, was a huge, terrific mask I had never seen before. As the moon rose, her slaves hung this mask on me; the thong cut into the back of my neck cruelly, and at the bottom the mask came to a point that pressed my belly; it was so wide my arms could only move laterally. It had no eyeholes; I broke into a sweat wondering how I would be able to follow the prophets into the Cave-Temple. It turned out to be no problem: the two moon slaves, one on each side, guided me by prodding spears in my ribs. Once in the cave, they guided me to the back side of The Stone and drove me to climb it, my feet groping for steps I could not see; once when I lost my balance, the spears' pressure kept me from falling backward. By the time I reached the top of The Stone, I was bleeding and dizzy. With one arm I kept the mask from gouging my belly while with the other I helped my aching neck support the mask. I did not know what to do next. Tears of pain and anger poured from my eyes. I began hopping. I should have been moving my arms in counterpoint to the rhythm of my hop, but I could not bear the thought of letting the mask cut into me more. I kept hopping in the same place, for fear of falling off; I had not been noticing the sounds of the other prophets, but suddenly I was aware they were making no sounds at all. In my alarm I lurched to the side, and cut my foot on a sharp break in the rock. Pain converted my panic to rage.

I lifted the mask and held it flat above my head. I threw my head back and howled as I had never howled in my life, through a constricted, gradually opening throat, until at the end I was roaring; when I gasped in my breath, I made a barking noise. I leaped and leaped, relieved of pain, confident. I punched my knee desecratingly through the brittle hide of the mask, and threw it behind me off The Stone. I tore off my cougar skin and, holding it with my claw by the tip of its tail, I whirled it around my head. The prophets, massed below me, fell onto their knees. I felt their fear. Howling, I soared the skin out over them; one of those on whom it landed screamed hideously. A commotion started; I could not see very well what was happening. I barked and they turned toward me again. I leaped three times and then, howling, jumped wide-armed off The stone. The twelve-foot drop hurt severely my already cut foot. I rolled exhausted into the channel in the cave floor.

Moon slaves with trembling hands mummied me in the deerskin and shoved me under The Stone with only my head sticking out. They brought two spears with darts tied to the points; rolling my head to watch them do this, I saw that the prophets were kneeling over and rubbing dirt into their hair; then the slaves laid the spears alongside the base of The Stone with the poisoned pricks pointed at my temples; exactly how close they were I could not be sure, but close enough so that I dared not move my head. In all my preparations I had, as I had been trained to do, rocked and wove at least my head; now, rigidity, live rigidity. A movement would scratch me and a scratch would kill me.

I pressed my hook into my thigh, curled my toes, and pressed my tongue against my teeth till my throat ached. I did not dare relieve myself even with a howl, for I might toss my head fatally. I strained against my thongs to the verge of apoplexy. For a while, I was unable to see, for sheer rage. Fatigue collapsed me. Yet I dared not relax my vigilance over my movements. My consciousness sealed me off. Those stone protuberances up between which I had to stare in the flickering light were merely chance processes on a boulder, similes to breasts. The one thing I might not become unconscious of was the pair of darts waiting for me to err. For a long time I thought of piercing my head against them, for relief, for spite. Hours passed. I was carefully watched.

I do not know what wild scheme I had had in mind when I had earlier resolved not to prophesy, what confrontation or escape; it had had the pure magnificence of a fantasy-resolution. But the reality, which I had not seriously tried to evade, was that I must prophesy or die. I kept lapsing from English into a delirium of Dang. By the greatest effort of will, I looked about me rationally: I wondered whether the return of Halley's Comet, at which time all the stakes should be mounted by skulls, would make the Dangs destroy the Cave-Temple and erect a new one; I observed the straight, indented seam of sandstone running slantwise up the boulder over me and wondered how many eons this rotting piece of granite had been tumbled about by water; I reflected that I was unworthy both as a Christian and as a Dang to prophesy the life of Jesus, but I convinced myself that it was a trivial matter since to the Christians it was the telling more than the teller that counted and to the Dangs this myth would serve as a civilizing force they needed. Surely, I thought, my hypocrisy could be forgiven me, especially since I resolved to punish myself for it by leaving the Dangs forever as soon as I could. Having reached this rational solution, I smiled and gestured to the high prophet with my eyes; he did not move a muscle. When I realized that nothing to do with hypocrisy would unbind me, desperation swarmed in my guts and mounted toward my brain; with this question it took me over: *How can I make myself believe it is true?* I needed to catch hold of myself again. I dug my hook so hard into my leg—it was the only action I was able to take—that I gasped with pain; the pain I wanted. I did not speculate on the consequences of gouging my leg, tearing a furrow in my thigh muscle, hurting by the same act the stump of my arm to which the hook was attached; just as I knew that the prophets, the torches, the poisoned darts were there in the cave, so also I knew that far far back in my mind I had good enough reasons to be hurting myself, reasons which I could find out if I wanted to, but which it was not worth my trouble to discover; I even allowed the knowledge that I myself was causing the pain to drift back in my mind. The pain itself, only the pain, became my consciousness, purging all else. Then, as the pain subsided, leaving me free and equipoised, awareness of the stone arched over me flooded my mind. Because it had been invested by the people with a great mystery, it was an incarnation; the power of their faith made it the moon, who was female; at the same time it was only a boulder. I understood Stone is Stone, and that understanding became my consciousness.

My muscles ceased straining against the bonds, nor did they slump; they ceased aching, they were at ease, they were ready. I said nothing, I did not change the upward direction of my glance, I did not smile; yet at this moment the high prophet removed the spears and had the moon slaves unbind me. I did not feel stiff nor did my wounds bother me, and when I put on my cougar skin and leaped, pulled the head over my face and roared, all the prophets fell onto their faces before me. I began chanting and I knew I was doing it all the better for knowing what I was about; I led them back out to the waiting people, and until dawn I chanted the story of the birth, prophesying, betrayal, sacrifice, and victory of the most high prophet. I am a good mimic, I was thoroughly trained, the story is the best: what I gave them was, for them, as good as a vision. I did not know the difference myself.

But the next evening I knew the difference. While I performed my ablutions and the routine ceremonies to the full moon, I thought with increasing horror of my state of mind during my conscious trance. What my state of mind actually had been I cannot with confidence now represent, for what I know of it is colored by my reaction against it the next day. I had remained conscious, in that I could recall what happened; yet that observer and commentator in myself, of whose existence I had scarcely been aware, but whom I had always taken for my consciousness, had vanished; I no longer had been thinking, but had lost control so that my consciousness had become what I was doing; and, almost worse, when I had been telling the story of Christ, I had done it not because I had wanted to or believed in it, but because, in some obscure sense, I had had to. Thinking about it afterward, I did not understand or want to understand what I was drifting toward, but I knew it was something that I feared. And I got out of there as soon as I was physically able.

Here in Sansom, what I have learned has provided me with material for an honorable contribution to knowledge, has given me a tenure to a professorship, thereby pleasing my wife; whereas if I had stayed there among the Dangs much longer, I would have reverted until I had become one of them, might not have minded when the time came to die under the sacrificial knife, would have taken in all ways the risk of prophecy, as my Dang son intends to do, until I had lost myself utterly.

[June 1958]

JOHN BARTH

The Remobilization of Jacob Horner

In September it was time to see the Doctor again: I drove out to the Remobilization Farm the morning during the first week of the month. Because the weather was fine, a number of the Doctor's other patients, quite old men and women, were taking the air, seated in their wheel chairs or in the ancient cane chairs along the porch. As usual, they greeted me a little suspiciously with their eyes; visitors of any sort, but particularly of my age, were rare at the farm, and were not welcomed. Ignoring their stony glances, I went inside to pay my respects to Mrs. Dockey, the receptionist-nurse. I found her in consultation with the Doctor himself.

"Good day, Horner," the Doctor beamed.

"Good morning, sir. Good morning, Mrs. Dockey."

That large, masculine woman nodded shortly without speaking—her custom—and the Doctor told me to wait for him in the Progress and Advice Room, which along with the dining room, the kitchen, the reception room, the bathroom, and the Treatment Room, constituted the first floor of the old frame house. Upstairs the partitions between the original bedrooms had been removed to form two dormitories, one for the men and one for the women. The Doctor had his own small bedroom upstairs, too, and there were two bathrooms. I did not know at that time where Mrs. Dockey slept, or whether she slept at the farm at all. She was a most uncommunicative woman.

182

I had first met the Doctor quite by chance on the morning of March 17, 1951, in what passes for the grand concourse of the Pennsylvania Railroad Station in Baltimore. It happened to be the day after my twenty-eighth birthday, and I was sitting on one of the benches in the station with my suitcase beside me. I was in an unusual condition: I couldn't move. On the previous day I had checked out of my room in an establishment on St. Paul and 33rd Streets owned by the university. I had roomed there since September of the year before when, halfheartedly, I matriculated as a graduate student and began work on the degree that I was scheduled to complete the following June.

But on March 16, my birthday, with my oral examination passed but my master's thesis not even begun, I packed my suitcase and left the room to take a trip somewhere. Because I have learned not to be much interested in causes and biographies, I shall ascribe this romantic move to simple birthday despondency, a phenomenon sufficiently familiar to enough people so that I need not explain it further. Birthday despondency, let us say, had reminded me that I had no self-convincing reason for continuing for a moment longer to do any of the things that I happened to be doing with myself as of seven o'clock on the evening of March 16, 1951. I had thirty dollars and some change in my pocket: when my suitcase was filled I hailed a taxi, went to Pennsylvania Station, and stood in the ticket line.

"Yes?" said the ticket agent when my turn came.

"Ah—this will sound theatrical to you," I said, with some embarrassment, "but I have thirty dollars or so to take a trip on. Would you mind telling me some of the places I could ride to from here for, say, twenty dollars?"

The man showed no surprise at my request. He gave me an understanding if unsympathetic look and consulted some sort of rate scales.

"You can go to Cincinnati, Ohio," he declared. "You can go to Crestline, Ohio. And let's see, now—you can go to Dayton, Ohio. Or Lima, Ohio. That's a nice town. I have some of my wife's people up around Lima, Ohio. Want to go there?"

"Cincinnati, Ohio," I repeated, unconvinced. "Crestline, Ohio; Dayton, Ohio; and Lima, Ohio. Thank you very much. I'll make up my mind and come back."

So I left the ticket window and took a seat on one of the benches in the middle of the concourse to make up my mind. And it was there that I simply ran out of motives, as a car runs out of gas. There was no reason to go to Cincinnati, Ohio. There was no reason to go to Crest-line, Ohio. Or Dayton, Ohio; or Lima, Ohio. There was no reason, either, to go back to the apartment hotel, or for that matter to go any-where. There was no reason to do anything. My eyes, as the German classicist Winckelmann said inaccurately of the eyes of Greek statues, were sightless, gazing on eternity, fixed on ultimacy, and when that is the case there is no reason to do anything—even to change the focus of one's eyes. Which is perhaps why the statues stand still. It is the malady *cosmopsis,* the cosmic view, that afflicted me. When one has it, one is frozen like the bullfrog when the hunter's light strikes him full in the eyes, only with *cosmopsis* there is no hunter, and no quick hand to terminate the moment—there's only the light.

Shortsighted animals all around me hurried in and out of doors leading down to the tracks; trains arrived and departed. Women, children, salesmen, soldiers, and redcaps hurried across the concourse toward immediate destinations, but I sat immobile on the bench. After a while Cincinnati, Crestline, Dayton, and Lima dropped from my mind, and their place was taken by that test-pattern of my con-sciousness, *Pepsi-Cola hits the spot,* intoned with silent oracularity. But it, too, petered away into the void, and nothing appeared in its stead.

If you look like a vagrant it is difficult to occupy a train-station bench all night, even in a busy terminal, but if you are reasonably well-dressed, have a suitcase at your side, and sit erect, policemen and rail-road employees will not disturb you. I was sitting in the same place, in the same position, when the sun struck the grimy station windows next morning, and in the nature of the case I suppose I would have remained thus indefinitely, but about nine o'clock a small, dapper fellow in his fifties stepped in front of me and stared directly into my eyes. He was bald, dark-eyed, and dignified, a Negro, and wore a greying mustache and a trim tweed suit to match. The fact that I did not stir even the pupils of my eyes under his gaze is an index to my condition, for ordinarily I find it next to impossible to return the stare of a stranger.

"Weren't you sitting here like this last night?" he asked me sharply. I did not reply. He came close, bent his face down toward mine, and moved an upthrust finger back and forth about two inches from my eyes. But my eyes did not follow his finger. He stepped back and regarded me critically, then snapped his fingers almost on the point of my nose. I blinked involuntarily, although my head did not jerk back.

"Ah," he said, satisfied, and regarded me again. "Does this happen to you often, young man?"

Perhaps because of the brisk assuredness of his voice, the *no* welled up in me like a belch. And I realized as soon as I deliberately held my tongue (there being in the last analysis no reason to answer his question at all) that as of that moment I was artificially prolonging what had been a genuine physical immobility. Not to choose at all is unthinkable: what I had done before was simply choose not to act, since I had been at rest when the situation arose. Now, however, it was harder—"more of a choice," so to speak—to hold my tongue than to croak out something that filled my mouth, and so after a moment I said, "No."

Then, of course, the trance was broken. I was embarrassed, and rose stiffly from the bench to leave.

"Where will you go?" my examiner asked with a smile.

"What?" I frowned at him. "Oh—get a bus home, I guess. See you around."

"Wait." His voice was mild, but entirely commanding. "Won't you have coffee with me? I'm a physician, and I'd be interested in discussing your case."

"I don't have any case," I said awkwardly. "I was just—sitting there for a minute or so."

"No. I saw you there last night at ten o'clock when I came in from New York," the Doctor said. "You were sitting in the same position. You *were* paralyzed, weren't you?"

I laughed. "Well, if you want to call it that; but there's nothing wrong with me. I don't know what came over me."

"Of course you don't, but I do. My specialty is various sorts of physical immobility. You're lucky I came by this morning."

"Oh, you don't understand—"

"I brought you out of it, didn't I?" he said cheerfully. "Here." He took a fifty-cent piece from his pocket and handed it to me and I accepted it before I realized what he'd done. "I can't go into that lounge over there. Go get two cups of coffee for us and we'll sit here a minute and decide what to do."

"No, listen, I—"

"Why not?" He laughed. "Go on, now. I'll wait here."

Why not, indeed?

"I have my own money," I protested lamely, offering him his fifty-cent piece back, but he waved me away and lit a cigar.

"Now, hurry up," he ordered around the cigar. "Move fast, or you might get stuck again. Don't think of anything but the coffee I've asked you to get."

"All right." I turned and walked with dignity toward the lounge, just off the concourse.

"Fast!" The Doctor laughed behind me. I flushed, and quickened my step.

While I waited for the coffee I tried to feel the curiosity about my invalidity and my rescuer that it seemed appropriate I should feel, but I was too weary in mind and body to wonder at anything. I do not mean to suggest that my condition had been unpleasant—it was entirely anesthetic in its advanced stage, and even a little bit pleasant in its inception—but it was fatiguing, as an overlong sleep is fatiguing, and one had the same reluctance to throw it off that one has to get out of bed when one has slept around the clock. Indeed, as the Doctor had warned (it was at this time, not knowing my benefactor's name, that I began to think of him with a capital D), to slip back into immobility at the coffee counter would have been extremely easy: I felt my mind begin to settle into rigidity, and only the clerk's peremptory, "Thirty cents, please," brought me back to action—luckily, because the Doctor could not have entered the white lounge to help me. I paid the clerk and took the paper cups of coffee back to the bench.

"Good," the Doctor said. "Sit down."

I hesitated. I was standing directly in front of him.

"Here!" he laughed. "On this side!"

I sat where ordered and we sipped our coffee. I rather expected to be asked questions about myself, but the Doctor ignored me.

"Thanks for the coffee," I said. He glanced at me impassively for a moment, as though I were a hitherto silent parrot who had suddenly blurted a brief piece of nonsense, and then he returned his attention to the crowd in the station.

"I have one or two calls to make before we catch the bus," he announced without looking at me. "Won't take long. I wanted to see if you were still here before I left town."

"What do you mean, catch the bus?"

"You'll have to come over to the farm—my Remobilization Farm near Wicomico—for a day or so, for observation," he explained coldly. "You don't have anything else to do, do you?"

"Well, I should get back to the university, I guess. I'm a student."

"Oh!" He chuckled. "Might as well forget about that for a while. You can come back in a few days if you want to."

"Say, you know, really, I think you must have a misconception about what was wrong with me a while ago. I'm not a paralytic. It's all just silly. I'll explain it to you if you want to hear it."

"No, you needn't bother. No offense intended, but the things you think are important probably aren't even relevant. I'm never very curious about my patients' histories. Rather not hear them, in fact—just clutters things up. It doesn't much matter what caused it anyhow, does it?" He grinned. "My farm's like a nunnery in that respect—I never bother about why my patients come there. Forget about causes; I'm no psychoanalyst."

"But that's what I mean, sir," I explained, laughing uncomfortably. "There's nothing physically wrong with me."

"Except that you couldn't move," the Doctor said. "What's your name?"

"Jacob Horner. I'm a graduate student up at Johns Hopkins—"

"Ah, ah," he warned. "No biography, Jacob Horner." He finished his coffee and stood up. "Come on, now, we'll get a cab. Bring your suitcase along."

"Oh, wait, now!"

"Yes?"

I fumbled for protests: the thing was absurd. "Well—this is absurd."

"Yes. So?"

I hesitated, blinking, wetting my lips.

"Think, think!" the Doctor said brusquely.

My mind raced like a car engine when the clutch is disengaged. There was no answer.

"Well, I—are you sure it's all right?" I asked, not knowing what my question signified.

The Doctor made a short, derisive sound (a sort of "Huf!") and turned away. I shook my head—at the same moment aware that I was watching myself act bewildered—and then fetched up my suitcase and followed after him, out to the line of taxicabs at the curb.

Thus began my *alliance* with the Doctor. He stopped first at an establishment on North Howard Street, to order two wheel chairs, three pairs of crutches, and certain other apparatus for the farm, and then at a pharmaceutical supply house on South Paca Street, where he also gave some sort of order. Then we went to the bus terminal and took the bus to the Eastern Shore. The Doctor's Mercury station wagon was parked at the Wicomico bus depot; he drove to the little settlement of Vineland, about three miles south of Wicomico, turned off onto a secondary road, and finally drove up a long, winding dirt lane to the Remobilization Farm, an aged but white-painted clapboard house in a clump of oaks on a knoll overlooking a creek. The patients on the porch, senile men and women, welcomed the Doctor with querulous enthusiasm, and he returned their greeting. Me they regarded with open suspicion, if not hostility, but the Doctor made no explanation of my presence; for that matter, I should have been hard put to explain it myself.

Inside, I was introduced to the muscular Mrs. Dockey and taken to the Progress and Advice Room for my first interview. I waited alone in that clean room—which, though bare, was not really clinical-looking—for some ten minutes, and then the Doctor entered and took his seat very much in front of me. He had donned a white medical-looking jacket and appeared entirely official and competent.

"I'll make a few things clear very quickly, Jacob," he said leaning forward with his hands on his knees and rolling his cigar around in his mouth between sentences. "The Farm, as you can see, is designed for the treatment of paralytics. Most of my patients are old people, but you mustn't infer from that that this is a nursing home for the aged. Perhaps you noticed when we drove up that my patients like me. They do. It has happened several times in the past that for one reason or another I have seen fit to change the location of the farm.

Once it was outside of Troy, New York; another time near Fond du Lac, Wisconsin; another time near Biloxi, Mississippi. And we've been other places, too. Nearly all the patients I have on the farm now have been with me at least since Fond du Lac, and if I should have to move tomorrow to Helena, Montana, or The Rockaways, most of them would go with me, and not because they haven't anywhere else to go. But don't think I have an equal love for them. They're just more or less interesting problems in immobility, for which I find it satisfying to work out therapies. I tell this to you, but not to them, because your problem is such that this information is harmless. And for that matter, you've no way of knowing whether anything I've said or will say is the truth, or just a part of my general therapy for you. You can't even tell whether your doubt in this matter is an honestly founded doubt or just a part of your treatment: access to the truth, Jacob, even belief that there is such a thing, is itself therapeutic or antitherapeutic, depending on the problem. The reality of your problem is all that you can be sure of."

"Yes, sir."

"Why do you say that?" the Doctor asked.

"Say what?"

" 'Yes, sir.' Why do you say 'Yes, sir'? "

"Oh—I was just acknowledging what you said before."

"Acknowledging the truth of what I said or merely the fact that I said it?"

"Well," I hesitated, flustered. "I don't know, sir."

"You don't know whether to say you were acknowledging the truth of my statements, when actually you weren't, or to say you were simply acknowledging that I said something, at the risk of offending me by the implication that you don't agree with any of it. Eh?"

"Oh, I agree with *some* of it," I assured him.

"What parts of it do you agree with? Which statements?" the Doctor asked.

"I don't know: I guess—" I searched my mind hastily to remember even one thing that he'd said. He regarded my floundering for a minute and then went on as if the interruption hadn't occurred.

"Agapotherapy—devotion-therapy—is often useful with older patients," he said. "One of the things that work toward restoring their mobility is devotion to some figure, a doctor or other kind of administrator. It keeps their allegiances from becoming divided. For that reason I'd move the farm occasionally even if other circumstances didn't make it desirable. It does them good to decide to follow me. Agapotherapy is one small therapy in a great number, some consecutive, some simultaneous, which are exercised on the patients. No two patients have the same schedule of therapies, because no two people are ever paralyzed in the same way. The authors of medical textbooks," he added with some contempt, "like everyone else, can reach generality only by ignoring enough particularity. They speak of paralysis, and the treatment of paralytics, as though one read the textbook and then followed the rules for getting paralyzed properly. There is no such thing as *paralysis,* Jacob. There is only paralyzed Jacob Horner. And I don't treat paralysis: I schedule therapies to mobilize John Doe or Jacob Horner, as the case may be. That's why I ignore you when you say you aren't paralyzed like the people out on the porch are paralyzed. I don't treat your paralysis; I treat paralyzed you. Please don't say 'Yes, sir.' "

The urge to acknowledge is an almost irresistible habit, but I managed to sit silent and not even nod.

"There are several things wrong with you, I think. I daresay you don't know the seating capacity of the Cleveland Municipal Stadium, do you?"

"*What?*"

The Doctor did not smile. "You suggest that my question is absurd, when you have no grounds for knowing whether it is or not—you obviously heard me and understood me. Probably you want to delay my learning that you *don't* know the seating capacity of Cleveland Municipal Stadium, since your vanity would be ruffled if the question *weren't* absurd, and even if it were. It makes no difference whether it is or not, Jacob Horner: it's a question asked you by your Doctor. Now, is there any ultimate reason why the Cleveland Stadium shouldn't seat fifty-seven thousand, four hundred, eighty-eight people?"

"None that I can think of." I grinned.

"Don't pretend to be amused. Of course there's not. Is there any reason why it shouldn't seat eighty-eight thousand, four hundred, seventy-five people?"

"No, sir."

"Indeed not. Then as far as Reason is concerned, its seating capacity could be almost anything. Logic will never give you the answer to my question. Only Knowledge of the World will answer it. There's no ultimate reason at all why the Cleveland Stadium should seat exactly seventy-three thousand, eight hundred and eleven people, but it happens that it does. There's no reason in the long run why Italy shouldn't be shaped like a sausage instead of a boot, but that doesn't happen to be the case. *The world is everything that is the case,* and what the case is is not a matter of logic. If you don't simply *know* how many people can sit in the Cleveland Municipal Stadium, you have no real reason for choosing one number over another, assuming you can make a choice at all—do you understand? But if you have some Knowledge of the World you may be able to say, 'Seventy-three thousand, eight hundred and eleven,' just like that. No choice is involved."

"Well," I said, "you'd still have to choose whether to answer the question or not, or whether to answer it correctly, even if you knew the right answer, wouldn't you?"

The Doctor's tranquil stare told me my question was somewhat silly, though it seemed reasonable enough to me.

"One of the things you'll have to do," he said dryly, "is buy a copy of the *World Almanac* for 1951 and begin to study it scrupulously. This is intended as a discipline, and you'll have to pursue it diligently, perhaps for a number of years. Informational Therapy is one of a number of therapies we'll have to initiate at once."

I shook my head and chuckled genially. "Do all your patients memorize the *World Almanac,* Doctor?"

I might as well not have spoken.

"Mrs. Dockey will show you to your bed," the Doctor said, rising to go. "I'll speak to you again presently." At the door he stopped and added, "One, perhaps two of the older men may attempt familiarities with you at night up in the dormitory. They're on Sexual Therapy. But unless you're accustomed to that sort of thing I don't think you should accept their advances. You should keep your life as uncomplicated as possible, at least for a while. Reject them gently, and they'll go back to each other."

There was little I could say. After a while Mrs. Dockey showed me my bed in the men's dormitory. I was not introduced to my roommates, nor did I introduce myself. In fact, during the three days that I remained at the farm not a dozen words were exchanged between us. When I left they were uniformly glad to see me go.

The Doctor spent two or three one-hour sessions with me each day. He asked me virtually nothing about myself; the conversations consisted mostly of harangues against the medical profession for its stupidity in matters of paralysis, and imputations that my condition was the result of defective character and intelligence.

"You claim to be unable to choose in many situations," he said once. "Well I claim that that inability is only theoretically inherent in situations, when there's no chooser. Given a particular chooser, it's unthinkable. So, since the inability *was* displayed in your case, the fault lies not in the situation but in the fact that there was no chooser. Choosing is existence: to the extent that you don't choose, you don't exist. Now, everything we do must be oriented toward choice and action. It doesn't matter whether this action is more or less reasonable than inaction; the point is that it is its opposite."

"But why should anyone prefer it?" I asked.

"There's no reason why you should prefer it, and no reason why you shouldn't. One is a patient simply because one chooses a condition that only therapy can bring one to, not because one condition is inherently better than another. My therapies for a while will be directed toward making you conscious of your existence. It doesn't matter whether you act constructively or even consistently, so long as you act. It doesn't matter to the case whether your character is admirable or not, so long as you think you have one."

"I don't understand why you should choose to treat anyone, Doctor," I said.

"That's my business, not yours."

And so it went. I was charged, directly or indirectly, with everything from intellectual dishonesty and vanity to nonexistence. If I protested, the Doctor observed that my protests indicated my belief in the truth of his statements. If I only listened glumly, he observed that my glumness indicated my belief in the truth of his statements.

"All right, then," I said at last, giving up. "Everything you say is true. All of it is the truth."

The Doctor listened calmly. "You don't know what you're talking about," he said. "There's no such thing as truth as you conceive it."

These apparently pointless interviews did not constitute my only activity at the farm. Before every meal all the patients were made to perform various calisthenics under the direction of Mrs. Dockey. For the older patients these were usually very simple—perhaps a mere nodding of the head or flexing of the arms—although some of the old folks could execute really surprising feats: one gentleman in his seventies was an excellent rope-climber, and two old ladies turned agile somersaults. For each patient Mrs. Dockey prescribed different activities; my own special prescription was to keep some sort of visible motion going all the time. If nothing else, I was constrained to keep a finger wiggling or a foot tapping, say, during mealtimes, when more involved movements would have made eating difficult. And I was told to rock from side to side in my bed all night long: not an unreasonable request, as it happened, for I did this habitually anyhow, even in my sleep—a habit carried over from childhood.

"Motion! Motion!" the Doctor would say, almost exalted. "You must be always *conscious* of motion!"

There were special diets and, for many patients, special drugs. I learned of Nutritional Therapy, Medicinal Therapy, Surgical Therapy, Dynamic Therapy, Informational Therapy, Conversational Therapy, Sexual Therapy, Devotional Therapy, Occupational and Preoccupational Therapy, Virtue and Vice Therapy, Theotherapy and Atheotherapy—and, later, Mythotherapy, Philosophical Therapy, Scriptotherapy, and many, many other therapies practiced in various combinations and sequences by the patients. Everything, to the Doctor, was either therapeutic, antitherapeutic, or irrelevant. He was a kind of superpragmatist.

At the end of my last session—it had been decided that I was to return to Baltimore experimentally, to see whether and how soon my immobility might recur—the Doctor gave me some parting instructions.

"It would not be well in your particular case to believe in God," he said. "Religion will only make you despondent. But until we work out something for you it will be useful to subscribe to some philosophy. Why don't you read Sartre and become an existentialist? It will keep you moving until we find something more suitable for you. Study the *World Almanac*: it is to be your breviary for a while. Take a day job, preferably factory work, but not so simple that you are able to think coherently while working. Something involving sequential operations would be nice. Go out in the evenings; play cards with people. I don't recommend buying a television set just yet. Exercise frequently. Take long walks, but always to a previously determined destination; and when you get there, walk right home again, briskly. And move out of your present quarters; the association is unhealthy for you. Don't get married or have love affairs yet, even if you aren't courageous enough to hire prostitutes. Above all, act impulsively: don't let yourself get stuck between alternatives, or you're lost. You're not that strong. If the alternatives are side by side, choose the one on the left; if they're consecutive in time, choose the earlier. If neither of these applies, choose the alternative whose name begins with the earlier letter of the alphabet. These are the principles of Sinistrality, Antecedence, and Alphabetical Priority—there are others, and they're arbitrary, but useful. Good-by."

"Good-by, Doctor," I said, and prepared to leave.

"If you have another attack and manage to recover from it, contact me as soon as you can. If nothing happens, come back in three months. My services will cost you ten dollars a visit—no charge for this one. I have a limited interest in your case, Jacob, and in the vacuum you have for a self. That *is* your case. Remember, keep moving all the time. Be *engagé*. Join things."

I left, somewhat dazed, and took the bus back to Baltimore. There, out of it all, I had a chance to attempt to decide what I thought of the Doctor, the Remobilization Farm, the endless list of therapies, and my own position. One thing seemed fairly clear: the Doctor was operating either outside the law or on its fringes. Sexual Therapy, to name only one thing, could scarcely be sanctioned by the American Medical Association. This doubtless was the reason for the farm's frequent relocation. It was also apparent that he was a crank—though perhaps not an ineffective one—and one wondered whether he had any sort of license to practice medicine at all. Because—his rationalizations aside—I was so clearly different from his other patients, I could only assume that he had some sort of special interest in my case: perhaps he was a frustrated psychoanalyst. At worst he was some combination of quack and prophet running a semi-legitimate rest home for senile eccentrics; and yet one couldn't easily laugh off his forcefulness, and his insights frequently struck home. As a matter of fact, I was unable to make any judgment one way or the other about him or the farm or the therapies.

A most extraordinary doctor. Although I kept telling myself that I was just going along with the joke, I actually did move to East Chase Street; I took a job as an assembler on the line of the Chevrolet factory out on Broening Highway, where I operated an air wrench that belted leaf springs on the left side of Chevrolet chassis, and I joined the UAW. I read Sartre, but had difficulty deciding how to apply him to specific situations. (How did existentialism help one decide whether to carry one's lunch to work or buy it in the factory cafeteria? I had no head for philosophy.) I played poker with my fellow assemblers, took walks from Chase Street down to the water front and back, and attended B movies. Temperamentally I was already pretty much of an atheist most of the time, and the proscription of women was a small burden, for I was not, as a rule, heavily sexed. I applied Sinistrality, Antecedence, and Alphabetical Priority religiously (though in some instances I found it hard to decide which of those devices best fitted the situation). And every quarter for the next two years I drove over to the Remobilization Farm for advice. It would be idle for me to speculate further on why I assented to this curious alliance, which more often than not was insulting to me—I presume that anyone interested in causes will have found plenty to pick from by now in this account.

I left myself sitting in the Progress and Advice Room, I believe, in September of 1953, waiting for the Doctor. My mood on this morning was an unusual one; as a rule I was almost "weatherless" the moment I entered the farmhouse, and I suppose that weatherlessness is the ideal condition for receiving advice, but on this morning, although I felt unemotional, I was not without weather. I felt dry, clear, and competent, for some reason or other—quite sharp and not a bit humble. In meteorological terms, my weather was *sec supérieur*.

"How are you these days, Horner?" the Doctor asked as he entered the room.

"Just fine, Doctor," I replied breezily. "How's yourself?"

The Doctor took his seat, spread his knees, and regarded me critically, not answering my question.

"Have you begun teaching yet?"

"Nope. Start next week. Two sections of grammar and two of composition."

"Ah." He rolled his cigar around in his mouth. He was studying me, not what I said. "You shouldn't be teaching composition."

"Can't have everything," I said cheerfully, stretching my legs out under his chair and clasping my hands behind my head. "It was that or nothing, so I took it."

The Doctor observed the position of my legs and arms.

"Who is this confident fellow you've befriended?" he asked. "One of the other teachers? He's terribly sure of himself!"

I blushed: it occurred to me that I was imitating one of my officemates, an exuberant teacher of history. "Why do you say I'm imitating somebody?"

"I didn't," the Doctor smiled. "I only asked who was the forceful fellow you've obviously met."

"None of your business, sir."

"Oh, my. Very good. It's a pity you can't take over that manner consistently—you'd never need my services again! But you're not stable enough for that yet, Jacob. Besides, you couldn't act like him when you're in his company, could you? Anyway I'm pleased to see you assuming a role. You do it, evidently, in order to face up to me: a character like your friend's would never allow itself to be insulted by some crank with his string of implausible therapies, eh?"

"That's right, Doctor," I said, but much of the fire had gone out of me under his analysis.

"This indicates to me that you're ready for Mythotherapy, since you seem to be already practicing it without knowing it, and therapeutically, too. But it's best you be aware of what you're doing, so that you won't break down through ignorance. Some time ago I told you to become an existentialist. Did you read Sartre?"

"Some things. Frankly I really didn't get to be an existentialist."

"No? Well, no matter now. Mythotherapy is based on two assumptions: that human existence precedes human essence, if either of the two terms really signifies anything; and that a man is free not only to choose his own essence but to change it at will. Those are both good existentialist premises, and whether they're true or false is no concern of us—they're *useful* in your case."

He went on to explain Mythotherapy.

"In life," he said, "there are no essentially major or minor characters. To that extent, all fiction and biography, and most historiography, is a lie. Everyone is necessarily the hero of his own life story. Suppose you're an usher in a wedding. From the groom's viewpoint he's the major character; the others play supporting parts, even the bride. From your viewpoint, though, the wedding is a minor episode in the very interesting history of *your* life, and the bride and groom both are minor figures. What you've done is choose to *play the part* of a minor character: it can be pleasant for you to *pretend to be* less important than you know you are, as Odysseus does when he disguises as a swineherd. And every member of the congregation at the wedding sees himself as the major character, condescending to witness the spectacle. So in this sense fiction isn't a lie at all, but a true representation of the distortion that everyone makes of life.

"Now, not only are we the heroes of our own life stories—we're the ones who conceive the story, and give other people the essences of minor characters. But since no man's life story as a rule is ever one story with a coherent plot, we're always reconceiving just the sort of hero we are, and consequently just the sort of minor roles the other people are supposed to play. This is generally true. If any man displays almost the same character day in and day out, all day long, it's either because he has no imagination, like an actor who can play only one role, or because he has an imagination so comprehensive that he sees each particular situation of his life as an episode in some grand over-all plot, and can so distort the situations that the same type of hero can deal with them all. But this is most unusual.

"This kind of role-assigning is mythmaking, and when it's done consciously or unconsciously for the purpose of aggrandizing or protecting your ego—and it's probably done for this purpose all the time—it become Mythotherapy. Here's the point: an immobility such as you experienced that time in Penn Station is possible only to a person who for some reason or other has ceased to participate in Mythotherapy. At that time on the bench you were neither a major nor a minor character: you were no character at all. It's because this has happened once that it's necessary for me to explain to you something that comes quite naturally to everyone else. It's like teaching a paralytic how to walk again.

"I've said you're too unstable to play any one part all the time—you're also too unimaginative—so for you these crises had better be met by changing scripts as often as necessary. This should come naturally to you; the important thing for you is to realize what you're doing so you won't get caught without a script, or with the wrong script in a given situation. You did quite well, for example, for a beginner, to walk in here so confidently and almost arrogantly a while ago, and assign me the role of a quack. But you must be able to change masks at once if by some means or other I'm able to make the one you walked in with untenable. Perhaps—I'm just suggesting an offhand possibility—you could change to thinking of me as The Sagacious Old Mentor, a kind of Machiavellian Nestor, say, and yourself as The Ingenuous But Promising Young Protégé, a young Alexander, who someday will put all these teachings into practice and far outshine the master. Do you get the idea? Or—this is repugnant, but it could be used as a last resort—The Silently Indignant Young Man, who tolerates the ravings of a Senile Crank but who will leave this house unsullied by them. I call this repugnant because if you ever used it you'd cut yourself off from much that you haven't learned yet.

"It's extremely important that you learn to assume these masks wholeheartedly. Don't think there's anything behind them: *ego* means *I,* and *I* means *ego,* and the ego by definition is a mask. Where there's no ego—this is you on the bench—there's no *I.* If you sometimes have the feeling that your mask is *insincere*—impossible word!—it's only because one of your masks is incompatible with another. You mustn't put on two at a time. There's a source of conflict; and conflict between masks, like absence of masks, is a source of immobility. The more sharply you can dramatize your situation and define your own role and everybody else's role, the safer you'll be. It doesn't matter in Mythotherapy for paralytics whether your role is major or minor, as long as it's clearly conceived, but in the nature of things it'll normally always be major. Now say something."

I could not.

"Say something!" the Doctor ordered. "Move! Take a role!"

I tried hard to think of one, but I could not.

"Damn you!" the Doctor cried. He kicked back his chair and leaped upon me, throwing me to the floor and pounding me roughly.

"Hey!" I hollered, entirely startled by his attack. "Cut it out! What the hell!" I struggled with him, and being both larger and stronger than he, soon had him off me. We stood facing each other warily, panting from the exertion.

"You watch that stuff!" I said belligerently. "I could make plenty of trouble for you if I wanted to, I'll bet!"

"Anything wrong?" asked Mrs. Dockey, sticking her head into the room. I would not want to tangle with her.

"No, not now." The Doctor smiled, brushing the knees of his white trousers. "A little Pugilistic Therapy for Jacob Horner. No trouble." She closed the door.

"Now, shall we continue our talk?" he asked me, his eyes twinkling. "You were speaking in a manly way about making trouble."

But I was no longer in a mood to go along with the whole ridiculous business. I'd had enough of the old lunatic for this quarter.

"Or perhaps you've had enough of The Old Crank for today, eh?"

"What would the sheriff in Wicomico think of this farm?" I grumbled. "Suppose the police were sent out to investigate Sexual Therapy?"

The Doctor was unruffled by my threats.

"Do you intend to send them?" he asked pleasantly.

"Do you think I wouldn't?"

"I've no idea," he said, still undisturbed.

"Do you dare me to?"

This question, for some reason or other, visibly upset him: he looked at me sharply.

"Indeed I do not," he said at once. "I'm sure you're quite able to do it. I'm sorry if my tactic for mobilizing you just then made you angry. I did it with all good intent. You *were* paralyzed again, you know."

"You and your paralysis!" I sneered.

"You *have* had enough for today, Horner!" the Doctor said. He too was angry now. "Get out! I hope you get paralyzed driving sixty miles an hour on your way home!" He raised his voice. "Get out of here, you damned moron!"

His obviously genuine anger immediately removed mine, which after the first instant had of course been only a novel mask.

"I'm sorry, Doctor," I said. "I won't lose my temper again."

We exchanged smiles.

"Why not?" He laughed. "It's both therapeutic and pleasant to lose your temper in certain situations." He relit his cigar, which had been dropped during our scuffle. "Two interesting things were demonstrated in the past few minutes, Jacob Horner. I can't tell you about them until your next visit. Good-by, now. Don't forget to pay Mrs. Dockey."

Out he strode, cool as he could be, and a few moments later out strode I: A Trifle Shaken, But Sure Of My Strength.

[July 1958]

JOHN CHEEVER

The Death of Justina

So help me God, it gets more and more preposterous, it corresponds less and less to what I remember and what I expect, as if the force of life were centrifugal and threw one further and further away from one's purest memories and ambitions; and I can barely recall the old house where I was raised, where in midwinter Parma violets bloomed in a cold frame near the kitchen door and down the long corridor, past the seven views of Rome—up two steps and down three—one entered the library where all the books were in order, the lamps were bright, where there was a fire and a dozen bottles of good bourbon, locked in a cabinet with a veneer like tortoise shell whose silver key my father wore on his watch chain. Just let me give you one example and if you disbelieve me look honestly into your own past and see if you can't find a comparable experience. On Saturday the doctor told me to stop smoking and drinking and I did. I won't go into the commonplace symptoms of withdrawal, but I would like to point out that, standing at my window in the evening, watching the brilliant afterlight and the spread of darkness, I felt, through the lack of these humble stimulants, the force of some primitive memory in which the coming of night with its stars and its moon was apocalyptic. I thought suddenly of the neglected graves of my three brothers on the mountainside and that death is a loneliness much crueler than any loneliness hinted at in life. The soul (I thought) does not leave the body, but lingers with it through every degrading stage of decomposition and neglect, through heat, through cold, through the long winter nights when no one comes with a wreath or a plant and no one says a prayer. This unpleasant premonition was followed by anxiety. We were going out for dinner and I thought that the oil burner would explode in our absence and burn the house. The cook would get drunk and attack my daughter with a carving knife, or my wife and I would be killed in a collision on the main highway, leaving our children bewildered orphans with nothing in life to look forward to but sadness. I was able to observe, along with these foolish and terrifying anxieties, a definite impairment to my discretionary poles. I felt as if I were being lowered by ropes into the atmosphere of my childhood. I told my wife—when she passed through the living room—that I had stopped smoking and drinking but she didn't seem to care and who would reward me for my privations? Who cared about the bitter taste in my mouth and that my head seemed to be leaving my shoulders? It seemed to me that men had honored one another with medals, statuary and cups for much less and that abstinence is a social matter. When I abstain from sin it is more often a fear of scandal than a private resolve to improve on the purity of my heart, but here was a call for abstinence without the worldly enforcement of society, and death is not the threat that scandal is. When it was time for us to go out I was so light-headed that I had to ask my wife to drive the car. On Sunday I sneaked seven cigarettes in various hiding places and drank two Martinis in the downstairs coat closet. At breakfast on Monday my English muffin stared up at me from the plate. I mean I *saw* a face there in the rough, toasted surface. The moment of recognition was fleeting, but it was deep, and I wondered who it had been. Was it a friend, an aunt, a sailor, a ski instructor, a bartender or a conductor on a train? The smile faded off the muffin, but it had been there for a second—the sense of a person, a life, a pure force of gentleness and censure, and I am convinced that the muffin had contained the presence of some spirit. As you can see, I was nervous.

On Monday my wife's old cousin, Justina, came to visit her. Justina was a lively guest, although she must have been crowding eighty. On Tuesday my wife gave her a lunch party. The last guest left at three and a few minutes later, Cousin Justina, sitting on the living-room sofa with a glass of brandy, breathed her last. My wife called me at the office and I said that I would be right out. I was clearing my desk when my boss, MacPherson, came in.

"Spare me a minute," he asked. "I've been bird-dogging all over the place, trying to track you down. Pierson had to leave early and I want you to write the last Elixircol commercial."

"Oh, I can't, Mac," I said. "My wife just called. Cousin Justina is dead."

"You write that commercial," he said. His smile was satanic. "Pierson had to leave early because his grandmother fell off a step-ladder."

Now I don't like fictional accounts of office life. It seems to me that if you're going to write fiction you should write about mountain-climbing and tempests at sea and I will go over my predicament with MacPherson briefly, aggravated as it was by his refusal to respect and honor the death of dear old Justina. It was like MacPherson. It was a good example of the way I've been treated. He is, I might say, a tall, splendidly groomed man of about sixty who changes his shirt three times a day, romances his secretary every afternoon between two and two-thirty and makes the habit of continuously chewing gum seem hygienic and elegant. I write his speeches for him and it has not been a happy arrangement for me. If the speeches are successful, Mac-Pherson takes all the credit. I can see that his presence, his tailor and his fine voice are all a part of the performance, but it makes me angry never to be given credit for what was said. On the other hand, if the speeches are unsuccessful—if his presence and his voice can't carry the hour—his threatening and sarcastic manner is surgical and I am obliged to contain myself in the role of a man who can do no good in spite of the piles of congratulatory mail that my eloquence sometimes brings in. I must pretend, I must, like an actor, study and improve on my pretension, to have nothing to do with his triumphs and I must bow my head gracefully in shame when we have both failed. I am forced to appear grateful for injuries, to lie, to smile falsely and to play out a role as asinine and as unrelated to the facts as a minor prince in an operetta, but if I speak the truth it will be my wife and my children who will pay in hardships for my outspokenness. Now he refused to respect or even to admit the solemn fact of a death in our family and if I couldn't rebel it seemed as if I could at least hint at it.

The commercial he wanted me to write was for a tonic called Elixircol and was to be spoken on television by an actress who was neither young nor beautiful, but who had an appearance of ready abandon and who was anyhow the mistress of one of the sponsor's uncles. *Are you growing old?* I wrote. *Are you falling out of love with your image in the looking glass? Does your face in the morning seem rucked and seamed with alcoholic and sexual excesses and does the rest of you appear to be a greyish-pink lump, covered all over with brindle hair? Walking in the autumn woods, do you feel that subtle distance has come between you and the smell of wood smoke? Have you drafted your obituary? Are you easily winded? Do you wear a girdle? Is your sense of smell fading, is your interest in gardening waning, is your fear of heights increasing and are your sexual drives as ravening and intense as ever and does your wife look more and more to you like a stranger with sunken cheeks who has wandered into your bedroom by mistake? If this or any of this is true you need Elixircol, the true juice of youth. The small economy size* (business with the bottle) *costs seventy-five dollars and the giant family bottle comes at two hundred and fifty. It's a lot of scratch, God knows, but these are inflationary times and who can put a price on youth? If you don't have the cash, borrow it from your neighborhood loan shark or hold up the local bank. The odds are three to one that with a ten-cent water pistol and a slip of paper you can shake ten thousand out of any fainthearted teller. Everybody's doing it.* (Music up and out.)

I sent this into MacPherson via Ralphie, the messenger boy, and took the 4:16 home, traveling through a landscape of utter desolation.

Now my journey is a digression and has no real connection to Justina's death, but what followed could only have happened in my country and in my time and since I was an American traveling across an American landscape, the trip may be part of the sum. There are some Americans who, although their fathers emigrated from the old world three centuries ago, never seem to have quite completed the voyage, and I am one of these. I stand, figuratively, with one wet foot on Plymouth Rock, looking with some delicacy, not into a formidable and challenging wilderness but onto a half-finished civilization embracing glass towers, oil derricks, suburban continents and abandoned movie houses and wondering why, in this most prosperous, equitable and accomplished world—where even the cleaning women practice the Chopin preludes in their spare time—everyone should seem to be so disappointed?

At Proxmire Manor I was the only passenger to get off the random, meandering and profitless local that carried its shabby lights off into the dusk like some game-legged watchman or beadle, making his appointed rounds. I went around to the front of the station to wait for my wife and to enjoy the traveler's fine sense of crises. Above me on the hill was my home and the homes of my friends, all lighted and smelling of fragrant wood smoke like the temples in a sacred grove, dedicated to monogamy, feckless childhood and domestic bliss, but so like a dream that I felt the lack of viscera with much more than poignance—the absence of that inner dynamism we respond to in some European landscapes. In short, I was disappointed. It was my country, my beloved country and there have been mornings when I could have kissed the earth that covers its many provinces and states. There was a hint of bliss—romantic and domestic bliss. I seemed to hear the jingle bells of the sleigh that would carry me to grandmother's house, although in fact grandmother spent the last years of her life working as a hostess on an ocean liner and was lost in the tragic sinking of the *S.S. Lorelei* and I was responding to a memory that I had not experienced. But the hill of light rose like an answer to some primitive dream of home-coming. On one of the highest lawns I saw the remains of a snow man who still smoked a pipe and wore a scarf and a cap, but whose form was wasting away and whose anthracite eyes stared out at the view with terrifying bitterness. I sensed some disappointing greenness of spirit in the scene, although I knew in my bones, no less, how like yesterday it was that my father left the old world to found a new; and I thought of the forces that had brought stamina to the image: the cruel towns of Calabria with their cruel princes, the badlands northwest of Dublin, ghettos, despots, whorehouses, bread lines, the graves of children. Intolerable hunger, corruption, persecution and despair had generated these faint and mellow lights and wasn't it all a part of the great migration that is the life of man?

My wife's cheeks were wet with tears when I kissed her. She was distressed, of course, and really quite sad. She had been attached to Justina. She drove me home where Justina was still sitting on the sofa. I would like to spare you the unpleasant details, but I will say that both her mouth and her eyes were wide open. I went into the pantry to telephone Dr. Hunter. His line was busy. I poured myself a drink—the first since Sunday—and lighted a cigarette. When I called the doctor again he answered and I told him what had happened. "Well, I'm awfully sorry to hear about it, Moses," he said. "I can't get over until after six and there isn't much that I can do. This sort of thing has come up before and I'll tell you all I know. You see you live in a B zone—two-acre lots, no commercial enterprises, and so forth.

A couple of years ago some stranger bought the old Plewett mansion and it turned out that he was planning to operate it as a funeral home. We didn't have any zoning provision at the time that would protect us and one was rushed through the village council at midnight and they overdid it. It seems that you not only can't have a funeral home in zone B—you can't bury anything there and you can't die there. Of course it's absurd, but we all make mistakes, don't we?

"Now there are two things you can do. I've had to deal with this before. You can take the old lady and put her into the car and drive her over to Chestnut Street where zone C begins. The boundary is just beyond the traffic light by the high school. As soon as you get her over to zone C, it's all right. You can just say she died in the car. You can do that or if this seems distasteful you can call the mayor and ask him to make an exception to the zoning laws. But I can't write you out a death certificate until you get her out of that neighborhood and of course no undertaker will touch her until you get a death certificate."

"I don't understand," I said, and I didn't, but then the possibility that there was some truth in what he had just told me broke against me or over me like a wave, exciting mostly indignation. "I've never heard such a lot of damned foolishness in my life," I said. "Do you mean to tell me that I can't die in one neighborhood and that I can't fall in love in another and that I can't eat. . . ."

"Listen. Calm down, Moses. I'm not telling you anything but the facts and I have a lot of patients waiting. I don't have the time to listen to you fulminate. If you want to move her, call me as soon as you get her over to the traffic light. Otherwise, I'd advise you to get in touch with the mayor or someone on the village council." He cut the connection. I was outraged, but this did not change the fact that Justina was still sitting on the sofa. I poured a fresh drink and lit another cigarette.

Justina seemed to be waiting for me and to be changing from an inert into a demanding figure. I tried to imagine carrying her out to the station wagon, but I couldn't complete the task in my imagination and I was sure that I couldn't complete it in fact. I then called the mayor, but this position in our village is mostly honorary and as I might have known he was in his New York law office and was not expected home until seven. I could cover her, I thought; that would be a decent thing to do, and I went up the back stairs to the linen

THE DEATH OF JUSTINA

closet and got a sheet. It was getting dark when I came back into the living room, but this was no merciful twilight. Dusk seemed to be playing directly into her hands and she had gained power and stature with the dark. I covered her with the sheet and turned on a lamp at the other end of the room, but the rectitude of the place with its old furniture, flowers, paintings, etc. was demolished by her monumental shape. The next thing to worry about was the children who would be home in a few minutes. Their knowledge of death, excepting their dreams and intuitions of which I know nothing, is zero and the bold figure in the parlor was bound to be traumatic. When I heard them coming up the walk I went out and told them what had happened and sent them up to their rooms. At seven I drove over to the mayor's.

He had not come home, but he was expected at any minute and I talked with his wife. She gave me a drink. By this time I was chainsmoking. When the mayor came in we went into a little office or library where he took up a position behind a desk, putting me in the low chair of a supplicant.

"Of course I sympathize with you, Moses," he said, settling back in his chair. "It's an awful thing to have happened, but the trouble is that we can't give you a zoning exception without a majority vote of the village council and all the members of the council happen to be out of town. Pete's in California and Jack's in Paris and Larry won't be back from Stowe until the end of the week."

I was sarcastic. "Then I suppose Cousin Justina will have to gracefully decompose in my parlor until Jack comes back from Paris."

"Oh, no," he said, "oh, *no*. Jack won't be back from Paris for another month, but I think you might wait until Larry comes from Stowe. Then we'd have a majority, assuming of course that they would agree to your appeal."

"For Christ's sake," I snarled.

"Yes, yes," he said, "it is difficult, but after all you must realize that this is the world you live in and the importance of zoning can't be overestimated. Why, if a single member of the council could give out zoning exceptions, I could give you permission right now to open a saloon in your garage, put up neon lights, hire an orchestra and destroy the neighborhood and all the human and commercial values we've worked so hard to protect."

"I don't want to open a saloon in my garage," I howled. "I don't want to hire an orchestra. I just want to bury Justina."

"I know, Moses, I know," he said. "I understand that. But it's just that it happened in the wrong zone and if I make an exception for you I'll have to make an exception for everyone, and this kind of morbidity, when it gets out of hand, can be very depressing. People don't like to live in a neighborhood where this sort of thing goes on all the time."

"Listen to me," I said. "You give me an exception and you give it to me now or I'm going home and dig a hole in my garden and bury Justina myself."

"But you can't do that, Moses. You can't bury anything in zone B. You can't even bury a cat."

"You're mistaken," I said. "I can and I will. I can't function as a doctor and I can't function as an undertaker, but I can dig a hole in the ground and if you don't give me my exception, that's what I'm going to do."

I got out of the low chair before I finished speaking and started for the door.

"Come back, Moses, come back," he said. "Please come back. Look, I'll give you an exception if you'll promise not to tell anyone. It's breaking the law, it's a forgery, but I'll do it if you promise to keep it a secret."

I promised to keep it a secret, he gave me the documents and I used his telephone to make the arrangements. Justina was removed a few minutes after I got home, but that night I had the strangest dream.

I dreamed that I was in a crowded supermarket. It must have been night because the windows were dark. The ceiling was paved with fluorescent light—brilliant, cheerful, but, considering our prehistoric memories, a harsh link in the chain of light that binds us to the past. Music was playing and there must have been at least a thousand shoppers pushing their wagons among the long corridors of comestibles and victuals. Now is there—or isn't there—something about the posture we assume when we push a wagon that unsexes us? Can it be done with gallantry? I bring this up because the multitude of shoppers seemed that evening, as they pushed their wagons, penitential and unsexed. There were all kinds, this being my beloved country. There were Italians, Finns, Jews, Negroes, Shropshiremen, Cubans—anyone who had heeded the voice of liberty—and they were dressed with that sumptuary abandon that European caricaturists record with such bitter disgust. Yes, there were grandmothers in shorts, big-butted women in knitted pants, and men wearing such an assortment of clothing that it looked as if they had dressed hurriedly in a burning building. But this, as I say, is my own country and in my opinion the caricaturist who vilifies the old lady in shorts, vilifies himself. I am a native and I was wearing buckskin jump boots, chino pants cut so tight that my sexual organs were discernible and a rayon acetate pajama top printed with representations of the *Pinta,* the *Nina* and the *Santa Maria* in full sail. The scene was strange—the strangeness of a dream where we see familiar objects in an unfamiliar light, but as I looked more closely I saw that there were some irregularities. Nothing was labeled. Nothing was identified or known. The cans and boxes were all bare. The frozen-food bins were full of brown parcels, but they were such odd shapes that you couldn't tell if they contained a frozen turkey or a Chinese dinner. All the goods at the vegetable and the bakery counters were concealed in brown bags and even the books for sale had no titles. In spite of the fact that the contents of nothing was known, my companions of the dream—my thousands of bizarrely dressed compatriots—were deliberating gravely over these mysterious containers as if the choices they made were critical. Like any dreamer, I was omniscient—I was with them and I was withdrawn—and stepping above the scene for a minute I noticed the men at the check-out counters. They were brutes. Now sometimes in a crowd, in a bar or a street, you will see a face so full-blown in its obdurate resistance to the appeals of love, reason and decency—so lewd, so brutish and unregenerate—that you turn away. Men like these were stationed at the only way out and as the shoppers approached them they tore their packages open—I still couldn't see what they contained—but in every case the customer, at the sight of what he had chosen, showed all the symptoms of the deepest guilt; that force that brings us to our knees. Once their choice had been opened, to their shame they were pushed—in some cases kicked—toward the door and beyond the door I saw dark water and heard a terrible noise of moaning and crying in the air. They waited at the door in groups to be taken away in some conveyance that I couldn't see. As

I watched, thousands and thousands pushed their wagons through the market, made their careful and mysterious choices and were reviled and taken away. What could be the meaning of this?

We buried Justina in the rain the next afternoon. The dead are not, God knows, a minority, but in Proxmire Manor their unexalted kingdom is on the outskirts, rather like a dump, where they are transported furtively as knaves and scoundrels and where they lie in an atmosphere of perfect neglect. Justina's life had been exemplary, but by ending it she seemed to have disgraced us all. The priest was a friend and a cheerful sight, but the undertaker and his helpers, hiding behind their limousines, were not, and aren't they at the root of most of our troubles with their claim that death is a violet-flavored kiss? How can a people who do not mean to understand death hope to understand love and who will sound the alarm?

I went from the cemetery back to my office.

The commercial was on my desk and MacPherson had written across it in large letters in grease pencil: "Very funny, you broken-down bore. Do again."

I was tired but unrepentent and didn't seem able to force myself into a practical posture of usefulness and obedience. I did another commercial.

Don't lose your loved ones because of excessive radioactivity. Don't be a wallflower at the dance because of strontium 90 in your bones. Don't be a victim of fallout. When the tart on 36th Street gives you the big eye, does your body stride off in one direction and your imagination in another? Does your mind follow her up the stairs and taste her wares in revolting detail while your flesh goes off to Brooks Brothers or the foreign-exchange desk of the Chase Manhattan Bank? Haven't you noticed the size of the ferns, the lushness of the grass, the bitterness of the string beans and the brilliant markings on the new breeds of butterfies? You have been inhaling lethal atomic waste for the last twenty-five years and only Elixircol can save you.

I gave this copy to Ralphie and waited perhaps ten minutes, when it was returned, marked again with grease pencil. "Do," he wrote, "or you'll be dead."

I felt very tired. I returned to the typewriter, put another piece of paper into the machine and wrote: *The Lord is my Shepherd, therefore can I lack nothing. He shall feed me in a green pasture and lead me forth beside the waters of comfort. He shall convert my soul and bring me forth in the paths of righteousness for his Name's sake. Yea, though I walk through the valley of the shadow of death I will fear no evil for thou art with me; thy rod and thy staff comfort me. Thou shalt prepare a table for me in the presence of them that trouble me; thou hast anointed my head with oil and my cup shall be full. Surely thy loving kindness and thy mercy shall follow me all the days of my life and I will dwell in the house of the Lord forever.* I gave this to Ralphie and went home.

[November 1960]

ISAAC BASHEVIS SINGER

The Spinoza of Market Street

Doctor Nahum Fischelson paced back and forth in his garret room in Market Street, Warsaw. Dr. Fischelson was a short, hunched man with a greyish beard, and was quite bald except for a few wisps of hair remaining at the nape of the neck. His nose was as crooked as a beak and his eyes were large, dark, and fluttering like those of some huge bird. It was a hot summer evening, but Dr. Fischelson wore a black coat which reached to his knees, and he had on a stiff collar and a bow tie. From the door he paced slowly to the dormer window set high in the slanting room and back again. One had to mount several steps to look out. A candle in a brass holder was burning on the table and a variety of insects and moths buzzed around the flame. Now and again one of the creatures would fly too close to the fire and sear its wings, or one would ignite and glow on the wick for an instant. At such moments Dr. Fischelson grimaced. His wrinkled face would twitch and beneath his disheveled mustache he would bite his lips. Finally he took a handkerchief from his pocket and waved it at the insects.

"Away from there, fools and imbeciles," he scolded. "You won't get warm here; you'll only burn yourself."

The insects scattered, but a second later returned and once more circled the trembling flame. Dr. Fischelson wiped the sweat from his wrinkled forehead and sighed. "Like men they desire nothing but the pleasure of the moment." On the table lay an open book printed in Latin, and on its broad-margined pages were notes and comments written in small letters by Dr. Fischelson. The book was Spinoza's *Ethics* and Dr. Fischelson had been studying it for the last thirty years. He knew every proposition, every proof, every corollary, every note by heart. When he wanted to find a particular passage, he generally opened to the place immediately without having to search for it. But, nevertheless, he continued to study the *Ethics* for hours every day with a magnifying glass in his bony hand, murmuring and nodding his head in agreement. The truth was that the more Dr. Fischelson studied, the more puzzling sentences, unclear passages, and cryptic remarks he found. Each sentence contained hints unfathomed by any of the students of Spinoza. Actually the philosopher had anticipated all of the criticisms of pure reason made by Kant and his followers. Dr. Fischelson was writing a commentary on the *Ethics*. He had drawers full of notes and drafts, but it didn't seem that he would ever be able to complete his work. The stomach ailment which had plagued him for years was growing worse from day to day. Now he would get pains in his stomach after only a few mouthfuls of oatmeal. "God in Heaven, it's difficult, very difficult," he would say to himself, using the same intonation as had his father, the late Rabbi of Tishevitz. "It's very, very hard."

Dr. Fischelson was not afraid of dying. To begin with, he was no longer a young man. Secondly, it is stated in the fourth part of the *Ethics* that "a free man thinks of nothing less than death and his wisdom is a meditation not of death, but of life." Thirdly, it is also said that "the human mind cannot be absolutely destroyed with the human body, but there is some part of it that remains eternal." And yet Dr. Fischelson's ulcer (or perhaps it was a cancer) continued to bother him. His tongue was always coated. He belched frequently and emitted a different foul-smelling gas each time. He suffered from heartburn and cramps. At times he felt like vomiting and at other times he was hungry for garlic, onions, and fried foods. He had long ago discarded the medicines prescribed for him by the doctors and had sought his own remedies. He found it beneficial to take grated radish after meals and lie on his bed, belly down, with his head hanging over the side. But these home remedies offered only temporary relief. Some of the doctors he consulted insisted there was nothing the matter with him. "It's just nerves," they told him. "You could live to be a hundred."

But on this particular hot summer night, Dr. Fischelson felt his strength ebbing. His head felt hollow, his knees were shaky, his pulse weak. He sat down to read and his vision blurred. The letters on the page turned from green to gold. The lines became waved and jumped over each other, leaving white gaps as if the text had disappeared in some mysterious way. The heat was unbearable, flowing down directly from the tin roof; Dr. Fischelson felt he was inside an oven. Several times he climbed the four steps to the window and thrust his head out into the cool of the evening breeze. He would remain in that position for so long his knees would become wobbly. "Oh, it's a fine breeze," he would murmur, "really delightful," and he would recall that, according to Spinoza, morality and happiness were identical, and that the most moral deed a man could perform was to indulge in some pleasure which was not contrary to reason.

Dr. Fischelson, standing on the top step at the window and looking out, could see into two worlds. Above him were the heavens, thickly strewn with stars. Dr. Fischelson had never seriously studied astronomy, but he could differentiate between the planets, those bodies which, like the earth, revolve around the sun, and the fixed stars, themselves distant suns, whose light reaches us a hundred or even a thousand years later. He recognized the constellations which mark the path of the earth in space and that nebulous sash, the Milky Way. Dr. Fischelson owned a small telescope he had bought in Switzerland where he had studied, and he particularly enjoyed looking at the moon through it. He could clearly make out on the moon's surface the volcanoes bathed in sunlight and the dark, shadowy craters. He never wearied of gazing at these cracks and crevasses. To him they seemed both near and distant, both substantial and insubstantial. Now and then he would see a shooting star trace a wide arc across the sky and disappear, leaving a fiery trail behind it. Dr. Fischelson would know then that a meteorite had reached our atmosphere, and perhaps some unburned fragment of it had fallen into the ocean or had landed in the desert or perhaps even in some inhabited region. Slowly the stars which had appeared from behind Dr. Fischelson's roof rose until they were shining above the house across the street. Yes, when Dr. Fischelson looked up into the heavens, he became aware of that infinite extension which is, according to Spinoza, one of God's attributes. It comforted Dr. Fischelson to think that, although he was only a weak, puny man, a changing mode of the absolutely infinite substance, he was nevertheless a part of the cosmos, made of the same matter as the celestial bodies; to the extent that he was a part of the Godhead, he knew he could not be destroyed. In such moments,

Dr. Fischelson experienced the *Amor Dei Intellectualis* which is, according to the philosopher of Amsterdam, the highest perfection of the mind. Dr. Fischelson breathed deeply, lifted his head as high as his stiff collar permitted, and actually felt he was whirling in company with the earth, the sun, the stars of the Milky Way, and the infinite host of galaxies known only to infinite thought. His legs became light and weightless and he grasped the window frame with both hands as if afraid he would lose his footing and fly out into eternity.

When Dr. Fischelson tired of observing the sky, his glance dropped to Market Street below. He could see a long strip extending from Yanash's market to Iron Street, with the gas lamps lining it merged into a string of fiery dots. Smoke was issuing from the chimneys on the black, tin roofs; the bakers were heating their ovens, and here and there sparks mingled with the black smoke. The street never looked so noisy and crowded as on a summer evening. Thieves, prostitutes, gamblers and fences loafed in the square, which looked from above like a pretzel covered with poppy seeds. The young men laughed coarsely and the girls shrieked. A peddler with a keg of lemonade on his back pierced the general din with his intermittent cries. A watermelon vendor shouted in a savage voice, and the long knife which he used for cutting the fruit dripped with the bloodlike juice. Now and again the street became even more agitated. Fire engines, their heavy wheels clanging, sped by; they were drawn by sturdy black horses which had to be tightly curbed to prevent them from running wild. Next came an ambulance, its siren screaming. Then some thugs had a fight among themselves, and the police had to be called. A passer-by was robbed and ran about, shouting for help. Some wagons loaded with firewood sought to get through into the courtyards where the bakeries were located, but the horses could not lift the wheels over the steep curbs and the drivers berated the animals and lashed them with their whips. Sparks rose from the clanging hoofs. It was not long after seven, which was the prescribed closing time for stores, but actually business had only begun. Customers were led in stealthily through back doors. The Russian policemen on the street, having been paid off, noticed nothing of this. Merchants continued to hawk their wares, each seeking to outshout the others.

"Gold, gold, gold," a woman who dealt in rotten oranges shrieked.

"Sugar, sugar, sugar," croaked a dealer in overripe plums.

"Heads, heads, heads," a boy who sold fish heads roared.

Through the window of a Chassidic study house across the way, Dr. Fischelson could see boys with long side locks swaying over holy volumes, grimacing and studying aloud in sing-song voices. Butchers, porters and fruit dealers were drinking beer in the tavern below. Vapor drifted from the tavern's open door like steam from a bath-house, and there was the sound of loud music. Outside of the tavern, streetwalkers snatched at drunken soldiers and workers on their way home from the factories. Some of the men carried bundles of wood on their shoulders, reminding Dr. Fischelson of the wicked who are con-demned to kindle their own fires in Hell. Husky record players poured out their raspings through open windows. The liturgy of the high holidays alternated with vulgar vaudeville songs.

Dr. Fischelson peered into the half-lit bedlam and cocked his ears. He knew that the behavior of this rabble was the very antithesis of reason. These people were immersed in the vainest of passions, were drunk with emotions, and, according to Spinoza, emotion was never good. Instead of the pleasure they ran after, all they succeeded in obtaining was disease and prison, shame and the suffering that re-sulted from ignorance. Even the cats which loitered on the roofs here seemed more savage and passionate than those in other parts of the town. They caterwauled with the voices of women in labor, and like demons scampered up walls and leaped onto eaves and balconies. One of the toms paused at Dr. Fischelson's window and let out a howl which made Dr. Fischelson shudder. The doctor stepped from the window and, picking up a broom, brandished it in front of the black beast's glowing, green eyes. "Scat, begone, you ignorant savage!"—and he rapped the broom handle against the roof until the tom ran off.

When Dr. Fischelson had returned to Warsaw from Zurich where he had studied philosophy, a great future had been predicted for him. His friends had known that he was writing an important book on Spinoza. A Jewish Polish journal had invited him to be a contributor; he had been a frequent guest at several wealthy households, and he had been made head librarian at the Warsaw Synagogue. Although even then he had been considered an old bachelor, the matchmakers had proposed several rich girls for him. But Dr. Fischelson had not taken advantage of these opportunities. He had wanted to be as independent as Spinoza himself. And he had been. But because of his heretical ideas he had come into conflict with the rabbi and had to resign his post as librarian. For years after that, he had supported himself by giving private lessons in Hebrew and German. Then, when he had become sick, the Berlin Jewish community had voted him a subsidy of five hundred marks a year. This had been made possible through the intervention of the famous Dr. Hildesheimer with whom he corresponded about philosophy. In order to get by on so small a pension, Dr. Fischelson had moved into the attic room and had begun cooking his own meals on a kerosene stove. He had a cupboard which had many drawers, and each drawer was labeled with the food it contained—buckwheat, rice, barley, onions, carrots, potatoes, mushrooms. Once a week Dr. Fischelson put on his wide-brimmed black hat, took a basket in one hand and Spinoza's *Ethics* in the other, and went off to the market for his provisions. While he was waiting to be served, he would open the *Ethics*. The merchants knew him and would motion him to their stalls.

"A fine piece of cheese, Doctor—just melts in your mouth."

"Fresh mushrooms, Doctor, straight from the woods."

"Make way for the Doctor, ladies," the butcher would shout. "Please don't block the entrance."

During the early years of his sickness, Dr. Fischelson had still gone in the evening to a café which was frequented by Hebrew teachers and other intellectuals. It had been his habit to sit there and play chess while drinking half a glass of black coffee. Sometimes he would stop at the bookstores on Holy Cross Street where all sorts of old books and magazines could be purchased cheap. On one occasion a former pupil of his had arranged to meet him at a restaurant one evening. When Dr. Fischelson arrived, he had been surprised to find a group of friends and admirers who forced him to sit at the head of the table while they made speeches about him. But these were things that had happened long ago. Now people were no longer interested in him. He had isolated himself completely and had become a forgotten man. The events of 1905, when the boys of Market Street had begun to organize strikes, throw bombs at police stations, and shoot strikebreakers so that the stores were closed even on weekdays, had greatly increased his isolation. He began to despise everything associated with the modern Jew—Zionism, socialism, anarchism. The young men in question seemed to him nothing but an ignorant rabble intent on destroying society, society without which no reasonable existence was possible. He still read a Hebrew magazine occasionally, but he felt contempt for modern Hebrew which had no roots in the Bible or the Mishnah. The spelling of Polish words had changed also. Dr. Fischelson concluded that even the so-called spiritual men had abandoned reason and were doing their utmost to pander to the mob. Now and again he still visited a library and browsed through some of the modern histories of philosophy, but he found that the professors did not understand Spinoza, quoted him incorrectly, attributed their own muddled ideas to the philosopher. Although Dr. Fischelson was well aware that anger was an emotion unworthy of those who walk the path of reason, he would become furious, and would quickly close the book and push it from him. "Idiots," he would mutter, "asses, upstarts." And he would vow never again to look at modern philosophy.

Every three months a special mailman who only delivered money orders brought Dr. Fischelson eighty rubles. He expected his quarterly allotment at the beginning of July, but as day after day passed, and the tall man with the blond mustache and the shiny buttons did not appear, the Doctor grew anxious. He had scarcely a groschen left. Who knows—possibly the Berlin Community had rescinded his subsidy; perhaps Dr. Hildesheimer had died, God forbid; the post office might have made a mistake. Every event has its cause, Dr. Fischelson knew. All was determined, all necessary, and a man of reason had no right to worry. Nevertheless, worry invaded his brain and buzzed about like the flies. If the worst came to the worst, it occurred to him, he could commit suicide, but then he remembered that Spinoza did not approve of suicide and compared those who took their own lives to the insane.

One day when Dr. Fischelson went out to a store to purchase a composition book, he heard people talking about war. In Serbia somewhere, an Austrian prince had been shot and the Austrians had delivered an ultimatum to the Serbs. The owner of the store, a young man with a yellow beard and shifty yellow eyes, announced, "We are about to have a small war," and he advised Dr. Fischelson to store up food because in the near future there was likely to be a shortage.

Everything happened so quickly. Dr. Fischelson had not even

decided whether it was worth-while to spend four groschen on a newspaper, and already posters had been hung up announcing mobilization. Men were to be seen walking on the street with round metal tags on their lapels, a sign that they were being drafted. They were followed by their crying wives. One Monday when Dr. Fischelson descended to the street to buy some food with his last kopecks, he found the stores closed. The owners and their wives stood outside and explained that merchandise was unobtainable. But certain special customers were pulled to one side and let in through back doors. On the street all was confusion. Policemen with swords unsheathed could be seen riding on horseback. A large crowd had gathered around the tavern where, at the command of the Tsar, the tavern's stock of whiskey was being poured into the gutter.

Dr. Fischelson went to his old café. Perhaps he would find some acquaintances there who would advise him. But he did not come across a single person he knew. He decided, then, to visit the rabbi of the synagogue where he had once been librarian, but the sexton with the six-sided skullcap informed him that the rabbi and his family had gone off to the spas. Dr. Fischelson had other old friends in town, but he found no one at home. His feet ached from so much walking; black and green spots appeared before his eyes and he felt faint. He stopped and waited for the giddiness to pass. The passersby jostled him. A dark-eyed high-school girl tried to give him a coin. Although the war had just started, soldiers eight abreast were marching in full battle dress; the men were covered with dust and were sunburned. Canteens were strapped to their sides, and they wore rows of bullets across their chests. The bayonets on their rifles gleamed with a cold green light. They sang with mournful voices. Along with the men came cannons, each pulled by eight horses; their blind muzzles breathed gloomy terror. Dr. Fischelson felt nauseous. His stomach ached; his intestines seemed about to turn themselves inside out. Cold sweat appeared on his face.

"I'm dying," he thought. "This is the end." Nevertheless, he did manage to drag himself home where he lay down on the iron cot and remained, panting and gasping. He must have dozed off because he imagined that he was in his home town, Tishevetz. He had a sore throat, and his mother was busy wrapping a stocking stuffed with hot salt around his neck. He could hear talk going on in the house; something about a candle and about how a frog had bitten him. He wanted to go out into the street, but they wouldn't let him because a Catholic procession was passing by. Men in long robes, holding double-edged axes in their hands, were intoning in Latin as they sprinkled holy water. Crosses gleamed; sacred pictures waved in the air. There was an odor of incense and corpses. Suddenly the sky turned a burning red and the whole world started to burn. Bells were ringing; people rushed madly about. Flocks of birds flew overhead, screeching. Dr. Fischelson awoke with a start. His body was covered with sweat, and his throat was now actually sore. He tried to meditate about his extraordinary dream, to find its rational connection with what was happening to him and to comprehend it *sub specie aeternitatis,* but none of it made sense. "Alas, the brain is a receptacle for nonsense," Dr. Fischelson thought.

And he once more closed his eyes; once more he dozed; once more he dreamt.

The eternal laws, apparently, had not yet ordained Dr. Fischelson's end.

There was a door to the left of Dr. Fischelson's attic room which opened off a dark corridor cluttered with boxes and baskets in which the odor of fried onions and laundry soap was always present. Behind this door lived a spinster whom the neighbors called Black Dobbe. Dobbe was tall and lean, and as black as a baker's shovel. She had a broken nose and there was a mustache on her upper lip. She spoke with the hoarse voice of a man, and she wore men's shoes. For years Black Dobbe had sold breads, rolls, and bagels which she had bought from the baker at the gate of the house. But one day she and the baker had quarreled, and she had moved her business to the market place, and now she dealt in what were called "wrinklers," which was a synonym for cracked eggs. Black Dobbe had no luck with men. Twice she had been engaged to bakers' apprentices, but in both instances they had returned the engagement contract to her. Some time afterward she had received an engagement contract from an old man, a glazier who claimed that he was divorced, but it had later come to light that he still had a wife. Black Dobbe had a cousin in America, a shoemaker, and repeatedly she boasted that this cousin was sending her passage, but she remained in Warsaw. She was constantly being teased by the women who would say, "There's no hope for you,

Dobbe. You're fated to die an old maid." Dobbe always answered, "I don't intend to be a slave for any man. Let them all rot."

That afternoon Dobbe received a letter from America. Generally she would go to Leizer the Tailor and have him read it to her. However, that day Leizer was out, and so Dobbe thought of Dr. Fischelson, whom the other tenants considered a convert since he never went to prayer. She knocked on the door of the doctor's room, but there was no answer. "The heretic is probably out," Dobbe thought. Nevertheless, she knocked once more, and this time the door moved slightly. She pushed her way in and stood there frightened. Dr. Fischelson lay fully clothed on his bed; his face was as yellow as wax; his Adam's apple stuck out prominently; his beard pointed upward. Dobbe screamed; she was certain that he was dead, but—no—his body moved. Dobbe picked up a glass which stood on the table, ran into the corridor, filled the glass with water from the faucet, hurried back, and threw the water into the face of the unconscious man. Dr. Fischelson shook his head and opened his eyes.

"What's wrong with you?" Dobbe asked. "Are you sick?"

"Thank you very much. No."

"Do you have a family? I'll call them."

"No family," Dr. Fischelson said.

Dobbe wanted to fetch the barber from across the street, but Dr. Fischelson signified that he didn't wish the barber's assistance. Since Dobbe was not going to the market that day, no "wrinklers" being available, she decided to do a good deed. She assisted the sick man to get off the bed and smoothed down the blanket. Then she undressed Dr. Fischelson and prepared some soup for him on the kerosene stove. The sun never entered Dobbe's room, but here squares of sunlight shimmered on the faded walls. The floor was painted red. Over the bed hung a picture of a man who was wearing a broad frill around his neck and had long hair. "Such an old fellow and yet he keeps his place so nice and clean," Dobbe thought approvingly. Dr. Fischelson asked for the *Ethics,* and she gave it to him disapprovingly. She was certain it was a gentile prayer book. Then she began bustling about, brought in a pail of water, swept the floor. Dr. Fischelson ate; after he had finished, he was much stronger, and Dobbe asked him to read her the letter.

He read it slowly, the paper trembling in his hands. It came from New York, from Dobbe's cousin. Once more he wrote that he was about to send her a "really important letter" and a ticket to America. By now Dobbe knew the story by heart, and she helped the old man decipher her cousin's scrawl. "He's lying," Dobbe said. "He forgot about me a long time ago." In the evening, Dobbe came again. A candle in a brass holder was burning on the chair next to the bed. Reddish shadows trembled on the walls and ceiling. Dr. Fischelson sat propped up in bed, reading a book. The candle threw a golden light on his forehead, which seemed as if cleft in two. A bird had flown in through the window and was perched on the table. For a moment Dobbe was frightened. This man made her think of witches, of black mirrors and corpses wandering around at night and terrifying women. Nevertheless, she took a few steps toward him and inquired, "How are you? Any better?"

"A little, thank you."

"Are you really a convert?" she asked, although she wasn't quite sure what the word meant.

"Me, a convert? No, I'm a Jew like any other Jew," Dr. Fischelson answered.

The doctor's assurances made Dobbe feel more at home. She found the bottle of kerosene and lit the stove, and after that she fetched a glass of milk from her room and began cooking kashe. Dr. Fischelson continued to study the *Ethics,* but that evening he could make no sense of the theorems and proofs with their many references to axioms and definitions and other theorems. With trembling hand he raised the book to his eyes and read, "The idea of each modification of the human body does not involve adequate knowledge of the human body itself. . . . The idea of each modification of the human mind does not involve adequate knowledge of the human mind."

Dr. Fischelson was certain he would die any day now. He made out his will, leaving all of his books and manuscripts to the synagogue library. His clothing and furniture would go to Dobbe since she had taken care of him. But death did not come. Rather his health improved. Dobbe returned to her business in the market, but she visited the old man several times a day, prepared soup for him, left him a glass of tea, and told him news of the war. The Germans had occupied Kalish, Bendin, and Cestechow, and they were marching on Warsaw. People said that on a particularly quiet morning, one could hear the rumblings of the cannon. Dobbe reported that the casualties were heavy. "They're falling like flies," she said. "What a terrible misfortune for the women."

She couldn't explain why, but the old man's attic room attracted her. She liked to remove the gold-rimmed books from the bookcase, dust them, and then air them on the window sill. She would climb the few steps to the window and look out through the telescope. She also enjoyed talking to Dr. Fischelson. He told her about Switzerland where he had studied, of the great cities he had passed through, of the high mountains that were covered with snow even in the summer. His father had been a rabbi, he said, and before he, Dr. Fischelson, had become a student, he had attended a yeshiva. She asked him how many languages he knew, and it turned out that he could speak and write Hebrew, Russian, German, and French, in addition to Yiddish. He also knew Latin. Dobbe was astonished that such an educated man should live in an attic room on Market Street. But what amazed her most of all was that, although he had the title "Doctor," he couldn't write prescriptions. "Why don't you become a real doctor?" she would ask him. "I am a doctor," he would answer. "I'm just not a physician." "What kind of a doctor?" "A doctor of philosophy." Although she had no idea of what this meant, she felt it must be very important. "Oh, my blessed mother," she would say, "where did you get such a brain?"

Then one evening after Dobbe had given him his crackers and his glass of tea with milk, he began questioning her about where she came from, who her parents were, and why she never married. Dobbe was surprised. No one had ever asked her such questions. She told him her story in a quiet voice and stayed until eleven o'clock. Her father had been a porter at the kosher butcher shops. Her mother had plucked chickens in the slaughterhouse. The family had lived in a cellar at No. 19 Market Street. When she was ten, she had become a maid. The man she had worked for had been a fence who bought stolen goods from thieves on the square. Dobbe had had a brother who had gone into the Russian army and had never returned. Her sister had married a coachman in Praga and had died in childbirth. Dobbe told of the battles between the underworld and the revolutionaries in 1905, of blind Ichte and his gang and how they collected protection money from the stores, of the thugs who attacked young boys and girls out on Saturday afternoon strolls if they were not paid money for security. She also spoke of the pimps who drove about in carriages and abducted women to be sold in Buenos Aires. Dobbe swore that some men had even sought to inveigle her into a brothel, but that she had run away. She complained of a thousand evils done to her. She had been robbed; her boy friend had been stolen; a competitor had once poured a pint of kerosene into her basket of bagels; her own cousin, the shoemaker, had cheated her out of a hundred rubles before he had left for America. Dr. Fischelson listened to her attentively. He asked her questions, then shook his head, and grunted.

"Well, do you believe in God?" he finally asked her.

"I don't know," she answered. "Do you?"

"Yes; I believe."

"Then why don't you go to a synagogue?" she asked.

"God is everywhere," he replied. "In the synagogue. In the market place. In this very room. We ourselves are parts of God."

"Don't say such things," Dobbe said, turning away. "You frighten me."

She left the room, and Dr. Fischelson was certain she had gone to bed. But he wondered why she had not said good night. "I probably drove her away with my philosophy," he thought. The very next moment he heard her footsteps. She came in carrying a pile of clothing like a peddler.

"I wanted to show you these," she said. "They're my trousseau."

And she began to spread out, on the chair, dresses—woolen, silk, velvet. Taking each dress up in turn, she held it to her body. She gave him an account of every item in her trousseau—underwear, shoes, stockings.

"I'm not wasteful," she said. "I'm a saver. I have enough money to go to America."

Then she was silent and her face turned brick-red. She looked at Dr. Fischelson out of the corners of her eyes, timidly, inquisitively. Dr. Fischelson's body suddenly began to shake as if he had the chills. He said, "Very nice, beautiful things." His brow furrowed and he pulled at his beard with two fingers. A sad smile appeared on his toothless mouth and his large fluttering eyes, gazing into the distance through the attic window, also smiled sadly.

The day that Black Dobbe came to the rabbi's chambers and announced that she was to marry Dr. Fischelson, the rabbi's wife thought she had gone mad. But the news had already reached Leizer the Tailor, and had spread to the bakery, as well as to other shops. There were those who thought that the "old maid" was very lucky; the doctor, they said, had a vast hoard of money. But there were others who took the view that he was a run-down degenerate who would give her syphilis. Although Dr. Fischelson had insisted that the wedding be a small, quiet one, a host of guests assembled in the rabbi's rooms. The baker's apprentices, who generally went about barefoot and in their underwear, with paper bags on the top of their heads, now put on light-colored suits, straw hats, yellow shoes, gaudy ties, and they brought with them huge cakes and pans filled with cookies. They had even managed to find a bottle of vodka, although liquor was forbidden in wartime. When the bride and groom entered the rabbi's chamber, a murmur arose from the crowd. The women could not believe their eyes. The woman that they saw was not one they had known. Dobbe wore a wide-brimmed hat which was amply adorned with cherries, grapes, and plums, and the dress that she had on was of white silk and was equipped with a train; on her feet were high-heeled shoes, gold in color, and from her thin neck hung a string of imitation pearls. Nor was this all: her fingers sparkled with rings and glittering stones. Her face was veiled. She looked almost like one of those rich brides who was married in the Vienna Hall. The baker's apprentices whistled mockingly. As for Dr. Fischelson, he was wearing his black coat and broad-toed shoes. He was scarcely able to walk; he was leaning on Dobbe. When he saw the crowd from the doorway, he became frightened and began to retreat, but Dobbe's former employer approached him saying, "Come in, come in, bridegroom. Don't be bashful. We are all brethren now."

The ceremony proceeded according to the law. The rabbi, in a worn satin gabardine, wrote the marriage contract and then had the bride and groom touch his handkerchief as a token of agreement; the rabbi wiped the point of the pen on his skullcap. Several porters, who had been called from the street to make up the quorum, supported the canopy. Dr. Fischelson put on a white robe as a reminder of the day of his death, and Dobbe walked around him seven times as custom required. The light from the braided candles flickered on the walls. The shadows wavered. Having poured wine into a goblet, the rabbi chanted the benedictions in a sad melody. Dobbe uttered only a single cry. As for the other women, they took out their lace handkerchiefs and stood with them in their hands, grimacing. When the baker's boys began to whisper wisecracks to each other, the rabbi put a finger to his lips and murmured, *"Eh, nu oh,"* as a sign that talking was forbidden. The moment came to slip the wedding ring on the bride's finger, but the bridegroom's hand started to tremble and he had trouble locating Dobbe's index finger. The next thing, according to custom, was the smashing of the glass, but though Dr. Fischelson kicked the goblet several times, it remained unbroken. The girls lowered their heads, pinched each other gleefully, and giggled. Finally one of the apprentices struck the goblet with his heel and it shattered. Even the rabbi could not restrain a smile. After the ceremony the guests drank vodka and ate cookies. Dobbe's former employer came up to Dr. Fischelson and said, *"Mazel tov,* bridegroom. Your luck should be as good as your wife." "Thank you, thank you," Dr. Fischelson murmured, "but I don't look forward to any luck." He was anxious to return as quickly as possible to his attic room. He felt a pressure in his stomach and his chest ached. His face had become greenish. Dobbe had suddenly become angry. She pulled back her veil and called out to the crowd, "What are you laughing at? This isn't a show." And without picking up the cushion cover in which the gifts were wrapped, she returned with her husband to their rooms on the fifth floor.

Dr. Fischelson lay down on the freshly made bed in his room and began reading the *Ethics.* Dobbe had gone back to her own room. The doctor had explained to her that he was an old man, that he was sick and without strength. He had promised her nothing. Nevertheless she returned wearing a silk nightgown, slippers with pompoms, and with her hair hanging down over her shoulders. There was a smile on her face, and she was bashful and hesitant. Dr. Fischelson trembled, and the *Ethics* dropped from his hands. The candle went out. Dobbe groped for Dr. Fischelson in the dark and kissed his mouth. "My dearest husband," she whispered to him. *"Mazel tov."*

What happened that night could be called a miracle. If Dr. Fischelson hadn't been convinced that every occurrence is in accordance with the laws of nature, he would have thought that Black Dobbe had bewitched him. Powers long dormant awakened in him. Although he had had only a sip of the benediction wine, he was as if intoxicated. He kissed Dobbe and spoke to her of love. Long forgotten quotations from Klopstock, Lessing, Goethe rose to his lips. The pressures and aches stopped. He embraced Dobbe, pressed her to himself, was again a man as in his youth. Dobbe was faint with delight; crying, she murmured things to him in a Warsaw slang which he did not understand. Later, Dr. Fischelson slipped off into the deep sleep young men know. He dreamt that he was in Switzerland and that he was climbing mountains—running, falling, flying. At dawn he opened his eyes; it seemed to him that someone had blown into his ears. Dobbe was snoring. Dr. Fischelson quietly got out of bed. In his long nightshirt he approached the window, walked up the steps and looked out in wonder. Market Street was asleep, breathing with a deep stillness. The gas lamps were flickering. The black shutters on the stores were fastened with iron bars. A cool breeze was blowing. Dr. Fischelson looked up at the sky. The black arch was thickly sown with stars: there were green, red, yellow, blue stars; there were large ones and small ones, winking and steady ones. There were those that were clustered in dense groups and those that were alone. In the higher spheres, apparently, little notice was taken of the fact that a certain Dr. Fischelson had, in his declining days, married someone called Black Dobbe. Seen from above, even the Great War was nothing but a temporary play of the modes. The myriads of fixed stars continued to travel their destined courses in unbounded space. The comets, planets, satellites, asteroids kept circling these shining centers. Worlds were born and died in cosmic upheavals. In the chaos of nebulae, primeval matter was being formed. Now and again a star tore loose and swept across the sky, leaving behind it a fiery streak. It was the month of August when there are showers of meteors. Yes, the divine substance was extended and had neither beginning nor end; it was absolute, indivisible, eternal, without duration, infinite in its attributes. Its waves and bubbles danced in the universal caldron, seething with change, following the unbroken chain of causes and effects, and he, Dr. Fischelson, with his unavoidable fate, was part of this. The doctor closed his eyelids and allowed the breeze to cool the sweat on his forehead and stir the hair of his beard. He breathed deeply of the midnight air, supported his shaky hands on the window sill and murmured, dreamily, "Divine Spinoza, forgive me. I have become a fool."

[October 1961]

PHILIP ROTH

Very Happy Poems

She grabbed a yellow pad that was on the floor beside the books and ran off with it to the kitchen; she sat down at the table and so excited was she that she simply swept her hand across the table, brushing away the breakfast crumbs. She would attend to them later—they were unimportant. She had never written a poem before (though sick and in bed in Reading she had tried a story), but the idea of poetry had always stirred her. Toward certain poems she had particularly tender feelings. She liked *To His Coy Mistress* and she loved *Ode to a Nightingale; Ode on Melancholy* too. She liked all of Keats, in fact; at least the ones that were anthologized.

She wrote on the pad:

Already with thee! Tender is the night

She liked *Tender Is the Night,* which of course wasn't a poem. She identified with Nicole; in college she had identified with Rosemary. She would have to read it over again. After Faulkner she would read all of Fitzgerald, even the books she had read before. But poetry. What other poems did she like?

She wrote:

Come live with me and be my love,
And we will all the pleasures prove.

Then directly below:

The expense of spirit in a waste of shame
Is lust in action—and till action, lust
Is perjured, murderous. . . .

She could not remember the rest. Those few lines, however, had always filled her with a headlong passion, even though she had to admit never having come precisely to grips with the meaning. Still, the sound.

She went on writing, with recollections of her three years of college, with her heart heaving and sighing appropriately.

Sabrina fair
Listen where thou are sitting
Under the glassy wave—
And I am black but o my soul is white
How sweetly flows
The liquefaction of her clothes
At last he rose, and twitch'd his mantle blue
Tomorrow to fresh woods and pastures new.
I am! Yet what I am none cares or knows
My friends forsake me like a memory lost,
I am the self-consumer of my woes.

And who had written those last lines? Keats again? What was the difference who had written them? She hadn't.

Oh, if she could sculpt, if she could paint, if she could write something! Anything—

The doorbell rang.

A *friend!* She ran to the door, pulling her belt tight around her. All I need is a friend to take my mind off myself and tell me how silly I'm being. A girl friend with whom I can go shopping and have coffee, in whom I can confide.

She opened the door. It was not a friend because she had had little opportunity, what with her job, her night classes, and generally watching out for herself, to make any friends since coming to Chicago. In the doorway was a pleasant-looking fellow of thirty or thirty-five—and simply from the thinness of his hair, the fragile swelling of his brown eyes, the narrowness of his body, the neatness of his clothes, she knew he would have a kind and modest manner. One was supposed to be leery of opening the door all the way in this neighborhood; Paul cautioned her to peer out over the latch first, but she was not sorry now that she had forgotten. You just couldn't distrust everybody and remain human.

His hat in one hand, a brief case in the other, the fellow asked, "Are you Mrs. Herz?"

"Yes." All at once she was feeling solid and necessary. The "Mrs.

Herz" had done it. Libby had, of course, a great talent for spiritual resurrection; when her fortunes finally changed, she knew they would change overnight. She did not really believe in unhappiness and privation and never would; it was an opinion, unfortunately, that did not make life any easier for her.

"I'm Marty Rosen," the young man said. "I wonder if I can come in. I'm from the Jewish Children's League."

Her moods came and went in flashes; now elation faded. Rosen smiled in what seemed to Libby both an easygoing and powerful way; clearly he was not on his first mission for a nonprofit organization. Intimidated, she stepped back and let him in, thinking: one *should* look over the latch first. Not only was she in her bathrobe (which hadn't been dry-cleaned for two years), but she was barefoot. "We didn't think you were coming," Libby said, "until next week. My husband isn't here. I'm sorry—didn't we get the date right? We've been busy, I didn't check the calendar—"

"That's all right," Rosen said. He looked down a moment, and there was nowhere she could possibly stick her feet. Oh, they should at least have laid the rug. So *what* if it was somebody else's! Now the floor stretched off, bare and cold, clear to the walls. "I will be coming around again next week," Rosen said. "I thought I'd drop in this morning for a few minutes, just to say hello."

"If you'd have called, my husband might have been able to be here."

"If we can work it out," Rosen was saying, "we do like to have sort of an informal session anyway, before the formal scheduled meeting."

"Oh, yes," said Libby, and her thoughts turned to her bedroom.

"—see the prospective parents—" he smiled—"in their natural habitat."

"Definitely, yes." The whole world was in conspiracy, even against her pettiest plans. "Let's sit down. Here." She pointed to the sofa. "Let me take your things."

"I hope I didn't wake you."

"God, no," she said, realizing it was almost ten. "I've been up for hours." After these words were out, they didn't seem right either.

With his topcoat over her arm, she went off to the bedroom, though by way of the sofa, where she slid into her slippers as glidingly as she could manage. She walked down the hall, shut the bedroom door, and then, having flung Mr. Rosen's stuff across a chair, she frantically set about whipping the sheets and blankets into some kind of shape. The clock on the half-painted dresser said not ten o'clock, but quarter to eleven. Up for hours! Still in her night clothes! She yanked at the sheets, hoisted the mattress (which seemed to outweigh her), and caught her fingernail in the springs. She ran to the other side, tugged on the blankets, but alas, too hard—they came slithering over at her and then were on the floor. Oh, Christ! She threw them back on the bed, raced around again—but five whole minutes had elapsed. At the dresser she pulled a comb through her hair, and came back into the living room, having slammed shut the bedroom door behind her. Mr. Rosen was standing before the Utrillo print. Beside him, their books were piled on the floor. "We're getting some bricks and boards for the books." He did not answer. "That's Utrillo," she said.

He did not answer again.

Of course it was Utrillo. Everybody knew Utrillo—that was the trouble. "It's corny, I suppose," said Libby. "My husband doesn't like the Impressionists that much either—but we've had it, I've had it, since college—and we carry it around and I guess we hang it whenever we move—not that we move that much, but, you know."

Turning, he said, "I suppose you like it, well, for sentimental reasons."

"Well . . . I just like it. Yes, sentiment—but aesthetics, of course, too."

She did not know what more to say. They both were smiling. He seemed like a perfectly agreeable man, and there was no reason for her to be giving him so frozen an expression. However, she soon discovered that the smile she wore she was apparently going to have to live with a while longer; the muscles of her face were working on their own.

"Yes," she said. "And—and this is our apartment. Please, sit down. I'll make some coffee."

"It's a very big apartment," he said, coming back to the sofa. "Spacious."

What did he mean—they didn't have enough furniture? "Well, yes—no," replied Libby. "There's this room and then down the hall is the kitchen. And my husband's study—"

Rosen, having already taken his trouser creases in hand, now rose and asked pleasantly, "May I look around?"

Libby did not believe that the idea had simply popped into his head. But he was so smooth-faced and soft-spoken and well-groomed, she was not yet prepared to believe him a sneak. He inclined toward her whenever she spoke, and, though it unnerved her some, she had preferred up till now to think of it as a kind of sympathetic lean.

"Oh, do," Libby said. "You'll have to excuse us, though; we were out to dinner last night. Not that we go out to dinner that much—however, we were out to dinner—" they proceeded down the hall and were in the kitchen—"and," she confessed, "I didn't get around to the dishes. . . . But," she said, cognizant of the sympathetic lean, though doing her best to avoid the sympathetic eyes, "this is the kitchen."

"Nice," he said. "Very nice."

There were the breakfast crumbs on the floor around the table. All she could think to say was, "It needs a paint job, of course."

"Very nice. Uh-huh."

He sounded genuine enough, she supposed. She went on. "We have plenty of hot water, of course, and everything."

"Does the owner live on the premises?"

"Pardon?"

"Does the owner of the building live on the premises?" he asked.

"It's an agency that manages the place," she said nervously.

"I was only wondering." He walked to the rear of the kitchen, crunching toast particles. Out the back window, through which he paused to look, there was no green yard. "There was just—" he lifted a hand to indicate that it was nothing—"a bulb out in the hallway, coming up. I wondered if the owner. . . ."

He dwindled off, and again she didn't know what to say. The bulb had been out since their arrival; she had never even questioned it—it came with the house. "You see," Libby said, "there are two Negro families in the building—" *What!* I don't have anything against Negroes! But what if the agency does—Why do I keep bringing up Negroes all the time! "And," she said, blindly, "the bulb went out last night, you see. My husband's going to pick one up today. Right now he's teaching. We don't like to bother the agency for little things. You know. . . ." But she could not tell whether he knew or not; he was leaning her way, but what of it? He turned and started back down the hall. Libby shut her eyes. I must stop lying. I must not lie again. He will be able to tell when I lie. They don't want liars for mothers, and they're perfectly right. Tell the truth. You have nothing to be ashamed of.

"My husband is a writer, aside from being a teacher," she said, running down the hall and slithering by Rosen, "and this—" she turned the knob to Paul's room, praying—"is his study."

Thank God. It was orderly; though there was not much that could be disordered. In the entire room—whose two tall winter-stained windows were set no further than ten feet from the apartment building next door—there was only a desk and a desk lamp, a chair and a typewriter, and a wastepaper basket. But the window shades were even and all the papers on the desk piled neatly. God bless Paul.

"My husband works in here." She flipped on the overhead light, but the room seemed to get no brighter; if anything, dingier. Whose fault was it that the sun couldn't come around that way? *They* hadn't constructed the building next door. "He's writing a novel," Libby told Mr. Rosen.

Rosen took quite an interest in that too. "Oh, yes? That must be some undertaking."

"Well, it's not finished yet—it is an undertaking, all right. But he's working on it. He works very hard. However, this," she said quickly, "this, of course, would be the baby's room. Will be the baby's room." She blushed. "Well, when we have a baby this will be—" Even while she spoke she was oppressed by the barren feebleness of the room. Where would a baby sleep? From what window would the lovely, healthy, natural light fall onto a baby's cheek? Where would one get the baby's crib? Catholic Salvage?

"Where will your husband work on his novel then?"

"I—" she wouldn't lie—"I don't know. We haven't talked about it. This has all happened very quickly. Our decision to have a baby."

"Of course."

"Not that we haven't thought about it—you see, it's not a problem. He can work anywhere. The bedroom. Anywhere. I'll discuss it with him tonight, if you like."

Rosen made a self-effacing gesture with his hands. "Oh, look, I don't care. That's all up to you folks." Even if there was something professional about his gentleness, she liked him for trying to put her at her ease. (Though that meant he knew about her nervousness; later he would mull over motives.) She had no real reason to be uneasy or overexcited or ashamed. Marty Rosen wouldn't kill her, wouldn't insult her—he wasn't even that much older than she—and what right, damn it, did he have to come unannounced! *That* was the trouble! What kind of business was this natural habitat business! *They have no right to trick people*—she was thinking, and the next thing she was opening the door to their own bedroom, and there was the bed, and the disheveled linens, and the half-painted dresser, and there were Paul's pajamas on the floor. There, in fact, was Rosen's coat, half on the floor. She closed the door and they went back into the living room.

"Actually," she said, addressing the back of his suit as they moved toward the sofa. "I was trying to write a poem. . . ."

"Really? A poem?" He sat down, and then instantly was leaning forward, his arms on his legs and his hands clasped, and he was smiling. It was as though nothing he had seen up until now meant a thing; as though there was an entirely different set of rules called into play when the prospective mother turned out to be a poet. "You write, too, do you?"

"Well," said Libby, "no." Then she did not so much sit down into their one easy chair as capitulate into it. Why had she told Rosen about the poem? What did that explain to anybody—did writing poetry excuse crumbs on the floor? It was the truth, but that was all it was. They may want poets for mothers, she thought, but they sure as hell don't want slobs.

"Well," said Rosen cheerily, "it's a nice-sized apartment." It seemed impossible to disappoint him. "How long have you been here, would you say?"

"Not long," the girl answered. "A few months. Since October."

Rosen was opening his brief case. "Do you mind if I take down a few things?"

"Oh, no, go right ahead." But her heart moved earthward. "We're going to paint, of course, as soon as—soon." Stop saying of course! "When everything's settled. When I get some time, I'll begin." The remark did not serve to make her any less conscious of her bathrobe and slippers. "You see," she went on, for Rosen had a way of listening even when no one was speaking—"I was working. I worked at the university. However I wasn't feeling well. Paul said I had better quit."

"That's too bad. Are you better now?"

"I'm fine. I feel fine—" she assured him. "I'm not pale, or sick, I just have very white skin—" Even as she spoke the white skin turned red.

Rosen smiled his smile. "I hope it wasn't serious."

"It wasn't anything really. I might have gotten quite sick—" *Why isn't Paul home? What good is he if he isn't here now?* "I had a kidney condition," she explained, starting in again. "It's why the doctors say I shouldn't have a baby. It would be too strong a risk. You see, I'm the one who can't have a baby. Not my husband."

"Well, there are many many couples that can't have babies, believe me."

His remark was probably intended to brace her, but tears nearly came to her eyes when she said, "Isn't that too bad. . . ."

He took a paper from his case and pushed out the tip of a ballpoint pen. The click sounded to Libby very official. She pulled herself up straight in her chair and waited for the questions. Rosen asked nothing; he jotted some words on the paper. Libby waited. He glanced up. "Just the number of rooms and so forth," he said.

"Oh, certainly. Go right ahead. I've just been having—" she yawned— "my lazy morning, you know—" she tried to stretch, but stifled the impulse halfway, she by no means wanted for a moment to appear in any way loose or provocative—"not making the bed or anything, just taking the day off, just doing nothing. With a baby, of course, it would be different."

"Oh, yes," His brow furrowed, even as he wrote. "Children are a responsibility."

"There's no doubt about that." And she could not help it—she did not care if that was so much simple ass-kissing. At least, at last, she'd said the right thing. All she had to do was to keep saying the right thing, and get him out of here, and the next time Paul would be home. There were so many Jewish families wanting babies, and so few Jewish babies, and so what if she was obsequious. As long as: one, she didn't lie; and two, she said the right thing. "They are a responsibility," she said. "We certainly know that."

"Your husband's an instructor then, isn't that right, in the college?"

"In English. He teaches English and he teaches Humanities."

"And he's got a Ph.D?"

He seemed to take it so for granted—wasn't he writing it down already?—that she suffered a moment of temptation. "An M.A. He's working on his Ph.D. Actually, he's just finishing up on it. He'll have it very soon, of course. Don't worry about that. Excuse me—I'm sorry, I don't mean to sound so instructive, I suppose I'm just a little nervous." She smiled, sweetly and spontaneously—a second later she thought that she must have charmed him. At least if he were someone else, if he were Gabe say, he would have been charmed; but this fellow seemed only to become more attentive. "I only meant," Libby said, "that I think Paul has a splendid career before him. Even if I am his wife." And didn't that have the ring of truth about it? Hadn't her words conveyed all the respect and admiration she had for Paul—and too all the love she still felt for him, and would feel forever? It had been a nice wifely remark uttered in a nice wifely way—why then, wasn't Rosen *moved* by it? Did he not see what a dedicated, doting, loving mother she would be?

"I'm sure he has," Rosen said, and he might just as well have been attesting to a belief in the process of evolution.

But one had to remember that he was here in an official capacity; you couldn't expect him to gush. He must see dozens of families every day and hear dozens of wives attest to their love for their husbands. He could probably even distinguish those who meant it, from those who didn't, from those who were no longer quite so sure. She tried then to stifle her disappointment, though it was clear to her she would probably not be able to get off so solid a remark again.

Rosen had set his paper down now. "And so you just—well, live here," he said, tossing the remark out with a little roll of the hands, "and see your friends, and your husband teaches and writes, and you keep house—"

"As I said, today is just my lazy day—"

"—and have a normal young people's life. That's about it then, would you say?"

"Well—" He seemed to have left something out, though she couldn't put her finger on it. "Yes. I suppose that's it."

He nodded. "And you go to the movies," he said, "and see an occasional play, and have dinner out once in a while, I suppose, and take walks—" his hands went round with each activity mentioned— "and try to put a few dollars in the bank, and have little spats, I suppose—"

She couldn't stand it—she was ready to scream. "We read, of

course." Though that wasn't precisely what she felt had been omitted, it was something.

He didn't seem at all to mind having been interrupted. "Are you interested in reading?"

"Well, yes. We read."

He considered further what she had said; or perhaps only waited for her to go on. He said finally, "What kind of books do you like best? Do you like fiction, do you like non-fiction, do you like biographies of famous persons, do you like how-to-do-it books, do you like who-done-its? What kind of books would you say you liked to read?"

"Books." She became flustered. "All kinds."

He leaned back now. "What books have you read recently?" To the question, he gave nothing more nor less than it had ever had before in the history of human conversation and its impasses.

It was her turn now to wave hands at the air. "God, I can't remember. It really slips my mind." She felt the color of her face changing again. "We're always reading something though—and well, Faulkner. Of course I read *The Sound and the Fury* in college, and *Light in August,* but I've been planning to read all of Faulkner, you know, chronologically. To get a sense of development."

His reply was slow in coming; he might have been waiting for her to break down and give the name of one thin little volume that she had read in the last year. "That sounds like a wonderful project, like a very worthwhile project."

In a shabby way she felt relieved.

"And your poetry," he asked, "what kind of poetry do you write?"

"What?"

"Do you write nature poems; do you write, oh, I don't know, rhymes; do you write little jingles? What kind of poetry would you say you write?"

Her eyes widened. "Well, I'm sorry, I don't write poetry," she said, as though he had stumbled into the wrong house.

"Oh, *I'm* sorry," he said, leaning forward to apologize. "I misunderstood."

"Ohhhh," Libby cried. "Oh, just this morning you mean."

Even Rosen seemed relieved. It was the first indication she had that the interview was wearing him down too. "Yes," he said, "this morning. Was that a nature poem, or, I don't know, philosophical? You know, your thoughts and so forth. I don't mean to be a nuisance, Mrs. Herz," he said, spreading his fingers over his foulard tie. "I thought we might talk about your interests. I don't want to pry, and if you—"

"Oh, yes, surely. Poetry, well, certainly," she said in a light voice.

"And this poem this morning, for instance—"

"Oh, that. I didn't know you meant that. That was—mostly my thoughts. I guess just a poem," she said, hating him, "about my thoughts."

"That sounds interesting." He looked down at the floor. "It's very interesting meeting somebody who writes poetry. Speaking for myself, I think, as a matter of fact, that there's entirely too much television and violence these days, that somebody who writes poetry would be an awfully good influence on a child."

"Thank you," Libby said softly. And now she didn't hate him. She closed her eyes—not the two shiny dark ones that Rosen could see. She closed her eyes, and she was back in that garden, and it was dusk, and her husband was with her, and in her arms was a child to whom she would later, by the crib, recite some of her poetry. "I think so too," she said.

"What makes poetry a fascinating subject," she heard Rosen saying, "is that people express all kinds of things in it."

"Oh, yes, it is fascinating. I'm very fond of poetry. I like Keats very much," and she spoke passionately now (as though her vibrancy concerning verse would make up for the books she couldn't remember having read recently). "And I like John Donne a great deal too, though I know he's the vogue, but still I do. And I like Yeats. I don't know a lot of Yeats, that's true, but I like some of him, what I know. I suppose they're mostly anthologized ones," she confessed, "but they're awfully good. 'The worst are full of passionate intensity, the best lack all conviction.' " A second later she said, "I'm afraid I've gotten that backward, or wrong, but I do like that poem, when I have it in front of me."

"Hmmmm," Rosen said, listening even after she had finished. "You seem really to be able to commit them to memory. That must be a satisfaction."

"It is."

"And how about your own poems? I mean would you say

they're, oh, I don't know, happy poems or unhappy poems? You know, people write all kinds of poems, happy poems, unhappy poems—what do you consider yours to be?"

"Happy poems," said Libby. "Very happy poems."

At the front door, while Mr. Rosen went around in a tiny circle as he wiggled into his coat, he said, "I suppose you know Rabbi Kuvin."

"Rabbi who?"

He was facing her, fastening buttons. "Bernie Kuvin. He's the rabbi over in the new synagogue. Down by the lake."

Libby urged up into her face what she hoped would be an untroubled look. "No. We don't."

Rosen put on his hat. "I thought you might know him." He looked down and over himself, as though he had something more important on his mind anyway, like whether he was wearing his shoes or not.

And Libby understood. "No, no, we don't go around here to the synagogue. We're New Yorkers, originally that is—we go when we're in New York. We have a rabbi in New York. You're right, though," she said, her voice beginning to reflect the quantity and quality of her hope, or hopelessness. "You're perfectly right—" her eyes teary now—"religion is very important—"

"I don't know. I suppose it's up to the individual couple—"

"Oh no, oh no," Libby said, and she was practically pushing the door shut in his face, and she was weeping, "oh no, you're perfectly right, you're a hundred-per-cent right, religion is very important to a child. But—" she shook and shook her tired head—"but my husband and I don't believe a God damn bit of it!"

And the door was closed, only by inches failing to chop off Rosen's coattails. She did not move away. She merely slid down right in the draft, right on the cold floor, and oh the hell with it. She sat there with her legs outstretched and her head in her hands. She was crying again. What had she done? *Why?* How could she possibly tell Paul? Why did she cry all the time? It was all wrong— *she* was all wrong. If only the bed had been made, if only it hadn't been for that stupid poetry writing— She had really ruined things now.

As far as she could see there was only one thing left to do.

Rushing up Michigan Boulevard in the unreasonable sunlight—unreasonable for this frost-bound city—she realized she was going to be late. She had gone into Saks with no intention of buying anything; she had with her only her ten-dollar bill (accumulated with pennies and nickels, then cashed in and hidden away for just such a crisis), and, besides, she knew better. She had simply not wanted to arrive at the office with fifteen minutes to spare. She did not intend to sit there perspiring and flushing, her body's victim. If you show up so very early, it's probably not too unfair of them to assume that you are weak and needy and pathetically anxious. And she happened to know she wasn't. She had been coping with her problems for some time now, and would, if she had to, continue to cope with them on into the future, until they just resolved themselves. She was by no means, she told herself, the most unhappy person in the world.

As a result, she had taken her time looking at sweaters. She had spent several minutes holding up against her a lovely white cashmere with a little tie at the neck. She had left the store (stopping only half a minute to look at a pair of black velveteen slacks) with the clock showing that it still wasn't one o'clock. And even if it had been, she would prefer not to arrive precisely as the big hand and the small hand came together on the hour. They would surely assume you were a compulsive then—which was another thing no one was simply going to *assume* about her.

But it was twelve minutes past the hour now, and even if she weren't a compulsive, she was nevertheless experiencing some of the more characteristic emotions of one. She clutched at her hat—which she had worn not to be warm, but attractive—and raced up the street. Having misjudged the distance, she was still some fifty numbers south of the building she was after. And it was no good to be this late, no good at all; in a way it was so aggressive of her (or defensive?) and God, she wasn't either! She was . . . what?

She passed a jewelry store; a golden clock in the window said fourteen after. She would miss her appointment. Where would she find the courage to make another? Oh, she *was* pathetically anxious—why hadn't she just gone ahead and been it! Why shopping? Clothes! Life was falling apart and she had to worry about velveteen slacks—and without even the money to buy them! She would miss her appointment. Then what? She could leave Paul. It was a mistake to think that he would ever take it upon himself to leave her. It must be she who says good-by to him. Go away. To where?

She ran as fast as she could. The doctor had to see her.

The only beard in the room was on a picture of Freud that hung on the wall beside the desk. Dr. Lumin, himself, was cleanshaven and accentless. What he had were steam-rolled Midwestern vowels and hefty South Chicago consonants, nothing at all that was European. Not that Libby had hung all her hopes on something as inconsequential as a bushy beard or a foreign intonation; nevertheless neither would by any means have shaken her confidence in his wisdom.

The doctor leaned across his desk and took her hand. He was a short, wide man with oversized head and hands. She had imagined before she met him that he would be tall; though momentarily disappointed, she was no less intimidated. He could have been a pygmy, and her hand when it touched his would have been no warmer. He gave her a nice meaty shake and she thought he looked like a butcher. She knew he wouldn't take any nonsense.

"I'm sorry I'm late." There were so many explanations she didn't give any.

"That's all right." He settled back into his chair. "I have someone coming in at two, so we won't have a full hour. Why don't you sit down?"

There was a straight-backed, red-leather chair facing his desk and a brownish leather couch along the wall. She did not know whether she was supposed to know enough to just go over and lie down on the couch and start right in telling her problems. . . . Who had problems anyway? She could not think of one. Except, if she lay down on the couch, should she step out of her shoes first?

Her shoulders drooped. "Where?" she asked finally.

"Wherever you like," he said.

"You won't mind," she said in a thin voice, "if I just sit for today."

He extended one of his hands, and said with a mild kind of force, "Why don't you sit." Oh, he was nice; a little crabby, but nice. She kept her shoes on and sat down in the straight chair.

And her heart took up a sturdy, martial rhythm. She looked

directly across the desk into a pair of grey and, to her, impenetrable eyes. She had had no intention of becoming evasive in his presence; not when she had suffered so in making the appointment. The room, however, was a good deal brighter than she had thought it would be, and on top of her fear settled a thin icing of shyness.

"I stopped off at Saks on the way up. I didn't mean to keep you."

With one of those meat-cutter's hands he waved her apology aside. "I'm interested—look, how did you get my name? For the record." It was the second time that day that she found herself settled down across from a perfect stranger who felt it necessary to be casual with her. . . . Dr. Lumin leaned back in his swivel chair, so that for a moment it looked as though he'd keep on going, and fall backward, sailing clear through the window, but not him. And go ahead, she thought, fall. *There goes Lumin.* . . . "How did you find out about me?" he asked.

With no lessening of her heartbeat, she blushed. It was like living with an idiot whose behavior was unpredictable from one moment to the next: what would this body of hers do then seconds from now? "I heard your name at a party at the University of Chicago." She figured the last would make it all more dignified, less accidental. Otherwise he might take it as an insult, her coming to him so arbitrarily. "My husband teaches at the university," she said.

"It says here—" the doctor was looking at a card—"Victor Honingfeld." His eyes were two nailheads. Would he turn out to be stupid? Did he read those books on the wall or were they just for public relations? She wished she could get up and go.

"Your secretary asked on the phone," she explained, "and I gave Victor's name. He's a colleague of my husband's. I—he mentioned your name in passing, and I remembered it, and when I thought I might like to—try something, I only knew you, so I called. I didn't mean to say that Victor had recommended you. It was just that I heard it—"

Why go on? Why bother? She had insulted him professionally now, she was sure. He would start off disliking her.

"I think," she said quickly, "I'm becoming very selfish."

Swinging back in his chair, his head framed in the silver light, he didn't answer.

"That's really my only big problem, I suppose," said Libby.

"Perhaps it's not even a problem. I suppose you could call it a foible or something along that line. But I thought, if I am *too* selfish, I'd like to talk to somebody. If I'm not, if it turns out it is just some sort of passing thing, circumstances you know, not me, well then I won't worry about it any more. Do you see?"

"Sure," he said, fluttering his eyelashes. He tugged undaintily at one of his fleshy ears and looked down in his lap, waiting. All day people had been waiting on her words. She wished she had been born self-reliant.

"It's been very confusing," she told him. "I suppose moving, a new environment. . . . It's probably a matter of getting used to things. And I'm just being impatient—" Her voice stopped, though not the rhythmic stroking in her breast. She didn't believe she had Lumin's attention. She was boring him. He seemed more interested in his necktie than in her. "Do you want me to lie down?" she asked, her voice quivering with surrender.

His big, raw face—the sharp, bony wedge of nose, the purplish, overdefined lips, those ears, the whole, huge, impressive red thing— tilted up in a patient, skeptical smile. "Look, come on, stop worrying about me. Worry about yourself," he said, almost harshly. "So how long have you been in Chicago, you two?"

She was no longer simply nervous; she was frightened. *You two.* If Paul were to know what she was doing, it would be his final disappointment. "October we came."

"And your husband's a teacher?"

"He teaches English at the university. He also writes."

"What? Books, articles, plays?"

"He's writing a novel now. He's still only a young man."

"And you—what about yourself?"

"I don't write," she said firmly. She was not going to pull her punches this second time. "I don't do anything."

He did not seem astonished. How could he, with that unexpressive butcher's face? He *was* dumb. Of course—it was always a mistake to take your troubles outside your house. You had to figure things out for yourself. *How?* "I was working," she said. "I was secretary to the Dean, and I was going to school, taking some courses at night downtown. But I've had a serious kidney condition."

"Which kind?"

"Nephritis. I almost died."

Lumin moved his head as though he were a clock ticking. "Oh, a nasty thing. . . ."

"Yes," she said. "I think it weakened my condition. Because I get colds, and every stray virus, and since it is really dangerous once you've had a kidney infection, Paul said I should quit my job. And the doctor, the medical doctor—" she regretted instantly having made such a distinction—"said perhaps I shouldn't take classes downtown at night, because of the winter. I suppose I started thinking about myself when I started being sick all the time. I was in bed, and I began to think of myself. Of course I'm sure everyone thinks of himself eighty per cent of the time. But, truly, I was up to about eighty-five."

She looked to see if he had smiled. Wasn't anybody going to be charmed today? Were people simply going to listen? She wondered if *he* found *her* dull. They tried to mask their responses, one expected that, but on the other hand it might be that she was no longer the delightful, bubbly girl she knew she once had been. Well, that's partly why she was here; to somehow get back to what she was. She wanted now to tell him only the truth. "I did become self-concerned, I think," she said. "Was I happy? was I this? was I that? and so forth, until I was self-absorbed. And it's hung on, in a way. Though I suppose what I need is an interest really, something to take my mind off myself. You simply can't go around all day saying I just had an orange, did that make me happy; I just typed a stencil, did that make me happy; because you only make yourself miserable."

The doctor rocked in his chair; he placed his hands on his belly, where it disappeared into his trousers like half a tent. "I don't know," he mumbled. "What, what does your husband think about all this?"

"I don't understand."

"About your going around all day eating oranges and asking yourself if they make you happy."

"I eat," she said, smiling, lying, "the oranges privately."

"Ah, hah." He nodded.

She found herself laughing, just a little. "Yes."

"So—go ahead. How privately? What privately?" He seemed suddenly to be having a good time.

"It's very involved," Libby said. "Complicated."

"I would imagine," Lumin said, a pleasant light in his eye.

"You've got all those pits to worry about." Then he was shooting toward her—he nearly sprang full-grown from his chair. Their faces might as well have been touching, his voice some string she herself had plucked. "Come on, Libby," Lumin said, "what's the trouble?"

For the second time that day, the fiftieth that week, she was at the mercy of her tears. "Everything," she cried. "Every rotten thing. Every rotten, despicable thing. Paul's the trouble—he's just a terrible, terrible trouble to me."

She covered her face and for a full five minutes her forehead shook in the palms of her hands. Secretly she was waiting, but she did not hear Lumin's gruff voice nor feel upon her shoulders anyone's hands. When she finally looked up he was still there.

She pleaded, "Please just psychoanalyze me and straighten me out. I cry so much."

"What about Paul?"

She almost rose from her seat. "He never makes love to me! I get laid once a month!" Some muscle in her—it was her heart—relaxed. Though by no means restored to permanent health, she felt unsprung.

"Well," said Lumin, with authority, "everybody's entitled to get laid more than that. Is this light in your eyes?" He raised an arm and tapped his nail on the bright pane of glass behind him.

"No, no," she said and, for no apparent reason, what she was to say next caused her to sob. "You can see the lake." She tried, however, to put some real effort into pulling herself together. She wanted to stop crying and make sense, but it was the crying that seemed finally to be more to the point than the explanations she began to offer him in the best of faith. "You see, I think I've been in love with somebody else for a very long time. And it isn't Paul's fault. Don't think that. It couldn't be. He's the most honest man, Paul—he's always been terribly good to me. I was a silly college girl, self-concerned and frivolous and unimportant, and brutally typical, and he was the first person I ever wanted to listen to. I used to go on dates, years ago this is, and never listen—just talk. But Paul gave me books to read and he told me thousands of things, and he was—well, he saved me really from being like all those other girls. And he's had the toughest life. Oh, honestly," she said, "my eyeballs are going to fall out of my skull, roll right on out. Between this and being sick . . . I never imagined everything was going to be like this, believe me. . . ." After a while she wiped her face with her fingers. "Is it time? Is it two?"

Lumin seemed not to hear. "What else?"

"I don't know." She drew in to clear her nose. "Paul—" Medical degrees and other official papers hung on either side of Freud's picture. Lumin's first name was Arnold. That little bit of information made her not want to go on. But he was waiting. "I'm not really in love with this old friend," she told him. "He's an old friend, we know him since graduate school. And he's—he's very nice, he's carefree, he's full of sympathy—"

"Isn't Paul?"

"Oh, yes," she said, in what came out like a whine. "Oh, *so* sympathetic. Dr. Lumin, I don't know what I want. I *don't* love Gabe. I really can't stand him, if you want to know the truth. He's not for me, he's not Paul—he never could be. Now he's living with some woman. She's so vulgar, I don't know what's gotten into him. We had dinner there—nobody said anything, and there was Gabe with that bitch."

"Why is she such a bitch?"

"Oh—" Libby wilted—"she's not that either. Do you want to know the bitch? Me. I was. But I knew it would be awful even before we got there. So, God, that didn't make it any easier."

He did not even have to bother; the next question she asked herself. "I don't *know* why. I just thought: why shouldn't we? We never go out to dinner, we hardly have been able to go out anywhere—and that's because of me too, and my health. Why shouldn't we? Do you see? And besides, I wanted to," she said. "It's as simple as that. I mean, isn't that still simple—to want to? But then I went ahead and behaved worse than anybody, I know I did. Oh, Gabe was all right— even she was all right, in a way. I understand all that. She's not a bitch probably. She's probably just a sexpot, good in bed or something, and why shouldn't Gabe live with her anyway? He's single, he can do whatever he wants to do. *I'm* the one who started the argument. All I do lately is argue with people. And cry. I mean that keeps me pretty busy, you can imagine."

Lumin remained Lumin; he didn't smile. In fact he frowned. "What do you argue about? Who are you arguing with?"

She raised two hands to the ceiling. "Everybody," she said. "Everything."

"Not Paul?"

"Not Paul—that's right, not Paul. *For* Paul," she announced.

"Everybody's just frustrating the hell out of him, and it makes me so angry, so *furious!* . . . Oh, I haven't even *begun* to tell you what's happened."

"Well, go on."

"What?" she said helplessly. "Where?"

"Paul. Why is this Paul so frustrated?"

She leaned forward, and her two fists came hammering down on his desk. "If he wasn't, Doctor, *oh, if they would just leave him alone!*" She fell back, breathless. "Isn't it two?"

At last he gave her a smile. "Almost."

"It must be. I'm so tired. I have such lousy resistance. . . ."

"It's a very tiring thing, this kind of talking," Lumin said. "Everybody gets tired."

"Doctor, can I ask you a question?"

"What?"

"What's the matter with me?"

"What do you think's the matter?"

"Please, Dr. Lumin, please don't pull that stuff. Really, that'll drive me nuts."

He shook a finger at her. "C'mon, Libby, don't threaten me." The finger dropped, and she thought she saw through his smile. "It's not my habit to drive people nuts."

She backed away. "I'm nuts already anyway."

For an answer he clasped and unclasped his hands.

"Well, I am," she said. "I'm cracked as the day is long."

He groaned. "What are you talking about. Huh? I'm not saying you should make light of these problems. These are real problems. Absolutely. Certainly. You've got every reason to be upset and want to talk to somebody. But—" he made a sour face—"what's this cracked business? How far does it get us. It doesn't tell us a hell of a lot, wouldn't you agree?"

She had, of course, heard of transference, and she wondered if it could be beginning so soon. She was beaming at him; her first friend in Chicago.

"So . . ." he said peacefully.

"Really, I haven't begun to tell you things."

"Sure, sure."

"When should I come again? I mean," she said, softer, with less bravado, "should I come again?"

"If you want to, of course. How's the day after tomorrow? Same time."

"That's fine. I think that would be perfect. Except—" Her heart, which had stopped its pounding earlier, started up again, like a band leaving the field. "How much will it be then?"

"Same as today—"

"I only brought," she rushed to explain, "ten dollars."

"We'll send a bill then. Don't worry about that."

"It's more than ten, for today?"

"The usual fee is twenty-five dollars."

"An hour?"

"An hour."

She had never in her life passed out; that she didn't this time probably indicated that she never would in her remaining years either. She lost her breath, voice, vision, sense, but managed to stay upright in her chair. "I—don't send a bill to the house."

"I'd rather you wouldn't," Lumin began, a kind of gaseous expression crossing his face, "worry about the money. We can talk about that too."

Libby had stood up. "I think I have to talk about it."

"All right. Sit down. We'll talk."

"It's after two, I think."

"That's all right."

What she meant was, would he charge for overtime? Twenty-five dollars an hour—forty cents a minute. "I can't pay twenty-five dollars." She tried to cry, but couldn't. She felt very dry, very tired.

"Perhaps we can work it out at twenty."

"I can't pay twenty. I can't pay fifteen. I can't pay anything."

"Of course," said Lumin firmly, "you didn't expect it would be for nothing."

"I suppose I did. I don't know—" She got up to go.

"Please sit down. Sit."

She almost crept back into the chair as though it were a lap. "Don't you see, it's all my doctor bills in the first place. Don't you see that?"

He nodded.

"Well, I can't pay!" But she couldn't cry either. *"I can't pay!"*

"Look, Libby, look here. I'm giving you an address. You go home, you give it some thought. It's right here on Michigan Avenue—the Institute. They have excellent people, the fee is less. You'll have an interview—"

"I married Paul," she said, dazed, "this is ridiculous—you're being ridiculous—excuse me, but you're being—"

He was writing something.

She shouted, "I don't want any Institute! *Why can't I have you!*"

He offered her the paper. "You can be interviewed at the Institute," he said, "and see if they'll be able to work you in right away. Come on, now," he said, roughly, "why don't you think about which you might prefer, which might better suit your circumstances—"

She stood up. "You don't even know they'll take me."

"It's research and training, so of course, yes, it depends—"

"I came to *you,* damn it!" She reached for the paper he had written on, and threw it to the floor. "I came to you and I told you all this. You listened. You just sat there, listening. And now I have to go tell somebody else all over again. Everything. I came to you—*I want you!*"

He stood up, showing his burly form, and that alone seemed to strip her of her force, though not her anger. "Of course," he said, "one can't always have everything one wants—"

"I don't want everything! I want *something!*"

He did not move, and she would not be intimidated; she had had enough for one day. Quite enough. "I want you," she said.

"Libby—"

"I'll jump out the window." She pointed over his shoulder. "I swear it."

He remained where he was, blocking her path. And Libby, run down, unwound, empty-minded suddenly, turned and went out his door. *He provoked me,* she thought in the elevator. *He provoked me. Him and that son-of-a-bitch Gabe. They led me on.*

Ten minutes later, in Saks, she bought a sweater; not the white cashmere, but a pale-blue lamb's-wool cardigan that was on sale. It was the first time in years she had spent ten dollars on herself. She left the store, walked a block south, toward the I.C. train, and then turned and ran all the way back to Saks.

Because the sweater had been on sale she had to plead with two floor managers and a buyer before they would give her her money back.

[January 1962]

TERRY SOUTHERN

The Road Out
of Axotle

There's an interesting road leading south out of Axotle, Mexico, that you might like to try sometime. It isn't on the Good Gulf Map, and it isn't on those issued by the Mexican Government. It is on one map—I wonder if you've seen it?—a map of very soft colors, scroll-edged, like some great exotic banknote; and the imprint of the publisher is in small black script along the lower left, "Ryder H. Raven and Son—San Jose, California." I came across it about a year ago.

The way it happened, I was with these two friends of mine in Mexico City—I say friends of mine though actually we'd met only a few days before, but anyway we were together this particular night, in their car—and the idea was to pick a town, such as the one we were in, and then to sort of drive away from it, in the opposite direction, so to speak. I knew what they had in mind, more or less, but it did seem that in being this strong on just-wanting-to-get-away-from, we might simply end up in the sea or desert. Then, too, at one point there was a kind of indecision as to the actual direction to take, like left or right—so I suggested that we look at a map. I knew there was a map in the car, because I had been with them earlier in the day when one of them, Emmanuel, bought a secondhand guidebook, of the kind that has folding maps in it.

"That is good, man," said the other one, who was driving, Pablo.

That was the way they talked, "That is good, man"; "This is bad, man." They were from Havana, and they spoke a fine, foppish sort of Spanish, but their English wasn't the greatest. Still, they insisted on speaking it, despite the fact that my own Spanish was good—in fact, the Mexican dialect part of it was so good that they preferred me to speak, whenever it was necessary, to the Mexicans—and it pleased their vanity to argue that, if *I* spoke, it was less obvious we were tourists.

Emmanuel got the guidebook from the glove compartment now and handed it to me in the backseat. We were at a corner southwest of the town, out beyond the stockyards and the slaughterhouse—at a crossroads. There was nothing happening here, only the yellow light from an arc lamp above, the yellow light that came dying down through the dead gauze of red dust which slowly rose and wound, or so it seemed, and bled around the car. That was the setting.

I had some trouble finding the right map and finally in seeing it, distracted, too, by the blast of California mambo from the radio; and it was then, while I was trying to hold the book up in a way to get more light, that something fell out of it.

"Let me see your lighter a minute, Pablo."

"What? What is?" He turned the radio down, just a bit. Sometimes he got quite excited if he heard his name.

What had fallen from the book was a map of Mexico, a map which had evidently been put there by the book's previous owner. One may say this because it was obvious the map was not a part of the guidebook; it was not of the same school of map making as were the maps in the guidebook. It was like something from another era, not handmade but somehow in that spirit: highly individual. It was large, but not as large as the ones given out by the gasoline stations— nor was it square; when opened, it was about eighteen by twenty-four inches, and was scaled 1:100.

The paper was extraordinarily thin—Bible paper, but much stronger, like rice paper or bamboo—and it was hazed with the slightest coloration of age which seemed to give a faint iridescence to those soft colors. They were Marie Laurencin colors, and it was like that as well, a map for a child, or a very nice woman.

"Where we are at this time?" asked Emmanuel, in a shout above the radio. Emmanuel was a year or two older than Pablo, and about one degree less self-centered.

I had looked at the map a few minutes without attempting the analogy, just tracing electric-blue rivers to cerulean seas, as they say, but I did know where we were, of course; and, almost at the same time, I saw where it might be interesting to go.

"Make a right," I said.

"A right, man," said Emmanuel. "Make a right." They had a

habit of repeating and relaying things to each other for no apparent reason.

Pablo gave a sigh, as of pain, as though he had known all along that's how it would be, and he lurched the car around the corner, sliding it like a top over the soft red dust, and up went the radio.

I continued to look at the map. We were going due west, and the map showed that about twenty miles ahead, on this same road, was a little town called Axotle. The road ran through the town east-west and then joined a highway, and this seemed to be all there was to it. But holding the lighter quite close, I had seen another road, a narrow, winding road, as thin as the blood vein of an eye, leading south out of the town. It seemed to go for about twenty-five miles, and on it there were two other towns, Corpus Christi and San Luiz, and there the road stopped. A blood-vein, dead-end road, with a town at the end of it; that was the place to go all right.

Pablo drove like a madman, except that he was quite a good driver actually. He was supposed to be upset, though, about not having found the kind of car he wanted to drive in Mexico. His story—or rather, his-story-through-Emmanuel, since Pablo himself didn't do much talking—was that he had a Mercedes at home and had been looking for a certain kind of car to drive in Mexico, a Pegaso, perhaps, but had finally bought this car we were in now, a '55 Oldsmobile, which had three carburetors and was supposed to do 145 on a straightaway, though, of course, there weren't too many of those.

"Man, this old wagon," he kept saying, "I dunt dig it."

But he drove it like the veritable wind, making funny little comments to himself and frowning, while Emmanuel sat beside him, wagging his closed-eyes head, shaking his shoulders and drumming his fingers along with the radio, or else was all hunched over in twisting up sticks of tea and lighting them. Sometimes he would sing along with the radio, too; not overdoing it, just a couple of shouts or a grunt.

We pulled in then at a Gulf station for gas. We were about halfway to Axotle now, and I was looking at the map again, outside the car, standing under the light of the station, when it suddenly occurred to me to check with the more recent map of the guidebook to see if perhaps the town had been built up in the last few years; it would put me in an embarrassing position with my new friends if we drove to the end of the line, only to smash headlong into a hot-dog stand. So I got out the guidebook and found a map of the corresponding region—quite detailed it was—and that was when the initial crevice of mystery appeared, because on this map there was *no* road leading south out of Axotle; there was only the east-west road which joined the highway. No road south and neither of the towns. I got a map then from the service station. It was a regular road map about two feet square, and was supposed to show every town with a population of 250 or more ... and the crevice became the proverbial fissure.

"This is bad, man," said Emmanuel, when I told him. Pablo didn't say anything, just stood there, scowling at the side of the car. Emmanuel and Pablo were both wearing dark prescription glasses, as they always did, even at night.

"No, man," I said, "this is *good.* They're ghost towns ... you dig? That will be interesting for you."

Emmanuel shrugged. Pablo was still frowning at the car.

"Ghost towns," I said, getting into the backseat again. "Sure, that's very good."

Then, as we got under way, Emmanuel turned to sit half-facing me, his back against the door, and he began to warm toward the idea, or was perhaps beginning to understand it.

"Yeah, man, that is very *good."* He nodded seriously. "Ghost town. *Crazy."*

"It is very good, man," he told Pablo, while the radio wailed and the car whined and floated over the long black road.

"What is this, man," Pablo demanded then in his abrupt irate way, half-turning around to me, "this goat town?"

"Goat town! Goat town!" shouted Emmanuel, laughing. "That's too much, man!"

"Man, I dunt dig it!" said Pablo, but he was already lost again, guiding his big rocket to the moon. And I lay back on the seat and dozed off for a while.

When I woke up, it was as though I had been on the edge of waking for a long time; the car was pitching about oddly, and I had half-fallen from the seat. The radio was still blasting, but behind it now was the rasping drone of Pablo's cursing. And I lay there, listening to that sound; it was like a dispassionate chant, a steady and unlinked inventory of all the profane images in Spanish. I assumed we had gotten off the road, except we seemed to be going unduly fast for that. Then I saw that Emmanuel had his hands up to his mouth and was shaking with laughter, and I realized that this had been going on for some time, with him saying softly over and over, "Man dig this . . . *road!* Dig this . . . *road!*"

So I raised up to have a look, and it was pretty incredible all right. It was more of a creek bed than a road, but occasionally there would be an open place to the side . . . a gaping, torn-off place that suggested we were on something like a Greek mountain pass. And then I saw as well, dishearteningly so, why we were going fast; it was because every now and then one of the side pockets stretched right up to the middle of the road, so that the back wheels would pull to that side, spinning a bit, as we passed over it. And, as we passed over it, you could see down . . . for quite a long way.

"What do you think it's like to the side?" I asked.

Emmanuel finally controlled his curious mirth long enough to turn around. "What do *I* think it's like?" he asked. "Man, it's *lions and tigers! And . . . big . . . pointy rocks!* Why? What do *you* think it's like?" And fairly shouting with laughter, he handed me another joint.

"*Goats,*" said Pablo with a grotesque snicker. "There are the goats there."

"All right, man," I said, and lay back with a groan to express my disquiet.

Pablo snorted. "Man, I'm swingin'!" he said, reassuringly.

Emmanuel broke up completely now and laid his head down laughing. "Pablo's swingin'!" he cried. He could hardly speak. He had to hold onto the rocking dashboard to keep from falling to the floorboards. "Ma-a-an, Pablo is . . . too . . . much!"

It was too much all right. I lay there smoking, my thoughts as bleak as the black rolling top I stared at, though gradually I did discern, or so it seemed, a certain rhythm and control taking hold of the erratic pitching of the car, and the next time I sat up the road, too, seemed in fairly good shape.

The moon had come out and you would get glimpses now and then of things alongside—strange dwarf trees and great round rocks, with patches of misty landscape beyond. It was just about then that the headlight caught a road sign in the distance, a rickety post akimbo with a board nailed to it (or maybe tied with a strand of vine) across which was painted, crudely to be sure, *"Puente,"* which, in these circumstances, would mean toll bridge.

"Crazy road," I heard Pablo say.

There was a bend in it just after the sign, and the glow of a kerosene lamp ahead—which proved to be from the window of an old tin shack; and in front of the shack there was a barrier across the road: a large, fairly straight tree limb. Beyond it, vaguely seen, was the small, strange bridge.

When we had stopped by the shack, we could see that there was someone inside, sitting at a table; and, after waiting a minute while nothing happened, Pablo jerked his head around at me.

"You make it, man," he said, handing me his billfold, "I can't make these greaser."

"Very well," I said, "you rotten little Fascist spic." And as I got out of the car I heard him explaining it again to Emmanuel: "Man, I can't make these greaser."

Inside the shack, the lamp was full up; but, with the chimney as jagged and black as a crater, I couldn't see too much of the room's appointments—only a shotgun leaning against the wall near the door, the barrel so worn and rust-scraped that it caught the yellow light in glints harder than brass. But I could see him all right—bigger than life, you might say, very fat, his sleeves twisted up, playing with cards. There was a bottle half filled with tequila on the table. I remember this because it occurred to me then, in a naïve, drug-crazed way, that we might have a pleasant exchange and finish off with a drink.

"Good evening," I said (with easy formality), then followed it up with something colloquial like, "What's the damage?"

He was squinting at me, and then beyond, to the car. And I recall first thinking that here was a man who had half lost his sight playing solitaire by a kerosene lamp; but he was something else as well, I realized, when I took it all in: he was a man with a *very* sinister look to him. He was smoking a homemade cigar, gnarled and knotted enough to have been comic, except that he kept baring his teeth around it, teeth which appeared to have been filed—and by humanity at large, one might presume, from the snarl with which he spoke, as he finally did:

"Where are you trying to go?"

"Corpus Christi," I said.

It occurred to me that it might be less involved, not to say cheaper, if I didn't divulge our full itinerary.

"Corpus Christi, eh?" He smiled, or it was something like a smile; then he got up, walked to the door, glanced at the car, spat out some of his cigar, and walked back to the table. "Five dollars a head," he said, sitting down again.

"Five dollars," I said, more in a thought aloud than a question, "Mexican dollars."

He made a sound, not unlike a laugh, and took up the cards again.

"You think you're Mexican?" He asked after a minute, without raising his head.

I had to consider it briefly. "Oh, *I* see—you mean, 'a-fool-and-his-money . . .' that sort of thing."

"You said it, my friend, I didn't."

"Yes. Well, you'll give me a receipt, of course."

"Receipt?" He laughed, spitting and wiping his mouth on his arm. "This isn't Monterrey, you know."

I hesitated, determined for the moment, in the responsibility to the rest of my party, not to be so misused; then I put my hands on the edge of the table and leaned forward a little. "I think you've probably picked the *wrong* crowd this time, Pancho," I said.

Whereas, actually, it was *I* who had picked the wrong party, for he laid his head back laughing with this—and an unpleasant laugh it was, as we know.

"Pancho," he said, getting up, "that's funny." Still laughing and wiping his hand across his mouth, his eyes half shut so that I couldn't quite see where he was looking, he walked around the table. "That's very funny," he said.

And you can appreciate how for a moment it was like a sequence in a film, where someone is supposed to be laughing or scratching his ear, and suddenly does something very aggressive to you—except that I stepped back a little then, and he walked on past me to the door . . . where it seemed my show of apprehension had given him not so much a fresh lease as a veritable deed on confidence.

"*You* don't need a receipt," he said, turning from the door, his eyes still two smoked slits, "you can trust me." Then he flicked his cigar with an air and gave his short, wild laugh, or cough, as it were.

But when he faced the car again, he sobered quickly enough. And Emmanuel and Pablo were sitting there, peering out, frowning terribly.

"What have you got inside?" he asked, and his tone indicated this might be the first of several rare cards he intended.

Somehow I felt it would not do to involve my friends, so I started reaching for the money.

He kept a cold, smoky silence as he watched me count it out. Then he took it, leaning back in the smug, smiling, closed-eyes strain against cigar smoke and the effort of pressing the loot deep into his tight trousers.

"Yes," I said. "Well, thanks for everything."

He grunted, then stepped out and raised the barrier. I started to get into the car, but he said something and turned back into the shack, motioning me with him.

"Wait," he said, as a quick afterthought, and from one dark side of the room he came up holding a cigar box.

"You want to buy some good marijuana?"

"What?"

"Marijuana," he said, letting the word out again like a coil of wet rope, and proffering the lid-raised box for my inspection.

"Very good," he said, "the best."

I leaned forward for a look and a sniff. It didn't appear to be the greatest; in fact, it didn't appear to be Mexican—and it looked like it was about fifteen years old.

"What is it, a spice of some kind?"

"Very good," he said.

"How much?"

"How much will you give?"

I took a pinch and tasted it.

He nodded toward the car. "Perhaps your friends.... I'll make you a good price. You tell me your price, I'll make you a good price. Okay?"

I stared at the box for a minute, then made an eccentric grimace. "You don't mean ... you don't mean marijuana ... the loco weed? What, to smoke?" I shook my head vigorously, backing away. "No, thanks!" I said, while his face went even more sour than one might have expected.

"Come back when you grow up!" he snarled, shutting the box;

and for the first time, as he turned into the shadow of the shack, he seemed slightly drunk.

The bridge itself was noteworthy. A bit longer than the car, but not a foot wider, it consisted of oil drums held together with barbed wire and covered with wooden planks, only the outer two of which seemed at all stationary. The device was secured at each bank by a rope attached to stakes driven into the ground.

We held back a few seconds before embarking, taking it all in. Then, as we crossed over, the whole thing sank about two feet, completely out of sight, swaying absurdly, as the black water rose up in swirls just above the running boards.

Nobody commented on the bridge; though once we were across, onto the road, and I was resting on the seat again, Emmanuel said:

"What happened back with the greaser, man?"

"Five dollars a head."

"That swine."

"That rotten greaser swine," said Pablo.

"You said it," I said, closing my eyes. I had not gotten to bed the night before; I was thinking, too, of a certain time-honored arrangement in Mexico whereby a cigar box full of marijuana is sold to a foreigner and then retrieved by the merchant at customs. I once heard that the amount of annual foreign revenue so gained in the consequent fines is second only to that from the tax on the shade-and-barrier seats at the bullfight. And I soon began to wonder, here on the soft-focus margin of sleep, how many, many times that particular box I just looked at had been sold. Ten? Twenty? How many miles? How many missions? Fifty missions to Laredo, and they would decorate the box and retire it. And smoke it. But, of course, it was no good. Why would they use anything good for a scheme like that? No, it would be like those bundles of newspaper money left for kidnapers; I suppose they send to New Jersey for it. Anyway, I decided not to mention the incident to my friends; it would only excite them unduly.

I must have been asleep when we reached Corpus Christi, because when I came up again to have a look, the car was already stopped. We were in the middle of the square, and Emmanuel was saying:

"Man, dig this . . . *scene*. Dig this . . . *scene,*" while Pablo was just sitting there, leaning forward over the wheel, his arms hanging to each side of it.

The town, if it may so be called, is simply this square of one-story frame buildings, fronted all around by a raised, wooden, sidewalk arcade. Besides the car we were in, there were two or three others parked in the square along with several small wagons that had mules or donkeys hitched to them.

"Now, this is your true Old West, Pablo," I began. "Notice the attempt at a rather formal—" But what *I* had failed to notice was that the shadowed arcades, all around the square, were lined with people. They were leaning against the storefronts, and lying on the wooden sidewalk, or sitting on the raised edge of it—not just grown people, but children as well; children, a number of whom were to be seen crawling about, in the manner of the very young indeed. This struck me as odd because it was now about two o'clock in the morning. But what was really more odd was the pure, unbroken torpor which seemed to overhang the crowd. For a large group of people—perhaps 200—their inactivity was marvelous to look upon like an oil painting. It seemed that all of them were leaning, sitting, or lying down; and it was not apparent that they were even talking to each other. And here and there was someone with a guitar, his head down, as though playing for only himself to hear.

As I was speculating about the possible reasons for this, my attention was suddenly caught by something that was happening to a wall nearby, the side of one of the buildings—it seemed to be soundlessly crumbling, and I thought now I must be out of my skull entirely. But it was not crumbling, it was simply oozing and changing color all over, *green,* and shades of green, changing from one instant to the next, from bottle-dark to shimmering-Nile; and this, in a strange and undulating way. Had we been in Rockefeller Plaza or the Gilbert Hall of Science . . . but here there was no accounting for it. But while I was assuring myself that first-rate hallucinations are only doubted in retrospect . . . Emmanuel saw it too. I knew he had seen it because he quickly leaned forward and began changing the radio stations. Then he turned around with an odd look on his face.

"Man, what is that? On that wall."

"Well," I said, "it must be *oil* . . . or something like that."

"Oil? Man, that's not oil. What's happening? That wall is *alive.*"

"Listen, let me get out of the car for a minute," I said, perhaps because of his tone. "I'm . . . curious, as a matter of fact, to see what it is myself."

As I got out of the car, I felt that if I took my eyes off the wall for a second, when I looked back it would have become just an ordinary wall—so I kept looking at it, and walked toward it then, very deliberately until I was there, leaning forward from two feet away to peer at it; and while I must have known before, it was not until my face was six inches from the wall that the field finally did narrow to the truth, a single moving inch: a green roach. For, true enough, that's how it was: alive—with a hundred thousand green-winged flying roaches, ever moving, back and forth, sideways and around, the wings in constant tremulous motion.

I looked around at the people then, sitting and leaning nearby. I started to say something—but I was distracted to see that they as well were covered with the roaches . . . not in quite the profusion of the wall, but only for the reason that from time to time they passed a hand in front of their faces, or shrugged. So I was not too surprised when I looked down at myself and saw that *I*, too, even as they and the immobile wall . . . and then I heard the sound, that which had been in the air all along—a heavy ceaseless whirling sound—and it was a sound which deepened intensely in the dark distance of the night above and around, and it seemed to say: *'You think there are quite a few of us down there—but if you only knew how many of us are out here!'*

I thought I understood why the people weren't talking: because the roaches would get in their mouths; or sleeping: because they would crawl up their noses. But I may have really felt that it was not so much because of this, but because of something else, past or impending.

I stuck my trousers into my socks, and my hands into my pockets, and started back to the car. I had heard about the green flying roaches, how they settle on a town like locusts, and now I felt a gleeful anticipation, like the first of a party to swim an icy stream— toward springing the phenomenon on Pablo and Emmanuel. I thought it might be good to pretend to have scarcely noticed: 'What, those? Why those are bugs, man. Didn't you ever see a bug before?'

When I got back to the car, however, I saw they had already surmised. Indeed, half the car was covered: the windshield wipers were sweeping, and inside, Pablo and Emmanuel were thumping wildly against the sideglass in trying to jar the creatures off.

"You finicky spics!" I shouted, snatching the door open and pretending to scoop and fan great armfuls in on them. Emmanuel jerked the door closed, and locked it; then he rolled the window a crack, and raised his mouth to it: "Man, what's happening?" he asked and quickly closed the glass.

I stood outside, gesticulating them out and pretending to shout some emergency information. Pablo had started the car, and was racing the engine, sitting all hunched over the wheel; I got a glimpse of his maniacal frown and it occurred to me that an experience like this might be enough to snap his brain.

After a second, Emmanuel rolled down the window just a bit again.

"Listen, man," he said, "we are going to drive over nearer to the bar, so we can make it into the bar—you know?"

I looked around the square. So they had already found the bar. None of the buildings had signs on them, but I suppose it wasn't too difficult to tell. I saw it then, too, on the side we had come in, and next to it, a café.

"Let's go to the café first," I said, "that would be much cooler."

Emmanuel nodded, and as I turned away, I knew he would be relaying it to Pablo: 'The café first, man, that's much cooler.'

We reached the door of the café at the same time, and went right in.

It was an oblong room, with a hard dirt floor and raw-wood walls; there were about ten tables, set two by two the length of the place—bare boards they were, nailed to four sticks, and accompanied by benches. We sat at the first one, near the door.

The place was not quite empty. There was a man, who was evidently the proprietor, sitting at a table at the end of the room, and a man who was evidently drunk, sitting at a table on the opposite side. The man who was drunk had his head down on the table, resting it there as in sleep; his head kept sliding off the table, causing him to shake and curse it, and then to replace it carefully, while the proprietor sat across the room, watching him. I construed the situation as this: that the proprietor was ready to close, and was waiting for the drunk to leave; this possibility seemed strengthened by the way he simply remained seated when we came in, staring at us until we ordered some coffee. When he had brought it, he went directly back to his table and sat down, there to resume watch on the drunk. There seemed to be a point of genuine interest for him in watching the drunk's head slide off the table. I noticed that it did, in fact, drop lower each time.

There were fewer roaches here, though still enough so that you might want to keep your hand over the coffee, or, in drinking it, hold it as though you were lighting a cigarette in the wind. Pablo didn't drink his coffee, however, and didn't bother to protect it, so that after a minute there were four roaches in it, thrashing about, not unlike tiny birds at bath. Whenever one of the roaches was scooped out to the rim of the cup, it would crawl along for an instant, fluttering like a thing possessed, and then jump back in. Pablo was poking about in the cup with a matchstick, and both he and Emmanuel regarded the roaches with manifest concern. Pretty soon they were talking about them as though they could distinguish one from another. "Dig this one, man, he's swinging!"

"Don't hold him under, man, he can't make it like that!"

For my own part, I was content to watch the drunk and the proprietor, and this was as well, for, very soon, there was a bit of action. The drunk straightened up and started looking around the room. When his eyes reached our party they stopped, and after a minute, he leaned toward us and vomited.

I turned to get the proprietor's reaction to this, he who was sitting, somewhat more stiffly in his chair now, still staring at the drunk, and frowning. Then he gave a short humorless laugh, and said in measured tones:

"Let's-see-you-do-that-again."

This caused the drunk to stop looking at us, and to turn around to the proprietor as though he hadn't seen him before; and after staring straight at him, he laid his head back down on the table.

The proprietor slapped the table and gave several short, barking laughs, then resumed his scrutinous vigil.

During this vignette, Pablo and Emmanuel had abandoned their cups, which, I saw now, were crowded with the drowned.

"Well, that seems to be that," I said, "shall we go to the bar?"

"Man, let's cut out of this place," said Emmanuel.

Pablo, with deeply furrowed brow, was staring at where the man had been sick. Finally he shook his shoulders violently.

"Man, I dunt dig . . . *vomit!*"

"Are you kidding?" I said, "I happen to know that you *do* dig good greaser vomit."

The remark amused Emmanuel. "Ha-ha-ha! Good greaser vomit! Pablo digs good greaser vomit! That's too much, man!"

"Listen," said Pablo, leaning forward in serious confidence, "let's go to the bar now, I think there are groovy chicks there."

Like the café, the bar was unpretentious; but, where the café had been sparse and fairly lighted, the bar was close and steeped in shadow—sinister enough, as dark places go, but there wasn't much happening, at least not to meet the eye. A few men at the tables, a few beat hustlers at the bar.

My friends, being at the head of our party now, chose a table in the very heart of things, and we ordered tequila.

Emmanuel nodded toward the bar, straightening his tie.

"See, man," he said, giving me a little nudge, "dig the chicks."

"Sure," I said, "you're swinging." Pablo kept involuntarily clearing his throat and making sporadic little adjustments to his person and attire, even touching his hair once or twice. But after a moment or two, this fidgeting turned into annoyance that the girls, though they had seen us come in, had not made a play; so very soon, he and Emmanuel got up and took their drinks to the bar.

The girls, there were four of them, appeared to be extremely beat—two, by way of example, not wearing shoes—and were each holding a glass, untouched it seemed, of dark brown drink.

It was interesting to see them and my friends at a distance, not hearing, only seeing the gestures of hands and mouth, the flash of teeth and the tilted glass—man at an ancient disadvantage.

Sipping my tequila, I began to pretend I had settled down around here—quite near the toll bridge, actually. And a few days after my arrival, there had been a nasty run-in with the fat roadblock greaser, who, it developed, was loathed and feared throughout the region, and was known as "Pigman." I heard the hushed whispers of the gathering crowd:

'Good Lord! The stranger's smashed his face away!'

'Did you see *that*—a single blow from the stranger sent the Pigman reeling!'

'Smashed his face entirely away! Good Lord! Etc., etc.'

I was going along with variations on this, when Pablo and Emmanuel came back to the table, sullen now and unrequited.

"Man, those chicks are the *worst,*" Emmanuel said, as they sat down. "Let's cut out of this place."

Pablo was looking as though he might black out momentarily.

When I asked what had happened, it was to learn that the girls had said they weren't working tonight, that they *never* worked on Tuesday night (or whatever night it was—it wasn't Sunday) and to come back tomorrow.

I took another look at them, and whatever rationale was behind their refusal, they were evidently satisfied with it, though it was obvious they could have made their entire month off my madcap friends.

As we rose in leaving though, one of them raised her dark glass in a toast of promise, and tomorrow.

Now we were off for the second lost city: San Luiz. It would be ten or twelve miles along the road that had brought us, so we recrossed the square and drove out on the opposite side we had come in.

The road here was just two tracks across a flat, rock-strewn plain. In five minutes we were in wilderness again, and after ten miles or so, when we finally reached the place where the town was supposed to be, the road stopped dead, at an extraordinary wire fence—a fence about 17 feet high and made of wire mesh the size of quarter-inch rope. We got out to have a look.

The fence was topped by four running strands of an odd-looking barbed wire, jutting outward, and along this, at intervals, was a large, white, professional sign which said in Spanish:

KEEP OUT
VERY HIGH VOLTAGE
DANGER OF DEATH

Beyond the fence, a trace of the old road's continuation was visible in our headlights for about fifty feet, before it disappeared into the night. On our side of the fence the road branched out left and right, and it ran alongside the fence in both directions for as far as one could see.

With the idea now of driving *around* the fence and picking up the road again, we got back into the car and took the right branch, following it until, shortly, at a ravine, it turned away from the fence and back toward the town. Retracing our route, we took the other branch of the road; again, after an eighth of a mile or so, the road turned away from the fence and back to the town, while the fence itself disappeared in the heavy growth.

Here it seemed to me that one might follow the fence on foot, and while I didn't think we could actually do it, having no flashlight, I was eager to try. So we left the car and walked alongside the fence, on a field of rock and stubble, but it was immediately so dense as to be almost impassable. The thicket grew right into the fence, and the fence had evidently been there for quite a while. Emmanuel soon turned back toward the car.

"It's a drag, man," he said.

Pablo, who had wandered off to the left, kept stopping and brushing at his clothes.

"Man, what is this? This is all scratch."

Finally he stopped completely and began striking matches; he seemed to be examining something in his hand. I beat my way through the brush to him.

"Man, this is bad," he said, "this is all scratch."

He was examining what appeared to be an invisible scratch on his hand.

"I couldn't see it," I said as the match died, "is it bleeding?"

"*Bleeding?*" He struck another match. "Man, is it *bleeding? Where?*"

We both peered at his hand.

"It looks all right," I said, "doesn't it?"

"Man I dunt *dig* this place? What is this?"

I suggested that he go back to the car and I would try to follow the fence a little farther.

I had become obsessed by the mystery of it. What was it behind this fence, in the vast area where one town used to exist and no town was supposed to? The fabulous estate of a mad billionaire? The testing ground for some fantastic weapon? Why had not the sign proclaimed the source of its authority? Why had it not strengthened itself with 'Private Property,' or 'Government Property'? No, here was a case of security so elaborate, so resolved upon, that even the power behind it would remain secret. Whatever it was—was so dreadful it was not supposed to exist.

Many are familiar with the story that infant-mortality (in childbirth) is not the figure it is represented to be—and that the discrepancy between the actual figure and the statistics are teratological cases—with the consequence that in every Christian country there is a monster-home, wholly secret, maintained by permanent appropriation, in the form of a "hidden-rider," self-perpetuating, and never revealed by the breakdown of any budget.

As I mused on this, moving cautiously along the edge of the black fence, and now at a considerable distance from the car, I stumbled against a rock and fell; I grabbed at the dry brush, but the terrain had changed, dropping away sharply from the fence, as did I with it now, about 15 feet down into a small gully. Here there was even less light than above, and as I sat there in pitch blackness, momentarily rubbing my forehead, I had a sudden uneasiness of something very menacing nearby and moving closer. And, as suddenly, I knew what it was.

Wild dogs have existed in Mexico for so long that they are a breed apart; the dissimilarity between them and ordinary dogs is remarkable. Wild dogs do not bark; the sound they produce comes from the uppermost part of the throat—a frantic and sustained snarl, and the strangeness of it is accentuated by its being directed *down,* for the reason that they run with their heads very low, nose almost touching the ground. Even in a pack, with blood dripping hot from their muzzles, they keep their backs arched and their tails between their legs. Their resemblance, in many ways, is less to the dog than to the hyena; they do not spring—their instinct is to chase a thing, biting at it, until it falls to break a leg . . . whereupon they hit it like piranha fish, taking bites at random, not going for the throat, but flailing it alive. It is improbable that wild dogs will attack a person who holds his ground—at least, so I was told later—so that it was a rather serious mistake that I began to run.

Through the snarls, before they caught me, I could hear the teeth snapping, as though they were so possessed by rage as to bite even the air itself. I half stumbled and turned when the first one bit the back of my leg and clung to it, in a loathsome knot, like a tarantula; I kicked it away violently, but so much more in a fit of repulsion than in adroitness that I took a nifty pratfall, there to grope for a frantic second or two for a rock or stick of defense, before scrambling to my feet again while being bitten again on the same leg. Exactly how many there were I don't know—at least six. I was bitten two or three times more, on the legs, before I fell again; and the bites, having come at just the moment before I fell, gave me the strong impression that they were now *closing in.*

But abruptly the scene was flooded with white light and the scream of twisting manbo, as our car came lurching and crashing down the ravine, headlights bouncing; then it suddenly stalled.

For an instant the action became a frozen tableau, the dogs petrified in strange attitudes of attack, and myself crouching at bay—a tableau at which my friends in the car simply sat and stared.

'Man, what's he doing?' I imagined Emmanuel saying, 'dig those weird *dogs.'*

And by the interior light of the car I could see Pablo's expression of exasperated amazement.

I was on the verge of shouting urgent instructions about completing my rescue, when Pablo, apparently at the end of his tether, began honking the horn wildly and lunged the car forward with a terrible roar, lights flashing—and the dogs scattered into the night.

"Come, man," said Pablo, gesturing impatiently, "we cut out now."

There was no sign of life as we crossed the square at Corpus Christi, so we drove on to the outskirts of Mexico City where we managed to rouse a doctor. He gave me a shot of tetanus, a couple of sutures, and some morphia tablets—which I had to share with Pablo and Emmanuel, after the doctor indignantly refused to sell them a hundred goofballs. Pablo was more indignant about it than the doctor, and as we drove away, he leaned out the window and shook his fist at the dark building:

"Go to devil, you greaser quack!" This broke Emmanuel up, but we got home without further incident.

My friends left the pension a few days after that, on a Sunday. I came out to the car and we shook hands lightly.

"You ought to make it," Emmanuel said. He had a thin, unlit cigar in his mouth. "Swinging chicks in Guadalajara, man."

"Guadalajara? I thought you were going to Acapulco."

"No, man, I don't think we'll go there. I don't think anything's happening there. Why? *You* want to go to *Acapulco?*"

"No," I said.

"How about Guadalajara? Crazy town, man."

"No, thanks."

Emmanuel nodded.

"Okay, man," he said.

Pablo raced the engine and leaned over the wheel, turning his head toward me; he looked like a progressive young missionary in his white linen suit and dark glasses.

"Later, man," he said.

"Yeah, man," said Emmanuel, "later."

"Later," I said.

They took off with a roar. At the corner, a very old woman with a great black shawl over her head, started across the street without looking. Pablo didn't slow down or perceptibly alter his course, and as she passed in front of the car, it looked like he missed her by the length of a matchstick. She hardly seemed to notice it though, only slowly turned her head after them, but by then they were almost out of sight.

So that was that; and the point of it all is, they left me the map—that is, should anyone ever care to make it, I mean, down to the big fence on that road out of Axotle.

[August 1962]

STANLEY ELKIN

I Look Out
For Ed Wolfe

He was an orphan, and, to him-
self, he seemed like one, looked like one. His orphan's features were
as true of himself as are their pale, pinched faces to the blind. At
twenty-seven he was a neat, thin young man in white shirts and light
suits with lintless pockets. Something about him suggested the ruthless isolation, the hard self-sufficiency of the orphaned, the peculiar
dignity of men seen eating alone in restaurants on national holidays.
Yet is was this perhaps which shamed him chiefly, for there was a
suggestion, too, that his impregnability was a myth, a smell not of the
furnished room which he did not inhabit, but of the three-room
apartment on a good street which he did. The very excellence of his
taste, conditioned by need and lack, lent to him the odd, maidenly
primness of the lonely.

He saved the photographs of strangers and imprisoned them behind clear plastic windows in his wallet. In the sound of his own voice
he detected the accent of the night school and the correspondence
course, and nothing of the fat, sunny ring of the world's casually af-
ternooned. He strove against himself, a supererogatory enemy, and
sought by a kind of helpless abrasion, as one rubs wood, the gleaming
self beneath. An orphan's thinness, he thought, was no accident.

Returning from lunch he entered the office building where he
worked. It was an old building, squat and gargoyled, brightly patched
where sandblasters had once worked and then quit before they had
finished. He entered the lobby, which smelled always of disinfectant,
and walked past the wide, dirty glass of the cigarette-and-candy
counter to the single elevator, as thickly barred as a cell.

The building was an outlaw. Low rents and a downtown address
and the landlord's indifference had brought together from the pe-

ripheries of business and professionalism a strange band of entrepreneurs and visionaries, men desperately but imaginatively failing: an eye doctor who corrected vision by massage; a radio evangelist; a black-belt judo champion; a self-help organization for crippled veterans; dealers in pornographic books, in paper flowers, in fireworks, in plastic jewelry, in the artificial, in the artfully made, in the imitated, in the copied, in the stolen, the unreal, the perversion, the plastic, the *schlock*.

On the sixth floor the elevator opened and the young man, Ed Wolfe, stepped out.

He passed the Association for the Indians, passed Plasti-Pens, passed *Coffin & Tombstone,* passed Soldier Toys, passed Prayer-a-Day. He walked by the opened door of C. Morris Brut, Chiropractor, and saw him, alone, standing at a mad attention, framed in the arching golden nimbus of his inverted name on the window, squeezing handballs.

He looked quickly away but Dr. Brut saw him and came toward him, putting the handballs in his shirt pocket where they bulged awkwardly. He held him by the elbow. Ed Wolfe looked at the yellowing tile beneath his feet, infinitely diamonded, chipped, the floor of a public toilet, and saw Dr. Brut's dusty shoes. He stared sadly at the jagged, broken glass of the mail chute.

"Ed Wolfe, take care of yourself," Dr. Brut said.

"Right."

"Regard your posture in life. A tall man like yourself looks terrible when he slumps. Don't be a *schlump.* It's not good for the organs."

"I'll watch it."

"When the organs get out of line the man begins to die."

"I know."

"You say so. How many guys make promises. Brains in the brainpan. Balls in the strap. The bastards downtown." He meant doctors in hospitals, in clinics, on boards, nonorphans with M.D. degrees and special license plates and respectable patients who had Blue Cross, charts, died in clean hospital rooms. They were the bastards downtown, his personal New Deal, his neighborhood Wall Street banker. A disease cartel. "They won't tell you. The white bread kills you. The cigarettes. The whiskey. The sneakers. The high heels. They won't tell you. Me, *I'll* tell you."

"I appreciate it."

"Wise guy. Punk. I'm a friend. I give a father's advice."

"I'm an orphan."

"I'll adopt you."

"I'm late for work."

"We'll open a clinic. 'C. Morris Brut and Adopted Son.' "

"It's something to think about."

"Poetry," Dr. Brut said and walked back to his office, his posture stiff, awkward, a man in a million who knew how to hold himself.

Ed Wolfe went on to his own office. He walked in. The sad-faced telephone girl was saying, "Cornucopia Finance Corporation." She pulled the wire out of the board and slipped her headset around her neck where it hung like a delicate horse collar. "Mr. La Meck wants to see you. But don't go in yet. He's talking to somebody."

He went toward his desk at one end of the big main office. Standing, fists on the desk, he turned to the girl. "What happened to my call cards?"

"Mr. La Meck took them," the girl said.

"Give me the carbons," Ed Wolfe said. "I've got to make some calls."

She looked embarrassed. The face went through a weird change, the sadness taking on an impossible burden of shame so that she seemed massively tragic, like a hit-and-run driver. "I'll get them," she said, moving out of the chair heavily. Ed Wolfe thought of Dr. Brut.

He took the carbons and fanned them out on the desk. He picked one in an intense, random gesture like someone drawing a number on a public stage. He dialed rapidly.

As the phone buzzed brokenly in his ear he felt the old excitement. Someone at the other end greeted him sleepily.

"Mr. Flay? This is Ed Wolfe at Cornucopia Finance." *(Can you cope, can you cope?* he hummed to himself.)

"Who?"

"Ed Wolfe. I've got an unpleasant duty," he began pleasantly. "You've skipped two payments."

"I didn't skip nothing. I called the girl. She said it was okay."

"That was three months ago. She meant it was all right to miss a few days. Listen, Mr. Flay, we've got that call recorded, too. Nothing gets by."

"I'm a little short."

"Grow."

"I couldn't help it," the man said. Ed Wolfe didn't like the cringing tone. Petulance and anger he could meet with his own petulance, his own anger. But guilt would have to be met with his own guilt and that, here, was irrelevant.

"Don't con me, Flay. You're a troublemaker. What are you, Flay, a Polish person? Flay isn't a Polish name, but your address. . . ."

"What's that?"

"What are you? Are you Polish?"

"What's that to you? What difference does it make?" That was more like it, Ed Wolfe thought warmly.

"That's what you are, Flay. You're a Pole. It's guys like you who give your race a bad name. Half our bugouts are Polish persons."

"Listen. You can't. . . ."

He began to shout. "*You* listen. You wanted the car. The refrigerator. The chintzy furniture. The sectional you saw in the funny papers. And we paid for it, right?"

"Listen. The money I owe is one thing, the way. . . ."

"We paid for it, right?"

"That doesn't. . . ."

"Right? Right?"

"Yes, you. . . ."

"Okay. You're in trouble, Warsaw. You're in terrible trouble. It means a lien. A judgment. We've got lawyers. You've got nothing. We'll pull the furniture the hell out of there. The car. Everything."

"Wait," he said. "Listen, my brother-in-law. . . ."

Ed Wolfe broke in sharply. "He's got some money?"

"I don't know. A little. I don't know."

"Get it. If you're short, grow. This is America."

"I don't know if he'll let me have it."

"Steal it. This is America. Good-by."

"Wait a minute. Please."

"That's it. There are other Polish persons on my list. This time it was just a friendly warning. Cornucopia wants its money. Cornucopia. Can you cope? Can you cope? Just a friendly warning, Polish-American. Next time we come with the lawyers and the machine guns. Am I making myself clear?"

"I'll try to get it to you."

Ed Wolfe hung up. He pulled a handkerchief from his drawer

and wiped his face. His chest was heaving. He took another call card. The girl came by and stood beside his desk. "Mr. La Meck can see you now," she mourned.

"Later. I'm calling." The number was already ringing.

"Please, Mr. Wolfe."

"Later, I said. In a minute." The girl went away. "Hello. Let me speak with your husband, madam. I am Ed Wolfe of Cornucopia Finance. He can't cope. Your husband can't cope."

The woman said something, made an excuse. "Put him on, goddamn it. We know he's out of work. Nothing gets by. Nothing." There was a hand on the receiver beside his own, the wide male fingers pink and vaguely perfumed, the nails manicured. For a moment he struggled with it fitfully, as though the hand itself were all he had to contend with. He recognized La Meck and let go. La Meck pulled the phone quickly toward his mouth and spoke softly into it, words of apology, some ingenious excuse Ed Wolfe couldn't hear. He put the receiver down beside the phone itself and Ed Wolfe picked it up and returned it to its cradle.

"Ed," La Meck said, "come into the office with me."

Ed Wolfe followed La Meck, his eyes on La Meck's behind.

La Meck stopped at his office door. Looking around he shook his head sadly and Ed Wolfe nodded in agreement. La Meck let Ed Wolfe pass in first. While La Meck stood, Ed Wolfe could discern a kind of sadness in his slouch, but once La Meck was seated behind his desk he seemed restored, once again certain of the world's soundness. "All right," La Meck began. "I won't lie to you."

Lie to me. Lie to me, Ed Wolfe prayed silently.

"You're in here for me to fire you. You're not being laid off. I'm not going to tell you that I think you'd be happier someplace else, that the collection business isn't your game, that profits don't justify our keeping you around. Profits are terrific, and if collection isn't your game it's because you haven't got a game. As far as your being happier someplace else, that's bullshit. You're not supposed to be happy. It isn't in the cards for you. You're a fall-guy type, God bless you, and though I like you personally I've got no use for you in my office."

I'd like to get you on the other end of a telephone some day, Ed Wolfe thought miserably.

"Don't ask me for a reference," La Meck said. "I couldn't give you one."

"No, no," Ed Wolfe said. "I wouldn't ask you for a reference." A helpless civility was all he was capable of. If you're going to suffer, *suffer,* he told himself.

"Look," La Meck said, his tone changing, shifting from brutality to compassion as though there were no difference between the two, "you've got a kind of quality, a real feeling for collection. I'm frank to tell you, when you first came to work for us I figured you wouldn't last. I put you on the phones because I wanted you to see the toughest part first. A lot of people can't do it. You take a guy who's down and bury him deeper. It's heart-wringing work. But you, you were amazing. An artist. You had a real thing for the deadbeat soul, I thought. But we started to get complaints, and I had to warn you. Didn't I warn you? I should have suspected something when the delinquent accounts started to turn over again. It was like rancid butter turning sweet. So I don't say this to knock your technique. Your technique's terrific. With you around we could have laid off the lawyers. But Ed, you're a gangster. A gangster."

That's it, Ed Wolfe thought. *I'm a gangster. Babyface Wolfe at nobody's door.*

"Well," La Meck said, "I guess we owe you some money."

"Two weeks' pay," Ed Wolfe said.

"And two weeks in lieu of notice," La Meck said grandly.

"And a week's pay for my vacation."

"You haven't been here a year," La Meck said.

"It would have been a year in another month. I've earned the vacation."

"What the hell," La Meck said. "A week's pay for vacation."

La Meck figured on a pad and tearing off a sheet handed it to Ed Wolfe. "Does that check with your figures?" he asked.

Ed Wolfe, who had no figures, was amazed to see that his check was so large. Leaving off the deductions he made $92.73 a week. Five $92.73's was evidently $463.65. It was a lot of money. "That seems to be right," he told La Meck.

La Meck gave him a check and Ed Wolfe got up. Already it was as though he had never worked there. When La Meck handed him the check he almost couldn't think what it was for. It was as if there

should have been a photographer there to record the ceremony. OR-
PHAN AWARDED CHECK BY BUSINESSMAN.

"Good-by, Mr. La Meck," he said. "It has been an interesting association," he added foolishly.

"Good-by, Ed," La Meck answered, putting his arm around Ed
Wolfe's shoulders and leading him to the door. "I'm sorry it had to
end this way." He shook Ed Wolfe's hand seriously and looked into
his eyes. He had a hard grip.

Quantity and quality, Ed Wolfe thought.

"One thing, Ed. Watch yourself. Your mistake here was that you
took the job too seriously. You hated the chiselers."

No, no, I loved them, he thought.

"You've got to watch it. Don't love. Don't hate. That's the secret.
Detachment and caution. Look out for Ed Wolfe."

"I'll watch out for him," he said giddily and in a moment he was
out of La Meck's office, and the main office, and the elevator, and the
building itself, loose in the world, as cautious and as detached as La
Meck could want him.

He took the car from the parking lot, handing the attendant the
two dollars. The man gave him fifty cents back. "That's right," Ed
Wolfe said, "it's only two o'clock." He put the half dollar in his
pocket, and, on an impulse, took out his wallet. He had twelve dollars. He counted his change. Eighty-two cents. With his finger, on the
dusty dashboard, he added $12.82 to $463.65. He had $476.47. *Does
that check with your figures?* he asked himself and drove into the
crowded traffic.

Proceeding slowly, past his old building, past garages, past bar
and grills, past second-rate hotels, he followed the traffic further
downtown. He drove into the deepest part of the city, down and
downtown to the bottom, the foundation, the city's navel. He watched
the shoppers and tourists and messengers and men with appointments. He was tranquil, serene. It was something he would be content
to do forever. He could use his check to buy gas, to take his meals at
drive-in restaurants, to pay tolls. It would be a pleasant life, a great
life, and he contemplated it thoughtfully. To drive at fifteen or twenty
miles an hour through eternity, stopping at stoplights and signs, pulling over to the curb at the sound of sirens and the sight of funerals,
obeying all traffic laws, making obedience to them his very code. Ed

Wolfe, the Flying Dutchman, the Wandering Jew, the Off and Running Orphan, "Look Out For Ed Wolfe," a ghostly wailing down the city's corridors. *What would be bad?* he thought.

In the morning, out of habit, he dressed himself in a white shirt and light suit. Before he went downstairs he saw that his check and his twelve dollars were still in his wallet. Carefully he counted the eighty-two cents that he had placed on the dresser the night before, put the coins in his pocket, and went downstairs to his car.

Something green had been shoved under the wiper blade on the driver's side.

YOUR CAR WILL NEVER BE WORTH MORE THAN IT IS WORTH RIGHT NOW! WHY WAIT FOR DEPRECIATION TO MAKE YOU AUTOMOTIVELY BANKRUPT? I WILL BUY THIS CAR AND PAY YOU CASH! I WILL NOT CHEAT YOU!

Ed Wolfe considered his car thoughtfully a moment and got in. He drove that day through the city playing the car radio softly. He heard the news each hour and each half hour. He listened to Arthur Godfrey far away and in another world. He heard Bing Crosby's ancient voice, and thought sadly, *Depreciation.* When his tank was almost empty he thought wearily of having to have it filled and could see himself, bored and discontented behind the bugstained glass, forced into a patience he did not feel, having to decide whether to take the Green Stamps the attendant tried to extend. *Put money in your purse, Ed Wolfe,* he thought. *Cash!* he thought with passion.

He went to the address on the circular.

He drove up onto the gravel lot but remained in his car. In a moment a man came out of a small wooden shack and walked toward Ed Wolfe's car. If he was appraising it he gave no sign. He stood at the side of the automobile and waited while Ed Wolfe got out.

"Look around," the man said. "No pennants, no strings of electric lights." He saw the advertisement in Ed Wolfe's hand. "I ran the ad off on my brother-in-law's mimeograph. My kid stole the paper from his school."

Ed Wolfe looked at him.

"The place looks like a goddamn parking lot. When the snow starts falling I get rid of the cars and move the Christmas trees right onto it. No overhead. That's the beauty of a volume business."

Ed Wolfe looked pointedly at the nearly empty lot.

"That's right," the man said. "It's slow. I'm giving the policy one more chance. Then I cheat the public just like everybody else. You're just in time. Come on, I'll show you a beautiful car."

"I want to sell my car," Ed Wolfe said.

"Sure, sure," the man said. "You want to trade with me. I give top allowances. I play fair."

"I want you to buy my car."

The man looked at him closely. "What do you want? You want me to go into the office and put on the ten-gallon hat? It's my only overhead so I guess you're entitled to see it. You're paying for it. I put on this big frigging hat, see, and I become Texas Willie Waxelman, the Mad Cowboy. If that's what you want, I can get it in a minute."

It was incredible, Ed Wolfe thought. *There were bastards everywhere who hated other bastards downtown everywhere.* "I don't want to trade my car in," Ed Wolfe said. "I want to sell it. I, too, want to reduce my inventory."

The man smiled sadly. "You want me to buy *your* car. You run in and put on the hat. I'm an automobile *salesman,* kid."

"No, you're not," Ed Wolfe said. "I was with Cornucopia Finance. We handled your paper. You're an automobile *buyer.* Your business is in buying up four- and five-year-old cars like mine from people who need dough fast and then auctioning them off to the trade."

The man turned away and Ed Wolfe followed him. Inside the shack the man said, "I'll give you two hundred."

"I need six hundred," Ed Wolfe said.

"I'll lend you the hat. Hold up a goddamn stagecoach."

"Give me five."

"I'll give you two fifty and we'll part friends."

"Four hundred and fifty."

"Three hundred. Here," the man said, reaching his hand into an opened safe and taking out three sheaves of thick, banded bills. He held the money out to Ed Wolfe. "Go ahead, count it."

Absently Ed Wolfe took the money. The bills were stiff, like money in a teller's drawer, their value as decorous and untapped as a sheet of postage stamps. He held the money, pleased by its weight. "Tens and fives," he said, grinning.

"You bet," the man said, taking the money back. "You want to sell your car?"

"Yes," Ed Wolfe said. "Give me the money," he said hoarsely.

He had been to the bank, had stood in the patient, slow, money-conscious line, had presented his formidable check to the impassive teller, hoping the four hundred and sixty-three dollars and sixty-five cents she counted out would seem his week's salary to the man who waited behind him. *Fool,* he thought, *it will seem two weeks' pay and two weeks in lieu of notice and a week for vacation for the hell of it, the three-week margin of an orphan.*

"Thank you," the teller said, already looking beyond Ed Wolfe to the man behind him.

"Wait," Ed Wolfe said. "Here." He handed her a white withdrawal slip.

She took it impatiently and walked to a file. "You're closing your savings account?" she asked loudly.

"Yes," Ed Wolfe answered, embarrassed.

"I'll have a cashier's check made out for this."

"No, no," Ed Wolfe said desperately. "Give me cash."

"Sir, we make out a cashier's check and cash it for you," the teller explained.

"Oh," Ed Wolfe said. "I see."

When the teller had given him the two hundred fourteen dollars and twenty-three cents, he went to the next window where he made out a check for $38.91. It was what he had in his checking account.

On Ed Wolfe's kitchen table was a thousand dollars. That day he had spent a dollar and ninety cents. He had twenty-seven dollars and seventy-one cents in his pocket. For expenses. "For attrition," he said aloud. "The cost of living. For streetcars and newspapers and half gallons of milk and loaves of white bread. For the movies. For a cup of coffee." He went to his pantry. He counted the cans and packages, the boxes and bottles. "The three weeks again," he said. "The orphan's nutritional margin." He looked in his icebox. In the freezer he poked around among white packages of frozen meat. He looked brightly into the vegetable tray. A whole lettuce. Five tomatoes. Several slices of cucumber. Browning celery. On another shelf four bananas. Three and a half apples. A cut pineapple. Some grapes, loose and collapsing darkly in a white bowl. A quarter pound of butter. A few eggs. Another egg, broken last week, congealing in a blue dish. Things in plastic bowls, in jars, forgotten, faintly mysterious leftovers, faintly rotten, vaguely futured, equivocal garbage. He closed the door, feeling a draft. "Really," he said, "it's quite cozy." He looked at the thousand dollars on the kitchen table. "It's not enough," he said. "It's not enough," he shouted. "It's not enough to be cautious on. La Meck, you bastard, detachment comes higher, what do you think? You think it's cheap?" He raged against himself. It was the way he used to speak to people on the telephone. "Wake up. Orphan! Jerk! Wake up. It costs to be detached."

He moved solidly through the small apartment and lay down on his bed with his shoes still on, putting his hands behind his head luxuriously. *It's marvelous,* he thought. *Tomorrow I'll buy a trench coat. I'll take my meals in piano bars.* He lighted a cigarette. *I'll never smile again,* he sang, smiling. "All right, Eddie, play it again," he said. "Mistuh Wuf, you don' wan' ta heah dat ol' song no maw. You know whut it do to you. She ain' wuth it, Mistuh Wuf." He nodded. "Again, Eddie." Eddie played his black ass off. "The way I see it, Eddie," he said, taking a long, sad drink of warm Scotch, "there are orphans and there are orphans." The overhead fan chuffed slowly, stirring the potted palmetto leaves.

He sat up in bed, grinding his heels across the sheets. "There are orphans and there are orphans," he said. "I'll move. I'll liquidate. I'll sell out."

He went to the phone and called his landlady and made an appointment to see her.

It was a time of ruthless parting from his things, but there was no bitterness in it. He was a born salesman, he told himself. A disposer, a natural dumper. He administered severance. As detached as a funeral director, what he had learned was to say good-by. It was a talent of a sort. And he had never felt quite so interested. He supposed he was doing what he had been meant for, what, perhaps, everyone was meant for. He sold and he sold, each day spinning off, reeling off little pieces of himself, like controlled explosions of the sun. Now his life was a series of speeches, of nearly earnest pitches. What he remembered of the day was what he had said. What others said to him, or even whether they spoke at all, he was unsure of.

Tuesday he told his landlady, "Buy my furniture. It's new. It's good stuff. It's expensive. You can forget about that. Put it out of your mind. I want to sell it. I'll show you bills for over seven hundred dollars. Forget the bills. Consider my character. Consider the man. Only the man. That's how to get your bargains. Examine. Examine. I could tell you about inner springs; I could talk to you of leather. But I won't. I don't. I smoke, but I'm careful. I can show you the ashtrays. You won't find cigarette holes in *my* tables. Examine. I drink. I'm a drinker. I drink. But I hold it. You won't find alcohol stains. May I be frank? I make love. Again, I could show you the bills. But I'm cautious. My sheets are virginal, white.

"Two hundred fifty dollars, landlady. Sit on that sofa. That chair. Buy my furniture. Rent the apartment furnished. Deduct what you pay from your taxes. Collect additional rents. Realize enormous profits. Wallow in gravy. Get it, landlady? Get it? Just two hundred fifty dollars. Don't disclose the figure or my name. I want to remain anonymous."

He took her into his bedroom. "The piece of resistance, landlady. What you're really buying is the bedroom stuff. I'm selling you your own bare floor. What charm. Charm? Elegance. Elegance! I throw in the livingroom rug. That I throw in. You have to take that or it's no deal. Give me cash and I move tomorrow."

Wednesday he said, "I heard you buy books. That must be interesting. And sad. It must be very sad. A man who loves books doesn't like to sell them. It would be the last thing. Excuse me. I've got no right to talk to you this way. You buy books and I've got books to sell. There. It's business now. As it should be. My library—" He smiled helplessly. "Excuse me. Such a grand name. Library." He began again slowly. "My books, my books are in there. Look them over. I'm afraid my taste has been rather eclectic. You see, my education has not been formal. There are over eleven hundred. Of course many are paperbacks. Well, you can see that. I feel as if I'm selling my mind."

The book buyer gave Ed Wolfe one hundred twenty dollars for his mind.

On Thursday he wrote a letter:

American Annuity & Life Insurance Company,
Suite 410,
Lipton-Hill Building,
2007 Beverl Street, S.W.,
Boston 19, Massachusetts

Dear Sirs,

I am writing in regard to Policy Number 593-00034-78, a $5,000, twenty-year annuity held by Edward Wolfe of the address below.

Although only four payments having been made, sixteen years remain before the policy matures, I find I must make application for the immediate return of my payments and cancel the policy.

I have read the "In event of cancellation" clause in my policy, and realize that I am entitled to only a flat three percent interest on the "total paid-in amount of the partial amortizement." Your records will show that I have made four payments of $198.45 each. If your figures check with mine this would come to $793.80. Adding three percent interest to this amount ($23.81), your company owes me $817.61.

Your prompt attention to my request would be gratefully appreciated, although I feel, frankly, as though I were selling my future.

On Monday someone came to buy his record collection. "What do you want to hear? I'll put something comfortable on while we talk. What do you like? Here, try this. Go ahead, put it on the machine. By the edges, man. By the edges! I feel as if I'm selling my throat. Never mind about that. Dig the sounds. Orphans up from Orleans singing the news of chain gangs to café society. You can smell the freight trains, man. Recorded during actual performance. You can hear the ice cubes clinkin' in the glasses, the waiters picking up their tips. I have jazz. Folk. Classical. Broadway. Spoken Word. Spoken Word, man! I feel as though I'm selling my ears. The stuff lives in my heart or I wouldn't sell. I have a one-price throat, one-price ears. Sixty dollars for the noise the world makes, man. But remember. I'll be watching. By the edges. Only by the edges!"

On Friday he went to a pawnshop in a Checker Cab.

"You? You buy gold? You buy clothes? You buy Hawaiian guitars? You buy pistols for resale to suicides? I wouldn't have recognized you. Where's the skullcap, the garters around the sleeves? The cigar I wouldn't ask you about. You look like anybody. You look like everybody. I don't know what to say. I'm stuck. I don't know how to deal with you. I was going to tell you something sordid, you know? You know what I mean? Okay, I'll give you facts.

"The fact is, I'm the average man. That's what the fact is. Eleven shirts, 15 neck, 34 sleeve. Six slacks, 32 waist. Five suits at 38 long. Shoes 10-C. A 7½ hat. You know something? Those marginal restaurants where you can never remember whether they'll let you in without a jacket? Well the jackets they lend you in those places always fit me. That's the kind of guy you're dealing with. You can have confidence. Look at the clothes. Feel the material. And there's one thing about me. I'm fastidious. Fastidious. Immaculate. You think I'd be clumsy. A fall guy falls down, right? There's not a mark on the clothes. Inside? Inside it's another story. I don't speak of inside. Inside it's all Band-Aids, plaster, iodine, sticky stuff for burns. But outside—fastidiousness, immaculation, reality! My clothes will fly off your racks. I promise. I feel as if I'm selling my skin. Does that check with your figures?

"So now you know. It's me, Ed Wolfe. Ed Wolfe, the orphan? I lived in the orphanage for sixteen years. They gave me a name. It was a Jewish orphanage so they gave me a Jewish name. Almost. That is they couldn't know for sure themselves so they kept it deliberately vague. I'm a foundling. A lostling. Who needs it, right? Who the hell needs it? I'm at loose ends, pawnbroker. I'm at loose ends out of looser beginnings. I need the money to stay alive. All you can give me.

"Here's a good watch. Here's a bad one. For good times and bad. That's life, right? You can sell them as a package deal. Here are radios, I'll miss the radios. A phonograph. Automatic. Three speeds. Two speakers. The politic bastard shuts itself off. And a pressure cooker. It's valueless to me, frankly. No pressure. I can live only on cold meals. Spartan. Spartan.

"I feel as if I'm selling—this is the last of it, I have no more things—I feel as if I'm selling my things."

On Saturday he called the phone company: "Operator? Let me speak to your supervisor, please.

"Supervisor? Supervisor, I am Ed Wolfe, your subscriber at TErrace 7-3572. There is nothing wrong with the service. The service has been excellent. No one calls, but you can have nothing to do with that. However, I must cancel. I find that I no longer have any need of a telephone. Please connect me with the business office.

"Business office? Business office, this is Ed Wolfe. My telephone number is TErrace 7-3572. I am closing my account with you. When the service was first installed I had to surrender a twenty-five-dollar deposit to your company. It was understood that the deposit was to be refunded when our connection with each other had been terminated. Disconnect me. Deduct what I owe on my current account from my deposit and refund the rest immediately. Business office, I feel as if I'm selling my mouth."

When he had nothing left to sell, when that was finally that, he stayed until he had finished all the food and then moved from his old apartment into a small, thinly furnished room. He took with him a single carton of clothing—the suit, the few shirts, the socks, the pajamas, the underwear and overcoat he did not sell. It was in preparing this carton that he discovered the hangers. There were hundreds of them. His own. Previous tenants'. Hundreds. In each closet on rods, in dark, dark corners was this anonymous residue of all their lives. He unpacked his carton and put the hangers inside. They made a weight. He took them to the pawnshop and demanded a dollar for them. They were worth, he argued, more. In an A&P he got another carton free and went back to repack his clothes.

At the new place the landlord gave him his key.

"You got anything else?" the landlord asked. "I could give you a hand."

"No," he said. "Nothing."

Following the landlord up the deep stairs he was conscious of the $2,479.03 he had packed into the pockets of the suit and shirts and pajamas and overcoat inside the carton. It was like carrying a community of economically viable dolls.

When the landlord left him he opened the carton and gathered all his money together. In fading light he reviewed the figures he had entered in the pages of an old spiral notebook:

Pay	$463.65
Cash	12.82
Car	300.00
Savings	214.23
Checking	38.91
Furniture (& bedding)	250.00
Books	120.00
Insurance	817.61
Records	60.00

Pawned:

Clothes	110.00
2 watches	18.00
2 radios	12.00
Phonograph	35.00
Pressure cooker	6.00
Phone deposit (less bill)	19.81
Hangers	1.00

Total	$2,479.03

So, he thought, that was what he was worth. That was the going rate for orphans in a wicked world. Something under $2,500. He took his pencil and lined through all the nouns on his list. He tore the list carefully from top to bottom and crumpled the half which inventoried his expossessions. Then he crumpled the other half.

He went to the window and pushed the loose, broken shade. He opened the window and set both lists on the ledge. He made a ring of his forefinger and thumb and flicked the paper balls into the street. "Look out for Ed Wolfe," he said softly.

In six weeks the season changed. The afternoons failed. The steam failed. He was as unafraid of the dark as he had been of the sunlight. He longed for a special grief, to be touched by anguish or terror, but when he saw the others in the street, in the cafeteria, in the theatre, in the hallway, on the stairs, at the newsstand, in the basement rushing their fouled linen from basket to machine, he stood, as indifferent to their errand, their appetite, their joy, their greeting, their effort, their curiosity, their grime, as he was to his own. No envy wrenched him, no despair unhoped him, but, gradually, he became restless.

He began to spend, not recklessly so much as indifferently. At first he was able to recall for weeks what he spent on a given day. It was his way of telling time. Now he had difficulty remembering and could tell how much his life was costing only by subtracting what he had left from his original two thousand four hundred seventy-nine dollars and three cents. In eleven weeks he had spent six hundred seventy-seven dollars and thirty-four cents. It was almost three times more than he had planned. He became panicky. He had come to think of his money as his life. Spending it was the abrasion again, the old habit of self-buffing to come to the thing beneath. He could not draw infinitely on his credit. It was limited. Limited. He checked his figures. He had eighteen hundred and one dollars, sixty-nine cents. He warned himself, "Rothschild, child. Rockefeller, feller. Look out, Ed Wolfe. Look out."

He argued with his landlord, won a five-dollar reduction in his rent. He was constantly hungry, wore clothes stingily, realized an odd reassurance in his thin pain, his vague fetidness. He surrendered his dimes, his quarters, his half-dollars in a kind of sober anger. In seven weeks he spent only one hundred thirty dollars, fifty-one cents. He checked his figures. He had sixteen hundred seventy-one dollars, eighteen cents. He had spent almost twice what he had anticipated. "It's all right," he said. "I've reversed the trend. I can catch up." He held the money in his hand. He could smell his soiled underwear. "Nah, nah," he said. "It's not enough."

It was not enough, it was not enough, it was not enough. He had painted himself into a corner. Death by *cul-de-sac*. He had nothing left to sell, the born salesman. The born champion, long-distance, Ed Wolfe of a salesman, and he lay in his room winded, wounded, wondering where his next pitch was coming from, at one with the ages.

He put on his suit, took his sixteen hundred, seventy-one dollars and eighteen cents and went down into the street. It was a warm night. He would walk downtown. The ice which just days before had covered the sidewalk was dissolved in slush. In darkness he walked through a thawing, melting world. There was, on the edge of the air, something, the warm, moist odor of the change of the season. He was, despite himself, touched. "I'll take a bus," he threatened. "I'll take a bus and close the windows and ride over the wheel."

He had dinner and some drinks in a hotel. When he finished he was feeling pretty good. He didn't want to go back. He looked at the bills thick in his wallet and went over to the desk clerk. "Where's the action?" he whispered. The clerk looked at him, startled. He went over to the bell captain. "Where's the action?" he asked and gave the man a dollar. He winked. The man stared at him helplessly.

"Sir?" the bell captain said, looking at the dollar.

Ed Wolfe nudged him in his gold buttons. He winked again. "Nice town you got here," he said expansively. "I'm a salesman, you understand, and this is new territory for me. Now if I were in Beantown or Philly or L.A. or Vegas of Big D or Frisco or Cincy, why I'd know what was what. I'd be okay, you know what I mean?" He winked once more. "Keep the buck, kid," he said. "Keep it, keep it," he said, walking off.

In the lobby a man sat in a deep chair, *The Wall Street Journal* opened widely across his face. "Where's the action?" Ed Wolfe said, peering over the top of the paper into the crown of the man's hat.

"What's that?" the man asked.

Ed Wolfe, surprised, saw that the man was a Negro.

"What's that?" the man repeated, vaguely nervous. Embarrassed, Ed Wolfe watched him guiltily, as though he had been caught in an act of bigotry.

"I thought you were someone else," he said lamely. The man smiled and lifted the paper to his face. Ed Wolfe stood before the man's opened paper, conscious of mildly teetering. He felt lousy, awkward, complicatedly irritated and ashamed, the mere act of hurting someone's feelings suddenly the most that could be held against him. It came to him how completely he had failed to make himself felt. "Look out for Ed Wolfe, indeed," he said aloud. The man lowered his paper. "Some of my best friends are Comanches," Ed Wolfe said. "Can I buy you a drink?"

"No," the man said.

"Resistance, eh?" Ed Wolfe said. "That's good. Resistance is good. A deal closed without resistance is no deal. Let me introduce myself. I'm Ed Wolfe. What's your name?"

"Please, I'm not bothering anybody. Leave me alone."

"Why?" Ed Wolfe asked.

The man stared at him and Ed Wolfe sat suddenly down beside him. "I won't press it," he said generously. "Where's the action? Where *is* it? Fold the paper, man. You're playing somebody else's gig." He leaned across the space between them and took the man by the arm. He pulled at him gently, awed by his own boldness. It was the first time since he had shaken hands with La Meck that he had touched anyone physically. What he was risking surprised and puzzled him. In all those months to have touched only two people, to have touched even two people! To feel their life, even, as now, through the unyielding wool of clothing, was disturbing. He was unused to it, frightened and oddly moved. The man, bewildered, looked at Ed Wolfe timidly and allowed himself to be taken toward the cocktail lounge.

They took a table near the bar. There, in the alcoholic dark, within earshot of the easy banter of the regulars, Ed Wolfe seated the Negro and then himself. He looked around the room and listened for a moment. He turned back to the Negro. Smoothly boozy, he pledged the man's health when the girl brought their drinks. He drank stolidly, abstractedly. Coming to life briefly, he indicated the men and women around them, their suntans apparent even in the dark. "Pilots," he said. "All of them. Airline pilots. The girls are all stewardesses and the pilots lay them." He ordered more drinks. He did not like liquor and liberally poured ginger ale into his bourbon. He ordered more drinks and forgot the ginger ale. *"Goyim,"* he said. "White *goyim.* American *goyim.*" He stared at the Negro. "These are the people, man. The mothered and fathered people." He leaned across the table. "Little Orphan Annie, what the hell kind of an orphan is that with all her millions and her white American *goyim* friends to bail her out?"

He watched them narrowly, drunkenly. He had seen them before—in good motels, in airports, in bars—and he wondered about them, seeing them, he supposed, as Negroes or children of the poor must have seen him when he had had his car and driven sometimes through slums. They were removed, aloof—he meant it—a different breed. He turned and saw the Negro and could not think for a moment what the man could have been doing there. The Negro slouched in his chair, his great white eyes hooded. "You want to hang around here?" Ed Wolfe asked him.

"It's your party," the man said.

"Then let's go someplace else," Ed Wolfe said. "I get nervous here."

"I know a place," the Negro said.

"*You* know a place. You're a stranger here."

"No, man," the Negro said. "This is my hometown. I come down here sometimes just to sit in the lobby and read the newspapers. It looks good, you know what I mean? It looks good for the race."

"*The Wall Street Journal?* You're kidding Ed Wolfe. Watch that."

"No," the Negro said. "Honest."

"I'll be damned," Ed Wolfe said. "I come for the same reasons."

"Yeah," the Negro said. "No shit."

"Sure, the same reaasons." He laughed. "Let's get out of here." He tried to stand, but fell back again in his chair. "Hey, help me up," he said loudly. The Negro got up and came around to Ed Wolfe's side of the table. Leaning over, he raised him to his feet. Some of the others in the room looked at them curiously. "It's all right," Ed Wolfe said. "He's my man. I take him with me everywhere. It looks good for the race." With their arms around each other's shoulders they stumbled out of the room and through the lobby.

In the street Ed Wolfe leaned against the building and the Negro hailed a cab, the dark left hand shooting up boldly, the long black body stretching forward, raised on tiptoes, the head turned sharply along the left shoulder. Ed Wolfe knew he had never done it before. The Negro came up beside Ed Wolfe and guided him toward the curb. Holding the door open he shoved him into the cab with his left hand. Ed Wolfe lurched against the cushioned seat awkwardly. The Negro gave the driver an address and the cab moved off. Ed Wolfe reached for the window handle and rolled it down rapidly. He shoved his head out the window of the taxi and smiled and waved at the people along the curb.

"Hey, man. Close the window," the Negro said after a moment. "Close the window. The cops, the cops."

Ed Wolfe lay his head along the edge of the taxi window and looked up at the Negro who was leaning over him and smiling and seemed trying to tell him something.

"Where we going, man?" he asked.

"We're there," the Negro said, sliding along the seat toward the door.

"One ninety-five," the driver said.

"It's your party," Ed Wolfe told the Negro, waving away responsibility.

The Negro looked disappointed, but reached into his pocket to pull out his wallet.

Did he see what I had on me? Ed Wolfe wondered anxiously. *Jerk, drunk, you'll be rolled. They'll cut your throat and then they'll leave your skin in an alley. Be careful.*

"Come on, Ed," the Negro said. He took him by the arm and got him out of the taxi.

Fake. Fake, Ed Wolfe thought. *Murderer. Nigger. Razor man.*

The Negro pulled Ed Wolfe toward a doorway. "You'll meet my friends," he said.

"Yeah, yeah," Ed Wolfe said. "I've heard so much about them."

"Hold it a second," the Negro said. He went up to the window and pressed his ear against the opaque glass.

Ed Wolfe watched him without making a move.

"Here's the place," the Negro said proudly.

"Sure," Ed Wolfe said. "Sure it is."

"Come on, man," the Negro urged him.

"I'm coming, I'm coming," Ed Wolfe mumbled, "but my head is bending low."

The Negro took out a ring of keys, selected one, and put it in the door. Ed Wolfe followed him through.

"Hey, Oliver," somebody called. "Hey, baby, it's Oliver. Oliver looks good. He looks *good.*"

"Hello, Mopiani," the Negro said to a short black man.

"How is stuff, Oliver?" Mopiani said to him.

"How's the market?" a man next to Mopiani asked, with a laugh.

"Ain't no mahket, baby. It's a *sto',*" somebody else said.

A woman stopped, looked at Ed Wolfe for a moment, and asked: "Who's the ofay, Oliver?"

"That's Oliver's broker, baby."

"Oliver's broker looks good," Mopiani said. "He looks *good.*"

"This is my friend, Mr. Ed Wolfe," Oliver told them.

"Hey, there," Mopiani said.

"Charmed," Ed Wolfe said.

"How's it going, man," a Negro said indifferently.

"Delighted," Ed Wolfe said.

He let Oliver lead him to a table.

"I'll get the drinks, Ed," Oliver said, leaving him.

Ed Wolfe looked at the room glumly. People were drinking

steadily, gaily. They kept their bottles under their chairs in paper bags. Ed Wolfe watched a man take a bag from beneath his chair, raise it, and twist the open end of the bag carefully around the neck of the bottle so that it resembled a bottle of champagne swaddled in its toweling. The man poured into his glass grandly. At the dark far end of the room some musicians were playing and three or four couples danced dreamily in front of them. He watched the musicians closely and was vaguely reminded of the airline pilots.

In a few minutes Oliver returned with a paper bag and some glasses. A girl was with him. "Mary Roberta, Ed Wolfe," he said, very pleased. Ed Wolfe stood up clumsily and the girl nodded.

"No more ice," Oliver explained.

"What the hell," Ed Wolfe said.

Mary Roberta sat down and Oliver pushed her chair up to the table. She sat with her hands in her lap and Oliver pushed her as though she were a cripple.

"Real nice little place here, Ollie," Ed Wolfe said.

"Oh, it's just the club," Oliver said.

"Real nice," Ed Wolfe said.

Oliver opened the bottle and poured liquor in their glasses and put the paper bag under his chair. Oliver raised his glass. Ed Wolfe touched it lamely with his own and leaned back, drinking. When he put it down empty, Oliver filled it again from the paper bag. He drank sluggishly, like one falling asleep, and listened, numbed, to Oliver and the girl. His glass never seemed to be empty anymore. He drank steadily but the liquor seemed to remain at the same level in the glass. He was conscious that someone else had joined them at the table. "Oliver's broker looks good," he heard somebody say. Mopiani. Warm and drowsy and gently detached, he listened, feeling as he had in barbershops, having his hair cut, conscious of the barber, unseen behind him, touching his hair and scalp with his warm fingers. "You see Bert? He looks good," Mopiani was saying.

With great effort Ed Wolfe shifted in his chair, turning to the girl.

"Thought you were giving out on us, Ed," Oliver said. "That's it. That's it."

The girl sat with her hands folded in her lap.

"Mary Roberta," Ed Wolfe said.

"Uh huh," the girl said.

"Mary Roberta."

"Yes," the girl said. "That's right."

"You want to dance?" Ed Wolfe asked.

"All right," she said. "I guess so."

"That's it, that's it," Oliver said. "Stir yourself."

He got up clumsily, cautiously, like one standing in a stalled Ferris wheel, and went around behind her chair, pulling it far back from the table with the girl in it. He took her warm, bare arm and moved toward the dancers. Mopiani passed them with a bottle. "Looks good, looks good," Mopiani said approvingly. He pulled her against him to let Mopiani pass, tightening the grip of his pale hand on her brown arm. A muscle leaped beneath the girl's smooth skin, filling his palm. At the edge of the dance floor Ed Wolfe leaned forward into the girl's arms and they moved slowly, thickly across the floor. He held the girl close, conscious of her weight, the life beneath her body, just under her skin. Sick, he remembered a jumping bean he had held once in his palm, awed and frightened by the invisible life, jerking and hysterical, inside the stony shell. The girl moved with him in the music, Ed Wolfe astonished by the burden of her life. He stumbled away from her deliberately. Grinning, he moved ungently back against her. "Look out for Ed Wolfe," he crooned.

The girl stiffened and held him away from her, dancing self-consciously. Ed Wolfe, brooding, tried to concentrate on the lost rhythm. They danced in silence for a while.

"What do you do?" she asked him finally.

"I'm a salesman," he told her gloomily.

"Door to door?"

"Floor to ceiling. Wall to wall."

"Too much," she said.

"I'm a pusher," he said, suddenly angry. She looked frightened. "But I'm not hooked myself. It's a weakness in my character. I can't get hooked. Ach, what would you *goyim* know about it?"

"Take it easy," she said. "What's the matter with you? Do you want to sit down?"

"I can't push sitting down," he said.

"Hey," she said, "don't talk so loud."

"Boy," he said, "you black Protestants. What's that song you people sing?"

"Come on," she said.

"Sometimes I feel like a motherless child," he sang roughly. The other dancers watched him nervously. "That's our national anthem, man," he said to a couple that had stopped dancing to look at him. "That's our song, sweethearts," he said, looking around him. "All right, mine then. I'm an orphan."

"Oh, come on," the girl said, exasperated, "an orphan. A grown man."

He pulled away from her. The band stopped playing. "Hell," he said loudly, "from the beginning. Orphan. Bachelor. Widower. Only child. All my names scorn me. I'm a survivor. I'm a goddamned survivor, that's what." The other couples crowded around him now. People got up from their tables. He could see them, on tiptoes, stretching their necks over the heads of the dancers. *No,* he thought. *No, no. Detachment and caution. The La Meck Plan. They'll kill you. They'll kill you and kill you.* He edged away from them, moving carefully backward against the bandstand. People pushed forward onto the dance floor to watch him. He could hear their questions, could see heads darting from behind backs and suddenly appearing over shoulders as they strained to get a look at him.

He grabbed Mary Roberta's hand, pulling her to him fiercely. He pulled and pushed her up onto the bandstand and then climbed up beside her. The trumpet player, bewildered, made room for him. "Tell you what I'm going to do," he shouted over their heads. "Tell you what I'm going to do."

Everyone was listening to him now.

"Tell you what I'm going to do," he began again.

Quietly they waited for him to go on.

"I don't *know* what I'm going to do," he shouted. "I don't *know* what I'm going to do. Isn't that a hell of a note?

"Isn't it?" he demanded.

"Brothers and sisters," he shouted, "and as an only child bachelor orphan I use the term playfully you understand. Brothers and sisters, I tell you what I'm *not* going to do. I'm no consumer. Nobody's death can make me that. I won't consume. I mean it's a question of identity, right? Closer, come up closer, buddies. You don't want to miss any of this."

"Oliver's broker looks good up there. Mary Roberta looks good. She looks good," Mopiani said below him.

"Right, Mopiani. She looks good, she looks *good.*" Ed Wolfe called loudly. "So I tell you what I'm going to do. What am I bid? What am I bid for this fine strong wench? Daughter of a chief, masters. Dear dark daughter of a dead dinge chief. Look at those arms. Those arms, those arms. What am I bid?"

They looked at him, astonished.

"What am I bid?" he demanded. "Reluctant, masters? Reluctant masters, masters? Say, what's the matter with you darkies? Come on, what am I bid?" He turned to the girl. "No one wants you, honey," he said. "Folks, folks, I'd buy her myself, but I've already told you. I'm not a consumer. Please forgive me, miss."

He heard them shifting uncomfortably.

"Look," he said patiently, "the management has asked me to remind you that this is a living human being. This is the real thing, the genuine article, the goods. Oh, I told them I wasn't the right man for this mob. As an orphan I have no conviction about the product. Now you should have seen me in my old job. I could be rough. Rough. I hurt people. Can you imagine? I actually caused them pain. I mean, what the hell, I was an orphan. I *could* hurt people. An orphan doesn't have to bother with love. An orphan's like a nigger in that respect. Emancipated. But you people are another problem entirely. That's why I came here tonight. There are parents among you. I can feel it. There's even a sense of parents behind those parents. My God, don't any of you folks ever die? So what's holding us up? We're not making any money. Come on, what am I bid?"

"Shut up, mister." The voice was raised hollowly someplace in the back of the crowd.

Ed Wolfe could not see the owner of the voice.

"He's not in," Ed Wolfe said.

"Shut up. What right you got to come down here and speak to us like that?"

"He's not in, I tell you. I'm his brother."

"You're a guest. A guest got no call to talk like that."

"He's out. I'm his father. He didn't tell me and I don't know when he'll be back."

"You can't make fun of us," the voice said.

"He isn't here. I'm his son."

"Bring that girl down off that stage!"

"Speaking," Ed Wolfe said.

"Let go of that girl!" someone called angrily.

The girl moved closer to him.

"She's mine," Ed Wolfe said. "I danced with her."

"Get her down from there!"

"Okay," he said giddily. "Okay. All right." He let go of the girl's hand and pulled out his wallet. The girl did not move. He took out the bills and dropped the wallet to the floor.

"Damned drunk!" someone shouted.

"That white man's crazy," someone else said.

"Here," Ed Wolfe said. "There's over sixteen hundred dollars here," he yelled, waving the money. It was, for him, like holding so much paper. "I'll start the bidding. I hear over sixteen hundred dollars once. I hear over sixteen hundred dollars twice. I hear it three times. Sold! A deal's a deal," he cried, flinging the money high over their heads. He saw them reach helplessly, noiselessly toward the bills, heard distinctly the sound of paper tearing.

He faced the girl. "Good-by," he said.

She reached forward, taking his hand.

"Good-by," he said again. I'm leaving."

She held his hand, squeezing it. He looked down at the luxuriant brown hand, seeing beneath it the fine articulation of bones, the rich sudden rush of muscle. Inside her own he saw, indifferently, his own pale hand, lifeless and serene, still and infinitely free.

[September 1962]

BERNARD MALAMUD

Life Is Better Than Death

She seemed to remember the man from the same day last year. He was standing at a nearby grave, occasionally turning to look around, while Etta, a rosary in her hand, prayed for the repose of the soul of her husband Armando. Sometimes she prayed Armando would move over and let her lie down with him so that her heart might be relieved. It was the second of November, All Souls' Day in the Cimitero Campo Verano, in Rome, and it had begun to drizzle after she had laid down the bouquet of yellow chrysanthemums on the grave Armando wouldn't have had if it weren't for a generous uncle, a doctor in Perugia. Without this uncle Etta had no idea where Armando would be buried, certainly in a much less attractive grave, though she would have resisted his often-expressed desire to be cremated.

Etta worked for meager wages in a draper's shop and Armando had left no insurance. The large bright yellow flowers, glowing in the November gloom on the faded grass, moved her and tears gushed forth for a moment. Although she felt uncomfortably feverish when she cried like that, Etta was glad she had, because crying seemed to be the only thing that relieved her. She was thirty, dressed in full mourning. Her figure was slim, her moist brown eyes red-rimmed and darkly ringed, the skin pale and the features grown thin. Since the accidental death of Armando, a few months more than a year ago, she came almost daily during the long Roman afternoon rest time to pray at his grave. She was devoted to his memory, ravaged within. Etta went to confession twice a week and took communion every Sunday. She lit candles for Armando at La Madonna Addolorata, and had a mass offered once a month—more often when she had a little extra money. Whenever she returned to the cold inexpensive flat she still lived in and could not give up because once it also had been his, Etta thought of Armando, recalling him as he had looked ten years ago, not as when he had died. Invariably she felt an oppressive pang and ate very little.

It was raining quietly when she finished her rosary. Etta dropped the beads into her purse and opened a black umbrella. The man from the other grave, wearing a darkish-green Borsalino and a tight black overcoat, had stopped a few feet behind her, cupping his small hands over a cigarette as he lit it. Seeing her turn from the grave, he touched his hat. He was a short man with dark eyes and a thin mustache. He had meaty ears but was handsome.

"Your husband?" he asked respectfully, letting the smoke flow out as he spoke, holding his cigarette cupped in his palm to keep it from getting wet.

She was momentarily nervous, undecided whether to do anything more than nod, then go her way, but the thought that he too was bereaved restrained her.

She said it was.

He nodded in the direction of the grave where he had stood. "My wife. One day while I was at my job she was hurryng to meet a lover and was killed in a minute by a taxi in the Piazza Bologna." He spoke without bitterness, without apparent emotion, but his eyes were troubled.

She noticed that he had put up his coat collar and was getting wet. Hesitantly she offered to share her umbrella with him on the way to the bus stop.

"Cesare Montaldo," he murmured, gravely accepting the umbrella and holding it high enough for both of them.

"Etta Oliva." She was, in her high heels, almost a head taller than he.

They walked slowly along an avenue of damp cypresses to the gates of the cemetery, Etta keeping from him that she had been so stricken by his story she could not get out even a sympathetic comment.

"Mourning is a hard business," Cesare said. "If people knew, there'd be less death."

She sighed with a slight smile.

Across the street from the bus stop was a "bar" with tables under a drawn awning. Cesare suggested coffee or perhaps an ice.

She thanked him and was about to refuse, but his sad serious expression changed her mind and she went with him across the street. He guided her gently by the elbow, the other hand firmly holding the umbrella over them. She said she felt cold and they went inside.

He ordered an espresso but Etta settled for a piece of pastry which she politely picked at. Between puffs of a cigarette he talked about himself. His voice was low and he spoke well. He was a freelance journalist, he said. Formerly he had worked in a government office, but the work was boring, so he had quit in disgust, although he was in line for the directorship. "I would have directed the boredom." Now he was toying with the idea of going to America. He had a brother in Boston who wanted him to come for a visit of several months and then decide whether he wanted to emigrate permanently. The brother thought they could arrange that Cesare might come in through Canada. He had considered the idea, but could not bring himself to break his ties with this kind of life for that. He seemed also to think that he would find it hard not to be able to come to his dead wife's grave when he was moved to do so. "You know how it is," he said, "with somebody you have once loved."

Etta felt in her purse for her handkerchief and touched her eyes with it.

"And you?" he asked sympathetically.

To her surprise she began to tell him her story. Though she had often related it to priests, she never had to anyone else, not even a friend. But she was telling it to a stranger because he seemed to be a man who would understand. And if later she regretted telling him, what difference would it make once he was gone?

She confessed she had prayed for her husband's death, and Cesare put down his coffee cup and sat with his cigarette between his lips, not puffing as she talked.

Armando, Etta said, had fallen in love with a cousin who had come during the summer from Perugia for a job in Rome. Her father had suggested that she live with them, and Armando and Etta, after talking it over, decided to let her stay for a while. They would save her rent to buy a used television set so they could watch *Lascia o Raddoppia*, the quiz program that everyone in Rome watched on Thursday nights, and that way save themselves the embarrassment of waiting for invitations and having to accept them from neighbors they didn't like. The cousin came, Laura Ansaldo, a big-boned, pretty girl of eighteen with thick brown hair and large eyes. She slept on the sofa in the living room, was easy to get along with, and made herself helpful in the kitchen before and after supper. Etta had liked her until she noticed that Armando had gone mad over the girl. She then tried to get rid of Laura, but Armando threatened he would leave her if she bothered the girl. One day she had come home from work and found them naked in the marriage bed, in the act. She had screamed and wept. She called Laura a stinking whore and swore she would kill her if she didn't leave the house that minute. Armando was contrite. He promised he would send the girl back to Perugia, and the next day in the Stazione Termini had put her on the train. But the separation from her was more than he could bear. He grew nervous and miserable. Armando confessed himself one Saturday night, and for the first time in ten years, took communion, but instead of calming down he desired the girl more strongly. After a week he told Etta that he was going to get his cousin and bring her back to Rome.

"If you bring that whore back," Etta shouted, "I'll pray to Christ that you drop dead before you get there."

"In that case," Armando said, "start praying."

When he left the house she fell on her knees and prayed with all her heart for his death.

That night Armando went with a friend to get Laura. The friend had a truck and was going to Assisi. On the way back he would pick them up in Perugia and drive to Rome. They started out when it was still twilight, but it soon grew dark. Armando drove for a while, then felt sleepy and crawled into the back of the truck. The Perugian hills were foggy after a hot September day and the truck hit a rock in the road a hard bump. Armando, in deep sleep, rolled out of the open tail gate of the truck, hitting the road with his head and shoulders, then rolling down the hill. He was dead before he stopped rolling. When she heard of this, Etta fainted away and it was two days before she could speak. After that she had prayed for her own death and often still did.

Etta turned her back to the other tables, though they were empty, and wept openly and quietly.

After a while Cesare squashed his cigarette. *"Calma, Signora.* If God had wanted your husband to live he would still be living. Prayers have little relevance to the situation. To my way of thinking the whole thing was no more than a coincidence. It's best not to go too far with religion or it becomes troublesome."

"A prayer is a prayer," she said. "I suffer for mine."

Cesare pursed his lips. "But who can judge these things? They're much more complicated than most of us know. In the case of my wife I didn't pray for her death, but I confess I might have wished it. Am I in a better position than you?"

"My prayer was a sin. You don't have that on your mind. It's worse than what you just might have thought."

"That's only a technical thing, *Signora.*"

"If Armando had lived," she said after a minute, "he would have been twenty-nine next month. I was a year older. But my life is useless now. I wait to join him."

He shook his head, seemed moved, and ordered an espresso for her.

Though Etta had stopped crying, for the first time in months she felt substantially relieved.

Cesare put her on the bus; as they were crossing the street he suggested they might meet now and then since they had so much in common.

"I live like a nun," she said.

He lifted his hat. *"Coraggio."* She smiled at him for his kindness.

When she returned home that night the anguish of life without Armando recommenced. She remembered him as he had been when he was courting her and felt uneasy for having talked about him to Cesare. And she vowed for herself continued prayers, rosaries, her own penitence to win him further indulgences in Purgatory.

Etta saw Cesare on a Sunday afternoon a week later. He had written her name in his little book and was able to locate her apartment in a house on the Via Nomentana through a friend in the gas and electric company.

When he knocked on her door she was surprised to see him, turned rather pale, though he hung back doubtfully. But she invited him in and he entered apologetically. He said he had found out by accident where she lived and she asked for no details. Cesare had brought a small bunch of violets which she embarrassedly accepted and put in water.

"You're looking better, *Signora,*" he said.

"My mourning for Armando goes on," she answered with a sad smile.

"*Moderazione,*" he counseled, flicking his meaty ear with his pinkie. "You're still a young woman, and at that not bad looking. You ought to acknowledge it to yourself. There are certain advantages to self-belief."

Etta made coffee and Cesare insisted on going out for a half-a-dozen pastries.

He said as they were eating that he was considering emigrating, if nothing better turned up soon. After a pause he said he had decided he had given more than his share to the dead. "I've been faithful to her memory, but I have to think of myself once in a while. There comes a time when one has to return to life. It's only natural. Where there's life there's life."

She lowered her eyes and sipped her coffee.

Cesare put down his cup and got up. He got on his coat and thanked her. As he was buttoning his overcoat he said he would drop by again when he was in the neighborhood. He had a journalist friend who lived close by.

"Don't forget I'm still in mourning," Etta said.

He looked up at her respectfully. "Who could forget that, *Signora?* Who would want to so long as you mourn?"

She then felt uneasy. "You know my story." She spoke as though she were explaining again.

"I know," he said, "that we were both betrayed. They died and we suffer. My wife ate flowers and I belch."

"They suffer too. At least let Armando suffer with a calm mind about me. I want him to feel that I'm still married to him." Her eyes were wet again.

"He's dead, *Signora.* The marriage is over," Cesare said. "There's no marriage without his presence unless you expect the Holy Ghost." He spoke dryly, adding quietly, "Your needs are different from a dead man's; you're a healthy woman. Let's face the facts."

"Not spiritually," she said quickly.

"Spiritually and physically, there's no love in death."

She blushed and spoke in excitement. "There's love for the dead. Let him feel that I'm paying for my sin at the same time he is for his. To help him into heaven I keep myself pure. Let him feel that."

Cesare nodded and left, but Etta, after he had gone, continued to be troubled. She felt uneasy, could not define her mood, and stayed longer than usual at Armando's grave the next day. She promised herself not to see Cesare again. In the next weeks she became a little miserly.

The journalist returned one evening almost a month later and Etta stood at the door in a way that indicated he would not be asked in. She had seen herself doing this if he appeared. But Cesare, with his hat in his hand, suggested a short stroll. The suggestion seemed so modest that she agreed. They walked down the Via Nomentana, Etta wearing her highest heels, Cesare unself-consciously talking. He wore small patent-leather shoes and smoked as they strolled.

It was already early December, still late autumn rather than winter. A few leaves clung to a few trees and a warmish mist hung in the air. For a while Cesare talked of the political situation, but after an espresso in a bar on the Via Venti Settembre, as they were walking back, he brought up the subject she had hoped to avoid. Cesare seemed suddenly to have lost his calm, not able to restrain what he had been planning to say. His voice was intense, his gestures impatient, his dark eyes restless. Although his outburst frightened her, she could do nothing to prevent it.

"*Signora,*" he said, "wherever your husband is, you're not helping him by putting this penance on yourself. To help him, the best thing you can do is take up your normal life. Otherwise he will continue to suffer doubly, once for something he was guilty of, and the second time for the unfair burden your denial of life imposes on him."

"I am repenting my sins, not punishing him." She was too disturbed to say more, considered walking home wordless, then slamming the front door in his face; but she heard herself hastily saying, "If we became intimate it would be like adultery to me. We would both be betraying the dead."

"Why is it you see everything in reverse?"

Cesare had stopped under a tree and almost jumped as he spoke. "They—*they* betrayed us. If you'll pardon me, *Signora,* the truth is my wife was a pig. Your husband was a pig. We mourn because we hate them. Let's have the dignity to face the facts."

"No more," she moaned, hastily walking on. "Don't say anything else, I don't want to hear it."

"Etta," said Cesare passionately, following her, "this is my last word and then I'll nail my tongue to my jaw. Just remember this. If Our Lord Himself this minute let Armando rise from the dead to take up his life on earth, tonight—this night—he would be lying in his cousin's bed."

Etta began to cry and walked on, crying, realizing the truth of his remark. Cesare seemed to have said all he had wanted to, and gently held her arm, breathing heavily as he escorted her back to her apartment. At the outer door, as she was trying to think how to get rid of him, how to end this, without waiting a minute he tipped his hat and walked off.

For more than a week Etta went through many torments. She felt a passionate desire to sleep with Cesare. Overnight her body became a torch. Her dreams were erotic. She saw Armando naked in bed with Laura, and in the same bed she saw herself naked with Cesare, clasping his small body to hers. But she resisted—prayed, confessed her most lustful thoughts, and stayed for hours at Armando's grave to calm her mind.

Cesare knocked at her door one night and, because she was repelled when he suggested the marriage bed, she went with him to his rooms. Though she felt guilty afterward, she continued to visit Armando's grave, though less frequently, and she didn't tell Cesare that she had been to the cemetery when she went to his flat afterward. Nor did he ask her, nor talk about his wife or Armando.

At first her uneasiness was intense. Etta felt as though she had committed adultery against the memory of her husband, but when she told herself, over and over, there was no husband, he was dead; there was no husband, she was alone; she began to believe it. There was no husband, there was only his memory. She was not committing adultery. She was a lonely woman who had a lover, a widower, a gentle and affectionate man.

One night as they were lying in bed, she asked Cesare about the possibility of marriage and he said that love was more important. They both knew how marriage destroyed love.

And when, two months later, she found she was pregnant and hurried that morning to Cesare's rooms to tell him, the journalist, in his pajamas, calmed her. "Let's not regret human life."

"It's your child," said Etta.

"Don't worry, I'll acknowledge it as mine," Cesare said, and Etta went home happy.

The next day, when she returned at her usual hour, after having told Armando at his grave that she was at last going to have a baby, Cesare was gone.

"Moved," the landlady said, with a poof of her hand, and she didn't know where.

Though Etta's heart hurt and she deeply mourned the loss of Cesare, try as she would she could not, even with the life in her belly, escape thinking of herself as an adulteress, and she never returned to the cemetery to stand once more at Armando's grave.

[May 1963]

BRUCE JAY FRIEDMAN

Black Angels

Smothered by debt, his wife and child in flight, Stefano held fast to his old house in the country, a life buoy in a sea of despair. Let him but keep up the house, return to it each day; before long, his wife would come to her senses, fly back to him. Yet he dreaded the approach of spring, which meant large teams of gardeners who would charge him killing prices to keep the place in shape. Cheapest of all had been the Angeluzzi Brothers who had gotten him off the ground with a two-hundred-and-fifty-dollar cleanup, then followed through with ninety dollars a month for maintenance, April through October, a hundred extra for the leaf-raking fall windup. Meticulous in April, the four Angeluzzis soon began to dog it; for his ninety, Stefano got only a few brisk lawn cuts and a swipe or two at his flower beds. This spring, unable to work, his life in shreds, Stefano held off on the grounds as long as he could. The grass grew to his shins until one day Swansdowne, a next-door neighbor who had won marigold contests, called on another subject, but with much lawn-mowing and fertilizing in his voice. Stefano dialed the Angeluzzis; then, on an impulse, he dropped the phone and reached for the local paper, running his finger along Home Services. A gardener named Please Try Us caught his fancy. He called the number, asked the deep voice at the other end to come by soon and give him an estimate. The following night, a return call came through.

"I have seen and checked out the place," said the voice, the tones heavy, resonant, solid.

"What'll you take for cleanup?" asked Stefano. "We'll start there."

Long pause. Lip smack. Then, "Thutty dollars."

"Which address did you go to? I'm at 42 Spring. Big old place on the corner of Spring and Rooter."

"That's correct. For fertilizing, that'll be eight extra, making thutty-eight."

"Awful lot of work here," said Stefano, confused, tingling with both guilt and relief. "All right, when can you get at it?"

"Tomorrow morning. Eight o'clock."

"You're on."

Stefano watched them arrive the next day, Sunday, a quartet of massive Negroes in two trucks and two sleek private cars. In stifling heat, they worked in checkered shirts and heavy pants, two with fedoras impossibly balanced on the backs of their great shaved heads. Stefano, a free-lance writer of technical manuals, went back to his work, stopping now and then to check the Negroes through the window. How could they possibly make out on thirty-eight dollars, he wondered. Divided four ways it came to nothing. Gas alone for their fleet of cars would kill their nine-fifty each. He'd give them forty-five dollars to salve his conscience, but still, what about their groceries, rent? Late in the afternoon, he ran out with beers for each. "Plenty of leaves, eh?" he said to Cotten, largest of them, the leader, expressionless in dainty steel-rimmed glasses.

"Take about two and a half days," said the Negro.

"I'm giving you forty-five dollars," said Stefano. "What the hell."

The job actually took three full days, two for the cleanup, a third for the lawn and fertilizing the beds. The last day was a bad one for Stefano. Through his window, he watched the black giants trim the lawn, then kneel in winter clothes and lovingly collect what seemed to be each blade of grass so there'd be no mess. He wanted to run out and tell them to do less work; certainly not at those prices. Yet he loved the prices, too. He could take it all out of expense money, not even bother his regular free-lance payments. At the end of the day, he walked up to Cotten, took out his wallet and said, "I'm giving you cash. So you won't have to bother with a check." It had occurred to him that perhaps the Negroes only did cleanups, no maintenance. By doing enough of them, thousands, perhaps they could sneak by, somehow make a living. "What about maintenance?" he asked the head gardener.

The man scratched his ear, shook his head, finally said, "Can't do your place for less than eighteen dollars a month."

"You guys do some work," said Stefano, shivering with glee. "Best I've seen. I think you're too low. I'll give you twenty-two."

The Negroes came back twice a week, turned Stefano's home

into a showplace, hacking down dead trees, planting new ones, filling in dead spots, keeping the earth black and loamy. Swansdowne, who usually let Stefano test-run new gardeners and then swooped down to sign them up if they were good, looked on with envy, yet called one day and said, "I would never let a colored guy touch my place."

"They're doing a great job on mine," said Stefano.

Maybe that explains it, he thought. All of the Swansdownes who won't have Negro gardeners. That's why their rates are low. Otherwise, they'd starve. He felt good, a liberal. Why shouldn't he get a slight break on money?

At the end of May, Stefano paid them their twenty-two dollars and distributed four American-cheese sandwiches. The three assistants took them back to a truck where one had mayonnaise. "You guys do other kinds of work?" Stefano asked Cotten, who leaned on a hoe. "What about painting? A house?"

The gardener looked up at Stefano's colonial. "We do," he said.

"How much would you take?" The best estimate on the massive ten-roomer had been seven hundred dollars.

"Fifty-eight dollars," said the huge Negro, neutral in his steel-rims.

"I'll pay for half the paint," said Stefano.

The following day, when Stefano awakened, the four Negroes, on high, buckling ladders, had half the house done, the paint deep brown, rich and gurgling in the sun. Their gardening clothes were spattered with paint. He'd pick up the cleaning bill, thought Stefano. It was only fair.

"It looks great!" he hollered up to Cotten, swaying massively in the wind.

"She'll shape up time we get the fourth coat on."

By mid-June, the four Negroes had cleaned out Stefano's attic for three dollars, waterproofed his basement for another sixteen; an elaborate network of drainage pipes went in for twelve-fifty. One day he came home to find the floors cleaned, sanded, shellacked, his cabinets scrubbed, linen closets dizzying in their cleanliness. Irritated for the first time—I didn't order this—he melted quickly when he saw the bill. A slip on the bread box read: "You owes us $2.80." Loving the breaks he was getting, Stefano threw them bonuses, plenty of sandwiches, all his old sports jackets, venetian blinds that had come out of the attic and books of fairly recent vintage on Nova Scotia tourism. Never in the thick of marriage had his place been so immaculate; cars slowed down to admire his dramatically painted home, his shrubs bursting with fertility. Enter any room; its cleanliness would tear your head off. With all these ridiculously cheap home services going for him, Stefano felt at times his luck had turned. Still, a cloak of loneliness rode his shoulders, aggravation clogged his throat. If only to hate her, he missed his wife, a young, pretty woman, circling the globe with her lover, an assistant director on daytime TV. He saw pictures of her, tumbling with lust, in staterooms, inns, the backs of small foreign cars. He missed his son, too, a boy of ten, needing braces. God only knows what shockers he was being exposed to. The pair had fled in haste, leaving behind mementos, toys lined up on shelves, dresses spilling out of chests. Aging quickly, his confidence riddled, Stefano failed in his quest for dates with young girls, speechless and uncertain on the phone. What could he do with himself. At these prices, he could keep his home spotless. But would that make everything all right. Would that haul back a disgruntled wife and son. One night, his heart weighing a ton, he returned from an "Over 28" dance to find the burly Negroes winding up their work. Sweating long into the night, they had rigged up an elaborate network of gas lamps, the better to show off a brilliantly laid out thicket of tea roses and dwarf fruit trees. Total cost for the lighting: Five dollars and fifty cents.

"Really lovely," said Stefano, inspecting his grounds, counting out some bills. "Here," he said to the head gardener. "Take another deuce. In my condition, money means nothing." The huge Negro toweled down his forehead, gathered up his equipment. "Hey," said Stefano. "Come on in for a beer. If I don't talk to someone I'll bust."

"Got to get on," said Cotten. "We got work to do."

"Come on, come on," said Stefano. "What can you do at this hour. Give a guy a break."

The Negro shook his head in doubt, then moved massively toward the house, Stefano clapping him on the back in a show of brotherhood.

Inside, Stefano went for flip-top beers. The gardener sat down in the living room, his great bulk caving deeply into the sofa. For a moment, Stefano worried about gardening clothes, Negro ones to boot, in contact with living-room furniture, then figured the hell with it, who'd complain.

"I've got the worst kind of trouble," said Stefano, leaning back on a Danish modern slat bench. "Sometimes I don't think I'm going to make it through the night. My wife's checked out on me. You probably figured that out already."

The Negro crossed his great legs, sipped his beer. The steel-rimmed glasses had a shimmer to them and Stefano could not make out his eyes.

"She took the kid with her," said Stefano. "That may be the worst part. You don't know what it's like to have a kid tearing around your house for ten years and then not to hear anything. Or maybe you do?" Stefano asked hopefully. "You probably have a lot of trouble of your own."

Silent, the Negro sat forward and shoved a cloth inside his flannel shirt to mop his chest.

"Anyway, I'll be goddamned if I know what to do. Wait around? Pretend she's never coming back? I don't know what in the hell to do with myself. Where do I go from here?"

"How long she gone?" asked the guest, working on the back of his neck now.

"What's that got to do with it?" asked Stefano. "About four months, I guess. Just before you guys came. Oh, I see what you mean. If she hasn't come back in four months, she's probably gone for good. I might as well start building a new life. That's a good point."

The Negro put away the cloth and folded his legs again, crossing his heavy, blunted fingers, arranging them on the point of one knee.

"It just happened out of the clear blue sky," said Stefano. "Oh, why kid around. It was never any good." He told the Negro about their courtship, the false pregnancy, how he had been "forced" to get married. Then he really started in on his wife, the constant primping, the thousands of ways she had made him jealous, the in-laws to support. He let it all come out of him, like air from a tire, talking with heat and fury; until he realized he had been talking nonstop for maybe twenty minutes, half an hour. The Negro listened to him, patiently, not bothering with his beer. Finally, when Stefano sank back to catch his breath, the gardener asked a question: "You think you any good?"

"What do you mean," said Stefano. "Of course I do. Oh, I get what you're driving at. If I thought I was worth anything, I wouldn't let all of this kill me. I'd just kind of brace myself, dig out and really build something fine for myself. Funny how you make just the right remark. It's really amazing. You know I've done the analysis bit. Never meant a damned thing to me. I've had nice analysts, tough ones, all kinds. But the way you just let me sound off and then asked that one thing. This is going to sound crazy, but what if we just talked this way, couple of times a week. I just sound off and then you come in with the haymaker, the way you just did. Just for fun, what would you charge me? An hour?"

"Fo' hundred," said the Negro.

"Four hundred. That's really a laugh. You must be out of your head. What are you, crazy? Don't you know I was just kidding around."

The Negro took a sip of the beer and rose to leave. "All right, wait a second," said Stefano. "Hold on a minute. Let's just finish up this hour, all right? Then we'll see about other times. This one doesn't count, does it?"

"It do," said the Negro, sinking into the couch and producing pad and pencil.

"That's not really fair, you know," said Stefano. "To count this one. Anyway, we'll see. Maybe we'll try it for awhile. That's some price. Where was I? Whew, all that money. To get back to what I was saying, this girl has been a bitch ever since the day I laid eyes on her. You made me see it tonight. In many ways, I think she's a lot like my mom. . . ."

[December 1964]

FLANNERY O'CONNOR

Parker's Back

Parker's wife was sitting on the front porch floor, snapping beans. Parker was sitting on the step, some distance away, watching her sullenly. She was plain, plain. The skin on her face was thin and drawn as tight as the skin on an onion and her eyes were grey and sharp like the points of two ice picks. Parker understood why he had married her—he couldn't have got her any other way—but he couldn't understand why he stayed with her now. She was pregnant and pregnant women were not his favorite kind. Nevertheless he stayed as if she had him conjured. He was puzzled and ashamed of himself.

The house they rented sat alone save for a single tall pecan tree on a high embankment overlooking a highway. At intervals a car would shoot past below and his wife's eyes would swerve suspiciously after the sound of it and then come back to rest on the newspaper full of beans in her lap. One of the things she did not approve of was automobiles. In addition to her other bad qualities, she was forever sniffing up sin. She did not smoke, dip, drink whiskey, use bad language or paint her face, and God knew some paint would have improved it, Parker thought. Her being against color, it was the more remarkable she had married him. Sometimes he supposed that she had married him because she meant to save him. At other times he had a suspicion that she actually liked everything she said she didn't. He could account for her one way or another; it was himself he could not understand.

She turned her head in his direction and said, "It's no reason you can't work for a man. It don't have to be a woman."

"Aw, shut your mouth for a change," Parker muttered.

If he had been certain she was jealous of the woman he worked for he would have been pleased, but more likely she was concerned with the sin that would result if he and the woman took a liking to each other. He had told her that the woman was a hefty young blonde; in fact she was nearly seventy years old and too dried up to have an interest in anything except getting as much work out of him as she could. Not that an old woman didn't sometimes get an interest in a young man, particularly if he was as attractive as Parker felt he was, but this old woman looked at him the same way she looked at her old tractor—as if she had to put up with it because it was all she had. The tractor had broken down the second day Parker was on it and she had set him at once to cutting bushes, saying out of the side of her mouth to the nigger, "Everything he touches, he breaks." She also asked him to wear his shirt when he worked; Parker had removed it even though the day was not sultry; he put it back on reluctantly.

This ugly woman Parker married was his first wife. He had had other women but he had planned never to get himself tied up legally. He had first seen her one morning when his truck broke down on the highway. He had managed to pull it off the road into a neatly swept yard on which sat a peeling two-room house. He got out and opened the hood of the truck and began to study the motor. Parker had an extra sense that told him when there was a woman nearby watching him. After he had leaned over the motor a few minutes, his neck began to prickle. He cast his eye over the empty yard and porch of the house. A woman he could not see was either nearby beyond a clump of honeysuckle or in the house, watching him out the window.

Suddenly Parker began to jump up and down and fling his hand about as if he had mashed it in the machinery. He doubled over and held his hand close to his chest. "Goddamnit!" he hollered. "Jesus Christ in hell! Jesus God Almightydamn! Goddamnit to hell!" he went on, flinging out the same few oaths over and over as loud as he could.

Without warning a terrible bristly claw slammed the side of his face and he fell backward on the hood of the truck. "You don't talk no filth here!" a voice close to him shrilled.

Parker's vision was so blurred that for an instant he thought he had been attacked by some creature from above, a giant hawk-eyed angel wielding a hoary weapon. As his sight cleared, he saw before him a tall rawboned girl with a broom.

"I hurt my hand," he said. "I *hurt* my hand." He was so incensed that he forgot that he hadn't hurt his hand. "My hand may be broke," he growled, although his voice was still unsteady.

"Lemme see it," the girl demanded.

Parker stuck out his hand and she came closer and looked at it. There was no mark on the palm and she took the hand and turned it over. Her own hand was dry and hot and rough and Parker felt himself jolted back to life by her touch. He looked more closely at her. I don't want nothing to do with this one, he thought.

The girl's sharp eyes peered at the back of the stubby reddish hand she held. There emblazoned in red and blue was a tattooed eagle perched on a cannon. Parker's sleeve was rolled to the elbow. Above the eagle a serpent was coiled about a shield and in the spaces between the eagle and the serpent there were hearts, some with arrows through them. Above the serpent there was a spread hand of cards. Every space on the skin of Parker's arm, from wrist to elbow, was covered in some loud design. The girl gazed at this with an almost stupefied smile of shock, as if she had accidentally grasped a poisonous snake; she dropped the hand.

"I got most of my other ones in foreign parts," Parker said. "These here I mostly got in the United States. I got my first one when I was only fifteen years old."

"Don't tell me," the girl said. "I don't like it. I ain't got any use for it."

"You ought to see the ones you can't see," Parker said and winked.

Two circles of red appeared like little apples on the girl's cheeks and softened her appearance. Parker was intrigued. He did not for a minute think that she didn't like the tattoos. He had never yet met a woman who was not attracted to them.

Parker was fourteen when he saw a man in a fair, tattooed from head to foot. Except for his loins which were girded with a panther hide, the man's skin was patterned in what seemed from Parker's distance—he was near the back of the tent, standing on a bench—a single intricate design of brilliant color. The man, who was small and sturdy, moved about on the platform, flexing his muscles so that the arabesque of men and beasts and flowers on his skin appeared to have a subtle motion of its own. Parker was filled with emotion, lifted up as some people are when the flag passes. He was a boy whose mouth habitually hung open. He was heavy and earnest, as ordinary as a loaf of bread. When the show was over, he had remained standing on the bench, staring where the tattooed man had been, until the tent was almost empty.

Parker had never before felt the least motion of wonder in himself. Until he saw the man at the fair, it did not enter his head that there was anything out of the ordinary about the fact that he existed. Even then it did not enter his head, but a peculiar unease settled in him. It was as if a blind boy had been turned so gently in a different direction that he did not know his destination had been changed.

He had his first tattoo sometime after—the eagle perched on the cannon. It was done by a local artist. It hurt very little, just enough to make it appear to Parker to be worth doing. This was peculiar too, for before he had thought that only what did not hurt was worth doing. The next year he quit school because he was sixteen and could. He went to the trade school for a while, and then he quit the trade school and worked for six months in a garage. The only reason he worked at all was to pay for more tattoos. His mother worked in a laundry and could support him, but she would not pay for any tattoo except her name on a heart, which he had put on, grumbling. However, her name was Betty Jean and nobody had to know it was his mother. He found out that the tattoos were attractive to the kind of girls he liked but who had never liked him before. He began to drink beer and get in fights. His mother wept over what was becoming of him. One night she dragged him off to a revival with her, not telling him where they were going. When he saw the big lighted church, he jerked out of her grasp and ran. The next day he lied about his age and joined the Navy.

Parker was large for the tight sailor's pants but the silly white cap, sitting low on his forehead, made his face by contrast look thoughtful and almost intense. After a month or two in the Navy, his mouth ceased to hang open. His features hardened into the features of a man. He stayed in the Navy five years and seemed a natural part of the grey mechanical ship, except for his eyes, which were the same pale slate color as the ocean and reflected the immense spaces around him as if they were a microcosm of the mysterious sea. In port Parker wandered about comparing the run-down places he was in to Birmingham, Alabama. Everywhere he went he picked up more tattoos.

He had stopped having lifeless ones like anchors and crossed rifles. He had a tiger and a panther on each shoulder, a cobra coiled about a torch on his chest, hawks over his thighs, Elizabeth II and Philip over where his stomach and liver were, respectively. He did not care much what the subject was so long as it was colorful; on his abdomen he had a few obscenities but only because that seemed the proper place for them. Parker would be satisfied with each tattoo about a month, then something about it that had attracted him would wear off. Whenever a decent-sized mirror was available, he would get in front of it and study his overall look. The effect was not of one intricate arabesque of colors but of something haphazard and botched. A huge dissatisfaction would come over him and he would go off and find another tattooist and have another space filled up. The front of Parker was almost completely covered but there were no tattoos on his back. He had no desire for one anywhere he could not readily see it himself. As the space on the front of him for tattoos decreased, his dissatisfaction grew and became general.

After one of his furloughs, he didn't go back to the Navy but remained away without official leave, drunk, in a rooming house in a city he did not know. His dissatisfaction, from being chronic and latent, had suddenly become acute and raged in him. It was as if the panther and the lion and the serpents and the eagles and the hawks had penetrated his skin and lived inside him in a raging warfare. The Navy caught up with him, put him in the brig for nine months and then gave him a dishonorable discharge.

After that Parker decided that country air was the only kind fit to breathe. He rented the shack on the embankment and bought the old truck and took various jobs which he kept as long as it suited him. At the time he met his future wife, he was buying apples by the bushel and selling them for the same price by the pound to isolated homesteaders on backcountry roads.

"All that there," the girl said, pointing to his arm, "is no better than what a fool Indian would do. It's a heap of vanity." She seemed to have found the word she wanted. "Vanity of vanities," she said.

Well what the hell do I care what she thinks of it? Parker asked himself, but he was plainly bewildered. "I reckon you like one of these better than another anyway," he said, dallying until he thought of something that would impress her. He thrust the arm back at her. "Which you like best?"

"None of them," she said, "but the chicken is not as bad as the rest."

"What chicken?" Parker almost yelled at her.

She pointed to the eagle.

"That's an eagle," Parker said. "What fool would waste their time having a chicken put on themself?"

"What fool would have any of it?" the girl said and turned away. She went slowly back to the house and left him there to get going. Parker remained for almost five minutes, looking agape at the dark door she had entered.

The next day he returned with a bushel of apples. He was not one to be outdone by anything that looked like her. He liked women with meat on them, so you didn't feel their muscles, much less their old bones. When he arrived, she was sitting on the top step and the yard was full of children, all as thin and poor as herself; Parker remembered it was Saturday. He hated to be making up to a woman when there were children around, but it was fortunate he had brought the bushel of apples off the truck. As the children approached him to see what he carried, he gave each child an apple and told it to get lost; in that way he cleared out the whole crowd.

The girl did nothing to acknowledge his presence. He might have been a stray pig or goat that had wandered into the yard and she too tired to take up the broom and send it off. He set the bushel of apples down next to her on the step. He sat down on a lower step.

"Hep yourself," he said, nodding at the basket; then he lapsed into silence.

She took an apple quickly as if the basket might disappear if she didn't make haste. Hungry people made Parker nervous. He had always had plenty to eat himself. He grew very uncomfortable. He reasoned he had nothing to say so why should he say it? He could not think now why he had come or why he didn't go before he wasted another bushel of apples on the crowd of children. He supposed they were her brothers and sisters.

She chewed the apple slowly but with a kind of relish of concentration, bent slightly but looking out ahead. The view from the porch stretched off across a long incline studded with ironweed and across the highway to a vast vista of hills and one small mountain. Long views depressed Parker. You look out into space like that and you begin to feel as if someone were after you, the Navy or the Government or Religion.

"Who them children belong to, you?" he said at length.

"I ain't married yet," she said. "They belong to momma." She said it as if it were only a matter of time before she would be married.

Who in God's name would marry her? Parker thought.

A large barefooted woman with a wide gap-toothed face appeared in the door behind Parker. She had apparently been there for several minutes.

"Good evening," Parker said.

The woman crossed the porch and picked up what was left of the bushel of apples. "We thank you," she said and returned with it into the house.

"That your old woman?" Parker muttered.

The girl nodded. Parker knew a lot of sharp things he could have said, like "You got my sympathy," but he was gloomily silent. He just sat there, looking at the view. He thought he must be coming down with something.

"If I pick up some peaches tomorrow I'll bring you some," he said.

"I'll be much obliged to you," the girl said.

Parker had no intention of taking any basket of peaches back there, but the next day he found himself doing it. He and the girl had almost nothing to say to each other. One thing he did say was, "I ain't got any tattoo on my back."

"What you got on it?" the girl said.

"My shirt," Parker said. "Haw."

"Haw haw," the girl said politely.

Parker thought he was losing his mind. He could not believe for a minute that he was attracted to a woman like this. She showed not the least interest in anything but what he brought until he appeared the third time with two cantaloupes. "What's your name?" she asked.

"O.E. Parker," he said.

"What does the O.E. stand for?"

"You can just call me O.E.," Parker said. "Or Parker. Don't nobody call me by my name."

"What's it stand for?" she persisted.

"Never mind," Parker said. "What's yours?"

"I'll tell you when you tell me what them letters are the short of," she said. There was just a hint of flirtatiousness in her tone and it went rapidly to Parker's head. He had never revealed the name to any man or woman, only to the files of the Navy and the Government, and it was on his baptismal record which he got at the age of a month; his mother was a Methodist. When the name leaked out of the Navy files, Parker narrowly missed killing the man who used it.

"You'll go blab it around," he said.

"I'll swear I'll never tell nobody," she said. "On God's holy word I swear it."

Parker sat for a few minutes in silence. Then he reached for the girl's neck, drew her ear close to his mouth and revealed the name in a low voice.

"Obadiah," she whispered. Her face slowly brightened as if the name came as a sign to her. "Obadiah," she said.

The name still stank in Parker's estimation.

"Obadiah Elihue," she said in a reverent voice.

"If you call me that aloud, I'll bust your head open," Parker said. "What's yours?"

"Sarah Ruth Cates," she said.

"Glad to meet you, Sarah Ruth," Parker said.

Sarah Ruth's father was a Straight Gospel preacher but he was away, spreading it in Florida. Her mother did not seem to mind Parker's attention to the girl so long as he brought a basket of something with him when he came. As for Sarah Ruth herself, it was plain to Parker after he had visited three times that she was crazy about him. She liked him even though she insisted that pictures on the skin were vanity of vanities and even after hearing him curse, and even after she had asked him if he was saved and he replied that he didn't see it was anything in particular to save him from. After that, inspired, Parker had said. "I'd be saved enough if you was to kiss me."

She scowled. "That ain't being saved," she said.

Not long after that she agreed to take a ride in his truck. Parker parked it on a deserted road and suggested to her that they lie down together in the back of it.

"Not until after we're married," she said—just like that.

"Oh, that ain't necessary," Parker said and as he reached for her, she thrust him away with such force that the door of the truck came off and he found himself flat on the ground. He made up his mind then and there to have nothing further to do with her.

They were married in the County Ordinary's office because Sarah Ruth thought churches were idolatrous. Parker had no opinion about that one way or the other. The Ordinary's office was lined with cardboard file boxes and record books with dusty yellow slips of paper hanging on out of them. The Ordinary was an old woman with red hair who had held office for forty years and looked as dusty as her books. She married them from behind the iron grille of a standup desk and when she finished, she said with a flourish, "Three dollars and fifty cents and till death do you part," and yanked some forms out of a machine.

Marriage did not change Sarah Ruth a jot and it made Parker gloomier than ever. Every morning he decided he had had enough and would not return that night; every night he returned. Whenever Parker couldn't stand the way he felt, he would have another tattoo, but the only surface left on him now was his back. To see a tattoo on his own back he would have to get two mirrors and stand between them in just the correct position and this seemed to Parker a good way to make an idiot of himself. Sarah Ruth who, if she had had sense, could have enjoyed a tattoo on his back, would not even look at the ones he had elsewhere. When he attempted to point out especial details of them, she would shut her eyes tight and turn her back as well. Except in total darkness, she preferred Parker dressed and with his sleeves rolled down.

"At the judgment seat of God, Jesus is going to say to you, 'What you been doing all your life besides have pictures drawn all over you?' " she said.

"You don't fool me none," Parker said. "You're just afraid that hefty girl I work for'll like me so much she'll say, 'Come on, Mr. Parker, let's you and me. . . .' "

"You're tempting sin," she said, "and at the judgment seat of God you'll have to answer for that too. You ought to go back to selling the fruits of the earth."

Parker did nothing much when he was at home but listen to what the judgment seat of God would be like for him if he didn't change his ways. When he could, he broke in with tales of the hefty girl he worked for. " 'Mr. Parker,' " he said she said, " 'I hired you for your brains.' " (She had added, "So why don't you use them?")

"And you should have seen her face the first time she saw me without my shirt," he said. " 'Mr. Parker,' she said, 'you're a walking panner-rammer!' " This had, in fact, been her remark but it had been delivered out of one side of her mouth.

Dissatisfaction began to grow so great in Parker that there was no containing it outside of a tattoo. It had to be his back. There was no help for it. A dim half-formed inspiration began to work in his mind. He visualized having a tattoo put there that Sarah Ruth would not be able to resist—a religious subject. He thought of an open book with HOLY BIBLE tattooed under it and an actual verse printed on the page. This seemed just the thing for a while; then he began to hear her say, "Ain't I already got a real Bible! What you think I want to read the same verse over and over for when I can read it all?" He needed something better even than the Bible! He thought about it so much that he began to lose sleep. He was already losing flesh—Sarah Ruth just threw the food in the pot and let it boil. Not knowing for certain why he continued to stay with a woman who was both ugly and pregnant and no cook made him generally nervous and irritable, and he developed a little tic in the side of his face.

Once or twice he found himself turning around abruptly as if someone were trailing him. He had had a granddaddy who had ended in the state mental hospital, although not until he was seventy-five, but as urgent as it might be for him to get a tattoo, it was just as urgent that he get exactly the right one to bring Sarah Ruth to heel. As he continued to worry over it, his eyes took on a hollow, preoccupied expression. The old woman he worked for told him that if he couldn't keep his mind on what he was doing, she knew where she could find a fourteen-year-old colored boy who could. Parker was too preoccupied even to be offended. At any time previous, he would have left her then and there, saying dryly, "Well, you go ahead on and get him then."

Two or three mornings later he was baling hay with the old woman's sorry baler and her broken-down tractor in a large field, cleared save for one enormous old tree standing in the middle of it. The old woman was the kind who would not cut down a large old tree just because it was a large old tree. She had pointed it out to Parker as if he didn't have eyes and told him to be careful not to hit it as the machine picked up hay near it. Parker began at the outside of the field and made circles inward toward it. He had to get off the tractor every now and then and untangle the baling cord or kick a rock out of the way. The old woman had told him to carry the rocks to the edge of the field, which he did when she was there watching. When he thought he could make it, he ran over them. As he circled the field his mind was on a suitable design for his back. The sun, the size of a golf ball, began to switch regularly from in front to behind him, but he appeared to see it both places as if he had eyes in the back of his head. All at once he saw the tree reaching out to grasp him. A ferocious thud propelled him into the air, and he heard himself yelling in an unbelievably loud voice, *"God above!"*

He landed on his back while the tractor crashed upside down into the tree and burst into flames. The first thing Parker saw were his shoes, quickly being eaten by the fire; one was caught under the tractor, the other was some distance away, burning by itself. He was not in them. He could feel the hot breath of the burning tree on his face. He scrambled backward, still sitting, his eyes cavernous, and if he had known how to cross himself he would have done it.

His truck was on a dirt road at the edge of the field. He moved toward it, still sitting, still backward, but faster and faster; halfway to it he got up and began a kind of forward-bent run from which he collapsed on his knees twice. His legs felt like two old rusted rain gutters. He reached the truck finally and took off in it, zigzagging up the road. He drove past his house on the embankment and straight for the city, fifty miles distant.

Parker did not allow himself to think on the way to the city. He only knew that there had been a great change in his life, a leap forward into a worse unknown, and that there was nothing he could do about it. It was for all intents accomplished.

The artist had two large cluttered rooms over a chiropodist's office on a back street. Parker, still barefooted, burst silently in on him at a little after three in the afternoon. The artist, who was about Parker's own age—twenty-eight—but thin and bald, was behind a small drawing table, tracing a design in green ink. He looked up with an annoyed glance and did not seem to recognize Parker in the hollow-eyed creature before him.

"Let me see the book you got with all the pictures of God in it," Parker said breathlessly. "The religious one."

The artist continued to look at him with his intellectual, superior stare. "I don't put tattoos on drunks," he said.

"You know me!" Parker cried indignantly. "I'm O.E. Parker! You done work for me before and I always paid!"

The artist looked at him another moment as if he were not altogether sure. "You've fallen off some," he said. "You must have been in jail."

"Married," Parker said.

"Oh," said the artist. With the aid of mirrors the artist had tattooed on the top of his head a miniature owl, perfect in every detail. It was about the side of a half-dollar and served him as a showpiece. There were cheaper artists in town but Parker had never wanted anything but the best. The artist went over to a cabinet in the back of the room and began to look over some art books. "Who are you interested in?" he said. "Saints, angels, Christs or what?"

"God," Parker said.

"Father, Son or Spirit?"

"Just God," Parker said impatiently. "Christ. I don't care. Just so it's God."

The artist returned with a book. He moved some papers off another table and put the book down on it and told Parker to sit down and see what he liked. "The up-t-date ones are in the back," he said.

Parker sat down with the book and wet his thumb. He began to go through it, beginning at the back where the up-to-date pictures were. Some of them he recognized—the Good Shepherd, Forbid Them Not, The Smiling Jesus, Jesus the Physician's Friend, but he kept turning rapidly backward and the pictures became less and less reassuring. One showed a gaunt green dead face streaked with blood. One was yellow with sagging purple eyes. Parker's heart began to beat faster and faster until it appeared to be roaring inside him like a great generator. He flipped the pages quickly, feeling that when he reached the one ordained, a sign would come. He continued to flip through until he had almost reached the front of the book. On one of the pages a pair of eyes glanced at him swiftly. Parker sped on, then stopped. His heart too appeared to cut off; there was absolute silence. It said as plainly as if silence were a language itself, *Go back.*

Parker returned to the picture—the haloed head of a flat stern Byzantine Christ with all-demanding eyes. He sat there trembling; his heart began slowly to beat again as if it were being brought to life by a subtle power.

"You found what you want?" the artist asked.

Parker's throat was too dry to speak. He got up and thrust the book at the artist, opened at the picture.

"That'll cost you plenty," the artist said. "You don't want all those little blocks though, just the outline and some better features."

"Just like it is," Parker said, "just like it is or nothing."

"It's your funeral," the artist said, "but I don't do that kind of work for nothing."

"How much?" Parker asked.

"It'll take maybe two days' work."

"How much?" Parker said.

"On time or cash?" the artist asked. Parker's other jobs had been on time, but he had paid.

"Ten down and ten for every day it takes," the artist said.

Parker drew ten one-dollar bills out of his wallet; he had three left in.

"You come back in the morning," the artist said, putting the money in his own pocket. "First I'll have to trace that out of the book."

"No, no!" Parker said. "Trace it now or gimme my money back," and his eyes blared as if he were ready for a fight.

The artist agreed. Anyone stupid enough to want a Christ on his back, he reasoned, would be just as likely as not to change his mind the next minute, but once the work was begun he could hardly do so.

While he worked on the tracing, he told Parker to go wash his back at the sink with the special soap he used there. Parker did it and returned to pace back and forth across the room, nervously flexing his shoulders. He wanted to go look at the picture again but at the same time he did not want to. The artist got up finally and had Parker lie down on the table. He swabbed his back with ethyl chloride and then began to outline the head on it with his iodine pencil. Another hour passed before he took up his electric instrument. Parker felt no particular pain. In Japan he had had a tattoo of the Buddha done on his upper arm with ivory needles; in Burma, a little brown root of a man had made a peacock on each of his knees using thin pointed sticks, two feet long; amateurs had worked on him with pins and soot. Parker was usually so relaxed and easy under the hand of the artist that he often went to sleep, but this time he remained awake, every muscle taut.

At midnight the artist said he was ready to quit. He propped one mirror, four feet square, on a table by the wall and took a smaller mirror of the lavatory wall and put it in Parker's hands. Parker stood with his back to the one on the table and moved the other until he saw a flashing burst of color reflected from his back. It was almost completely covered with little red and blue and ivory and saffron squares; from them he made out the lineaments of the face—a mouth, the beginnings of heavy brows, a straight nose, but the face was empty; the eyes had not yet been put in. The impression for the moment was almost as if the artist had tricked him and done the Physician's Friend.

"It don't have eyes," Parker cried out.

"That'll come," the artist said, "in due time. We have another day to go on it yet."

Parker spent the night on a cot at the Haven of Light Christian Mission. He found these the best places to stay in the city because they were free and included a meal of sorts. He got the last available cot and because he was still barefooted, he accepted a pair of second-hand shoes which, in his confusion, he put on to go to bed; he was still shocked from all that had happened to him. All night he lay awake in the long dormitory of cots with lumpy figures on them. The only light was from a phosphorescent cross glowing at the end of the room. The tree reached out to grasp him again, then burst into flame; the shoe burned quietly by itself; the eyes in the book said to him distinctly *Go back* and at the same time did not utter a sound. He wished that he were not in this city, not in this Haven of Light Mission, not in a bed by himself. He longed miserably for Sarah Ruth. Her sharp tongue and ice-pick eyes were the only comfort he could bring to mind. He decided he was losing it. Her eyes appeared soft and dilatory compared with the eyes in the book, for even though he could not summon up the exact look of those eyes, he could still feel their penetration. He felt as though, under their gaze, he was as transparent as the wing of a fly.

The tattooist had told him not to come until ten in the morning, but when he arrived at that hour, Parker was sitting in the dark hallway on the floor, waiting for him. He had decided upon getting up that, once the tattoo was on him, he would not look at it, that all his sensations of the day and night before were those of a crazy man and that he would return to doing things according to his own sound judgment.

The artist began where he left off. "One thing I want to know," he said presently as he worked over Parker's back, "why do you want this on you? Have you gone and got religion? Are you saved?" he asked in a mocking voice.

Parker's voice felt salty and dry. "Naw," he said, "I ain't got no use for none of that. A man can't save his self from whatever it is he don't deserve none of my sympathy." These words seemed to leave his mouth like wraiths and to evaporate at once as if he had never uttered them.

"Then why. . . ."

"I married this woman that's saved," Parker said. "I never should have done it. I ought to leave her. She's done gone and got pregnant."

"That's too bad," the artist said. "Then it's her making you have this tattoo."

"Naw," Parker said, "she don't know nothing about it. It's a surprise for her."

"You think she'll like it and lay off you a while?"

"She can't hep herself," Parker said. "She can't say she don't like the looks of God." He decided he had told the artist enough of his business. Artists were all right in their place but he didn't like them poking their noses into the affairs of regular people. "I didn't get no sleep last night," he said. "I think I'll get some now."

That closed the mouth of the artist but it did not bring him any sleep. He lay there, imagining how Sarah Ruth would be struck speechless by the face on his back and every now and then this would be interrupted by a vision of the tree of fire and his empty shoe burning beneath it.

The artist worked steadily until nearly four o'clock, not stopping to have lunch, hardly pausing with the electric instrument except to wipe the dripping dye off Parker's back as he went along. Finally he finished. "You can get up and look at it now," he said.

Parker sat up, but he remained on the edge of the table.

The artist was pleased with his work and wanted Parker to look at it at once. Instead Parker continued to sit on the edge of the table, bent forward slightly but with a vacant look. "What ails you?" the artist said. "Go look at it."

"Ain't nothing ail me," Parker said in a sudden belligerent voice. "That tattoo ain't going nowhere. It'll be there when I get there." He reached for his shirt and began gingerly to put it on.

The artist took him roughly by the arm and propelled him between the two mirrors. "Now *look*," he said, angry at having his work ignored.

Parker looked, turned white and moved away. The eyes in the reflected face continued to look at him—still, straight, all-demanding, enclosed in silence.

"It was your idea, remember," the artist said. "I would have advised something else."

Parker said nothing. He put on his shirt and went out the door while the artist shouted, "I'll expect all of my money!"

Parker headed toward a package shop on the corner. He bought a pint of whiskey and took it into a nearby alley and drank it all in five minutes. Then he moved on to a pool hall nearby which he frequented when he came to the city. It was a well-lighted barnlike place with a bar up one side and gambling machines on the other and pool tables in the back. As soon as Parker entered, a large man in a red-and-black checkered shirt hailed him by slapping him on the back and yelling, "Yeyyyyyy boy! O.E. Parker!"

Parker was not yet ready to be struck on the back. "Lay off," he said, "I got a fresh tattoo there."

"What you got this time?" the man asked and then yelled to a few at the machine, "O.E.'s got him another tattoo."

"Nothing special this time," Parker said and slunk over to a machine that was not being used.

"Come on," the big man said, "let's have a look at O.E.'s tattoo," and while Parker squirmed in their hands, they pulled up his shirt. Parker felt all the hands drop away instantly and his shirt fell again like a veil over the face. There was a silence in the poolroom which seemed to Parker to grow from the circle around him until it extended to the foundations under the building and upward through the beams in the roof.

Finally someone said, "Christ!" Then they all broke into noise at once. Parker turned around, an uncertain grin on his face.

"Leave it to O.E.!" the man in the checkered shirt said. "That boy's a real card!"

"Maybe he's gone and got religion," someone yelled.

"Not on your life," Parker said.

"O.E.'s got religion and is witnessing for Jesus, ain't you, O.E.?" a little man with a piece of cigar in his mouth said wryly. "An o-riginal way to do it if I ever saw one."

"Leave it to Parker to think of a new one!" the fat man said.

"Yyeeeeeeyyyyyyyy boy!" someone yelled and they all began to whistle and curse in compliment until Parker said, "Aaa shut up."

"What'd you do it for?" somebody asked.

"For laughs," Parker said. "What's it to you?"

"Why ain't you laughing then?" somebody yelled.

Parker lunged into the midst of them and like a whirlwind on a summer's day there began a fight that raged amid overturned tables and swinging fists until two of them grabbed him and ran to the door with him and threw him out. Then a calm descended on the pool hall as nerve shattering as if the long barnlike room were the ship from which Jonah had been cast into the sea.

Parker sat for a long time on the ground in the alley behind the pool hall, examining his soul. He saw it as a spider web of facts and lies that was not at all important to him but which appeared to be necessary in spite of his opinion. The eyes that were now forever on his back were eyes to be obeyed. He was as certain of it as he had ever been of anything. Throughout his life, grumbling and sometimes cursing, often afraid, once in rapture, Parker had obeyed whatever instinct of this kind had come to him—in rapture when his spirit had lifted at the sight of the tattooed man at the fair, afraid when he had joined the Navy, grumbling when he had married Sarah Ruth.

The thought of her brought him slowly to his feet. She would know what he had to do. She would clear up the rest of it, and she would at least be pleased. His truck was still parked in front of the building where the artist had his place, but it was not far away. He got in it and drove out of the city and into the country night. His head was almost clear of liquor and he observed that his dissatisfaction was gone, but he felt not quite like himself. It was as if he were himself but a stranger to himself, driving into a new country though everything he saw was familiar to him, even at night.

He arrived finally at the house on the embankment, pulled the truck under the pecan tree and got out. He made as much noise as possible to assert that he was still in charge here, that his leaving her for a night without word meant nothing except it was the way he did things. He slammed the car door, stamped up the two steps and across the porch and rattled the doorknob. It did not respond to his touch. "Sarah Ruth!" he yelled, "let me in."

There was no lock on the door and she had evidently placed the back of a chair against the knob. He began to beat on the door and rattle the knob.

He heard the bedsprings creak and bent down and put his head to the keyhole, but it was stopped up with paper. "Let me in!" he hollered, bamming on the door again. "What you got me locked out for?"

A sharp voice close to the door said, "Who's there?"

"Me," Parker said. "O.E."

He waited a moment.

"Me," he said impatiently. "O.E."

Still no sound from inside.

He tried once more. "O.E.," he said, bamming the door two or three more times. "O.E. Parker. You know me."

There was a silence. Then the voice said slowly, "I don't know no O.E."

"Quit fooling," Parker pleaded. "You ain't got any business doing me this way. It's me, old O.E., I'm back. You ain't afraid of me."

"Who's there?" the same unfeeling voice said.

Parker turned his head as if he expected someone behind him to give him the answer. The sky had lightened slightly and there were two or three streaks of yellow floating above the horizon. Then as he stood there, a tree of light burst over the skyline.

Parker fell back against the door as if he had been pinned there by a lance.

"Who's there?" the voice from inside said and there was a quality about it now that seemed final. The knob rattled and the voice said peremptorily, "Who's there, I ast you?"

Parker bent down and put his mouth near the stuffed keyhole. "Obadiah," he whispered and all at once he felt the light pouring through him, turning his spider-web soul into a perfect arabesque of colors, a garden of trees and birds and beasts.

"Obadiah Elihue!" he whispered.

The door opened and he stumbled in. Sarah Ruth loomed there, hands on her hips. She began at once, "That was no hefty blonde woman you was working for and you'll have to pay her every penny on her tractor you busted up. She don't keep insurance on it. She came here and her and me had us a long talk and I. . . ."

Trembling, Parker set about lighting the kerosene lamp.

"What's the matter with you, wasting that kerosene this near daylight?" she demanded. "I ain't got to look at you."

A yellow glow enveloped them. Parker put the match down and began to unbutton his shirt.

"And you ain't going to have none of me this near morning," she said.

"Shut your mouth," he said quietly. "Look at this and then I don't want to hear no more out of you." He removed the shirt and turned his back to her.

"Another picture," Sarah Ruth growled. "I might have known you was off after putting some more trash on yourself."

Parker's knees went hollow under him. He wheeled around and cried, "Look at it! Don't just say that! *Look* at it!"

"I done looked," she said.

"Don't you know who it is?" he cried in anguish.

"No, who is it?" Sarah Ruth said. "It ain't anybody I know."

"It's Him," Parker said.

"Him who?"

"God!" Parker cried.

"God? God don't look like that!"

"What do you know how he looks?" Parker moaned. "You ain't seen him."

"He don't *look*," Sarah Ruth said. "He's a spirit. No man shall see his face."

"Aw listen," Parker groaned, "this is just a picture of Him."

"Idolatry!" Sarah Ruth screamed. "Idolatry. Enflaming yourself with idols under every green tree! I can put up with lies and vanity but I don't want no idolator in this house!" and she grabbed up the broom and thrashed him across the shoulders with it.

Parker was too stunned to resist. He sat there and let her beat him until she had nearly knocked him senseless and large welts had formed on the face of the tattooed Christ. Then he staggered up and made for the door.

She stamped the broom two or three times on the floor and went to the window and shook it out to get the taint of him off it. Still gripping it, she looked toward the pecan tree and her eyes hardened still more. There he was—who called himself Obadiah Elihue—leaning against the tree, crying like a baby.

[April 1965]

BARRY TARGAN

Harry Belten and the Mendelssohn Violin Concerto

Alice Belten labored up the thin wooden outer stairway leading to Josephine Goss's tiny apartment above Fulmer's dress shop. She opened the weather-stained door, streamed into the limited sitting room, and cried, "Oh, Josie. I think my Harry's going crazy." From the day thirty-one years before, when Alice and Harry had married, Josephine Goss, Alice's best friend, had suspected that Harry Belten was crazy. Thirty-one years' knowledge of him fed the suspicion. Her friend's announcement came now as no surprise.

"The violin again?" she asked, but as though she knew.

"Yes," Alice said, almost sobbing, "but worse this time, much worse. Oh God!" She put her hands to her head. "Why was I born?"

"Well, what is it?" Josephine asked.

"Oh God," Alice moaned.

"*What is it?*" Josephine lanced at her.

Alice snapped her head up, to attention. "A concert. He's going to give a concert. He's going to play in front of people."

Josephine slumped a little in her disappointment. "Is that all? He's played in front of people before, the jerk. Do you want some tea?" she asked in a tone which considered the subject changed.

"No, I don't want any tea. Who could drink? Who could eat? It's not the same. This time it's for *real.* Don't you understand?" Alice waved her hands upward. "This time he thinks he's Heifetz. He's renting an orchestra, a hall. He's going to a big city. He's going to advertise. Oh God! Oh God!" She collapsed into the tears she had sought all day.

Josephine revived. "Well I'll be. . . ." She smiled. "So the jerk has finally flipped for real. Where's he getting the money?"

"A mortgage," Alice managed. "A second mortgage." Although not relieved, she was calming. "Harry figures it'll cost about three thousand dollars."

"Three thousand dollars!" Josephine shouted. It was more serious than she had thought. "Does he stand to make anything?"

"No."

"No?"

"Nothing."

"Nothing? Nothing? Get a lawyer," she said and she rose to do it.

Harry Belten sold hardware and appliances for Alexander White, whose store was located in the town of Tyler, population four thousand, southwest New York—the Southern Tier. He had worked for Alexander White for thirty-two years, ever since he came up from the Appalachian coal country of western Pennsylvania on his way to Buffalo and saw the little sign in the general-store window advertising for a clerk. Harry had had the usual young-man dreams of life in the big city, but he had come up in the Depression. He had figured quickly on that distant afternoon that a sure job in Tyler was better than a possible soup line in Buffalo, so he stopped and he stayed. Within a year he had married Alice Miller, the young waitress and cashier at what was then Mosely's filling station, bus depot, and restaurant—the only one in Tyler. Two years later Alice was pregnant and gave birth in a hot August to a son, Jackson (after Andrew Jackson, a childhood hero of Harry's). Two years after that Harry started to pay for a house. That was in 1939. He didn't have the down payment, but in 1939, in or around Tyler, a bank had to take some risk if it wanted to do any business at all. And Harry Belten, after six years in Tyler and at the same job, was considered by all to be, and in fact was, reliable.

His life had closed in upon him quickly. But, he sometimes reflected, he would not have arranged it to be anything other than what it was.

In 1941 Harry Belten bought a violin and began to learn to play it. Once a week, on Sunday afternoon, he would take the short bus ride over to neighboring Chamsford to Miss Houghton, a retired schoolteacher who gave music lessons to an occasional pupil. A couple of jokes were made about it in Tyler at the time, but the war was starting and all interest went there. Alice was pregnant again, and in 1942 gave birth to a daughter, Jane. Harry started working part time in a ball-bearing factory in Buffalo. He drove up with four other men from Tyler three times a week. Mr. White didn't object, for there wasn't much to sell in the hardware line anymore, and besides, it was patriotic. Through it all Harry practiced the violin. Hardly anyone knew and no one cared, except maybe Josephine Goss, who never tired of remembering that Harry's violin playing and the Second World War started together.

"Harry," Alexander White called out from his little cubbyhole office in the back of the store, "could you come back here a minute please?"

"Right away, Alex," Harry answered. He took eighty cents out of a dollar for nails, handed the customer his change, and walked to the back of the store. "Keep an eye on the front," he said to Martin Bollard, who was stacking paint cans, as he passed him. While not technically a manager—besides himself and White there were only two others—Harry was by far the senior clerk. Frequently he would open and close the store, and more than once, when the boss took a vacation or had an operation, he had run the entire business, from ordering stock to making the bank deposits and ledger entries. Over the accumulating years White had sometimes reminded himself that you don't find a Harry Belten every day of the week or around some corner.

Harry squeezed into the office and sat down in the old ladder-back chair. "What can I do for you, Alex?"

"Oh, nothing . . . nothing," the older man said. He was looking at a household-supplies catalog on the desk, thumbing through it. After a few seconds he said, "You know these new ceramic-lined garbage pails? You think we should try a gross?"

"Too many," Harry said. "We don't sell a gross of pails in a year."

"Yeah, yeah. That's right, Harry. It was just that the discount looked so good." He thumbed the catalog some more. "Harry," he started again, "yesterday at lunch down at Kiwanis I heard a couple of guys saying you was going to give a violin concert?"

"Yes sir, Alex. That's correct. As a matter of fact," he continued, "I'd been meaning to talk to you about it." Harry rushed on into his own interest and with an assurance that left his employer out. He made it all seem so "done," so finished, so accomplished. "You see, I figure I'll need a year to get ready, to really get ready. I mean I know all the fingerings and bowings of the pieces I'll be playing. But what I need is *polish*. So I've contacted a teacher—you know, a really top professional teacher. And, well, my lessons are on Monday afternoons starting in a month. The end of April that is." Alexander White looked sideways and up at Harry.

"Harry," he said slowly, smilingly, "the store isn't closed on Mondays. It's closed on Wednesday afternoons. Can't you take your lessons on Wednesday?"

"No," Harry said. "Karnovsky is busy on Wednesday. Maybe," he offered, "we could close the store on Monday and open on Wednesday instead?" White gave a slight start at such a suggestion. "Anyway, I've got to have off Monday afternoons. Without pay, of course." Alexander White shook his hand in front of his eyes and smiled again.

"Harry, when did you say the concert was? In a year, right? And you said just now that you knew all the fingers and bows?"

"Fingerings and bowings," Harry corrected.

"Fingerings and bowings. Yeah. You said so yourself all you need was polish. Okay. Good! But Harry, why a *year*? I mean how much polish do you need for Tyler anyway?"

"Oh," Harry said, "the concert isn't going to be in Tyler. Oh no sir." Harry was igniting. It was something that Alexander White did not behold easily: this fifty-one-year-old man—his slightly crumpled face, the two deep thrusts of baldness on his head, the darkening and sagging flesh beneath the eyes—beginning to burn, to be lustrous. "This isn't going to be like with the quartet that time or like with Tingle on the piano. No sir, Alex. This is *it!* I'm giving the concert in Oswego."

"Uuuh," White grunted as though he had been poked sharply above the stomach.

"I'm renting the Oswego Symphony Orchestra—two days for rehearsals, one day for the performance," Harry continued.

"Uuuh. Aaah," White grunted and wheezed again, nodding, his eyes wincing and watering a little.

"Are you okay, Alex?" Harry asked.

"Harry!" Martin Bollard shouted from the front of the store. It meant that there were customers waiting.

"Be right there," Harry shouted back. He stood to leave and started to squeeze his way out. "And I'm renting the auditorium there," he said over his shoulder and was gone back to work.

"Eeeh. Uuuh," White grunted in conclusion, his breath escaping him. The corners of his mouth turned down. He had blanched and the color had not come back. He said softly to himself, "Then it's true," and waited as if for refutation from a spirit more benign than Harry's demonic one. "But Harry," he rose up, "you're not that kind of fiddler!"

"Mr. Belten, in all candor, you are not a concert-caliber violinist." Karnovsky was speaking. His English was perfect, tempered by a soft, prewar Viennese lilt which could bring delicate memories of music and a time past. Harry had just finished playing a Spanish dance by Sarasate. He put his violin down on top of the piano and turned to the old, gentle man. It was the first time Karnovsky had heard him play.

"I know," Harry said. "I know. But I don't want to be a concert violinist. All I want to do is to give this one concert." Somewhere Karnovsky sighed. Harry went on. "I know all the notes for all the pieces I'm going to play, all the fingerings and bowings. What I need now is polish."

"Mr. Belten, what you need is . . ." but Karnovsky did not finish. "Mr. Belten, there is more to concertizing than all the notes, all the fingerings and bowings. There is a certain . . ." and again he did not finish. "Mr. Belten, have you ever heard Heifetz? Milstein? Stern? Either on records or live?" Harry nodded. "Well that, Mr. Belten, that kind of polish you aren't . . . I'm not able to give you." Karnovsky ended, embarrassed by his special exertion. He was a small man, bald and portly. His eyebrows flickered with every nuance of meaning or emotion, either when he spoke or when he played.

He stood now before Harry, slightly red, his eyes wide. Harry soothed him.

"Ah, Mr. Karnovsky, that kind of playing no man can give to another. I don't ask so much from you. Just listen and suggest. Do to me what you would do to a good fiddler." Karnovsky could not look at him longer this way. He turned around.

"What do you propose to play for your concert, Mr. Belten?" Suspicions began to rise in Karnovsky's mind.

"I thought I'd start with the Vivaldi *Concerto in A Minor.*" Karnovsky nodded. "Then Chausson's *Poème,* then the two Beethoven *Romances,* then something by Sarasate. . . ." Karnovsky's head continued to bob. "And finish up with the Mendelssohn." Karnovsky could not help it. He spun around on Harry.

"The *Mendelssohn?*"

"Yes."

"The Mendelssohn? The Mendelssohn *Violin Concerto?* You are going to play the Mendelssohn? You know the Mendelssohn?"

"Yes," Harry said. "Yes. Yes." He was himself excited by the excitement of the older man, but in a different way.

"How do you know the Mendelssohn?" Karnovsky asked him. His tone was tougher. A fool was a fool, but music was music. Some claims you don't make. Some things you don't say.

"I've studied it," Harry answered.

"How long?" Karnovsky probed. "With whom?"

"Eighteen years. With myself. Ever since I learned how to play in all the positions, I've worked on the Mendelssohn. Every day a little bit. Phrase by phrase. No matter what I practiced, I always saved a little time for the Mendelssohn. I thought the last forty measures of the third movement would kill me. It took me four and a half years." Harry looked up at Karnovsky, but that innocent man had staggered back to the piano bench and collapsed. "It's taken a long time," Harry smiled. No matter what else, he was enjoying talking about music.

"Eighteen *years?*" Karnovsky croaked from behind the piano.

"Eighteen years," Harry reaffirmed, "and now I'm almost ready." *But is the world?* Karnovsky thought to himself. His own wryness softened him toward this strange and earnest man.

"It's fifteen dollars an hour, you know," he tried finally.

"Right," Harry said. Karnovsky fumbled in his pocket and

withdrew a white Life-Saver. He rubbed it in his fingers and then flipped it like a coin in the air. He caught it in his hand and put it into his mouth. Outside, March rain slicked the grimy streets.

"Okay," he muttered. "Like we agreed before you . . . when we spoke . . . on the. . . ." The eyebrows fluttered. "Go," he said. "Get the fiddle. We begin." Harry obeyed.

"Then you're really going through with it?" Alice asked.

"Of course," Harry said, swallowing quickly the last of his Jell-O. He pushed his chair back and stood up.

"Where are you going?" Alice asked.

"I've got something Karnovsky showed me that I want to work on. It's terrific." He smiled. "Already I'm learning stuff I never dreamed of." He started to leave.

"Harry," Alice said, getting up too, "first let's talk a little, huh?"

"Okay," he said, "talk."

"Come into the living room," she said, and walked into it. Harry followed. They both sat down on the sofa. Alice said, "Harry, tell me. Why are you doing it?"

"Doing what?" he asked.

"Throwing three thousand bucks out the window, is what," Alice said, her voice beginning to rise, partly in offended surprise at his question, at his innocence.

"What are you talking about, 'throw out the window'? What kind of talk is that? Is lessons from Louis Karnovsky throwing money away? Is performing the Mendelssohn *Violin Concerto* with a full, professional orchestra behind you throwing money away? What are you talking about? Drinking! That's throwing money away. Gambling! That's throwing money away. But the Mendolssohn *Violin Concerto?* Jeezzz," he concluded turning away his head, not without impatience.

Alice sat there trying to put it together. Something had gotten confused, switched around. It had all seemed so obvious at first. But now it was she who seemed under attack. *What had drinking to do with anything?* she wondered. *Who was doing what wrong?* She gave it up to try another way.

"Do you remember when you and the other guys played together and sometimes put on a show . . . concert . . . in the Grange Hall?"

Harry smiled and then laughed. "Yeah," he said. "Boy, were we a lousy string quartet." But it was a pleasant memory and an important one, and it released him from both his excitement and his scorn.

Shortly after the war some gust of chance, bred out of the new mobility enforced upon the land, brought to Tyler a cellist in the form of a traveling salesman. His name was Fred Miller and he represented a company which sold electric milking machines, their necessary supporting equipment, and other dairy sundries. It was not the first merchandise Fred Miller had hawked across America; it proved not to be the last—only one more item of an endless linkage of products which seemed to gain their reality more from such as he than from their own actual application. Who, after all, can believe in the abstraction of an electric milking machine, of plastic dolls, of suppositories, of Idaho? But Fred Miller was real, full of some American juice that pumped vitality into whatever he touched. And he had brought his cello with him.

After they played, over beer and sandwiches, Fred Miller would tell them about America and about music. "Once," he would begin, "when I was selling automobile accessories [or brushes or aluminum storm windows or animal food] in Denver, one night after supper I was outside the hotel when looking up the street I saw on the movie marquee, instead of the usual announcement of 'Fair star in a country far,' the single word 'Francescatti.' " (The other three would look at each other knowingly.) "Of course, I hurried to the theatre." And then he would take them through the music, through the performance, piece by piece, gesture by gesture, play by play.

"And there he was, not more than twenty bars away from his entrance, big as life and cool as day, wiping his hands on his handkerchief, that forty-grand Strad sticking out from under his chin. *And then he starts to mess with the bow.* Yep. He's got both hands on the bow tightening the hairs. It's a bar to go. It's two beats away. You're sure he's missed it and *wham.* Faster than the speed of light he's whacked that old bow down on the cleanest harmonic A you've ever heard, and it's off to the races, playing triple stops all the way and never missing nothing. Hand me a beer will you, Harry?" And only then would the three of them breathe.

There was the one about when Milstein lost his bow and it almost stabbed a lady in the eighth row. Or the Heifetz one, where he didn't move anything but his fingers and his bow arm, not even his eyes, through the entire Beethoven *Concerto*. There was Stern and Rosand and Oistrakh and Fuchs and Ricci and Piatigorsky and Feuermann and Rose and the Juilliard and the Hungarian and the Budapest and Koussevitsky and Toscanini and Ormandy and the gossip and the feuds and the apocryphal. All of music came to Tyler on those Thursday nights mixed gloriously with the exotic names of Seattle and Madison and Butte and Tucson and with the rubber, steel, plastic, and edible works of all our hands and days.

One Tuesday Fred Miller came into the hardware store to tell Harry that he was leaving. The electric-milking-machine business hadn't made it and he was off to Chicago to pick up a new line. There wasn't even time for a farewell performance. For a few weeks after, Harry, Tingle, and the reconstructed viola player from Bath had tried some improvised trios, but the spirit had gone out of the thing. Harry would sometimes play to Tingle's piano accompaniment or to Music Minus One records. But mostly he played alone.

"Harry," Alice broke in upon him gently, for she sensed where he had been, "Harry, all I'm trying to say is that for people who don't have a lot of money, three thousand dollars is a lot of money to spend . . . on anything!"

"I'll say," Harry agreed, getting up. "I'll be five years at least paying this thing off." He walked away to the room at the back of the house in which he had practiced for twenty-four years. Alice sat, miserable in her dumbness, frustrated and frightened. Something was catching and pulling at her which she couldn't understand. What was she worried about? When he had spent the eight hundred dollars on the new violin, she had not flinched. She had taken the six hundred dollars of hi-fi equipment in her wifely stride, indeed, had come to like it. All their married life they had lived in genteel debt. She looked then as she had in other anxious times for reference and stability to the bedrock of her life, but what she found there only defeated her further: the children were grown and married, the boy, even, had gone to college; all the insurance and the pension plans were paid to date; the second mortgage on the house—which would pay for all of this concertizing—would only push back the final ownership slightly, for the house, on a thirty-year mortgage to begin with, had only four more years to go. The impedimenta of existence were under control.

As Alice sat in the midst of this, the phone rang. She rose to answer it. What was the problem? Was there a problem? Whose problem? It was all so hard. Alice could have wept.

"Hello, Alice." It was Josephine Goss.

"Yes."

"I've been talking to the lawyer." Josephine sounded excited in the way people do who act after obliterating ages of inaction have taught them to forget the taste—giddy, high-pitched, trying to outrun the end of it. "He says you can't do anything legal to stop Harry unless he really is crazy, and if he really is crazy, you've got to be able to prove it."

"So?" Alice said, bracing for the lash of her friend's attitude her questions always earned.

"*So?* So you got to get him to a psychiatrist, so that's what." All at once Alice was deeply frightened, only to discover in the center of her fear the finest speck of relief. Terrible as it was to contemplate, was this the answer? Was this why nothing made sense with Harry anymore? Was he really mad?

From the back of the house Harry's violin sounded above it all.

Harry came out of the storeroom with an armload of brooms.

"Well, if it ain't Pangini himelf," Billy Rostend shouted out.

"Paganini," Harry corrected him, laughing, "the greatest of them all." He put the brooms down. "What can I do for you, Billy?"

"I came for some more of that off-white caulking compound I bought last week. But what I'd really like is to know what is all this about you giving a concert in Oswego. You really going to leave all us poor people and become a big star?"

"Not a chance," Harry said. "How many tubes do you want?"

"Eight. But no kidding, Harry, what's the story?" Alexander White put down the hatchet he had been using to break open nail kegs to listen. The shy, ubiquitous Tingle, a frequent visitor to the store, slipped quietly behind a rack of wooden handles for picks and axes. Martin Bollard and Mrs. George Preble, who had been talking closely and earnestly about an electric toaster at the front of the store, paused at the loudness of Billy's voice and at the question too. There were many in Tyler who wanted to know the story.

"No story," Harry answered him. "I've got this feeling, you see, that I've always wanted to give a real, big-time concert. And now I'm going to do it. That's all. It's that simple." He had been figuring on a pad. "That'll be $3.12, Billy. Do you want a bag?" Billy became conspiratorial. He dropped his voice to a whisper, but it was sharp and whistling.

"Come on, Harry, what gives?" It was more a command than a question, the kind of thing living for three decades in a small town permits, where any sense of secret is affront.

"It's nothing more than what I just told you, Billy. It's something I've always wanted to do, and now I'm going to do it."

"Yeah!" Billy spat at him. "Well, I'll believe that when I believe a lot of other things." He scooped up the tubes of caulking and slammed out of the store. Mrs. George Preble followed, either unnerved by the encounter or bent on gossip, without buying the toaster. Harry looked at Martin Bollard and shrugged his shoulders, but what could Martin say, who also wanted answers to the question Billy had asked. Only the wraithlike Tingle, glancing quickly about himself twice, looked at Harry, smiled, and then was gone.

"Harry, could I see you a minute," Alexander White called to him.

In back, in the little office, White explained to Harry that "it" was all over the town, indeed, all over the entire area of the county that had contact with Tyler. He explained to Harry that business was a "funny thing" and that people were "fickle." He explained that if a man didn't like you he would drive (county roads being so good now) ten miles out of his way to do his business elsewhere. After more than thirty years people didn't distinguish between Harry Belten and White's Hardware. What Harry did reflected on the business. And what Harry was doing, whatever it was, wasn't good for it. Harry listened carefully and attentively, as he always had. In thirty-two years he had never sassed the boss or had a cross word with him. He wasn't going to start now. Whatever was bugging Alexander White and the town of Tyler was something they were going to have to learn to live with until April twenty-eight, eight months away.

"Yes, sir," Harry said. After almost a minute, when Alexander White didn't say anything more, Harry went back to work. And Alexander White went back to opening nail kegs, smashing vigorously and repeatedly at the lids, splintering them beyond necessity.

When Harry came into Karnovsky's studio and said hello, Karnovsky's expressive eyebrows pumped up and down four times before he said a thing. The grey-and-yellow sallowness of the old man's skin took on an illusory undercast of healthy pink from the blood that had risen.

"Mr. Belten, from the beginning I have felt strangely about our relationship. I never minced words. I told you from the beginning that you didn't have it to be a concert violinist. That the idea of you concertizing, beginning to concertize, you, a man your age, was . . . was . . . *crazy!*" Harry had never seen the gentle Karnovsky sputter before. It affected him deeply. "But okay, I thought," Karnovsky continued, "so who cares. So a man from the Southern Tier wants to put on a performance with the local high-school orchestra or something. So okay, I thought. So who cares." He was using his arms to form his accusation the way that a conductor forms a symphony. Karnovsky brought his orchestra to a climax. "But now I find that you have engaged the Oswego Symphony Orchestra and are going to perform in . . . in public! *You are doing this thing for real!*" Not in years, perhaps never before, had Karnovsky shouted so loudly. The sound of his reaching voice surprised him, shocked him, and he fell silent, but he continued to look at Harry, his eyebrows bouncing.

After a moment Harry asked, "Am I committing some crime? What is this terrible thing I am about to do?"

Karnovsky hadn't thought about it in those terms. Six weeks earlier he had told Bronson, his stuffy colleague at the university where he was Professor of Violin, about Harry. A frustrated Heifetz, he had called him. He had also used the word "nut," but gently and with humor. So it was that when at lunch that very day, Bronson had told him that his Harry Belten had hired a professional orchestra and had rented a hall in the middle of the downtown of a large city, Karnovsky felt unjustly sinned against, like the man who wakens belatedly to the fact that "the joke's on him." He considered, and reasonably, the effect that this might have upon his reputation. To be linked with this mad venture was not something you could easily explain away to the musical world. And Karnovsky had a reputation big enough to be shot at by the droning snipers who, living only off of wakes, do what they can to bring them about. Finally, there was the central offense of his musicianship. After fifty-five years of experience as performer and teacher, he knew what Harry's performance would sound like. It wouldn't be unbearably bad, but it didn't belong where Harry was intent on putting it. Maybe, he thought, that would be the best approach.

"Mr. Belten, the musicians will laugh at you. Anyone in your audience—if you even have an audience—who has heard a professional play the Mendelssohn will laugh at you."

"So." Harry shrugged it off. "What's so terrible about that? They laughed at you once."

"What?" Karnovsky started. "What are you talking about?"

"In 1942, when you played the Schoenberg *Violin Concerto* for the first time in Chicago. Worse than laugh at you, they booed and shouted and hissed, even. And one lady threw her pocketbook and it hit you on the knee. I read about it all in *Grant's History of Music Since 1930.*"

Who could help but be softened? Karnovsky smiled. "Believe me, that performance I'll never forget. Still, in Italy in 1939, in Milan, it was worse. Three guys in the audience tried to get up on the stage, to kill me I guess, at least from the way they were screaming and shaking their fists. Thank God there were some police there. I was touring with the Schoenberg *Concerto* then, so I guess they had heard about the trouble it was causing and that's why the police were there." He was warming to his memory and smiling broadly now. *It is a good thing,* he thought, *to have a big, good thing to remember.*

"So what's the difference?" Harry asked.

"What?" Karnovsky came back to the room slowly.

"They laughed at you. They'll laugh at me. What's the difference?"

Repentantly softened, Karnovsky gently said, "It wasn't me they were laughing at, it was the music." He looked away from Harry. "With you it will be you."

"Oh, of course," Harry agreed. "What I meant was what is the difference to the performer?" Harry really wanted to know. "Does the performer take the cheers for himself but leave the boos for the composer? In Italy they were going to kill *you,* not Schoenberg."

Karnovsky had moved to the large window and looked out, his back to Harry. March had turned to May. He heard Harry unzip the canvas cover of his violin case.

"No lesson," he said without turning. He heard Harry zip the case closed again. "Next week," he whispered, but Harry heard and left. Karnovsky stood before the window a long time. Auer had Heifetz, he thought. Kneisel had Fuchs. And I got Harry Belten.

"You're home early," Alice called out.

"Yeah. It's too hot to sell, too hot to buy. White closed up early," He had the evening paper under his arm and in his hand the mail.

"Oh, the mail," Alice said. "I forgot to get it. Anything?"

Harry was looking. He saw a letter addressed to him from the Oswego Symphony, opened it and read.

"Ha!" he shouted, flinging his hand upward.

"What is it?" Alice came over to him.

"It's from the Oswego Symphony. They want to cancel the agreement. They say they didn't know I was going to use the orchestra to give my own public performance." Harry hit the letter with his fist. "They want out. Listen." Harry read from the letter.

". . . given the peculiar nature of the circumstances surrounding your engagement of the orchestra and considering that it is a civically sponsored organization which must consider the feelings and needs both present and future of the community, I am sure that you will be sensitive to the position in which we find ourselves. It has taken many years to establish in the minds and hearts of our people here a sense of respect and trust in the orchestra, and while this is not to say that your intended performance would violate that trust, yet it must be obvious to you that it would perhaps severely qualify it. It goes without saying that upon receipt of the contract, your check will be returned at once along with a cash consideration of fifty dollars for whatever inconvenience this will have involved you in."

Somewhere in the middle of the first ponderous sentence, Alice had gotten lost. "Harry," she asked, "what does it mean?"

"Wait," Harry said as he read the letter again. And then he laughed, splendidly and loud. "It means," he gasped out to her, "that they are offering me my first chance to make money from the violin—by *not* playing." He roared. "Well, the hell with them!" he shouted up at the ceiling. "A contract is a contract. We play!" And he thundered off to his music room to write a letter saying so.

"Harry," Alice called after him. "Harry," she trailed off. But he was gone. She had meant to tell him that the children were coming that night for supper. And she had meant to tell him that Tingle had quietly left at the front door that morning a bundle of large maroon-and-black posters announcing the debut of Harry Belten in Oswego. But, then, it seemed that it was not important to tell him, that until all of this was settled one way or another she would not be able to tell what was important or what was not. Under her flaming flesh, she felt heavy, sodden, cold.

Throughout supper he regaled them with his excitement. Although neither of his children had become musicians, Jackson had learned the piano and Jane the violin. But once past high school they had left their instruments and their skill in that inevitable pile of lost things heaped up by the newer and for a time more attractive urgencies. College had engulfed the boy, marriage and babies the girl. As children they had made their music and had even liked it, but the vital whip of love had never struck them. Still, they had lived too long in that house and with that man not to be sympathetic to his joy. It was, then, wrenchingly difficult when, after supper, after the ice cream on the summer porch which he and his father had built, Jackson told his father that everyone was concerned by what they thought was Harry's strange behavior. Would he consent to be examined?

"Examined?" Harry asked.

"By a doctor," his son answered.

The daughter looked away.

"What's the matter?" Harry looked around surprised. "I feel fine."

"By a different kind of doctor, Dad."

"Oh," Harry said, and quickly understood. "By a ... uh ... a psychiatrist?"

"Yes." Jackson's voice hurried on to add, to adjust, to soften. "Dad ... it's not that we...."

But Harry cut him off. "Okay," he said.

They all turned and leaned toward him as though they expected him to fall down.

"Daddy?" his daughter began, putting her hand out to him. She didn't think that he had understood. She wanted him to be certain that he understood what was implied. But he forstalled her, them.

"It's okay," he said, nodding. "I understand. A psychiatrist. Make the arrangements." And then, to help them out of their confused silence and their embarrassment, he said, "Look. I really may be nuts or something, but not," he added, "the way everybody thinks." And with the confidence of a man who knows a thing or two about his own madness, he kissed them all good night and went to bed.

By the middle of September all kinds of arrangements had been made or remained to be made. First of all, there was the Oswego Symphony. A series of letters between Mr. Arthur Stennis, manager of the orchestra, and Harry had accomplished nothing. It was finally suggested that Harry meet with the Board of Directors personally. A date, Tuesday afternoon, September 21, was set. Then there was the psychiatrist. For convenience, an appointment had been made for Tuesday morning. The psychiatrist was in Rochester. Harry's plan was to have his lesson as usual Monday afternoon, sleep over in Buffalo, drive to Rochester and the psychiatrist the following morning, and then on to Oswego and the Board of the Symphony in the afternoon; home that night and back to work on Wednesday. That was the way he explained it to Alexander White at the store.

After lunch on the twentieth of September Harry prepared to enter upon his quest. He knew it was off to a battle that he went, so he girded himself and planned. And it was the first time he would be sleeping away from home without his wife since he took his son camping fourteen years before. He was enjoying the excitement.

"Is everything in the suitcase?" he asked Alice.

"Yes," she said.

"Are you sure?"

"Yes, yes. I've checked it a dozen times." She held up the list and read it off. "Toothbrush, shaving, underwear, shirt, handkerchief."

"Tie?"

"Tie."

"Okay," he said. "Tonight I'll call you from the Lake View Hotel and tomorrow after the doctor I'll call you too. I won't call after the meeting. I'll just drive right home." He picked up the suitcase and walked toward the door. "Wish me luck," he said.

"Oh, Harry," Alice called and ran to him. She kissed him very hard on his cheek and hugged him to her. "Good luck," she said.

Harry smiled at the irony. "With whom?" he asked.

"With . . . with *all* of them," she said, laughing and squeezing his arm.

At the door he picked up his violin case and, hoisting it under his arm in exaggerated imitation of an old-time movie gangster, turned and sprayed the room. "Rat-a-tat-tat."

They both laughed. Harry kissed his wife and left the house, his weapon ready in his hand.

The psychiatrist was fat and reddish, his freckles still numerous and prominent. He sat behind an expensive looking desklike table and smoked a large, curved pipe. Harry thought that he looked like a nice man.

"Good morning, Mr. Belten," he said, gesturing for Harry to be seated. "Please, be comfortable."

"That pipe smells wonderful," Harry said. The doctor wrote on a legal-size yellow pad on the desk. "Did you write that down?" Harry asked.

The doctor looked up and smiled. "Not exactly. I wrote down something about what you said."

"Oh," Harry nodded.

"Mr. Belten, do you know why you're here?" the psychiatrist asked.

"Certainly," Harry answered. "For you to see if I'm crazy."

"Not exactly. In fact, not at all." The word "crazy" made the doctor's ears redden. "Your family felt that your behavior in the past six months exhibited a definite break with your behavior patterns of the past and felt that, with your consent, an examination now would be useful in determining any potential developments of an aberrated nature. Are you laughing?" he asked Harry, a bit put off.

"I was just thinking, my family felt that, all that?"

The doctor laughed too.

"Doctor, do you know why my family felt whatever it was you said they felt and wanted me examined? I'll tell you. One: Because they can't understand why I want to give this big, public concert. Two: Because it's costing me three thousand dollars, which for me is a lot of money. And three: Because my wife's best friend, who has always disliked me for no good reason, put the bug into my wife."

"Supppose you tell me about it," the doctor said.

Although not certain what the doctor meant by "it," Harry told him plenty. He told him about Alexander White and the hardware business and about Tyler, about Fred Miller and about Miss Houghton, the old violin teacher, and about Karnovsky, the new one, and about the teachers in-between. He told him about Josephine Goss and about his children, about his wife and about the gentle Tingle and about when he bought the new violin. It took a long time to tell all the things that Harry was telling. The doctor was writing rapidly.

"Are you writing down things about that too?" Harry asked.

The doctor paused and looked up at Harry. "Do you want to see what I'm writing?" he asked.

"No," Harry said. "I trust you."

The doctor leaned forward. "Good," he said. "Now, what do you mean by 'trust me'?"

"I mean," Harry answered, "that you'll see I'm not craz . . . not . . . ah . . ." he gave it up with a shrug . . . *"crazy* and that you'll tell my family that and they'll feel better and won't try to stop me from giving the concert."

The doctor leaned back heavily. His pipe had gone out. "Mr. Belten, I can tell you right now that you're not *crazy*—as you put it— and that I have nothing to do with stopping you from giving your concert. Even if I thought you were *crazy* I couldn't stop you. It would have to go through the courts, there would have to be a trial. . . ."

"Fine," Harry interrupted. He stood up. "Just tell them that nothing's wrong with me."

"I didn't say that," the doctor said.

Harry sat down. "What do you mean?" he asked.

"Well." The doctor lit his pipe at length. "Sometimes people can be 'sane' and still 'have something wrong with them.' " He was uncomfortable with Harry's phrasing but decided to use it for the sake of clarity. "By helping the individual to find out what that thing is, we help him to lead a . . . a . . . *happier* life."

"Oh, I get it." Harry brightened. "We find out why I want to give the concert so that when I do give it I'll enjoy it even more?"

"Not exactly." The doctor smiled, but something in what Harry had said lurked dangerously over him. He stiffened slightly as he said, "By finding out why you want to give it maybe we discover that it isn't so important after all, that maybe, finally, you don't really need to give it, that you would be just as happy, maybe happier, by *not* giving it." He continued, his pipe steaming, "There are all kinds of possibilities. It might easily be that your apparent compulsion to give this concert is in reality a way of striking back at the subconscious frustrations of a small life, a way of grasping out for some of the excitement, some of the thrill that you never had."

"Sure," Harry said. "Now that you put it that way, I can see where it could be that too." Harry smiled. "That's pretty good." The doctor smiled. "Still, I don't see where that means that I *shouldn't* have the thrill, the excitement of giving the concert. Maybe after the concert I won't have anymore—what did you call them—'subconscious frustrations.' Maybe the best thing for me *is* to give the concert."

There was a long silence. The doctor let his pipe go out and stared at Harry. At last he said, "Why not?"

It didn't take the Board, or more precisely, Mr. Arthur Stennis, manager of the orchestra and secretary to the Board, more than ten minutes to come to the point. To wit: even though they (he) had executed a contract with one Harry Belten, the Board felt that the reputation of the orchestra had to be protected and that there were sufficient grounds to charge misrepresentation on his part and take the whole thing to court if necessary, which action could cost Harry Belten a small fortune. Why didn't he take their generous offer (now up to two hundred dollars) for returning the contract and forget the whole thing?

"Because," Harry explained again, "I don't want the money. I want to give a concert with a professional orchestra." But that simple answer, which had alienated others, did not aid him here.

He looked around him at the other eight members of the Board. Five were women, all older than Harry, all looking identical in their rinsed-grey hair and in those graceless clothes designed to capture women in their age. They all wore rimless glasses and peered out at Harry, silently, flatly, properly. No help there, he thought. There was the conductor, Morgenstern, a good minor-leaguer. He had said nothing and had not even looked at Harry from the time both had entered the room. Next to him was the treasurer, elected to the Board but, Harry knew, strictly a hired hand. He would take no opposite side. Finally there was Mr. Stanley Knox, eighty-three years old and one of the wealthier men in Oswego, improbably but defiantly present. Although Harry had never seen this ancient man before that afternoon, he knew instinctively that he knew him well. Stanley Knox wore the high-button boot of the past. The too-large check of his unlikely shirt, the width of his tie, the white, green-lined workman's suspenders which Harry glimpsed under the Montgomery Ward suit marked Stanley Knox for what he basically was: for all that counted, just one more of Harry's customers. He had dealt with Stanley Knoxes for more than thirty years. Had he learned anything in all that time that would matter now? Yes.

"It isn't fair," Harry said.

"It might not seem fair to you," Stennis countered, "but would it be fair to the people of Oswego?" He looked around the table in that kind of bowing gesture which suggested that he spoke for them all.

But Harry pursued. "You start by being fair one man at a time." He paused for that to work. Then he continued. "But *besides* me," he said, waving himself out of the picture, "it isn't fair to the musicians. You talk about the good of the orchestra, but you take bread out of the musicians' mouths. Do you think *they* would mind playing with me?"

"What does each man lose?" Stanley Knox asked of anyone. His eyes were rheumy and his teeth chattered in his head.

"For two rehearsals and the performance, between thirty and forty dollars a man," Harry answered.

Stanley Knox looked at Stennis. "Hee, hee," he began. His head lolled for a moment and then straightened. "That's a lot of money for a man to lose."

"Mr. Knox," Stennis explained in the tone affected for the young and the senile, "the thirty dollars lost now could mean much more to the individual members of the orchestra in the years to come. The thirty dollars now should be looked at as an investment in the future, a future of faith and trust that the Oswego Symphony will bring to its people the *best* in music *all* of the time." He said the last looking, glaring, at Harry.

The old man leaned forward in his chair, shaking, and said, "Forty bucks now is forty bucks now." His spittle flew around him. He slapped his open palm down upon the sleek conference table. And then he asked Stennis, "Have you ever heard him play?" Stennis told him no. "Then how do you know he's so bad?" The old ladies, who had been watching either Harry or Stanley Knox, now turned to Stennis. It was the first sign that Harry had a chance.

Then Stennis said, too prissily, too impatiently, "Because at fifty-one years of age you *don't* start a career as a concert violinist. You *don't* start giving concerts."

But that was exactly the wrong thing to say.

"Get your fiddle and play for us," the old man said to Harry. Harry got up and walked to the back of the room where his violin case rested on a table. He took the violin out of the case. Behind him he could hear Stennis squawk:

"Mr. Knox. This is *still* a Board meeting and we are *still* subject to the rules of parliamentary procedure."

"Shut up, Stennis," Stanley Knox said. Harry came forward and played. After he finished a pleasant little minuet of Haydn's he saw the old ladies smiling.

"Very nice," Stanley Knox said.

Stennis interrupted him, feverishly. "But Haydn minuets don't prove anything. My twelve-year-old *daughter* can play that, for God's sake."

Stanley Knox paid him no heed. "Do you know *Turkey in the Straw?*"

Harry nodded and played. Stennis was frantic. As Harry finished, he stood up. "Mr. Knox. I must insist on order." He looked around him for support, and, much as they were enjoying the music, the old ladies nodded, reluctantly, in agreement—Board business was, after all, Board business.

But Stanley Knox slapped the table for his own order. "Quiet," he commanded. "Let the boy play. Play *The Fiddler's Contest,*" he ordered Harry.

"Mr. Knox!" Stennis shouted.

"Quiet!" Knox shouted back. "Let the boy play."

Harry played.

Stennis hit his hand to his head and rushed noisily from the room.

One by one the old ladies tiptoed out, and then the treasurer left, and then Morgenstern, who walked by Harry and neither looked at him nor smiled nor frowned. Harry played on.

"Let the boy play," Stanley Knox roared, pounding the table. "Let the boy play."

By the time Alexander White ate lunch on Monday, April 24, Harry was halfway to Buffalo and his last lesson with Karnovsky. "Well, this is the week," he had cheerfully observed for White that morning. "It sure is," his wearied boss had replied. Although it was spring and the busier time of the year in the hardware business, he had suggested that Harry take off Tuesday as well as the other three and a half days of the week. Harry had objected that he didn't mind working Tuesday. "I know," White told him. "It's me. I object. Go. Get this thing over with." So Harry went. Now Alexander White sat in the Tyler Arms coffee shop-restaurant on Route 39 eating a chicken-salad sandwich. It was two in the afternoon, but he couldn't have gotten away sooner. Louis Bertrand came into the shop and walked over to where Alexander White was sitting.

"Mind if I join you, Alex?" he asked.

"No, no. Sit down," White said, gesturing to the seat opposite him. But even before Bertrand had settled creakingly down into the cane chair, White regretted it.

"So Harry's gone and left you," he observed lightly.

For a fact, White thought, everything travels fast in a small town. "No, no. He had three and a half days off so I gave him the fourth too. Let him get it out of his sytem. Thank God when this week is over." He went to bite into the other half of his sandwich but found that he didn't want it. He sipped at his coffee several times. Thank God when this week is over, he thought.

"But will it be over? Will he get it out of his system?"

"What? What do you mean? You don't think he's going to become a musician, do you? A gypsy?" With his voice Alexander White turned the idea down. He knew his man.

"Why not?" Louis Bertrand asked.

"*Why not? Why not?* Because a man lives and works in a place all his life, he doesn't just like that leave it. Because . . . because he likes it here, the people, his job and everything. And besides, he couldn't afford it even if he wanted to."

"Couldn't he?"

In all the weeks, in all the months that Alexander White had been engulfed and upset by the impinging consequences of Harry's action, he had never been frightened because he had never imagined conclusions more complex than the return to normal which he expected to take place after the concert. But now, for the first time, he imagined more largely.

"What does that mean?" he asked Louis Bertrand steadily and hard.

"I don't say it means anything." He looked away from White over to where George Latham, owner of the Tyler Arms, was sitting drinking coffee. He raised his voice to attract an ally. There had been something in Alexander White's tone. "But when a clerk starts spending three thousand bucks on nothing and takes off a week just like that and buys fancy violins, well. . . ." George Latham had come over and so had George Smiter, who had just entered. Bertrand looked up at them.

"Well *what?*" White demanded.

"Now take it easy, Alex," George Latham soothed him. "Lou didn't mean anything."

"The hell he didn't. Are you accusing Harry of something? Are you saying he's been stealing from me?" No one had said it and none of them thought that it was so, but anger breeds its kind, and mystery compounds it. It wasn't long before they were all arguing heatedly, not to prove a point but to attack an enigma. All except Alexander White, who found out that in thirty-two years men could be honest and loyal and even courageous, and that in the face of that exciting truth violin concerts or what have you for whatever reasons didn't matter much. Uncertain of Harry's compelling vision, unnerved by the ardor of his dream, certain only of the quality of the man and what that demanded of himself, he defended Harry and his concert stoutly. He was surprised to hear the things he was saying, surprised that he was saying them. But he felt freed and good.

In the Green Room Karnovsky paced incessantly.

"Relax," Harry said to him. Karnovsky looked up to see if it was a joke. Harry was tuning his violin.

"I'm relaxed," he said. "I'm relaxed. Here. Give me that," he commanded Harry and grabbed the violin away from him. He began to tune it himself, but it was in tune. He gave it back to Harry. "And don't forget, in the *tutti* in the second movement of the Vivaldi, you have got to come up *over* the orchestra, *over* it."

An electrician knocked at the door. "How do you want the house lights?" he asked Harry.

"What?" Harry said, turning to Karnovsky.

"Halfway," Karnovsky said to the electrician, who left. "Never play in a dark house," he explained to Harry. "You should always be able to see them or else you'll forget that they're there and then the music will die. But don't look at them," he rushed to add.

Harry laughed. "Okay," he said. Then he heard the merest sound of applause. The conductor had taken his place. Harry moved for the door.

"Good luck," Karnovsky said from back in the room.

"Thanks," Harry said. And then, turning, he asked, "You care?"

"I care," Karnovsky said slowly. "I care."

In the great auditorium, built to seat some five thousand, scattered even beyond random were, here and there, a hundred twenty-seven people. Most had come from Tyler, but at least thirty were people who would come to hear a live performance, especially a live performance of the Mendelssohn, anywhere, anytime. In their time they had experienced much. But what, they wondered this night as Morgenstern mounted the podium, was this? Certainly it was Morgenstern and indeed that was the orchestra and there, walking gaily out upon the stage, was a man with a violin in his hand. The house lights were sinking, as in all the concerts of the past. But where were the people? What was going on? Some four or five, unnerved by the hallucinated spectacle, stood up and raced out of the auditorium. But it was only after Harry had been playing (the Vivaldi) for three or four minutes, had wandered for ten measures until he and the orchestra agreed upon the tempo, had come in flat on two successive entrances, and had scratched loudly once, that the others—the strangers—began to get nervous. Now a fine anxiety sprang up in them. Their minds raced over the familiar grounds of their expectations—the orchestra, the conductor, the hall, the music—but nothing held together and no equation that they could imagine explained anything. One woman felt in herself the faint scurryings of hysteria, the flutters of demonic laughter, but she struggled out of the hall in time. Among the other strangers there was much nudging of neighbors and shrugs of unknowing. Then, each reassured that he was not alone in whatever mad thing it was that was happening, they sank down into the wonder of it all. And Harry got, if not good, better. He played through the rest of the first half of the concert pleasantly enough and without incident.

There was no intermission. The time for the Mendelssohn had come.

The Mendelssohn *Concerto in E minor for Violin and Orchestra, Op. 64* was completed September 16, 1844, and was first performed by the celebrated virtuoso Ferdinand David in Leipzig, March 13, 1845. From its first performance and ever after it was and is greatly received in its glory. Every major violinist since David has lived long enough to perform it well. And of concerti for the violin it is preeminent, for it combines a great display of violin technique with lyric magnificence, holding the possibilities of ordered sound at once beyond and above satisfying description. Nowhere in all the vast world of violin literature does the instrument so perfectly emerge as a disciple of itself. No one performs the Mendelssohn *Violin Concerto* publicly without entering into, at least touching upon, its tradition.

After a measure and a half, the violin and the orchestra engage each other and stay, throughout the piece, deeply involved in the other's fate. But the music is for the violin after all, so it is important that the violinist establish at once his mastery over the orchestra, determine in his entrance the tempo and the dynamic pattern that the orchestra must bow to. This Harry did. But he did not do much more. Playing with a reasonable precision and, even, polish; with, even, a certain technical assurance which allowed his tone to bloom, he played well enough but not grandly. As he concluded the first movement he thought to himself, with neither chagrin nor surprise, "Well, Belten. You're no Heifetz," and at the end of the lovely, melancholy second movement, "You're no Oistrakh, either." It was really just as he expected it would be. He was enjoying it immensely.

In the Mendelssohn *Violin Concerto* there are no pauses between the three movements. Part of the greatness of the piece lies in its extraordinary sense of continuity, in its terrific pressure of building, in its tightening, mounting pace (even the cadenza is made an integral part of the overall development). Because there are no pauses and because of the length of the piece and because of the great physical stress put upon the instrument by the demands of the music, there is an increased possibility for one of the strings to lose that exact and

353

critical degree of tautness which gives it—and all the notes played upon it—the correct pitch. If such a thing happens, then the entire harmonic sense of the music is thrown into jeopardy.

Deep into the third movement, at the end of the recapitulation in the new key, Morgenstern heard it happen. He glanced quickly over at Harry. And Glickman, the concertmaster, heard it. He glanced up at Morgenstern. And Karnovsky heard it too. In the many times that he himself had performed the Mendelssohn, this same thing had happened to him only two terrible times. He remembered them like nightmares, perfectly. There was only one thing to do. The performer must adjust his fingering of the notes played on the weakened string. In effect, he must play all the notes on that one string slightly off, slightly wrong, while playing the notes on all the other three strings correctly. Karnovsky tightened in his seat while his fingers twitched with the frustrated knowledge that he could not give to Harry up on the stage. He was suffocating in his black rage at the injustice about to overtake this good man. That the years of absurd dreaming, the months of aching practice should be cast away by the failure of a miserable piece of gut strangled Karnovsky almost to the point of fainting.

Even before Morgenstern had looked at him (and with the first real emotion Harry had seen on that man's face), Harry had heard the pitch drop on the D string. Only his motor reponses formed out of his eighteen years of love carried him through the next three speeding measures as terror exploded in him. He had time to think two things: *I know what should be done,* and *Do it.* He did it. It almost worked.

Harry Belten played the worst finale to the Mendelssohn *Violin Concerto* probably ever played with a real orchestra and before the public, any public. But it was still recognizably the Mendelssohn, it was not too badly out of tune, and if he was missing here and there on the incredibly difficult adjustments to the flatted D string, there were many places where he wasn't missing at all. Besides Karnovsky, Morgenstern, and Glickman, nobody in the tiny audience in the Coliseum knew what was going on. What they knew was what they heard: to most, sounds which could not help but excite; to the more knowledgeable, a poor performance of a great piece of music. But what Karnovsky knew made him almost weep in his pride and in his joy. And then, in that wonder-filled conclusion, violin and orchestra welded themselves together in an affirming shout of splendor and success. The Mendelssohn *Concerto in E minor for Violin and Orchestra, Op. 64,* was over.

In all his life Harry did not remember shaking as he was shaking now as Morgenstern and then the concertmaster grasped his hand in the traditional gesture made at concert's end. His sweat was thick upon them. He turned, smiling, to the world. Out of the great silence someone clapped. One clap. It rang like a shot through the empty hall, ricocheting from high beam to vacant seat and back. And then another clap. And then a clapping, an uncoordinated, hesitant buzz of sound rising up into the half gloom of the hollow dome. Then someone shouted out, "Hey, Harry. That was terrific."

"Yeah," fourteen rows back a voice agreed, "terrific." Two on either distant side of the auditorium whistled shrilly their appreciation. Someone pounded his feet. Joe Lombardy remembered a picture he had seen on TV once where after a concert they had shouted *bravo.*

"Bravo," he shouted. He was on his feet, waving to the stage. "Hey, Harry. Bravo." He looked around him to bring in the others. "Bravo," he shouted again. Other joined, almost chanting: "Bravo. Bravo. Bravo. Bravo." And the sounds flew upward like sparks from fire glowing and dying in the dark.

"Encore," Joe Lombardy, remembering more, shouted out. "Encore," he screamed, pleased with himself. "Encore," he knifed through the thinly spread tumult.

"Encore," the others yelled. "Encore. Encore." What there was there of Tyler cheered.

Alice Belten, sitting between her two children, holding their hands, her eyes full, laughing, was at ease. She looked up at the man on the stage. He threw her a kiss. And she kissed him back.

Then Harry Belten tuned his violin, placed it under his chin, and played his encore. And then he played another one.

[July 1966]

RAYMOND CARVER

Neighbors

Bill and Arlene Miller were a happy couple. But now and then they felt they alone among their circle had been passed by somehow, leaving Bill to attend to his bookkeeping duties and Arlene occupied with secretarial chores. They talked about it sometimes, mostly in comparison with the lives of their neighbors, Harriet and Jim Stone. It seemed to the Millers that the Stones lived a fuller and brighter life, one very different from their own. The Stones were always going out for dinner, or entertaining at home, or traveling about the country somewhere in connection with Jim's work.

The Stones lived across the hall from the Millers. Jim was a salesman for a machine-parts firm and often managed to combine business with a pleasure trip, and on this occasion the Stones would be away for ten days, first to Cheyenne, then on to St. Louis to visit relatives. In their absence, the Millers would look after the Stones' apartment, feed Kitty, and water the plants.

Bill and Jim shook hands beside the car. Harriet and Arlene held each other by the elbows and kissed lightly on the lips.

"Have fun," Bill said to Harriet.

"We will," said Harriet. "You kids have fun too."

Arlene nodded.

Jim winked at her. " 'Bye, Arlene. Take good care of the old man."

"I will," Arlene said.

"Have fun," Bill said.

"You bet," Jim said, clipping Bill lightly on the arm. "And thanks again, you guys."

The Stones waved as they drove away, and the Millers waved too.

"Well, I wish it was us," Bill said.

"God knows, we could use a vacation," Arlene said. She took his arm and put it around her waist as they climbed the stairs to their apartment.

After dinner Arlene said, "Don't forget. Kitty gets liver flavoring the first night." She stood in the kitchen doorway folding the hand-made tablecloth that Harriet had bought for her last year in Santa Fe.

Bill took a deep breath as he entered the Stones' apartment. The air was already heavy and it was always vaguely sweet. The sunburst clock over the television said half-past eight. He remembered when Harriet had come home with the clock, how she crossed the hall to show it to Arlene, cradling the brass case in her arms and talking to it through the tissue paper as if it were an infant.

Kitty rubbed her face against his slippers and then turned onto her side, but jumped up quickly as Bill moved to the kitchen and se-lected one of the stacked cans from the gleaming drainboard. Leaving the cat to pick at her food, he headed for the bathroom. He looked at himself in the mirror and then closed his eyes and then opened them. He opened the medicine chest. He found a container of pills and read the label: *Harriet Stone. One each day as directed,* and slipped it into his pocket. He went back to the kitchen, drew a pitcher of water and returned to the living room. He finished watering, set the pitcher on the rug, and opened the liquor cabinet. He reached in back for the bottle of Chivas Regal. He took two drinks from the bottle, wiped his lips on his sleeve and replaced the bottle in the cabinet.

Kitty was on the couch sleeping. He flipped the lights, slowly closing and checking the door. He had the feeling he had left some-thing.

"What kept you?" Arlene said. She sat with her legs turned under her, watching television.

"Nothing. Playing with Kitty," he said, and went over to her and touched her breasts.

"Let's go to bed, honey," he said.

The next day Bill took only ten of the twenty minutes' break allotted for the afternoon, and left at fifteen minutes before five.

He parked the car in the lot just as Arlene hopped down from the bus. He waited until she entered the building, then ran up the stairs to catch her as she stepped out of the elevator.

"Bill! God, you scared me. You're early," she said.

He shrugged. "Nothing to do at work," he said.

She let him use her key to open the door. He looked at the door across the hall before following her inside.

"Let's go to bed," he said.

"Now?" She laughed. "What's gotten into you?"

"Nothing. Take your dress off." He grabbed for her awkwardly, and she said, "Good God, Bill."

He unfastened his belt.

Later they sent out for Chinese food, and when it arrived they ate hungrily, without speaking, and listened to records.

"Let's not forget to feed Kitty," she said.

"I was just thinking about that," he said. "I'll go right over."

He selected a can of fish for the cat, then filled the pitcher and went to water. When he returned to the kitchen the cat was scratching in her box. She looked at him steadily for a minute before she turned back to the litter. He opened all the cupboards and examined the canned goods, the cereals, the packaged foods, the cocktail and wine glasses, the china, the pots and pans. He opened the refrigerator. He sniffed some celery, took two bites of cheddar cheese, and chewed on an apple as he walked into the bedroom. The bed seemed enormous, with a fluffy white bedspread draped to the floor. He pulled out a nightstand drawer, found a half-empty package of cigarettes and stuffed them into his pocket. Then he stepped to the closet and was opening it when the knock sounded at the front door.

He stopped by the bathroom and flushed the toilet on his way.

"What's been keeping you?" Arlene said. "You've been over here more than an hour."

"Have I really?" he said.

"Yes, you have," she said.

"I had to go to the toilet," he said.

"You have your own toilet," she said.

"I couldn't wait," he said.

That night they made love again.

In the morning he had Arlene call in for him. He showered, dressed, and made a light breakfast. He tried to start a book. He went out for a walk and felt better, but after a while, hands still in his pockets, he returned to the apartment. He stopped at the Stones' door on the chance he might hear the cat moving about. Then he let himself in at his own door and went to the kitchen for the key.

Inside it seemed cooler than his apartment, and darker too. He wondered if the plants had something to do with the temperature of the air. He looked out the window, and then he moved slowly through each room considering everything that fell under his gaze, carefully, one object at a time. He saw ashtrays, items of furniture, kitchen utensils, the clock. He saw everything. At last he entered the bedroom, and the cat appeared at his feet. He stroked her once, carried her into the bathroom and shut the door.

He lay down on the bed and stared at the ceiling. He lay for a while with his eyes closed, and then he moved his hand into his pants. He tried to recall what day it was. He tried to remember when the Stones were due back, and then he wondered if they would ever return. He could not remember their faces or the way they talked and dressed. He sighed, and then with effort rolled off the bed to lean over the dresser and look at himself in the mirror.

He opened the closet and selected a Hawaiian shirt. He looked until he found Bermudas, neatly pressed and hanging over a pair of brown twill slacks. He shed his own clothes and slipped into the shorts and the shirt. He looked in the mirror again. He went to the living room and poured himself a drink and sipped it on his way back to the bedroom. He put on a dark suit, a blue shirt, a blue and white tie, black wing-tip shoes. The glass was empty and he went for another drink.

In the bedroom again he sat on a chair, crossed his legs, and smiled, observing himself in the mirror. The telephone rang twice and fell silent. He finished the drink and took off the suit. He rummaged the top drawers until he found a pair of panties and a brassiere. He stepped into the panties and fastened the brassiere, then looked through the closet for an outfit. He put on a black and white checkered skirt which was too snug and which he was afraid to zipper, and a burgundy blouse that buttoned up the front. He considered her shoes, but understood they would not fit. For a long time he looked out the living-room window from behind the curtain. Then he returned to the bedroom and put everything away.

He was not hungry. She did not eat much either, but they looked at each other shyly and smiled. She got up from the table and checked that the key was on the shelf, then quickly cleared the dishes.

He stood in the kitchen doorway and smoked a cigarette and watched her pick up the key.

"Make yourself comfortable while I go across the hall," she said. "Read the paper or something." She closed her fingers over the key. He was, she said, looking tired.

He tried to concentrate on the news. He read the paper and turned on the television. Finally he went across the hall. The door was locked.

"It's me. Are you still there, honey?" he called.

After a time the lock released and Arlene stepped outside and shut the door. "Was I gone so long?" she said.

"Well you were," he said.

"Was I?" she said. "I guess I must have been playing with Kitty."

He studied her, and she looked away, her hand still resting on the doorknob.

"It's funny," she said. "You know, to go in someone's place like that."

He nodded, took her hand from the knob, and guided her toward their own door. He let them into their apartment. "It is funny," he said. He noticed white lint clinging to the back of her sweater, and the color was high in her cheeks. He began kissing her on the neck and hair and she turned and kissed him back.

"Oh, damn," she said. "Damn, damn," girlishly clapping her hands. "I just remembered. I really and truly forgot to do what I went over there for. I didn't feed Kitty or do any watering." She looked at him. "Isn't that stupid?"

"I don't think so," he said. "Just a minute, I'll get my cigarettes and go back with you."

She waited until he had closed and locked their door, and then she took his arm at the muscle and said, "I guess I should tell you. I found some pictures."

He stopped in the middle of the hall. "What kind of pictures?"

"You can see for yourself," she said, and watched him.

"No kidding." He grinned. "Where?"

"In a drawer," she said.

"No kidding," he said.

And then she said, "Maybe they won't come back," and was at once astonished at her words.

"It could happen," he said. "Anything could happen."

"Or maybe they'll come back and," but she did not finish.

They held hands for the short walk across the hall, and when he spoke she could barely hear his voice.

"The key," he said. "Give it to me."

"What?" she said. She gazed at the door.

"The key," he said, "you have the key."

"My God," she said, "I left the key inside."

He tried the knob. It remained locked. Then she tried the knob, but it would not turn. Her lips were parted, and her breathing was hard, expectant. He opened his arms and she moved into them.

"Don't worry," he said into her ear. "For God's sake, don't worry." They stayed there. They held each other. They leaned into the door as if against a wind, and braced themselves.

[June 1971]

GAIL GODWIN

A Sorrowful Woman

One winter evening she looked at them: the husband durable, receptive, gentle; the child a tender golden three. The sight of them made her so sad and sick she did not want to see them ever again.

She told her husband these thoughts. He was attuned to her; he understood such things. He said he understood. What would she like him to do? "If you could put the boy to bed and read him the story about the monkey who ate too many bananas, I would be grateful." "Of course," he said. "Why, that's a pleasure." And he sent her off to bed.

The next night it happened again. Putting the warm dishes away in the cupboard, she turned and saw the child's grey eyes approving her movements. In the next room was the man, his chin sunk in the open collar of his favorite wool shirt. He was dozing after her good supper. The shirt was the grey of the child's trusting gaze. She began yelping without tears, retching in between. The man woke in alarm and carried her in his arms to bed. The boy followed them up the stairs, saying, "It's all right, Mommy," but this made her scream. "Mommy is sick," the father said, "go and wait for me in your room."

The husband undressed her, abandoning her only long enough to root beneath the eiderdown for her flannel gown. She stood naked except for her bra, which hung by one strap down the side of her body; she had not the impetus to shrug it off. She looked down at the right nipple, shriveled with chill, and thought, How absurd, a vertical bra. "If only there were instant sleep," she said, hiccuping, and the husband bundled her into the gown and went out and came back with a sleeping draught guaranteed swift. She was to drink a little glass of cognac followed by a big glass of dark liquid and afterwards there was just time to say Thank you and could you get him a clean pair of pajamas out of the laundry, it came back today.

The next day was Sunday and the husband brought her breakfast in bed and let her sleep until it grew dark again. He took the child for a walk, and when they returned, red-cheeked and boisterous, the father made supper. She heard them laughing in the kitchen. He brought her up a tray of buttered toast, celery sticks and black bean soup. "I am the luckiest woman," she said, crying real tears. "Nonsense," he said. "You need a rest from us," and went to prepare the sleeping draught, find the child's pajamas, select the story for the night.

She got up on Monday and moved about the house till noon. The boy, delighted to have her back, pretended he was a vicious tiger and followed her from room to room, growling and scratching. Whenever she came close, he would growl and scratch at her. One of his sharp little claws ripped her flesh, just above the wrist, and together they paused to watch a thin red line materialize on the inside of her pale arm and spill over in little beads. "Go away," she said. She got herself upstairs and locked the door. She called the husband's office and said, "I've locked myself away from him. I'm afraid." The husband told her in his richest voice to lie down, take it easy, and he was already on the phone to call one of the baby-sitters they often employed. Shortly after, she heard the girl let herself in, heard the girl coaxing the frightened child to come and play.

After supper several nights later, she hit the child. She had known she was going to do it when the father would see. "I'm sorry," she said, collapsing on the floor. The weeping child had run to hide. "What has happened to me, I'm not myself anymore." The man picked her tenderly from the floor and looked at her with much concern. "Would it help if we got, you know, a girl in? We could fix the room downstairs. I want you to feel freer," he said, understanding these things. "We have the money for a girl. I want you to think about it."

And now the sleeping draught was a nightly thing, she did not have to ask. He went down to the kitchen to mix it, he set it nightly beside her bed. The little glass and the big one, amber and deep rich brown, the flannel gown and the eiderdown.

The man put out the word and found the perfect girl. She was young, dynamic and not pretty. "Don't bother with the room, I'll fix it up myself." Laughing, she employed her thousand energies. She painted the room white, fed the child lunch, read edifying books, raced the boy to the mailbox, hung her own watercolors on the fresh-painted walls, made spinach soufflé, cleaned a spot from the mother's coat, made them all laugh, danced in stocking feet to music in the white room after reading the child to sleep. She knitted dresses for herself and played chess with the husband. She washed and set the mother's soft ash-blonde hair and gave her neck rubs, offered to.

The woman now spent her winter afternoons in the big bedroom. She made a fire in the hearth and put on slacks and an old sweater she had loved at school, and sat in the big chair and stared out the window at snow-ridden branches, or went away into long novels about other people moving through other winters.

The girl brought the child in twice a day, once in the late afternoon when he would tell of his day, all of it tumbling out quickly because there was not much time, and before he went to bed. Often now, the man took his wife to dinner. He made a courtship ceremony of it, inviting her beforehand so she could get used to the idea. They dressed and were beautiful together again and went out into the frosty night. Over candlelight he would say, "I think you are better, you know." "Perhaps I am," she would murmur. "You look . . . like a cloistered queen," he said once, his voice breaking curiously.

One afternoon the girl brought the child into the bedroom. "We've been out playing in the park. He found something he wants to give you, a surprise." The little boy approached her, smiling mysteriously. He placed his cupped hands in hers and left a live dry thing that spat brown juice in her palm and leapt away. She screamed and wrung her hands to be rid of the brown juice. "Oh, it was only a grasshopper," said the girl. Nimbly she crept to the edge of a curtain, did a quick knee bend and reclaimed the creature, led the boy competently from the room.

"The girl upsets me," said the woman to her husband. He sat frowning on the side of the bed he had not entered for so long. "I'm sorry, but there it is." The husband stroked his creased brow and said he was sorry too. He really did not know what they would do without that treasure of a girl. "Why don't you stay here with me in bed," the woman said.

Next morning she fired the girl, who cried and said, "I loved the little boy, what will become of him now?" But the mother turned away her face and the girl took down the watercolors from the walls, sheathed the records she had danced to and went away.

"I don't know what we'll do. It's all my fault, I know. I'm such a burden, I know that."

"Let me think. I'll think of something." (Still understanding these things.)

"I know you will. You always do," she said.

With great care he rearranged his life. He got up hours early, did the shopping, cooked the breakfast, took the boy to nursery school. "We will manage," he said, "until you're better, however long that is." He did his work, collected the boy from the school, came home and made the supper, washed the dishes, got the child to bed. He managed everything. One evening, just as she was on the verge of swallowing her draught, there was a timid knock on her door. The little boy came in wearing his pajamas. "Daddy has fallen asleep on my bed and I can't get in. There's not room."

Very sedately she left her bed and went to the child's room. Things were much changed. Books were rearranged, toys. He'd done some new drawings. She came as a visitor to her son's room, wakened the father and helped him to bed. "Ah, he shouldn't have bothered you," said the man, leaning on his wife. "I've told him not to." He dropped into his own bed and fell asleep with a moan. Meticulously she undressed him. She folded and hung his clothes. She covered his body with the bedclothes. She flicked off the light that shone in his face.

The next day she moved her things into the girl's white room. She put her hairbrush on the dresser; she put a note pad and pen beside the bed. She stocked the little room with cigarettes, books, bread and cheese. She didn't need much.

At first the husband was dismayed. But he was receptive to her needs. He understood these things. "Perhaps the best thing is for you to follow it through," he said. "I want to be big enough to contain whatever you must do."

All day long she stayed in the white room. She was a young queen, a virgin in a tower; she was the previous inhabitant, the girl with all the energies. She tried these personalities on like costumes, then discarded them. The room had a new view of streets she'd never seen that way before. The sun hit the room in late afternoon and she took to brushing her hair in the sun. One day she decided to write a poem. "Perhaps a sonnet." She took up her pen and pad and began working from words that had lately lain in her mind. She had choices for the sonnet, ABAB or ABBA for a start. She pondered these possibilities until she tottered into a larger choice: she did not have to write a sonnet. Her poem could be six, eight, ten, thirteen lines, it could be any number of lines, and it did not even have to rhyme.

She put down the pen on top of the pad.

In the evenings, very briefly, she saw the two of them. They knocked on her door, a big knock and a little, and she would call Come in, and the husband would smile though he looked a bit tired, yet somehow this tiredness suited him. He would put her sleeping draught on the bedside table and say, "The boy and I have done all right today," and the child would kiss her. One night she tasted for the first time the power of his baby spit.

"I don't think I can see him anymore," she whispered sadly to the man. And the husband turned away, but recovered admirably and said, "Of course, I see."

So the husband came alone. "I have explained to the boy," he said. "And we are doing fine. We are managing." He squeezed his wife's pale arm and put the two glasses on her table. After he had gone, she sat looking at the arm.

"I'm afraid it's come to that," she said. "Just push the notes under the door; I'll read them. And don't forget to leave the draught outside."

The man sat for a long time with his head in his hands. Then he rose and went away from her. She heard him in the kitchen where he mixed the draught in batches now to last a week at a time, storing it in a corner of the cupboard. She heard him come back, leave the big glass and the little one outside on the floor.

Outside her window the snow was melting from the branches, there were more people on the streets. She brushed her hair a lot and seldom read anymore. She sat in her window and brushed her hair for hours, and saw a boy fall off his new bicycle again and again, a dog chasing a squirrel, an old woman peek slyly over her shoulder and then extract a parcel from a garbage can.

In the evening she read the notes they slipped under her door. The child could not write, so he drew and sometimes painted his. The notes were painstaking at first; the man and boy offering the final strength of their day to her. But sometimes, when they seemed to have had a bad day, there were only hurried scrawls.

One night, when the husband's note had been extremely short, loving but short, and there had been nothing from the boy, she stole out of her room as she often did to get more supplies, but crept upstairs instead and stood outside their doors, listening to the regular breathing of the man and boy asleep. She hurried back to her room and drank the draught.

She woke earlier now. It was spring, there were birds. She listened for sounds of the man and the boy eating breakfast; she listened for the roar of the motor when they drove away. One beautiful noon, she went out to look at her kitchen in the daylight. Things were changed. He had bought some new dish towels. Had the old ones worn out? The canisters seemed closer to the sink. She inspected the cupboard and saw new things among the old. She got out flour, baking powder, salt, milk (he bought a different brand of butter), and baked a loaf of bread and left it cooling on the table.

The force of the two joyful notes slipped under her door that evening pressed her into the corner of the little room; she had hardly space to breathe. As soon as possible, she drank the draught.

Now the days were too short. She was always busy. She woke with the first bird. Worked till the sun set. No time for hair brushing. Her fingers raced the hours.

Finally, in the nick of time, it was finished one late afternoon. Her veins pumped and her forehead sparkled. She went to the cupboard, took what was hers, closed herself into the little white room and brushed her hair for a while.

The man and boy came home and found: five loaves of warm bread, a roast stuffed turkey, a glazed ham, three pies of different fillings, eight molds of the boy's favorite custard, two weeks' supply of fresh-laundered sheets and shirts and towels, two hand-knitted sweaters (both of the same grey color), a sheath of marvelous watercolor beasts accompanied by mad and fanciful stories nobody could ever make up again, and a tablet full of love sonnets addressed to the man. The house smelled redolently of renewal and spring. The man ran to the little room, could not contain himself to knock, flung back the door.

"Look, Mommy is sleeping," said the boy. "She's tired from

doing all our things again." He dawdled in a stream of the last sun for that day and watched his father roll tenderly back her eyelids, lay his ear softly to her breast, test the delicate bones of her wrist. The father put down his face into her fresh-washed hair.

"Can we eat the turkey for supper?" the boy asked.

[August 1971]

JOY WILLIAMS

The Lover

The girl is twenty-five. It has not been very long since her divorce but she cannot remember the man who used to be her husband. He was probably nice. She will tell the child this, at any rate. Once he lost a fifty-dollar pair of sunglasses while surf casting off Gay Head and felt badly about it for days. He did like kidneys, that was one thing. He loved kidneys for weekend lunch. She would voyage through the supermarkets, her stomach sweetly sloped, her hair in a twist, searching for fresh kidneys for this young man, her husband. When he kissed her, his kisses, or so she imagined, would have the faint odor of urine. Understandably, she did not want to think about this. It hardly seemed that the same problem would arise again, that is, with another man. Nothing could possibly be gained from such an experience! The child cannot remember him, this man, this daddy, and she cannot remember him. He had been with her when she gave birth to the child. Not beside her, but close by, in the corridor. He had left his work and come to the hospital. As they wheeled her by, he said, "Now you are going to have to learn how to love something, you wicked woman." It is difficult for her to believe he said such a thing.

The girl does not sleep well and recently has acquired the habit of listening all night to the radio. It is a weak, not very good radio and at night she can only get one station. From midnight until four she listens to *Action Line*. People call the station and make comments on the world and their community and they ask questions. Music is played and a brand of beef and beans is advertised. A woman calls up and says, "Could you tell me why the filling in my lemon meringue pie is runny?" These people have obscene materials in their mailboxes. They want to know where they can purchase small flags suitable for waving on Armed Forces Day. There is a man on the air who answers these questions right away. Another woman calls. She says, "Can you get us a report on the progress of the collection of Betty Crocker coupons for the lung machine?" The man can and does. He answers the woman's question. Astonishingly, he complies with her request. The girl thinks such a talent is bleak and wonderful. She thinks this man can help her.

The girl wants to be in love. Her face is thin with the thinness of a failed lover. It is so difficult! Love is concentration, she feels, but she can remember nothing. She tries to recollect two things a day. In the morning with her coffee, she tries to remember and in the evening, with her first bourbon and water, she tries to remember as well. She has been trying to remember the birth of her child now for several days. Nothing returns to her. Life is so intrusive! Everyone was talking. There was too much conversation! The doctor was above her, waiting for the pains. "No, I still can't play tennis," the doctor said. "I haven't been able to play for two months. I have spurs on both heels and it's just about wrecked our marriage. Air conditioning and concrete floors is what does it. Murder on your feet." A few minutes later, the nurse had said, "Isn't it wonderful to work with Teflon? I mean for those arterial repairs? I just love it." The girl wished that they would stop talking. She wished that they would turn the radio on instead and be still. The baby inside her was hard and glossy as an ear of corn. She wanted to say something witty or charming so that they would know she was fine and would stop talking. While she was thinking of something perfectly balanced and amusing to say, the baby was born. They fastened a plastic identification bracelet around her wrist and the baby's wrist. Three days later, after they had come home, her husband sawed off the bracelets with a grapefruit knife. The girl had wanted to make it an occasion. She yelled, "I have a lovely pair of tiny silver scissors that belonged to my grandmother and you have used a grapefruit knife!" Her husband was flushed and nervous but he smiled at her as he always did. "You are insecure," she said tearfully. "You are insecure because you had mumps when you were eight." Their divorce was one year and two months away. "It was not mumps," he said carefully. "Once I broke my arm while swimming is all."

The girl becomes a lover to a man she met at a dinner party. He calls her up in the morning. He drives over to her apartment. He drives a white convertible which is all rusted out along the rocker panels. They do not make convertibles anymore, the girl thinks with alarm. He asks her to go sailing. They drop the child off at a nursery school on the way to the pier. She is two years old now. Her hair is an odd color, almost grey. It is braided and pinned up under a big hat with mouse ears that she got on a visit to Disney World. She is wearing a striped jersey stuffed into striped shorts. She kisses the girl and she kisses the man and goes into the nursery carrying her lunch in a Wonder bread bag. In the afternoon, when they return, the girl has difficulty recognizing the child. There are so many children, after all, standing in the rooms, all the same size, all small, quizzical creatures, holding pieces of wooden puzzles in their hands.

It is late at night. A cat seems to be murdering a baby bird in a nest somewhere outside the girl's window. The girl is listening to the child sleep. The child lies in her varnished crib, clutching a bear. The bear has no tongue. Where there should be a small piece of red felt there is nothing. Apparently, the child had eaten it by accident. The crib sheet is in a design of tiny yellow circus animals. The girl enjoys looking at her child but cannot stand the sheet. There is so much going on in the crib, so many colors and patterns. It is so busy in there! The girl goes into the kitchen. On the counter, four palmetto bugs are exploring a pan of coffee cake. The girl goes back to her own bedroom and turns on the radio. There is a great deal of static. The Answer Man on *Action Line* sounds very annoyed. An old gentleman is asking something but the transmission is terrible because the old man refuses to turn off his rock tumbler. He is polishing stones in his rock tumbler like all old men do and he refuses to turn it off while speaking. Finally, the Answer Man hangs up on him. "Good for you," the girl says. The Answer Man clears his throat and says in a singsong way, "The wine of this world has caused only satiety. Our homes suffer from female sadness, embarrassment and confusion. Absence, sterility, mourning, privation and separation abound throughout the land." The girl puts her arms around her knees and begins to rock back and forth on the bed. The child murmurs in sleep. More palmetto bugs skate across the Formica and into the cake. The girl can hear them. A woman's voice comes on the radio now. The girl is shocked. It seems to be her mother's voice. The girl leans toward the radio. There is a terrible weight on her chest. She can scarcely breathe. The voice says, "I put a little pan under the air-conditioner outside my window and it catches the condensation from the machine and I use that water to water my ivy. I think anything like that makes one a better person."

The girl has made love to nine men at one time or another. It does not seem like many but at the same time it seems more than necessary. She does not know what to think about them. They were all very nice. She thinks it is wonderful that a woman can make love to a man. When lovemaking, she feels she is behaving reasonably. She is well. The man often shares her bed now. He lies sleeping, on his stomach, his brown arm across her breasts. Sometimes, when the child is restless, the girl brings her into bed with them. The man shifts position, turns on his back. The child lies between them. The three lie, silent and rigid, earnestly conscious. On the radio, the Answer Man is conducting a quiz. He says, "The answer is: the time taken for the fall of the dashpot to clear the piston is four seconds, and what is the question? The answer is: when the end of the pin is five-sixteenths of an inch below the face of the block, and what is the question?"

She and the man travel all over the South in his white convertible. The girl brings dolls and sandals and sugar animals back to the child. Sometimes the child travels with them. She sits beside them, pretending to do something gruesome to her eyes. She pretends to dig out her eyes. The girl ignores this. The child is tanned and sturdy and affectionate although sometimes, when she is being kissed, she goes limp and even cold, as though she has suddenly, foolishly died. In the restaurants they stop at, the child is well-behaved although she takes only butter and ice water. The girl and the man order carefully but do not eat much either. They move the food around on their plates. They take a bite now and then. In less than a month the man has spent many hundreds of dollars on food that they do not eat. *Action Line* says that an adult female consumes seven hundred pounds of dry food in a single year. The girl believes this of course but it has nothing to do with her. Sometimes, she greedily shares a bag of Fig Newtons with the child but she seldom eats with the man. Her stomach is hard, flat, empty. She feels hungry always, dangerous to herself, and in love. They leave large tips on the tables of restaurants and then they reenter the car. The seats are hot from the sun. The child sits on the girl's lap while they travel, while the leather cools. She seems to ask for nothing. She makes clucking, sympathetic sounds when she sees animals smashed flat on the side of the road. When the child is not with them, they travel with the man's friends.

The man has many friends whom he is devoted to. They are clever and well-off; good-natured, generous people, confident in their pro-longed affairs. They have known each other for years. This is dis-comforting to the girl who has known no one for years. The girl fears that each has loved the other at one time or another. These relation-ships are so complex, the girl cannot understand them! There is such flux, such constancy among them. They are so intimate and so calm. She tries to imagine their embraces. She feels that theirs differ from her own. One afternoon, just before dusk, the girl and man drive a short way into the Everglades. It is very dull. There is no scenery, no prospect. It is not a swamp at all. It is a river, only inches deep! An-other couple rides in the back of the car. They have very dark tans and have pale yellow hair. They look almost like brother and sister. He is a lawyer and she is a lawyer. They are drinking gin and tonics, as are the girl and the man. The girl has not met these people before. The woman leans over the back seat and drops another ice cube from the cooler into the girl's drink. She says, "I hear that you have a little daughter." The girl nods. She feels funny, a little frightened. "The child is very *sortable*," the girl's lover says. He is driving the big car very fast and well but there seems to be a knocking in the engine. He wears a long-sleeved shirt buttoned at the wrists. His thick hair needs cutting. The girl loves to look at him. They drive, and on either side of them, across the slim canals or over the damp saw grass, speed air-boats. The sound of them is deafening. The tourists aboard wear huge earmuffs. The man turns his head toward her for a moment. "I love you," she says. "Ditto," he says loudly, above the clatter of the air-boats. "Double-ditto." He grins at her and she begins to giggle. Then she sobs. She has not cried for many months. There seems something wrong with the way she is doing it. Everyone is astounded. The man drives a few more miles and then pulls into a gas station. The girl feels desperate about this man. She would do the unspeakable for him, the unforgivable, anything. She is lost but not in him. She wants herself lost and never found, in him. "I'll do anything for you," she cries. "Take an aspirin," he says. "Put your head on my shoulder."

The girl is sleeping alone in her apartment. The man has gone on a business trip. He assures her he will come back. He'll always come back, he says. When the girl is quite alone she measures her drink out carefully. Carefully, she drinks twelve ounces of bourbon in two and a half hours. When she is not with the man, she resumes her habit of listening to the radio. Frequently, she hears only the replies of *Action Line.* "Yes," the Answer Man says, "in answer to your question, the difference between rising every morning at six or at eight in the course of forty years amounts to 29,200 hours or three years, two hundred twenty-one days and sixteen hours which are equal to eight hours a day for ten years. So that rising at six will be the equivalent of adding ten years to your life." The girl feels, by the Answer Man's tone, that he is a little repulsed by this. She washes her whiskey glass out in the sink. Balloons are drifting around the kitchen. They float out of the kitchen and drift onto the balcony. They float down the hall and bump against the closed door of the child's room. Some of the balloons don't float but slump in the corners of the kitchen like mounds of jelly. These are filled with water. The girl buys many balloons and is always blowing them up for the child. They play a great deal with the balloons, breaking them over the stove or smashing the water-filled ones against the walls of the bathroom. The girl turns off the radio and falls asleep.

The girl touches her lover's face. She runs her fingers across the bones. "Of course I love you," he says. "I want us to have a life together." She is so restless. She moves her hand across his mouth. There is something she doesn't understand, something she doesn't know how to do. She makes them a drink. She asks for a piece of

374

gum. He hands her a small crumpled stick, still in the wrapper. She is sure that it is not the real thing. The Answer Man has said that Lewis Carroll once invented a substitute for gum. She fears that this is that. She doesn't want this! She swallows it without chewing. "Please," she says. "Please what?" the man replies, a bit impatiently.

Her former husband calls her up. It is autumn and the heat is unusually oppressive. He wants to see the child. He wants to take her away for a week to his lakeside house in the middle of the state. The girl agrees to this. He arrives at the apartment and picks up the child and nuzzles her. He is a little heavier than before. He makes a little more money. He has a different watch, wallet and key ring. "What are you doing these days?" the child's father asks. "I am in love," she says.

The man does not visit the girl for a week. She doesn't leave the apartment. She loses four pounds. She and the child make Jell-O and they eat it for days. The girl remembers that after the baby was born, the only food the hospital gave her was Jell-O. She thinks of all the water boiling in hospitals everywhere for new mothers' Jell-O. The girl sits on the floor and plays endlessly with the child. The child is bored. She dresses and undresses herself. She goes through everything in her small bureau drawer and tries everything on. The girl notices a birthmark on the child's thigh. It is very small and lovely, in the shape, the girl thinks, of a wineglass. A doll's wineglass. The girl thinks about the man constantly but without much exactitude. She does not even have a photograph of him! She looks through old magazines. He must resemble someone! Sometimes, late at night, when she thinks he might come to her, she feels that the Answer Man arrives instead. He is like a moving light, never still. He has the high temperature and metabolism of a bird. On *Action Line,* someone is saying, "And I live by the airport, what is this that hits my house, that showers my roof on takeoff? We can hear it. What is this, I demand to know! My lawn is healthy, my television reception is fine but something is going on without my consent and I am not well, my wife's had a stroke and someone stole my stamp collection and took the orchids off my trees." The girl sips her bourbon and shakes her head. The greediness and wickedness of people, she thinks, their rudeness and lust. "Well," the Answer Man says, "each piece of earth is bad for something. Something is going to get it on it and the land itself is no longer safe. It's weakening. If you dig deep enough to dip your seed, beneath the crust you'll find an emptiness like the sky. No, nothing's compatible to living in the long run. Next caller, please." The girl goes to the telephone and dials hurriedly. It is very late. She whispers, not wanting to wake the child. There is static and humming. "I can't make you out," the Answer Man shouts. "Are you a phronemophobiac?" The girl says more firmly, "I want to know my hour." "Your hour came, dear," he says. "It went when you were sleeping. It came and saw you dreaming and it went back to where it was."

The girl's lover comes to the apartment. She throws herself into his arms. He looks wonderful. She would do anything for him! The child grabs the pocket of his jacket and swings on it with her full weight. "My friend," the child says to him. "Why yes," the man says with surprise. They drive the child to the nursery and then go out for a wonderful lunch. The girl begins to cry and spills the roll basket on the floor.

"What is it?" he asks. "What's wrong?" He wearies of her, really. Her moods and palpitations. The girl's face is pale. Death is not so far, she thinks. It is easily arrived at. Love is further than death. She kisses him. She cannot stop. She clings to him, trying to kiss him. "Be calm," he says.

The girl no longer sees the man. She doesn't know anything about him. She is a gaunt, passive girl, living alone with her child. "I love you," she says to the child. "Mommy loves me," the child murmurs, "and Daddy loves me and Grandma loves me and Granddaddy loves me and my friend loves me." The girl corrects her, "Mommy loves you," she says. The child is growing. In not too long the child will be grown. When is this happening! She wakes the child in the middle of the night. She gives her a glass of juice and together they listen to the radio. A woman is speaking on the radio. She says, "I hope you will not think me vulgar." "Not at all," the Answer Man replies. "He is never at a loss," the girl whispers to the child. The woman says, "My husband can only become excited if he feels that some part of his body is missing." "Yes," the Answer Man says. The girl shakes the sleepy child. "Listen to this," she says. "I want you to know about these things." The unknown woman's voice continues, dimly. "A finger or an eye or a leg. I have to pretend it's not there."

"Yes," the Answer Man says.

[July 1973]

WILLIAM KOTZWINKLE

Horse Badorties
Goes Out

I am all alone in my pad, man, my piled-up-to-the-ceiling-with-junk pad. Piled with sheet music, piled with garbage bags bursting with rubbish, piled with unnameable flecks of putrified wretchedness in grease. My pad, my own little Lower East Side Horse Badorties pad.

I just woke up, man. Horse Badorties just woke up and is crawling around in the sea of abominated filth, man, which he calls home. Walking through the rooms of my pad, man, from which I shall select my wardrobe for the day. Here, stuffed in a trash basket, is a pair of incredibly wrinkled-up muck-pants. And here, man, beneath a pile of wet newspapers is a shirt, man, with one sleeve. All I need now, man, is a tie, and here is a perfectly good rubber Japanese toy snake, man, which I can easily form into an acceptable knot.

SPAGHETTI! MAN! Now I remember. That is why I have arisen from my cesspool bed, man, because of the growlings of my stomach. It is time for breakfast, man. But first I must make a telephone call to Alaska.

Must find telephone. Important deal in the making. Looking around for telephone, man. And here is an electric extension cord, man, which will serve perfectly as a belt to hold up my falling-down Horse Badorties pants, simply by running the cord through the belt loops and plugging it together.

Looking through the shambles wreckage busted chair old sardine can with a roach in it, empty piña-colada bottle, gummy something on the wall, broken egg on the floor, some kind of coffee grounds sprinkled around. What's this under here, man?

It's the sink, man. I have found the sink. Wait a second, man . . .

it is not the sink but my Horse Badorties easy chair piled with dirty dishes. I must sit down here and rest, man, I'm so tired from getting out of bed. Throw dishes onto the floor, crash break shatter. Sink down into the damp cushions, some kind of fungus on the armrest, possibility of smoking it.

I'm in my little Horse Badorties pad, man, looking around. It's the nicest pad I ever had, man, and I'm getting another one just like it down the hall. Two pads, man. The rent will be high but it's not so bad if you don't pay it. And with two pads, man, I will have room to rehearse the Love Chorus, man, and we will sing our holy music and record it on my battery-powered portable falling-apart Japanese tape recorder with the corroded worn-out batteries, man. How wonderful, man.

Sitting in chair, staring at wall, where paint is peeling off and jelly is dripping and hundreds of telephone numbers are written. I must make a telephone call immediately, man, that is a MUST.

Sitting in chair, staring at wall. Unable to move, man, feeling the dark heavy curtain of impassable numbness settling on me, man.

Falling back to sleep, head nodding down to chest, arm falling off side of chair. I've found the phone, man. It was right beside me all the time, man, and I am holding it up, man, and there is margarine in the dial holes. This, man, is definitely my telephone.

". . . hello? . . . hello, man, this is Horse Badorties . . . right, man, I'm putting together a little deal, man. Acapulco artichoke hearts, man, lovely stuff . . . came across the Colorado River on a raft, man, it's a little damp, but other than that . . . can you hold on a second, man, I think I hear somebody trying to break through the window. . . ."

I cannot speak a moment longer, man, without something to eat. I am weak from hunger, man, and must hunt for my refrigerator through sucked oranges, dead wood, old iron, scum-peel. Here it is, man, with the garbage table wedged against it. Tip the table, man, Horse Badorties is starving.

Some kind of mysterious vegetable, man, is sitting in the refrigerator, shriveled, filthy, covered with fungus, a rotten something, man, and it is my breakfast.

Rather than eat it, man, I will return to my bed of pain. I will go back to my bed, man, if I can locate my bed. It's through this door and back in here somewhere, man. I must get some more sleep, I realize that now. I cannot function, cannot move forward, man, until I have retreated into sleep.

Crawling, man, over the bureau drawers which are bursting with old rags and my used-sock collection, and slipping down, man, catching a piece of the bed, man, where I can relax upon a pile of books old pail some rocks floating around. Slipping onto my yellow smeared still mortified ripped wax-paper scummy sheets, man. And the last thing I do, man, before I sleep, is turn on my battery-powered hand-held Japanese fan. The humming note it makes, man, the sweet and constant melodic droning lulls me to sleep, man, where I will dream symphonies, man, and wake up with a stiff neck.

Horse Badorties waking up again, man. Man, what planet am I on? I seem to be contained in some weird primeval hideous grease. Wait a second, man, this is my Horse Badorties pillowcase. I am alive and well in my own Horse Badorties abominable life.

Time to get up, to get out. Get up, man, you've got to get up and go out into the day and bring fifteen-year-old chicks into your life.

I'm moving my Horse Badorties feet, man, getting my stuff together, collecting the various precious contents of my pad, man, which I MUST take along with me. I have the Japanese fan in my hand, man, and I am marching forward through my rubbish heap. Cooling myself, man, on a hot summer morning or afternoon, one of the two.

Over to the window, man, which looks far out over the rooftops to a distant tower, where the time is showing four o'clock in the afternoon. Late, man. I've got to get out of the pad or I will circle around in it again, uncovering lost treasures and I will get hung up and stuck here all day.

Here is my satchel, man. Now I must stuff it with essential items for survival on the street: sheet music, fan, alarm clock, tape recorder. The only final and further object which must be packed in my survival satchel is the Korean ear-flap cap in case I happen to hear Puerto Rican music along the way.

There are countless thousands of other things in these rooms, man, I should take along with me, in case of emergency, and since it is summertime, I MUST take my overcoat. I have a powerful intuition it will come in handy.

Many other things, man, would I like to jam in my satchel. All of it, man, I want to take it all with me, and that is why I must, after getting a last drink of water, get out of here.

Roaches scurrying over the gigantic pile of caked and stuck-together greasy dishes in my Horse Badorties sink. The water is not yet cold enough. I'm going to let the water run here, man, for a second, while it gets cold. Don't let me forget to turn it off.

I've got everything I need, man. Everything I could possibly want for a few hours on the street is already in my satchel. If it gets much heavier, man, I won't be able to carry it.

"I'm turning on the tape recorder, man, to record the sound of the door closing as I go out of my pad. It is the sound of liberation, man, from my compulsion to delay over and over again my departure ... wait just a second, man, I forgot to make sure if there's one last thing I wanted to take."

Back into pad once more, man. Did I forget to do anything, take anything? There is just one thing and that is to change my shoes, man, removing these plastic Japanese shoes which kill my feet, because here, man, is a Chinese gum rubber canvas shoe for easy Horse Badorties walking. Where is the other one, man? Here it is, man, with some kind of soggy wet beans, man, sprouting inside it. I can't disturb nature's harmony, man, I'll have to wear two different shoes, man, one yellow plastic Japanese, the other red canvas Chinese, and my walking, man, will be hopelessly unbalanced. I'd better not go out at all, man.

Look, man, you have to go out. Once you go outside, man, you can always buy a fresh pair of Lower East Side Ukrainian cardboard bedroom slippers. Let's go, man, out the door, everything is cool.

Out the door again, man, and down the steps, down the steps, down ... one ... two ... three flights of stairs. ...

Jesus, man, I forgot my walkie-talkies. I've gone down three flights of steps, man. And I am turning around and going back up them again.

I am climbing back up the stairs because, though I am tired and falling apart, I cannot be without my walkie-talkies, man. Common sense, man.

"It is miraculous, man. I am making a special tape-recorded announcement of this miracle, man, so that I will never forget this moment of superb unconscious intuition. Ostensibly, man, I returned for my walkie-talkies, but actually it was my unconscious mind luring me back, man, because I left the door to my pad wide open. Anyone might have stepped in and carried away the valuable precious contents of my pad, man. And so I am back in the scrap heap, man, the wretched tumbled-down strewn-about everything of my pad, man, and I am seeing a further miracle, man. It is the miracle of the water in the sink, man, which I left running. Man, do you realize that if I had not returned here for my walkie-talkies, I would have flooded the pad, creating tidal waves among my roaches, and also on the roaches who live downstairs with the twenty-six Puerto Rican chickens? A catastrophe has been averted, man. And what is more, now the water is almost cold, man. It just needs to run a few more minutes, man, and I can have my drink of water."

But first, man, I see that I forgot to take my moon-lute, man, hanging here inside the stove. The moon-lute, man, the weirdest instrument on earth, man. Looks like a Chinese frying pan, man, and I am the only one in the Occidental world who would dare to play it, man, as it sounds like a Chinaman falling down a flight of stairs. Which reminds me, man, I'd better get out of this pad, man, and down the stairs. I'm going, man, I'm on the way, out of the door. I am closing up the pad, man, without further notice.

No, man, on second thought, I am not closing up my pad, man, I am returning to it once again for the last time, man, to make a single telephone call to my junkman, man, who is going to sell me a perfectly good used diving bell with a crack in it, man. It will only take the smallest part of a moment, man, for me to handle this important piece of business.

My telephone, man, how wonderful to get back to my telephone again, linking myself once more to the outer world.

"Hello, man . . . there's a shipment of organic carrots on the way, man, are you interested in a few bunches. . . ."

"Hello, man, will you get out your *I Ching*, man, and look up this hexagram I just threw, number 51, nine in the fourth place, what is it . . . *shock is mired?* Right, man, I'm hip, I lost my school bus in a swamp. . . ."

"Hello, baby, this is Horse Badorties . . . sing this note for me will you, baby, I need to have my tympanic cavity blown out: *Boooooooooooooooooooooop!*"

"Hello, Mother, this is Horse. Did I, by any chance, on my last visit, leave a small container of vitamin C tablets, little white tablets in an unmarked bottle . . . yes, I did? Good, I'll be up to get them soon, man, but don't under any circumstances take one of them."

"Hello, man, Horse Badorties here . . . listen, man, I'm sorry I didn't get over to your pad with the Swiss chard, man, but I was unavoidably derailed for three days, man. I was walking along, man, and I saw these kids, man, in the street, playing with a *dead rat,* man. I had to go back to my pad to get a shovel and bury it, man. You understand, man, kids must not be imprinted with such things. Look, man, I'll be over soon, I'll be there at . . . hold on a second, man, just a second. . . ."

"Hello, man . . . this is Horse Badorties, I've got a deal cooking, man . . . stop shouting, man . . . right, man, now I remember—I already have your bread, that is, man, I had your bread until today, man, when a strange thing happened, man, which you will find hard to believe . . . don't go away, man, I'll call you back in five minutes."

". . . hello? . . . hello, man, Horse Badorties here, man. Man, I'm sorry I didn't get over to you with the tomato surprise, man, but dig, a very strange thing happened, man. I was walking in Van Cortlandt Park, man, and suddenly I saw this airplane overhead, man, running out of gas. The cat was circling low, man, looking for a place to land. I had to guide him in, man, for a forced landing, man, and it took quite a long time, which is why I'll be late getting to your pad, man. . . ."

". . . hello, man, listen, man, I've been having fantastically precognitive dreams lately, man, I am digging the future every night, and last night I had a definite signal, man, that the flying saucers are about to land. That's right, man, I wouldn't kid you, and dig, man, I am getting everyone I know to come up to the roof of my pad, man, to watch the saucers land, as there is a possibility I'll be carried away, man, into the sky and taken to another planet. . . ."

Tired, man, I am getting so tired telephoning. I will just close my eyes for a brief nap, man. I have trained myself through the years, man, to close my eyes and sleep for exactly ten minutes, man, no more no less, and wake up perfectly refreshed.

It is morning, Horse Badorties, what a wonderful sunshining morning, wait a second, man, it is afternoon, I overslept. I must hurry, man, *Horse Badorties must go out!*

No, no, it's dorky day again!

"Dorky dorky . . ."

(Dorky day again, man, and I am stumbling around my pad, repeating over and over):

" . . . dorky dorky dorky dorky dorky dorky dorky dorky . . ."

(Constant repetition of the word *dorky* cleans out my consciousness, man, gets rid of all the rubble and cobwebs piled up there. It is absolutely necessary for me to do this once a month and today is dorky day):

" . . . dorky dorky dorky dorky dorky dorky dorky dorky . . ."

(There is a knock at the door, man, go answer it.)

" . . . dorky dorky dorky dorky dorky dorky dorky . . ."

(It is a knapsack blonde chick, man! I wave her in but I cannot stop my dorky now.)

" . . . dorky dorky dorky dorky dorky dorky dorky dorky . . ."

"I got a VD shot."

" . . . dorky dorky dorky dorky dorky dorky dorky dorky . . ."

"I tried hitchhiking out through the Lincoln Tunnel and the cops stopped me."

" . . . dorky dorky dorky dorky dorky dorky dorky dorky . . ."

"I figured maybe I should stay in the city a while longer. I thought it must be a sign."

" . . . dorky dorky dorky dorky dorky dorky dorky dorky . . ."

"What's going on, man, what's all this dorky?"

" . . . dorky dorky dorky dorky dorky dorky dorky dorky . . ."

"I brought some breakfast . . . some bread and jelly."

" . . . dorky dorky dorky dorky dorky dorky dorky dorky dorky dorky dorky dorky dorky dorky dorky dorky dorky . . ."

"Christ, man, knock it off, will you?"

" . . . dorky dorky dorky dorky dorky dorky dorky dorky dorky dorky dorky dorky dorky dorky dorky dorky dorky dorky dorky . . ."

"You're driving me up the wall, man."

" . . . dorky dorky dorky dorky dorky dorky dorky dorky . . ."

(Another knock at the door, man. It always happens on dorky day. It is a saxophone player, man.)

" . . . dorky dorky dorky dorky dorky dorky dorky dorky . . . "

"How's it going, Horse?"

" . . . dorky dorky dorky dorky dorky dorky dorky dorky . . . "

"What's up with Horse, baby?"

" . . . dorky dorky dorky dorky dorky dorky dorky dorky . . . "

"I don't know. He was like this when I got here."

" . . . dorky dorky dorky dorky dorky dorky dorky dorky dorky dorky dorky dorky dorky dorky dorky dorky . . ."

"Hey, Horse, what's all this dorky, man?"

" . . . dorky dorky dorky dorky dorky dorky dorky dorky . . ."

"I have some bread and jelly in my knapsack. Do you want some?"

" . . . dorky dorky dorky dorky dorky dorky dorky dorky dorky dorky dorky dorky dorky dorky dorky dorky dorky . . ."

"What is it, raspberry?"

" . . . dorky dorky dorky dorky dorky dorky dorky . . ."

"Strawberry."

" . . . dorky dorky dorky dorky dorky dorky dorky dorky . . . "

"Hey, Horse, man, knock it off, man, and we'll play some music."

" . . . dorky dorky dorky dorky dorky dorky dorky dorky dorky dorky dorky dorky dorky dorky dorky dorky . . . "

"He won't answer you. I know he won't answer you."

" . . . dorky dorky dorky dorky dorky dorky dorky dorky . . . "

"I think maybe he's composin' some kind of song, baby."

" . . . dorky dorky dorky dorky dorky dorky dorky dorky . . ."

"I thought I might stay here for a while, but I can't stay here, not with all this dorky."

" . . . dorky dorky dorky dorky dorky dorky dorky dorky dorky dorky dorky dorky dorky dorky dorky dorky dorky . . ."

"Dig, baby, you can stay with me if you want. My pad's just around the corner."

" . . . dorky dorky dorky dorky dorky dorky dorky dorky . . . "

"Can we go there right now? I can't take any more of this dorky."

" . . . dorky dorky dorky dorky dorky dorky dorky dorky . . . "

"Sure, baby, let's go."

" . . . dorky dorky dorky dorky dorky dorky dorky dorky dorky dorky dorky dorky dorky . . . "

"Do you think . . . he'll be all right?"

" . . . dorky dorky dorky dorky . . . "

"Yeah, he just has to work it on out. Come on, baby, let's go. So long, man, take it easy with your dorky."

" . . . dorky . . ."

Dorky day, man, has changed my life, I see that now. Because now that it is the day after dorky day, I have a clear picture of what I must do with my life. I must, man, and this is absolute necessity, *Horse Badorties must go out!* The time, man, has come to get out of the pad NOW, man, right now!

Okay, man, I am going straight out the door, without breakfast, without looking around, without further ado. I will be in actual sunlight, man, walking along. Man, I must be straightening out my life, I must be shaping up, man.

Have I forgotten anything?

Sunglasses, tape recorder, fan, umbrella, satchel, used tea bag, disgusting blobular something, my tire pump, man, and this medicinal herb from the Himalayas, the leaves of which bloom only once in a thousand years and I have a shipment of it waiting for me in a subway tunnel, go Horse, go man, out into the real world.

Wait a second, man, I've got to smoke a few of these dandelion stalks to accelerate my brain waves. However, before I make that important step, I must use the stopped-up toilet, man, down which someone flushed a Turkish bath mat by mistake. How wonderful, man, to attend to vital bodily needs before anything else. I should be out buying a dogsled, man, but first I must rearrange my piles of completely disordered everything imaginable, so I can find the toilet. That is a *must* man.

And then I'll go out.

[September 1973]

GRACE PALEY

The Long-Distance Runner

One day, before or after forty-two, I became a long-distance runner. Thought I was stout and in many ways inadequate to this desire, I wanted to go far and fast, not as fast as bicycles and trains, not as far as Taipei, Hingwan, places like that, but round and round the county from the seaside to the bridges, along the old neighborhood streets a couple of times, before old age and urban renewal ended them and me.

I tried the country first, Connecticut, which, being wooded, is always full of buds in spring. All creation is secret, isn't that true? So I trained in the wide-zoned suburban hills where I wasn't known. I ran all spring in and out of dogwood bloom, then laurel.

People sometimes stopped and asked me why I ran, a lady in silk shorts halfway down over her fat thighs. In training, I replied, and rested only to answer if closely questioned. I wore a white sleeveless undershirt as well, with excellent support, not to attract the attention of old men and prudish children.

The summer came, my legs seemed strong. I kissed the kids good-bye. They were quite old by then. It was near the time for parting anyway. I told Mrs. Raftery to look in now and then and give them some of that rotten Celtic supper she makes.

I told them they could take off any time they wanted to. Go lead your private lives, I said. Only leave me out of it.

A word to the wise, said Richard.

You're depressed, Faith, Mrs. Raftery said. Your boyfriend

Jack, the one you think's so hotsy-totsy, hasn't called and you're as gloomy as a tick on Sunday.

Cut the folk shit with me, Raftery, I muttered. Her eyes filled with tears because that's who she is: folk shit from bunion to topknot. That's how she got liked by me, loved, invented, and endured.

When I walked out the door they were all reclining before the television set, Richard, Tonto, and Mrs. Raftery, gazing at the news. Which proved with moving pictures that there *had* been a voyage to the moon, and Africa and South America hid in a furious whorl of clouds.

I said, Good-bye. They said, Yeah, okay, sure.

If that's how it is, forget it, I hollered, and took the Independent Subway to Brighton Beach.

At Brighton Beach I stopped at the Salty Breezes Locker Room to change my clothes. Twenty-five years ago my father invested $500 in its future. In fact, he still clears about $3.50 a year, which goes directly (by law) to The Children of Judea to cover their deficit.

No one paid too much attention when I started to run, easy and light on my feet. I ran on the boardwalk first, past my mother's leafleting station—between a soft ice cream stand and a degenerated dune. There she had been assigned by her comrades to halt the tides of cruel American enterprise with simple socialist sense.

I wanted to stop and admire the long beach. I wanted to stop in order to think admiringly about New York. There aren't many rotting cities so tan and sandy and speckled with citizens at their salty edges. But I had already spent a lot of life lying down or standing and staring. I had decided to run.

After about a mile and a half I left the boardwalk and began to trot into the old neighborhood. I was running well. My breath was long and deep. I was thinking pridefully about my form.

Suddenly I was surrounded by about three hundred blacks.

Who you?

Who that?

Look at her! Just look! When you seen a fatter ass?

Poor thing. She ain't right. Leave her, you boys, you bad boys.

I used to live here, I said.

Oh yes, they said, in the white old days. That time too bad to last.

But we loved it here. We never went to Flatbush Avenue or Times Square. We loved our block.

Tough black titty.

I like your speech, I said. Metaphor and all.

Right on. We get that from talking.

Yes, my people also had a way of speech. And don't forget the Irish. The gift of gab.

Who they? said a small boy.

Cops.

Nowadays, I suggested, there's more than Irish on the police force.

You right, said two ladies. More more, much much more. They's French Chinamen Russkies Congoleans. Oh missee, you too right.

I lived in that house, I said. That apartment house. All my life. Till I got married.

Now that *is* nice. Live in one place. My mother live that way in South Carolina. One place. Her daddy farmed, she said. They ate. No matter winter war bad times. Roosevelt. Something! Ain't that wonderful! And it weren't cold! Big trees!

That apartment. I looked up and pointed. There. The third floor.

They all looked up. So what! You blubberous devil! said a dark young man. He wore horn-rimmed glasses and had that intelligent look that City College boys used to have when I was eighteen and first looked at them.

He seemed to lead them in contempt and anger, even the littlest ones who moved toward me with dramatic stealth singing "Devil, oh Devil." I don't think the little kids had bad feeling because they poked a finger into me, then laughed.

Still, I thought it might be wise to keep my head. So I jumped right in with some facts. I said, How many flowers' names do you know? Wild flowers, I mean. My people only knew two. That's what they say now, anyway. Rich or poor, they only had two flowers' names. Rose and violet.

Daisy, said one boy immediately.

Weed, said another. That *is* a flower, I thought. But everyone else got the joke.

Saxifrage, lupine, said a lady. Viper's bugloss, said a small Girl Scout in medium green with a dark green sash. She held up a *Handbook of Wild Flowers*.

How many you know, fat mama? a boy asked warmly. He wasn't against my being a mother or fat. I turned my attention to him.

Oh, sonny, I said, I'm way ahead of my people. I know in yellows alone: common cinquefoil, trout lily, yellow adder's-tongue, swamp buttercup and common buttercup, golden sorrel, yellow or hop clover, devil's paintbrush, evening primrose, black-eyed Susan, golden aster, also the yellow pickerelweed growing down by the water if not in the water, and dandelions of course. I've seen all these myself. Seen them.

You could see China from the boardwalk, a boy said. When it's nice.

I know more flowers than countries. Mostly young people these days have traveled in many countries.

Not me. I ain't been nowhere.

Not me either, said about seventeen of the boys.

I'm not allowed, said a little girl. There's drunken junkies.

But *I! I!* cried out a tall black youth, very handsome and well-dressed, I am an African. My father came from the high stolen plains. *I* have been everywhere. I was in Moscow six months, learning machinery. I was in France, learning French. I was in Italy, observing the peculiar Renaissance and the people's sweetness. I was in England, where I studied the common law and the urban blight. I was at the Conference of Dark Youth in Cuba to understand our passion. I am now here. Here am I to become an engineer and return to my people, around the Cape of Good Hope in a Norwegian sailing vessel. In this way I will learn the fine old art of sailing in case the engines of the new society of my old inland country should fail.

We had an extraordinary amount of silence after that.

Then one old lady in a black dress and high, white lace collar said to another old lady dressed exactly the same way, Glad tidings when someone got brains in the head, not fish juice. Amen, said a few.

Whyn't you go up to Mrs. Luddy living in your house, you lady, huh? The Girl Scout asked this.

Why she just groove to see you, said some sarcastic snickerer.

She got palpitations. Her man, he give it to her.

That ain't all, he a natural gift-giver.

I'll take you, said the Girl Scout. My name in Cynthia. I'm in Troop 355, Brooklyn.

I'm not dressed, I said, looking at my lumpy knees.

You shouldn't wear no undershirt like that without no runnin number or no team writ on it. It look like a undershirt.

Cynthia! Don't take her up there, said an important boy. Her head strange. Don't you take her. Hear?

Lawrence, she said softly, you tell me once more what to do, I'll wrap you round that lamppost.

Git! she said, powerfully addressing *me*.

In this way I was led into the hallway of the whole house of my childhood.

The first door I saw was still marked in flaky gold, 1A. That's where the janitor lived, I said. He was a Negro.

How come like that? Cynthia made an astonished face. How come the janitor was a black man?

Oh, Cynthia, I said. Then I turned to the opposite door, first floor front, 1B. I remembered. Now, here, this was Mrs. Goreditsky, very very fat. All her children died at birth. Born, then one, two, three. Dead. Five children, then Mr. Goreditsky said, I'm bad luck on you, Tessie, and he went away. He sent fifteen dollars a week for seven years. Then no one heard.

I know her, poor thing, said Cynthia. The city come for her summer before last. The way they knew, it smelled. They wrapped her up in a canvas. They couldn't get through the front door. It scraped off a piece of her. My uncle Ronald had to help them, but he got disgusted.

Only two years ago. She was still here! Wasn't she scared?

So we all, said Cynthia. White ain't everything.

Who lived up here, she asked, 2B? Right now, my best friend, Nancy Rosalind, lives here. She got two brothers, and her sister married and got a baby. She very light-skinned. Not her mother. We got all colors amongst us.

Your best friend? That's funny. Because it was *my* best friend. Right in that apartment. Joanna Rosen.

What become of her? Cynthia asked. She got a running shirt too?

Come on, Cynthia, if you really want to know, I'll tell you. She married this man, Marvin Steirs.

Who's he?

I recollected his achievements. Well, he's the president of a big corporation, JoMar Plastics. This corporation owns a steel company, a radio station, a new Xerox-type machine that lets you do twenty-five different pages at once. This corporation has a foundation, the JoMar Fund for Research in Conservation. Capitalism is like that, I added, in order to be politically useful.

How come you know, you go up their house?

I happened to read all about them on the financial page, just last week. It made me think: a different life. That's all.

Different spokes for different folks, said Cynthia.

I sat down on the cool marble steps and remembered Joanna's cousin Ziggie. He was older than we were. He wrote a poem which told us we were lovely flowers and our legs were petals, which nature would force open no matter how many times we said no.

Then I had several other interior thoughts that I couldn't share with a child, the kind that give your face a blank or melancholy look.

Now you're not interested, said Cynthia. Now you're not gonna say a thing. Who lived here, 2A? Who? Two men lives here now. Women comin and women goin. My mother says, Danger sign: Stay away, my darling, stay away.

I don't remember, Cynthia. I really don't.

You got to. What'd you come for, anyways?

Then I tried. 2A. 2A. Was it the twins? I felt a strong obligation as though remembering was in charge of the *existence* of the past. This is not so.

Cynthia, I said, I don't want to go any farther. I don't even want to remember.

Come on, she said, tugging at my shorts, don't you want to see Mrs. Luddy, the one lives in your old house? That be fun, no?

No. No, I don't want to see Mrs. Luddy.

Now you shouldn't pay no attention to those boys downstairs. She will like you. I mean, she is kind. She don't like most white people, but she might like you.

No, Cynthia, it's not that, but I don't want to see my father and mother's house now.

I didn't know what to say. I said, Because my mother's dead. This was a lie, because my mother lives in her own room with my father in The Children of Judea. With her hand over her socialist heart, she reads the paper every morning after breakfast. Then she says sadly to my father, Every day the same, dying, dying, dying from killing.

Oh oh, the poor thing, Cynthia said, looking into my eyes. Oh, if my mama died, I don't know what I'd do. Even if I was as old as you. I could kill myself. Tears filled her eyes and started down her cheeks. If my mother died, what would I do? She is my protector, she won't let the pushers get me. She hold me tight. She gonna hide me in the cedar box if my uncle Rudford comes try to get me back. She *can't* die, my mother.

Cynthia—honey—she won't die. She's young. I put my arm out to comfort her. You could come live with me, I said. I got two boys, they're nearly grown up. I missed it, not having a girl.

What? What you mean now, live with you and boys. She pulled away and ran for the stairs. Stay way from me, honky lady. I know them white boys. They just gonna try and jostle my black woman-hood. My mother told me about that, keep you white honky devil boys to your devil self, you just leave me be, you old bitch you. Somebody help me, she started to scream, you hear? Somebody help. She gonna take me away.

She flattened herself to the wall, trembling. I was too frightened by her fear of me to say, Honey, I wouldn't hurt you, it's me. I heard her helpers, the voices of large boys crying, We coming, we coming, hold your head up, we coming. I ran past her fear to the stairs and up them two at a time. I came to my old own door. I knocked like the landlord, loud and terrible.

Mama not home, a child's voice said, No, no. I said. It's me! A lady! Someone's chasing me, let me in. Mama not home, I ain't al-lowed to open up for nobody.

It's me! I cried out in terror. Mama! Mama! Let me in!

The door opened. A slim woman whose age I couldn't invent looked at me. She said, Get in and shut that door tight. She took a hard pinching hold on my upper arm. Then she bolted the door her-self. Them hustlers after you. They make me pink. Hide this white lady now, Donald. Stick her under our bed, you got a high bed.

Oh, that's okay. I'm fine now, I said. I felt safe and at home.

You in my house, she said. You do as I say. For two cents, I throw you out.

I squatted under a small kid's pissy mattress. Then I heard the knock. It was tentative and respectful. My mama don allow me to open. Donald! someone called. Donald!

Oh no, he said. Can't do it. She gonna wear me out. You know her. She already tore up my ass this morning once. Ain't *gonna* open up.

I lived there for about three weeks with Mrs. Luddy and Donald and three little baby girls nearly the same age. I told her a joke about Irish twins. Ain't Irish, she said.

Nearly every morning the babies woke us up at about six-forty-five. We gave them all a bottle and went back to sleep till eight. I made coffee and she changed diapers. Then it really stank for a while. At this time I usually said, Well, listen, thanks really, but I've got to go I guess. I guess I'm going. She'd usually say, Well, guess again. *I* guess you ain't. Or if she was feeling disgusted she'd say, Go on now! Get! You wanna go, I guess by now I have snorted enough white stink to choke a horse. Go on!

I'd get to the door and then I'd hear voices. I'm ashamed to say I'd become fearful. Despite my geographical love of mankind, I would be attacked by local fears.

There was a sentimental truth that lay beside all that going and not going. It *was* my house where I'd lived long ago my family life. There was a tile on the bathroom floor that I myself had broken, dropping a hammer on the toe of my brother Charles as he stood dreamily shaving, his prick halfway up his undershorts. Astonishment and knowledge first seized me right there. The kitchen was the same. The table was the enameled table common to our class, easy to clean, with wooden under-corners for indigent and old cockroaches that couldn't make it to the kitchen sink. (However, it was not the same table, because I have inherited that one, chips and all.)

The living room was something like ours, only we had less plastic. There may have been less plastic in the world at that time. Also, my mother had set beautiful cushions everywhere, on beds and chairs. It was the way she expressed herself, artistically, to embroider at night or take strips of flowered cotton and sew them across ordinary white or blue muslin in the most delicate designs, the way women have always used materials that live and die in hunks and tatters, to say, This is my place.

Mrs. Luddy said, Uh huh!

Of course, I said, men don't have that outlet. That's how come they run around so much.

Till they drunk enough to lay down, she said.

Yes, I said, on a large scale you can see it in the world. First they make something, then they murder it. Then they write a book about how interesting it is.

You got something there, she said. Sometimes she said, Girl, you don't know nothin.

We often sat at the window looking out and down. Little tufts of breeze grew on that windowsill. The blazing afternoon was around the corner and up the block.

You say men, she said. Is that men? she asked. What you call—a man?

Four flights below us, leaning on the stoop, were about a dozen people and around them devastation. Just a minute, I said. I had seen devastation on my way, running, gotten some of the pebbles of it in my running shoe and the dust of it in my eye. I had thought with the indignant courtesy of a citizen, This is a disgrace to the City of New York, which I love and am running through.

But now, from the commanding heights of home, I saw it clearly. The tenement in which Jack, my old and present friend, had come to gloomy manhood had been destroyed, first by fire, then by demolition (which is a swinging ball of steel that cracks bedrooms and kitchens). Because of this work, we could see several blocks wide and a block and a half long. Crazy Eddy's house still stood, famous 1510, gutted, with black window frames, no glass, open laths, the stubbornness of the suppporting beams! Some persons or families still lived on the lowest floors. In the yards between, a couple of old sofas lay on their fat faces, their springs sticking up into the air. Just as in wartime, a half dozen ailanthus trees had already found their first quarter inch of earth and begun a living attack on the dead yards. At night, I knew animals roamed the place, squalling and howling, furious New York dogs and street cats and mighty rats. You would think you were in Bear Mountain Park, the terror of venturing forth.

Someone ought to clean that up, I said.

Mrs. Luddy said, Who you got in mind? Mrs. Kennedy?

Donald made a stern face. He said, That just what I gonna do when I get big. Gonna get the sanitary man in and show it to him. You see that, you big guinea you, you clean it up right now! Then he stamped his feet and fierced his eyes.

Mrs. Luddy said, Come here, you little nigger. She kissed the top of his head and gave him a whack on the backside all at one time.

Well, said Donald, encouraged, look out there now, you all! Go on, I say, look! Though we had already seen, to please him we looked. On the stoop men and boys lounged, leaned, hopped about, stood on one leg, then another, took their socks off and scratched their toes, talked, sat on their haunches, heads down, dozing.

Donald said, Look at them. They ain't got self-respect. They got Afros *on* they heads, but they don't know they black *in* they heads.

I thought he ought to learn to be more sympathetic. I said, There are reasons that people are that way.

Yes, ma'am, said Donald.

Anyway, how come you never go down and play with the other kids, how come you're up here so much?

My mama don't like me do that. Some of them is bad. Bad. I might become a dope addict. I got to stay clear.

You just a dope, that's a fact, said Mrs. Luddy.

He ought to be with kids his age more, I think.

He see them in school, miss. Don't trouble your head about it, if you don't mind.

Actually, Mrs. Luddy didn't go down into the street either. Donald did all the shopping. She let the welfare investigator in; the meterman came into the kitchen to read the meter. I saw him from the back room where I hid. She picked up her check. She cashed it. She returned to wash the babies, change their diapers, wash clothes, iron, feed people, and then in free half hours she sat by that window. She was waiting.

I believed she was watching and waiting for a man. I wanted to discuss this with her, talk lovingly like sisters. But before I could freely say, Forget about that son of a bitch, he's a pig, I did have to offer a few solid facts about myself, my kids, about fathers, husbands, passersby, evening companions, and the life of my father and mother in this room by this exact afternoon window.

I told her, for instance, that in my worst times I had given myself one extremely simple physical pleasure. This was cream cheese for breakfast. In fact, I insisted on it, sometimes depriving the children of very important articles and foods.

Girl, you don't know nothin, she said.

Then for a little while she talked gently as one does to a person who is innocent and insane and incorruptible because of stupidity. She had had two such special pleasures for hard times, she said. The first men, but they turned rotten, white women had ruined the best, give them the idea their dicks made of solid gold. The second pleasure she had tried was wine. She said, I do like wine. You *has* to have something just for yourself by yourself. Then she said, But you can't raise a decent boy when you liquor-dazed every night.

White or black, I said, returning to men, they did think they were bringing a rare gift, whereas it was just sex, which is common like bread, though essential.

Oh, you can do without, she said. There's folks does without.

I told her Donald deserved the best. I loved him. If he had flaws, I hardly noticed them. It's one of my beliefs that children do not have flaws, even the worst do not.

Donald was brilliant, like my boys, except that he had an easier disposition. For this reason, I decided, almost the second moment of my residence in that household, to bring him up to reading level at once. I told him we would work with books and newspapers. He went immediately to his neighborhood library and brought some hard books to amuse me. *Black Folktales* by Julius Lester and *Pushcart War*, which is about another neighborhood but relevant.

Donald always agreed with me when we talked about reading and writing. In fact, when I mentioned poetry, he told me he knew all about it, that David Henderson, a known black poet, had visited his second-grade class. So Donald was, as it turned out, well ahead of my nosy tongue. He was usually very busy shopping or making faces to force the little serious baby girls into laughter. But if the subject came up, he could take *the* poem right out of the air into which language and event had just gone.

An example: That morning, his mother had said, Whew, I just got too much piss and diapers and wash. I wanna just sit down by that window and rest myself. He wrote a poem:

Just got too much pissy diapers
and wash and wash.
Just wanna sit down by that window
and look out.
    Ain't nothing there.

Donald, I said, you are plain brilliant. I'm never going to forget you. For God's sake, don't you forget me.

You fool with him too much, said Mrs. Luddy. He already don't even remember his grandma, you never gonna meet someone like her, a curse never come past her lips.

I do remember, Mama, I remember. She lying in bed, right there. A man standing in the door. She say, Esdras, I put a curse on you head. You worsen tomorrow. How come she said like that?

Gomorrah, I believe Gomorrah, she said. She know the Bible inside out.

Did she live with you?

No, no, she visiting. She come up to see us all, her children, how we doing. She come up to see sights. Then she lay down and died. She was old.

I was quiet because of the death of mothers. Mrs. Luddy looked at me thoughtfully. Then she said:

My mama had stories to tell, she raised me on. *Her* mama was a little thing, no sense. Stand in the door of the cabin all day, suckin her thumb. It was slave times. One day a young field boy come stormin along. He knock on the door of the first cabin hollerin, Sister, come out, it's freedom. She come out; she say, Yeah? When? He say, Now! It's freedom now! From one cabin he run to the next cabin, cryin out, Sister, it's freedom now!

Oh, I remember that story, said Donald. Freedom now! Freedom now! He jumped up and down.

You don't remember nothin, boy. Go on, get Eloise, she want to get into the good times.

Eloise was two but undersized. We got her like that, said Donald. Mrs. Luddy let me buy her ice cream and green vegetables. She was waiting for kale and chard, but it was too early. The kale liked cold. You not about to be here November, she said. No, no. I turned away, lonesomeness touching me, and sang our Eloise song:

Eloise loves the bees
The bees they buzz
Like Eloise does.

Then Eloise crawled all over the splintery floor, buzzing wildly.
Oh, you crazy baby, said Donald, buzz buzz buzz.
Mrs. Luddy sat down by the window.
You all make a lot of noise, she said sadly. You just right on
noisy.

The next morning Mrs. Luddy woke me up.
Time to go, she said.
What?
Home.
What? I said.
Well, don't you think you little boys cryin for you? Where's
Mama? They standin in the window. Time to go, lady. This ain't Free
Vacation Farm. Time we was by ourself a little.
Oh Ma, said Donald, she ain't a lot of trouble.
Go on, get Eloise, she hollerin. And button up your lip.
She didn't offer me coffee. She looked at me strictly all the time.
I tried to look strictly back, but I failed because I loved the sight of
her.
Donald was teary, but I didn't dare turn my head to him, until
the parting minute at the door. Even then, I kissed the top of his head
a little too forcefully and said, Well, I'll see you.
On the front stoop there were about half a dozen midmorning
family people and kids arguing about who had dumped garbage out
of which window. They were very disgusted with one another.
Two young men in handsome dashikis stood in counsel and
agreement on the street corner. They divided a comment. How come
white womens got rotten teeth? And look so old? A girl near them
said, Hush.
I walked past them and didn't begin my run until the road
opened somewhere along Ocean Parkway. I was a little stiff because
my way of life had used only small movements, an occasional stretch
to put a knife or teapot out of reach of the babies. I ran about ten, fifteen blocks. Then my second wind came, which is classical, famous
among runners, it's the beginning of flying.

In the three weeks I'd been off the street, jogging had become popular. It seemed that I was only one person doing her thing, which happened, like most American eccentric acts, to be the most "in" thing I could have done. In fact, two young men ran alongside of me for nearly a mile. They ran silently beside me and turned off at Avenue H. A gentleman with a moustache, running poorly in the opposed direction, waving. He called out, "Hi, señora."

Near home I ran through our park, where I had aired my children on weekends and late-summer afternoons. I stopped at the northeast playground, where I met a dozen young mothers intelligently handling their little ones. In order to prepare them, meaning no harm, I said, In fifteen years, you girls will be like me, wrong in everything.

At home it was Saturday morning. Jack had returned, looking as grim as ever, but he'd brought cash and a vacuum cleaner. While the coffee perked, he showed Richard how to use it. They were playing tic-tac-toe on the dusty wall.

Richard said, Well! Look who's here! Hi!

Any news? I asked.

Letter from Daddy, he said. From the lake and water country in Chile. He says it's like Minnesota.

He's never been to Minnesota, I said. Where's Anthony?

Here I am, said Tonto, appearing. But I'm leaving.

Oh yes, I said. Of course. Every Saturday he hurries through breakfast or misses it. He goes to visit his friends in institutions. These are well-known places like Bellevue, Hillside, Rockland State, Central Islip, Manhattan. These visits take him all day and sometimes half the night.

I found some chocolate chip cookies in the pantry. Take them, Tonto, I said. I remember nearly all his friends as little boys and girls always hopping, skipping, jumping, and cookie-eating. He was annoyed. He said, No! Chocolate cookies is what the commissaries are full of. How about money?

Jack dropped the vacuum cleaner. He said, No!

They have parents for that.

I said, Here, five dollars for cigarettes, one dollar each.

Cigarettes! said Jack. Goddamnit! Black lungs and death!

Cancer! Emphysema! He stomped out of the kitchen, breathing. He took the bike from the back room and started for Central Park, which has been closed to cars but opened to bicycle riders. When he'd been gone about ten minutes, Anthony said, It's really open only on Sundays.

Why didn't you say so? Why can't you be decent to him? I asked. It's important to me.

Oh, Faith, he said, patting me on the head because he'd grown so tall, all that air. It's good for his lungs. And his muscles! He'll be back soon.

You should ride too, I said. You don't want to get mushy in your legs. You should go swimming once a week.

I'm too busy, he said. I have to see my friends.

Then Richard, who had been vacuuming under his bed, came into the kitchen. You still here, Tonto?

Going going gone, said Anthony, don't bat your eye.

Now, listen, Richard said, here's a note. It's for Lydia, if you get as far as Rockland. Don't forget it. Don't open it. Don't read it. I know he'll read it.

Anthony smiled and slammed the door.

Did I lose weight? I asked.

Yes, said Richard. You look okay. You never look too bad. But where were you? I got sick of Raftery's boiled potatoes. Where were you, Faith?

Well! I said. Well! I stayed a few weeks in my old apartment, where Grandpa and Grandma and me and Hope and Charlie lived when we were little. I took you there long ago. Not so far from the ocean where Grandma made us very healthy with sun and air.

What are you talking about? said Richard. Cut the baby talk.

Anthony came home earlier than expected because some people were in shock therapy and someone else had run away. He listened to me for a while. Then he said, I don't know what she's talking about either.

Neither did Jack, despite the understanding often produced by love after absence. He said, Tell me again. He was in a good mood. He said, You can even tell it to me twice.

I repeated the story. They all said, What?

Because it isn't usually so simple. Have you known it to happen much nowadays? A woman inside the steamy energy of middle age runs and runs. She finds the houses and streets where her childhood happened. She lives in them. She learns as though she were still a child what in the world is coming next.

[March 1974]

T. CORAGHESSAN BOYLE

Heart of a Champion

Here are the corn fields and the wheat fields winking gold and goldbrown and yellowbrown in midday sun. Up the grassy slope we go, to the barn redder than red against sky bluer than blue, across the smooth stretch of the barnyard with its pecking chickens, and then right on up to the screen door at the back of the house. The door swings open, a black hole in the sun, and Timmy emerges with his cornsilk hair. He is dressed in crisp overalls, striped T-shirt, stubby blue Keds. There must be a breeze—and we are not disappointed—his clean fine cup-cut hair waves and settles as he scuffs across the barnyard to the edge of the field. The boy stops there to gaze out over the wheat-manes, eyes unsquinted despite the sun, eyes blue as tinted lenses. Then he brings three fingers to his lips in a neat triangle and whistles long and low, sloping up sharp to cut off at the peak. A moment passes: he whistles again. And then we see it—out there at the far corner of the field—the ripple, the dashing furrow, the blur of the streaking dog, white chest, flashing feet.

They are in the woods now. The boy whistling, hands in pockets, kicking along with his short darling strides, the dog beside him wagging the white tip of her tail, an all-clear flag. They pass beneath an arching black-barked oak. It creaks, and suddenly begins to fling itself down on them: immense, brutal: a panzer strike. The boy's eyes startle and then there's the leap, the smart snout clutching his trousers, the thunder-blast of the trunk, the dust and spinning leaves. "Golly, Lassie, I didn't even see it," says the boy, sitting safe in a mound of moss. The collie looks up at him—the svelte snout, the deep gold logician's eyes—and laps at his face.

Now they are down by the river. The water is brown with angry suppurations, spiked with branches, fence posts, tires, and logs. It rushes like the sides of boxcars, chews deep and insidious at the bank under Timmy's feet. The roar is like a jetport—little wonder the boy cannot hear the dog's warning bark. We watch the crack appear, widen to a ditch, then the halves splitting—snatch of red earth, writhe of worm—the poise and pitch, and Timmy crushing down with it. Just a flash—but already he is way downstream, his head like a plastic jug, dashed and bobbed, spinning toward the nasty mouth of the falls. But there is the dog—fast as a flashcube—bursting along the bank, all white and gold, blended in motion, hair sleeked with the wind of it . . . yet what can she hope to do? The current surges on, lengths ahead, sure bet to win the race to the falls. Timmy sweeps closer, sweeps closer, the falls loud as a hundred timpani now, the war drums of the Sioux, Africa gone bloodlust mad! The dog forges ahead, lashing over the wet earth like a whipcrack, straining every ganglion, until at last she draws abreast of the boy. Then she is in the air, then the foaming yellow water. Her paws churning like pistons, whiskers chuffing with exertion—oh, the roar!—and there, she's got him, her sure jaws clamping down on the shirt collar, her eyes fixed on the slip of rock at falls' edge. The black brink of the falls, the white paws digging at the rock—and they are safe. The dog sniffs at the inert little form, nudges the boy's side until she manages to roll him over. She clears his tongue and begins mouth-to-mouth.

Night: the barnyard still, a bulb burning over the screen door. Inside, the family sits at dinner, the table heaped with pork chops, mashed potatoes, applesauce and peas, home-baked bread, a pitcher of immaculate milk. Mom and Dad, good-humored and sympathetic, poised at attention, forks in mid-swoop, while Timmy tells his story.

"So then Lassie grabbed me by the collar and, golly, I guess I blanked out because I don't remember anything more till I woke up on the rock—"

"Well, I'll be," says Mom.

"You're lucky you've got such a good dog, son," says Dad, gazing down at the collie where she lies serenely, snout over paw, tail wapping the floor. She is combed and washed and fluffed, her lashes mascaraed and curled, chest and paws white as soap. She looks up humbly. But then her ears leap, her neck jerks around—and she's up at the door, head cocked, alert. A high yipping yowl, like a stuttering fire whistle, shudders through the room. And then another. The dog whines.

"Darn," says Dad. "I thought we were rid of those coyotes. Next thing you know they'll be after the chickens again."

The moon blanches the yard, leans black shadows on trees, the barn. Upstairs in the house, Timmy lies sleeping in the pale light, his hair gorgeously mussed, his breathing gentle. The collie lies on the throw rug beside the bed, her eyes open. Suddenly she rises and slips to the window, silent as shadow, and looks down the long elegant snout to the barnyard below, where the coyote slinks from shade to shade, a limp pullet dangling from his jaws. He is stunted, scabious, syphilitic, his forepaw trap-twisted, eyes running. The collie whimpers softly from the window. The coyote stops in mid-trot, frozen in a cold shard of light, ears high on his head—then drops the chicken at his feet, leers up at the window and begins a crooning, sad-faced song.

The screen door slaps behind Timmy as he bolts from the house, Lassie at his heels. Mom's head pops forth on the rebound. "Timmy!" The boy stops as if jerked by a rope, turns to face her. "You be home before lunch, hear?"

"Sure, Mom," the boy says, already spinning off, the dog at his side.

In the woods, Timmy steps on a rattler and the dog bites its head off. "Gosh," he says. "Good girl, Lassie." Then he stumbles and flips over an embankment, rolls down the brushy incline and over a sudden precipice, whirling out into the breathtaking blue space, a sky diver. He thumps down on a narrow ledge twenty feet below—and immediately scrambles to his feet, peering timorously down the sheer wall to the heap of bleached bones at its base. Small stones break loose, shoot out like asteroids. Dirt-slides begin. But Lassie yarps reassuringly from above, sprints back to the barn for winch and cable, hoists the boy to safety.

On their way back for lunch Timmy leads them through a still and leaf-darkened copse. But notice that birds and crickets have left off their cheeping. How puzzling! Suddenly, around a bend in the path before them, the coyote appears. Nose to the ground, intent. All at once he jerks to a halt, flinches as if struck, hackles rising, tail dipping between his legs. The collie, too, stops short, yards away, her chest proud and shaggy and white. The coyote cowers, bunches like a cat, glares. Timmy's face sags with alarm. The coyote lifts his lip. But the collie prances up and stretches her nose out to him, her eyes liquid. She is balsamed and perfumed; her full chest tapers to sleek haunches and sculpted legs. The coyote is puny, runted, half her size, his coat a discarded doormat. She circles him now, sniffing. She whimpers, he growls, throaty and tough—and stands stiff while she licks at his whiskers, noses his rear, the bald black scrotum. Timmy is horror-struck as the coyote slips behind her, his black lips tight with anticipation.

"What was she doing, Dad?" Timmy asks over his milk, good hot soup, and sandwich.

"The sky was blue today, son," Dad says. "The barn was red."

Late afternoon: the sun mellow, orange. Purpling clots of shadow hang from the branches, ravel out from tree trunks. Bees and wasps and flies saw away at the wet full-bellied air. Timmy and the dog are far out beyond the north pasture, out by the old Indian burial ground, where the boy stoops to search for arrowheads. The collie is pacing the crest above, whimpering voluptuously, pausing from time to time to stare out across the forest, eyes distant and moonstruck. Behind her, storm clouds, dark exploding brains, spread over the horizon.

We observe the wind kicking up: leaves flapping like wash, saplings quivering. It darkens quickly now, clouds scudding low and smoky over treetops, blotting the sun from view. Lassie's white is whiter than ever, highlighted against the heavy horizon, wind-whipped hair foaming around her. Still, she does not look down at the boy as he digs.

The first fat random drops, a flash, the volcanic blast of thunder. Timmy glances over his shoulder at the noise just in time to see the scorched pine plummeting toward the constellated freckles in the center of his forehead. Now the collie turns—too late!—the *swoosh-whack* of the tree, the trembling needles. She is there in an instant, tearing at the green welter, struggling through to his side. The boy lies unconscious in the muddying earth, hair cunningly arranged, a thin scratch painted on his cheek. The trunk lies across his back, the tail of a brontosaurus. The rain falls.

Lassie tugs doggedly at a knob in the trunk, her pretty paws slipping in the wet—but it's no use—it would take a block and tackle, a crane, a corps of engineers to shift that stubborn bulk. She falters, licks at the boy's ear, whimpers. See the troubled look in Lassie's eye as she hesitates, uncertain, priorities warring: stand guard—or dash for help? Her decision is sure and swift—eyes firm with purpose, she's off like shrapnel, already up the hill, shooting past dripping trees, over river, cleaving high wet banks of wheat.

A moment later she dashes through the puddled and rain-screened barnyard, barking right on up to the back door, where she pauses to scratch daintily, her voice high-pitched, insistent. Mom swings open the door and Lassie pads in, toenails clacking on the shiny linoleum.

"What is it, girl? What's the matter? Where's Timmy?"

"Yarf! Yarfata-yarf-yarf!"

"Oh, my! Dad! Dad, come quickly!"

Dad rushes in, face stolid and reassuring. "What is it, dear? . . . Why, Lassie!"

"Oh, Dad, Timmy's trapped under a pine tree out by the old Indian burial ground—"

"Arpit-arp."

"—a mile and a half past the north pasture."

Dad is quick, firm, decisive. "Lassie, you get back up there and stand watch over Timmy. Mom and I will go for Doc Walker. Hurry now!"

The dog hesitates at the door: "Rarfarrar-ra!"

"Right!" says Dad. "Mom, fetch the chain saw."

See the woods again. See the mud-running burial ground, the fallen pine, and there: Timmy! He lies in a puddle, eyes closed, breathing slow. The hiss of the rain is nasty as static. See it work: scattering leaves, digging trenches, inciting streams to swallow their banks. It lies deep now in the low areas, and in the mid areas, and in the high areas. Now see the dam, some indeterminate distance off, the yellow water, like urine, churning over its lip, the ugly earthen belly distended, bloated with the pressure. Raindrops pock the surface like a plague.

Now see the pine once more . . . and . . . what is it? There! The coyote! Sniffing, furtive, the malicious eyes, the crouch, the slink. He stiffens when he spots the boy—but then he slouches closer, a rubbery dangle drooling from between his mismeshed teeth. Closer. Right over the prone figure now, stooping, head dipping between shoulders, irises caught in the corners of his eyes: wary, sly, predatory: a vulture slavering over fallen life.

But wait! Here comes Lassie! Sprinting out of the wheat field, bounding rock to rock across the crazed river, her limbs contourless with speed and purpose.

The jolting front seat of the Ford. Dad, Mom, the Doctor, all dressed in slickers and flap-brimmed hats, sitting shoulder to shoulder behind the clapping wipers, their jaws set with determination, eyes aflicker with downright gumption.

The coyote's jaws, serrated grinders, work at the bones of Timmy's hand. The boy's eyelids flutter with the pain, and he lifts his head feebly—but slaps it down again, flat, lifeless, in the mud. Now see Lassie blaze over the hill, show-dog indignation aflame in her eyes. The scrag of a coyote looks up at her, drooling blood, choking down choice bits of flesh. He looks up from eyes that go back thirty million years. Looks up unmoved, uncringing, the ghastly snout and murderous eyes less a physical than a philosophical challenge. See the collie's expression alter in mid-bound—the countenance of offended A.K.C. morality giving way, dissolving. She skids to a halt, drops her tail and approaches him, a buttery gaze in her golden eyes. She licks the blood from his vile lips.

The dam. Impossibly swollen, the rain festering the yellow surface, a hundred new streams rampaging in, the pressure of those millions of gallons hard-punching millions more. There! The first gap, the water flashing out, a boil splattering. The dam shudders, splinters, blasts to pieces like crockery. The roar is devastating.

The two animals start at the terrible rumbling. Still working their gummy jaws, they dash up the far side of the hill. See the white-tipped tail retreating side by side with the hacked and tick-crawling one—both tails like banners as the animals disappear into the trees at the top of the rise. Now look back to the rain, the fallen pine in the crotch of the valley, the spot of the boy's head. Oh, the sound of it, the wall of water at the far end of the valley, smashing through the little declivity, a God-sized fist prickling with shattered trunks and boulders, grinding along, a planet dislodged. And see Timmy: eyes closed, hair plastered, arm like meatmarket leftovers.

But now see Mom and Dad and the Doctor struggling over the rise, the torrent seething closer, booming and howling. Dad launches himself in full charge down the hillside—but the water is already sweeping over the fallen pine, lifting it like paper. There is a confusion, a quick clip of a typhoon at sea—is that a flash of golden hair?—and it is over. The valley fills to the top of the rise, the water ribbed and rushing.

But we have stopped looking. For we go sweeping up and out of the dismal rain, back to magnificent wheat fields in midday sun. There is a boy cupping his hands to his mouth and he is calling: "Laahh-sie! Laahh-sie!"

Then we see what we must see—way out there at the end of the field—the ripple, the dashing furrow, the blur of the streaking dog, white chest, flashing feet.

[January 1975]

HAROLD BRODKEY

His Son, In His Arms, In Light, Aloft

My father is chasing me.

My God, I feel it up and down my spine, the thumping on the turf, the approach of his hands, his giant hands, the huge ramming increment of his breath as he draws near: a widening effort. I feel it up and down my spine and in my mouth and belly—Daddy is so swift: who ever heard of such swiftness? Just as in stories. . . .

I can't escape him, can't fend him off, his arms, his rapidity, his will. His interest in me.

I am being lifted into the air—and even as I pant and stare blurredly, limply, mindlessly, a map appears, of the dark ground where I ran: as I hang limply and rise anyway on the fattened bar of my father's arm, I see that there's the grass, there's the path, there's a bed of flowers.

I straighten up. There are the lighted windows of our house, some distance away. My father's face, full of noises, is near: it looms: his hidden face: is that you, old money-maker? My butt is folded on the trapeze of his arm. My father is as big as an automobile.

In the oddly shrewd-hearted torpor of being carried home in the dark, a tourist, in my father's arms, I feel myself attached by my heated-by-running dampness to him: we are attached, there are binding oval stains of warmth.

In most social talk, most politeness, most literature, most religion, it is as if violence didn't exist—except as sin, something far away. This is flattering to women. It is also conducive to grace—because the heaviness of fear, the shadowy henchmen selves that fear attaches to us, that fear sees in others, is banished.

Where am I in the web of jealousy that trembles at every human movement?

What detectives we have to be.

What if I am wrong? What if I remember incorrectly? It does not matter. This is fiction—a game—of pleasures, of truth and error, as at the sensual beginning of a sensual life.

My father, Charley, as I knew him, is invisible in any photograph I have of him. The man I hugged or ran toward or ran from is not in any photograph: a photograph shows someone of whom I think: *Oh, was he like that?*

But in certain memories, *he* appears, a figure, a presence, and I think, *I know him.*

It is embarrassing to me that I am part of what is unsayable in any account of his life.

When Momma's or my sister's excesses, of mood, or of shopping, angered or sickened Daddy, you can smell him then from two feet away: he has a dry, achy little stink of a rapidly fading interest in his life with us. At these times, the women in a spasm of wit turn to me; they comb my hair, clean my face, pat my bottom or my shoulder, and send me off; they bid me to go cheer up Daddy.

Sometimes it takes no more than a tug at his newspaper: the sight of me is enough; or I climb on his lap, mimic his depression; or I stand on his lap, press his head against my chest. . . . His face is immense, porous, complex with stubble, bits of talcum on it, unlikely colors, unlikely features, a bald brow with a curved square of lamplight in it. About his head there is a nimbus of sturdy wickedness, of unlikelihood. If his mood does not change, something tumbles and goes dead in me.

Perhaps it is more a nervous breakdown than heartbreak: I have failed him: his love for me is very limited: I must die now. I go somewhere and shudder and collapse—a corner of the dining room, the back stoop or deck: I lie there, empty, grief-stricken, literally unable to move—I have forgotten my limbs. If a memory of them comes to me, the memory is meaningless. . . .

Momma will then stalk in to wherever Daddy is and say to him, "Charley, you can be mad at me, I'm used to it, but just go take a look and see what you've done to the child. . . ."

My uselessness toward him sickens me. Anyone who fails toward him might as well be struck down, abandoned, eaten.

Perhaps it is an animal state: I-have-nothing-left, I-have-no-place-in-this-world.

Well, this is his house. Momma tells me in various ways to love him. Also, he is entrancing—he is so big, so thunderish, so smelly, and has the most extraordinary habits, reading newspapers, for instance, and wiggling his shoe: his shoe is gross: kick someone with that and they'd fall into next week.

Some memories huddle in a grainy light. What it is is a number of similar events bunching themselves, superimposing themselves, to make a false memory, a collage, a mental artifact. Within the boundaries of one such memory one plunges from year to year, is small and helpless, is a little older: one remembers it all but it is nothing that happened, that clutch of happenings, of associations, those gifts and ghosts of a meaning.

I can, if I concentrate, whiten the light—or yellow-whiten it, actually—and when the graininess goes, it is suddenly one afternoon.

I could not live without the pride and belonging-to-himness of being that man's consolation. He had the disposal of the rights to the out-of-doors—he was the other, the other-not-a-woman: he was my strength, literally, my strength if I should cry out.

Flies and swarms of the danger of being unfathered beset me when I bored my father: it was as if I were covered with flies on the animal plain where some ravening wild dog would leap up, bite and grip my muzzle, and begin to bring about my death.

I had no protection: I was subject now to the appetite of whatever inhabited the dark.

A child collapses in a sudden burst of there-is-nothing-here, and that is added onto nothingness, the nothing of being only a child concentrating on there being nothing there, no hope, no ambition: there is a despair but one without magnificence except in the face of its completeness: *I am a child and am without strength of my own.*

I have—in my grief—somehow managed to get to the back deck: I am sitting in the early evening light; I am oblivious to the light. I did and didn't hear his footsteps, the rumble, the house thunder dimly (behind and beneath me), the thunder of his-coming-to-rescue-me.... I did and didn't hear him call my name.

I spoke only the gaping emptiness of grief—that tongue—I understood I had no right to the speech of fathers and sons.

My father came out on the porch. I remember how stirred he was, how beside himself that I was so unhappy, that a child, a child he liked, should suffer so. He laid aside his own mood—his disgust with life, with money, with the excesses of the women—and he took on a broad-winged, malely flustering, broad-winged optimism—he was at the center of a great beating (of the heart, a man's heart, of a man's gestures, will, concern), dust clouds rising, a beating determination to persuade me that the nature of life, of *my* life, was other than I'd thought, other than whatever had defeated me—he was about to tell me there was no need to feel defeated, he was about to tell me that I was a good, or even a wonderful, child.

He kneeled—a mountain of shirt-front and trousers; a mountain that poured, clambered down, folded itself, re-formed itself: a disorderly massiveness, near to me, fabric-hung-and-draped: Sinai. He said, "Here, here, what is this—what is a child like you doing being so sad?" And: "Look at me.... It's all right.... Everything is all right...." The misstatements of consolation are lies about the absolute that require faith—and no memory: the truth of consolation can be investigated if one is a proper child—that is to say, affectionate—only in a non-skeptical way.

"It's not all right!"

"It is—it is." It was and wasn't a lie: it had to do with power—

and limitations: my limitations and his power: he could make it all right for me, everything, provided my everything was small enough and within his comprehension.

Sometimes he would say, "Son—" He would say it heavily— "Don't be sad—I don't want you to be sad—I don't like it when you're sad—"

I can't look into his near and, to me, factually incredible face— incredible because so large (as at the beginning of a love affair): I mean as a *face:* it is the focus of so many emotions and wonderments: he could have been a fool or was—it was possibly the face of a fool, someone self-centered, smug, an operator, semi-criminal, an intelligent psychoanalyst; it was certainly a mortal face—but what did the idea or word mean to me then—*mortal?*

There was a face; it was as large as my chest; there were eyes, inhumanly big, humid—what could they mean? How could I read them? How do you read eyes? I did not know about comparisons: how much more affectionate he was than other men, or less, how much better than common experience or how much worse in this area of being fathered my experience was with him: I cannot say even now: it is a statistical matter, after all, a matter of averages: but who at the present date can phrase the proper questions for the poll? And who will understand the hesitations, the blank looks, the odd expressions on the faces of the answerers?

The odds are he was a—median—father. He himself had usually a conviction he did pretty well: sometimes he despaired—of himself: but blamed me: my love: or something: or himself as a father: he wasn't good at managing stages between strong, clear states of feeling. Perhaps no one is.

Anyway, I knew no such terms as *median* then: I did not understand much about those parts of his emotions which extended past the rather clear area where my emotions were so often amazed. I chose, in some ways, to regard him seriously: in other ways, I had no choice—he was what was given to me.

I cannot look at him, as I said: I cannot see anything: if I look at him without seeing him, my blindness insults him: I don't want to hurt him at all: I want nothing: I am lost and have surrendered and am really dead and am waiting without hope.

He knows how to rescue people. Whatever he doesn't know, one of the things he knows in the haste and jumble of his heart, among the blither of tastes in his mouth and opinions and sympathies in his mind and so on, is the making yourself into someone who will help someone who is wounded. The dispersed and unlikely parts of him come together for a while in a clucking and focused arch of abiding concern. Oh how he plows ahead; oh how he believes in rescue! He puts—he *shoves*—he works an arm behind my shoulders, another under my legs: his arms, his powers shove at me, twist, lift and jerk me until I am cradled in the air, in his arms: "You don't have to be unhappy—you haven't hurt anyone—don't be sad—you're a *nice* boy. . . ."

I can't quite hear him, I can't quite believe him. I can't be *good*—the confidence game is to believe him, is to be a good child who trusts him—we will both smile then, he and I. But if I hear him, I have to believe him still. I am set up that way. He is so big; he is the possessor of so many grandeurs. If I believe him, hope and pleasure will start up again—suddenly—the blankness in me will be relieved, broken by these—meanings—that it seems he and I share in some big, attaching way.

In his pride he does not allow me to suffer: I belong to him.

He is rising, jerkily, to his feet and holding me at the same time. I do not have to stir to save myself—I only have to believe him. He rocks me into a sad-edged relief and an achingly melancholy delight with the peculiar lurch as he stands erect of establishing his balance and rectifying the way he holds me, so he can go on holding me, holding me aloft, against his chest: I am airborne: I liked to have that man hold me—in the air: I knew it was worth a great deal, the embrace, the gift of altitude. I am not exposed on the animal plain. I am not helpless.

The heat his body gives off! It is the heat of a man sweating with regret. His heartbeat, his burning, his physical force: ah, there is a large rent in the nothingness: the mournful apparition of his regret, the proof of his loyalty wake me: I have a twin, a massive twin, mighty company: Daddy's grief is at my grief: my nothingness is echoed in him (if he is going to have to live without me): the rescue was not quite a secular thing. The evening forms itself, a classroom, a brigade of shadows, of phenomena—the tinted air slides: there are shadowy skaters everywhere; shadowy cloaked people step out from behind things which are then hidden behind their cloaks. An alteration in the air proceeds from openings in the ground, from leaks in the sunlight which is being disengaged, like a stubborn hand, or is being stroked shut like my eyelids when I refuse to sleep: the dark rubs and bubbles noiselessly—and seeps—into the landscape. In the rubbed distortion of my inner air, twilight soothes: there are two of us breathing in close proximity here (he is telling me that grownups sometimes have things on their minds, he is saying mysterious things which I don't comprehend); I don't want to look at him: it takes two of my eyes to see one of his—and then I mostly see myself in his eye: he is even more unseeable from here, this holder: my head falls against his neck: "I know what you like—you'd like to go stand on the wall—would you like to see the sunset?" Did I nod? I think I did: I nodded gravely: but perhaps he did not need an answer since he thought he knew me well.

We are moving, this elephant and I, we are lumbering, down some steps, across grassy, uneven ground—the spoiled child in his father's arms—behind our house was a little park—we moved across the grass of the little park. There are sun's rays on the dome of the moorish bandstand. The evening is moist, fugitive, momentarily sneaking, half welcomed in this hour of crime. My father's neck. The stubble. The skin where the stubble stops. Exhaustion has me: I am a creature of failure, a locus of childishness, an empty skull: I am this being-young. We overrun the world, he and I, with his legs, with our eyes, with our alliance. We move on in a ghostly torrent of our being like this.

My father has the smell and feel of wanting to be my father. Guilt and innocence stream and re-stream in him. His face, I see now in memory, held an untiring surprise: as if some grammar of deed and purpose—of comparatively easy tenderness—startled him again and again, startled him continuously for a while. He said, "I guess we'll just have to cheer you up—we'll have to show you life isn't so bad—I guess we weren't any too careful of a little boy's feelings, were we?" I wonder if all comfort is alike.

A man's love is, after all, a fairly spectacular thing.

He said—his voice came from above me—he spoke out into the air, the twilight—"We'll make it all right—just you wait and see. . . ."

He said, "This is what you like," and he placed me on the wall that ran along the edge of the park, the edge of a bluff, a wall too high for me to see over, and which I was forbidden to climb: he placed me on the stubbed stone mountains and grouting of the wall-top. He put his arm around my middle: I leaned against him: and faced outward into the salt of the danger of the height, of the view (we were at least one hundred and fifty feet, we were, therefore, hundreds of feet in the air); I was flicked at by narrow, abrasive bands of wind, evening wind, veined with sunset's sun-crispness, strongly touched with coolness.

The wind would push at my eyelids, my nose, my lips. I heard a buzzing in my ears which signaled how high, how alone we were: this view of a river valley at night and of parts of four counties was audible. I looked into the hollow in front of me, a grand hole, an immense, bellying deep sheet or vast sock. There were numinous fragments in it—birds in what sunlight was left, bits of smoke faintly lit by distant light or mist, hovering inexplicably here and there: rays of yellow light, high up, touching a few high clouds.

It had a floor on which were creeks (and the big river), a little dim, a little glary at this hour, rail lines, roads, highways, houses, silos, bridges, trees, fields, everything more than half hidden in the enlarging dark: there was the shrinking glitter of far-off noises, bearded and stippled with huge and spreading shadows of my ignorance: it was panorama as a personal privilege. The sun at the end of the large, sunset-swollen sky was a glowing and urgent orange; around it were the spreading petals of pink and stratospheric gold: on the ground were occasional magenta flarings; oh it makes you stare and gasp; a fine, astral (not a crayon) red rode in a broad, magnificent band across the middlewestern sky: below us, for miles, shadowiness tightened as we watched (it seemed); above us, tinted clouds spread across the vast shadowing sky: there were funereal lights and sinkings everywhere. I stand on the wall and lean against Daddy, only somewhat awed and abstracted: the view does not own me as it usually does: I am partly in the hands of the jolting—amusement—the conceit—of having been resurrected—by my father.

I understood that he was proffering me oblivion plus pleasure, the end of a sorrow to be henceforth remembered as Happiness. This was to be my privilege. This amazing man is going to rescue me from any anomaly or barb or sting in my existence: he is going to confer happiness on me: as a matter of fact, he has already begun.

"Just you trust me—you keep right on being cheered up—look at that sunset—that's some sunset, wouldn't you say?—everything is going to be just fine and dandy—you trust me—you'll see—just you wait and see. . . ."

Did he mean to be a swindler? He wasn't clear-minded—he often said, "I mean well." He did not think other people meant well.

I don't feel it would be right to adopt an Oedipal theory to explain what happened between him and me: only a sense of what he was like as a man, what certain moments were like, and what was said.

It is hard in language to get the full, irregular, heavy sound of a man.

He liked to have us "all dressed and nice when I come home from work," have us wait for him in attitudes of serene all-is-well contentment. As elegant as a Spanish prince I sat on the couch toying with an oversized model truck—what a confusion of social pretensions, technologies, class disorder there was in that. My sister would sit in a chair, knees together, hair brushed: she'd doze off if Daddy was late. Aren't we happy! Actually, we often are.

One day he came in plungingly, excited to be home and to have us as an audience rather than outsiders who didn't know their lines and who often laughed at him as part of their struggle to improve their parts in his scenes. We were waiting to have him approve of our tableau—he usually said something about what a nice family we looked like or how well we looked or what a pretty group or some such thing—and we didn't realize he was the tableau tonight. We held our positions, but we stared at him in a kind of mindless what-should-we-do-besides-sit-here-and-be-happy-and-nice? Impatiently he said, "I have a surprise for you, Charlotte—Abe Last has a heart after all." My father said something on that order: or "—a conscience after all"; and then he walked across the carpet, a man somewhat jerky with success—a man redolent of vaudeville, of grotesque and sentimental movies (he liked grotesquerie, prettiness, sentiment). As he walked, he pulled banded packs of currency out of his pockets, two or three in each hand. "There," he said, dropping one, then three in Momma's dressed-up lap. "There," he said, dropping another two: he uttered a "there" for each subsequent pack. "Oh, let me!" my sister cried and ran over to look—and then she grabbed two packs and said, "Oh, Daddy, how much *is* this?"

It was eight or ten thousand dollars, he said. Momma said, "Charley, what if someone sees—we could be robbed—why do you take chances like this?"

Daddy harrumphed and said, "You have no sense of fun—if you ask me, you're afraid to be happy. I'll put it in the bank tomorrow—if I can find an honest banker—here, young lady, put that money down: you don't want to prove your mother right, do you?"

Then he said, "I know one person around here who knows how to enjoy himself—" and he lifted me up, held me in his arms.

He said, "We're going outside, this young man and I."

"What should I do with this money!"

"Put it under your mattress—make a salad out of it: you're always the one who worries about money," he said in a voice solid with authority and masculinity, totally pieced out with various self-satisfactions—as if he had gained a kingdom and the assurance of appearing as glorious in the histories of his time; I put my head back and smiled at the superb animal, at the rosy—and cowardly—panther leaping; and then I glanced over his shoulder and tilted my head and looked sympathetically at Momma.

My sister shouted, "I know how to enjoy myself—I'll come too! . . ."

"Yes, yes," said Daddy, who was *never* averse to enlarging spheres of happiness and areas of sentiment. He held her hand and held me on his arm.

"Let him walk," my sister said. And: "He's getting bigger—you'll make a sissy out of him, Daddy. . . ."

Daddy said, "Shut up and enjoy the light—it's as beautiful as Paris and in our own backyard."

Out of folly, or a wish to steal his attention, or greed, my sister kept on: she asked if she could get something with some of the money; he dodged her question; and she kept on; and he grew peevish, so peevish, he returned to the house and accused Momma of having never taught her daughter not to be greedy—he sprawled, im-

petuous, displeased, semi-frantic in a chair: "I can't enjoy myself—
there is no way a man can live in this house with all of you—I swear
to God this will kill me soon. . . ."

Momma said to him, "I can't believe in the things you believe
in—I'm not a girl anymore: when I play the fool, it isn't convincing—you get angry with me when I try. You shouldn't get angry with
her—you've spoiled her more than I have—and how do you expect
her to act when you show her all that money—how do you think
money affects people?"

I looked at him to see what the answer was, to see what he would
answer. He said, "Charlotte, try being a rose and not a thorn."

At all times, and in all places, there is always the possibility that I will
start to speak or will be looking at something and I will feel his face
covering mine, as in a kiss and as a mask, turned both ways like that:
and I am inside him, his presence, his thoughts, his language: *I* am
languageless then for a moment, an automaton of repetition, a
bagged piece of an imaginary river of descent.

I can't invent everything for myself: some always has to be what
I already know: some of me always has to be him.

When he picked me up, my consciousness fitted itself to that position: I remember it—clearly. He could punish me—and did—by refusing to lift me, by denying me that union with him. Of course, the
union was not one-sided: I was his innocence—as long as I was not an
accusation, that is. I censored him—in that when he felt himself
being, consciously, a father, he held back part of his other life, of his
whole self: his shadows, his impressions, his adventures would not
readily fit into me—what a gross and absurd rape that would have
been.

So he was *careful*—he *walked on eggs*—there was an odd courtesy of his withdrawal behind his secrets, his secret sorrows and horrors, behind the curtain of what-is-suitable-for-a-child.

Sometimes he becomes simply a set of limits, of walls, inside
which there is the caroming and echoing of my astounding sensibility
amplified by being his son and in his arms and aloft; and he lays his
sensibility aside or models his on mine, on my joy, takes his emotional coloring from me, like a mirror or a twin: his incomprehensible
life, with its strengths, ordeals, triumphs, crimes, horrors, his sadness

and disgust, is enveloped and momentarily assuaged by my direct and indirect childish consolation. My gaze, my enjoying him, my willingness to be him, my joy at it, supported the baroque tower of his necessary but limited and maybe dishonest optimism.

One time he and Momma fought over money and he left: he packed a bag and went. Oh it was sad and heavy at home. I started to be upset, but then I retreated into an impenetrable stupidity: not knowing was better than being despairing. I was put to bed and I did fall asleep: I woke in the middle of the night; he had returned and was sitting on my bed—in the dark—a huge shadow in the shadows. He was stroking my forehead. When he saw my eyes open, he said in a sentimental, heavy voice, "I could never leave *you*—"

He didn't really mean it: I was an excuse: but he did mean it—the meaning and not-meaning were like the rise and fall of a wave in me, in the dark outside of me, between the two of us, between him and me (at other moments he would think of other truths, other than the one of he-couldn't-leave-me sometimes). He bent over sentimentally, painedly, not nicely, and he began to hug me; he put his head down, on my chest; my small heartbeat vanished into the near, sizable, anguished, angular, emotion-swollen one that was his. I kept advancing swiftly into wakefulness, my consciousness came rushing and widening blurredly, embracing the dark, his presence, his embrace. It's Daddy, it's Daddy—it's dark still—wakefulness rushed into the dark grave or grove of his hugely extended presence. His affection. My arms stumbled: there was no adequate embrace in me—I couldn't lift *him*—I had no adequacy yet except that of my charm or what-have-you, except things the grown-ups gave me—not things: traits, qualities. I mean my hugging his head was nothing until he said, "Ah, you love me. . . . You're all right. . . ."

Momma said: "They are as close as two peas in a pod—they are just alike—that child and Charley. That child is God to Charley. . . ."

He didn't always love me.

In the middle of the night that time, he picked me up after a while, he wrapped me in a blanket, held me close, took me downstairs in the dark; we went outside, into the night; it was dark and chilly but there was a moon—I thought he would take me to the wall but he just stood on our back deck. He grew tired of loving me; he grew abstracted and forgot me: the love that had just a moment before been so intently and tightly clasping and nestling went away, and I found myself released, into the cool night air, the floating damp, the silence, with the darkened houses around us.

I saw the silver moon, heard my father's breath, felt the itchiness of the woolen blanket on my hands, noticed its wool smell. I did this alone and I waited. Then when he didn't come back, I grew sleepy and put my head down against his neck: he was nowhere near me. Alone in his arms, I slept.

Over and over a moment seems to recur, something seems to return in its entirety, a name seems to be accurate: and we say it always happens like this. But we are wrong, of course.

I was a weird choice as someone for him to love.

So different from him in the way I was surprised by things.

I am a child with this mind. I am a child he has often rescued.

Our attachment to each other manifests itself in sudden swoops and grabs and rubs of attention, of being entertained, by each other, at the present moment.

I ask you, how is it possible it's going to last?

Sometimes when we are entertained by each other, we are bold about it, but just as frequently, it seems embarrassing, and we turn our faces aside.

His recollections of horror are more certain than mine. His suspicions are more terrible. There are darknesses in me I'm afraid of, but the ones in him don't frighten me but are like the dark in the yard, a dark a child like me might sneak into (and has)—a dark full of unseen shadowy almost-glowing presences—the fear, the danger—are desirable—difficult—with the call-to-be-brave: the childish bravura of *I must endure this* (knowing I can run away if I choose).

The child touches with his pursed, jutting, ignorant lips the large, handsome, odd, humid face of his father who can run away too. More dangerously.

He gave away a car of his that he was about to trade in on a new one: he gave it to a man in financial trouble; he did it after seeing a movie about crazy people being loving and gentle with each other and everyone else: Momma said to Daddy, "You can't do anything you want—you can't listen to your feelings—you have a family. . . ."

After seeing a movie in which a child cheered up an old man, he took me to visit an old man who probably was a distant relative, and who hated me at sight, my high coloring, the noise I might make, my father's affection for me: "Will he sit still? I can't stand noise. Charley, listen, I'm in bad shape—I think I have cancer and they won't tell me—"

"Nothing can kill a tough old bird like you, Ike. . . ."

The old man wanted all of Charley's attention—and strength— while he talked about how the small threads and thicker ropes that tied him to life were being cruelly tampered with.

Daddy patted me afterward, but oddly he was bored and disappointed in me as if I'd failed at something.

He could not seem to keep it straight about my value to him or to the world in general; he lived at the center of his own intellectual shortcomings and his moral price: he needed it to be true, as an essential fact, that goodness—or innocence—was in him or was protected by him, and that, therefore, he was a good *man* and superior to other men, and did not deserve—certain common masculine fates— horrors—tests of his courage—certain pains. It was necessary to him to have it be true that he knew what real goodness was and had it in his life.

Perhaps that was because he didn't believe in God, and because he felt (with a certain self-love) that people, out in the world, didn't appreciate him and were needlessly difficult—"unloving": he said it often—and because it was true he was shocked and guilty and even enraged when he was "forced" into being unloving himself, or when he caught sight in himself of such a thing as cruelty, or cruel nosiness, or physical cowardice—God, how he hated being a coward—or hatred, physical hatred, even for me, if I was coy or evasive or disinterested or tired of him: it tore him apart literally—bits of madness, in varying degrees, would grip him as in a Greek play: I see his mouth, his salmon-colored mouth, showing various degrees of sarcasm—sarcasm mounting into bitterness and even a ferocity without tears that always suggested to me, as a child, that he was near tears but had forgotten in his ferocity that he was about to cry.

Or he would catch sight of some evidence, momentarily inescapable—in contradictory or foolish statements of his or in unkept promises that it was clear he had never meant to keep, had never made any effort to keep—that he was a fraud; and sometimes he would laugh because he was a fraud—a good-hearted fraud, he believed—or he would be sullen or angry, a fraud caught either by the tricks of language so that in expressing affection absentmindedly he had expressed too much; or caught by greed and self-concern: he hated the evidence that he was mutable as hell: that he loved sporadically and egotistically, and often with rage and vengeance, and that madness I mentioned earlier: he couldn't stand those things: he usually forgot them; but sometimes when he was being tender, or noble, or self-sacrificing, he would sigh and be very sad—maybe because the good stuff was temporary. I don't know. Or sad that he did it only when he had the time and was in the mood. Sometimes he forgot such things and was superbly confident—or was that a bluff?

I don't know. I really can't speak for him.

I look at my hand and then at his; it is not really conceivable to me that both are hands: mine is a sort of a hand. He tells me over and over that I must not upset him—he tells me of my power over him—I don't know how to take such a fact—is it a fact? I stare at him. I gasp with the ache of life stirring in me—again: again: *again*—I ache with tentative and complete and then again tentative belief.

For a long time piety was anything at all sitting still or moving slowly and not rushing at me or away from me but letting me look at it or be near it without there being any issue of safety-about-to-be-lost.

This world is evasive.

But someone who lets you observe him is not evasive, is not hurtful, at that moment: it is like in sleep where *the other* waits—the Master of Dreams—and there are doors, doorways opening into farther rooms where there is an altered light, and which I enter to find—what? That someone is gone? That the room is empty? Or perhaps I find a vista, of rooms, of archways, and a window, and a peach tree in flower—a tree with peach-colored flowers in the solitude of night.

I am dying of grief, Daddy. I am waiting here, limp with abandonment, with exhaustion: perhaps I'd better believe in God. . . .

My father's virtues, those I dreamed about, those I saw when I was awake, those I understood and misunderstood, were, as I felt them, in dreams or wakefulness, when I was a child, like a broad highway opening into a small dusty town that was myself; and down that road came bishops and slogans, Chinese processions, hasidim in a dance, the nation's honor and glory *in its young people,* baseball players, singers who sang "with their whole hearts," automobiles and automobile grilles, and grave or comic bits of instruction. This man is attached to me and makes me light up with festal affluence and oddity; he says, "I think you love me."

He was right.

He would move his head—his giant face—and you could observe in his eyes the small town which was me in its temporary sophistication, a small town giving proof on every side of its arrogance and its prosperity and its puzzled contentment.

He also instructed me in hatred: he didn't mean to, not openly: but I saw and picked up the curious buzzing of his puckered distastes, a nastiness of dismissal that he had: a fetor of let-them-all-kill-each-other. He hated lots of people, whole races: he hated ugly women.

He conferred an odd inverted splendor on awfulness—because *he* knew about it: he went into it every day. He told me not to want that, not to want to know about that: he told me to go on being just the way I was—"a nice boy."

When he said something was unbearable, he meant it; he meant he could not bear it.

In my memories of this time of my life, it seems to be summer all the time, even when the ground is white: I suppose it seems like summer because I was never cold.

Ah: I wanted to see. . . .

My father, when he was low (in spirit) would make rounds, inside his head, checking on his consciousness, to see if it was safe from inroads by *"the unbearable":* he found an all-is-well in a quiet emptiness. . . .

In an uninvadedness, he found the weary complacency and self-importance of All is Well.

(The woman liked invasions—up to a point).

One day he came home, mysterious, exalted, hatted and suited, roseate, handsome, a little sweaty—it really was summer that day. He was exalted—as I said—but nervous toward me—anxious with promises.

And he was, oh, somewhat angry, justified, toward the world, toward me, not exactly as a threat (in case I didn't respond) but as a jumble.

He woke me from a nap, an uneasy nap, lifted me out of bed, me, a child who had not expected to see him that afternoon—I was not particularly happy that day, not particularly pleased with him, not pleased with him at all, really.

He dressed me himself. At first he kept his hat on. After a while, he took it off. When I was dressed, he said, "You're pretty sour today," and he put his hat back on.

He hustled me down the stairs; he held my wrist in his enormous palm—immediate and gigantic to me and blankly suggestive of a meaning I could do nothing about except stare at blankly from time to time in my childish life.

We went outside into the devastating heat and glare, the blathering, humming afternoon light of a midwestern summer day: a familiar furnace.

We walked along the street, past the large, silent houses, set, each one, in hard, pure light. You could not look directly at anything, the glare, the reflections were too strong.

Then he lifted me in his arms—aloft.

He was carrying me to help me because the heat was bad—and worse near the sidewalk which reflected it upward into my face—and because my legs were short and I was struggling, because he was in a hurry and because he liked carrying me, and because I was sour and blackmailed him with my unhappiness, and he was being kind with a certain—limited—mixture of exasperation-turning-into-a-degree-of-mortal-love.

Or it was another time, really early in the morning, when the air was partly asleep, partly adance, but in veils, trembling with heavy moisture. Here and there, the air broke into a string of beads of pastel colors, pink, pale green, small rainbows, really small, and very narrow. Daddy walked rapidly. I bounced in his arms. My eyesight was unfocused—it bounced too. Things were more than merely present: they pressed against me: they had the aliveness of myth, of the beginning of an adventure when nothing is explained as yet.

All at once we were at the edge of a bankless river of yellow light. To be truthful, it was like a big, wooden beam of fresh, unweathered wood: but we entered it: and then it turned into light, cooler light than in the hot humming afternoon but full of bits of heat that stuck to me and then were blown away, a semi-heat, not really friendly, yet reassuring: and very dimly sweaty; and it grew, it spread: this light turned into a knitted cap of light, fuzzy, warm, woven, itchy: it was pulled over my head, my hair, my forehead, my eyes, my nose, my mouth.

So I turned my face away from the sun—I turned it so it was pressed against my father's neck mostly—and then I knew, in a childish way, knew from the heat (of his neck, of his shirt collar), knew by childish deduction, that his face was unprotected from the luminousness all around us: and I looked; and it was so: his face, for the moment unembarrassedly, was caught in that light. In an accidental glory.

[August 1975]

TRUMAN CAPOTE

La Côte Basque 1965

Overheard in a cowboy bar in Roswell, New Mexico. . . .

FIRST COWBOY: Hey, Jed. How are you? How you feeling?
SECOND COWBOY: Good! Real good. I feel so good I didn't have to jack off this morning to get my heart started.

"Carissimo!" she cried. "You're just what I'm looking for. A lunch date. The duchess stood me up."

"Black or white?" I said.

"White," she said, reversing my direction on the sidewalk.

White is Wallis Windsor, whereas the black duchess is what her friends call Perla Appfeldorf, the Brazilian wife of a notoriously racist South African diamond industrialist. As for the lady who also knew the distinction, she was indeed a lady—Lady Ina Coolbirth, an American married to a British chemicals tycoon and a lot of woman in every way. Tall, taller than most men, Ina was a big breezy peppy broad, born and raised on a ranch in Montana.

"This is the second time she's canceled," Ina Coolbirth continued. "She says she has hives. Or the duke has hives. One or the other. Anyway, I've still got a table at Côte Basque. So, shall we? Because I do so need someone to talk to, really. And, thank God, Jonesy, it can be you."

Côte Basque is on East Fifty-fifth Street, directly across from the St. Regis. It was the site of the original Le Pavillon, founded in 1940 by the honorable restaurateur Henri Soulé. M. Soulé abandoned the premises because of a feud with his landlord, the late president of Columbia Pictures, a sleazy Hollywood hood named Harry Cohn (who, upon learning that Sammy Davis, Jr. was "dating" his blond star Kim Novak, ordered a hit man to call Davis and tell him: "Listen, Sambo, you're already missing one eye. How'd you like to try for none?" The next day Davis married a Las Vegas chorus girl—colored). Like Côte Basque, the original Pavillon consisted of a small entrance area, a bar to the left of this, and in the rear, through an archway, a large red-plush dining room. The bar and main room formed in Outer Hebrides, an Elba to which Soulé exiled second-class patrons. Preferred clients, selected by the proprietor with unerring *snobisme*, were placed in the banquette-lined entrance area—a practice pursued by every New York restaurant of established chic: Lafayette, The Colony, La Grenouille, La Caravelle. These tables, always nearest the door, are drafty, afford the least privacy, but nevertheless to be seated at one, or not, is a status-sensitive citizen's moment of truth. Harry Cohn never made it at Pavillon. It didn't matter that he was a hotshot Hollywood hottentot or even that he was Soulé's landlord. Soulé saw him for the shoulder-padded counter-jumper Cohn was and accordingly ushered him to a table in the sub-zero regions of the rear room. Cohn cursed, he huffed, puffed, revenged himself by upping and upping the restaurant's rent. So Soulé simply moved to more regal quarters in the Ritz Tower. However, while Soulé was still settling there, Harry Cohn cooled (Jerry Wald, when asked why he attended the funeral, replied: "Just to be sure the bastard was dead"), and Soulé, nostalgic for his old stamping ground, again leased the address from the new custodians and created, as a second enterprise, a sort of boutique variation on Le Pavillon: La Côte Basque.

Lady Ina, of course, was allotted an impeccable position—the fourth table on the left as you enter. She was escorted to it by none other than M. Soulé, distrait as ever, pink and glazed as a marzipan pig.

"Lady Coolbirth. . . ." he muttered, his perfectionist eyes spinning about in search of cankered roses and awkward waiters. "Lady Coolbirth . . . umn . . . very nice . . . umn . . . and Lord Coolbirth? . . . umn . . . today we have on the wagon a very nice saddle of lamb. . . ."

She consulted me, a glance, and said: "I think not anything off the wagon. It arrives too quickly. Let's have something that takes forever. So that we can get drunk and disorderly. Say a soufflé Furstenberg. Could you do that, Monsieur Soulé?"

He tutted his tongue—on two counts: he disapproves of customers dulling their taste buds with alcohol, and also: "Furstenberg is a great nuisance. An uproar."

Delicious though: a froth of cheese and spinach into which an assortment of poached eggs has been sunk strategically, so that, when struck by your fork, the soufflé is moistened with golden rivers of egg yolk.

"An uproar," said Ina, "is exactly what I want," and the proprietor, touching his sweat-littered forehead with a bit of handkerchief, acquiesced.

Then she decided against cocktails, saying: "Why not have a proper reunion?" From the wine steward she ordered a bottle of Roederer's Cristal. Even for those who dislike Champagne, myself among them, there are two Champagnes one can't refuse: Dom Pérignon and the even superior Cristal, which is bottled in a natural-colored glass that displays its pale blaze, a chilled fire of such prickly dryness that, swallowed, seems not to have been swallowed at all, but instead to have turned to vapors on the tongue and burned there to one damp sweet ash.

"Of course," said Ina, "Champagne does have one serious drawback: swilled as a regular thing, a certain sourness settles in the tummy, and the result is permanent bad breath. Really incurable. Remember Arturo's breath, bless his heart? And Cole adored Champagne. God, I do miss Cole so, dotty as he was those last years. Did I ever tell you the story about Cole and the stud wine steward? I can't remember quite where he worked. He was Italian, so it couldn't have been here or Pav. The Colony? Odd: I see him clearly—a nut-brown man, beautifully flat, with oiled hair and the sexiest jawline—but I can't see *where* I see him. He was a southern Italian, so they called him Dixie, and Teddie Whitestone got knocked up by him—Bill Whitestone aborted her himself under the impression it was his doing. And perhaps it was—in quite another context—but still I think it rather dowdy, unnatural, if you will, a doctor aborting his own wife. Teddie Whitestone wasn't alone; there was a queue of gals greasing Dixie's palm with billets-doux. Cole's approach was creative: he invited Dixie to his apartment under the pretext of getting advice on the laying in of a new wine cellar—Cole! who knew more about wine than that dago ever dreamed. So they were sitting there on the couch—the lovely suede one Billy Baldwin made for Cole—all very informal, and Cole kisses this fellow on the cheek, and Dixie grins and says: 'That will cost you five hundred dollars, Mr. Porter.' Cole just laughs and squeezes Dixie's leg: 'Now that will cost you a thousand dollars, Mr. Porter.' Then Cole realized this piece of pizza was serious; and so he unzippered him, hauled it out, shook it and said: 'What will be the full price on the use of that?' Dixie told him two thousand dollars. Cole went straight to his desk, wrote a check and handed it to him. And he said: 'Miss Otis regrets she's unable to lunch today. Now get out.' "

The Cristal was being poured. Ina tasted it. "It's not cold enough. But ahhh!" She swallowed again. "I do miss Cole. And Howard Sturgis. Even Papa; after all, he did write about me in *Green Hills of Africa*. And Uncle Willie. Last week in London I went to a party at Drue Heinz's and got stuck with Princess Margaret. Her mother's a darling, but the rest of that family!—though Prince Charles may amount to something. But basically royals think there are just three categories: colored folk, white folk, and royals. Well, I was about to doze off, she's such a drone, when suddenly she announced, apropos of nothing, that she had decided she really didn't like 'poufs'! An extraordinary remark, source considered. Remember the joke about who got the first sailor? But I simply lowered my eyes, *très* Jane Austen, and said: 'In that event, ma'am, I fear you will spend a very lonely old age.' Her expression!—I thought she might turn me into a pumpkin."

There was an uncharacteristic bite and leap to Ina's voice, as though she were speeding along helter-skelter to avoid confiding what it was she wanted, but didn't want, to confide. My eyes and ears were drifting elsewhere. The occupants of a table placed catty-corner to ours were two people I'd met together in Southampton last summer, though the meeting was not of such import that I expected them to recognize me—Gloria Vanderbilt di Cicco Stokowski Lumet Cooper and her childhood chum Carol Marcus Saroyan Saroyan (she married *him* twice) Matthau: women in their late thirties, but looking not much removed from those deb days when they were grabbing Lucky Balloons at the Stork Club.

"But what can you say," inquired Mrs. Matthau of Mrs. Cooper, "to someone who's lost a good lover, weighs two hundred pounds and is in the dead center of a nervous collapse? I don't think she's been out of bed for a month. Or changed the sheets. 'Maureen'—this is what I *did* tell her—'Maureen, I've been in a lot worse condition than you. I remember once when I was going around stealing sleeping pills out of other people's medicine cabinets, saving up to bump myself off. I was in debt up to here, every penny I had was borrowed. . . .'"

"*Dar*ling." Mrs. Cooper protested with a tiny stammer, "why didn't you come to *me?*"

"Because you're rich. It's much less difficult to borrow from the poor."

"But *dar*ling. . . ."

Mrs. Matthau proceeded: "So I said, 'Do you know what I did, Maureen? Broke as I was, I went out and hired myself a *personal* maid. My fortunes rose, my outlook changed completely, I felt loved and pampered. So if I were you, Maureen, I'd go into hock and hire some very expensive creature to run my bath and turn down the bed.' Incidentally, did you go to the Logans' party?"

"For an hour."

"How was it?"

"Marvelous. If you've never been to a party before."

"I wanted to go. But you know Walter. I never imagined I'd marry an actor. Well, *marry* perhaps. But not for love. Yet here I've been stuck with Walter all these years and it still makes me curdle if I see his eye stray a fraction. Have you seen this new Swedish cunt called Karen something?"

"Wasn't she in some spy picture?"

"Exactly. Lovely face. Divine photographed from the bazooms up. But the legs are strictly redwood forest. Absolute tree trunks. Anyway, we met her at the Widmarks' and she was moving her eyes around and making all these little noises for Walter's benefit, and I stood it as long as I could, but when I heard Walter say, 'How old are you, Karen?' I said: 'For God's sake, Walter, why don't you chop off her legs and read the rings?'"

"Carol! You didn't."

"You know you can always count on me."

"And she heard you?"

"It wouldn't have been very interesting if she hadn't."

Mrs. Matthau extracted a comb from her purse and began drawing it through her long albino hair: another leftover from her World War Two debutante nights—an era when she and all her *compères,* Gloria and Honeychile and Oona and Jinx, slouched against El Morocco upholstery ceaselessly raking their Veronica Lake locks.

"I had a letter from Oona this morning," Mrs. Matthau said.

"So did I," Mrs. Cooper said.

"Then you know they're having another baby."

"Well, I assumed so. I always do."

"That Charlie is a lucky bastard," said Mrs. Matthau.

"Of course, Oona would have made any man a great wife."

"Nonsense. With Oona, only geniuses need apply. Before she met Charlie, she wanted to marry Orson Welles . . . and she wasn't even seventeen. It was Orson who introduced her to Charlie; he said: 'I know just the guy for you. He's rich, he's a genius, and there's nothing that he likes more than a dutiful young daughter.'"

Mrs. Cooper was thoughtful. "If Oona hadn't married Charlie, I don't suppose I would have married Leopold."

"And if Oona hadn't married Charlie, and you hadn't married Leopold, I wouldn't have married Bill Saroyan. Twice yet."

The two women laughed together, their laughter like a naughty but delightfully sung duet. Though they were not physically similar—Mrs. Matthau being blonder than Harlow and as lushly white as a gardenia, while the other had brandy eyes and a dark dimpled brilliance markedly present when her negroid lips flashed smiles—one sensed they were two of a kind: charmingly incompetent adventuresses.

Mrs. Matthau said: "Remember the Salinger thing?"

"Salinger?"

"A Perfect Day for Banana Fish. That Salinger."

"Franny and Zooey."

"Umn huh. You don't remember about him?"

Mrs. Cooper pondered, pouted; no, she didn't.

"It was while we were still at Brearley," said Mrs. Matthau. "Before Oona met Orson. She had a mysterious beau, this Jewish boy with a Park Avenue mother, Jerry Salinger. He wanted to be a writer, and he wrote Oona letters ten pages long while he was overseas in the Army. Sort of love-letter essays, very tender, tenderer than God. Which is a bit too tender. Oona used to read them to me, and when she asked what I thought, I said it seemed to me he must be a boy who cried very easily; but what she wanted to know was whether I thought he was brilliant and talented or really just silly, and I said both, he's both, and years later when I read *Catcher in the Rye* and realized the author was Oona's Jerry, I was still inclined to that opinion."

"I never heard a strange story about Salinger," Mrs. Cooper confided.

"I've never heard anything about him that wasn't strange. He's certainly not your normal everyday Jewish boy from Park Avenue."

"Well, it isn't really about *him*, but about a friend of his who went to visit him in New Hampshire. He does live there, doesn't he? On some very remote farm? Well, it was February and terribly cold. One morning Salinger's friend was missing. He wasn't in his bedroom or anywhere around the house. They found him finally, deep in a snowy woods. He was lying in the snow wrapped in a blanket and holding an empty whiskey bottle. He'd killed himself by drinking the whiskey until he'd fallen asleep and frozen to death."

After a while Mrs. Matthau said: "That *is* a strange story. It must have been lovely, though—all warm with whiskey, drifting off into the cold starry air. Why did he do it?"

"All I know is what I told you," Mrs. Cooper said.

An exiting customer, a florid-at-the-edges swarthy balding Charlie sort of fellow, stopped at their table. He fixed on Mrs. Cooper a gaze that was intrigued, amused and ... a trifle grim. He said: "Hello, Gloria"; and she smiled: "Hello, darling"; but her eyelids twitched as she attempted to identify him; and then he said: "Hello, Carol. How are ya, doll?" and she knew who he was all right: "Hello, darling. Still living in Spain?" He nodded; his glance returned to Mrs. Cooper: "Gloria, you're as beautiful as ever. More beautiful. See ya. . . ." He waved and walked away.

Mrs. Cooper stared after him, scowling.

Eventually Mrs. Matthau said: "You didn't recognize him, did you?"

"N-n-no."

"Life. Life. Really, it's too sad. There was nothing familiar about him at all?"

"Long ago. Something. A dream."

"It wasn't a dream."

"Carol. Stop that. Who is he?"

"Once upon a time you thought very highly of him. You cooked his meals and washed his socks—" Mrs. Cooper's eyes enlarged, shifted "—and when he was in the Army you followed him from camp to camp, living in dreary furnished rooms—"

"No!"

"Yes!"

"No."

"Yes, Gloria. Your first husband."

"That . . . man . . . was . . . Pat di Cicco?"

"Oh, darling. Let's not brood. After all, you haven't seen him in almost twenty years. You were only a child. Isn't that," said Mrs. Matthau, offering a diversion, "Jackie Kennedy?"

And I heard Lady Ina on the subject, too: "I'm almost blind with these specs, but just coming in there, isn't that Mrs. Kennedy? And her sister?"

It was; I knew the sister because she had gone to school with Kate McCloud, and when Kate and I were on Abner Dustin's yacht at the Feria in Seville she had lunched with us, then afterward we'd gone water-skiing together, and I've often thought of it, how perfect she was, a gleaming gold-brown girl in a white bathing suit, her white skis hissing smoothly, her brown-gold hair whipping as she swooped and skidded between the waves. So it was pleasant when she stopped to greet Lady Ina ("Did you know I was on the plane with you from London? But you were sleeping so nicely I didn't dare speak") and seeing me remembered me: "Why, hello there, Jonesy," she said, her rough whispery warm voice very slightly vibrating her, "how's your sunburn? Remember, I warned you, but you wouldn't listen." Her laughter trailed off as she folded herself onto a banquette beside her sister, their heads inclining toward each other in whispering Bouvier conspiracy. It was puzzling how much they resembled one another without sharing any common feature beyond identical voices and wide-apart eyes and certain gestures, particularly a habit of staring deeply into an interlocutor's eyes while ceaselessly nodding the head with a mesmerizingly solemn sympathy.

Lady Ina observed: "You can see those girls have swung a few big deals in their time. I know many people can't abide either of them, usually women, and I can understand that, because they don't like women and almost never have anything good to say about *any* woman. But they're perfect with men, a pair of Western geisha girls; they know how to keep a man's secrets and how to make him feel important. If I were a man, I'd fall for Lee myself. She's marvelously made, like a Tanagra figurine; she's feminine without being effeminate; and she's one of the few people I've known who can be both candid and cozy—ordinarily one cancels the other. Jackie—no, not on the same planet. Very photogenic, of course; but the effect is a little . . . unrefined, exaggerated."

I thought of an evening when I'd gone with Kate McCloud and a gang to a drag-queen contest held in a Harlem ballroom: hundreds of young queens sashaying in hand-sewn gowns to the funky honking of saxophones: Brooklyn supermarket clerks, Wall Street runners, black dishwashers and Puerto Rican waiters adrift in silk and fantasy, chorus boys and bank cashiers and Irish elevator boys got up as Marilyn Monroe, as Audrey Hepburn, as Jackie Kennedy. Indeed, Mrs. Kennedy was the most popular inspiration; a dozen boys, the winner among them, wore her high-rise hairdo, winged eyebrows, sulky, palely painted mouth. And, in life, that is how she struck me—not as a bona fide woman, but as an artful female impersonator impersonating Mrs. Kennedy.

I explained what I was thinking to Ina, and she said: "That's what I meant by . . . exaggerated." Then: "Did you ever know Rosita Winston? Nice woman. Half Cherokee, I believe. She had a stroke some years ago, and now she can't speak. Or, rather, she can say just one word. That very often happens after a stroke, one's left with one word out of all the words one has known. Rosita's word is 'beautiful.' Very appropriate, since Rosita has always loved beautiful things. What reminded me of it was old Joe Kennedy. He, too, has been left with one word. And his word is: 'Goddammit!' " Ina motioned the waiter to pour Champagne. "Have I ever told you about the time he assaulted me? When I was eighteen and a guest in his house, a friend of his daughter Kek . . ."

Again, my eye coasted the length of the room, catching, *en passant,* a bluebearded Seventh Avenue brassiere hustler trying to con a closet-queen editor from the New York *Times*; and Diana Vreeland, the pomaded, peacock-iridescent editor of *Vogue*, sharing a table with an elderly man who suggested a precious object of discreet *ex-*

travagance, perhaps a fine grey pearl—Mainbocher; and Mrs. William S. Paley lunching with her sister, Mrs. John Hay Whitney. Seated near them was a pair unknown to me: a woman forty, forty-five, no beauty but very handsomely set up inside a brown Balenciaga suit with a brooch composed of cinnamon-colored diamonds fixed to the lapel. Her companion was much younger, twenty, twenty-two, a hearty sunbrowned statue who looked as if he might have spent the summer sailing alone across the Atlantic. Her son? But no, because . . . he lit a cigarette and passed it to her and their fingers touched significantly; then they were holding hands.

". . . the old bugger slipped into my bedroom. It was about six o'clock in the morning, the ideal hour if you want to catch someone really slugged out, really by complete surprise, and when I woke up he was already between the sheets with one hand over my mouth and the other all over the place. The sheer ballsy gall of it—right there in his own house with the whole family sleeping all around us. But all those Kennedy men are the same; they're like dogs, they have to pee on every fire hydrant. Still, you had to give the old guy credit, and when he saw I wasn't going to scream he was *so* grateful. . . ."

But they were not conversing, the older woman and the young seafarer; they held hands, and then he smiled and presently she smiled, too.

"Afterward, can you imagine? he pretended nothing had happened, there was never a wink or a nod, just the good old daddy of my schoolgirl chum. It was uncanny and rather cruel; after all, he'd had me and I'd even pretended to enjoy it; there should have been some sentimental acknowledgment, a bauble, a cigarette box. . . ." She sensed my other interest, and her eyes strayed to the improbable lovers. She said: "Do you know that story?"

"No," I said. "But I can see there has to be one."

"Though it's not what you think. Uncle Willie could have made something divine out of it. So could Henry James—better than Uncle Willie, because Uncle Willie would have cheated, and, for the sake of a movie sale, would have made Delphine and Bobby lovers."

Delphine Austin from Detroit; I'd read about her in the columns—an heiress married to a marbleized pillar of New York clubman society. Bobby, her companion, was Jewish, the son of hotel magnate S.L.L. Semenenko and first husband of a weird young movie cutie who had divorced him to marry his father (and whom the father had divorced when he caught her in flagrante with a German shepherd—dog. I'm not kidding).

According to Lady Ina, Delphine Austin and Bobby Semenenko had been inseparable the past year or so, lunching every day at Côte Basque and Lutèce and L'Aiglon, traveling in winter to Gstaad and Lyford Cay, skiing, swimming, spreading themselves with utmost vigor considering the bond was not June-and-January frivolities but really the basis for a double-bill, double-barreled, three-handkerchief variation on an old Bette Davis weeper like *Dark Victory:* they both were dying of leukemia.

"I mean, a worldly woman and a beautiful young man who travel together with death as their common lover and companion. Don't you think Henry James could have done something with that? Or Uncle Willie?"

"No. It's too corny for James, and not corny enough for Maugham."

"Well, you must admit, Mrs. Hopkins would make a fine tale."

"Who?" I said.

"Standing there," Ina Coolbirth said.

That Mrs. Hopkins. A redhead dressed in black; black hat with a veil trim, a black Mainbocher suit, black crocodile purse, crocodile shoes. M. Soulé had an ear cocked as she stood whispering to him; and suddenly everyone was whispering. Mrs. Kennedy and her sister had elicited not a murmur, nor had the entrances of Lauren Bacall and Katharine Cornell and Clare Boothe Luce. However, Mrs. Hopkins was *une autre chose:* a sensation to unsettle the suavest Côte Basque client. There was nothing surreptitious in the attention allotted her as she moved with head bowed toward a table where an escort already awaited her—a Catholic priest, one of those high-brow, malnutritional, Father D'Arcy clerics who always seems most at home when absent from the cloisters and while consorting with the very grand and very rich in a wine-and-roses stratosphere.

"Only," said Lady Ina, "Ann Hopkins would think of that. To advertise your search for spiritual 'advice' in the most public possible manner. Once a tramp, always a tramp."

"You don't think it was an accident?" I said.

"Come out of the trenches, boy. The war's over. Of course it wasn't an accident. She killed David with malice aforethought. She's a murderess. The police know that."

"Then how did she get away with it?"

"Because the family wanted her to. David's family. And, as it happened in Newport, old Mrs. Hopkins had the power to prevail. Have you ever met David's mother? Hilda Hopkins?"

"I saw her once last summer in Southampton. She was buying a pair of tennis shoes. I wondered what a woman her age, she must be eighty, wanted with tennis shoes. She looked like—some very old goddess."

"She is. That's why Ann Hopkins got away with cold-blooded murder. Her mother-in-law is a Rhode Island goddess. *And* a saint."

Ann Hopkins had lifted her veil and was now whispering to the priest who, servilely entranced, was brushing a Gibson against his starved blue lips.

"But it *could* have been an accident. If one goes by the papers. As I remember, they'd just come home from a dinner party in Watch Hill and gone to bed in separate rooms. Weren't there supposed to have been a recent series of burglaries thereabouts?—and she kept a shotgun by her bed, and suddenly in the dark her bedroom door opened and she grabbed the shotgun and shot at what she thought was a prowler. Only it was her husband. David Hopkins. With a hole through his head."

"That's what she said. That's what her lawyer said. That's what the police said. And that's what the papers said . . . even the *Times*. But that isn't what happened." And Ina, inhaling like a skin diver, began: "Once upon a time a jazzy little carrottop killer rolled into town from Wheeling or Logan—somewhere in West Virginia. She was eighteen, she'd been brought up in some country-slum way, and she had already been married and divorced; or she *said* she'd been married a month or two to a Marine and divorced him when he disappeared (keep that in mind: it's an important clue). Her name was Ann Cutler, and she looked rather like a malicious Betty Grable. She worked as a call girl for a pimp who was a bell captain at the Waldorf; and she saved her money and took voice lessons and dance lessons and ended up as the favorite lay of one of Frankie Costello's shysters, and he always took her to El Morocco. It was during the war—1943—and Elmer's was always full of gangsters and military brass. But one night an ordinary young Marine showed up there; except that he wasn't ordinary: his father was one of the stuffiest men in the East—and richest. David had sweetness and great good looks, but he was just like old Mr. Hopkins really—an anal-oriented Episcopalian. Stingy. Sober. Not at all café society. But there he was at Elmer's, a soldier on leave, horny and a bit stoned. One of Winchell's stooges was there, and he recognized the Hopkins boy; he bought David a drink, and said he could fix it up for him with any one of the girls he saw, just pick one, and David, poor sod, said the redhead with the button nose and big tits was okay by him. So the Winchell stooge sends her a note, and at dawn little David finds himself writhing inside the grip of an expert Cleopatra's clutch. I'm sure it was David's first experience with anything less primitive than a belly rub with his prep-school roomie. He went bonkers, not that one can blame him; I know some very grown-up Mr. Cool Balls who've gone bonkers over Ann Hopkins. She was clever with David; she knew she'd hooked a biggie, even if he was only a kid, so she quit what she was doing and got a job in lingerie at Saks; she never pressed for anything, refused any gift fancier than a handbag, and all the while he was in the service she wrote him every day, little letters cozy and innocent as a baby's layette. In fact, she *was* knocked up; and it *was* his kid; but she didn't tell him a thing until he next came home on leave and found his girl four months pregnant. Now here is where she showed that certain venomous *élan* that separates truly dangerous serpents from mere chicken snakes: she told him she didn't want to marry him. Wouldn't marry him under any circumstances because she had no desire to lead a Hopkins life; she had neither the background nor innate ability to cope with it, and she was sure neither his family nor friends would ever accept her. She said all she would ever ask would be a modest amount of child support. David protested, but of course he was relieved, even though he would still have to go to his father with the story—David had no money of his own. It was then that Ann made her smartest move; she had been doing her homework, and she knew everything there was to know about David's parents; so she said: 'David, there's just one thing I'd like. I want to meet your family. I never had much family of my own, and I'd like my child to have some occasional contact with his grandparents. They might like that, too.' *C'est très joli, très diabolique, non?* And it worked. Not that Mr. Hopkins was fooled. Right from the start he said the girl was a tramp, and she would never see a nickel of his; but Hilda Hopkins fell for it—she believed that gorgeous hair and those blue malarkey eyes, the whole poor-little-match-girl pitch Ann was tossing her. And as David was the oldest son, and she was in a hurry for a grandchild, she did exactly what Ann had gambled on: she persuaded David to marry her, and her husband to, if not condone it, at least not forbid it. And for some while it seemed as if Mrs. Hopkins had been very wise: each year she was rewarded with another grandchild until there were three, two girls and a boy; and Ann's social pickup was incredibly quick—she crashed right through, not bothering to observe any speed limits. She certainly grasped the essentials, I'll say that. She learned to ride and became the horsiest horse-hag in Newport. She studied French and had a French butler and campaigned for the Best Dressed List by lunching with Eleanor Lambert and inviting her for week-ends. She learned about furniture and fabrics from Sister Parish and Billy Baldwin; and little Henry Geldzahler was pleased to come to tea (Tea! Ann Cutler! My God!) and to talk to her about modern paint-ings. But the deciding element in her success, leaving aside the fact she'd married a great Newport name, was the duchess. Ann realized something that only the cleverest social climbers ever do. If you want to ride swiftly and safely from the depths to the surface, the surest way is to single out a shark and attach yourself to it like a pilot fish. This is as true in Keokuk, where one massages, say, the local Mrs. Ford Dealer, as it is in Detroit, where you may as well try for Mrs. Ford herself—or in Paris or Rome. But why should Ann Hopkins, being by marriage a Hopkins and the daughter-in-law of *the* Hilda Hopkins, need the duchess? Because she needed the blessing of some-one with presumably high standards, someone with international im-pact whose acceptance of her would silence the laughing hyenas. And who better than the duchess? As for the duchess, she has high toler-ance for the flattery of rich ladies-in-waiting, the kind who always pick up the check; I wonder if the duchess has *ever* picked up a check. Not that it matters. She gives good value. She's one of that unusual female breed who are able to have a genuine friendship with another woman. Certainly she was a marvelous friend to Ann Hopkins. Of course she wasn't taken in by Ann—after all, the duchess is too much of a con artist not to twig another one; but the idea amused her of taking this cool-eyed cardplayer and lacquering her with a little real style, launching her on the circuit, and the young Mrs. Hopkins be-came quite notorious—though without the style. The father of the second Hopkins girl was Fon Portago, or so everyone says, and God knows she does look very *espagnole;* however that may be, Ann Hopkins was definitely racing her motor in the Grand Prix manner. One summer she and David took a house at Cap Ferrat (she was trying to worm her way in with Uncle Willie: she even learned to play first-class bridge; but Uncle Willie said that while she was a woman he might enjoy writing about, she was not someone he trusted to have at his card table), and from Nice to Monte she was known by every male past puberty as Madame Marmalade—her favorite *petit déjeuner* being hot cock buttered with Dundee's best. Although I'm told it's actually strawberry jam she prefers. I don't think David guessed the full measure of these fandangos, but there was no doubt he was miserable, and after a while he fell in with the very girl he ought to have married originally—his second cousin, Mary Kendall, no beauty but a sensible, attractive girl who had always been in love with him. She was engaged to Tommy Bedford but broke it off when David asked her to marry him. *If* he could get a divorce. And he *could:* all it would cost him, according to Ann, was five million dollars tax-free. David still had no glue of his own, and when he took this proposition to his father, Mr. Hopkins said *never!* and said he'd always warned that Ann was what she was, bad baggage, but David hadn't listened, so now that was his burden, and as long as the father lived she would never get a subway token. After this, David hired a detective and within six months had enough evidence, including Polaroids of her being screwed front and back by a couple of jockeys in Saratoga, to have her jailed, much less divorce her. But when David confronted her, Ann laughed and told him his father would never allow him to take such filth into court. She was right. It was interesting, because when discussing the matter, Mr. Hopkins told David that, under the circumstances, he wouldn't object to the son killing the wife, then keeping his mouth shut, but certainly David couldn't divorce her and supply the press with that kind of manure.

"It was at this point that David's detective had an inspiration; an unfortunate one, because if it had never come about, David might still be alive. However, the detective had an idea: he searched out the Cutler homestead in West Virginia—or was it Kentucky?—and interviewed relatives who had never heard from her after she'd gone to New York, had never known her in her grand incarnation as Mrs. David Hopkins but simply as Mrs. Billy Joe Barnes, the wife of a hillbilly jarhead. The detective got a copy of the marriage certificate from the local courthouse, and after that he tracked down this Billy Joe Barnes, found him working as an airplane mechanic in San Diego, and persuaded him to sign an affidavit saying he had married one Ann Cutler, never divorced her, not remarried, that he simply had returned from Okinawa to find she had disappeared, but as far as he knew she was still Mrs. Billy Joe Barnes. Indeed she was!—even the cleverest criminal minds have a basic stupidity. And when David presented her with the information and said to her: 'Now we'll have no more of those round-figure ultimatums, since we're not legally married,' surely it was then she decided to kill him: a decision made by her genes, the inescapable white-trash slut inside her, even though she knew the Hopkinses would arrange a respectable 'divorce' and provide a very good allowance; but she also knew if she murdered David, and got away with it, she and her children would eventually receive his inheritance, something that wouldn't happen if he married Mary Kendall and had a second family. So she pretended to acquiesce and told David there was no point arguing as he obviously had her by the snatch, but would he continue to live with her for a month while she settled her affairs? He agreed, idiot; and immediately she began preparing the legend of the prowler—twice she called police, claiming a prowler was on the grounds; soon she had the servants and most of the neighbors convinced that prowlers were everywhere in the vicinity, and actually Nini Wolcott's house was broken into, presumably by a burglar, but now even Nini admits that Ann must have done it. As you may recall, if you followed the case, the Hopkinses went to a party at the Wolcotts' the night it happened. A Labor Day dinner dance with about fifty guests; I was there, and I sat next to David at dinner. He seemed very relaxed, full of smiles, I suppose because he thought he'd soon be rid of the bitch and married to his cousin Mary; but Ann was wearing a pale green dress, and she seemed almost green with tension—she chattered on like a lunatic chimpanzee about prowlers and burglars and how she always slept now with a shotgun by her bedside. According to the *Times,* David and Ann left the Wolcotts' a bit after midnight, and when they reached home, where the servants were on holiday and the children staying with their grandparents in Bar Harbor, they retired to separate bedrooms. Ann's story was, and is, that she went straight to sleep but was wakened within half an hour by the noise of her bedroom door opening: she saw a shadowy figure—the prowler! She grabbed her shotgun and in the dark fired away, emptying both barrels. Then she turned on the lights and, oh, horror of horrors, discovered David sprawled in the hallway nicely cooled. But that isn't where the cops found him. Because that isn't where or how he was killed. The police found the body inside a glassed-in shower, naked. The water was still running, and the shower door was shattered with bullets."

"In other words—" I began.

"In other words—" Lady Ina picked up but waited until a captain, supervised by a perspiring M. Soulé, had finished ladling out the soufflé Furstenberg "—none of Ann's story was true. God knows what she expected people to believe; but she just, after they reached home and David had stripped to take a shower, followed him there with a gun and shot him through the shower door. Perhaps she intended to say the prowler had stolen her shotgun and killed him. In that case, why didn't she call a doctor, call the police? Instead, she telephoned her *lawyer*. Yes. And *he* called the police. But not until *after* he had called the Hopkinses in Bar Harbor."

The priest was swilling another Gibson; Ann Hopkins, head bent, was still whispering at him confessionally. Her waxy fingers, unpainted and unadorned except for a stark gold wedding band, nibbled at her breast as though she were reading rosary beads.

"But if the police *knew* the truth—"

"Of course they knew."

"Then I don't see how she got away with it. It's not conceivable."

"I told you," Ina said tartly, "she got away with it because Hilda Hopkins wanted her to. It was the children: tragic enough to have lost their father, what purpose could it serve to see the mother convicted of murder? Hilda Hopkins, and old Mr. Hopkins, too, wanted Ann to go scot-free; and the Hopkinses, within their terrain, have the power to brainwash cops, reweave minds, move corpses from shower stalls to hallways; the power to control inquests—David's death was declared an accident at an inquest that lasted less than a day." She looked across at Ann Hopkins and her companion—the latter, his clerical brow scarlet with a two-cocktail flush, not listening now to the imploring murmur of his patroness but staring rather glassy-gaga at Mrs. Kennedy, as if any moment he might run amok and ask her to autograph a menu. "Hilda's behavior has been extraordinary. Flaw-less. One would never suspect she wasn't truly the affectionate, griev-ing protector of a bereaved and very legitimate widow. She never gives a dinner party without inviting her. The one thing I wonder is what everyone wonders—when they're alone, just the two of them, what do they talk about?" Ina selected from her salad a leaf of Bibb lettuce, pinned it to a fork, studied it through her black spectacles. "There is at least one respect in which the rich, the really very rich, *are* different from ... other people. They understand *vegetables.* Other people—well, anyone can manage roast beef, a great steak, lobsters. But have you ever noticed how, in the homes of the very rich, at the Wrightsmans' or Dillons', at Bunny's and Babe's, they al-ways serve only the most beautiful vegetables, and the greatest vari-ety? The greenest petits pois, infinitesimal carrots, corn so baby-kerneled and tender it seems almost unborn, lima beans tinier than mice eyes, and the young asparagus! the limestone lettuce! the raw red mushrooms! zucchini. . . ." Lady Ina was feeling her Champagne.

Mrs. Matthau and Mrs. Cooper lingered over *café filtre.* "I know," mused Mrs. Matthau, who was analyzing the wife of a midnight-TV clown/hero, "Jane *is* pushy: all those telephone calls—Christ, she could dial Answer Prayer and talk an hour. But she's bright, she's fast on the draw, and when you think what she has to put up with. This last episode she told me about: hair-raising. Well, Bobby had a week off from the show—he was so exhausted he told Jane he wanted just to stay home, spend the whole week slopping around in his pajamas, and Jane was ecstatic; she bought hundreds of magazines and books and new LPs and every kind of goody from Maison Glass. Oh, it was going to be a lovely week. Just Jane and Bobby sleeping and screwing and having baked potatoes with caviar for breakfast. But after one day he evaporated. Didn't come home that night or call. It wasn't the first time, Jesus be, but Jane was out of her mind. Still, she couldn't report it to the police; what a sensation that would be. Another day passed, and not a word. Jane hadn't slept for forty-eight hours. Around three in the morning the phone rang. Bobby. Smashed. She said: 'My God, Bobby, where are you?' He said he was in Miami, and she said, losing her temper now, how the fuck did you get in Miami, and he said, oh, he'd gone to the airport and taken a plane, and she said what the fuck for, and he said just because he felt like being alone. Jane said: 'And *are* you alone?' Bobby, you know what a sadist he is behind that huckleberry grin, said: 'No. There's someone lying right here. She'd like to speak to you.' And on comes this scared little giggling peroxide voice: 'Really, is this really Mrs. Baxter, hee hee? I thought Bobby was making a funny, hee hee. We just heard on the radio how it was snowing there in New York—I mean, you ought to be down here with us where it's ninety degrees!' Jane said, very chiseled: 'I'm afraid I'm much too ill to travel.' And peroxide, all fluttery distress: 'Oh, gee, I'm sorry to hear that. What's the matter, honey?' Jane said: 'I've got a double dose of syph and the old clap-clap, all courtesy of that great comic, my husband, Bobby Baxter—and if you don't want the same I suggest you get the hell out of there.' And she hung up."

Mrs. Cooper was amused, though not very; puzzled rather. "How can any woman tolerate that? I'd divorce him."

"Of course you would. But, then, you've got the two things Jane hasn't."

"Ah?"

"One: dough. And two: identity."

Lady Ina was ordering another bottle of Cristal. "Why not?" she asked, defiantly replying to my concerned expression. "Easy up, Jonesy. You won't have to carry me piggyback. I just feel like it: shattering the day into golden pieces." Now, I thought, she's going to tell me what she wants, but doesn't want, to tell me. But no, not yet. Instead: "Would you care to hear a truly vile story? Really vomitous? Then look to your left. That sow sitting next to Betsy Whitney."

She *was* somewhat porcine, a swollen muscular baby with a freckled Bahamas-burnt face and squinty-mean eyes; she looked as if she wore tweed brassieres and played a lot of golf.

"The governor's wife?"

"The governor's wife," said Ina, nodding as she gazed with melancholy contempt at the homely beast, legal spouse of a former New York governor. "Believe it or not, but one of the most attractive guys who ever filled a pair of trousers used to get a hard-on every time he looked at that bull dyke. Sidney Dillon—" the name, pronounced by Ina, was a caressing hiss.

To be sure. Sidney Dillon. Conglomateur, adviser to Presidents, an old flame of Ina's. I remember once picking up a copy of what was, after the Bible and *The Murder of Roger Ackroyd*, Ina's favorite book, Isak Dinesen's *Out of Africa;* from between the pages fell a Polaroid picture of a swimmer standing at water's edge, a wiry well-constructed man with a hairy chest and a twinkle-grinning tough-Jew face; his bathing trunks were rolled to his knees, one hand rested sexily on a hip, and with the other he was pumping a dark fat mouth-watering dick. On the reverse side a notation, made in Ina's boyish script, read: *Sidney. Lago di Garda. En route to Venice. June, 1962.*

"Dill and I have always told each other everything. He was my lover for two years when I was just out of college and working at *Harper's Bazaar.* The only thing he ever specifically asked me never to repeat was this business about the governor's wife; I'm a bitch to tell it, and maybe I wouldn't if it wasn't for all these blissful bubbles risin' in my noggin—" She lifted her Champagne and peered at me through its sunny effervescence. "Gentlemen, the question is: why would an educated, dynamic, very rich and well-hung Jew go bonkers for a cretinous Protestant size forty who wears low-heeled shoes and lavender water? Especially when he's married to Cleo Dillon, to my mind the most beautiful creature alive, always excepting the Garbo of even ten years ago (incidentally, I saw her last night at the Gunthers', and I must say the whole setup has taken on a very weathered look, dry and drafty, like an abandoned temple, something lost in the jungles at Angkor Wat; but that's what happens when you spend most of a life loving only yourself, and that not very much). Dill's in his sixties now; he could still have any woman he wants, yet for years he yearned after yonder porco. I'm sure he never entirely understood this ultra-perversion, the reason for it; or if he did he never would admit it, not even to an analyst—that's a thought! Dill at an analyst! Men like that can never be analyzed because they don't consider any other man their equal. But as for the governor's wife, it was simply that for Dill she was the living incorporation of everything denied him, forbidden to him as a Jew, no matter how beguiling and rich he might be: the Racquet Club, Le Jockey, the Links, White's—all those places he would never sit down to a table of backgammon, all those golf courses where he would never sink a putt—the Everglades and the Seminole, the Maidstone, and St. Paul's and St. Mark's et al., the saintly little New England schools his sons would never attend. Whether he confesses to it or not, that's why he wanted to fuck the governor's wife, revenge himself on that smug hog-bottom, make her sweat and squeal and call him daddy. He kept his distance, though, and never hinted at any interest in the lady, but waited for the moment when the stars were in their correct constellation. It came unplanned—one night he went to a dinner party at the Cowleses'; Cleo had gone to a wedding in Boston. The governor's wife was seated next to him at dinner; she, too, had come alone, the governor off campaigning somewhere. Dill joked, he dazzled; she sat there pigeyed and indifferent, but she didn't seem surprised when he rubbed his leg against hers, and when he asked if he might see her home she nodded, not with much enthusiasm but with a decisiveness that made him feel she was ready to accept whatever he proposed. At that time Dill and Cleo were living in Greenwich; they'd sold their town house on Riverview Terrace and had only a two-room pied-à-terre at the Pierre, just a living room and a bedroom. In the car, after they'd left the Cowleses', he suggested they stop by the Pierre for a nightcap: he wanted her opinion of his new Bonnard. She said she would be pleased to give her opinion; and why shouldn't the idiot have one? Wasn't her husband on the board of directors at the Modern? When she'd seen the painting, he offered her a drink, and she said she'd like a brandy; she sip-sipped it, sitting opposite him across a coffee table, nothing at all happening between them, except that suddenly she was very talkative—about the horse sales in Saratoga, and a hole-by-hole golf game she'd played with Doc Holden at Lyford Cay; she talked about how much money Joan Payson had won from her at bridge and how the dentist she'd used since she was a little girl had died and now she didn't know *what* to do with her teeth; oh, she jabbered on until it was almost two, and Dill kept looking at his watch, not only because he'd had a long day and was anxious but because he expected Cleo back on an early plane from Boston: she'd said she would see him at the Pierre before he left for the office. So eventually, while she was rattling on about root canals, he shut her up: 'Excuse me, my dear, but do you want to fuck or not?' There is something to be said for aristocrats, even the stupidest have had some kind of class bred into them; so she shrugged—'Well, yes, I suppose so'—as though a salesgirl had asked if she liked the look of a hat. Merely resigned, as it were, to that old familiar hard-sell Jewish effrontery. In the bedroom she asked him not to turn on the lights. She was quite firm about that—and in view of what finally transpired, one can scarcely blame her. They undressed in the dark, and she took forever—unsnapping, untying, unzipping—and said not a word except to remark on the fact that the Dillons obviously slept in the same bed since there was only the one; and he told her yes, he was affectionate, a mama's boy who couldn't sleep unless he had something soft to cuddle against. The governor's wife was neither a cuddler nor a kisser. Kissing her, according to Dill, was like playing post office with a dead and rotting whale: she really did need a dentist. None of his tricks caught her fancy, she just lay there, inert, like a missionary being outraged by a succession of sweating Swahilis. Dill couldn't come. He felt as though he were sloshing around in some strange puddle, the whole ambience so slippery he couldn't get a proper grip. He thought maybe if he went down on her—but the moment he started to, she hauled him up by his hair: 'Nonnonono, for God's sake, don't do that!' Dill gave up, he rolled over, he said: 'I don't suppose you'd blow me?' She didn't bother to reply, so he said okay, all right, just jack me off and we'll call it scratch, okay? But she was already up, and asked him please not to turn on the light, please, and she said no, he need not see her home, stay where he was, go to sleep, and while he lay there listening to her dress he reached down to finger himself, and it felt . . . it felt . . . he jumped up and snapped on the light. His whole paraphernalia had felt sticky and strange. As though it were covered with blood. And it was. So was the bed. The sheets bloodied with stains the size of Brazil. The governor's wife had just picked up her purse, had just opened the door, and Dill said: 'What the hell is this? Why did you do it?' Then he knew why, not because she told him, but because of the glance he caught as she closed the door: like Carino, the cruel maître d' at the old Elmer's—leading some blue-suit brown-shoes hunker to a table in Siberia. She had mocked him, punished him for his Jewish presumption.

"Jonesy, you're not eating?"

"It isn't doing much for my appetite. This conversation."

"I warned you it was a vile story. And we haven't come to the best part yet."

"All right. I'm ready."

"No, Jonesy. Not if it's going to make you sick."

"I'll take my chances," I said.

Mrs. Kennedy and her sister had left; the governor's wife was leaving, Soulé beaming and bobbing in her wide-hipped wake. Mrs. Matthau and Mrs. Cooper were still present but silent, their ears perked to our conversation; Mrs. Matthau was kneading a fallen yellow rose petal—her fingers stiffened as Ina resumed: "Poor Dill didn't realize the extent of his difficulties until he'd stripped the sheets off the bed and found there were no clean ones to replace them. Cleo, you see, used the Pierre's linen and kept none of her own at the hotel. It was three o'clock in the morning and he couldn't reasonably call for maid service: what would he say, how could he explain the loss of his sheets at that hour? The particular hell of it was that Cleo would be sailing in from Boston in a matter of hours, and regardless of how much Dill screwed around he'd always been scrupulous about never giving Cleo a clue; he really loved her, and, my God, what could he say when she saw the bed? He took a cold shower and tried to think of some buddy he could call and ask to hustle over with a change of sheets. There was me, of course; he trusted me, but I was in London. And there was his old valet, Wardell. Wardell was queer for Dill and had been a slave for twenty years just for the privilege of soaping him whenever Dill took his bath; but Wardell was old and arthritic, Dill *couldn't* call him in Greenwich and ask him to drive all the way in to town. Then it struck him that he had a hundred chums but really no friends, not the kind you ring at three in the morning. In his own company he employed more than six thousand people, but there was not one who had ever called him anything except *Mr. Dillon.* I mean, the guy was feeling sorry for himself. So he poured a truly stiff Scotch and started searching in the kitchen for a box of laundry soap, but he couldn't find any and in the end had to use a bar of Guerlain's *Fleurs des Alpes.* To wash the sheets. He soaked them in the tub in scalding water. Scrubbed and scrubbed. Rinsed and scrubadubdubbed. There he was, the powerful Mr. Dillon, down on his knees and flogging away like a Spanish peasant at the side of a stream. It was five o'clock, it was six, the sweat poured off him, he felt as if he were trapped in a sauna; he said the next day when he weighed himself he'd lost eleven pounds. Full daylight was upon him before the sheets looked credibly white. But wet. He wondered if hanging them out the window might help—or merely attract the police? At last he thought of drying them in the kitchen oven. It was only one of those little hotel stoves, but he stuffed them in and set them to bake at four hundred fifty degrees. And they baked, brother: smoked and steamed—the bastard burned his hand pulling them out. Now it was eight o'clock and there was no time left. So he decided there was nothing to do but make up the bed with the steamy soggy sheets, climb between them and say his prayers. He really *was* praying when he started to snore. When he woke up it was noon, and there was a note on the bureau from Cleo: 'Darling, you were sleeping so soundly and sweetly that I just tiptoed in and changed and have gone on to Greenwich. Hurry home.' "

The Mesdames Cooper and Matthau, having heard their fill, self-consciously prepared to depart.

Mrs. Cooper said: "D-darling, there's the most m-m-marvelous auction at Parke Bernet this afternoon—Gothic tapestries."

"What the fuck," asked Mrs. Matthau, "would I do with a Gothic tapestry?"

Mrs. Cooper replied: "I thought they might be amusing for picnics at the beach. You know, spread them on the sands."

Lady Ina, after extracting from her purse a Bulgari vanity case made of white enamel sprinkled with diamond flakes, an object remindful of snow prisms, was dusting her face with a powder puff. She started with her chin, moved to her nose, and the next thing I knew she was slapping away at the lenses of her dark glasses.

And I said, "What are you doing, Ina?"

She said: "Damn! damn!" and pulled off the glasses and mopped them with a napkin. A tear had slid down to dangle like sweat at the tip of a nostril—not a pretty sight; neither were her eyes—red and veined from a heap of sleepless weeping. "I'm on my way to Mexico to get a divorce."

One wouldn't have thought that would make her unhappy; her husband was the stateliest bore in England, an ambitious achievement, considering some of the competition: the Earl of Derby, the Duke of Marlborough, to name but two. Certainly that was Lady Ina's opinion; still, I could understand why she married him—he was rich, he was technically alive, he was a "good gun" and for that reason reigned in hunting circles, boredom's Valhalla. Whereas Ina . . . Ina was fortyish and a multiple divorcée on the rebound from an affair with a Rothschild who had been satisfied with her as a mistress but hadn't thought her grand enough to wed. So Ina's friends were relieved when she returned from a shoot in Scotland engaged to Lord

Coolbirth; true, the man was humorless, dull, sour as port decanted too long—but, all said and done, a lucrative catch.

"I know what you're thinking," Ina remarked, amid more tearful trickling. "That if I'm getting a good settlement I ought to be congratulated. I don't deny Cool was tough to take. Like living with a suit of armor. But I did . . . feel safe. For the first time I felt I had a man I couldn't possibly lose. Who else would want him? But I've now learned this, Jonesy, and hark me well: there's always someone around to pick up an old husband. *Always.*" A crescendo of hiccups interrupted her: M. Soulé, observing from a concealed distance, pursed his lips. "I was careless. Lazy. But I just couldn't bear any more of those wet Scottish weekends with the bullets whizzing round, so he started going alone, and after a while I began to notice that everywhere he went Elda Morris was sure to go—whether it was a grouse shoot in the Hebrides or a boar hunt in Yugoslavia. She even tagged along to Spain when Franco gave that huge hunting party last October. But I didn't make too much of it—Elda's a great gun, but she's also a hard-boiled fifty-year-old virgin; I *still* can't conceive of Cool wanting to get into those rusty knickers." Her hand weaved toward the Champagne glass but, without arriving at its destination, drooped and fell like a drunk suddenly sprawling flat on the street. "Two weeks ago," she began, her voice slowed, her Montana accent becoming more manifest, "as Cool and I were winging to New York, I realized that he was staring at me with a, hmnnn, *ser*pentine scowl. Ordinarily he looks like an egg. It was only nine in the morning; nevertheless, we were drinking that loathsome airplane champagne, and when we'd finished a bottle and I saw he was still looking at me in this . . . homicidal . . . way, I said: 'What's bugging you, Cool?' And *he* said: 'Nothing that a divorce from you wouldn't cure.' Imagine the wickedness of it! springing something like that on a plane!—when you're stuck together for hours, and can't get away, can't shout or scream. It was doubly nasty of him because he knows I'm terrified of flying—he *knew* I was full of pills and booze. So now I'm on my way to Mexico." At last her hand retrieved the glass of Cristal; she sighed, a sound despondent as spiraling autumn leaves. "My kind of woman needs a man. Not for sex. Oh, I like a good screw. But I've had my share; I can do without it. But I can't live without a man. Women like me have no other focus, no other way of scheduling our lives; even if we hate him, even if he's an iron head with a cotton heart, it's better than this footloose routine. Freedom may be the most important thing in life, but there's such a thing as too much freedom. And I'm the wrong age now, I can't face all that again, the long hunt, the sitting up all night at Elmer's or Annabel's with some fat greaser swimming in a sea of stingers. All the old gal pals asking you to their little black-tie dinners and not really wanting an extra woman and wondering where they're going to find a 'suitable' extra man for an aging broad like Ina Coolbirth. As though there *were* any suitable extra men in New York. *Or* London. Or Butte, Montana, if it comes to that. They're all queer. Or *ought* to be. That's what I meant when I told Princess Margaret it was too bad she didn't like fags because it meant she would have a very lonely old age. Fags are the only people who are kind to worldly old women; and I adore them, I always have, but I really am not *ready* to become a full-time fag's moll; I'd rather go dyke. No, Jonesy, that's never been part of my repertoire, but I can see the appeal for a woman my age, someone who can't abide loneliness, who needs comfort and admiration: some dykes can ladle it out good. There's nothing cozier or safer than a nice little lez-nest. I remember when I saw Anita Hohnsbeen in Sante Fe. How I envied her. But I've always envied Anita. She was a senior at Sarah Lawrence when I was a freshman. I think everyone had a crush on Anita. She wasn't beautiful, even pretty, but she was so bright and nerveless and *clean*—her hair, her skin, she always looked like the first morning on earth. If she hadn't had all that glue, and if that climbing Southern mother of hers had stopped pushing her, I think she would have married an archaeologist and spent a happy lifetime excavating urns in Anatolia. But why disinter Anita's wretched history?—five husbands and one retarded child, just a waste until she'd had several hundred breakdowns and weighed ninety pounds and her doctor sent her out to Santa Fe. Did you know Santa Fe is the dyke capital of the United States? What San Francisco is to *les garçons,* Santa Fe is to the Daughters of Bilitis. I suppose it's because the butchier ones like dragging up in boots and denim. There's a delicious woman there, Megan O'Meaghan, and Anita met her and, baby, that was *it.* All she'd ever needed was a good pair of motherly tits to suckle. Now she and Megan live in a rambling abode in the foothills, and Anita looks . . . almost as clear-eyed as she did when we were at school together. Oh, it's a bit corny—the piñon fires, the Indian fetish dolls, Indian rugs, and the two ladies fussing in the kitchen over homemade tacos and the 'perfect' Margarita. But say what you will, it's one of the pleasantest homes I've ever been in. Lucky Anita!"

She lurched upward, a dolphin shattering the surface of the sea, pushed back the table (overturning a Champagne glass), seized her purse, said: "Be right back"; and careened toward the mirrored door of the Côte Basque powder room.

Although the priest and the assassin were still whispering and sipping at their table, the restaurant's rooms had emptied, M. Soulé had retired. Only the hatcheck girl and a few waiters impatiently flicking napkins remained. Stewards were resetting the tables, sprucing the flowers for the evening visitors. It was an atmosphere of luxurious exhaustion, like a ripened, shedding rose, while all that waited outside was the failing New York afternoon.

[November 1975]

WILLIAM STYRON

Shadrach

My tenth summer on earth, in the year 1935, will never leave my mind because of Shadrach and the way he brightened and darkened my life then and thereafter. He turned up as if from nowhere, arriving at high noon in the village where I grew up in Tidewater, Virginia. He was a black apparition of unbelievable antiquity, palsied and feeble, blue-gummed and grinning, a caricature of a caricature at a time when every creaky, superannuated Negro grandsire was (in the eyes of society, not alone the eyes of a small southern white boy) a combination of Stepin Fetchit and Uncle Remus. On that day when he seemed to materialize before us, almost out of the ether, we were playing marbles. Little boys rarely play marbles nowadays but marbles were an obsession in 1935, somewhat predating the yo-yo as a kids' craze. One could admire these elegant many-colored spheres as potentates admire rubies and emeralds; they had a sound yet slippery substantiality, evoking the tactile delight— the same aesthetic yet opulent pleasure—of small precious globes of jade. Thus, among other things, my memory of Shadrach is bound up with the lapidary mineral feel of marbles in my fingers and the odor of cool bare earth on a smoldering hot day beneath a sycamore tree, and still another odor (ineffaceably a part of the moment): a basic fetor, namely the axillary and inguinal smell which that squeamish decade christened B.O., and which radiated from a child named Little Mole Dabney, my opponent at marbles. He was ten years old, too, and had never been known to use Lifebuoy soap, or any other cleansing agent.

Which brings me soon enough to the Dabneys. For I realize I must deal with the Dabneys in order to try to explain the encompassing mystery of Shadrach—who after a fashion was a Dabney himself. The Dabneys were not close neighbors; they lived nearby down the road in a rambling weatherworn house which lacked a lawn. On the grassless, graceless terrain of the front yard was a random litter of eviscerated Frigidaires, electric generators, stoves, and the remains of two or three ancient automobiles whose scavenged carcasses lay abandoned beneath the sycamores like huge rusted insects. Poking up through these husks were masses of weeds and hollyhocks, dandelions gone to seed, sunflowers. Junk and auto parts were a sideline of Mr. Dabney, he also did odd jobs; but his primary pursuit was bootlegging.

Like such noble Virginia family names as Randolph and Peyton and Tucker and Harrison and Lee and Fitzhugh and a score of others, the patronym Dabney is an illustrious one, but with the present Dabney, born Vernon, the name had lost almost all of its luster. He should have gone to the University of Virginia; instead, he dropped out of school in the fifth grade. It was not his fault; nor was it his fault that the family had so declined in status. It was said that his father (a true scion of the distinguished old tree but a man with a "character defect" and a weakness for the bottle) had long ago slid down the social ladder, forfeiting his F.F.V. status by marrying a half-breed Mattaponi or Pamunkey Indian girl from the York River, accounting perhaps for the black hair and sallowish muddy complexion of the son.

Mr. Dabney—at this time, I imagine he was in his forties—was a runty, hyperactive entrepreneur with a sourly intense, purse-lipped, preoccupied air and a sometimes rampaging temper. He also had a ridiculously foul mouth, from which I learned my first dirty words. It was with delectation, with the same sickishly delighted apprehension of evil which beset me about eight years later when I was accosted by my first prostitute, that I heard Mr. Dabney in his frequent transports of rage use those words forbidden to me in my own home. His blasphemies and obscenities, far from scaring me, caused me to shiver with their splendor. I practiced his words in secret, deriving from their amalgamated filth what, in a dim pediatric way, I could perceive was erotic inflammation. "Son of a bitch whorehouse bat shit Jesus Christ pisspot asshole!" I would screech into an empty closet, and feel my little ten-year-old pecker rise. Yet as ugly and threatening as Mr. Dabney might sometimes appear, I was never really daunted by him for he had a humane and gentle side. Although he might curse like a stevedore at his wife and children, at the assorted mutts and cats that thronged the place, at the pet billy goat which he once caught in the act of devouring his new three dollar Thom McAn shoes, I soon saw that even his most murderous fits were largely bluster.

Oh how I loved the Dabneys! I visited the Dabney homestead as often as I could, basking in its casual squalor. I must avoid giving the impression of Tobacco Road, the Dabneys were of better quality. Yet there were similarities. The mother, named Trixie, was a huge sweaty generous sugarloaf of a woman, often drunk. It was she, I am sure, who propagated the domestic sloppiness. But I loved her passionately just as I loved and envied the whole Dabney tribe and that total absence in them of the bourgeois aspirations and gentility which were my own inheritance. I envied the sheer teeming multitude of the Dabneys—there were seven children—which made my status as an only child seem so effete, spoiled and lonesome. Only illicit whiskey kept the family from complete destitution, and I envied their near poverty. Also their religion. They were Baptists: as a Presbyterian I envied that. To be totally immersed—how wet and natural! They lived in a house devoid of books or any reading matter except funny papers—more envy. I envied their abandoned slovenliness, their sour unmade beds, their roaches, the cracked linoleum on the floor, the homely cur dogs leprous with mange that foraged at will through house and yard. My perverse longings were—to turn around a phrase unknown at the time—downwardly mobile. Afflicted at the age of ten by *nostalgie de la boue,* I felt deprived of a certain depravity. I was too young to know, of course, that one of the countless things of which the Dabneys were victim was the Great Depression.

Yet beneath this scruffy facade, the Dabneys were a family of some property. Although their ramshackle house was rented, as were most of the dwellings in our village, they owned a place elsewhere, and there was occasionally chatter in the household about "the Farm," far upriver in King and Queen County. Mr. Dabney had inherited the place from his dissolute father and it had been in the family for generations. It could not have been much of a holding, or else it would have been sold years before, and when, long afterwards, I came to absorb the history of the Virginia Tidewater—that primordial American demesne where the land was sucked dry by tobacco, laid waste and destroyed a whole century before golden California became an idea, much less a hope or a westward dream—I realized that the Dabney farm must have been as nondescript and as pathetic a relic as any of the scores of shrunken, abandoned "plantations" scattered for a hundred miles across the tidelands between the Potomac and the James. The chrysalis, unpainted, of a dinky, thrice-rebuilt farmhouse with a few mean acres in corn and second-growth timber—that was all. Nonetheless it was to this ancestral dwelling that the nine Dabneys, packed like squirming eels into a fifteen-year-old Model T Ford pockmarked with the ulcers of terminal decay, would go forth for a month's sojourn each August, as seemingly bland and blasé about their customary estivation as Rockefellers decamping to Pocantico Hills. But they were not entirely vacationing. I did not know then but discovered later that the woodland glens and lost glades of the depopulated land of King and Queen were every moonshiner's dream for hideaways in which to decoct white lightning, and the exodus to "the Farm" served a purpose beyond the purely recreative: each Dabney of whatever age and sex had at least a hand in the operation of the still, even if it was simply shucking corn.

All of the three Dabney boys bore the nickname of Mole, being differentiated from each other by a logical nomenclature—Little, Middle, and Big Mole; I don't think I ever knew their real names. It was the youngest of the three Moles I was playing marbles with when Shadrach made his appearance. Little Mole was a child of stunning ugliness, sharing with his brothers an inherited mixture of bulging thyroid eyes, mashed-in, spoon-like nose and jutting jaw which (I say in retrospect) might have nicely corresponded to Cesare Lombroso's description of the criminal physiognomy. Something more remarkable—accounting surely for their collective nickname—was the fact that save for their graduated sizes they were nearly exact replicas of each other, appearing less related by fraternal consanguinity than as monotonous clones, as if Big Mole had reproduced Middle who in turn had created Little, my evil-smelling playmate. None of the Moles ever wished or was ever required to bathe and this accounted for another phenomenon. At the vast and dismal consolidated rural school we attended, one would mark the presence of any of the three Dabney brothers in a classroom by the circumambience of empty desks which caused each Mole to be isolated from his classmates who, edging away without apology from the effluvium, would leave the poor Mole abandoned in his aloneness, like some species of bacteria on a microscope slide whose noxious discharge has destroyed all life in a circle around it.

By contrast—the absurdity of genetics!—the four Dabney girls were fair, fragrant in their Woolworth perfumes, buxom, lusciously ripe of hindquarter, at least two of them knocked up and wed before attaining full growth. Oh, those lost beauties. . . .

That day Little Mole took aim with a glittering taw of surreal chalcedony; he had warts on his fingers, his odor in my nostrils was quintessential Mole. He sent my agate spinning into the weeds.

Shadrach appeared then. We somehow sensed his presence, looked up and found him there. We had not heard him approach, he had come as silently and portentously as if he had been lowered on some celestial apparatus operated by unseen hands. He was astoundingly black. I had never seen a Negro of that impenetrable hue: it was blackness of such intensity that it reflected no light at all, achieving a virtual obliteration of facial features and taking on a mysterious undertone which had the blue-gray of ashes. Perched on a fender, he was grinning at us from the rusted frame of a demolished Pierce-Arrow. It was a blissful grin which revealed deathly purple gums, the yellowish stumps of two teeth and a wet mobile tongue. For a long while he said nothing but, continuing to grin, contentedly rooted at his crotch with a hand warped and wrinkled with age: the bones moved beneath his black skin in clear skeletal outline. With his other hand he firmly grasped a walking stick.

It was then that I felt myself draw a breath in wonder at his age, which was surely unfathomable. He looked older than all the patriarchs of *Genesis* whose names flooded my mind in a Sunday school litany: Lamech, Noah, Enoch, and that perdurable old Jewish fossil, Methuselah. Little Mole and I drew closer, and I saw then that the old man had to be at least partially blind; cataracts clouded his eyes like milky cauls, the corneas swam with rheum. Yet he was not entirely without sight, I sensed the way he observed our approach; above the implacable sweet grin there were flickers of wise recognition. His presence remained worrisomely Biblical; I felt myself drawn to him with an almost devout compulsion, as if he were the prophet Elijah sent to bring truth, light, the Word. The shiny black mohair mail order suit he wore was baggy and frayed, streaked with dust; the cuffs hung loose, and from one of the ripped ankle-high clodhoppers protruded a naked black toe. Even so, the presence was thrillingly ecclesiastical and fed my piety.

It was midsummer, the very trees seemed to hover on the edge of combustion; a mockingbird began to chant nearby in notes rippling and clear. I walked closer to the granddaddy through a swarm of fat green flies supping hungrily on the assorted offal carpeting the Dabney yard. Streams of sweat were pouring off the ancient black face. Finally I heard him speak in a senescent voice so faint and garbled that it took moments for it to penetrate my understanding. But I understood: "Praise de Lawd. Praise His sweet name! Ise arrived in Ole Virginny!"

He beckoned to me with one of his elongated, bony, bituminous fingers; at first it alarmed me but then the finger seemed to move appealingly, like a small harmless snake. "Climb up on ole Shad's knee," he said. I was beginning to get the hang of his gluey diction, realized that it was a matter of listening to certain internal rhythms; even so, with the throaty gulping sound of Africa in it, it was nigger talk I had never heard before. "Jes climb up," he commanded. I obeyed. I obeyed with love and eagerness, it was like creeping up against the bosom of Abraham. In the collapsed old lap I sat happily, fingering a brass chain which wound across the grease-shiny vest; at the end of the chain, dangling, was a nickel-plated watch upon the face of which the black mitts of Mickey Mouse marked the noontime hour. Giggling now, snuggled against the ministerial breast, I inhaled the odor of great age—indefinable, not exactly unpleasant but stale like a long-unopened cupboard—mingled with the smell of unlaundered fabric and dust. Only inches away the tongue quivered like a pink clapper in the dark gorge of a cavernous bell. "You jes a sweetie," he crooned. "Is you a Dabney?" I replied with regret, "No," and pointed to Little Mole. "That's a Dabney," I said.

"You a sweetie, too," he said, summoning Little Mole with the outstretched forefinger, black, palsied, wiggling. "Oh, you jes de sweetest thing!" The voice rose joyfully. Little Mole looked perplexed. I felt Shadrach's entire body quiver; to my mystification he was overcome with emotion at beholding a flesh and blood Dabney and as he reached toward the boy I heard him breathe again: "Praise de Lawd! Ise arrived in Ole Virginny!"

Then at that instant Shadrach suffered a cataclysmic crisis—one that plainly had to do with the fearful heat. He could not, of course, grow pallid but something enormous and vital did dissolve within the black eternity of his face; the wrinkled old skin of his cheeks sagged, his milky eyes rolled blindly upward, and uttering a soft moan he fell back across the car's ruptured seat with its naked springs and its holes disgorging horsehair.

"Watah!" I heard him cry feebly, *"Watah!"* I slid out of his lap, watched the scrawny black legs no bigger around than pine saplings begin to shake and twitch. "Watah, please!" I heard the voice implore, but Little Mole and I needed no further urging; we were gone—racing headlong to the kitchen and the cluttered, reeking sink. "That old nigger's dying!" Little Mole wailed. We got a cracked jelly glass, ran water from the faucet in a panic, speculating as we did: Little Mole ventured the notion of a heat stroke, I theorized a heart attack. We screamed and babbled, we debated whether the water should be at body temperature or iced. Little Mole added half a cupful of salt, then decided that the water should be hot. Our long delay was fortunate, for several moments later, as we hurried with the terrible potion to Shadrach's side, we found that the elder Dabney had appeared from a far corner of the yard and, taking command of the emergency, had pried Shadrach away from the seat of the Pierce-Arrow, dragged or carried him across the plot of bare earth and propped him up against a tree trunk where he now stood sluicing water from a garden hose into Shadrach's gaping mouth. The old man gulped his fill. Then Mr. Dabney, small and fiercely intent in his baggy overalls, hunched down over the stricken patriarch, whipped out a pint bottle from his pocket and poured a stream of crystalline whiskey down into Shadrach's gorge. While he did this he muttered to himself in tones of incredulity and inwardly tickled amazement: "Well, kiss my ass! Who are you, old uncle? Just who in the goddamned hell *are* you?"

We heard Shadrach give a strangled cough, then he began to try out something resembling speech. But the word he was almost able to produce was swallowed and lost in the hollow of his throat.

"What did he say? What did he say?" Mr. Dabney demanded impatiently.

"He said his name is Shadrach!" I shouted, proud that I alone seemed able to fathom this obscure Negro dialect further muddied by the crippled cadences of senility.

"What's he want?" Mr. Dabney said.

I bent my face toward Shadrach's, which looked contented again. His voice in my ear was at once whispery and sweet, a gargle of beatitude: "Die on Dabney ground."

"I think he said," I told Mr. Dabney at last, "that he wants to die on Dabney ground."

"Well I'll be God damned," said Mr. Dabney.

"Praise de Lawd!" Shadrach cried suddenly, in a voice that even Mr. Dabney could understand. "Ise arrived in Ole Virginny!"

Mr. Dabney roared at me: "Ask him where he came from!"

Again I inclined my face to that black shrunken visage upturned to the blazing sun; I whispered the question and the reply came back after a long silence, in fitful stammerings. At last I said to Mr. Dabney: "He says he's from Clay County down in Alabama."

"*Alabama!* Well, kiss my ass!"

I felt Shadrach pluck at my sleeve and once more I bent down to listen. Many seconds passed before I could discover the outlines of the words struggling for meaning on the flailing ungovernable tongue. But finally I captured their shapes, arranged them in order.

"What did he say now?" Mr. Dabney said.

"He said he wants you to bury him."

"*Bury him!*" Mr. Dabney shouted. "How can I bury him? He ain't even dead yet!"

From Shadrach's breast there now came a gentle keening sound which, commencing on a note of the purest grief, startled me by the way it resolved itself suddenly into a mild faraway chuckle; the moonshine was taking hold. The pink clapper of a tongue lolled in the cave of the jagged old mouth. Shadrach grinned.

"Ask him how old he is," came the command. I asked him. "Nimenime," was the glutinous reply.

"He says he's ninety-nine years old," I reported, glancing up from the ageless abyss.

"*Ninety-nine!* Well, kiss my ass! Just kiss my ass!"

Now other Dabneys began to arrive, including the mother Trixie and
the two larger Moles, along with one of the older teen-age daughters,
whale-like but meltingly beautiful as she floated on the crest of her
pregnancy, and accompanied by her hulking, acne-cratered teen-age
spouse. There also came a murmuring clutch of neighbors—sun-
reddened shipyard workers in cheap sport shirts, scampering towhead
children, a quartet of scrawny housewives in sacklike dresses, bluish
crescents of sweat beneath their arms. In my memory they make an
aching tableau of those exhausted years. They jabbered and clucked
in wonder at Shadrach who, immobilized by alcohol, heat, infirmity
and his ninety-nine Augusts, beamed and raised his rheumy eyes to
the sun. "Praise de Lawd!" he quavered.

We hoisted him to his feet and supported the frail, almost
weightless old frame as he limped on dancing tiptoe to the house,
where we settled him down upon a rumpsprung glider which squatted
on the back porch in an ambient fragrance of dog urine, tobacco
smoke and mildew. "You hungry, Shad?" Mr. Dabney bellowed.
"Mama, get Shadrach something to eat!" Slumped in the glider, the
ancient visitor gorged himself like one plucked from the edge of critical starvation: he devoured three cantaloupes, slurped down bowl
after bowl of Rice Krispies, and gummed his way through a panful of
hot cornbread smeared with lard. We watched silently, in wonder-
ment. Before our solemnly attentive eyes he gently and carefully
eased himself back on the malodorous pillows and with a soft sigh
went to sleep.

Some time after this—during the waning hours of the afternoon,
when Shadrach woke up, and then on into the evening—the mystery
of the old man's appearance became gradually unlocked. One of the
Dabney daughters was a fawn-faced creature of twelve named Edmonia; her fragile beauty (especially when contrasted with ill-favored
brothers) and her precocious breasts and bottom had caused me—
young as I was—a troubling, unresolved itch. I was awed by the ease
and nonchalance with which she wiped the drool from Shadrach's
lips. Like me, she possessed some inborn gift of interpretation, and
through our joint efforts there was pieced together over several hours

an explanation for this old man—for his identity and his bizarre and inescapable coming.

He stayed on the glider, we put another pillow under his head. Nourishing his dragon's appetite with Hershey bars and, later on, with nips from Mr. Dabney's bottle, we were able to coax from those aged lips a fragmented, abbreviated but reasonably coherent biography. After a while it became an anxious business for, as one of the adults noticed, old Shad seemed to be running a fever; his half-blind eyes swam about from time to time, and the clotted phlegm which rose in his throat made it all the more difficult to understand anything. But somehow we began to divine the truth. One phrase, repeated over and over, I particularly remember: "Ise a Dabney." And indeed those words provided the chief clue to his story.

Born a slave on the Dabney plantation in King and Queen County, he had been sold down to Alabama in the decades before the Civil War. Shadrach's memory was imperfect regarding the date of his sale. Once he said "fifty," meaning 1850, and another time he said "fifty-five," but it was an item of little importance; he was probably somewhere between fifteen and twenty-five years old when his master—Vernon Dabney's great-grandfather—disposed of him, selling him to one of the many traders prowling the worn-out Virginia soil of that stricken bygone era; and since in his confessional to us, garbled as it was, he used the word "coffle" (a word beyond my ten-year-old knowledge but one whose meaning I later understood), he must have journeyed those six hundred miles to Alabama on foot and in the company of God knows how many other black slaves, linked together by chains.

So now, as we began slowly to discover, this was Shadrach's return trip home to Ole Virginny—three-quarters of a century or thereabouts after his departure from the land out of which he had sprung, which had nurtured him, and where he had lived his happy years. Happy? Who knows? But we had to assume they were his happy years—else why this incredible pilgrimage at the end of his life? As he had announced with such abrupt fervor earlier, he wanted only to die and be buried on "Dabney ground."

We learned that after the war he had become a sharecropper, that he had married three times and had had many children (once he said twelve, another time fifteen; no matter, they were legion); he had

outlived them all, wives and offspring. Even the grandchildren had
died off, or had somehow vanished. "Ah was dibested of all mah
plenty," was another statement I can still record verbatim. Thus di-
vested and (as he cheerfully made plain to all who gathered around
him to listen) sensing mortality in his own shriveled flesh and bones,
he had departed Alabama on foot—just as he had come there—to
find the Virginia of his youth.

Six hundred miles! The trip, we were able to gather, took over
four months, since he said he set out from Clay County in the early
spring. He walked nearly the entire way, although now and then he
would accept a ride—almost always, one can be sure, from the few
Negroes who owned cars in the rural South of those years. He had
saved up a few dollars, which allowed him to provide for his stomach.
He slept on the side of the road or in barns, sometimes a friendly
Negro family would give him shelter. The trek took him across
Georgia and the Carolinas and through Southside Virginia. His itinerary is still anyone's conjecture. Because he could not read either
road sign or road map, he obviously followed his own northward-
questing nose, a profoundly imperfect method of finding one's way
(he allowed to Edmonia with a faint cackle) since he once got so far
astray that he ended up not only miles away from the proper highway
but in a city and state completely off his route—Chattanooga, Tennessee. But he circled back and moved on. And how, once arrived in
Virginia with its teeming Dabneys, did he discover the only Dabney
who would matter, the single Dabney who was not merely the proprietor of his birthplace but the one whom he also unquestioningly expected to oversee his swiftly approaching departure, laying him to
rest in the earth of their mutual ancestors? How did he find *Vernon
Dabney?* Mr. Dabney was by no means an ill-spirited or ungenerous
man (despite his runaway temper), but was a soul nonetheless beset
by many woes in the dingy threadbare year 1935, being hard pressed
not merely for dollars but for dimes and quarters, crushed beneath an
elephantine and inebriate wife along with three generally shiftless
sons and two knocked-up daughters plus two more in the offing, and
living with the abiding threat of revenue agents swooping down to
terminate his livelihood and, perhaps, get him sent to the Atlanta
penitentiary for five or six years. He needed no more cares or bur-
dens, and now in the hot katydid-shrill hours of summer night I saw
him gaze down at the leathery old dying black face with an expres-

sion that mingled compassion and bewilderment and stoppered-up rage and desperation, and then whisper to himself: "He wants to die on Dabney ground! Well, kiss my ass, just kiss my ass!" Plainly he wondered how, among all his horde of Virginia kinfolk, Shadrach found *him,* for he squatted low and murmured: "Shad! Shad, how come you knew who to look for?" But in his fever Shadrach had drifted off to sleep, and so far as I ever knew there was never any answer to that.

The next day it was plain that Shadrach was badly off. During the night he had somehow fallen from the glider, and in the early morning hours he was discovered on the floor, leaking blood. We bandaged him up. The wound just above his ear was superficial, as it turned out, but it had done him no good; and when he was replaced on the swing he appeared to be confused and at the edge of delirium, plucking at his shirt, whispering and rolling his gentle opaque eyes at the ceiling. Whenever he spoke now his words were beyond the power of Edmonia or me to comprehend, faint high-pitched mumbo-jumbo in a drowned dialect. He seemed to recognize no one. Trixie, leaning over the old man as she sucked at her first Pabst Blue Ribbon of the morning, decided firmly that there was no time to waste. "Shoog," she said to Mr. Dabney, using her habitual pet name (diminutive form of Sugar), "you better get out the car if we're goin' to the Farm. I think he ain't gone last much longer." And so, given unusual parental leave to go along on the trip, I squeezed myself into the back seat of the Model T, privileged to hold in my lap a huge greasy paper bag full of fried chicken which Trixie had prepared for noontime dinner at the Farm.

Not all of the Dabneys made the journey—the two older daughters and the largest Mole were left behind—but we still comprised a multitude. We children were packed sweatily skin to skin and atop each other's laps in the rear seat, which reproduced in miniature the messiness of the house with this new litter of empty RC Cola and Nehi bottles, funny papers, watermelon rinds, banana peels, greasy jack handles, oil-smeared gears of assorted sizes and wads of old Kleenex. On the floor beneath my feet I even discerned (to my intense discomfort, for I had just learned to recognize such an object) a crumpled, yellowish used condom, left there haphazardly, I was certain, by one of the older daughters' boyfriends who had been able to borrow the heap for carnal sport. It was a bright summer day, scorchingly hot like the day preceding it, but the car had no workable windows and we were pleasantly ventilated. Shadrach sat in the middle of the front seat. Mr. Dabney was hunched over the wheel, chewing at a wad of tobacco and driving with black absorption; he had stripped to his undershirt, and I thought I could almost see the rage and frustration in the tight bunched muscles of his neck. He muttered curses at the balky gearshift but otherwise said little, rapt in his guardian misery. So voluminous that the flesh of her shoulders fell in a freckled cascade over the back of her seat, Trixie loomed on the other side of Shadrach; the corpulence of her body seemed in some way to both enfold and support the old man, who nodded and dozed. The encircling hair around the shiny black head was, I thought, like a delicate halo of the purest frost or foam. Curiously, for the first time since Shadrach's coming, I felt a stab of grief and achingly wanted him not to die.

"Shoog," said Trixie, standing by the rail of the dumpy little ferry that crossed the York River, "what kind of big birds do you reckon those are behind that boat there?" The Model T had been the first car aboard, and all of us had flocked out to look at the river, leaving Shadrach to sit there and sleep during the fifteen minute ride. The water was blue, sparkling with whitecaps, lovely. A huge gray naval tug with white markings chugged along to the mine depot at Yorktown, trailing eddies of garbage and a swooping flock of frantic gulls. Their squeals echoed across the peaceful channel.

"Seagulls," said Mr. Dabney. "Ain't you never recognized seagulls before? I can't believe such a question. Seagulls. Dumb greedy bastards."

"Beautiful things," she replied softly, "all big and white. Can you eat one?"

"So tough you'd like to choke to death."

We were halfway across the river when Edmonia went to the car to get a ginger ale. When she came back she said hesitantly: "Mama, Shadrach has made a fantastic mess in his pants."

"Oh Lord," said Trixie.

Mr. Dabney clutched the rail and raised his small, pinched, tormented face to heaven. "Ninety-nine years old! Christ almighty! He ain't nothin' but a ninety-nine years old *baby!*"

"It smells just awful," said Edmonia.

"Why in the God damned hell didn't he go to the bathroom before we left?" Mr. Dabney said. "Ain't it bad enough we got to drive three hours to the Farm without—"

"*Shoosh!*" Trixie interrupted, moving ponderously to the car. "Poor ol' thing, he can't help it. Vernon, you see how you manage your bowels fifty years from now."

Once off the ferry we children giggled and squirmed in the back seat, pointedly squeezed our noses, and scuffled amid the oily rubbish of the floorboards. It was an awful smell. But a few miles up the road in the hamlet of Gloucester Court House, drowsing in eighteenth-century brick and ivy, Trixie brought relief to the situation by bidding Mr. Dabney to stop at an Amoco station. Shadrach had partly awakened from his slumbrous trance. He stirred restlessly in his pool of discomfort, and began to make little fretful sounds, so softly restrained as to barely give voice to what must have been his real and terrible distress. "There now, Shad," Trixie said gently, "Trixie'll look after you." And this she did, half-coaxing, half-hoisting the old man from the car and into a standing position, then with the help of Mr. Dabney propelling his skinny scarecrow frame in a suspended tiptoe dance to the rest room marked COLORED, where to the muffled sound of rushing water she performed some careful rite of cleansing and diapering. Then they brought him back to the car. For the first time that morning Shadrach seemed really aroused from that stupor into which he had plunged so swiftly hours before. "Praise de Lawd!" we heard him say, feebly but with spirit, as the elder Dabneys maneuvered him back onto the seat, purified. He gazed about him with glints of recognition, responding with soft chuckles to our little pats of attention. Even Mr. Dabney seemed in sudden good humor. "You comin' along all right now, Shad?" he howled over the rackety cluttering sound of the motor. Shadrach nodded and grinned but remained silent. There was a mood in the car of joy and revival. "Slow down, Shoog," Trixie murmured indolently, gulping at a beer, "there might be a speed cop." I was filled with elation, and hope tugged at my heart as the flowering landscape rushed by, green and lush with summer and smelling of hay and honeysuckle.

The Dabney country retreat, as I have said, was dilapidated and rudimentary, a true downfall from bygone majesty. Where there once stood a plantation house of the Palladian stateliness required of its kind during the Tidewater dominion in its heyday, there now roosted a dwelling considerably grander than a shack yet modest by any reckoning. Box-like, paintless, supported by naked concrete blocks and crowned by a roof of glistening sheet metal, it would have been an eyesore almost anywhere except in King and Queen County, a bailiwick so distant and underpopulated that the house was scarcely ever viewed by human eyes. A tilted privy out back lent another homely note, junk littered the yard here too. But the soft green acres that surrounded the place were Elysian; the ancient fields and the wild woods rampant with sweet gum and oak and redbud had reverted to the primeval glory of the time of Pocahontas and Powhatan; grapevines crowded the emerald-green thickets which bordered the house on every side, a delicious winey smell of cedar filled the air, and the forest at night echoed with the sound of whippoorwills. The house itself was relatively clean, thanks not to any effort on the part of the Dabneys but to the fact that it remained unlived in by Dabneys for most of the year.

That day after our fried chicken meal we placed Shadrach between clean sheets on a bed in one of the sparsely furnished rooms, then turned to our various recreations. Little Mole and I played marbles all afternoon just outside the house, seeking the shade of a majestic old beech tree; after an hour of crawling in the dirt our faces were streaked and filthy. Later we took a plunge in the millpond which, among other things, purged Little Mole of his B.O. The other children went fishing for perch and bream in the brackish creek which ran through the woods. Mr. Dabney drove off to get provisions at the crossroads store, then vanished into the underbrush to tinker around his well-hidden still. Meanwhile Trixie tramped about with heavy footfalls in the kitchen and downed half a dozen Blue Ribbons, pausing occasionally to look in on Shadrach. Little Mole and I peered in, too, from time to time. Shadrach lay in a deep sleep and seemed to be at peace, even though now and then his breath came in a ragged gasp and his long black fingers plucked convulsively at the hem of the sheet which covered him to his breast like a white shroud. Then the afternoon was over. After a dinner of fried perch and bream we all went to bed with the setting of the sun. Little Mole and I lay sprawled naked in the heat on the same mattress, separated by a paper-thin wall from Shadrach's breathing which rose and fell in my ears against the other night sounds of this faraway and time-haunted place: katydids and crickets and hoot owls and the reassuring cheer—now near, now almost lost—of a whippoorwill.

Late the next morning the county sheriff paid a visit on Mr. Dabney. We were not at the house when he arrived, and so he had to wait for us; we were at the graveyard. Shadrach still slept, with the children standing watch one by one. After our watch Little Mole and I had spent an hour exploring the woods and swinging on the grapevines, and when we emerged from a grove of pine trees, a quarter of a mile or so behind the house, we came upon Mr. Dabney and Trixie. They were poking about in a bramble-filled plot of land which was the old Dabney family burial ground. It was a sunny, peaceful place, where grasshoppers skittered in the tall grass. Choked with briars and nettles and weeds and littered with tumbledown stone markers, unfenced and untended for countless decades, it had been abandoned to the encroachments of summer after summer like this one, when even granite and marble had to give way against the stranglehold of spreading roots and voracious green growing things.

All of Mr. Dabney's remote ancestors lay buried here, together with their slaves, who slept in a plot several feet off to the side—inseparable from their masters and mistresses, but steadfastly apart in death as in life. Mr. Dabney stood amid the tombstones of the slaves, glaring gloomily down at the tangle of vegetation and at the crumbling lopsided little markers. He held a shovel in his hand but had not begun to dig. The morning had become hot, and the sweat streamed from his brow. I peered at the headstones, read the given names, which were as matter-of-fact in their lack of patronymic as spaniels or cats: *Fauntleroy, Wakefield, Sweet Betty, Mary, Jupiter, Lulu. Requiescat in*

Pace. Anno Domini 1790 . . . 1814 . . . 1831. All of these Dabneys, I thought, like Shadrach.

"I'll be God damned if I believe there's a square inch of space left," Mr. Dabney observed to Trixie, and spat a russet gob of tobacco juice into the weeds. "They just crowded all the old dead uncles and mammies they could into this piece of land here. They must be shoulder to shoulder down there." He paused and made his characteristic sound of anguish—a choked dirgelike groan. "Christ Almighty! I hate to think of diggin' about half a ton of dirt!"

"Shoog, why don't you leave off diggin' until this evenin'?" Trixie said. She was trying to fan herself with a soggy handkerchief, and her face—which I had witnessed before in this state of drastic summer discomfort—wore the washed-out bluish shade of skim milk. It usually preceded a fainting spell. "This sun would kill a mule."

Mr. Dabney agreed, saying that he looked forward to a cool glass of iced tea, and we made our way back to the house along a little path of bare earth that wound through a field glistening with goldenrod. Then, just as we arrived at the back of the house we saw the sheriff waiting. He was standing with a foot on the running board of his Plymouth sedan; perched on its front fender was a hulkingly round, intimidating silver siren (in those days pronounced si-*reen*). He was a potbellied middle-aged man with a sun-scorched face fissured with delicate seams and he wore steel-rimmed spectacles. A gold-plated star was pinned to his civilian shirt, which was soaked with sweat. He appeared hearty, made an informal salute and said: "Mornin', Trixie. Mornin', Vern."

"Mornin', Tazewell," Mr. Dabney replied solemnly, though with an edge of suspicion. Without pause he continued to trudge toward the house. "You want some ice tea?"

"No thank you," he said. "Vern, hold on a minute. I'd like a word with you."

I was knowledgeable enough to fear in a vague way some involvement with the distillery in the woods, and I held my breath, but then Mr. Dabney halted, turned, and said evenly: "What's wrong?"

"Vern," the sheriff said, "I hear you're fixin' to bury an elderly colored man on your property here. Joe Thornton down at the store said you told him that yesterday. Is that right?"

Mr. Dabney put his hands on his hips and glowered at the sheriff. Then he said: "Joe Thornton is a God damned incurable blabber-mouth. But that's right. What's wrong with that?"

"You can't," said the sheriff.

There was a pause. "Why not?" said Mr. Dabney.

"Because it's against the law."

I had seen rage, especially in matters involving the law, build up within Mr. Dabney in the past. A pulsing vein always appeared near his temple, along with a rising flush in cheeks and brow; both came now, the little vein began to wiggle and squirm like a worm. "What do you mean, it's against the law?"

"Just that. It's against the law to bury anybody on private property."

"*Why* is it against the law?" Mr. Dabney demanded.

"I don't *know* why, Vern," said the sheriff, with a touch of exasperation. "It just *is,* that's all."

Mr. Dabney flung his arm out—up and then down in a stiff, adamant, unrelenting gesture, like a railroad semaphore.

"Down in that field, Tazewell, there have been people buried for nearabout two hundred years. I got an old senile man on my hands. He was a slave and he was born on this place. Now he's dyin' and I've got to bury him here. And I am."

"Vern, let me tell you something," the sheriff said with an attempt at patience. "You will not be permitted to do any such a thing, so please don't try to give me this argument. He will have to be buried in a place where it's legally permitted, like any of the colored church-yards around here, and he will have to be attended to by a licensed colored undertaker. That's the *law,* Commonwealth of Virginia, and there ain't any which whys or wherefores about it."

Trixie began to anticipate Mr. Dabney's fury and resentment even before he erupted. "Shoog, keep yourself calm—"

"*Bat shit!* It is an *outrage!*" he roared. "Since when did a tax-paying citizen have to answer to the gov'ment in order to bury a harmless sick old colored man on his own property! It goes against every bill of rights I ever heard of—"

"Shoog!" Trixie put in. "*Please—*" She began to wail.

The sheriff put out placating hands and loudly commanded: "*Quiet!*" Then when Mr. Dabney and Trixie fell silent he went on: "Vern, me an' you have been acquainted for a long time, so please don't give me no trouble. I'm tellin' you for the last time, this. Namely, you have *got* to arrange to get that old man buried at one of the colored churches around here, and you will also have to have him taken care of by a licensed undertaker. You can have your choice. There's a well-known colored undertaker in Tappahannock and also I heard of one over in Middlesex, somewhere near Urbanna or Saluda. If you want, I'll give them a telephone call from the courthouse."

I watched as the red rage in Mr. Dabney's face was overtaken by a paler, softer hue of resignation. After a brooding long silence, he said: "All right then. *All right!* How much you reckon it'll cost?"

"I don't know exactly, Vern, but there was an old washer woman worked for me and Ruby died not long ago, and I heard they buried her for thirty-five dollars."

"Thirty-five dollars!" I heard Mr. Dabney breathe. "Christ have mercy!"

Perhaps it was only his rage which caused him to flee, but all afternoon Mr. Dabney was gone and we did not see him again until that evening. Meanwhile, Shadrach rallied for a time from his deep slumber, so taking us by surprise that we thought that he might revive completely. Trixie was shelling peas and sipping beer while she watched Little Mole and me at our marble game. Suddenly Edmonia, who had been assigned to tend to Shadrach for an hour, came running from the house. "Come here you all, real quick!" she said in a voice out of breath. "Shadrach's wide awake and talking!" And he was: when we rushed to his side we saw that he had hiked himself up in bed and his face for the first time in many hours wore an alert and knowing expression, as if he were at least partially aware of his surroundings. He had even regained his appetite. Edmonia had put a daisy in the buttonhole of his shirt, and at some point during his amazing resurrection, she said, he had eaten part of it.

"You should have heard him just now," Edmonia said, leaning over the bed. "He kept talking about going to the millpond. What do you think he meant?"

"Well, could be he just wants to go see the millpond," Trixie replied. She had brought Shadrach a bottle of RC Cola from the kitchen and now she sat beside him, helping him to drink it through a paper straw. "Shad," she asked in a soft voice, "is that what you want? You want to go see the millpond?"

A look of anticipation and pleasure spread over the black face and possessed those old rheumy eyes. And his voice was high-pitched but strong when he turned his head to Trixie and said: "Yes ma'am, I does. I wants to see de millpond."

"How come you want to see the millpond?" Trixie said gently.

Shadrach offered no explanation, merely said again: "I wants to see de millpond."

And so, in obedience to a wish whose reason we were unable to plumb but could not help honor, we took Shadrach to see the millpond. It lay in the woods several hundred yards to the east of the house—an ageless murky dammed-up pool bordered on one side by a glade of moss and fern, spectacularly green, and surrounded on all its other sides by towering oaks and elms. Fed by springs and by the same swiftly rushing stream in which the other children had gone fishing, its water mirrored the overhanging trees and the changing sky and was a pleasurable ordeal to swim in, possessing the icy cold that shocks a body to its bones. For a while we could not figure out how to transport Shadrach down to the place; it plainly would not do to try to let him hobble that long distance, propelled, with our clumsy help, on his nearly strengthless legs in their dangling gait. Finally someone thought of the wheelbarrow, which Mr. Dabney used to haul corn to the still. It was fetched from its shed, and we quickly made of it a not unhandsome and passably comfortable sort of a wheeled litter, filling it with hay and placing a blanket on top.

On this mound Shadrach rested easily, with a look of composure, as we moved him gently rocking down the path. I watched him on the way: in my memory he still appears to be a half-blind but self-possessed and serene African potentate being borne in the fullness of his many years to some longed-for, inevitable reward.

We set the wheelbarrow down on the mossy bank, and there for a long time Shadrach gazed at the millpond, alive with its skating waterbugs and trembling beneath a copper-colored haze of sunlight where small dragonflies swooped in nervous filmy iridescence. Standing next to the wheelbarrow, out of which the shanks of Shadrach's skinny legs protruded like fragile black reeds, I turned and stared into the ancient face, trying to determine what it was he beheld now that created such a look of wistfulness and repose. His eyes began to follow the Dabney children, who had stripped to their underdrawers and had plunged into the water. That seemed to be an answer, and in a bright gleam I was certain that Shadrach had once swum here too, during some unimaginable August nearly a hundred years before.

I had no way of knowing that if his long and solitary journey from the Deep South had been a quest to find this millpond and for a recaptured glimpse of childhood, it may just as readily have been a final turning of his back on a life of suffering. Even now I cannot say for certain, but I have always had to assume that the still-young Shadrach who was emancipated in Alabama those many years ago was set loose, like most of his brothers and sisters, into another slavery perhaps more excruciating than the sanctioned bondage. The chronicle has already been a thousand times told about those people liberated into their new and incomprehensible nightmare: of their poverty and hunger and humiliation, of the crosses burning in the night, random butchery and, above all, the unending dread. None of that madness and mayhem belongs in this story, but without at least a reminder of these things I would not be faithful to Shadrach. Despite the immense cheerfulness with which he had spoken to us of being "dibested of mah plenty," he must have endured unutterable adversity. Yet his return to Virginia, I can now see, was out of no longing for the former bondage, but to find an earlier innocence. And as a small boy at the edge of the millpond I saw Shadrach not as one who had fled darkness, but had searched for light refracted within a flashing moment of remembered childhood. As Shadrach's old clouded eyes gazed at the millpond with its plunging and calling children, his face was suffused with an immeasurable calm and sweetness, and I sensed that he had recaptured perhaps the one pure, untroubled moment in his life. "Shad, did you go swimming here too?" I said. But there was no answer. And it was not long before he was drowsing again; his head fell to the side and we rolled him back to the house in the wheelbarrow.

On Saturday nights in the country the Dabneys usually went to bed as late as ten o'clock. That evening Mr. Dabney returned at suppertime, still sullen and fretful but saying little, still plainly distraught and sick over the sheriff's mandate. He did not himself even pick up a fork. But the supper was one of those ample and blessed meals of Trixie's I recall so well. Only the bounty of a place like the Tidewater backcountry could provide such a feast for poor people in those hard-pressed years: ham with red-eye gravy, grits, collard greens, okra, sweet corn, huge red tomatoes oozing juice in a salad with onions and herbs and vinegar. For dessert there was a delectable bread pudding drowned in fresh cream. Afterward, a farmer and bootlegging colleague from down the road named Mr. Seddon R. Washington arrived in a broken-down pickup truck to join with Mr. Dabney at the only pastime I ever saw him engage in—a game of dominoes. Twilight fell and the oil lanterns were lit. Little Mole and I went back like dull slugs to our obsessive sport, scratching a large circle in the dust beside the porch and crouching down with our crystals and agates in a moth-crazed oblong of lantern light, tiger-yellow and flickering. A full moon rose slowly out of the edge of the woods like an immense, bright, faintly smudged balloon. The clicking of our marbles alternated with the click-click of the dominoes on the porch bench.

"If you wish to know the plain and simple truth about whose fault it is," I heard Mr. Dabney explain to Mr. Washington, "you can say it is the fault of your Franklin D for Disaster Roosevelt. The Dutchman millionaire. And his so-called New Deal ain't worth a jug full of warm piss. You know how much I made last year—legal, that is?"

"How much?" said Mr. Washington.

"I can't even tell you. It would shame me. They are colored people sellin' deviled crabs for five cents a piece on the streets in Newport News made more than me. There is an injustice somewhere with this system." He paused. "Eleanor's near about as bad as he is." Another pause. "They say she fools around with colored men and Jews. Preachers mainly."

"Things bound to get better," Mr. Washington said.

"They can't get no worse," said Mr. Dabney.

Footsteps made a soft slow padding sound across the porch and I looked up and saw Edmonia draw near her father. She parted her lips, hesitated for a moment, then said: "Daddy, I think Shadrach has passed away."

Mr. Dabney said nothing, attending to his dominoes with his expression of pinched, absorbed desperation and muffled wrath. Edmonia put her hand lightly on his shoulder. "Daddy, did you hear what I said?"

"I heard."

"I was sitting next to him, holding his hand, and then all of a sudden his head—it just sort of rolled over and he was still and not breathing. And his hand—it just got limp and—well, what I mean, cold." She paused again. "He never made a sound."

Mr. Washington rose with a cough and walked to the far edge of the porch where he lit a pipe and gazed up at the blazing moon. When again Mr. Dabney made no response, Edmonia lightly stroked the edge of his shoulder and said gently: "Daddy, I'm afraid."

"What're you afraid about?" he replied.

"I don't know," she said with a tremor. "Dying. It scares me. I don't know what it means—death. I never saw anyone—like that before."

"Death ain't nothin' to be afraid about," he blurted in a quick, choked voice. "It's life that's fearsome! *Life!*" Suddenly he arose from the bench, scattering dominoes to the floor, and when he roared *"Life!"* again I saw Trixie emerge from the black hollow of the front door and approach with footfalls that sent a shudder through the porch timbers. "Now, *Shoog*—" she began.

"Life is where you've got to be terrified!" he cried as the unplugged rage spilled forth. "Sometimes I understand why men commit suicide! Where in the God damned hell am I goin' to get the money to put him in the ground? Niggers have always been the biggest problem! God damn it, I was brought up to have a certain respect and say *colored* instead of *niggers* but they are always a problem, these niggers! They will just drag you down, God damned black bastards! Nigger assholes! I ain't got thirty-five dollars! I ain't got *twenty-five* dollars! I ain't got *five* dollars!"

"Vernon!" Trixie's voice rose, and she entreatingly spread out her great creamy arms. "Someday you're goin' to get a *stroke!"*

"And one other thing! Franklin D. Roosevelt is the worse nigger lover of them all!"

Then suddenly his fury—or the harsher, wilder part of it— seemed to evaporate, sucked up into the moonlit night with its soft summery cricketing sounds and its scent of warm loam and honeysuckle. For an instant he looked shrunken, runtier than ever, so light and frail that he might blow away like a leaf, and he ran a nervous, trembling hand through his shock of tangled black hair. "I know, I know," he said in a faint unsteady voice edged with grief. "Poor old man, he couldn't help it. He was a decent, pitiful old thing, probably never done anybody the slightest harm. I ain't got a thing in the world against Shadrach. Poor old man."

Crouched below the porch I felt an abrupt, smothering misery. The tenderest gust of wind blew from the woods and I shivered at its touch on my cheek, mourning for Shadrach and Mr. Dabney, and slavery and destitution, and all the human discord swirling around me in a time and place I could not understand. As if to banish my fierce unease, I began to try—in a seizure of concentration—to count the fireflies sparkling in the night air. Eighteen, nineteen, twenty. . . .

"And anyway," Trixie said, touching her husband's hand, "he died on Dabney ground like he wanted to. Even if he's got to be put away in a strange graveyard."

"Well, he won't know the difference," said Mr. Dabney. "When you're dead nobody knows the difference. Death ain't much."

[November 1978]

VANCE BOURJAILY

The Amish Farmer

A couple of weeks ago in class, I told the Amish farmer story again. I hadn't thought I would and never planned at all to write it down. I guess this was because I used to think it a simple story, which I understood so well that, with any further telling, my own interest in it would be used up. But this particular class had people in it whom I liked, we had an hour of open time, and the Amish farmer story had got people into lively discussions in the past.

The class is a workshop in writing fiction; I got my storytelling energy up for them. Often it helps to pick a particular student, from whom my teaching ego happens to crave a little response, and then to think in terms of summoning energy for him or for her. On this day, the student I held in mind and with whom I had eye contact as I started talking was one we call Katie Jay; she is smart, searching, scathing sometimes, very talented, a leader though not without enemies, cool, almost elegant in her blond slimness. Is Katie Jay. It is because of her that I am writing the story now.

"Listen to this," I said. "What I'm going to try to illustrate is the remarkable power of point of view. I'm going to tell you a story in which I think you'll recognize the kind of material a writer might decide to use. I'll tell it pretty much as it came to me, and then let's talk about how it would change in tone, mood, meaning—in the basic kind of piece it would make—just from changing the point of view from which it's told from that of one character in it to that of another."

Katie Jay smiled and nodded at me slightly; I smiled back and started catching other eyes.

On a spring morning (I said) about ten years ago, I got a call from a friend and student named Noel Butler, asking if he could come to the house. He sounded upset.

"Come along," I said. "You in trouble, Noel?"

"I think somebody just tried to kill me," Noel said.

I stepped outside, onto the lawn, to wait for him. The temperature was up around 60. The dirt glittered and steamed where it showed, wet and black beneath the grass plants. I didn't have much doubt that the situation had to do with Noel's wife.

At that time I had seen Dawn Butler only twice, and four months earlier, but she was vivid to me as she was to all men.

Let me explain that Noel had come to Indiana from Boston to start graduate school the previous September without Dawn and nervous about it. He was someone we'd recruited for the graduate program, an engaging, articulate young writer with a couple of publications, a year of prep school teaching, and a year in publishing. We'd offered him an assistantship, something we rarely do for first-year students; he was going to start right in teaching core lit to sophomores, as well as taking his graduate hours.

It seemed plain from the first look at Noel that we'd made a good move. He was poised, talkative, nice-looking in a horn-rimmed, wavy-haired, Brooks Brothers way. He probably looked archaic to some of his peers, but he looked just right to me; and if his flow of persuasive speech was a little glib at times, he was still a pleasure to have in class. He kept things moving. We heard that his undergraduate students doted on him from the first "Good morning, people."

I was just starting to get to know Noel. It wasn't really quite appropriate yet for intimate matters to come up between us, but he just couldn't keep himself from telling me about Dawn: she was beautiful and wild, and he loved her desperately, and he might even have to leave us if she kept on refusing to join him here in our midwestern city, which she supposed must be pretty dull. He said that at first Dawn had promised to come along as soon as he found them a decent place to live; he had a place located, but she kept delaying. He also told me that she had a child, a boy, born illegitimately when she was seventeen, the son of a celebrated choreographer whose protégée Dawn had been. She'd been scared of the man, who was also a celebrated bisexual and capable of violence, had run away from him, given up dancing, and had the child. But that was only part of it, Noel said. I'd have to see Dawn to believe her.

Midway through October he got himself excused from classes for a week, got friends to cover his core lit meetings, and flew to Boston. He phoned me excitedly from there to ask me to check on his academic arrangements but really to say, triumphantly, that she'd agreed to come. I reminded him that the director of our program was giving a cocktail party Friday for the staff and teaching assistants, and Noel said proudly that he'd be there with Mrs. Butler.

So. It was in the rather formal living room at the director's house that I first saw Dawn. I can almost say, without a sense of exaggeration, that I felt her. She had that kind of insistent sexual presence that men think they perceive as a wave of heat. It makes your cheeks tingle and the hair bristle at the back of your neck. I'd met a few women with that brute magnetism before, but none who had more of it than Dawn Butler and only one, an actress, who combined it, as Dawn did, with more physical beauty than seemed fair.

I remember that I guessed which room she'd be in before I saw her, because every other man at the party was in that room already.

Dawn had dark hair, which she wore brushed back in long, soft waves down to below her shoulder blades. Her face was round and her brown, protruding eyes so large they made the other features seem more delicate than they probably were, and the skin paler. Her mouth, on second look, and one certainly did look twice, was actually quite wide. It was also very mobile, open much of the time, with the small, conspicuously white teeth parted. She had an unsettling way of flicking her tongue forward so that you were aware of the tip of it striking the upper front teeth.

She was not quite tall, but willowy, which gave an impression of height. Her arms were rather short, her shoulders quite square, and she stood dancer-style with her feet spread and toed out, which brought her pelvis forward and her head back and up, there in the director's living room. She had the look of a woman standing her ground and at the same time enticing you to share it with her.

She was wearing black with a silver belt. The dress bared her neck and collarbones but was not cut low. Instead it was slit, down to the diaphragm, and under it she must have been wearing one of those wire brassieres that create a look of nudity down the center of the chest while providing a slightly unnatural amount of breast separation. It was provocative enough.

She also grabbed my hand with both of hers when we were introduced, not quite pulling me toward her, and exhaled a small sound of some sort. Noel stood beaming at her side.

Say she was overdoing, if you like; that form of greeting wasn't used on me alone, I'd better add. As the evening went on, she was conducting public dalliance simultaneously with as many of us as could crowd around, four or five at a time.

"I don't know if I can get to like it here," she said. "Noel has us at that Holiday Inn so far, up on the hill. It makes me apprehensive, looking down at your lights, not knowing what to expect." Suddenly she showed us her right palm, ran the fingertips of her left hand over it. "Damp. That's how lie detectors work, isn't it? I couldn't fool a lie detector."

Then she touched the damp palm to her cheek, smiled, flicked her tongue, and wiped the hand on her hip lightly. I remember being both smitten, as were all the other men, and struck by the thought that there was something wrong, something consonant with the overdone greeting. It was what was missing from the voice—a young, light, reasonably well educated, Eastern-city voice. It didn't have, in spite of the smiles and the flicking tongue, much fun in it.

Generally a good coquette, doing her magic publicly, will spurt, shimmer, and sparkle with a kind of laughter, now open, now repressed, a laughter both at the men for being gulled and at herself for spending all that gorgeous candlepower on gulling them. Brilliance, raillery, self-mockery, all of it in fun: Dawn Butler's performance didn't have those qualities. It was as if she had already passed on, with each man who listened to her, beyond flirtation, to some further stage in a relationship already intimate, about to be serious, even dangerous.

The next thing would almost have to be a note, folded very small, pressed into your hand, to be read urgently, secretly, and the note would say, "Where is your car parked?" or even "Save me."

I have splendid resistance to people who dramatize themselves. So when Dawn said, to someone offering her a whiskey, "Oh, but I only drink wine," I collided with the director in the living room doorway, both of us rushing to the kitchen, where I'd left a bottle of wine and he had several on the shelf. Dawn was twenty-two years old.

The other time I saw her that fall was the next evening; she was more relaxed. She and Noel were with some of his student friends, drinking beer at Hickey's Tavern. They asked me to join them, and I did for a few minutes, sitting down by Dawn, asking her about the place Noel had found for them to live in. She replied by taking my wrist between her thumb and forefinger, looking into my eyes, holding on for a couple of beats, and then squeezing quite hard. But her voice, when she let go, was sultry and amused: "Don't you know? Don't you really know? I'm being taken out to a farm, miles away. I'll never see you again."

She came close to being right about that, but before I go on I want to be fair to Dawn. She did display, there with the student group, a little gaiety. It wasn't sparkling, perhaps, but it wasn't stagy, either—a sort of sweet naughtiness that was quite engaging and that had the student males riding around no-hands and standing on their heads, at about the same junior high school level to which she'd reduced the staff the night before.

Then she was gone. Noel did take her far from this city, more than twenty miles, but not just in distance. He came as close as you can to taking her away in time as well, about three centuries.

He took her to an Amish farm, where he had rented the small, spare house intended for the parents when the inheriting son took the place in charge. I will have to tell you a little more about the Amish in a moment. They are, of course, the people who call themselves "plain," the lace-capped women and bearded men who drive buggies and still farm with horses.

"Are you surprised Dawn was willing to go down there?" Noel asked me, visiting one day soon afterward in my office. "I admit I didn't give her much choice."

I said something dumb, like "It should be an interesting experience for both of you."

"We've had enough interesting experiences," Noel said, and

then, not very smooth for once: "Dawn agrees. She does now. After Boston—well, look. Otherwise I wouldn't have brought her and Jimmer out here in spite of missing her so much. I told her."

Jimmer, I remembered, was her little boy, but I didn't actually see him until spring.

And now you've got to hear about the winter, and more about the Amish, too.

The winter that Dawn and Noel Butler, and Dawn's son—strange changeling child of a passionate adolescent girl and a perverse, creative man, much older—never mind. That winter was a bitch.

It snowed early, got cold, stayed cold. The country roads were often impassable, and it was a struggle for Noel to get back and forth to meet his classes. But he would tell me, from time to time, that it was worth it to him, and I understood him to mean that he and Dawn were happy and cozy and trusting.

About the Amish I'll try not to tell you any more than you need to know. They include several conservative splinter groups from the Mennonite Church, and of them all the most conservative are the Old Order Amish. Like all Mennonites, they are pacifist, believe in nonresistance, refuse to take oaths, and are very strict in matters of recreation and self-indulgence. The Old Order Amish, in addition, try to live just as the first of their faith did in 1650—wearing similar clothing, hairstyles, and face-hair styles, farming by the same methods, without the use of engines or electricity. They are a God-and-family-centered people, and their way of life endures, in its enclaves in Indiana, Pennsylvania, Iowa, and Oregon, because of its tight structure in which the children are brought up believing that they are, like their parents, among the chosen very, very few. They are not quaint; they are proud. They own excellent small farms, farm them well, and pass them along carefully through the generations.

They maintain their own schools, which go only through the eighth grade. They take a distant, not altogether unworldly, interest in us, whom they must meet in bargaining situations, and a very intense interest in one another. Community is hardly less important to them than family.

On the Old Order Amish farm where Dawn, Noel, and Dawn's child spent the winter, there was a patriarch as head of the household, a widower in his late sixties. His older sons were established with

families on farms of their own, which he'd helped buy; the youngest
son, of whom, Noel said, the old man was particularly proud, was
heir designate to the family farm. This heir was called Daniel.

Daniel was thirty-two, with a wife and seven children. Noel
found him a scrupulous landlord. Though Daniel worked an extremely long, hard day, he would always take time to make sure
Dawn and Noel's cottage was snug and in repair. But though he had
provided the cottage with electricity, as well as a telephone, when he
and his father had decided to rent it, he would not use power tools
nor himself turn off or on a light.

"Strong arms, bright blue eyes, and a reddish-brown beard,"
Noel said. "With that upper lip shaved clean the way they do. He's
always so solemn when we see him, and he won't let his wife or any of
the kids come in our door."

That was as much as I knew about the family when Noel arrived
at my house, just before noon on a spring day, to say that Daniel, the
Amish farmer, had tried to kill him.

Every story has its relatives. This one is some sort of cousin, in my
mind, to a play I saw as a boy, called *Rain*. In the play, as I remember
it, a missionary and a loose woman are trapped in a hotel in the trop-
ics by incessant rain, which becomes her ally in the temptation and
seduction of the man. Dawn's allies were cold, wind, snow, and ice,
perhaps, but I don't want to push the comparison with the old play
too far: Dawn, after all, was still quite girlish, and Daniel's rectitude
was of a personal, not a missionary, kind.

Noel said that as a matter of fact, Dawn first reacted to Daniel
with some awe. Noel couldn't say just when Dawn had started regarding Daniel as either an interesting possibility or an actual attraction. Noel admitted quite abjectly his own stupidity. He and the winter had made Dawn and Daniel the only man and woman in the
world.

My guess is that she was simply, in the beginning, unable to keep
from making just a very slight test of Daniel, a little test of herself as
well, with no serious motive except curiosity—I'm willing to see it as
innocent curiosity, if it wasn't actually unconscious—just to see if
he'd respond to her at all. And once he'd responded just a little—was
it with a stammer, or a blush, or a clumsy pressing back against a

pressing hand?—then it may suddenly have been too late for both of them.

She had to go on with it. The ice and snow insisted, and her imprisonment. Daniel, I imagine, fought and prayed—and came back for another press of the hand, and one day a hug, and—how much later?—something that was barely the first kiss.

It would all have been very gradual, very difficult, very absorbing to the two imaginations, in a rhythm deliberate as seasons changing. I thought of Dawn, passing her winter days that way, moving toward him, guardedly, the excitement allowed to grow very slowly, having to keep the embraces, as they intensified little by little, out of sight of her child, her husband, the Amish family. The potential lovers were as hemmed in, as hard put to find times of privacy, as any couple could be.

"I know when it finally happened," Noel said. It clearly hurt him to tell me, but he had to. "The first time. Dawn and I drove into Yodertown one afternoon to shop and didn't start back until after dark. It was storming by then, a wet, wild, late-winter storm, with ruts and mud frozen on the surface, soft and treacherous underneath, and the wind howling and freezing and the snow blowing. We got to within about three miles of the place before the windshield wouldn't clear anymore and I ran off the road and got us stuck in the ditch.

"I was wearing boots and outdoor clothing, though not really enough of it. Dawn would never dress for winter when we were going somewhere in a heated car. Her shoes were thin and even had heels on them. She was wearing a kind of high-fashion wool cloak that looked romantic as hell, but nothing to keep the wind out. I'd have given her my hat and jacket, but there was no way to beat the shoe problem.

"We had most of a tank of gas. I might have stayed with her, but Jimmer was home and hungry and the night was scary. The car'd be twice as hard to get out in the morning, when I had to get to school. We decided I'd better go for help. Dawn was to run the motor periodically for heat and to turn on the headlights for half a minute out of every five, to show where she was. So I left.

"God, it was a terrible walk. It kept getting colder. The wind got higher, and the snowfall was the heaviest I've ever been out in. I could hardly see. Luckily, it was coming at my back, but I still stumbled and struggled in the bad footing, and once I got so far off the road I ran into barbed-wire fence. It probably took me an hour to go three miles. I was going to phone . . ." Noel hesitated. "As a matter of fact, Vance, I was going to phone you, because I knew you had a four-wheel-drive truck. I hoped when the storm let up, you could find the place and wouldn't mind coming after me so we could get Dawn and try to pull the car out."

I nodded.

"When I finally got there, the phone was out. The lights, too. Jimmer was terrified. I didn't know what to do. I lit candles and tried to comfort the boy. The stove worked all right, so I fixed him some soup. I remember standing there, stirring it, with my teeth chattering. I couldn't get warm.

"I thought of putting Jimmer to bed under blankets, taking Dawn's winter boots and jacket, and walking back, but I wasn't too sure I could make it, going against that wind, or that she could, coming back. I decided I was going to have to get Daniel's help and advice. I should be able to say that some damn warning voice told me not to, but it isn't so. Whatever'd been happening, they'd concealed it very well.

"Anyway, I didn't know if his team of horses and the closed carriage—a sort of van they use in the winter—could go through the weather. I was wondering about that when he knocked at the door. He'd seen the candlelight. He knew the car hadn't come in. He came to check up, and I explained.

"When he learned that Dawn was out there alone, Daniel got quite upset. Especially, I suppose, because, not being familiar with cars, he couldn't believe that she was safe and comfortable.

"I asked if his team could go out, and he said no.

"I asked what he thought we should do, and he said, 'Likely I'll take tractor to pull out. Sure.' I was almost shocked. There was this monstrous, big old iron-wheeled tractor in the barn. One of Daniel's older brothers had bought it years before, when some of the Old Order people argued that a tractor was permissible on the farm so long as it didn't have rubber tires. Instead, these tractors had lugs, almost spikes, and they tore up the country roads so bad the Secondary

Roads Department banned them. Daniel himself didn't use the tractor, but he'd learned to drive it as a boy—an act of rebellion, I suppose, if not real wickedness. A couple of times a year the older brother would come over and start the thing up and do maintenance on it.

"I asked if I should ride along. Daniel didn't even answer. I was in no shape to go out again, anyway. The night was getting worse. Jimmer was there. I gave Daniel Dawn's boots and things to take along, and out he went in his coat and overalls. They're not allowed to use buttons. Their clothes are held together with safety pins. He had a scarf and a black, broadbrimmed hat, knit gloves and galoshes. After a while I heard the big old machine start, and then I heard it lumber past our little house. It didn't have any lights."

Here I paused, as Noel had paused. I looked around the class and seemed to have their attention; but it was hard to tell about Katie Jay, my smart student. Her eyes were down and away, studying her tabletop.

Wouldn't Daniel's father and the Amish family (I asked the class) have heard that tractor moving out? They might have taken it for the county snowplow passing on the road.

The rest is much too easy to imagine: Daniel on his iron tractor seat, laboring against the unfamiliar steering wheel, turning into the wind, chugging through the night. Snow and dark, forces of nature storming in his face, trying to turn him back; the scarf tight, facial skin around his beard getting numb, hands and feet freezing as the slow machine gripped and bumped. But after a time he'd have started to see the faint glimmering of the headlights at long intervals, calling him to her. I don't know whether in his own mind he was damned before he got there; but the great, clanking, spike-wheeled thing he rode was an engine of sin, no question. And it failed him, going into the ditch itself a hundred yards before he reached the car, so that he finished getting there on foot.

Imagine Daniel knocking, then, on the deeply frosted window, and Dawn opening the door to what must have looked like a man of ice.

"Is it Daniel?"

"Are you all right, missus?"

"Daniel, get in. Get in. You'll die out there."

"But it's you worries me."

"Please. Get in."

He does. The door closes. And they are trapped together in the night. There is a nearly frozen man to thaw. She holds him. She croons to him. She wipes his hair and beard with her cloak. I think that an embrace develops out of this, gets almost violent before, perhaps with a sob, he pulls away. And the wind howls, the snow blows and piles. Dawn waits. Perhaps she touches him, and, with another sob, he hurls himself at her again and is, after how many engagements, received into a warmth like no other.

That this happened, Noel was quite sure—whatever guilts and indecisions followed, whatever withdrawals and renewals—because of what took place the next night. It was clear and extremely cold, and in the morning there was a curious frozen smudge in the center of one of the panes of glass in their bedroom window. Jimmer said someone had looked in, very late. Dawn said it was the boy's imagination. But Noel felt sure that the smudge was made, and others like it as other nights came and went, by the Amish farmer pressing his cheek against the cold glass that separated him from the woman he loved.

"God, how we've fought since then," Noel said. "I knew. Dawn has a crazy-lady act that goes with having an affair. I'd seen it before. So I accused her.

" 'Oh, what fun, Noel darling, who?'

" 'Daniel,' I said, and she almost had hysterics laughing at me. She pulled a handful of her hair around and held it to her chin for a beard, and ran around being Daniel, getting drunk on carrot juice and pinching pumpkins on the fanny.... I said to cut it out, that I knew for sure, and she said oh, then she'd run and get Daniel so I could tell him all about it.

"Yesterday I got home an hour before she expected me. I saw Daniel leave the house. I went in, and Jimmer was napping. Dawn said Daniel was getting the sink unclogged. This morning I looked, and then I showed her, there's no way that sink could clog up because the drain's so big. You couldn't stop it up with a sweater.

"So she grabbed a sweater of mine and started stuffing it into the drain, and I told her to go to hell, I was leaving. I got out a suitcase and started to pack it. She grabbed the clothes out of it and ran out the door, screaming and dropping my stuff all over the yard. I was furious. I ran out after her, and there was Daniel, over by the barn, working on that monstrous tractor with a wrench as long as your arm.

"Dawn ran over and got behind him, pointing at me, and right away Daniel started for me with that wrench. First I couldn't believe it. Then I ran. I ran to the car with Daniel after me, and he pounded the car with the wrench as I drove away. You can see the dents, Vance. Look."

Well (I said to the class), Noel needed his clothes and his books. He was afraid to go back. I said I'd go, and my phone rang.

"Is Noel there?" It was Dawn.

"Yes."

"Will he talk to me?"

I asked. Noel shook his head. "I'm sorry," I said.

"Tell him Daniel has to see him."

I did. Noel turned pale and whispered, "Oh, my God."

I covered the mouthpiece and said, "Noel, I don't know the man, but I'll bet you anything he wants to beg your pardon."

"Ask Dawn," Noel said, and I did.

"Daniel's in an agony of shame," Dawn said. "I think he wants to get down on his knees to Noel."

I passed that along. "She's such a liar," Noel said, but he agreed to a meeting with Daniel. I went too. It took place in a local filling station, owned by a backslid uncle of Daniel's. The young farmer was pretty close to tears, if not quite on his knees. He wanted Noel to forgive him and to pray for him, but afterward Noel still felt wary about going for his stuff. I went, after all, and saw Dawn again.

Her appearance was strained—we none of us come out of the winters here looking terrific—but her manner was curiously relaxed. I found her, this time, easy to talk to. She seemed to be waiting, without any great anxiety, to see what would happen. None of the Amish family was in sight when I drove in, nor were they when I drove out again.

Noel graduated and left eight years ago. But Dawn and Jimmer are still in Indiana, as far as I know, living between Gary and Michigan City, by the shore of the big lake. They went there with Daniel.

He gave it all up, his God, his inheritance, his family, his community. He's working up there as a truck driver, I understand.

I paused and said, "Okay. True story." Then I looked toward Katie Jay, the bright student I spoke of, who often asserts the privilege of first comment; but her eyes were on her hands and her hands were still on the table in front of her. "Who wants to pick a point-of-view character for it?"

Dave, who is fast and sedulous, said, "Yours. I don't see anything wrong with the way you told it."

"But it stays a raconteur's story," I said. "A pastime. What happens if you use one of the characters?"

"The raconteur could be more involved," Dave said. "Something could happen to him, as a consequence. Or he could be more of a commentator, more cynical or more compassionate or more open about drawing a moral."

"Let's drop him, anyway," I said. "And tell it from Noel's point of view. What happens?"

Ernie's hand went up—but let me summarize rather than try to quote our discussion.

No acceptable serious story could be told from Noel's point of view, the class felt, because he would be weak and a loser, just one more sensitive young man betrayed and asking for our pity. But there were comic possibilities—a mean, ironic one if Noel were the kind of flawed narrator who, thinking he has the reader's sympathy, shows that he really drove Dawn straight into Daniel's arms. Or, said someone, give Noel enough perspective to be aware of that himself now and it could be a farce, about the smart guy who outsmarts himself but comes out a winner anyway because he's free of an impossible situation.

The talk of flawed narrators led to some discussion of having the story seen and heard through the eyes and ears of Jimmer, the child, whose understanding of certain things might be precocious and exceed the reader's, the reader in turn seeing other things of which Jimmer would be unaware. Several in the class saw that solution as being too literary and as taking away a certain harsh dignity the story might have if it were Daniel's.

From Daniel's point of view, we'd have a serious psychological melodrama to write, full of guilt, struggle, and prayer. We would have to decide whether to regard him as a victim or not, and the piece could be pretty heavy going. What about doing it as Dawn would see it?

"A sappy romance," someone said, a male.

"Depends on Dawn," said one of the women. "It could be a sophisticated romance if she's sophisticated. It could even be another kind of comedy, you know, if you make her able to deal with his religion thing."

Again I looked at Katie Jay. I really wanted to hear her get going on Dawn Butler. I expected a strong, funny attack. This was because Katie Jay had once explained to me, when we were speaking about a very cool man-woman piece she'd written, that sex was something she could not take seriously. When she was fifteen, Katie Jay said, and had her first boyfriend, her mother had simply put an extra pillow on the bed. That was all sex meant to slim-necked, caustic Katie Jay, with her shiny blond head and sharp tongue: the essence of no big deal.

When she had nothing to say, I asked my final question: "Is there any way this story could be written as a serious tragedy?" Then I answered myself: Yes, again as a function of choosing a particular point of view. Recently, I explained, I have come to know a very old Amish farmer, a fine, thoughtful man in his seventies. He is, although he interests himself a little in worldly matters, essentially and attractively an innocent man, if not naive. His name is Aaron, and I can admire if not quite envy him. He has lived that life structured for him by fanatical Dutch peasants three centuries ago, and has been fulfilled by it.

"Suppose," I said, "we think of Daniel's father as a man like Aaron, which he must have been. A man who, if only because of his years, is aware before the rest, before Daniel even, of what might happen, yet too appalled to think it really will. He is a man who can truly and simply use a word like *Jezebel* and feel the damnation in it. And he's a patriarch, waiting to be consulted and obeyed, but he will hesitate a long time, too long, to acknowledge so great a sin as actual. Suppose we saw through Aaron's eyes not just the loss, day by day, of his finest son, but the way in which it foretells the whole structure

492

breaking down, the wearing away of order in the world—wouldn't that point of view give you a chance to build some tragic power?"

The class couldn't disagree, because I wouldn't let them. It was one of those days when I felt like having the last word, and it was time to dismiss them anyway. But as they went out, free and clamorous, Katie Jay was still sitting as she had been, not jumping up in her usual way to cry out sharply to her friends, proclaim where they were to go to have a beer. She sat there, uncharacteristically still, but finally she did look up at me.

I went around the table to her and smiled. Katie Jay's hand moved up and took my arm above the elbow, and the grip, between thumb and forefinger, reminded me of another's grip, ten years before, on my wrist.

"Yes, Katie?"

She continued looking at me for a moment. Then her eyes went away, her face turned back toward the table, and she released my arm.

"Katie Jay?"

She shook her head. She gathered up her books and stood. I moved aside, concerned, confused, a little cross, and watched her walk to the door of the classroom where she turned back to look at me again.

"I need him," Katie Jay said, and there was nothing cool, nothing detached, nothing even very smart about her voice. "Oh, I need that Amish farmer. Don't you see?"

[October 1980]

TIM O'BRIEN

The Ghost Soldiers

I was shot twice. The first time, out by Tri Binh, it knocked me against the pagoda wall, and I bounced and spun around and ended up on Teddy Thatcher's lap. Lucky thing, because Teddy was the medic. He tied on a compress and told me to take a nap, then he ran off toward the fighting. For a long time I lay there all alone, listening to the battle, thinking, *I've been shot, I've been shot.* Winged, grazed, creased: all those Gene Autry movies I'd seen as a kid. In fact, I even laughed. Except then I started to think I might bleed to death. It was the fear, mostly, but I felt awful wobbly, and then I had a sinking sensation, ears all plugged up, as if I'd gone deep under water. Thank God for Teddy Thatcher. Every so often, maybe four times altogether, he trotted back to check me out. Which took guts. It was a wild fight, lots of noise, guys running and laying down fire, regrouping, running again, no front or rear, real chaos, but Teddy took the risks. "Easy does it," he said. "Just a side wound—no problem unless you're pregnant. You pregnant, buddy?" He ripped off the compress, applied a fresh one, and told me to clamp it in place with my fingers. "Press hard," he said. "Don't worry about the baby; too late to save it." Teddy wiped the blood off his hands. "No more house calls, pal. Gotta run." Then he took off. It was almost dark before the fighting petered out and the chopper came to take me and two dead guys away. "Adios, amigo," Teddy said in his fake Mexican accent. "Happy trails to you." I was barely feeling up to it, but I said, "Oh, Cisco," and Teddy wrapped his arms around me and kissed my neck and said, "Oh, Pancho!" Then the bird took off. On the ride in to Chu Lai, I kept waiting for the pain to come. I squeezed my fists tight and bit down, but actually I couldn't feel much. A throb, that's all. Even in the hospital it wasn't bad.

When I got back to Delta Company twenty-six days later, in mid-March, Teddy Thatcher was dead, and a new medic named Jorgenson had replaced him. Jorgenson was no Teddy. Incompetent and wimpy and scared. So when I got shot the second time, in the butt, along the Song Tra Bong, it took the son of a bitch almost ten minutes to work up the courage to crawl over to me. By then I was gone with the pain. Later I found out I'd almost died of shock. Jorgenson didn't know about shock, or if he knew, the fear made him forget. To make it worse, the guy bungled the patch job, and a couple of weeks later my ass started to rot away. You could actually peel off chunks of meat with your fingernail.

I was borderline gangrene. I spent a month flat on my belly—couldn't play cards, couldn't sleep. I kept seeing Jorgenson's scared-green face. Those buggy eyes, the way his lips twitched, that silly excuse for a moustache. After the rot cleared up, once I could think straight, I devoted a lot of time to figuring ways to get back at him.

Getting shot should be an experience from which you can draw a little pride. I'm not talking macho crap; I'm not saying you should strut around with your Purple Hearts on display. All I mean is that you should be able to *talk* about it: the stiff thump of the bullet, the way it knocks the air out of you and makes you cough, the sound of the shot when it comes about ten decades later, the dizzy feeling, the disbelief, the smell of yourself, the stuff you think about and say and do right afterward, the way your eyes focus on a tiny pebble or a blade of grass and how you think, man, that's the last thing I'll ever see, *that* pebble, *that* blade of grass, which makes you want to cry. Pride isn't the right word; I don't know the right word. All I know is, you shouldn't feel embarrassed. Humiliation shouldn't be part of it.

Diaper rash, the nurses called it. They sprinkled me with talcum powder and patted my ass and said "Git-cha-goo, git-cha-goo." Male nurses, too. That was the worst part. It made me hate Jorgenson the way some guys hated Charlie—ear-cutting hate, the kind atrocities are made of.

I guess the higher-ups decided I'd been shot enough. In early May, when I was released from the Ninety-first Evac Hospital, they transferred me over to headquarters company—S-4, the battalion supply section. Compared with the boonies, of course, it was cushy duty. Regular hours, movies, floor shows, the blurry slow motion of the rear. Fairly safe, too. The battalion firebase was built into a big hill just off Highway One, surrounded on all sides by flat paddy land, and between us and the paddies there were plenty of bunkers and sandbags and rolls of razor-tipped barbed wire. Sure, you could still die there—once a month or so we'd get hit with some mortar fire—but what the hell, you could die in the bleachers at Fenway Park, bases loaded, Yaz coming to the plate. Safety is relative; it's never permanent.

I wasn't complaining. Naturally there were times when I halfway wanted to head back to the field; I missed adventure, the friendships, even the danger. A hard thing to explain to somebody who hasn't felt it. Danger, it makes things vivid. When you're afraid, really afraid, you taste your own spit, you see things you never saw before, you pay attention. On the other hand, though, I wasn't crazy. I'd already taken two bullets; the odds were deadly. So I just settled in, took it easy, counted myself lucky. I figured my war was over. If it hadn't been for the constant ache in my butt, I guess things would've worked out fine.

But Jesus, it *hurt*. Torn-up muscle, nerves like live electric wires: it was pain.

Pain, you know?

At night, for example, I had to sleep on my belly. Doesn't sound so terrible until you consider that I'd been a back-sleeper all my life. It got to where I was almost an insomniac. I'd lie there all fidgety and tight, then after a while I'd get angry. I'd squirm around on my cot, cussing, half-nuts with hurt, then I'd start remembering stuff. Jorgenson. I'd think, Jesus Christ, I almost died. Shock—how could the bastard forget to treat for shock? Diaper rash, butt rot. I'd remember how long it took him to get to me, how his fingers were all jerky and nervous, the way his lips twitched under that ridiculous moustache. The nights were miserable.

Sometimes I'd roam around the base. I'd head down to the wire and stare out at the darkness, out where the war was, all those ghosts, and I'd count ways to make Jorgenson suffer.

One thing for sure. You forget how much you use your butt until you can't use it anymore.

In July, Delta Company came in for stand-down. I was there on the helipad to meet the choppers. Curtis and Lemon and Azar slapped hands with me—jokes, dirty names, disguised affection—then I piled their gear in my jeep and drove them down to the Delta hootches. We partied until chow time. Afterward, we kept on partying. It was one of the rituals. Even if you weren't in the mood, you did it on principle.

By midnight it was story time.

"Morty Becker wasted his luck," said Lemon. "No lie," said Azar.

I smiled and waited. There was a tempo to how stories got told. Lemon peeled open a finger blister and sucked on it and wagged his head sadly.

"Go on," Azar said. "Tell it."

"Becker used up his luck. Pissed it away."

"On *nothin'*," Azar said.

Lemon nodded, started to speak, then stopped and got up and moved to the cooler and shoved his hands deep into the ice. He was naked except for his socks and his dog tags. In a way, I envied him—all of them. Those deep bush tans, the jungle sores and blisters, the stories, the in-it-togetherness. I felt close to them, yes, but I also felt separate.

Bending forward, Lemon scooped ice up against his chest, pressing it there for a moment, eyes closed; then he fished out a beer and snapped it open.

"It was out by My Khe," he said. "Remember My Khe? Bad-ass country, right? A blister of a day, hot-hot, and we're just sort of groovin' it, lyin' around, nobody bustin' ass or anything. I mean, listen, it's *hot*. We're poppin' salt tabs just to stay conscious. Finally somebody says, 'Hey, where's Becker?' The captain does a head count, and guess what? No Becker."

"Gone," Azar said. "Vanished."

"Ghosts."

"Poof, no fuckin' Becker."

"We send out two patrols—no dice. Not a trace." Lemon poured beer on his open blister, slowly licked the foam off. "By then it's getting dark. Captain's about ready to have a fit—you know how he gets, right?—and then, guess what? Take a guess."

"Becker shows," I said.

"You got it, man. Becker shows. We've almost chalked him up as MIA, and then, bingo, he shows."

"Soaking wet," Azar said.

"Hey—"

"Okay, it's your story, but *tell* it."

Lemon frowned. "Soaking wet," he said.

"Ha!"

"Turns out he went for a swim. You believe that? All by himself, the moron just takes off, hikes a couple klicks, finds himself a river, strips, hops in, no security, no *nothin'.* Dig it? He goes swimming."

Azar giggled. "A hot day."

"Not that hot," murmured Curtis Young. "Not that fuckin' hot."

"Hot, though."

"Get the picture?" Lemon said. "I mean, this is My Khe we're talking about. Doomsville, and the guy goes for a *swim.*"

"Yeah," I said. "Crazy."

I looked across the hootch. Thirty or forty guys were there, some drinking, some passed out, but I couldn't find Morty Becker among them.

Lemon grinned. He reached out and put his hand on my knee and squeezed.

"That's the kicker, man. No more Becker."

"No?"

"The kicker's this," Lemon said, "Morty Becker's luck gets all used up. See? On a lousy swim."

"And that's the truth. That's the truth," said Azar.

Lemon's hand still rested on my knee, very gently. The fingers were quivering a little

"What happened?"

"Ah, shit."

"Go on, tell."

"Fatality," Lemon said. "Couple days later, maybe a week, Becker gets real dizzy. Pukes a lot, temperature zooms way up. Out of sight, you know? Jorgenson says he must've swallowed bad water on that swim. Swallowed a virus or something."

"Jorgenson," I said. "Where is my good buddy Jorgenson?"

"Hey, look—"

"Just tell me where to find him."

Lemon made a quick clicking sound with his tongue. "You want to *hear* this? Yes or no?"

"Sure, but where's—"

"Listen up. Becker gets sick, right? Sick, sick, sick. Never seen nobody so bad off, *never*. Sicko! Arms jerkin' all over hell, can't walk, can't talk, can't fart, can't nothin'. Like he's paralyzed. Can't move. Polio, maybe."

Curtis Young shook his head. "Not polio. You got it wrong."

"Maybe polio."

"No way," Curtis said. "Not polio."

"*Maybe*," Lemon said. "I'm just saying what Jorgenson says. Maybe fuckin' polio. Or that elephant disease. Elephantiasshole or whatever."

"But not polio."

Azar smiled and snapped his fingers. "Either way," he said, "it goes to show. Don't throw away luck on little stuff. Save it up."

"That's the lesson, all right."

"Becker was due."

"There it is. Overdue. Don't fritter away your luck."

"Fuckin' polio."

Lemon closed his eyes.

We sat quietly. No need to talk, because we were thinking about the same things: about Mort Becker, the way luck worked and didn't work, how it was impossible to gauge the odds. Maybe the disease was lucky. Who knows? Maybe it saved Morty from getting shot.

"Where's Jorgenson?" I said.

"Ease off on that," Lemon whispered. "Let it go."

"Sure. No sweat, no sweat. But where's the son of a bitch hiding?"

Another thing: Three times a day, no matter what, I had to stop whatever I was doing, go find a private place, drop my pants, bend over, and apply this antibacterial ointment to my ass. No choice—I had to do it. And the worst part was how the ointment left yellow stains on the seat of my trousers, big greasy splotches. Herbie's hemorrhoids, that was one of the jokes. There were plenty of other jokes, too—plenty.

During the first full day of Delta's stand-down, I didn't run into Jorgenson once. Not at chow, not at the flicks, not during our long booze sessions in the hootch.

I didn't hunt him down, though. I just waited.

"Forget it," Lemon said. "Granted, the man messed up bad, real bad, but you got to take into account how green he was. Just a tenderfoot. Brand new. Remember?"

"I forget. Remind me."

"You survived."

I showed Lemon the yellow stain on my britches. "I'm in terrific shape. Really funny, right?"

"Not exactly," Lemon said.

But he was laughing. He started snapping a towel at my backside. I laughed—I couldn't help it—but I didn't see the big joke.

Later, after some dope, Lemon said: "The thing is, Jorgenson's doing all right. Better and better. People change, they adapt. I mean, okay, he's not a Teddy Thatcher, he won't win medals or anything, but the poor dude hangs in there, he knows his shit. Kept Becker alive."

"My sore ass."

Lemon nodded. He shrugged, leaned back, popped the hot roach into his mouth, chewed for a long time. "You've lost touch, man. Jorgenson . . . he's *with* us now."

"I'm not."

"No," he said. "I guess you're not."

"Good old loyalty."

"War."

"Friends in need, friends get peed on."

Lemon shook his head. "We're friends, Herbie. You and me. But look, you're not *out* there anymore, and Jorgenson is. If you'd just seen him the past couple of weeks—the way he handled Becker, then when Pinko hit the mine—I mean, the kid did some good work. Ask anybody. So . . . I don't know. If it was me, Herbie, I'd say screw it. Leave it alone."

"I won't hurt him."

"Right."

"I won't. Show him some ghosts, that's all."

In the morning I spotted Jorgenson. I was up on the helipad, loading the resupply choppers, and then, when the last bird took off, while I was putting on my shirt, I looked up, half-squinting, and there he was. In a way, it was a shock. His size, I mean. Even smaller than I remembered—a little squirrel of a guy, five and a half feet tall, skinny and mousy and sad.

He was leaning against my jeep, waiting for me.

"Herb," he said, "can we talk?"

At first I just looked at his boots.

Those boots: I remembered them from when I got shot. Out along the Song Tra Bong, a bullet in my ass, all that pain, and the funny thing was that what I remembered, now, were those new boots—no scuffs; smooth, unblemished leather. One of those last details, Jorgenson's boots.

"Herb?"

I looked at his eyes—a long, straight-on stare—and he blinked and made a stabbing motion at his nose and backed off a step. Oddly, I felt some pity for him. A bona fide card-carrying twit. The tiniest arms and wrists I'd ever seen—a sparrow's nervous system. He made me think of those sorry kids back in junior high who used to spend their time collecting stamps and butterflies, always off by themselves, no friends, no hope.

He took another half-step backward and said, very softly, "Look, I just wanted . . . I'm sorry, Herb."

I didn't move or look away or anything.

"Herb?"

"Talk, talk, talk."

"What can I say? It was—"

"Excuses?"

Jorgenson's tongue flicked out, then slipped away. He shook his head. "No, it was a bungle, and I don't . . . I was *scared*. All the noise and everything, the shooting, I'd never seen that before. I couldn't make myself move. After you got hit, I kept telling myself to move, move, but I couldn't *do* it. Like I was full of Novocain or something. You ever feel like that? Like you can't even move?"

"Anyway," I said.

"And then I heard how you . . . the shock, the gangrene. Man, I felt like . . . couldn't sleep, couldn't eat. Nightmares, you know? Kept seeing you lying out there, heard you screaming, and . . . it was like my legs were filled up with cement. I *couldn't.*"

His lip trembled, and he made a weird moaning sound—not quite a moan, feathery and high—and for a second I was afraid he might start crying. That would've ended it. I was a sucker for tears. I would've patted his shoulder, told him to forget it. Thank God he tried to shake my hand. It gave me an excuse to spit.

"Kiss it," I said.

"Herb, I can't go back and do it over."

"Lick it, kiss it."

But Jorgenson just smiled. Very tentatively, like an invalid, he kept pushing his hand out at me. He looked so mournful and puppy-doggish, so damned hurt, that I made myself spit again. I didn't feel like spitting—my heart wasn't in it—but somehow I managed, and Jorgenson glanced away for a second, still smiling a weary little smile, resigned-looking, as if to show how generous he was, how big-hearted and noble.

It almost made me feel guilty.

I got into the jeep, hit the ignition, left him standing there.

Guilty, for Chrissake. Why should it end up with *me* feeling the guilt? I hated him for making me stop hating him.

Thing is, it had been a vow. *I'll get him, I'll get him*—it was down inside me like a stone. Except now I couldn't generate the passion. Couldn't feel the anger. I still had to get back at him, but now it was a need, not a want. An obligation. To rev up some intensity, I started drinking a little—more than a little, a lot. I remembered the river, getting shot, the pain, how I kept calling out for a medic, waiting and waiting and waiting, passing out once, waking up, screaming, how the scream seemed to make new pain, the awful stink of myself, the sweating and shit and fear, Jorgenson's clumsy fingers when he finally got around to working on me. I remembered it all, every detail. *Shock,* I thought. *I'm dying of shock.* I tried to tell him that, but my tongue didn't connect with my brain. All I could do was go, "Ough! Ough!" I wanted to say, "You *jerk!* I'm *dying!* Treat for shock, treat for shock!" I remembered all that, and the hospital, and those giggling nurses. I even remembered the rage. Except I couldn't feel it anymore. Just a word—*rage*—spelled out in my head. No *feeling.* In the end, all I had were the facts. Number one: the guy had almost killed me. Number two: there had to be consequences. Only thing was, I wished I could've gotten some pleasure out of them.

I asked Lemon to give me a hand.

"No pain," I said. "Basic psy-ops, that's all. We'll just scare him. Mess with his head a little."

"Negative," Lemon said.

"Just show him some ghosts."

"Sick, man."

"Not all *that* sick." I stuck a finger in Lemon's face. "Sick is getting shot. Try it sometime, you'll see what genuine sick is."

"No," he said.

"Comrade-in-arms. Such crap."

"I guess."

Stiffly, like a stranger, Lemon looked at me for a long time. Then he moved across the hootch and lay down with a comic book and pretended to read. His lips were moving, but that didn't fool me a bit.

I had to get Azar in on it.

Azar didn't have Lemon's intelligence, but he had a better sense of justice.

"Tonight?" he said.

"Just don't get carried away."

"Me?"

Azar grinned and snapped his fingers. It was a tic. Snap, snap—whenever things got tight, whenever there was a prospect of action.

"Understand?"

"Roger-dodger," Azar said. "Only a game, right?"

We called the enemy "ghosts." "Bad night," we'd murmur. "Ghosts are out." To get spooked, in the lingo, meant not only to get scared but to get killed. "Don't get spooked," we'd say. "Stay cool, stay alive." The countryside was spooky; snipers, tunnels, ancestor worship, ancient papa-sans, incense. The land was haunted. We were fighting forces that didn't obey the laws of twentieth-century science. Deep in the night, on guard, it seemed that all of Nam was shimmering and swaying—odd shapes swirling in the dark; phantoms; apparitions; spirits in the abandoned pagodas; boogeymen in sandals. When a guy named Olson was killed, in February, everybody started saying, "The Holy Ghost took him." And when Ron Ingo hit the booby trap, in April, somebody said he'd been made into a deviled egg—no arms, no legs, just a poor deviled egg.

It was ghost country, and Charlie was the main ghost. The way he came out at night. How you never really saw him, just thought you did. Almost magical—appearing, disappearing. He could levitate. He could pass through barbed wire. He was invisible, blending with the land, changing shape. He could fly. He could melt away like ice. He could creep up on you without sound or footsteps. He was scary.

In the daylight, maybe, you didn't believe in all this stuff. You laughed, you made jokes. But at night you turned into a believer: no skeptics in foxholes.

Azar was wound up tight. All afternoon, while we made preparations, he kept chanting, "Halloween, Halloween." That, plus the finger snapping, almost made me cancel the whole operation. I went hot and cold. Lemon wouldn't speak to me, which tended to cool it off, but then I'd start remembering things. The result was a kind of tepid numbness. No ice, no heat. I went through the motions like a sleepwalker—rigidly, by the numbers, no real emotion, no heart. I rigged up my special effects, checked out the battle terrain, measured distances, gathered the ordnance and gear we'd need. I was professional enough about it, I didn't miss a thing, but somehow it felt as if I were gearing up to fight somebody else's war. I didn't have that patriotic zeal.

Who knows? If there'd been a dignified way out, I might've taken it.

During evening chow, in fact, I kept staring across the mess hall at Jorgenson, and when he finally looked up at me, a puzzled frown on his face, I came very close to smiling. Very, very close. Maybe I was fishing for something. A nod, a bow, one last apology—anything. But Jorgenson only gazed back at me. In a strange way, too. As if he didn't *need* to apologize again. Just a straight, unafraid gaze. No humility at all.

To top if off, my ex-buddy Lemon was sitting with him, and they were having this chummy-chummy conversation, all smiles and sweetness.

That's probably what cinched it.

I went back to my hootch, showered, shaved, threw my helmet against the wall, lay down awhile, fidgeted, got up, prowled around, applied some fresh ointment, then headed off to find Azar.

Just before dusk, Delta Company stood for roll call. Afterward the men separated into two groups. Some went off to drink or sleep or catch a movie; the others trooped down to the base perimeter, where, for the next eleven hours, they would pull night guard duty. It was SOP—one night on, one night off.

The was Jorgenson's night on.

I knew that in advance, of course. And I knew his bunker assignment: number six, a pile of sandbags at the southwest corner of the perimeter. That morning I'd scouted every inch of his position; I knew the blind spots, the ripples of land, the places where he'd take cover in case of trouble. I was ready. To guard against freak screwups, though, Azar and I tailed him down to the wire. We watched him lay out his bedroll, connect the Claymores to their firing devices, test the radio, light up a cigarette, yawn, then sit back with his rifle cradled to his chest like a teddy bear.

"A pigeon," Azar whispered. "Roast pigeon on a spit. I smell it cookin'."

"Remember, though. This isn't for real."

Azar shrugged. He touched me on the shoulder, not roughly but not gently either. "What's real?" he said. "Eight months in Fantasyland, it tends to blur the line. Honest to God, I sometimes can't remember what real *is*."

Psychology—that was one thing I knew. I never went to college, and I wasn't exactly a whiz in high school either, but all my life I've paid attention to how things operate inside the skull. Example: You don't try to scare people in broad daylight. You wait. Why? Because the darkness squeezes you inside yourself, you get cut off from the outside world, the imagination takes over. That's basic psychology. I'd pulled enough night guard to know how the fear factor gets multiplied as you sit there hour after hour, nobody to talk to, nothing to do but stare blank-eyed into the Big Black Hole. The hours pile up. You drift; your brain starts to roam. You think about dark closets, madmen, murderers hiding under the bed, all those childhood fears. Fairy tales with gremlins and trolls and one-eyed giants. You try to block it all out but you can't. You see ghosts. You blink and laugh and shake your head. Bullshit, you say. But then you remember the guys who died: Teddy, Olson, Ingo, maybe Becker, a dozen others whose faces you can't see anymore. Pretty soon you begin to think about the stories you've heard about Charlie's magic. The time some guys cornered two VC in a dead-end tunnel, no way out, but how, when the tunnel was fragged and searched, nothing was found but dead rats. A hundred stories. A whole bookful: ghosts swinging from the trees, ghosts wiping out a whole Marine platoon in twenty seconds flat, ghosts rising from the dead, ghosts behind you and in front of you and inside you. Your ears get ticklish. Tiny sounds get heightened and distorted, crickets become monsters, the hum of the night takes on a weird electronic tingle. You try not to breathe. You coil and tighten up and listen. Your knuckles ache, and your pulse ticks like an alarm clock. What's *that?* You jerk up. Nothing, you say, nothing. Unless. . . . You check to be sure your weapon is loaded. Put it on full automatic. Count your grenades, make sure the pins are bent for quick throwing. Crouch lower. Listen, listen. And then, after enough time passes, things start to get bad.

"Come on, man," Azar said. "Let's *do* it." But I told him to be patient. "Waiting, that's half the trick," I said. "Give him time, let him simmer." So we went to the movies, *Barbarella* again, the sixth straight night. But it kept Azar happy—he was crazy about Jane Fonda. "Sweet Janie," he kept saying, over and over. "Sweet Janie boosts a man's morale." Then, with his hand, he showed me which part of his morale got boosted. An old joke. Everything was old. The movie, the heat, the booze, the war. I fell asleep during the second reel—a hot, angry sleep—and forty minutes later I woke up to a sore ass and a foul temper.

It wasn't yet midnight.

We hiked over to the EM club and worked our way through a six-pack. Lemon was there, at another table, but he pretended not to see me.

Around closing time, I made a fist and showed it to Azar. He smiled like a little boy. "Goody," he said. We picked up the gear, smeared charcoal on our faces, then moved down to the wire.

"Let's hurt him," Azar whispered. "Pain time for ol' Jorgy."

"No, man, listen to me—"

But Azar lifted his thumb and grinned and peeled away from me and began circling behind Bunker Six. For a second I couldn't move. Not fear, exactly; I don't know what it was. My boots felt heavy.

In a way, it was purely mechanical. I didn't think. I just shouldered the gear and crossed quietly over to a heap of boulders that overlooked Jorgenson's bunker.

I was directly behind him. Thirty-two meters away, exactly. My measurements were precise.

Even in the heavy darkness, no moon yet, I could make out Jorgenson's silhouette: a helmet, his shoulders, the rifle barrel. His back was to me. That was the heart of the psychology: he'd be looking out at the wire, the paddies, where the danger was; he'd figure his back was safe; only the chest and belly were vulnerable.

Quiet, quiet.

I knelt down, took out the flares, lined them up in front of me, unscrewed the caps, then checked my wristwatch. Still five minutes to go. Edging over to my left, I groped for the ropes, found them wedged in the crotch of two boulders. I separated them and tested the tension and checked the time again. One minute.

My head was light. Fluttery and taut at the same time. It was the feeling I remembered from the boonies, on ambush or marching at night through ghost country. Peril and doubt and awe, all those things and a million more. You wonder if you're dreaming. Unreal, unreal. As if molting, you seem to slip outside yourself. It's like you're in a movie. There's a camera on you, so you begin acting, following the script: "Oh, Cisco!" You think of all the films you've seen, Audie Murphy and Gary Cooper and Van Johnson and Roy Rogers, all of them, and certain lines of dialogue come back to you—"I been plugged!"—and then, when you get shot, you can't help falling back on them. "Jesus, Jesus," you say, half to yourself, half to the camera.

"I been fuckin' *plugged!*" You expect it of yourself. On ambush, poised in the dark, you fight to control yourself. Not too much fidgeting; it wouldn't look good. You try to grin. Eyes open, be alert— old lines, old movies. It all swirls together, clichés mixing with your own emotions, and in the end you can't distinguish. . . .

It was time. I fingered one of the ropes, took a breath, then gave it a sharp jerk.

Instantly there was a clatter outside the wire.

I expected the noise, I was even tensed for it, but still my heart took a funny little hop. I winced and ducked down.

"Now," I murmured. "Now it starts." Eight ropes altogether. I had four, Azar had four. Each rope was hooked up to a homemade noisemaker out in front of Jorgenson's bunker—eight tin cans filled with rifle cartridges. Simple devices, but they worked.

I waited a moment, and then, very gently, I gave all four of my ropes a little tug. Delicate—nothing loud. If you weren't listening, listening hard, you might've missed it. But Jorgenson was listening. Immediately, at the first low rattle, his silhouette seemed to freeze. Then he ducked down and blended in with the dark.

There—another rattle. Azar this time.

We kept at it for ten minutes. Noise, silence, noise, silence. Stagger the rhythm. Start slowly, gradually build the tension.

Crouched in my pile of boulders, squinting down at Jorgenson's position, I felt a swell if immense power. It was the feeling Charlie must have: full control, mastery of the night. Like a magician, a puppeteer. Yank on the ropes, watch the silly wooden puppet jump and twitch. It made me want to giggle. One by one, in sequence, I pulled on each of the ropes, and the sound came bouncing back at me with an eerie, indefinite formlessness: a rattlesnake, maybe, or the creak of a closet door or footsteps in the attic—whatever you made of it.

"There now," I whispered, or thought. "There, there."

Jorgenson wasn't moving. Not yet. He'd be coiled up in his circle of sandbags, fists tight, blinking, listening.

Again I tugged on my ropes.

I smiled. Eyes closed, I could almost *see* what was happening down there.

Bang. Jorgenson would jerk up. Rub his eyes, bend forward.

Eardrums fluttering like wings, spine stiff, muscles hard, brains like Jell-O. I could *see* it. Right now, at this instant, he'd glance up at the sky, hoping for a moon, a few stars. But no moon, no stars. He'd start talking to himself: "Relax, relax." Desperately he'd try to bring the night into focus, but the effort would only cause distortions: objects would seem to pick themselves up and twist and wiggle; trees would creep forward like an army on midnight maneuvers; the earth itself would begin to sway. Funhouse country. Trick mirrors and trapdoors and pop-up monsters. Lord, I could *see* it! It was as if I were down there *with* him, *beside* him. "Easy," he was muttering, "easy, easy, easy," but it didn't get easier. His ears were stiff, his eyeballs were dried up and hard, like stones, and the ghosts were coming out.

"Creepy," Azar cackled. "Wet pants, goose bumps. We *got* him. Ghost town!" He held a beer out to me, but I shook my head.

We sat in the dim quiet of my hootch, boots off, smoking, listening to Mary Hopkin.

"So what next?"

"Wait," I said. "More of the same."

"Well, sure, but—"

"Shut up and *listen.*"

That high elegant voice. That melody. "Those were the days, my friend. . . ." Someday, when the war was over, I'd go to London and ask Mary Hopkin to marry me. "We'd sing and dance forever and a day. . . ." Nostalgic and mawkish, but so what? That's what Nam does to you. Turns you sentimental, makes you want to marry girls like Mary Hopkin. You learn, finally, that you'll die. You see the corpses, sometimes you even kick them, feel the boot against meat, and you always think, *Me, me.* "We'd fight and never lose, those were the days, oh yes. . . ." That's what war does to you.

Azar switched off the tape.

"Shit, man," he said. "Don't you got some *music?*"

And now, finally, the moon was out. It was a white moon, mobile, clouded, nearly full. We slipped back to our positions and went to work again with the ropes. Louder, now, more insistently. The moon added resonance. Starlight shimmied in the barbed wire; reflections, layerings of shadow. Slowly, slowly we dragged the tin cans closer to Jorgenson's bunker, and this, plus the moon, gave a sense of creeping peril, the slow tightening of a noose.

At 0300 hours, the very deepest part of the night, Azar set off the first trip flare.

There was a light popping sound out in front of Bunker Six. Then a sizzle. And then the night seemed to snap itself in half. The flare burned ten paces from the bunker: like the Fourth of July, white-hot magnesium, a thousand sparklers exploding in a single cluster.

As the flare died, I fired three more.

It was instant daylight. For a moment I was paralyzed—blinded, struck dumb.

Then Jorgenson moved. There was a short, squeaky cry—not even a cry, really, just a sound of terror—and then a blurred motion as he jumped up and ran a few paces and rolled and lay still. His silhouette was framed like a cardboard cutout against the burning flares.

He was weeping.

A soft, musical sound. Like a long hollow sigh. As the flares burned themselves out, the weeping became raspy and painful. I sympathized. I really did. In fact, I almost trotted over to console him: "I know, I know. Scary business. You just want to cry and cry and cry."

In the dark outside my hootch, even though I bent toward him, nose to nose, all I could see were Azar's white eyes.

"Enough," I told him.

"Oh, sure."

"Seriously."

"Serious?" he said. "That's too serious for me; I'm a fun lover. A party boy on Halloween."

When Azar smiled I saw the quick glitter of teeth, but then the smile went away, and I knew it was hopeless. I tried, though. I told him the score was even—no need to rub it in. I was firm. I explained, very bluntly, that it was my game, beginning to end, and now I wanted to end it. I even got belligerent.

Azar just peered at me, almost dumbly.

"Poor Herbie," he said.

Nothing dramatic. The rest was inflection and those electric white-white eyes.

An hour before dawn we moved up for the last phase. Azar was in command now. I tagged after him, thinking maybe I could keep a lid on.

"Don't take this personal," Azar whispered. "You know? It's just that I like to finish things."

I didn't look at him; I looked at my fingernails, at the moon. When we got down near the wire, Azar gently put his hand on my shoulder, guiding me over toward the boulder pile. He knelt down and inspected the ropes and flares, nodded, peered out at Jorgenson's bunker, nodded again, removed his helmet and sat on it.

He was smiling again.

"Herbie?" he whispered.

I ignored him. My lips had a waxy, cold feel, like polished rock. I kept running my tongue over them. I told myself to stop it and I did, but then a second later I was doing it again.

"You know something?" Azar said, almost to himself. "Sometimes I feel like a little kid again. Playing war, you know? I get into it. I mean, wow, I *love* this shit."

"Look, why don't we—"

"Shhhh."

Smiling, Azar put a finger to his lips, partly as a warning, partly as a nifty gesture.

We waited another twenty minutes. It was cold now, and damp. My bones ached. I had a weird feeling of brittleness, as if somebody could reach out and grab me and crush me like a Christmas tree ornament. It was the same feeling out along the Song Tra Bong, when I got shot: I tried to grin wryly, like Bogie or Gable, and I thought about all the zingers Teddy Thatcher and I would use—except now Teddy was dead. Except when I called out for a medic, loud, nobody came. I started whimpering. The blood was warm, like dishwater, and I could feel my pants filling up with it. God, I thought, all this blood; I'll be *hollow*. Then the brittle feeling came over me. I passed out, woke up, screamed, tried to crawl but couldn't. I felt alone. All around me there was rifle fire, voices yelling, and yet for a moment I thought I'd gone deaf: the sounds were in my head, they weren't real. I smelled myself. The bullet had smashed through the colon, and the stink of my own shit made me afraid. I was crying. Leaking to death, I thought—blood and crap leaking out—and I couldn't quit crying. When Jorgenson got to me, all I could do was go "Ough! Ough!" I tightened up and pressed and grunted, trying to stop the leak, but that only made it worse, and Jorgenson punched me and told me to cut it out, ease off. *Shock,* I thought. I tried to tell him that: "Shock, man! Treat for shock!" I was lucid, things were clear, but my tongue wouldn't make the right words. And I was squirming. Jorgenson had to put his knee on my chest, turn me over, and when he did that, when he ripped my pants open, I shouted something and tried to wiggle away. I was hollowed out and cold. It was the *smell* that scared me. He was pressing down on my back—sitting on me, maybe, holding me down—and I kept trying to buck him off, rocking and moaning, even when he stuck me with morphine, even when he used his shirt to wipe my ass, even when he plugged the hole. Shock, I kept thinking. And then, like magic, things suddenly clicked into slow motion. The morphine, maybe: I focused on those brand-new black boots of his, then on a pebble, then on a single wisp of dried grass— the last things I'd ever see. I couldn't look away, I didn't dare, and I couldn't stop crying.

Even now, in the dark, I felt the sting in my eyes.

Azar said, "Herbie."

"Sure, man, I'm solid."

Down below, the bunker was silent. Nothing moved. The place looked almost abandoned, but I knew Jorgenson was there, wide awake, and I knew he was waiting.

Azar went to work on the ropes.

It began gently, like a breeze: a soft, lush, sighing sound. The ghosts were out. I was blinking, shivering, hugging myself. You can *die* of fright; it's possible, it can happen. I'd heard stories about it, about guys so afraid of dying that they died. You freeze up, your muscles snap, the heart starts fluttering, the brain floats away. It can *happen.*

"Enough," I whispered. "Stop it."

Azar looked at me and winked. Then he yanked sharply on all four ropes, and the sound made me squeal and jerk up.

"Please," I said. "Call it quits, right now. Please, man."

Azar wasn't listening. His white eyes glowed as he shot off the first flare. "Please," I murmured, but then I watched the flare arc up over Jorgenson's bunker, very slowly, pinwheeling, exploding almost without noise, just a sudden red flash.

There was a short, anguished whimper in the dark. At first I thought it was Jorgenson, or maybe a bird, but then I knew it was my own voice. I bit down and folded my hands and squeezed.

Twice more, rapidly, Azar fired off red flares, and then he turned and looked at me and lifted his eyebrows.

"Herbie," he said softly, "you're a sad case. Sad, sad."

"Look, can't we—"

"Sad."

I was frightened—of him, of us—and though I wanted to do something, wanted to stop him, I crouched back and watched him pick up the tear-gas grenade, pull the pin, stand up, smile, pause, and throw. For a moment the night seemed to stop as if bewitched; then the gas puffed up in a smoky cloud that partly obscured the bunker. I was moaning. Even from thirty meters away, upwind, I could smell the gas: not really *smell* it, though. I could *feel* it, like breathing razor blades. CS gas, the worst. Chickenshit gas, we called it, because that was what it turned you into—a mindless, squawking chickenshit.

"Jesus, please," I moaned, but Azar lobbed over another one, waited for the hiss, then scrambled over to the rope we hadn't used yet. *"Please,"* I said. Azar grabbed the rope with both hands and pulled.

It was my idea. That morning I'd rigged it up: a sandbag painted white, a pulley system, a rope.

Show him a ghost.

Azar pulled, and out in front of Bunker Six, as if rising up from a grave, the white sandbag lifted itself up and hovered in the misty swirl of gas.

Jorgenson began firing. Just one round at first—a single red tracer that thumped into the sandbag and burned.

"Ooooooh!" Azar murmured. "Star light, star bright. . . ."

Quickly, talking to himself, Azar hurled the last gas grenade, shot up another flare, then snatched the rope and made the white sandbag dance.

Jorgenson did not go nuts. Quietly, almost with dignity, he stood up and took aim and fired at the sandbag. I could see his profile against the red flares. His face seemed oddly relaxed. No twitching, no screams. With a strange, calm deliberation, he gazed out at the sandbag for several seconds, as if deciding something, and then he shook his head and smiled. Very slowly, he began marching out toward the wire. He did not crouch or run or crawl. He walked. He moved with a kind of graceful ease—resolutely, bravely, straight at the sandbag—firing with each step, stopping once to reload, then resuming his stately advance.

. "Guts," Azar said.

Azar yanked on the rope and the sandbag bobbed and shimmied, but Jorgenson kept moving forward. When he reached the sandbag he stopped and turned, then he shouted my name, then he placed his rifle muzzle directly against the bag.

"Herbie!" he hollered, and he fired. The sandbag seemed to explode.

Azar dropped the rope.

"Show's over," he said. He looked down at me with pity. "Sad, sad, sad."

I was weeping. Distantly, as if from another continent, I heard Jorgenson pumping rounds into the sandbag.

"Disgusting," Azar said. "Herbie, Herbie. Saddest fucking case I ever seen."

Azar smiled. He looked out at Jorgenson, then at me. Those eyes—falcon eyes, ghost eyes. He moved toward me as if to help me up, but then, almost as an afterthought, he kicked me. My kneecap seemed to snap.

"Sad," he murmured, then he turned and headed off to bed.

"No big deal," I told Jorgenson. "Leave it alone. I'll live."

But he hooked my arm over his shoulder and helped me down to the bunker. My knee was hurting bad, but I didn't say anything. We sat facing each other.

It was almost full dawn now, a hazy silver dawn, and you could tell by the color and smells that rain wasn't far off.

For a while we didn't speak.

"So," he finally said.

"Right."

We shook hands, but neither of us put much emotion in it, and we didn't look at each other's eyes.

Jorgenson pointed out at the shot-up sandbag.

"That was a nice touch," he said. "No kidding, it had me . . . a nice touch. You've got a real sense of drama, Herbie. Someday you should go into the movies or something."

"I've thought about that."

"Another Hitchcock."

I nodded.

"*The Birds.* You ever see it?"

"Scary shit, man."

We sat for a while longer, then I started to get up, but my knee wasn't working right. Jorgenson had to give me a hand.

"Even?" he asked.

"Pretty much."

We touched—not a hug or anything, but something like that— then Jorgenson picked up his helmet, brushed it off, touched his funny little moustache, and looked out at the sandbag. His face was filthy. There were still tear splotches on his cheeks.

Up at the medic's hootch, he cleaned and bandaged my knee, then we went to chow. We didn't have much to say. Chitchat, some jokes. Afterward, in an awkward moment, I said, "Let's kill Azar."

Jorgenson smiled. "Scare him to death, right?"

"Right," I said.

"What a movie!"

I shrugged. "Sure. Or just kill him."

[March 1981]

RICHARD FORD

Rock Springs

Edna and I had started down from Kalispell heading for Tampa–St. Pete, where I still had some friends from the old glory days who wouldn't turn me in to the police. I had managed to scrape with the law in Kalispell over several bad checks—which is a prison crime in Montana. And I knew Edna was already looking at her cards and thinking about a move, since it wasn't the first time I'd been in law scrapes in my life. She herself had already had her own troubles, losing her kids and keeping her ex-husband, Danny, from breaking in her house and stealing her things while she was at work, which was really why I had moved in in the first place, that and needing to give my little daughter, Cheryl, a better shake in things.

I don't know what was between Edna and me, just beached by the same tides when you got down to it. Though love has been built on frailer ground than that, as I well know. And when I came in the house that afternoon, I just asked her if she wanted to go to Florida with me, leave things where they sat, and she said, "Why not? My datebook's not that full."

Edna and I had been a pair eight months, more or less man and wife, some of which time I had been out of work, and some when I'd worked at the dog track as a lead-out and could help with the rent and talk sense to Danny when he came around. Danny was afraid of me because Edna had told him I'd been in prison in Florida for killing a man once, though that wasn't true. I had once been in jail in Tallahassee for stealing tires and had gotten into a fight on the county farm where a man had lost his eye. But I hadn't done the hurting, and Edna just wanted the story worse than it was so Danny wouldn't act crazy and make her have to take her kids back, since she had made a good adjustment to not having them, and I already had Cheryl with me. I'm not a violent person and would never put a man's eye out, much less kill someone. My former wife, Helen, would come all the way from Waikiki Beach to testify to that. We never had violence, and I believe in crossing the street to stay out of trouble's way. Though Danny didn't know that.

But we were half down through Wyoming, going toward I-80 and feeling good about things, when the oil light flashed on in the car I'd stolen, a sign I knew to be a bad one.

I'd gotten us a good car, a cranberry Mercedes I'd stolen out of an ophthalmologist's lot in Whitefish, Montana. I stole it because I thought it would be comfortable over a long haul, because I thought it got good mileage, which it didn't, and because I'd never had a good car in my life, just old Chevy junkers and used trucks back from when I was a kid swamping citrus with Cubans.

The car made us all high that day. I ran the windows up and down, and Edna told us some jokes and made faces. She could be lively. Her features would light up like a beacon and you could see her beauty, which wasn't ordinary. It all made me giddy, and I drove clean down to Bozeman, then straight on through the park to Jackson Hole. I rented us the bridal suite in the Quality Court in Jackson and left Cheryl and her little dog, Duke, sleeping while Edna and I drove to a rib barn and drank beer and laughed till after midnight.

It felt like a whole new beginning for us, bad memories left behind and a new horizon to build on. I got so worked up, I had a tattoo done on my arm that said FAMOUS TIMES, and Edna bought a Bailey hat with an Indian feather band and a little turquoise-and-silver bracelet for Cheryl, and we made love on the seat of the car in the Quality Court parking lot just as the sun was burning up on the Snake River, and everything seemed then like the end of the rainbow.

It was that very enthusiasm, in fact, that made me keep the car one day longer instead of driving it into the river and stealing another one, like I should have done and *had* done before.

Where the car went bad there wasn't a town in sight or even a house, just some low mountains maybe fifty miles away or maybe a hundred, a barbed-wire fence in both directions, hardpan prairie, and some hawks sailing through the evening air seizing insects.

I got out to look at the motor, and Edna got out with Cheryl and the dog to let them have a pee by the car. I checked the water and checked the oil stick, and both of them said perfect.

"What's that light mean, Earl?" Edna said. She had come and stood by the car with her hat on. She was just sizing things up for herself.

"We shouldn't run it," I said. "Something's not right in the oil."

She looked around at Cheryl and Little Duke, who were peeing on the hardtop side by side like two little dolls, then out at the mountains, which were becoming black and lost in the distance. "What're we doing?" she said. She wasn't worried yet, but she wanted to know what I was thinking about.

"Let me try it again," I said.

"That's a good idea," she said, and we all got back in the car.

When I turned the motor over, it started right away and the red light stayed off and there weren't any noises to make you think something was wrong. I let it idle a minute, then pushed the accelerator down and watched the red bulb. But there wasn't any light on, and I started wondering if maybe I hadn't dreamed I saw it, or that it had been the sun catching an angle off the window chrome, or maybe I was scared of something and didn't know it.

"What's the matter with it, Daddy?" Cheryl said from the back seat. I looked back at her, and she had on her turquoise bracelet and Edna's hat set back on the back of her head and that little black-and-white Heinz dog on her lap. She looked like a little cowgirl in the movies.

"Nothing, honey, everything's fine now," I said.

"Little Duke tinkled where I tinkled," Cheryl said, and laughed.

"You're two of a kind," Edna said, not looking back. Edna was usually good with Cheryl, but I knew she was tired now. We hadn't had much sleep, and she had a tendency to get cranky when she didn't sleep. "We oughta ditch this damn car first chance we get," she said.

"What's the first chance we got?" I said, because I knew she'd been at the map.

"Rock Springs, Wyoming," Edna said with conviction. "Thirty miles down this road."

She pointed out ahead. I had wanted all along to drive the car into Florida like a big success story. But I knew Edna was right about it, that we shouldn't take crazy chances. I had kept thinking of it as my car and not the ophthalmologist's, and that was how you got caught in these things.

"Then my belief is we ought to go to Rock Springs and negotiate ourselves a new car," I said. I wanted to stay upbeat, like everything was panning out right.

"That's a great idea," Edna said, and she leaned over and kissed me hard on the mouth.

"That's a great idea," Cheryl said. "Let's pull on out of here right now."

The sunset that day I remember as being the prettiest I'd ever seen. Just as it touched the rim of the horizon, it all at once fired the air into jewels and red sequins the precise likes of which I had never seen before and haven't seen since. The West has it all over everywhere for sunsets, even Florida, where it's supposedly flat but where half the time trees block your view.

"It's cocktail hour," Edna said after we'd driven awhile. "We ought to have a drink and celebrate something." She felt better thinking we were going to get rid of the car. It certainly had dark troubles and was something you'd want to put behind you.

Edna had out a whiskey bottle and some plastic cups and was measuring levels on the glove-box lid. She liked drinking, and she liked drinking in the car, which was something you got used to in Montana, where it wasn't against the law, where, though, strangely enough, a bad check would land you in Deer Lodge Prison for a year.

"Did I ever tell you I once had a monkey?" Edna said, setting my drink on the dashboard where I could reach it when I was ready. Her spirits were already picked up. She was like that, up one minute and down the next.

"I don't think you ever did tell me that," I said. "Where were you then?"

"Missoula," she said. She put her bare feet on the dash and rested the cup on her breasts. "I was waitressing at the Amvets. It was before I met you. Some guy came in one day with a monkey. A spider monkey. And I said, just to be joking, 'I'll roll you for that monkey.' And the guy said, 'Just one roll?' And I said, 'Sure.' He put the monkey down on the bar, picked up the cup, and rolled out boxcars. I picked it up and rolled out three fives. And I just stood there looking at the guy. He was just some guy passing through, I guess a vet. He got a strange look on his face—I'm sure not as strange as the one I had—but he looked kind of sad and surprised and satisfied all at once. I said, 'We can roll again.' But he said, 'No, I never roll twice for anything.' And he sat and drank a beer and talked about one thing and another for a while, about nuclear war and building a stronghold somewhere up in the Bitterroot, whatever it was, while I just watched the monkey, wondering what I was going to do with it when the guy left. And pretty soon he got up and said, 'Well, good-bye, Chipper'; that was this monkey's name, of course. And then he left before I could say anything. And the monkey just sat on the bar all that night. I don't know what made me think of that, Earl. Just something weird. I'm letting my mind wander."

"That's perfectly fine," I said. I took a drink of my drink. "I'd never own a monkey," I said after a minute. "They're too nasty. I'm sure Cheryl would like a monkey, though, wouldn't you, honey?" Cheryl was down on the seat playing with Little Duke. She used to talk about monkeys all the time then. "What'd you ever do with that monkey?" I said, watching the speedometer. We were having to go slower now because the red light kept fluttering on. And all I could do to keep it off was go slower. We were going maybe thirty-five and it was an hour before dark, and I was hoping Rock Springs wasn't far away.

"You really want to know?" Edna said. She gave me a quick, sharp glance, then looked back at the empty desert as if she was brooding over it.

"Sure," I said. I was still upbeat. I figured *I* could worry about breaking down and let other people be happy for a change.

"I kept it a week," she said. She seemed gloomy all of a sudden, as if she saw some aspect of the story she had never seen before. "I took it home and back and forth to the Amvets on my shifts. And it didn't cause any trouble. I fixed a chair up for it to sit on, back of the bar, and people liked it. It made a nice little clicking noise. We changed its name to Mary because the bartender figured out it was a girl. Though I was never really comfortable with it at home. I felt like it watched me too much. Then one day a guy came in, some guy who'd been in Vietnam, still wore a fatigue coat. And he said to me, 'Don't you know that a monkey'll kill you? It's got more strength in its fingers than you got in your whole body.' He said people had been killed in Vietnam by monkeys, bunches of them marauding while you were asleep, killing you and covering you with leaves. I didn't believe a word of it, except that when I got home and got undressed I started looking over across the room at Mary on her chair in the dark watching me. And I got the creeps. And after a while I got up and went out to the car, got a length of clothesline wire, and came back in and wired her to the doorknob through her little silver collar, and went back and tried to sleep. And I guess I must've slept the sleep of the dead—though I don't remember it—because when I got up I found Mary had tipped off her chair back and hanged herself on the wire line. I'd made it too short."

Edna seemed badly affected by that story and slid low in the seat so she couldn't see out over the dash. "Isn't that a shameful story, Earl, what happened to that poor little monkey?"

"I see a town! I see a town!" Cheryl started yelling from the back seat, and right up Little Duke started yapping and the whole car fell into a racket. And sure enough she had seen something I hadn't, which was Rock Springs, Wyoming, at the bottom of a long hill, a little glowing jewel in the desert with I-80 running on the north side and the black desert spread out behind.

"That's it, honey," I said. "That's where we're going. You saw it first."

"We're hungry," Cheryl said. "Little Duke wants some fish, and I want spaghetti." She put her arms around my neck and hugged me.

"Then you'll just get it," I said. "You can have anything you want. And so can Edna and so can Little Duke." I looked over at Edna, smiling, but she was staring at me with eyes that were fierce with anger. "What's wrong?" I said.

"Don't you care anything about that awful thing that happened to me?" she said. Her mouth was drawn tight, and her eyes kept cutting back at Cheryl and Little Duke, as if they had been tormenting her.

"Of course, I do," I said. "I thought that was an awful thing." I didn't want her to be unhappy. We were almost there, and pretty soon we could sit down and have a real meal without thinking somebody might be hurting us.

"You want to know what I did with that monkey?" Edna said.

"Sure I do," I said.

She said, "I put her in a green garbage bag, put it in the trunk of my car, drove to the dump, and threw her in the trash." She was staring at me darkly, as if the story meant something to her that was real

521

important but that only she could see and that the rest of the world was a fool for.

"Well, that's horrible," I said. "But I don't see what else you could do. You didn't mean to kill it. You'd have done it differently if you had. And then you had to get rid of it, and I don't know what else you could have done. Throwing it away might seem unsympathetic to somebody, probably, but not to me. Sometimes that's all you can do, and you can't worry about what somebody else thinks." I tried to smile at her, but the red light was staying on if I pushed the accelerator at all, and I was trying to gauge if we could coast to Rock Springs before the car gave out completely. I looked at Edna again. "What else can I say?" I said.

"Nothing," she said, and stared back at the dark highway. "I should've known that's what you'd think. You've got a character that leaves something out, Earl. I've known that a long time."

"And yet here you are," I said. "And you're not doing so bad. Things could be a lot worse. At least we're all together here."

"Things could always be worse," Edna said. "You could go to the electric chair tomorrow."

"That's right," I said. "And somewhere somebody probably will. Only it won't be you."

"I'm hungry," said Cheryl. "When're we gonna eat? Let's find a motel. I'm tired of this. Little Duke's tired of it too."

Where the car stopped rolling was some distance from the town, though you could see the clear outline of the interstate in the dark with Rock Springs lighting up the sky behind. You could hear the big tractors hitting the spacers in the overpass, revving up for the climb to the mountains.

I shut off the lights.

"What're we going to do now?" Edna said irritably, giving me a bitter look.

"I'm figuring it," I said. "It won't be hard, whatever it is. You won't have to do anything."

"I'd hope not," she said, and looked the other way.

Across the road and across a dry wash a hundred yards was what looked like a huge mobile-home town, with a factory or a refinery of some kind lit up behind it and in full swing. There were lights on in a lot of the mobile homes, and there were cars moving along an access road that ended near the freeway overpass a mile the other way. The lights in the mobile homes seemed friendly to me, and I knew right then what I should do.

"Get out," I said, and opened my door.

"Are we walking?" Edna said.

"We're pushing," I said.

"I'm not pushing," Edna said, and reached up and locked her door.

"All right," I said. "Then you just steer."

"You pushing us to Rock Springs, are you, Earl? It doesn't look like it's more than about three miles," Edna said.

"I'll push," Cheryl said from the back.

"No, hon. Daddy'll push. You just get out with Little Duke and move out of the way."

Edna gave me a threatening look, just as if I'd tried to hit her. But when I got out she slid into my seat and took the wheel, staring angrily ahead straight into the cottonwood scrub.

"Edna can't drive that car," Cheryl said from out in the dark. "She'll run it in the ditch."

"Yes, she can, hon. Edna can drive it as good as I can. Probably better."

"No, she can't," Cheryl said. "No, she can't either." And I thought she was about to cry, but she didn't.

I told Edna to keep the ignition on so it wouldn't lock up and to steer into the cottonwoods with the parking lights on so she could see. And when I started, she steered it straight off into the trees, and I kept pushing until we were twenty yards into the cover and the tires sank in the soft sand and nothing at all could be seen from the road.

"Now where are we?" she said, sitting at the wheel. Her voice was tired and hard, and I knew she could have put a good meal to use. She had a sweet nature, and I recognized that this wasn't her fault but mine. Only I wished she could be more hopeful.

"You stay right here, and I'll go over to that trailer park and call us a cab," I said.

"What cab?" Edna said, her mouth wrinkled as if she'd never heard anything like that in her life.

"There'll be cabs," I said, and tried to smile at her. "There's cabs everywhere."

"What're you going to tell him when he gets here? Our stolen car broke down and we need a ride to where we can steal another one? That'll be a big hit, Earl."

"I'll talk," I said. "You just listen to the radio for ten minutes and then walk on out to the shoulder like nothing was suspicious. And you and Cheryl act nice. She doesn't need to know about this car."

"Like we're not suspicious enough already, right?" Edna looked up at me out of the lighted car. "You don't think right, did you know that, Earl? You think the world's stupid and you're smart. But that's not how it is. I feel sorry for you. You might've *been* something, but things just went crazy someplace."

I had a thought about poor Danny. He was a vet and crazy as a shit-house mouse, and I was glad he wasn't in for all this. "Just get the baby in the car," I said, trying to be patient. "I'm hungry like you are."

"I'm tired of this," Edna said. "I wish I'd stayed in Montana."

"Then you can go back in the morning," I said. "I'll buy the ticket and put you on the bus. But not till then."

"Just get on with it, Earl," she said, slumping down in the seat, turning off the parking lights with one foot and the radio on with the other.

The mobile-home community was as big as any I'd ever seen. It was attached in some way to the plant that was lighted up behind it, because I could see a car once in a while leave one of the trailer streets, turn in the direction of the plant, then go slowly into it. Everything in the plant was white, and you could see that all the trailers were painted white and looked exactly alike. A deep hum came out of the plant, and I thought as I got closer that it wouldn't be a location I'd ever want to work in.

I went right to the first trailer where there was a light and knocked on the metal door. Kids' toys were lying in the gravel around the little wood steps, and I could hear talking on TV that suddenly went off. I heard a woman's voice talking, and then the door opened wide.

A large Negro woman with a wide, friendly face stood in the doorway. She smiled at me and moved forward as if she was going to come out, but she stopped at the top step. There was a little Negro boy behind her peeping out from behind her legs, watching me with his eyes half closed. The trailer had that feeling that no one else was inside, which was a feeling I knew something about.

"I'm sorry to intrude," I said. "But I've run up on a little bad luck tonight. My name's Earl Middleton."

The woman looked at me, then out into the night toward the freeway as if what I had said was something she was going to be able to see. "What kind of bad luck?" she said, looking down at me again.

"My car broke down out on the highway," I said. "I can't fix it myself, and I wondered if I could use your phone to call for help."

The woman smiled down at me knowingly. "We can't live without cars, can we?"

"That's the honest truth," I said.

"They're like our hearts," she said firmly, her face shining in the little bulb light that burned beside the door. "Where's your car situated?"

I turned and looked over into the dark, but I couldn't see anything because of where we'd put it. "It's over there," I said. "You can't see it in the dark."

"Who all's with you now?" the woman said. "Have you got your wife with you?"

"She's with my little girl and our dog in the car," I said. "My daughter's asleep or I would have brought them."

"They shouldn't be left in the dark by themselves," the woman said, and frowned. "There's too much unsavoriness out there."

"The best I can do is hurry back," I said. I tried to look sincere, since everything except Cheryl being asleep and Edna being my wife was the truth. The truth is meant to serve you if you'll let it, and I wanted it to serve me. "I'll pay for the phone call," I said. "If you'll bring the phone to the door I'll call from right here."

The woman looked at me again as if she was searching for a truth of her own, then back out into the night. She was maybe in her sixties, but I couldn't say for sure. "You're not going to rob me, are you, Mr. Middleton?" she said, and smiled like it was a joke between us.

"Not tonight," I said, and smiled a genuine smile. "I'm not up to it tonight. Maybe another time."

"Then I guess Terrel and I can let you use our phone with Daddy not here, can't we, Terrel? This is my grandson, Terrel Junior, Mr. Middleton." She put her hand on the boy's head and looked down at him. "Terrel won't talk. Though if he did he'd tell you to use our phone. He's a sweet boy." She opened the screen for me to come in.

The trailer was a big one with a new rug and a new couch and a living room that expanded to give the space of a real house. Something good and sweet was cooking in the kitchen, and the trailer felt like it was somebody's comfortable new home instead of just temporary. I've lived in trailers, but they were just snail backs with one room and no toilet, and they always felt cramped and unhappy—though I've thought maybe it might've been me that was unhappy in them.

There was a big Sony TV and a lot of kids' toys scattered on the floor. I recognized a Greyhound bus I'd gotten for Cheryl. The phone was beside a new leather recliner, and the Negro woman pointed for me to sit down and call and gave me the phone book. Terrel began fingering his toys, and the woman sat on the couch while I called, watching me and smiling.

There were three listings for cab companies, all with one number different. I called the numbers in order and didn't get an answer until the last one, which answered with the name of the second company. I said I was on the highway beyond the interstate and that my wife and family needed to be taken to town and I would arrange for a tow later. While I was giving the location, I looked up the name of a tow service to tell the driver in case he asked.

When I hung up, the Negro woman was sitting looking at me with the same look she had been staring with into the dark, a look that seemed to want truth. She was smiling, though. Something pleased her and I reminded her of it.

"This is a very nice home," I said, resting in the recliner, which felt like the driver's seat of the Mercedes and where I'd have been happy to stay.

"This isn't *our* house, Mr. Middleton," the Negro woman said. "The company owns these. They give them to us for nothing. We have our own home in Rockford, Illinois."

"That's wonderful," I said.

"It's never wonderful when you have to be away from home, Mr. Middleton, though we're only here three months, and it'll be easier when Terrel Junior begins his special school. You see, our son was killed in the war, and his wife ran off without Terrel Junior. Though you shouldn't worry. He can't understand us. His little feelings can't be hurt." The woman folded her hands in her lap and smiled in a satisfied way. She was an attractive woman and had on a blue-and-pink floral dress that made her seem bigger than she could've been, just the right woman to sit on the couch she was sitting on. She was good nature's picture, and I was glad she could be, with her little brain-damaged boy, living in a place where no one in his right mind would want to live a minute. "Where do *you* live, Mr. Middleton?" she said politely, smiling in the same sympathetic way.

"My family and I are in transit," I said. "I'm an ophthalmologist, and we're moving back to Florida, where I'm from. I'm setting up practice in some little town where it's warm year-round. I haven't decided where."

"Florida's a wonderful place," the woman said. "I think Terrel would like it there."

"Could I ask you something?" I said.

"You certainly may," the woman said. Terrel had begun pushing his Greyhound across the front of the TV screen, making a scratch that no one watching the set could miss. "Stop that, Terrell Junior," the woman said quietly. But Terrel kept pushing his bus on the glass, and she smiled at me again as if we both understood something sad. Except I knew Cheryl would never damage a television set. She had respect for nice things, and I was sorry for the lady that Terrel didn't. "What did you want to ask?" the woman said.

"What goes on in that plant or whatever it is back there beyond these trailers, where all the lights are on?"

"Gold," the woman said, and smiled.

"It's what?" I said.

"Gold," the Negro woman said, smiling as she had for almost all the time I'd been there. "It's a gold mine."

"They're mining gold back there?" I said, pointing.

"Every night and every day," she said, smiling in a pleased way.

"Does your husband work there?" I said.

"He's the assayer," she said. "He controls the quality. He works three months a year, and we live the rest of the time at home in Rockford. We've waited a long time for this. We've been happy to have our grandson, but I won't say I'll be sorry to have him go. We're ready to start our lives over." She smiled broadly at me and then at

Terrel, who was giving her a spiteful look from the floor. "You said you had a daughter," the Negro woman said. "And what's her name?"

"Irma Cheryl," I said. "She's named for my mother."

"That's nice," she said. "And she's healthy, too. I can see it in your face." She looked at Terrel Junior with pity.

"I guess I'm lucky," I said.

"So far you are," she said. "But children bring you grief, the same way they bring you joy. We were unhappy for a long time before my husband got his job in the gold mine. Now, when Terrel starts to school, we'll be kids again." She stood up. "You might miss your cab, Mr. Middleton," she said, walking toward the door, though not to be forcing me out. She was too polite. "If *we* can't see your car, the cab surely won't be able to."

"That's true," I said, and got up off the recliner, where I'd been so comfortable. "None of us have eaten yet, and your food makes me know how hungry we probably all are."

"There are fine restaurants in town, and you'll find them," the Negro woman said. "I'm sorry you didn't meet my husband. He's a wonderful man. He's everything to me."

"Tell him I appreciate the phone," I said. "You saved me."

"You weren't hard to save," the woman said. "Saving people is what we were all put on earth to do. I just passed you on to whatever's coming to you."

"Let's hope it's good," I said, stepping back into the dark.

"I'll be hoping, Mr. Middleton. Terrel and I will both be hoping."

I waved to her as I walked out into the darkness toward the car where it was hidden in the night.

The cab had already arrived when I got there. I could see its little red and green roof lights all the way across the dry wash, and it made me worry that Edna was already saying something to get us in trouble, something about the car or where we'd come from, something that would cast suspicion on us. I thought, then, how I never planned things well enough. There was always a gap between my plan and what happened, and I only responded to things as they came along and hoped I wouldn't get in trouble. I was an offender in the law's eyes. But I always *thought* differently, as if I weren't an offender and had no intention of being one, which was the truth. But as I read on a napkin once, between the idea and the act a whole kingdom lies. And I had a hard time with my acts, which were oftentimes offender's acts, and my ideas, which were as good as the gold they mined there where the bright lights were blazing.

"We're waiting for you, Daddy," Cheryl said when I crossed the road. "The taxicab's already here."

"I see, hon," I said, and gave Cheryl a big hug. The cabdriver was sitting in the driver's seat having a smoke with the lights on inside. Edna was leaning against the back of the cab between the taillights, wearing her Bailey hat. "What'd you tell him?" I said when I got close.

"Nothin'," she said. "What's there to tell?"

"Did he see the car?"

She glanced over in the direction of the trees where we had hid the Mercedes. Nothing was visible in the darkness, though I could hear Little Duke combing around in the underbrush tracking something, his little collar tinkling. "Where're we going?" she said. "I'm so hungry I could pass out."

"Edna's in a terrible mood," Cheryl said. "She already snapped at me."

"We're tired, honey," I said. "So try to be nicer."

"She's never nice," Cheryl said.

"Run go get Little Duke," I said. "And hurry back."

"I guess *my* questions come last here, right?" Edna said.

I put my arm around her. "That's not true," I said.

"Did you find somebody over there in the trailers you'd rather stay with? You were gone long enough."

"That's not a thing to say," I said. "I was just trying to make things look right, so we don't get put in jail."

"So *you* don't, you mean," Edna said and laughed a little laugh I didn't like hearing.

"That's right. So I don't," I said. "I'd be the one in Dutch." I stared out at the big, lighted assemblage of white buildings and white lights beyond the trailer community, plumes of white smoke escaping up into the heartless Wyoming sky, the whole company of buildings looking like some unbelievable castle, humming away in a distorted dream. "You know what all those buildings are there?" I said to

Edna, who hadn't moved and who didn't really seem to care if she ever moved anymore ever.

"No. But I can't say it matters, 'cause it isn't a motel and it isn't a restaurant," she said.

"It's a gold mine," I said, staring at the gold mine, which, I knew now from walking to the trailer, was a greater distance from us than it seemed, though it seemed huge and near, up against the cold sky. I thought there should've been a wall around it with guards instead of just the lights and no fence. It seemed as if anyone could go in and take what they wanted, just the way I had gone up to that woman's trailer and used the telephone, though that obviously wasn't true.

Edna began to laugh then. Not the mean laugh I didn't like, but a laugh that had something caring behind it, a full laugh that enjoyed a joke, a laugh she was laughing the first time I laid eyes on her, in Missoula in the Eastgate bar in 1979, a laugh we used to laugh together when Cheryl was still with her mother and I was working steady at the track and not stealing cars or passing bogus checks to merchants. A better time all around. And for some reason it made me laugh just hearing her, and we both stood there behind the cab in the dark, laughing at the gold mine in the desert, me with my arm around her and Cheryl out rustling up Little Duke and the cabdriver smoking in the cab and our stolen Mercedes-Benz, which I'd had such hopes for in Florida, stuck up to its axle in sand, where I'd never get to see it again.

"I always wondered what a gold mine would look like when I saw it," Edna said, still laughing, wiping a tear from her eye.

"Me too," I said. "I was always curious about it."

"We're a couple of fools, ain't we, Earl?" she said, unable to quit laughing completely. "We're two of a kind."

"It might be a good sign, though," I said.

"How could it be?" she said. "It's not our gold mine. There aren't any drive-up windows." She was still laughing.

"We've seen it," I said, pointing. "That's it right there. It may mean we're getting closer. Some people never see it at all."

"In a pig's eye, Earl," she said. "You and me see it in a pig's eye."

And she turned and got into the cab to go.

The cabdriver didn't ask anything about our car or where it was, to mean he'd noticed something queer. All of which made me feel like we had made a clean break from the car and couldn't be connected with it until it was too late, if ever. The driver told us a lot about Rock Springs while he drove, that because of the gold mine a lot of people had moved there in just six months, people from all over, including New York, and that most of them lived out in the trailers. Prostitutes from New York City, who he called "B-girls," had come into town, he said, on the prosperity tide, and Cadillacs with New York plates cruised the little streets every night, full of Negroes with big hats who ran the women. He told us that everybody who got in his cab now wanted to know where the women were, and when he got our call he almost didn't come because some of the trailers were brothels operated by the mine for engineers and computer people away from home. He said he got tired of running back and forth out there just for vile business. He said that *60 Minutes* had even done a program about Rock Springs and that a blowup had resulted in Cheyenne, though nothing could be done unless the prosperity left town. "It's prosperity's fruit," the driver said. "I'd rather be poor, which is lucky for me."

He said all the motels were sky-high, but since we were a family he could show us a nice one that was affordable. But I told him we wanted a first-rate place where they took animals, and the money didn't matter because we had had a hard day and wanted to finish on a high note. I also knew that it was in the little nowhere places that the police look for you and find you. People I'd known were always being arrested in cheap hotels and tourist courts with names you'd never heard of before. Never in Holiday Inns or Travelodges.

I asked him to drive us to the middle of town and back out again so Cheryl could see the train station, and while we were there I saw a pink Cadillac with New York plates and a TV aerial being driven slowly by a Negro in a big hat down a narrow street where there were just bars and a Chinese restaurant. It was an odd sight, nothing you could ever expect.

"There's your pure criminal element," the cabdriver said, and seemed sad. "I'm sorry for people like you to see a thing like that. We've got a nice town here, but there're some that want to ruin it for everybody. There used to be a way to deal with trash and criminals, but those days are gone forever."

"You said it," Edna said.

"You shouldn't let it get *you* down," I said to the cabdriver. "There's more of you than them. And there always will be. You're the best advertisement this town has. I know Cheryl will remember you and not *that* man, won't you, honey?" But Cheryl was asleep by then, holding Little Duke in her arms on the taxi seat.

The driver took us to the Ramada Inn on the interstate, not far from where we'd broken down. I had a small pain of regret as we drove under the Ramada awning that we hadn't driven up in a cranberry-colored Mercedes but instead in a beat-up old Chrysler taxi driven by an old man full of complaints. Though I knew it was for the best. We were better off without that car, better, really, in any other car but that one, where the signs had turned bad.

I registered under another name and paid for the room in cash so there wouldn't be any questions. On the line where it said "Representing" I wrote "ophthalmologist" and put "M.D." after the name. It had a nice look to it, even though it wasn't my name.

When we got to the room, which was in the back where I'd asked for it, I put Cheryl on one of the beds and Little Duke beside her so they'd sleep. She'd missed dinner, but it only meant she'd be hungry in the morning, when she could have anything she wanted. A few missed meals don't make a kid bad. I'd missed a lot of them myself and haven't turned out completely bad.

"Let's have some fried chicken," I said to Edna when she came out of the bathroom. "They have good fried chicken at the Ramadas, and I noticed the buffet was still up. Cheryl can stay right here, where it's safe, till we're back."

"I guess I'm not hungry anymore," Edna said. She stood at the window staring out into the dark. I could see out the window past her some yellowish foggy glow in the sky. For a moment I thought it was the gold mine out in the distance lighting the night, though it was only the interstate.

"We could order up," I said. "Whatever you want. There's a menu on the phone book. You could just have a salad."

"You go ahead," she said. "I've lost my hungry spirit." She sat on the bed beside Cheryl and Little Duke and looked at them in a sweet way and put her hand on Cheryl's cheek just as if she'd had a fever. "Sweet little girl," she said. "Everybody loves you."

"What do you want to do?" I said. "I'd like to eat. Maybe *I'll* order up some chicken."

"Why don't you do that?" she said. "It's your favorite." And she smiled at me from the bed.

I sat on the other bed and dialed room service. I asked for chicken, garden salad, potato, and a roll, plus a piece of hot apple pie and ice tea. I realized I hadn't eaten all day. When I put down the phone I saw that Edna was watching me, not in a hateful way or a loving way, just in a way that seemed to say she didn't understand something and was going to ask me about it.

"When did watching me get so entertaining?" I said, and smiled at her. I was trying to be friendly. I knew how tired she must be. It was after nine o'clock.

"I was just thinking how much I hated being in a motel without a car that was mine to drive. Isn't that funny? I started feeling like that last night when that purple car wasn't mine. That purple car just gave me the willies, I guess, Earl."

"One of those cars *outside* is yours," I said. "Just stand right there and pick it out."

"I know," she said. "But that's different, isn't it?" She reached and got her blue Bailey hat, put it on her head, and set it way back like Dale Evans. She looked sweet. "I used to like to go to motels, you know," she said. "There's something secret about them and free—I was never paying, of course. But you felt safe from everything and free to do what you wanted because you'd made the decision to be there and paid that price, and all the rest was the good part. Fucking and everything, you know." She smiled at me in a good-natured way.

"Isn't that the way this is?" I said. I was sitting on the bed, watching her, not knowing what to expect her to say next.

"I don't guess it is, Earl," she said, and stared out the window. "I'm thirty-two and I'm going to have to give up on motels. I can't keep that fantasy going anymore."

"Don't you like this place?" I said, and looked around at the room. I appreciated the modern paintings and the lowboy bureau and the big TV. It seemed like a plenty nice enough place to me, considering where we'd been already.

"No, I don't," Edna said with real conviction. "There's no use in my getting mad at you about it. It isn't your fault. You do the best you can for everybody. But every trip teaches you something. And I've learned I need to give up on motels before some bad thing happens to me. I'm sorry."

"What does that mean?" I said, because I really didn't know what she had in mind to do, though I should've guessed.

"I guess I'll take that ticket you mentioned," she said, and got up and faced the window. "Tomorrow's soon enough. We haven't got a car to take me anyhow."

"Well, that's a fine thing," I said, sitting on the bed, feeling like I was in a shock. I wanted to say something to her, to argue with her, but I couldn't think what to say that seemed right. I didn't want to be mad at her, but it made me mad.

"You've got a right to be mad at me, Earl," she said, "but I don't think you can really blame me." She turned around and faced me and sat on the windowsill, her hands on her knees. Someone knocked on the door. I just yelled for them to set the tray down and put it on the bill.

"I guess I *do* blame you," I said. I was angry. I thought about how I could have disappeared into that trailer community and hadn't, had come back to keep things going, had tried to take control of things for everybody when they looked bad.

"Don't. I wish you wouldn't," Edna said, and smiled at me like she wanted me to hug her. "Anybody ought to have their choice in things if they can. Don't you believe that, Earl? Here I am out here in the desert where I don't know anything, in a stolen car, in a motel room under an assumed name, with no money of my own, a kid that's not mine, and the law after me. And I have a choice to get out of all of it by getting on a bus. What would you do? I know exactly what you'd do."

"You think you do," I said. But I didn't want to get into an argument about it and tell her all I could've done and didn't do. Because it wouldn't have done any good. When you get to the point of arguing, you're past the point of changing anybody's mind, even though it's supposed to be the other way, and maybe for some classes of people it is, just never mine.

Edna smiled at me and came across the room and put her arms around me where I was sitting on the bed. Cheryl rolled over and looked at us and smiled, then closed her eyes, and the room was quiet. I was beginning to think of Rock Springs in a way I knew I would always think of it, a lowdown city full of crimes and whores and disappointments, a place where a woman left me, instead of a place where I got things on the straight track once and for all, a place I saw a gold mine.

"Eat your chicken, Earl," Edna said. "Then we can go to bed. I'm tired, but I'd like to make love to you anyway. None of this is a matter of not loving you, you know that."

Sometime late in the night, after Edna was asleep, I got up and walked outside into the parking lot. It could've been anytime because there was still the light from the interstate frosting the low sky and the big red Ramada sign humming motionlessly in the night and no light at all in the east to indicate it might be morning. The lot was full of cars all nosed in, most of them with suitcases strapped to their roofs and their trunks weighed down with belongings the people were taking someplace, to a new home or a vacation resort in the mountains. I had laid in bed a long time after Edna was alseep, watching the Atlanta Braves on cable television, trying to get my mind off how I'd feel when I saw that bus pull away the next day, and how I'd feel when I turned around and there stood Cheryl and Little Duke and no one to see about them but me alone, and that the first thing I had to do was get hold of some automobile and get the plates switched, then get them some breakfast and get us all on the road to Florida, all in the space of probably two hours, since that Mercedes would certainly look less hid in the daytime than the night, and word travels fast. I've always taken care of Cheryl myself as long as I've had her with me. None of the women ever did; most of them didn't even seem to like her, though they took care of me in a way so that I could take care of her. And I knew that once Edna left, all that was going to get harder. Though what I wanted most to do was not think about it just for a little while, try to let my mind go limp so it could be strong for the rest of what there was. I thought that the difference between a successful life and an unsuccessful one, between me at that moment and all the people who owned the cars that were nosed in to their proper places in the lot, maybe between me and that woman out in the trailers by the gold mine, was how well you were able to put things like this out of your mind and not be bothered by them, and maybe, too, by how many troubles like this one you had to face in a lifetime.

Through luck or design they had all faced fewer troubles, and by their own characters, they forgot them faster. And that's what I wanted for me. Fewer troubles, fewer memories of trouble.

I walked over to a car, a Pontiac with Ohio tags, one of the ones with bundles and suitcases strapped to the top and a lot more in the trunk, by the way it was riding. I looked inside the driver's window. There were maps and paperback books and sunglasses and the little plastic holders for cans that hang on the window wells. And in the back there were kids' toys and some pillows and a cat box with a cat sitting in it staring up at me like I was the face of the moon. It all looked familiar to me, the very same things I would have in my car if I had a car. Nothing seemed surprising, nothing different. Though I had a funny sensation at that moment and turned and looked up at the windows along the back of the Ramada Inn. All were dark except two. Mine and another one. And I wondered, because it seemed funny, what would you think a man was doing if you saw him in the middle of the night looking in the windows of cars in the parking lot of the Ramada Inn? Would you think he was trying to get his head cleared? Would you think he was trying to get ready for a day when trouble would come down on him? Would you think his girlfriend was leaving him? Would you think he had a daughter? Would you think he was anybody like you?

[February 1982]

JOHN UPDIKE

More Stately Mansions

Its webs of living gauze no more unfurl;
Wrecked is the ship of pearl!
And every chambered cell,
Where its dim dreaming life was wont to dwell,
As the frail tenant shaped his growing shell,
Before thee lies revealed,—
Its irised ceiling rent, its sunless crypt unsealed!
—Oliver Wendell Holmes,
"The Chambered Nautilus"

One of my students the other day brought into class a nautilus shell that had been sliced down the middle to make a souvenir from Hawaii. That's how far some of these kids' parents get on vacation, though from the look of the city (Mather, Massachusetts; population 47,000) you wouldn't think there was any money in town at all.

I held the souvenir in my hand, marveling at the mathematics of it—the perfect logarithmic spiral and the parade of increasing chambers, each sealed with a curved septum. I held it up to show the class. "What the poem doesn't tell you," I told them, "is that the nautilus is a nasty, hungry blob that uses its deserted chambers as propulsion tanks to maneuver up and down as it chases prey."

I sounded sore; the students widened their eyes, those that had been listening. They know their insides better than you do, often. The shell had reminded me of Karen. She had loved Nature, its fervent little intricacies. There was a sheen to the white-and-pale-orange nacre, here in the staring light of the tall classroom windows, that was hers. As I diagramed on the blackboard the spiral and up and down arrows and the dainty siphuncle whereby the nautilus performs its predatory hydrostatic magic I was remembering how she, to arouse me in the brightness of the big spare bedroom at the back of her house, would softly drag her pale-orange hair and her small white breasts across my penis.

Arousal wasn't always instant; I would be nervous, sweaty, guilty, stealing time from the lunch hour or even—so urgent did it all seem—ducking out of the school in a free period (classes run fifty minutes in our system) to drive across town to spend twenty minutes with her and then drive the fifteen minutes back again, screeching that old Falcon Monica's parents had given us into the high school parking lot under the eyes of the kids loafing and sneaking cigarettes out by the bike racks. They may have wondered, but teachers come and go, kids have no idea what it takes or doesn't take to keep the world running, and though studying us is one of their main ways of using up energy, they can't really believe the abyss that adult life is; that what they dream, we do. They couldn't know, no matter what their lavatory walls said, that Karen's musk was really on my finger-tips and face and that behind my fly my own little siphuncle sported a pearly ache of satisfaction.

She and Alan lived in the Elm Hill section, where the millowners and their managers had built big Victorian clapboard houses. The high school, new in 1950, had been laid out on an old farm on the other side of the river. With less than the whole dying downtown between us, we might have had time to share a cigarette afterward or talk, so that I might have come to understand better what our affair meant from her side, what she got out of it and the place she gave it in her life. My father had worked in those empty mills. He had me late and had coughed and drunk himself to death by the time I was twenty, and a kind of rage at the mills and him and all of Mather would come over me when, in a panic to be back to my next class, I would get stuck in the overshadowed streets down in the factory district. The city fathers had made them all one-way in some hopeless redevelopment scheme.

My grandfather came over from Italy to help build those mills. My oldest brother is a former auto mechanic who now owns a one-third share in a parts-and-supplies store and never touches a tool ex-

cept to sell it. Our middle brother sells insurance. They had me set to
become a Boston doctor, but with the lint's getting my father's lungs
so early I was lucky to get through college. I picked up the education
credits and a quick Master's and now teach general science to ninth
and tenth graders. A while ago I was made assistant principal, which
means two classes a day less and afternoons in the office. I had hoped
originally to get out of Mather, but here is where our connections
were—my father's old foreman was on the school board when they
hired me—so here I still am. Fall is the nicest season, and in recent
years some high-tech has overflowed Route 128 and come into the
local economy.

Alan's father, old Jake Owens, had owned Pilgrim, one of the
smaller mills and about the last along the river to close down. That
was the late Forties, twenty or more years after the bigger outfits had
sold their machinery south. Some in town said Jake showed a touching loyalty to Mather and its workers; others said the Owenses never
had had much head for business. They were drinking and shooting
men, with a notion of themselves as squires, at home in their little
piece of dirty valley with its country club, its Owens Avenue, its
hunting and skiing an hour or two north in New Hampshire. When
his father died in the mid-Sixties, Alan came home from the West
Coast with his Stanford law degree and his red-haired wife.

Karen was from Santa Barbara, thirtyish, pretty, but parched
somehow. All that Pacific sun was beginning to produce crow's-feet
and tiny little lines fanning out from her quick, maybe too-frequent
smile. She was small, with a tight small figure that had been on a lot
of beaches. She had majored in psychology and had a California
teacher's certificate, and put her name in at the high school office as a
substitute. That was where I first saw her, striding along our long,
noisy halls, her orange hair bouncing down her back. She was no
taller than many of the girls but different from them, a different animal. The corded throat and seasoned voice of a woman.

When we did talk, Karen and I, it was in the open, on opposite
sides of the fence, about the war. There was a condescending cer-
tainty about her pacifism that infuriated me, and a casual, bright edge
of militance that perhaps frightened me. I can't imagine now why I
imagined then the U.S.A. couldn't take care of itself. I felt so damn
motherly toward, of all people, LBJ. He looked so hangdog, even if
he was a bully.

"Why do you talk of people being *for* the war?" I would ask Karen in the teachers' room, amid the cigarette smoke and between-the-acts euphoria of teachers off-stage for fifty minutes. "It puts you people in such a smug no-lose position, being *not* for the war. Nobody's for any war, in the abstract; it's just sometimes judged to be the least of available evils."

"When is it the least?" she asked. "Tell me, Frank." She had a tense way of intertwining her crossed legs with the legs of the straight wooden school-supply chair so that her kneecaps jutted out, rimmed in white. This was the heyday of the mini-skirt, when female underpants, sure of being seen, sprouted patterns of flowers. When she crossed her legs like that, her skirt slid up to reveal an oval vaccination scar her childhood doctor had never thought would show. There were a number of awkward, likable things about Karen in spite of the politics: she smoked a lot, and her teeth were stained and slightly crooked, in an age of universal orthodontia. Her hands had the rising blue veins of middle age, and a tremor. I loved the expensive clothes she couldn't help but wear. Though her sweaters were cashmere, they always looked tugged slightly awry, so that a background of haste and distress invitingly seemed to lie behind her smooth public pose.

"Maybe you don't realize the kind of town you've moved to," I told her. "The VFW is where we have our dances. Our kids aren't pouring pig blood into draft board files. Their grandparents were glad to get here, and when their country asks them to go fight, they just go. They're scared, but they go."

"Why does that make it right?" Karen asked gently. "Explain it to me." The old psychology major. She was giving up the argument and babying me, as a kind of crazy man.

Her hair in its long brushed flower-child fall was not exactly either orange or red, it was the deep flesh color of a whelk shell's lip; and the more you looked, the more freckles she had. She was giving me an out, of sorts—a chance to shift out of this angry gear that discussion of the war always shoved me into. Johnson had been a schoolteacher, as I was now, and it seemed to me in the late Sixties that the entire class from coast to coast just wasn't *listening*.

"It just *does*," I told Karen, in my very lameness accepting her offer, surrendering. "I love these kids." This was a lie. "I grew up just like them." This was half a lie; I had been the youngest child, pampered, prepared for something better, out of Mather. "They give us great football teams." This was the truth.

The peace movement in Mather amounted to a few candle-bearing parades led by the local clergy, the same clergymen who would invoke the blessings on Memorial Day before the twenty-one-gun salute shattered the peace of the cemetery. When the first local boy died in Vietnam, he got a new elementary school named after him. When the second died, they took a street intersection in his part of town, called it a square, and named it after him. For the third and the fourth, there wasn't even an intersection.

The Owenses' house on the hill had a big living room lined with walnut wainscoting and wonderful ball-and-stick woodwork above the entranceways; the room could easily hold meetings of fifty or sixty, and did. At Karen's invitation, black men imported from Boston spoke here, and angry women imported from Cambridge. Civil rights and feminism and the perfidy of the Pentagon and the scheming, polluting corporations had become one big issue, and the Owenses had become the local chieftains of discontent, at least in the little circle Monica and I were drawn into. CMC, we called ourselves: Concerned Mather Citizens.

Monica and I had both been raised Catholic; I let it go in about my sophomore year of college, when my father died, but Monica kept it up until she went on the Pill. Our three children had been born in the first four years of our marriage. At first she attended mass, though she couldn't take communion; then she stopped even that. I was sorry to see it—it had been a part of her I had understood—and to hear her talk about the Church with such bitterness. That's how women can be, mulling something over and getting madder and madder about it, all in secret, and then making a sudden quantum jump. Revolutionaries. My impression was that Karen had courted Monica at the teachers' Christmas party, asking her to come over during the holidays and help address circulars. Monica jumped right in. She stopped getting perms and painting her fingernails. She pulled her springy black hair back into a ponytail and wore sneakers and jeans not only around the house but out to shop. She stopped struggling against her weight. Monica bloomed, I suppose; she had been a jock at Mather High (field hockey, girls' basketball) and a cheerleader, and now, ten years later and fifteen pounds heavier, that old girlish push, that egging-on fierceness, had come back. I didn't much like it but wasn't consulted. Somehow in all this I had become the oppressor, part of "the system," and the three children we had "given" each other had been some kind of dirty trick. She said the Pill was carcinogenic and I should get my tubes tied. I told her to go get her own tubes tied and she said that was what Karen Owens had advised. I asked angrily if that was what Karen Owens had done to herself and Monica replied with a certain complacence that, no, that wasn't the reason Karen and Alan didn't have children, she knew that much, and knew I'd be interested. I ignored the innuendo, excited to think of Karen in this intimate way and alarmed by Monica's tone. It was one thing to stop going to mass—after all, the Church had betrayed us, taking away Latin and Saint Christopher and fish on Friday—but there were limits, surely.

Still, I went to the meetings with her, across town through the factory district and up Elm Hill. Support the Blacks, Stop the War, Save the Ecology—Karen often sat up beside the speaker, entwining her legs with the chair legs so her kneecaps made white squares and, with a thoughtful V gesture, resting the tips of her middle and index fingers at the corners of her lips, as if enjoining herself not to say too much. When she did talk, she would keep tucking her blond hair behind her ears, a gesture I came to associate with our lovemaking. Sometimes she laughed, showing her engagingly imperfect teeth. Alan would sit in one of the back rows of the chairs they had assembled, looking surly and superior, already by that time of evening stupid with booze but backing her up in his nasal drawl when she needed it. As a lawyer in town he had already taken on enough fair-housing and draft-resistance cases to hurt his practice with the people who could pay. It was hard to know how unhappy this made him; it was hard to decipher what he saw, slumped down in the back, watching with sleepy eyes. He had great long lashes, and prematurely bushy eyebrows, and a high, balding forehead, nicely tanned.

I disliked him. He took up my oxygen when he was in the room. He was tall, tall as the rich get, plants with no weeds around them. When he looked down at me, it wasn't as if he didn't see me, he saw me too well; his eyes—with their lashes that looked artificial and a yellowish cast to the whites—flicked through and away, having seen it all and been instantly bored. Whatever had happened to him out there on the West Coast, it had left him wise in a way that made the world no longer very useful to him. He had death in his glance. Yet he also had Karen, and this Victorian mansion, and golf clubs and shotguns and tennis presses in the closets, and his father's deer heads in the library, and a name in the town that would still be worth something when this war and its protest had blown over.

In fairness, Alan could be entertaining, if he hadn't drunk too much. After the meetings a favored few of us would stay to tidy up, and Alan might get out his banjo and play. As a teenager, off at private schools since he was eleven, he had been a bluegrass freak and had taught himself this lonely music, fashionable then. When he got going, I would see green hills, and a lone hawk soaring, and the mouths of coal mines, and feel so patriotic that tears would sting my corneas; all the lovely country that had been in America would come rushing back, as it was before we had filled the land too full. Tipping back his head to howl the hillbilly chorus, Alan exposed his skinny throat as if to be cut.

While Monica and I would sit enthralled, joining in on the choruses, Karen would keep moving about, picking up the glasses and ashtrays, her determined manner and small set smile implying that this was an act Alan saved for company. First it had been her turn to howl; now it was his. When his repertoire ran out, she took over again, organizing word games, or exercises to enhance our perceptions. One Saturday night, I remember, all the women there hid behind a partition of blankets and extended one hand for the men to identify, and to my embarrassment I recognized Karen's and couldn't find Monica's—it was thicker and darker than it should have been, with a hairier wrist.

In many ways I did not recognize my wife; her raised consciousness licensed her to drink too much, to stay up too late. She never wanted to go home. The Owenses, the times, had corrupted her. However my own heart was wandering, I wanted to have her home, raising the children, keeping order against the day when all this disturbance, this reaching beyond ourselves, blew over. I had been attracted to the mother in her, the touch of heaviness already there when she was seventeen, her young legs glossy and chunky in the white cheerleader socks. She had an athlete's slow heartbeat and fell asleep early. When I came to sleep with Karen, in the bright back bedroom of her big ornate house, I had trouble accepting the twittery fervor she brought to acts that with Monica had a certain solemn weight, as of something yielded. Monica had once confessed to me that she held back out of dread of losing her identity in the act of sex; Karen seemed, contrariwise, to be pushing toward such a loss. Her quick dry lips, kissing mine for the first time in the hazardous privacy of the teachers' room, had an avidity borrowed (it crossed my mind) from the adolescents thundering all around us. I couldn't be worth, surely, quite such an agitation of lips and tongue, quite so hard a hug from this slender, overheated person, whose heart I could feel tripping against my own through the twin cages of our ribs and the wool of her sweater. Even in this moment of first surrender I noted that the wool was cashmere. I wondered if she had mistaken me, working-class one generation removed, for a redneck stud, an obediently erect conscript from the suffering, steady poor. I was a little repelled by the something *schooled* in her embrace—something prereadied and too good to be true. But in time I accepted this as simply her metabolism, her natural way. She was love-starved. So was I.

Days when she didn't substitute became our days, set up with sweaty phone calls from the pay phone outside the cafeteria, which the kids had usually clogged with gum or clumsy slugs. The Owenses' house backed up to some acres of woods that they owned. Bird-chirp and pine-scent would sift through her windows. The light was almost frightening; I was used to the uxorious dark. She kept an aquarium and a terrarium back here, to take advantage of the sun, and wildlife posters all around; *we* were wildlife, naked and endangered. The bestial efficiency of our encounters had to do for tenderness. She knew to the minute when I would arrive and was ready, clothes off and phone off the hook. She knew to the minute when I must go. When one of my free periods backed onto the lunch hour, and we had more time, we wasted it in bickering. When LBJ announced he would not run, I told her this would bring in Nixon, and hoped she was happy. This while the happiness of our lovemaking was still making her eyes shine. She had a way of looking me over, of examining me as reverently as she did the toad and garter snake in her terrarium. Somehow, I, with my sexual hunger and blue-collar snarl, was simply life to her, a kind of treasure.

And she to me? Heaven, of a sort. When I sneaked in the back door, past the plastic trash cans smelling of Alan's empties, Karen would be standing at the head of the back stairs like a bright, torn piece of sky. Up close, her body was a star map, her shoulders and shins crowded with freckles constellated too thick to be counted. Even those patches of skin shaped like the pieces of a bathing suit revealed to inspection a dark dot or two where the sun had somehow pricked.

"You really ought to go, darling," Karen would say. More practiced than I, I suppose, she was the enforcer of our affair. I began to resent this, this sense of being disciplined. At school, when she came to substitute, I loved seeing her in the halls, her red hair bouncing on her back, her compact little body full of our secrets. The Movement was in the air even here now; our young Poles and Portuguese were no longer prepared to be drafted unquestioningly, and the classes in government and history, even in general science, had become battlefields. At Columbia and in Paris that spring, students were rioting. I felt whole masses of rooted presumption being torn up around me, but no longer cared. I felt so proud, linking myself with Karen in those minutes between classes, in the massive shuffle smelling of perfume and chewing gum and bodily warmth.

She warned me, "I love your touch, but, Frank, you mustn't touch me in public."

"When did I?"

"Just now. In the hall." We were in the teachers' room. She had lit a cigarette. She seemed extra nervous, indignant.

"I wasn't aware," I told her. "I'm sure nobody noticed."

"Don't be stupid. The children notice everything."

It was true. I had seen our names penciled together, with the correct verb, on a lavatory wall. "You care?"

"Of course I care. So should you. We could both be hurt."

"By whom? The school board? The American Legion? I thought the revolution was on and there was naked dancing in the streets. I'm all for it; watch."

"*Frank.* Someone could come in that door any second."

"We used to neck in here like mad."

"That was before we had our days."

"Our half hours. I'm sick of rushing back to the table of elements in a postcoital daze."

"You are?"

The fear in her eyes insulted me. "Yes," I told her, "and I'm sick of the hypocrisy. I'm sick of insomnia. I can't sleep anymore, I want you beside me so much. I thrash around, I take aspirin. Sometimes I cry, for a change of pace."

She tucked her hair behind her ears. Her face looked narrow, its skin tight at the sides of her eyes, a glaze across the tiny wrinkles. "Has Monica noticed?"

"No, she slumbers on. Nothing wakes her up. Why?—has Alan noticed any difference in you?"

"No, and I don't want him to."

"You don't? Why not?"

"Need you ask?" The sarcasm made her face look quite evil. There was a set of assumptions behind it that I hated.

My voice got loud. "You bet your sweet ass I need." I repeated, "Why the hell not?"

"*Shh.* He's my husband, that's why."

"That seems simplistic. And rather conservative, if I may say so."

Betty Kurowski, first-year algebra and business math, opened the door, looked at our faces, and said, "Oh. Well, I'll go smoke in the girls' lavatory." As she was closing the door we both begged her to come back.

"We were just arguing about Vietnam," Karen told her. "Frank wants to bomb South China now."

For summer employment, Monica and I were counselors at a summer camp in New Hampshire, about forty minutes' drive from Mather. As if this were not separation enough, Alan and Karen spent a month in Santa Barbara visiting her family. They lived in a million-dollar house near the beach. Amid the *plockety-plock* of table tennis and the shouts of horseplay from our little brown lake, I could not stop thinking of Karen—her flesh, the sunlight, the way she fed on me with her eyes and mouth. I was weary of children, including my own, yet part of my fantasy was that I would give her a child.

When the Owenses returned from their month away, toward the end of August, Monica called them and arranged to have Karen come to the camp to lead a nature walk. Karen fixed up a bottle with a jeweler's loupe so that the children could peer into a sample of pond water and see the frenzy of tiny life there. In the aftermath of this visit, this glimpse of her functioning with such sweet earnestness as a teacher, I wrote her on camp stationery a letter full of remembered details of our lovemaking and proposing we break out and get married. More a violent dream than a proposal: the surge of writing, in a corner of the picnic pavilion while Monica was out on the lake with a canoeing class, carried me into it, and I had enough prescience to hold off mailing it a day. But on rereading, it all seemed frightening but true, like the cruel facts of pond life. Once the blue mailbox had closed its iron mouth, I sensed I had overstepped. Not that there was much danger of Alan intercepting; I knew the mail arrived at the Owenses' around noon, when he would be at his office or still in bed from the night before. Alcohol was worming deeper into his system and making it hard for him to sleep at night, too.

Days of silence went by; at first I was relieved. But I had expected some message from Karen, at least a gesture toward the two of us on the social plane. Camp was over. Summer muddle—New England squeezing the last drops of fun out of its few warm months—was all around us, and I longed for school to begin again.

In Chicago, at August's end, the Democrats were nominating Humphrey while Johnson cowered in the White House. That Wednesday night a call from Karen came through; the Owenses were having a crowd over to watch the speeches and the riots on television. The convention went on and on, everything sacred unraveling before our eyes, and we kept pace with brandy and beer and white wine. Instead of junk-food snacks, Karen served little saucers of health foods—raisins, sesame and sunflower seeds. Alan was concentrating on the bourbon, and somehow around eleven I was delegated to go downtown and get him another bottle. The package stores were closed, but the Owenses told me they were sure I could wangle a fifth from the bartender at Rudy's, where my father had been a regular. I resented the errand—I had resented my father's long evenings at Rudy's—but performed it, counting out Alan his change to the penny. Around midnight the other concerned citizens began to drift home; around one-thirty the four of us were left sitting at the four sides of the kitchen table. The night was hot, with a last-gasp heat; along the coast, sea breezes lighten the summer, but in our river valley it hangs heavy until the maples start to turn. Crickets were singing outside the screen door.

"So where are we?" Alan abruptly asked. He seemed to be focused on Karen, across the table from him. Monica and I sat on his either side.

"Here and there," Monica said, giggling. She had had plenty to drink and was more mischievous, more wakeful, than I was used to seeing her. Out of her ponytail, her hair had a bushy outward thrust that was the coming look—tough, cheerful, ethnic. Karen's look, the long ironed hair, the nervous vulnerability, belonged to a fading past.

"Let's talk turkey," Alan persisted through his blur, his long lashes blinking, his rather pretty mouth fixed, as it were, helplessly in a sneer.

"Oh, goody, let's," Monica said, glancing at me to see how I was taking things.

"Alan, explain what you *mean*," Karen said. Her voice could take on a wheedling tone. She was the least drunk of us all and I saw her, in a flash of alcoholic illumination, as pedantic. He was being naughty and she was set to baby him Socratically as she had babied me about the kids going off to fight. Using her psychology. "Don't hide behind your liquor," she went on after Alan. "Explain what you *mean*." Some old grievance between them seemed to be surfacing.

It appeared to me he didn't mean very much, was just making conversation. I was so interested in the tremor of Karen's hands as she maneuvered a cigarette to her mouth that I was slow to notice Monica's substantial hand on top of Alan's bony one. I was so used to seeing her comfort children at the camp that I dismissed it as more Alan-babying.

"He's a Virgo," Karen told Monica, smiling now that her cigarette was lit. "Virgos are *so* withholding."

He looked at his wife with his fishy starry stunned eyes and I saw that he loathed the brightness that I loved. Much as I disliked him, my thought was that he must have reasons. He opened his mouth to speak and she prompted "Yes?" too eagerly; her sharp smile chased him back into his shell.

Alan hunched lower over the table, and Hubert Humphrey's high-pitched old-womanish voice came out of his mouth. "Let's put America back on track," he said, imitating the acceptance speech we had heard, interspersed with shots of the violence outside. "Let's not talk about the green belt." Karen's latest project had been to arouse community interest in creating a green belt around our tired little city. "Let's talk about—"

"Below the belt," Monica finished for him, and she and I laughed. Across the table from me she looked enlarged, her hair puffed out and her face broadening under its genial film of alcohol. Her mother was fat, with a distinct moustache, but I had never thought Monica would grow to resemble her. Now that she had, I didn't mind; I felt she would take care of me, even though I had recently flung into the mailbox a letter offering to leave her. Her glances toward me were like holes in the haze the Owenses were generating, working something out between themselves. She and I and, in his way, Alan were in tune with the crickets and the occasional swish of cars passing, but our camaraderie was lamed by something uncomprehending in Karen and dampened by our common fatigue; watching too much television, we too had become staticky and blurred. We were grateful when Karen stood up and shut us off. She announced that tomorrow was another day and she was going to bed. Monica said yes, and she had to take Tommy to the orthodontist.

We kissed each other good night then, Karen and I primly, Alan not wanting to let go of Monica's hand. A warm drizzle had begun outdoors. My wife fell asleep in the car beside me as the windshield wipers swept away the speckles of rain. Downtown was deserted, the great empty factories looking majestic and benevolent, asleep. We lived across the river, in a development beyond the high school.

That was our last evening with the Owenses. Next morning, Karen called the house when she knew Monica would be off with Tommy. "I told him," she told me.

"You did?" A great numbness hit my heart and merged with my hangover. "But why?" I had answered on the upstairs phone and could see on the street below a few yellow leaves, the first fallen, lying in spots of damp from last night's rain.

Karen's voice, husky with lack of sleep, picked its way carefully, as if spelling out things to a child. "Didn't you under*stand* what Alan"—I hated the slightly strengthened way she pronounced *Alan*—"was *say*ing last night? He was saying he wanted to go to bed with your wife."

"Well, something like that. How does that signify?"

Karen didn't answer.

I supplied, "You think he should have asked her in private, instead of making it a committee matter."

She said, "The reason he couldn't get it out, he didn't think you'd accept me in exchange." Her voice snagged, then continued, roughened by tears, "He'd only ever seen us quarrel."

"That's touching," I said. I didn't find Alan touching, actually. But she was enrolling me in her decision.

"I couldn't bear it, Frank. His being so innocent."

"How did he take the news?"

"Oh, he was exhilarated. He kept me up all night with it. He couldn't believe—I shouldn't tell you this—he couldn't believe I'd sleep with a townie."

Downstairs my two younger children had grown bored with television and were punching each other, quarreling. I said, "But with a nontownie he'd believe it? How many nontownies have you slept with?"

"Frank, don't." She hesitated. "You know how I am. He doesn't give me shit, Frank. He's *sink*ing."

"Well, let him." A coldness, the cold of deadness, had come over me.

"I can't."

"Okay. I don't think it was very nice of you to turn us in without even warning me," I said, all weary dignity.

"You would have argued."

"You bet. I love you."

"I did it for you too. For you and Monica."

"Thanks." The day outside was bright, with a rinsed brightness, and I thought, *When she hangs up, I must open the window and let some air in.* "Did you get my letter?" I asked her.

"Yes. That was another thing. It frightened me."

"I meant it to be a nice letter."

"It was nice. Only—a little possessive?"

"Oh. Pardon me." *I'll never sleep with her again, never, ever,* I thought, and the window whose panes I stared through seemed a translucent seal barring me from great volumes of possibility, I on one side and my life on the other, the naked bright day.

Karen was crying again, less in grief, I thought, than in exasperation. "I *wanted* to talk to you about it, but there wasn't any way to get *to* you; I haven't even had a chance to give you the present I brought from Santa Barbara."

"What was it?"

"A shell. A beautiful shell."

"That you found on the beach?"

"No, those are too ordinary and small. I bought it in a shop, a shell from the South Seas. A top shell, silvery white outside with pink freckles underneath. You know how you go on about my freckles."

"Your dear, wild freckles," I said.

Karen didn't substitute-teach that fall; she went into Boston and worked long days for the peace movement. Friends of ours who had remained in the Owenses' inner circle told us that some nights she didn't come home at all. If you look at the memoirs of the celebrity-radicals of that time, a lot of it was sex. Liberals drink, radicals use dope and have sex. Karen and Alan split up finally sometime between when Nixon and Kissinger engineered our troop withdrawal and when South Vietnam collapsed. His drinking became famously worse; he ceased to function as a lawyer at all, though the name stayed up in the lobby of the office block downtown where he had rented space. She went back to the West Coast; he stayed with us, like the gutted factories. Though I didn't see him from one year to the next, I thought of him often, always with joy at his fall. Monica and I had moved, actually, into his neighborhood; we allowed ourselves a fourth child before she got herself sterilized, and, with heating oil going higher and higher, we were able to pick up very reasonably a big turn-of-the-century house on Elm Hill. We've closed off some of the rooms and burn a lot of wood.

Betty Kurowski's mother cleaned, twice a week, the Owens house two blocks further up the hill, and it was Betty who told me how bad Alan was getting. "A skeleton," she said. "You should go see him, Frank. I went in there last week and talked with him and he asked about you. He saw in the paper how you've become assistant principal."

"Why would I want to go see that snide bastard?"

Betty looked at me knowingly, under those straight black eyebrows that don't go with her bleached hair. "For old times' sake," she said, straight-faced.

I asked Monica to go with me and she said, "It's not me he wants to see."

"He did once, as you remember."

"That was pathetic, that was just him trying to fight back. He's not fighting back anymore. Poor Alan Owens. That whole family was just too good for this world." That's the sort of thing her mother would say. But Monica hasn't gotten fat. She counts those calories and is taking a night course in computer science. She's been working mornings as receptionist and biller for a photo-developing lab that has taken half a floor of the old Pilgrim mill, and they want her to learn to use the computer. I'm proud of her, seeing her go off nights in her trim programmer's suit. She's tough. Old cheerleaders keep that toughness. Win or lose is the way they figure. The facts about Karen and me, when they came out, just made her determined to win.

Karen sends mimeographed Christmas letters. She's remarried, has had a son and a daughter, and got a degree in landscape architecture. Alan had been holding her back, but a dozen years ago she was too timid to know that.

Nobody answered my knock. The Owens house has a front door as wide as a billiard table, with gray glass sidelights into which an arabesque pattern of frosting has been etched, so people can peek in only in spots. The clapboards in the shelter of the porch were pumpkin-colored, but those out in the weather were faded pale as wheat, and peeling. Advertising handouts had been allowed to pile up on the welcome mat. The door was unlocked and swung open easily. The downstairs showed Mrs. Kurowski's work; indeed, it was uncannily clean and tidy in the big rooms, as if no one ever walked through. The long kitchen, with its little square cherry drop-wing table, looked innocent of meals. Two tangerines in a pewter bowl had turned half green with mold. "Alan?" I was sorry I had come; being in this house again after so many years awakened in my stomach the sour nervousness of those noontime visits that would never be again. Sunlight slanted in at the kitchen windows the way it always had, making the scratched lip of the aluminum sink sparkle, putting a sheen on the dry bar of soap in a cracked rubber dish. I stood at the foot of the dark-stained back stairs at whose head naked Karen used to flicker like a piece of sky, and called again, "Alan?"

Frighteningly, his voice came. "Come on up, Frank." He had had a deeper, more melodious voice than one would have expected out of his skinny, slumped frame, and there was still timbre in his voice, though it sounded frayed and quavery, like an old woman's—like his imitation of Hubert Humphrey. I climbed the stairs, my belly remembering how my eyes would possess her—ankles, knees, amber maidenhair—every step carrying me higher toward the level of her keen, fluttering, excessively pleased embrace, her heart through her lifted, stretched ribs thumbing against my classroom clothes, my tie and the coarse cotton of my button-down shirt crushed against the silk of her.

"In here," his voice came, already weaker. I had feared he would be in the bright back room that she and I had used, but he was in the bedroom that had been theirs, at the front of the house, clouded by the mass of the two big beeches outside. And the shades were drawn. The dim room was soaked in a smell that at first I took to be medicinal but that then came clear as whiskey, the flat and shameful smell it has in the empty bottle. Alan was sitting in the center of his tousled bed in striped pajamas and an untied pale-blue bathrobe, in the yoga position, pertly smoking a cigarette. He looked dreadful—emaciated, with a patchy black beard inches long. He had lost the hair on the top of his head in a clean swath, but the rest hung down with a biblical lankness nearly to his shoulders. His skin was as dull and thin as tracing paper, with something translucent about the pure-white tops of his bare feet. The room was hot, the thermostat turned way up—in this day and age, a bit of swank in that.

"God, Alan. How do you feel?"

"Not bad, Frank. How do I look?"

"Well, thin. Aren't you eating?"

He put the cigarette to his lips the way children learning to smoke do, trying to follow the tip with his eyes. Yet the gesture with which he took it away and exhaled was debonair. "I've been having a little war with my stomach," he said. "I can't keep anything down."

"Have you seen a doctor?"

"*Aaah.*" A little flip of his hand, all bones now. His gestures had become effete, unduly flexible. "They always say the same thing. I know what I've got, a stomach bug that's been going around. A touch of flu."

"What is it that they always say?" I asked. "The doctors."

His hands had become so frail the hairs on their backs seemed to be growing with a separate life. He turned his head away, toward the dusty frame of light coming in around the drawn shade nearest his bed; dim as it was, the light made him squint, and a cutting edge of bone was declared by a shadow scooped at his temple. He turned back toward me and tipped his head flirtatiously. "You know, you son of a bitch," he drawled, trying to be pleasant. "To taper off on the sauce. But the sauce has never hurt me. It's when I taper off that the horrors begin." This last seemed honest; his voice had flattened in tone.

There must be terror in there somewhere, I thought. But as a gentleman he wanted to shelter me from it. The result was grisly parody, a kind of puppetry. So gaunt, yet, his face spread wide by alcohol and middle age, he looked like a lollipop, with a Rasputin beard. Terror was *my* emotion, mixed in with that thrill of importance eyewitnesses have.

I found the courage to tell him, "Alan, you can't keep on like this. You really must do something."

It was what he had wanted me to say, so he could spurn it. He sneered and made a soft hawking noise that put me in my place. "I'm not that much of a doer. Let's talk about you. I hear you got a promotion."

"It happens, if you're there long enough."

"Always modest," he said. "And you've moved in down the street."

"You mind?"

It wasn't clear that he heard me. His next speech came out as if it had been prepared on a ribbon; his head wobbled as he drawled it out. "I always knew you'd make it as a townie. One of those sleek slobs in three-piece suits eating out at Scudellari's every Friday night, hopping up from your table to go across and say hello to a school board member, all jolly, heading up the door-to-door drive for the new hospital wing, the K of C clambake and all that. That's what I used to tell Karen, he'll wind up one of those sleek wop slobs in a three-piece suit. Where's the third piece?"

His twitching head, his eyes looking theatrical with their lashes, seemed actually to be searching the corners near the ceiling for the third piece. The atmosphere in this room was rich with the gloom, the bad smells, the majesty of his ruin, none of his scorn bottled up anymore. I laughed with him. "Yeah," I said. "Karen said at the time you couldn't believe she'd sleep with a townie."

"Wop. I think I said wop."

"Probably."

"You owe me one for that. You owe me one, brother."

"It was a long time ago. What happened between you two then?"

He looked toward the window shade again, as if he could see out. "Karen was—greedy." The words came out of him as if dictated from behind, by a voice he had to squint to hear and then echo, missing some words. "You owe me one, brother," he repeated, fuddled.

"Alan, what can I do for you?" My own voice seemed to boom. "I'm not a doctor, but I'd say you need one." That third piece he mentioned, the vest, seemed to be on my chest, making me thicker, armored, ruthless in my health; it's wonderful to feel your life on you like a suit in perfect press.

He fended me off with effeminate, flustered gestures. "You can do a little shopping for me," he said. "This damn flu, I can hardly make it to the john. My legs don't want to work right."

"Can't Betty's mother shop for you?"

"She drags in loathsome stuff. Breakfast cereal. Orange juice. She doesn't know . . ."

"Doesn't know what, Alan?"

"What's good for flu."

"What is? Bourbon?"

He gave me a straight dark helpless look. "Just to tide me over until I get my legs back."

"On one condition, Alan. You call your doctor."

"Oh, sure. Absolutely. I know he'll just say it's the flu. My wallet's on the bureau over there—"

"My treat." As he said, I owed him one. No embarrassing deal with the bartender at Rudy's this time; I paid $8.98 over the counter for a fifth of Wild Turkey's best at the liquor supermart at the new shopping mall on the other side of Elm Hill. Back up the hill, back up the stairs: my siphuncle was working overtime. He wasn't in his bed, he was in the bathroom; I listened a moment and heard the noise of dry heaves. I left the bottle on the bedside table.

Who can say that that was the bottle that killed him? A parade of bottles killed him, going back to his spoiled teens. It was not the next morning but the next that they found him curled over, stiffened in the yoga position beside the toilet bowl. When they opened the door (Betty's mother had called the police, guessing what was behind it), his body fell over in one piece, like a husk. Dehydration, internal bleeding, heart failure. Betty told us there were empty bottles every-where—under the bed, in the closet. I picture mine in my mind's eye, drained, lying on its side on the floor, gleaming when they raised the shades at last. Maybe it was that bottle I thought of when the student brought in the nautilus shell. Or the shell Karen never got to give me. Or that big house with all its rooms and this naked freckled woman waiting in one of its chambers. That was forever ago. It has taken all of the Seventies to bury the Sixties.

[October 1982]

JOYCE CAROL OATES

Ich Bin ein Berliner

As the younger brother—indeed, the only sibling—of a "notorious" deceased, I have frequently been interviewed; but I will give no more interviews. It was thought indiscreet of me to say certain things. Such as "The advantage of being a younger brother is that one generally *outlives.*" Such as "The advantage of being younger is that one eventually becomes elder." Such as "The distinction between suicide and murder might be overrated."

When I flew to Berlin the first time, to "claim" my brother's body and arrange to ship it home, a disagreeably public flurry attended my departure. Now, a year later, nearly a year later, approaching the exact anniversary of his death, my journey to make other claims goes unreported. *"Some things are performed in secret,"* I seem to recall my brother saying, *"or not at all."*

"Did you anticipate his death?" I ask one of my brother's acquaintances, shouting to make my voice heard over the din in the Flash Point Discothek on the Kurfürstendamm. "Did he seem, well, you know—suicidal?"

Here is Rudi, young and shaggily blond and very much a Berliner, a sullen boyishness about his features, a prettily evoked brutal aura not to be taken altogether seriously, a manner of fashion, costume (tight, scarlet velour shirt unbuttoned to mid-chest, tighter blue jeans, cattleman's boots that come to mid-calf), sheer style. A thug who is in fact a university student, a male prostitute who is in fact only a waiter at the Flash Point, costumed like the other waiters and waitresses. His embarrassment is good manners as well as surprise, his pretense of not having exactly heard is to be attributed to the deafening rock music and not to the thin timbre of my American voice.

So he hunches forward and cups his ear and asks me to repeat my question, and the ruddy flush overtakes his throat and face in a most becoming way, and then he says, not altogether willing to bring his luminous, steely-gray gaze up to mine: "Did I anticipate your brother's death, his death in particular, in those weeks? No, I would say no. But did I anticipate Death—that is another question, sir—to which the answer is: *Yes, I think so, yes, maybe, yes, who knows?*" Sniffing loudly enough for me to hear over the noise, releasing a soupçon, not altogether disagreeable, of cologne and hearty male sweat and an unidentified acrid-sweet drug, though perhaps it is only the odor of grief, though perhaps it is only the odor of fear, for who am I, after all, to be making inquiries about *that particular death* once again.

To win my heart, perhaps, he wipes at his nose with the cuff of his velvety scarlet sleeve and says in a voice blurred by the din on all sides, or by his own internal agitation: "Who can know, who can be sure of these things? Premonitions—anticipating suicide—death? That same day your brother walked into their bullets another friend of mine died, a friend of twelve years, our mothers had known each other since they were schoolgirls, she was my age exactly, she was found in a telephone booth in the Pankstrasse Station, a stupid death, a death I hate her for. . . . I had knowledge of *some death* about to happen, *someone's death,* but I cannot pretend now, so long afterward, to know whose it would be. She died, this friend of mine, of an accident so stupid I would like to grab hold of her, to stop her, to hurt her," he says angrily, making a gesture toward one forearm with the fingers of the other, gripping a ghost-syringe so that I cannot help but wince. That other death is too sad, too ugly—more ridiculous, perhaps, than my brother's.

"I know," I tell Rudi, consoling him. "I understand," I say to him, drawing back from his harsh acrid panting breath. "It's so hard to forgive them. And impossible to forget."

Afterward, in my sanitized bunker of a hotel room, I wondered whether I should be angry that the Berliner Rudi had deflected my line of questioning so skillfully and imposed his somewhat sordid grief upon my own.

That other death, after all, might be judged contemptible. But my brother's death might be judged—or so certain persons have argued—heroic.

I assure them all, as if there were any conceivable doubt: Of course I know how he died. Everyone knows how he died. *Time,* after all, reported on the number of bullets and the general condition of "vital organs." In fact, I have memorized the official reports issued by both sets of police, on both sides of the Wall. I have memorized the documented facts, the testimonies under oath, the protestations of regret from high-ranking officials of both governments. I often murmur to myself—I can't quite imagine why—that masterpiece of scolding and commiseration from the German Democratic Republic.

"Of course I know how he died," I tell Mr. G____, the seemingly helpful State Department lackey of junior rank who works closely with Amerika Haus and with visiting Fulbright fellows at the Free University. "But *how* doesn't translate into *why.*"

A beat of some seconds. An uncongenial silence. Then he says, with a just-perceptible glance at his wristwatch, "As you know, your brother became very interested in certain subjects—Berlin now, Berlin in the Forties, Berlin in the Thirties, Berlin when it became *Berlin,* in the Twenties. And he became very interested in Germany, and the Germanys, and the Reich, and the Republic, and of course the Wall. And so he neglected his work at the university. He disappointed quite a few of us. And gradually the fixation increased, the obsessive thoughts. Conversations with him became difficult. He might be said to have become *disturbed,* and it enraged him that other people were perhaps less disturbed, less *morbid.* But all this," the youngish Mr. G_____ says in his accentless Foreign Service English, "you certainly know."

Politely I inquire: "How would you define *morbid,* in this context? A *morbid interest* in Berlin, and in German history, and in the Wall—?"

"Any interest at all," he says, amiably enough, though with no semblance of a smile. "Any interest at all, pursued beyond a certain point, in this particular context."

Midnight on the Hardenbergstrasse. Tourist-gaiety, tourist-euphoria, a little frenzy is good for the soul. Automobiles, taxis, the usual amplified music. It is America. But no, it is Berlin. West Berlin. Germany. But no, it is America. No? Yes? America? But with such strong accents?

Everyone is a tourist here, in this part of the city, in this part of Europe. We are Westerners in the East. An oasis of sparkling West in the glum barbed-wire East. Everyone is infected with tourist-gaiety, everyone strolling tonight on the Hardenbergstrasse, arms linked, "wild" young people with spiky dyed hair, well-fed gentlemen in tailored clothes, solitary "foreigners" like myself. Look: The radiant Mercedes-Benz cross, rotating nobly overhead! A sacred vision beamed over the Wall into the shadowy East.

The Wall. Why did it interest my doomed brother to the point of sickness but interests me scarcely at all (save as a point of geographical and historical information)? For I am not an obsessive personality; the morbid I find commonplace.

For instance, the starkness of the Wall and the terror it allegedly engenders—all quite exaggerated. Here we haven't the stink of Gothic centuries, boulders dragged out of the fields by peasants, bleeding hands, backs flayed under the whip, that sort of thing. Here we have monotony, a look of the modern: gray concrete, a structure approximately twelve feet high, resistant to subtlety and fine-spun poetry, a matter of statistics. Always statistics. The Wall isolates, as my guidebook says, some 480 square kilometers of the 880 square kilometers of Greater Berlin.

We have only a dotted line on my tourist map to acknowledge it. It's even difficult to locate that line of tiny, pale-blue dots aswim in a typographical picnic of more garish colors. As a point of personal reference I added a tourist-attraction asterisk of my own, in red ink, at that point in the Pankow district where the Wall borders the Reinickendorf district, where my brother died. On "Eastern" soil.

What is the Wall but a distant fantasy, an irrelevant fact here on the Hardenbergstrasse at midnight? Sauna Paradies, the New Crazy Shock Revue ("Herren als Damen"), the Weingarten family restaurant. Not at all like Times Square, not America, simple frank robust goodnatured Germanic spirits, altogether healthy, a tonic dose of the pagan. Why did my scholarly brother seek out morbid diversions, why did he betray his commitment to American optimism, why do his former students at the Free University still protect him, even from his own brother? I wonder what sort of "research" he did those last six or seven weeks.

The Flash Point Discothek again, where I had best not return so soon. Would not want to embarrass, or alarm, or annoy, or intimidate, or—most of all—*bore* dear shag-haired Rudi.

Perhaps his research took him to the Internationale Spitzengirls Salon, and to the Cabaret Chez Nous, and the Big Eden Peep Show, and the Chalet Noir. Non-Stop-Sex-Shop. Drugged teenage girls, very pretty. But skeletal-thin. Something has happened to the robust Aryan mammalian form.

Lounging about the much-photographed tourist attraction, the bombed and never-repaired Kaiser Wilhelm Memorial Church (forever a monument, a luridly visible monument, to their suicidal zeal and our zealous bombs), here are very young girls, such familiar girls, skin-tight blue jeans, silky shorts, halter tops, spiky dyed hair, eyes outlined in hopeful circus colors: sit with us awhile, have you change, have you dollar, *bitte* deutsche marks, cigarette please, sir, thank you, you are very kind.

Did you know my brother? I ask, supplying the name, but they are too young and too recent, memory fades swiftly in this part of the world.

Courteous, though. The blank smooth foreheads crinkling in a pretense of solemn thought.

Nein, I think. No. Sorry, no.

Why are there so many shoes for sale in West Berlin, I asked the girls, why marvelous gleaming pyramids of shoes, show windows brilliantly illuminated all hours of the night, stores like cathedrals?—but meaning no harm, jocose sort of chatter, friendly American passing the time, no danger. X-Rated Playtime, Colonel Sanders Kentucky Fried Chicken, I move on to prescribed tourist pleasures, baby prostitutes in open-toed platform shoes, robust singing in beer gardens, old-world charm, marching songs, Salon Massage ("Boys & Girls All"), a floor show called "Welcome to Hell" in helpful English.

All in the spirit of jest.

My research brings me back to festive Kantstrasse at three-thirty in the morning. Odors of grease-fried foods, spilled beer, the companionable blare of American acid rock, ruddy thug-faces cruising in their Mercedeses, pigs' snouts, small blinking beady eyes. But I am being unfair. Am I being unfair? I am reporting what I see and failing to alter a syllable.

Among the debris in his room, photographs of this very street. This kiosk where the History of the Wall (as seen from the West) is on perpetual display in the usual tourist-languages. His photographs of their photographs of the Brandenburg Gate, and Checkpoint Charlie, and the dying eighteen-year-old Peter Fechter, many years dead.

Obviously this martyred youth gave my brother the idea. The inspiration. The goad.

He was shot down—Peter Fechter, that is—on 17 August 1962. As all the Free World knows, or should know. Shot down by East Berlin guards at the foot of the Wall and allowed to bleed to death for a long, a very long, a famously long time.

He is bleeding to death still: you can see the snaky black blood on the pavement. Propaganda hero amid the neon traffic, the outdoor cafés, X-rated *Kino,* summer strollers licking fat ice-cream cones, business as usual. Granted, you die only once. But how long does it take?

Photographs of my brother were taken too, of course. But by then he was already dead.

He was interested—I surmise, morbidly interested—in the origins of Berlin, in the early thirteenth century; and in the history of the Prussian eagle, and the terrible triumph of Napoleon, and the founding of the German Empire, and Kaiser Wilhelm II, and the Thousand-Year Reich, and the Berlin blockade, and the erection, at last, of the Wall in 1961. In 1961, when my brother was in the eighth grade at St. Ursula's on Gratiot Avenue in Detroit and I was in fourth grade in the same school, which is still in session, though the nuns do not look like nuns any longer. How peculiar that he was older than I in those days. And now seems younger. And soon *will* be younger.

"Imagine the surprise of the East Berlin guards," I find myself saying to Mr. G____, whom I have coerced into having a drink with me at the well-lit Weingarten, "that any East Berliner, at this point in history, would approach the Wall on foot. Just walking. Maybe swaying a little—staggering—d'you think? Because he must have been drunk—euphoric—with the daring of it. The theatrics. Because the bullets can't have hurt, there were so many."

Time of death, 4:25 A.M., 17 June 1981, said to be a fairly cold northern European night.

Mr. G___ has heard it all before, Mr. G___ yearns for a respite from West Berlin, a respite from Germany, from history. Doubtless he is very much moved by my brother's silly death, but he cannot avoid yawning behind his hand and glancing covertly at his watch. Clearly we aren't chums. The Foreign Service has refined his American weaknesses out of him. We share a common language but no common memory. My last name—my brother's last name—is a distinct embarrassment to him. It was "an international incident," after all!

"Suicide is the triumph of the will over biology, don't you think?" I ask him, but he mistakes my twitchy sardonic smile for the first signs of weeping. And explains nervously that he must get home.

Was it a drunken prank; was it an exploit for publicity's sake (he had published a few poems, translated from English into German by one of his colleagues at the Free University: he was therefore a "poet" and a problematic character known as a Leftist sympathizer); was it a simple mistake; was it a heroic political gesture; was it—just suicide?

In any case the member of his family who had to fly to Berlin to "claim" the body and arrange to ship it back home was most inconvenienced. And finds it very hard to forgive suicide as a *witty gesture.*

It should be mentioned that I have been personally affected by none of this. My temperament is not morbid. I celebrate health. I celebrate clarity. If it amuses me to indulge in certain philosophical speculations, that is only because I presume they are of general—which is to say, allegorical—interest.

N.B. Since West Berlin is a walled city in the East, an escape from "East" to "West" might involve an attempt to scale the Wall in an *easterly direction.*

The "escape" from the Pankow district to the populous Reinickendorf district, however, would have been ordinary enough—from "East" to "West."

Is a certain crisis in history past? There are fewer escapes by way of the river now—fewer drownings, bullet-riddled bodies. Land mines detonated along the great stretch of the border between the two Germanys are apt to be set off these days by such innocent creatures as hares, deer, stray dogs, etc. "The Wall is forever," my brother scrawled across one of the letters he never sent.

I am about to leave. My curiosity hasn't been satisfied but rather numbed. The Wall may be forever but I have no interest in it. As I said, my temperament is not naturally morbid.

I am about to leave, but here is a box of his personal effects: loose papers, crumpled letters, dog-eared paperback books. In my sealed hotel room I lie upon my bed and examine the evidence. My eyes begin to smart from so much print, orange Penguin spines, exclamation points and question marks in red ballpoint ink, perhaps this person was not my brother after all but a stranger whose passion would embarrass me.

"The Wall is forever," he wrote. But nothing is forever.

Here is a paperback edition of *Beyond the Pleasure Principle* with passages underscored on every page: *"A drive is an urge inherent in organic life to restore an earlier state of being."* One must imagine the dead man striding purposefully forward to his death, ignoring the shouted commands in German. *The aim of all life is death,* substantiating the State Department's suspicions of Leftist sympathizing and general morbidity, hadn't one of his terse little poems been an elegy for the "martyred" Meinhof who hanged herself in her prison cell *("Sadism is in fact a death instinct which, under the influence of the narcissistic libido, has been forced away from the ego")*? Rumors suggested he must have been in contact with East German agitators; rumors hinted he might have been a spy. What are the journalistic terms—dupe, pawn? All very teasing, all very enigmatic, which doesn't solve the problem of why he died, why by that particular method. *"Our views have from the very first been dualistic, and today they are even more definitely dualistic than before—now that we describe the opposition as being, not between ego instincts and sexual instincts, but between life instincts and death instincts."*

I shall burn his personal effects—including as many pages of his books as I have the patience to tear out—in a tidy little funeral pyre in the aluminum wastebasket close at hand. Thus all evidence is erased. Thus even the offensive smoke is whirled and sucked out of the room by the wonderfully efficient German ventilation system.

I shall fly from West Berlin to Frankfurt (by special air access route) to New York City to home, my flight leaves at 11:25 A.M., in the meantime I am too restless to stay in one place, in the meantime I must walk quickly in case I am being followed.

Gretel with silver eyelids and kinked lavender hair and long skinny slug-white legs, giggling, squirming, certain it is all a joke and I am a very amusing gentleman. Gretel, who knows me, at the moment, far more intimately than my brother did: which is to say, more intimately than any brother could.

Handsome brute of a girl! Face shaped like a shovel, enormous smiling teeth, Pan-Cake makeup in skillful layers of beige, beige-rose, and ivory, those amazing slow-blinking silver eyelids, each eyelash fastidiously painted black and curled. No wasteful coy motions—no morbid tendencies. I find myself shivering at her Berliner accent. It really *is* a remarkable accent. The quintessence of German? The quintessence. Of German. Ah, German! Speak to me, I beg her, speak, tell me a riddle, a joke, a story, a legend, scold, tease, punish, anything you will: *Speak to me in Berliner.*

The anniversary of his birth is approaching. 17 June.

An error: I meant to say the anniversary of his death is approaching. 17 June. I shall have returned to the States by then. Don't you think? At the hotel they evinced surprise—it seemed quite sincere—that I had decided to extend my stay by another week.

"Surprise" is rendered more convincing in a foreign accent.

"Surprise," "regret," "suspicion"—the usual. More convincing in a foreign accent in which primary tones are emphasized and subtleties are cheerily abandoned. *Speak to me in Berliner,* I beg.

Arabesques of light that glitter like a massive snake's scales along the Hardenbergstrasse . . .

I am standing in that street or in another, shouting after two

German girls who have passed me by, bitches, sluts, pigs, cunts, I shouted, krauts, I shouted, I'll make you regret laughing at me! Laughing at an American!

My brother's wallet contained only a few deutsche marks when his body was found. Snapshots of home, of childhood? Gone. Identification? Gone. He had thrown away his passport but it was later discovered in some very ordinary place—a trash container in a railway station. He had thrown away being American, it seems, preparatory to throwing away being human, preparatory to throwing away being alive. I hate him for that logic.

How dare they laugh at an American, how dare they unlock the door of my room in my absence and investigate my belongings and the findings of my research? A violation so skillfully performed they have left no trace except an unmistakable disturbance of the air.

My hotel room in the Berliner Hospiz: a sealed capsule, a bunker, ventilated by a ceaselessly humming mechanism, which might from time to time emit its own subtle gases and which causes everything to vibrate in a most disagreeable, though hardly perceptible, manner. Consider my hands. So finely trembling. My inner organs— they, too, vibrate and have begun to grow exhausted with the strain. A foreign pulse beat is evident, a hard thrusting sexual rhythm, not my own, an infection from without: Gretel and Rudi and the others whom my research must encompass.

The doorknobs should be remarked upon: they are unusually small, perhaps five inches in circumference, solid steel, very difficult to turn, particularly if your hand is damp, or weak, or shaking. And the telephone?—I cannot think it might be trusted.

A ludicrous fate, to die locked in a windowless bathroom in a sealed hotel room, my invaluable passport only a few yards away, and the telephone, too: but the door will not open because the doorknob will not turn. Help help I cry, *bitte, danke,* I cry absurdly, oh help, I know you are listening, is the doorknob riveted in place? Are the poisonous gases being filtered in? Mr. G____, of our State Department: ". . . Of course we have not forgotten your brother, yes we remain concerned, yes it is a tragedy, we spoke of little else here at the Institute for weeks, but you must understand that a year has passed, or nearly, and naturally we have other matters to concern ourselves with, there are new developments, new crises, the young Germans' hatred of our current administration is unfortunate, their demonstrations against nuclear power, there are invariably new problems, and, yes, new tragedies, but of course we have not forgotten your brother, please do not take offense, no the Berlin police are certainly not watching you, no you are not in danger, yes I must admit we would advise you to return home, yes it is generally believed your brother had been emotionally disturbed for some time before the accident, no I couldn't offer any particular reason, he spoke to me a few times about the claustrophobic atmosphere here, but this is a common reaction, not just among visiting Americans but among Berliners too, the younger Germans especially, the students, unfortunately it isn't a phenomenon widely discussed, there are some things that simply cannot be discussed, no I cannot share your loathing for Berlin, I think you are being unnecessarily harsh, of course we all need a recovery period from it, back in the States, but we are devoted to Berlin it is a very special city it is a phenomenon unparalleled in diplomatic history a stateless city a 'Western city' in 'Eastern Europe' under our protection you must recall John F. Kennedy's famous words *I am a Berliner* in the very geography of totalitarianism the glittering city survives the jewel afloat upon the sea of darkness survives and flourishes under our protection for it will not be attacked by the Enemy an armed attack on Berlin is *precisely the same* as an armed attack on Chicago or New York or Washington. . . . But of course we have not forgotten your brother."

Light, and morning, and the comforting beat of the streets, a marvelous sexual urgency to the displays, the surface, bright bold plastic colors, festive crowds, nothing to fear. Berlin was reduced to rubble and rubble has no memory so one cannot expect a poignant sense of history—and in any case, does history exist? Everyone appears to have been born after 30 April 1945. If not, if they are older folk, they certainly served courageously in the Resistance; they may have been wounded, imprisoned, tortured—the usual. They are Americans at heart. They are patriotic. If they want the two Germanys united, it is only in the interest of world peace, a bulwark, as the saying goes, against the real Enemy.

My ticket has been secured for the flight to Frankfurt at 13.00

hours. Everything is in readiness except what does it mean, Rudi at the Flash Point wriggling his hips and placing a forefinger against his smiling lips, and then against mine. *Nein! Not a word! No more, mein Herr! Not to me!*

At the checkpoint it is remarkably easy to cross over: one is simply a tourist, an interested and sympathetic traveler, the passport is all, the passport is indispensable, one travels from West to East with agreeable ease, machine guns are doubtless manned in those tall deserted buildings, but one feels little apprehension: look at the pots of pansies arranged prettily along the curb, the usual pansy-hues, sweet little imperturbable faces, a welcome treat for the eye amidst all this gray concrete and barbed wire.

I shall not cross over, however. They are waiting for me to do so. Hence, I shall disappoint them. I need not repeat my brother's exact procedure. And it seems I have an engagement elsewhere, with both Birgit and Heidi, at the Salon Mandy.

The logic of the groin, the wordless satisfactions of the groin, billboard nudes iridescent and fleshy as if alive, baby giantesses undulating in the night sky. Consider the eternal wisdom of the groin, which opposes that of the Wall: for the Wall is Death.

No, *mein Herr,* I believe you are mistaken: the Wall is Life.

For consider: While it appears to be nothing but tiresome concrete and electrified wire, guarded by bored young soldiers and German shepherd attack dogs (top of the breed, needless to say), while it appears to be merely a political expediency required by both sides, it is, in fact, Life. Like Gretel, like Rudi, like that *Herr* at the Salon who was in truth *eine Dame,* like many others too numerous to list. For, as one approaches the Wall, even from the "Western" sector, through one of those amazing rubble lots off Friedrichstrasse, note how the pulse helplessly quickens, no matter how the mind intones, *You are safe on this side, they have no reason to fire upon you coming from this side,* note how the heart grows tumescent, how vision is sharpened, the very air rings with delight.

The Wall is Life. Especially when you are drunk, or euphoric, or too depressed to raise your head. *Why did he die* matters less now than *how precisely did he die* but if they imagine (for certainly they are watching) I am going to repeat his performance as 17 June advances they are mistaken. History cannot imitate itself without human participation.

Mid-June. Nearing the solstice. N.B. In certain areas, tall wire-mesh fences have been erected as well, in front of the (concrete) Wall; and these fences are topped with barbed wire, through which Death silently and secretly and ceaselessly pulses. One touch—! One touch.
    A way of making an end.

Once upon a time, in the remote days of the Holy Roman Empire, there was a cruel landowner, a nobleman of immense wealth, who built a great castle in the Bavarian Alps and instituted so terrifying a means of punishing wrongdoers among his peasants that for many centuries his name was associated with a certain species of tyranny: dreaded, and yet respected. And known throughout the land.
    His ingenious method was: the wrongdoer was locked in a high tower in the remotest wing of the castle, and the promise made, under God, that he would not be put to death, or even tortured; and that the nobleman, who was a Christian, would see that he was fed never less than once daily for the remainder of his natural life. The prisoner could never hope to taste freedom again: for even should a civil war bring about the fall of the castle, or should a younger and weaker (which is to say, less punitive) heir come into power, the prisoner would be summarily executed by the keeper of the dungeon. Thus it was that a covenant was forged: and the criminal was granted the privilege, most unusual in those barbaric times, of knowing that the nobleman was bound to his pledge; and that the future, in a manner of speaking, was assured. Never freedom, but a natural span of life. In a manner of speaking.
    The tower dungeon measured some fifteen feet in diameter, and its ceiling was perhaps twenty feet high. It was windowless, save for a single aperture, a hole struck through the stone wall, some eighteen inches across, at the level of the floor. Through this crude opening light shone, and "fresh air" circulated. The opening offered, as well, an apparent means of escape.
    Now, it happened that the prisoner could not see what lay directly below the hole in the wall unless he managed to force his

shoulders through and to squirm partway free, into the daylight: for the tower wall was some five feet thick, and the opening itself constituted a kind of tunnel, to be burrowed into, if the prisoner's strength was great enough. Once the prisoner made this bid for freedom, however, it was unlikely that he could retreat into the dungeon. (Indeed, there are no recorded instances of such a feat.)

Without exception, prisoners became obsessed with the aperture in the wall and spent all their waking hours (and, doubtless, their sleeping hours as well) in contemplation of it. Gradations of sunlight, or dusk, or dark: the faint luminous aura of the moon: mist, or rain, or pelting sleet, or snow: how wonderfully various the elements of the world beyond the aperture! Many a prisoner lay directly before it; others crouched against the far wall, staring in fascination until they were nearly blind; or they squatted with fists pressed against their eyes, that they might see nothing, and be tempted by nothing. They soon forgot to pray, because their apprehension of the opening was in itself a ceaseless prayer.

Now, through the crude "window" they could breathe the unmistakable odor of ripened, rotting flesh; but they could also breathe, when the wind was exactly right, the bright fresh magnificent air of high meadows, and steppes, and snow-ridged mountains—and sometimes even the odors of home: the comforting smell of woodsmoke, and familiar food being prepared by solicitous hands.

The curious thing was, though these prisoners were, as we have seen, treated with considerable mercy, being provided with food, clothing, shelter, and protection from injury through their lives, it nonetheless transpired—sometimes within the space of a scant day or two!—that they would go berserk and choose "freedom," and force themselves through the narrow hole in the wall, despite the physical pain involved and their ignorance of what lay outside. Unhappy wretches! Foolish peasants! They abandoned the guarantee of undisturbed animal existence for the possibility—no, the probability—of nonexistence: so displaying, it might be said, the very same willfulness, and rebelliousness, and lack of discretion that angered their lord in the first place and brought them to the tower.

For how could they, granted even their madness, close their senses against the blatant fact of rotting corpses, whose stench was wafted to them on every breeze, save when freezing temperatures locked all decaying phenomena in place; and how could they fail to comprehend the screams of scavenger birds, and the circling and darting shadows that so often brushed against the mouth of the aperture?

Yet the old legend would have it—and, indeed, our knowledge of human nature concurs—that the perversity of even the most ignorant peasant was such that "freedom" (though also Death) exerted its ineluctable attraction over that of imprisonment (though also Life) through many and many a year.

[December 1982]

DON DeLILLO

Human Moments in World War III

A note about Vollmer. He no longer describes the earth as a library globe or a map that has come alive, as a cosmic eye staring into deep space. This last was his most ambitious fling at imagery. The war has changed the way he sees the earth. The earth is land and water, the dwelling place of mortal men, in elevated dictionary terms. He doesn't see it anymore (storm-spiraled, sea-bright, breathing heat and haze and color) as an occasion for picturesque language, for easeful play or speculation.

At two hundred and twenty kilometers we see ship wakes and the larger airports. Icebergs, lightning bolts, sand dunes. I point out lava flows and cold-core eddies. That silver ribbon off the Irish coast, I tell him, is an oil slick.

This is my third orbital mission, Vollmer's first. He is an engineering genius, a communications and weapons genius, and maybe other kinds of genius as well. As mission specialist I'm content to be in charge. (The word "specialist," in the peculiar usage of Colorado Command, refers here to someone who does not specialize.) Our spacecraft is designed primarily to gather intelligence. The refinement of the quantum burn technique enables us to make frequent adjustments of orbit without firing rockets every time. We swing out into high wide trajectories, the whole earth as our psychic light, to inspect unmanned and possibly hostile satellites. We orbit tightly, snugly, take intimate looks at surface activities in untraveled places.

The banning of nuclear weapons has made the world safe for war.

I try not to think big thoughts or submit to rambling abstractions. But the urge sometimes comes over me. Earth orbit puts men into philosophical temper. How can we help it? We see the planet complete, we have a privileged vista. In our attempts to be equal to the experience, we tend to meditate importantly on subjects like the human condition. It makes a man feel *universal,* floating over the continents, seeing the rim of the world, a line as clear as a compass arc, knowing it is just a turning of the bend to Atlantic twilight, to sediment plumes and kelp beds, an island chain glowing in the dusky sea.

I tell myself it is only scenery. I want to think of our life here as ordinary, as a housekeeping arrangement, an unlikely but workable setup caused by a housing shortage or spring floods in the valley.

Vollmer does the systems checklist and goes to his hammock to rest. He is twenty-three years old, a boy with a longish head and close-cropped hair. He talks about northern Minnesota as he removes the objects in his personal preference kit, placing them on an adjacent Velcro surface for tender inspection. I have a 1901 silver dollar in my personal preference kit. Little else of note. Vollmer has graduation pictures, bottle caps, small stones from his backyard. I don't know whether he chose these items himself or whether they were pressed on him by parents who feared that his life in space would be lacking in human moments.

Our hammocks are human moments, I suppose, although I don't know whether Colorado Command planned it that way. We eat hot dogs and almond crunch bars and apply lip balm as part of the pre-sleep checklist. We wear slippers at the firing panel. Vollmer's football jersey is a human moment. Outsized, purple and white, of polyester mesh, bearing the number 79, a big man's number, a prime of no particular distinction, it makes him look stoop-shouldered, abnormally long-framed.

"I still get depressed on Sundays," he says.

"Do we have Sundays here?"

"No, but they have them there and I still feel them. I always know when it's Sunday."

"Why do you get depressed?"

"The slowness of Sundays. Something about the glare, the smell of warm grass, the church service, the relatives visiting in nice clothes. The whole day kind of lasts forever."

"I didn't like Sundays either."

"They were slow but not lazy-slow. They were long and hot, or long and cold. In summer my grandmother made lemonade. There was a routine. The whole day was kind of set up beforehand and the routine almost never changed. Orbital routine is different. It's satisfying. It gives our time a shape and substance. Those Sundays were shapeless despite the fact you knew what was coming, who was coming, what we'd all say. You knew the first words out of the mouth of each person before anyone spoke. I was the only kid in the group. People were happy to see me. I used to want to hide."

"What's wrong with lemonade?" I ask.

A battle management satellite, unmanned, reports high-energy laser activity in orbital sector Dolores. We take out our laser kits and study them for half an hour. The beaming procedure is complex and because the panel operates on joint control only we must rehearse the sets of established measures with the utmost care.

A note about the earth. The earth is the preserve of day and night. It contains a sane and balanced variation, a natural waking and sleeping, or so it seems to someone deprived of this tidal effect.

This is why Vollmer's remark about Sundays in Minnesota struck me as interesting. He still feels, or claims he feels, or thinks he feels, that inherently earthbound rhythm.

To men at this remove, it is as though things exist in their particular physical form in order to reveal the hidden simplicity of some powerful mathematical truth. The earth reveals to us the simple awesome beauty of day and night. It is there to contain and incorporate these conceptual events.

Vollmer in his shorts and suction clogs resembles a high-school swimmer, all but hairless, an unfinished man not aware he is open to cruel scrutiny, not aware he is without devices, standing with arms folded in a place of echoing voices and chlorine fumes. There is something stupid in the sound of his voice. It is too direct, a deep voice from high in the mouth, well back in the mouth, slightly insistent, a little loud. Vollmer has never said a stupid thing in my presence. It is just his voice that is stupid, a grave and naked bass, a voice without inflection or breath.

We are not cramped here. The flight deck and crew quarters are thoughtfully designed. Food is fair to good. There are books, videocassettes, news and music. We do the manual checklists, the oral checklists, the simulated firings with no sign of boredom or carelessness. If anything, we are getting better at our tasks all the time. The only danger is conversation.

I try to keep our conversations on an everyday plane. I make it a point to talk about small things, routine things. This makes sense to me. It seems a sound tactic, under the circumstances, to restrict our talk to familiar topics, minor matters. I want to build a structure of the commonplace. But Vollmer has a tendency to bring up enormous subjects. He wants to talk about war and the weapons of war. He wants to discuss global strategies, global aggressions. I tell him now that he has stopped describing the earth as a cosmic eye, he wants to see it as a game board or computer model. He looks at me plain-faced and tries to get me in a theoretical argument: selection space-based attacks versus long drawn-out well-modulated land-sea-air engagements. He quotes experts, mentions sources. What am I supposed to say? He will suggest that people are disappointed in the war. The war is dragging into its third week. There is a sense in which it is worn out, played out. He gathers this from the news broadcasts we periodically receive. Something in the announcer's voice hints at a let-down, a fatigue, a faint bitterness about—*something*. Vollmer is probably right about this. I've heard it myself in the tone of the broadcaster's voice, in the voice of Colorado Command, despite the fact that our news is censored, that they are not telling us things they feel we shouldn't know, in our special situation, our exposed and sensitive position. In his direct and stupid-sounding and uncannily perceptive way, young Vollmer says that people are not enjoying this war to the same extent that people have always enjoyed and nourished themselves on war, as a heightening, a periodic intensity. What I object to in Vollmer is that he often shares my deep-reaching and most reluctantly held convictions. Coming from that mild face, in that earnest resonant run-on voice, these ideas unnerve and worry me as they never do when they remain unspoken. Vollmer's candor exposes something painful.

It is not too early in the war to discern nostalgic references to earlier wars. All wars refer back. Ships, planes, entire operations are named after ancient battles, simpler weapons, what we perceive as conflicts of nobler intent. This recon-interceptor is called Tomahawk II. When I sit at the firing panel I look at a photograph of Vollmer's granddad when he was a young man in sagging khakis and a shallow helmet, standing in a bare field, a rifle strapped to his shoulder. This is a human moment and it reminds me that war, among other things, is a form of longing.

We dock with the command station, take on food, exchange video-cassettes. The war is going well, they tell us, although it isn't likely they know much more than we do.

Then we separate.

The maneuver is flawless and I am feeling happy and satisfied, having resumed human contact with the nearest form of the outside world, having traded quips and manly insults, traded voices, traded news and rumors—buzzes, rumbles, scuttlebutt. We stow our supplies of broccoli and apple cider and fruit cocktail and butterscotch pudding. I feel a homey emotion, putting away the colorfully packaged goods, a sensation of prosperous well-being, the consumer's solid comfort.

Volmer's T-shirt bears the word *Inscription.*

"People had hoped to be caught up in something bigger than themselves," he says. "They thought it would be a shared crisis. They would feel a sense of shared purpose, shared destiny. Like a snow-storm that blankets a large city—but lasting months, lasting years, carrying everyone along, creating fellow-feeling where there was only suspicion and fear. Strangers talking to each other, meals by candle-light when the power fails. The war would ennoble everything we say and do. What was impersonal would become personal. What was solitary would be shared. But what happens when the sense of shared crisis begins to dwindle much sooner than anyone expected? We begin to think the feeling lasts longer in snowstorms."

A note about selective noise. Forty-eight hours ago I was monitoring data on the mission console when a voice broke in on my report to Colorado Command. The voice was unenhanced, heavy with static. I checked my headset, checked the switches and lights. Seconds later the command signal resumed and I heard our flight dynamics officer ask me to switch to the redundant sense frequencer. I did this but it only caused the weak voice to return, a voice that carried with it a strange and unspecifiable poignancy. I seemed somehow to recognize it. I don't mean I knew who was speaking. It was the tone I recognized, the touching quality of some half-remembered and tender event, even through the static, the sonic mist.

In any case, Colorado Command resumed transmission in a matter of seconds.

"We have a deviate, Tomahawk."

"We copy. There's a voice."

"We have gross oscillation here."

"There's some interference. I have gone redundant but I'm not sure it's helping."

"We are clearing an outframe to locate source."

"Thank you, Colorado."

"It is probably just selective noise. You are negative red on the step-function quad."

"It was a voice," I told them.

"We have just received an affirm on selective noise."

"I could hear words, in English."

"We copy selective noise."

"Someone was talking, Colorado."

"What do you think selective noise is?"

"I don't know what it is."

"You are getting a spill from one of the unmanneds."

"If it's an unmanned, how could it be sending a voice?"

"It is not a voice as such, Tomahawk. It is selective noise. We have some real firm telemetry on that."

"It sounded like a voice."

"It is supposed to sound like a voice. But it is not a voice as such. It is enhanced."

"It sounded unenhanced. It sounded human in all sorts of ways."

"It is signals and they are spilling from geosynchronous orbit. This is your deviate. You are getting voice codes from twenty-two thousand miles. It is basically a weather report. We will correct, Tomahawk. In the meantime, advise you stay redundant."

About ten hours later Vollmer heard the voice. Then he heard two or three other voices. They were people speaking, people in conversation. He gestured to me as he listened, pointed to the headset, then raised his shoulders, held his hands apart to indicate surprise and bafflement. In the swarming noise (as he said later), it wasn't easy to get the drift of what people were saying. The static was frequent, the references were somewhat elusive, but Vollmer mentioned how intensely affecting these voices were, even when the signals were at their weakest. One thing he did know: it wasn't selective noise. A quality of purest, sweetest sadness issued from remote space. He wasn't sure but he thought there was also a background noise integral to the conversation. Laughter. The sound of people laughing.

In other transmissions we've been able to recognize theme music, an announcer's introduction, wisecracks and bursts of applause, commercials for products whose long-lost brand names evoke the golden antiquity of great cities buried in sand and river silt.

Somehow we are picking up signals from radio programs of forty, fifty, sixty years ago.

Our current task is to collect imagery data on troop deployment. Vollmer surrounds his Hasselblad, engrossed in some microadjustment. There is a seaward bulge of stratocumulus. Sunglint and littoral drift. I see blooms of plankton in a blue of such Persian richness it seems an animal rapture, a color-change to express some form of intuitive delight. As the surface features unfurl, I list them aloud by name. It is the only game I play in space, reciting the earth-names, the nomenclature of contour and structure. Glacial scour, moraine debris. Shatter-coning at the edge of a multi-ring impact site. A resurgent caldera, a mass of castellated rimrock. Over the sand seas now. Parabolic dunes, star dunes, straight dunes with radial crests.

The emptier the land, the more luminous and precise the names for its features. Vollmer says the thing science does best is name the features of the world.

He has degrees in science and technology. He was a scholarship winner, an honors student, a research assistant. He ran science projects, read technical papers in the deep-pitched earnest voice that rolls off the roof of his mouth. As mission specialist (generalist), I sometimes resent his nonscientific perceptions, the glimmerings of maturity and balanced judgment. I am beginning to feel slightly preempted. I want him to stick to systems, onboard guidance, data parameters. His human insights make me nervous.

"I'm happy," he says.

These words are delivered with matter-of-fact finality and the simple statement affects me powerfully. It frightens me in fact. What does he mean he's happy? Isn't happiness totally outside our frame of reference? How can he think it is possible to be happy here? I want to say to him, "This is just a housekeeping arrangement, a series of more or less routine tasks. Attend to your tasks, do your testing, run through your checklists." I want to say, "Forget the measure of our vision, the sweep of things, the war itself, the terrible death." Forget the overarching night, the stars as static points, as mathematical fields. Forget the cosmic solitude, the upwelling awe and dread."

I want to say, "Happiness is not a fact of this experience, at least not to the extent that one is bold enough to speak of it."

Laser technology contains a core of foreboding and myth. It is a clean sort of lethal package we are dealing with, a well-behaved beam of photons, an engineered coherence, but we approach the weapon with our minds full of ancient warnings and fears. (There ought to be a term for this ironic condition: primitive fear of the weapons we are advanced enough to design and produce.) Maybe this is why the project managers were ordered to work out a firing procedure that depends on the coordinated actions of two men—two temperaments, two souls—operating the controls together. Fear of the power of light, the pure stuff of the universe.

A single dark mind in a moment of inspiration might think it liberating to fling a concentrated beam at some lumbering humpbacked Boeing making its commercial rounds at thirty thousand feet.

Vollmer and I approach the firing panel. The panel is designed in such a way that the joint operators must sit back to back. The reason for this, although Colorado Command never specifically said so, is to keep us from seeing each other's face. Colorado wants to be sure that weapons personnel in particular are not influenced by each other's tics and perturbations. We are back to back, therefore, harnessed in our seats, ready to begin. Vollmer in his purple and white jersey, his fleeced pad-abouts.

This is only a test.

I start the playback. At the sound of a prerecorded voice command, we each insert a modal key in its proper slot. Together we count down from five and then turn the keys one-quarter left. This puts the system in what is called an open-minded mode. We count down from three. The enhanced voice says, *You are open-minded now.*

Vollmer speaks into his voiceprint analyzer.

"This is code B for bluegrass. Request voice identity clearance."

We count down from five and then speak into our voiceprint analyzers. We say whatever comes into our heads. The point is simply to produce a voiceprint that matches the print in the memory bank. This ensures that the men at the panel are the same men authorized to be there when the system is in an open-minded mode.

This is what comes into my head: "I am standing at the corner of Fourth and Main, where thousands are dead of unknown causes, their scorched bodies piled in the street."

We count down from three. The enhanced voice says, *You are cleared to proceed to lock-in position.*

We turn our modal keys half right. I activate the logic chip and study the numbers on my screen. Vollmer disengages voiceprint and puts us in voice circuit rapport with the onboard computer's sensing mesh. We count down from five. The enhanced voice says, *You are locked in now.*

"Random factor seven," I say. "Problem seven. Solution seven."

Vollmer says, "Give me an acronym."

"BROWN, for Bearing Radius Oh White Nine."

My color-spec lights up brown. The numbers on my display screen read 2, 18, 15, 23, 14. These are the alphanumeric values of the letters in the acronym BROWN as they appear in unit succession.

The logic-gate opens. The enhanced voice says, *You are logical now.*

As we move from one step to the next, as the colors, numbers, characters, lights and auditory signals indicate that we are proceeding correctly, a growing satisfaction passes through me—the pleasure of elite and secret skills, a life in which every breath is governed by specific rules, by patterns, codes, controls. I try to keep the results of the operation out of my mind, the whole point of it, the outcome of these sequences of precise and esoteric steps. But often I fail. I let the image in, I think the thought, I even say the word at times. This is confusing, of course. I feel tricked. My pleasure feels betrayed, as if it had a life of its own, a childlike or intelligent-animal existence independent of the man at the firing panel.

We count down from five. Vollmer releases the lever that unwinds the systems-purging disc. My pulse marker shows green at three-second intervals. We count down from three. We turn the modal keys three-quarters right. I activate the beam sequencer. We turn the keys one-quarter right. We count down from three. Bluegrass music plays over the squawk box. The enhanced voice says, *You are moded to fire now.*

We study our world map kits.

"Don't you sometimes feel a power in you?" Vollmer says. "An extreme state of good health, sort of. An *arrogant* healthiness. That's it. You are feeling so good you begin thinking you're a little superior to other people. A kind of life-strength. An optimism about yourself that you generate almost at the expense of others. Don't you sometimes feel this?"

(Yes, as a matter of fact.)

"There's probably a German word for it. But the point I want to make is that this powerful feeling is so—I don't know—*delicate*. That's it. One day you feel it, the next day you are suddenly puny and doomed. A single little thing goes wrong, you feel doomed, you feel utterly weak and defeated and unable to act powerfully or even sensibly. Everyone else is lucky, you are unlucky, hapless, sad, ineffectual and doomed."

(Yes, yes.)

By chance we are over the Missouri River now, looking toward the Red Lakes of Minnesota. I watch Vollmer go through his map kit, trying to match the two worlds. This is a deep and mysterious happiness, to confirm the accuracy of a map. He seems immensely satisfied. He keeps saying, *"That's it, that's it."*

Vollmer talks about childhood. In orbit he has begun to think about his early years for the first time. He is surprised at the power of these memories. As he speaks he keeps his head turned to the window. Minnesota is a human moment. Upper Red Lake, Lower Red Lake. He clearly feels he can see himself there.

"Kids don't take walks," he says. "They don't sunbathe or sit on the porch."

He seems to be saying that children's lives are too well-supplied to accommodate the spells of reinforced being that the rest of us depend on. A deft enough thought but not to be pursued. It is time to prepare for a quantum burn.

We listen to the old radio shows. Light flares and spreads across the blue-banded edge, sunrise, sunset, the urban grids in shadow. A man and woman trade well-timed remarks, light, pointed, bantering. There is a sweetness in the tenor voice of the young man singing, a simple vigor that time and distance and random noise have enveloped in eloquence and yearning. Every sound, every lilt of strings has this veneer of age. Vollmer says he remembers these programs, although of course he has never heard them before. What odd happenstance, what flourish or grace of the laws of physics, enables us to pick up these signals? Traveled voices, chambered and dense. At times they have the detached and surreal quality of aural hallucination, voices in attic rooms, the complaints of dead relatives. But the sound effects are full of urgency and verve. Cars turn dangerous corners, crisp gunfire fills the night. It was, it is, wartime. Wartime for Duz and Grape-Nuts Flakes. Comedians make fun of the way the enemy talks. We hear hysterical mock German, moonshine Japanese. The cities are in light, the listening millions, fed, met comfortably in drowsy rooms, at war, as the night comes softly down. Vollmer says he recalls specific moments, the comic inflections, the announcer's fat-man laughter. He recalls individual voices rising from the laughter of the studio audience, the cackle of a St. Louis businessman, the brassy wail of a high-shouldered blonde, just arrived in California, where women wear their hair this year in aromatic bales.

Vollmer drifts across the wardroom, upside-down, eating an almond crunch.

He sometimes floats free of his hammock, sleeping in a fetal crouch, bumping into walls, adhering to a corner of the ceiling grid.

"Give me a minute to think of the name," he says in his sleep.

He says he dreams of vertical spaces from which he looks, as a boy, at—*something*. My dreams are the heavy kind, the kind that are hard to wake from, to rise out of. They are strong enough to pull me back down, dense enough to leave me with a heavy head, a drugged and bloated feeling. There are episodes of faceless gratification, vaguely disturbing.

"It's almost unbelievable when you think of it, how they live there in all that ice and sand and mountainous wilderness. Look at it," he says. "Huge barren deserts, huge oceans. How do they endure all those terrible things? The floods alone. The earthquakes alone make it crazy to live there. Look at those fault systems. They're so big, there's so many of them. The volcanic eruptions alone. What could be more frightening than a volcanic eruption? How do they endure avalanches, year after year, with numbing regularity? It's hard to believe people live there. The floods alone. You can see whole huge discolored areas, all flooded out, washed out. How do they survive, where do they go? Look at the cloud buildups. Look at that swirling storm center. What about the people who live in the path of a storm like that? It must be packing incredible winds. The lightning alone. People exposed on beaches, near trees and telephone poles. Look at the cities with their spangled lights spreading in all directions. Try to imagine the crime and violence. Look at the smoke pall hanging low. What does that mean in terms of respiratory disorders? It's crazy. Who would live there? The deserts, how they encroach. Every year they claim more and more arable land. How enormous those snow-fields are. Look at the massive storm fronts over the ocean. There are ships down there, small craft some of them. Try to imagine the waves, the rocking. The hurricanes alone. The tidal waves. Look at those coastal communities exposed to tidal waves. What could be more frightening than a tidal wave? But they live there, they stay there. Where could they go?"

I want to talk to him about calorie intake, the effectiveness of the earplugs and nasal decongestants. The earplugs are human moments. The apple cider and the broccoli are human moments. Vollmer himself is a human moment, never more so than when he forgets there is a war.

The close-cropped hair and longish head. The mild blue eyes that bulge slightly. The protuberant eyes of long-bodied people with stooped shoulders. The long hands and wrists. The mild face. The easy face of a handyman in a panel truck that has an extension ladder fixed to the roof and a scuffed license plate, green and white, with the state motto beneath the digits. That kind of face.

He offers to give me a haircut. What an interesting thing a haircut is, when you think of it. Before the war there were time slots reserved for such activities. Houston not only had everything scheduled well in advance but constantly monitored us for whatever meager feedback might result. We were wired, taped, scanned, diagnosed, and metered. We were men in space, objects worthy of the most scrupulous care, the deepest sentiments and anxieties.

Now there is a war. Nobody cares about my hair, what I eat, how I feel about the spacecraft's decor, and it is not Houston but Colorado we are in touch with. We are no longer delicate biological specimens adrift in an alien environment. The enemy can kill us with its photons, its mesons, its charged particles faster than any calcium deficiency or trouble of the inner ear, faster than any dusting of micrometeoroids. The emotions have changed. We've stopped being candidates for an embarrassing demise, the kind of mistake or unforeseen event that tends to make a nation grope for the appropriate response. As men in war we can be certain, dying, that we will arouse uncomplicated sorrows, the open and dependable feelings that grateful nations count on to embellish the simplest ceremony.

A note about the universe. Vollmer is on the verge of deciding that our planet is alone in harboring intelligent life. We are an accident and we happened only once. (What a remark to make, in egg-shaped orbit, to someone who doesn't want to discuss the larger questions.) He feels this way because of the war.

The war, he says, will bring about an end to the idea that the universe swarms, as they say, with life. Other astronauts have looked past the star-points and imagined infinite possibility, grape-clustered worlds teeming with higher forms. But this was before the war. Our view is changing even now, his and mine, he says, as we drift across the firmament.

Is Vollmer saying that cosmic optimism is a luxury reserved for periods between world wars? Do we project our current failure and despair out toward the star clouds, the endless night? After all, he says, where are they? If they exist, why has there been no sign, not one, not any, not a single indication that serious people might cling to, not a whisper, a radio pulse, a shadow? The war tells us it is foolish to believe.

Our dialogues with Colorado Command are beginning to sound like computer-generated tea-time chat. Vollmer tolerates Colorado's jargon only to a point. He is critical of their more debased locutions and doesn't mind letting them know. Why, then, if I agree with his views on this matter, am I becoming irritated by his complaints? Is he too young to champion the language? Does he have the experience, the professional standing to scold our flight dynamics officer, our conceptual paradigm officer, our status consultants on waste-management systems and evasion-related zonal options? Or is it something else completely, something unrelated to Colorado Command and our communications with them? Is it the sound of his voice? Is it just his *voice* that is driving me crazy?

Vollmer has entered a strange phase. He spends all his time at the window now, looking down at the earth. He says little or nothing. He simply wants to look, do nothing but look. The oceans, the continents, the archipelagos. We are configured in what is called a cross-orbit series and there is no repetition from one swing around the earth to the next. He sits there looking. He takes meals at the window, does checklists at the window, barely glancing at the instruction sheets as we pass over tropical storms, over grass fires and major ranges. I keep waiting for him to return to his prewar habit of using quaint phrases to describe the earth. It's a beach ball, a sun-ripened fruit. But he simply looks out the window, eating almond crunches, the wrappers floating away. The view clearly fills his consciousness. It is powerful enough to silence him, to still the voice that rolls off the roof of his mouth, to leave him turned in the seat, twisted uncomfortably for hours at a time.

The view is endlessly fulfilling. It is like the answer to a lifetime of questions and vague cravings. It satisfies every childlike curiosity, every muted desire, whatever there is in him of the scientist, the poet, the primitive seer, the watcher of fire and shooting stars, whatever obsessions eat at the night side of his mind, whatever sweet and dreamy yearning he has ever felt for nameless places faraway, whatever earth-sense he possesses, the neural pulse of some wilder awareness, a sympathy for beasts, whatever belief in an immanent vital force, the Lord of Creation, whatever secret harboring of the idea of human oneness, whatever wishfulness and simplehearted hope, whatever of too much and not enough, all at once and little by little, whatever burning urge to escape responsibility and routine, escape his own overspecialization, the circumscribed and inward-spiraling self, whatever remnants of his boyish longing to fly, his dreams of strange spaces and eerie heights, his fantasies of happy death, whatever indolent and sybaritic leanings, lotus-eater, smoker of grasses and herbs, blue-eyed gazer into space—all these are satisfied, all collected and massed in that living body, the sight he sees from the window.

"It is just so interesting," he says at last. "The colors and all." The colors and all.

[July 1983]